THE PROCESS OF CREATION

That year and a half was one of the most exciting and delightful I have ever experienced. Working on scripts in association with Gene Roddenberry and Gene Coon was stimulating and challenging. All the actors were wonderful in taking time to share ideas they had developed about their characters. Playing the same person week after week on a series can become deadly dull for the actors and the audience if it's the same every week. The secret to keeping everyone interested is akin to slowly peeling an onion. Each time another layer is exposed, something new is revealed about the character. It's like sharing a surprise gift with the audience—something fresh and special. The actors had given their characters real thought; and from that shared information springboards for new stories often developed. Sometimes it was only an attitude like the Spock-McCoy verbal sparring or a physical trait such as the Famous Spock Neck Pinch, referred to in scripts as the "FNSP"—but ali of it colored and flavored the scripts and the characters.

—From the introduction
by D. C. Fontana

Please be sure to ask your bookseller for the Bantam Spectra Books you have missed:

The Trinity Paradox
by Kevin J. Anderson and Doug Beason
Nightfall
by Isaac Asimov and Robert Silverberg
What Might Have Been, Volume 3: Alternate Wars
edited by Gregory Benford and Martin H. Greenberg
Rendezvous with Rama
by Arthur C. Clarke
The Garden of Rama
by Arthur C. Clarke and Gentry Lee
The Mutant Season
by Karen Haber and Robert Silverberg
The Mutant Prime
by Karen Haber
Shivering World
by Kathy Tyers
Star of the Guardians by Margaret Weis
Volume One: **The Lost King**
Volume Two: **King's Test**
Volume Three: **King's Sacrifice**
Star Wars, Volume One: Heir to the Empire
by Timothy Zahn
The Next Wave #1: Red Genesis
by S.C. Sykes
The Next Wave #2: Alien Tongues
by Stephen Leigh

STAR TREK®

THE CLASSIC EPISODES 1

adapted by James Blish

with J. A. Lawrence

Introduction by D. C. FONTANA

BANTAM BOOKS

NEW YORK • TORONTO • LONDON • SYDNEY • AUCKLAND

STAR TREK: THE CLASSIC EPISODES 1
A Bantam Spectra Book

PRINTING HISTORY
Stories appearing in this volume were published in a slightly different form by Bantam Books.
Special Bantam edition / September 1991

SPECTRA and the portrayal of a boxed "s" are trademarks of Bantam Books, a division of Bantam Doubleday Dell Publishing Group, Inc.

ISBN 0-553-29138-6

Published simultaneously in the United States and Canada

Bantam Books are published by Bantam Books, a division of Bantam Doubleday Dell Publishing Group, Inc. Its trademark, consisting of the words "Bantam Books" and the portrayal of a rooster, is Registered in U.S. Patent and Trademark Office and in other countries. Marca Registrada. Bantam Books, 666 Fifth Avenue, New York, New York 10103.

PRINTED IN THE UNITED STATES OF AMERICA

OPM *0 9 8 7 6 5 4 3 2 1*

CONTENTS

INTRODUCTION

BY D. C. FONTANA

A framed cartoon by William Rotzler hangs on the wall in my home. It depicts a woman talking to a man. On her ankle is a manacle attached to a short chain—on the end of which is the U.S.S. *Enterprise* (NCC 1701). The caption reads: "It follows me everywhere." That, in a nutshell, is the effect *Star Trek* has had on my life.

If I pay for something in a store with a check or credit card, it is not uncommon for the salesperson to stare at the name and then say, "Are you *the* D. C. Fontana?"

"Uh . . . yes."

"Star Trek?"

"That's right."

Following that comes (take your pick): (1) compliments of the scripts I wrote, (2) questions about the show and/or the stars, (3) the future of the show (there always seems to be one), or (4) questions on how he/she can sell a script to the show. Frequently the person comments that he or she grew up watching *Star Trek*. Depending on the age of the person, that can mean he or she is actually a third- or fourth-generation fan, having seen it in one of its many reincarnations on syndicated television, not in its original broadcast years.

One of the many phenomena attached to "*Trek* Classic" is that it has never been *out* of syndication. Somewhere in the world *Star Trek* is always running for a still-fascinated audience. (Sometimes I wonder how translations into other languages handle the show. "He's dead, Jim" probably translates easily, but references to "colladium trioxide in an algobarium solution'' might be more difficult to get across.) There have been many incidents of a station removing *Trek* Classic from its programming and agitated viewers sending in a blizzard of protest mail until it is restored. The original show still gets fan mail, and many people write to say how *Star Trek* has changed or influenced their lives for the better. Certainly it influenced mine.

I remember the day I first heard the name *Star Trek*. It was spring of 1964, and I was one of the secretaries on Gene Roddenberry's *Lieutenant* series at Metro-Goldwyn-Mayer. We knew that *The Lieutenant* would not be renewed by NBC, and Gene was working on the creation of a new series. Gene was aware I was a member of the Writers Guild at that time and that I had script credits. He was one of the people who encouraged me to keep writing and working toward a full-time career as a writer. One afternoon, he handed me a small sheaf of typed pages and said, ''That's what I'm doing for the next one. Let me know what you think.''

I took it home to read that evening. There wasn't much on paper yet, but the ship (then the U.S.S. *Yorktown*) jumped off the page as an exciting vehicle to the stars, captained by a young, energetic Captain Robert April and carrying a science officer named Spock who was half-human and half-Martian. (His skin was reddish in cast in that early draft.) I didn't even like science fiction in particular at that time—but I was hooked. When I returned the pages the next day, I said to Gene, ''I have only one question. Who's going to play Spock?'' He nudged an eight-by-ten photograph across his desk toward me. It was the picture of an actor who had recently played a role on *The Lieutenant* and whom I knew well, because he had guest starred in the first story I sold to television four years before. Leonard Nimoy. Everything else about the show turned out to be wide open, but Leonard Nimoy as Mr. Spock never changed.

MGM, which had a ''first look'' deal with Gene on his projects, passed on *Star Trek*. (Ever since, I have visualized the company and its then-executives gnashing their teeth in agony and frustration over that decision.) Thus freed of his obligation to Metro, Gene and his agent took *Star Trek* shopping. The enlightened consumers turned out to be Oscar Katz, head of Desilu Productions, and Herb Solow, who succeeded

Mr. Katz. They made a deal with Gene's Norway Productions to coproduce *Star Trek*—if it could be sold to a network. Then began the odyssey to the Big Three—CBS, ABC, and NBC. Gene tells stories of how he would outline the project, describe its potential, the characters, the adventures—and receive stony silence. At last, in frustration in a meeting with NBC executives, he burst out, "It's *Wagon Train* to the stars!" *This* they could understand, and *Star Trek* was bought by NBC in the late spring of 1964.

Two long years were to pass before *Star Trek* became a series. First an hour-length pilot script had to develop from the original short format. Over the summer, as the script was written, the U.S.S. *Yorktown* became the U.S.S. *Enterprise*. Captain Robert April changed to Robert Winter and finally to Christopher Pike. He acquired a crew in addition to Mr. Spock, including a mysterious female first officer simply called Number One. Mr. Spock himself changed from a half Martian/half human to a Vulcan/human half-breed. The ship and the crew were armed with lasers, and the transporter was created. Franz Bachelin, the art director, and his assistant, Matt Jeffries, designed the look of the show and, especially, the look of the *Enterprise*. (An interesting side note here is that Franz was of German birth and had flown for Germany in World War I. Matt Jeffries was a private pilot and had copiloted B17's during World War II. Gene himself was a veteran pilot of the war in the Pacific and an ex-airline pilot. All that aviation experience made the *Enterprise* an interesting "bird.") An old friend of mine, William Theiss, had impressed Gene with his costume designs and had come aboard as costume designer. And the inimitable Robert H. Justman was the first assistant director when the first *Star Trek* pilot went to stage at Desilu Culver in the winter of 1964–65.

NBC rejected the finished pilot as "too cerebral."

But they also felt there was something there that would make a successful series, and they gave Gene the order to do a second pilot, a move almost unprecedented in network history. Samuel A. Peeples was signed to write the second pilot script based on Gene's format. Jeff Hunter bowed out of the lead role, and the hunt was on for a new captain. Costumes changed in style and color. The look of the ship altered slightly, and the reference to weaponry became phasers instead of lasers. Gene revised his characters, except for Mr. Spock; and the entire show was recast. After a great deal of consideration, the new commander of the *Enterprise* was William Shatner as Captain James R. Kirk. (Yes, James *R.* Kirk.) The second pilot was shot in the summer of 1965. It was early 1966 before we heard the word that NBC definitely would go with *Star Trek* as a series.

The production staff consisted of Gene Roddenberry as producer/writer and John D. F. Black as story editor/writer. Bob Justman had moved up from production manager on the second pilot to associate producer of the series. Bill Theiss was again retained as costume designer, and Matt Jeffries became the art director. Almost all the other personnel were new to the show.

During this time, I not only worked for Gene as his production secretary, I continued my writing career that had begun in 1960 with the sale of several scripts to a western series titled *The Tall Man*. Other scripts followed *(slowly)* so that in early 1966, I had nine writing credits to my name. As the series began production, Gene asked me if I would like to do a script for it. I chose a story from the detailed Writers/ Directors Guide titled "Charlie X."

The series was well into production before someone (I believe it was Bob Justman) realized new scripts referred to the captain as James *T.* Kirk—and the headstone Gary Mitchell had carved for the captain in "Where No Man Has Gone Before" clearly read James *R.* Kirk. Gene thought about it and decided that if pressed for an answer on the discrepancy, the response was to be: "Gary Mitchell had godlike powers, but at base he was human. *He made a mistake.*"

We never did come up with a really plausible explanation for the non-use of the shuttlecraft in the early Richard Matheson script "The Enemy Within." The plot called for members of the crew to be stranded on an icy planet due to transporter malfunction. The simple fact was, the shuttlecraft had not been built yet. The AMT Company finally delivered the large shuttlecraft about a third of the way through the first season, in time for it to be featured in the "Galileo Seven" script by Oliver Crawford. Once it was established there *were* shuttlecraft aboard the *Enterprise*, fans wrote in to ask about the discrepancy. We finally had to admit that it was our mistake. We hadn't seen the need for the shuttlecraft until a story came along that used one.

In fact, the *Enterprise* tended to grow as story points created new rooms and areas we could use again. As the seasons progressed, more corridors were added; the "Jeffries Tube" and the auxiliary control room appeared. Sick bay and engineering changed and expanded.

"How'd that happen on a five-year mission into space?" someone would ask.

"The Enterprise put into space dock at a Federation planet for maintenance and equipment upgrade," we'd reply straight-faced.

An NBC executive once said, "The trouble with you *Star Trek* people is you believe that damn ship is really up there."

Bob Justman looked him in the eye and snapped, "It *is*."

In September, John D. F. Black, who had been serving as story editor, received an offer to write a movie and opted to leave *Star Trek*. He was replaced by Steven Carabatsos. At the same time, Gene L. Coon joined the show as producer, and Gene Roddenberry took on the title of executive producer. I left my job as production secretary to write free-lance and completed my second script, "Tomorrow Is Yesterday." By early November, Gene knew he would not renew Carabatsos's thirteen-week contract. He brought me a script titled "The Way of the Spores," which he said was not working. If I could rewrite it to his satisfaction and to Desilu's and NBC's, he would back me for the position of story editor. I took on the rewrite, starting with a reworking of the story. It had originally involved Sulu meeting his old love, Leila Kalomi—hence Jill Ireland's exotic name. After thinking about it, I told Gene Roddenberry, "This should be a love story—for Mr. Spock." Gene nodded and told me to write it. The result was "This Side of Paradise," which did indeed satisfy Gene, Desilu, and NBC that I could handle rewrites. In mid-December of 1966, I was awarded the job of story editor on *Star Trek*.

The next year and a half was one of the most exciting and delightful I have ever experienced. Working on scripts in association with Roddenberry and Coon was stimulating and challenging. All the actors were wonderful in taking time to share ideas they had developed about their characters. Playing the same person week after week on a series can become deadly dull for the actors and the audience if it's the same every week. The secret to keeping everyone interested is akin to slowly peeling an onion. Each time another layer is exposed, something new is revealed about the character. It's like sharing a surprise gift with the audience—something fresh and special. The actors had given their characters real thought; and from that shared information, springboards for new stories often developed. Sometimes it was only an attitude (like the Spock-McCoy verbal sparring) or a physical trait (such as the Famous Spock Neck Pinch, referred to in scripts as the "FSNP")—but all of it colored and flavored the scripts and the characters.

The crew was talented and ingenious at saving time (and therefore money) and in putting the best images possible on screen. They were proud of the fact that no crew on the lot was faster at moving from one set to another and getting ready to resume shooting. Even the carpenters, plasterers, painters, and greensmen who created the sets took special pride in their association with *Star Trek*. After all, they were the only crew in Hollywood who built a different planet on Stage 10 every other week.

And, of course, we all experienced a certain sense of pleasure in seeing how much Bill Theiss could get away with in his costuming. There were times when his designs drove Jean Messerschmidt, the NBC censor, up the wall. The "Theiss Theory of Titillation" involved taking an essentially nonsexual part of the body (such as the back or the side of the leg) and revealing a lot of it. Added to this was the *promise* that a section of costume would fall or part and reveal all. Those who believed the promise were doomed to disappointment. The costumes never failed—the actresses were glued into them!

We were rewarded personally by the fact that although the Nielsen ratings were not the highest for the show, fans by the thousands were writing every week to tell us they loved *Star Trek*. The mail had begun to arrive after the initial show was aired. At first, it was bundles of mail, then a full bag, and then a *lot* of full mailbags. Although some of the more unique and interesting letters were referred back to the staff for personal response, most of it was handled by a mail-reply service. Curiously, for the first time anyone could remember, the writers of the show received fan mail. This indicated the high level of intelligence of viewers. They actually read the credits, and they realized writers created the scripts and that the actors didn't just get up there and "make it up as they went along." NBC was not impressed. At the end of the first season, they decided to cancel the show.

The fans, however, had other ideas. They just couldn't accept the fact that NBC planned to cancel *Star Trek*. A mail campaign began, a campaign that eventually deluged NBC and its affiliates with protest mail. Since the networks traditionally believed that each letter received expressed the opinion of one hundred others who hadn't taken the time to write, the sheer numbers convinced them *Star Trek* had enough audience to justify keeping it on another season. And when the show apparently was under threat at the end of the second season, the mail began again. That was when NBC made its unprecedented on-air announcement that *Star Trek would* be on for a third season. They renewed it. They also planned to kill it.

Most people know what happened in the third season. The show was given a time slot that at that time was certain death, especially for a series with the audience *Star Trek* attracted—Friday night at 10:00 P.M. The *Trek* loyalists were not just a core of science fiction fans or children, but additionally consisted of high school and college students, young marrieds, business and professional people. Unfortunately, they didn't have Nielsen boxes on their TV sets. (Several years after *Star Trek* went off prime time, a thorough demographics analysis revealed it had had exactly the type of audience NBC most wanted to draw.) Gene Roddenberry, who had returned to the series to actively produce, made another decision to disengage himself from the production and executive-produce from afar. The series became less philosophic and began to follow the formula of "a creature a week." The ratings declined past the point where any massive letter-writing campaign could save it, and *Star Trek* went off prime-time television in 1969.

I had met many friends on *Star Trek*. I had written eight scripts and two stories and successfully completed my first stint as a story editor. The show was well thought of in the industry, so credits on it were stepping stones to other assignments. But it was sad to see a well-loved series die of terminal network neglect.

I left *Star Trek* at the end of its second season to write free-lance again. In that year, I did scripts for *Big Valley*, *Lancer*, and *The High Chaparral*, as well as two stories and a script for *Star Trek*'s third season. The years after that saw me stay busy as a writer, including receiving a nomination for a Writers Guild award; and *Trek* slipped into the world of syndication. About 1971, the *Star Trek* conventions began.

Prior to this, *Trek* had been included in the programming for general science fiction cons. At this time, however, conventions devoted solely to *Star Trek* came into being. I believe they not only prolonged *Star Trek*'s syndication life, but also acquainted new fans with the "complete *Trek*." If one had only seen the series in syndication, one saw severely edited films. Local stations cut as much as five minutes from each segment to accommodate the greater number of commercials they ran. Frequently, it was the teaser that set up the entire plot that was clipped, but each individual station editor could cut the segments any way he thought best. Therefore, the same episode shown in, say, San Francisco, Los Angeles, and San Diego could be cut three entirely different ways. The convention committees were able to rent copies of the episodes from Paramount and run them in their entirety. The famous "blooper reel" also made its appearance and became a staple feature at most conventions.

I made guest appearances at some conventions. (Writers are appreciated more by *Star Trek* fans, a fact we writers cherish; and we could tell stories of how a plot originated and developed while the actors delivered anecdotes of onstage life.) The *Star Trek* Welcommittee was a national organization that served as coordinator and news dispenser for many individual fans and fan clubs and kept them informed of convention activity. I met a lot of fans, some of whom also became friends.

One of the ones who impressed everyone connected with *Star Trek* was young George LaForge. Stricken with a crippling disease early in life and confined to a wheelchair, George attended many *Star Trek* conventions. At one of them, Gene Roddenberry formally made George an Admiral of the Fleet. George's mother once remarked that she firmly believed his interest and enthusiasm for *Star Trek* had given George strength for more years of life than he might have had otherwise. *Star Trek* can be proud of that, as well as of the many young people who have written to say that the show (or specific episodes of it) encouraged them to pursue a productive career, an education, or to change a destructive way of life to a positive one. Sometimes they say it gave them hope or pulled them out of a suicidal depression. Sometimes episodes just made them *think*. *Star Trek* can be proud of that, too.

The conventions during that period of time were big, drawing thousands of people. Some conventions donated their profits to charitable organizations; others simply made money for the promoters. That kind of attraction must have started someone thinking, because in the spring of 1973, Gene Roddenberry and Lou Scheimer, president of Filmation, took me to lunch. They told me NBC was interested in doing an animated version of *Star Trek* for their Saturday morning lineup. Filmation would do the animation; Gene would executive-produce; and I was asked to join the team. Again, I signed on—this time as associate producer and story editor.

Gene was determined that *Star Trek Animated* would not be a kiddie show. It would be true to the original series, and we would tell stories adult in theme and concept despite the Saturday morning audience consisting mostly of children. We hoped to draw older viewers into the time period. Additionally, animation allowed a new dimension impossible to live action filming. Stories could be set in hostile environments (underwater, for instance). More varied and more intricate settings could be drawn than could have been built on stage; and unusual aliens could be utilized without the difficulties of masks, prosthetics, or revealing zippers. Only on the animated show could we have portrayed so well Larry Niven's seven-foot-tall felinoid carnivores, the Kzin. Animation made possible the depiction of regular alien crew members such as navigator Arex, with his three arms and three legs, and Lieutenant M'Ress, another felinoid. It also allowed fans to see for the first (and only) time what a "Vulcan teddy bear," the sehlat, really looked like. Voices were provided by *Trek* regulars Bill Shatner, Leonard Nimoy, DeForest Kelley, George Takei, Jimmy Doohan, Nichelle Nichols, and Majel Barrett with an occasional guest voice like Mark Lenard, who portrayed Sarek.

I attended the World Science Fiction Convention in Toronto that Labor Day weekend with a very small reel of film in my hand and great trepidation in my heart. We had no finished episodes yet, and all I could show was a brief (one minute!) title sequence for the new show. It was scheduled to be shown late on Saturday night (very late, as it turned out), and all day I heard resentful murmurs of how poor an opinion the fans had of an animated version of *Trek*. Dire predictions and scathing comments about *kiddie cartoons* were voiced, and the feeling very definitely was cool when I asked the projectionist to roll the scant piece of film for a large roomful of fans.

And then there was magic. The familiar music swelled out over the speakers, and the *Enterprise* flashed across the screen against a sparkling background of stars. The title and the actors' names came up as the ship quartered the screen. It didn't matter that it was an animation. It didn't matter that for animation purposes the light silver-gray vessel had to be done in dark gray so it wouldn't "wash out" in animation. The faithfulness to the original of that one minute of film won over the fans. The screen went to black as the audience applauded and cheered. Word of mouth began to spread. *Trek*—the *real Trek*—was back, even if it was animated.

We were aided in our insistence on quality material by the fact that the Writers Guild of America was on strike between March and June of that year. Excellent writers who would normally be unavailable to us were not working—and animation was a perfectly legal field for them to write in as it is not covered by the Writers Guild contract. We called in *Star Trek* veterans Sam Peeples, David Gerrold, Margaret Armen, Stephen Kandel, Paul Schneider, and David Harmon to do scripts for that first season. Walter Koenig wrote a script for us. And I wrote "Yesteryear."

NBC was very nervous about "Yesteryear." After all, there I was depicting Saturday morning cartoon characters not only talking about euthanatizing a pet, but actually doing so on screen! "Don't worry," Gene told them. "Trust Dorothy." The resulting film contains what I feel is a moving case for death with dignity for animals suffering with painful diseases or severe injury. To my knowledge, NBC did not receive one letter of protest in regard to the episode's content.

Although the animated series ran for two seasons, I stayed with it only for its first year. Due to the nature of animation and the extraordinary amount of time and money it takes to do one half-hour episode, the first season consisted of only sixteen new shows. The second season was primarily reruns with six new ones mixed in. This short series, like its predecessor, has had a rebirth and extended life cycle in syndication and now has been issued on videocassette and laser disk.

I went back to writing prime-time television for series such as *Streets of San Francisco*, *The Six-Million-Dollar Man*, *Land of the Lost*, and *Police Woman*. In 1976, I was approached to become story editor on the *Fantastic Journey* series. Immediately thereafter I served as story editor on *Logan's Run*. Both these jobs were directly attributable to the reputation I had acquired on *Star Trek*. Script assignments on *The Waltons*, *Dallas*, and other series ushered me toward the end of the seventies.

Along the way there was an attempt to produce another prime-time *Star Trek* series. I don't know why it was not put into production—unless someone at Paramount noted the enormous success of *Star Wars* in 1977 and realized they had their own property on which to base a science fiction adventure movie. We all know where that led—especially since, at this writing, a script is in preparation for the sixth *Star Trek* feature. The movies have been popular and solid money makers, and I believe they served to bring about the announcement of a new *Star Trek* series shortly after *Trek* Classic celebrated its twentieth anniversary.

The new concept called for a different kind of crew, especially the captain, and an expanded vision of the *Star Trek* universe for the eighties and nineties. The loyal fans hated the idea in the beginning. For the first time, mail began to be received that protested the changes that had leaked to the public. Perhaps they felt reassured when they learned that not only would Gene Roddenberry be in charge, but familiar names would again grace the staff—Bob Justman, Bill Theiss, John Dwyer, Charles Washburn, David Gerrold—and D. C. Fontana.

But a bald captain? A ship carrying over a thousand, including families? A fifteen-year-old boy genius—and his physician mother? A woman security chief? An android? A *Klingon* officer on the bridge? I don't wonder the fans had their doubts. It was so different from the beloved *Trek* they supported so faithfully all those years. After all, that was *their Trek*.

Those of us involved in the evolution of *Star Trek: The Next Generation* privately had our doubts, too. The effort was compared to trying to catch lightning in a bottle—difficult to do once. Impossible to do twice. But even though everyone else said it was impossible, the staff, cast, and crew of *Star Trek: The Next Generation* were determined to catch the lightning.

Producing a television series of any kind is an exercise in madness. You might have a lot of fun doing it, but it requires long, grueling hours of work—evenings and weekends included. It demands total dedication of mind and energy. Creative people often are high-strung people, and production of a series can mean tense relationships and personality conflicts. Everyone wants the project to succeed; they just might not agree on the road to take to get to success. However, the day comes when the infant show toddles out to face the audience—and, however it got there, it's either going to fall flat on its face or keep on walking. *Star Trek: The Next Generation* is now in its fourth successful season.

I left the show at the completion of production of the first thirteen episodes, and I'm now concentrating on the writing of motion picture scripts. I'm very proud of the fact that I contributed to all three television versions of *Star Trek*. I'm also proud of the fact that I wrote more *Trek* scripts than anyone else, and most of them have been well received and fondly remembered by the audience.

Just the other day, I stopped in a bookstore to purchase a reference book. When I handed over my credit card, the clerk glanced at it perfunctorily and then more closely.

"You're D. C. Fontana?"

"Uh . . . yes."

"Gosh, I really loved your work on *Star Trek*. . . ."

Me too, friends. Me too.

December, 1990

PREFACE TO *STAR TREK 3*

Some Awards for *Star Trek*—and an Open Letter

Science fiction fans hold an annual World Convention, which is held in a different city every year (though it has been outside the United States only once so far, in London in 1965[1]). The most recent one, in Berkeley, Calif., was the twenty-sixth.

One of the many items on the program is the giving of achievement awards for the best SF novel, novelette, short story, and so on of the preceding year. These awards are statuettes called "Hugos," after the late Hugo Gernsback, who founded the first science fiction magazine *(Amazing Stories)* in 1926.

In recent years, one of the categories has been "Best Dramatic Presentation," but there have seldom been many nominations for this category, and at at least one convention the decision was, "No award."

But since *Star Trek* came along, things have been different. At the 1967 convention in New York, the winner for Best Dramatic Presentation was Gene Roddenberry, not as originator and producer of *Star Trek* (though he was both) but as the author of the episode called "The Menagerie," which appeared during the show's first season.

And in 1968, *all four* of the nominees for Best Dra-

[1]Since 1965, the World Science Fiction Convention has gone truly international, with conventions in Heidelberg, Germany (1970); Toronto, Canada (1973); Melbourne, Australia (1975, 1985); Brighton, England (1979, 1987); and The Hague, thc Netherlands (1990).

matic Presentation were from *Star Trek.* Three of those scripts are adapted in this collection; I have indicated them by asterisks.

What about the fourth? Well, the fourth was the actual Hugo winner, "The City on the Edge of Forever," by Harlan Ellison. It is not in this collection for the simple reason that I had already put it in the preceding book, *Star Trek Two.*[2] And judging by my mail, it was the heavy favorite there, too—which is a separate matter, since SF fandom and *Star Trek* fandom do not seem to overlap very much, certainly by no more than 10 percent.

The Hugo, by the way, was not Mr. Ellison's first award for that script; it was also voted the best single TV script of the year, regardless of category, by the television writers themselves. This award was given, however, not for the script as it ran on *Star Trek*, but for Mr. Ellison's original version, which had to be edited for the show—for one thing, it was too long. I mention this because readers of *Star Trek Two* may remember that in doing the adaptation of the script I tried to preserve what I thought were the best features of both versions. I feared that I might just have spoiled the whole thing in the process, but the readers' letters said not (and Mr. Ellison said not, too).[3]

There is more that ought to be said about the fan mail, partly because it is, I think, interesting in itself, and partly in the hope that the facts might influence those sponsors and network officials who put too much faith in TV rating services. Beginning in 1951, I have written twenty-seven published novels and short-story collections (and including a volume of essays on science fiction). All of these books are still in print but one, and one of them was itself a Hugo

[2]"The City on the Edge of Forever" appears in this omnibus volume.

[3]The award mentioned here is the Writers Guild award for Best Dramatic Episode Teleplay of the 1967–68 season. Harlan Ellison's original script appeared in print in a collection called *Six Science Fiction Plays* (Pocket Books, 1976) edited by Roger Elwood. The aired version of "The City on the Edge of Forever" was awarded not only the Hugo, but a George Méliès Fantasy Award at the International Film Festival in Los Angeles, California, in 1973.

winner.[4] In addition, I've written many short stories and other kinds of material; the first one of these appeared early in 1940, and many have been anthologized—several of them repeatedly—in fifty-eight different collections at last count. In twenty-nine years my work has appeared in eighteen different countries.

I note these figures not to brag—well, not entirely, anyhow—but as background for one astonishing fact: I have received more mail about my two previous *Star Trek* books than I have about *all my other work put together.*

I don't have to count the letters to establish this. All I have to do is look at the comparative thickness of two accordion file folders.

These letters have been arriving at an average rate of two a day ever since January 1967. They make an astonishing collection. The writers range from children under ten, through college undergraduates (a large subgroup), to housewives. Not all the writers give their ages, of course, but enough of them do to make an adequate statistical sample, so I can say with fair confidence that the average age is thirteen. The *median* age, however, is fifteen—that is, there are just as many writers over that age as there are under it.*

Most of them say that they have never read, or seen, any science fiction before *Star Trek,* or if they have, that they hadn't liked it. Some ask me to recommend other SF books, or name some other books I have written. Still others announce a strong urge to write the stuff themselves, sometimes documented by accompanying manuscripts. In short, the evidence is strong that *Star Trek* has created an almost entirely new audience.

For over a year I tried to answer every one of these letters, however briefly, but the inroads this made on my creative writing time became a serious matter and I had to give it up, with regrets. (To give up answering the letters, that is!) However, there is one answer that I found myself making over and over that I would like to repeat here. That is the answer

[4] *A Case of Conscience* (1958).

*This difference shows that those over fifteen are mostly young adults. The top *stated* age is twenty-eight.

I gave to people who sent me *Star Trek* short stories, outlines, suggestions for scripts for the show, or even complete scripts:

"I have nothing to do with any aspect of the *Star Trek* show, including the selection of scripts. All I do is adapt some of the scripts into short stories. Furthermore, it is a firm rule of the producers that anyone even vaguely connected with the show who receives any sort of submission from anybody other than a recognized agent must return it unread, which is what I am doing in your case too. There are sound legal reasons for this that I'm sure you will understand.

"Furthermore, if you want to sell science fiction, your chances would be considerably greater if you tried to write a completely original story for one of the magazines, rather than basing your work on the characters and background of an already famous TV show. Originality is valued more highly in science fiction than in any other branch of literature. Hence, no matter what your affection for the *Star Trek* characters—which I share—you will in the long run be better off creating your own."

I have written those two paragraphs so many times that I could practically set them to music. Another I have written almost as often goes like this:

"I'm sorry, but I have no pictures from *Star Trek* to offer, nor can I send you a sample script—the scripts I have are the show's property, not mine. The place to write for further information is STAR TREK Enterprises, P.O. Box 38429, Hollywood, Calif. 90038.[5] I myself have never been on the set, nor met any of the actors; and I have seen Mr. Roddenberry exactly three times, each time on a convention speaker's platform, along with about 800 other spectators."

Today I would like to add to this: Before you write, try a book called *The Making of Star Trek*, by Stephen E. Whitfield and Gene Roddenberry. It almost surely contains the information you are looking for—and lots of pictures, too.

Finally: Thanks to all of you who suggested what scripts I might include in this book; I kept a tally, and abided by the

[5]This is an old address, however *Star Trek* materials are available from hundreds of sources today. *Star Trek* conventions are held nationwide on a nearly weekly basis and they are a collector's best source for photographs and memorabilia.

voting. Thanks, too, to those who asked that I write an original *Star Trek* novel. Both the studio and Bantam agreed, somewhat to my surprise, that this was a good idea, so it's in the works.

So, to those of you who have written to me and haven't gotten an answer, I hope you will accept this as an apology and an explanation. At the least, I think it answers the most frequently asked questions.

JAMES BLISH
Brooklyn, N.Y.
1968

PREFACE TO *STAR TREK 4*

As I mentioned in the preface to *Star Trek Three*, I get a staggering amount of fan mail from the readers of the *Star Trek* books—far more than I can possibly answer. I'm still getting more and more. I also get letters asking me to adapt particular stories. I keep a running tally of them, to help me make up the table of contents for the next book.

This time, "The Menagerie," an episode by Gene Roddenberry himself, was high on the list. It won the Hugo award for Best Dramatic Presentation of 1967 at the 25th World Science Fiction Convention in New York. A *Star Trek* episode won the year after that, too—Harlan Ellison's "The City on the Edge of Tomorrow," (sic) which appeared in *Star Trek Two*. Now, alas, no new episodes of *Star Trek* are being produced, so it wasn't in competition for the 1970 awards.

Even though *Star Trek* is no longer a network television show, it is as popular as ever. As a syndicated show, it is presently being exhibited on over a hundred stations throughout the United States, and in England, too.

And I'm going on with the books, as almost all your letters have asked me to do. As matters stand now, there will be at least four more of them, all within the next year or so.

JAMES BLISH
Harpsden (Henley)
Oxon, England

PREFACE TO *STAR TREK 5*

After the announcement in *Star Trek 4* that I would be doing more of these books a year, a number of fans wrote to suggest scripts to be included—for which, again, many thanks—and in some cases to ask for a schedule of when the books would appear.

That's a question I just can't answer. I write full-time for my living, and that of assorted relatives and cats, and right at this moment I have ten books in my job jar, counting this one. They all have deadlines attached, two of which I've already missed, thanks to social engagements and all the other small-shot calls of everyday life. I tend to work on two or three books concurrently, but I can't *finish* more than one at a time, and even after thirty years in this business, I find I can't predict how long any given book will take.

All that I can say for sure is that I have contracted to do four *Star Trek* books in the coming year, and that I'll deliver them—but exactly when each successive one will show up is something that is pretty much in the lap of the gods. I have all the scripts here, and I'll write the books, but I'll have to leave it up to you to do the watching for them.

Also, may I remind you once more that the volume of mail I get about these books is completely unprecedented in my experience, and far more than I can cope with. I read all the letters with attention and am happy to have them; but were I to try to answer them, I'd never get any books written at all. Please don't stop writing, but please also accept my apologies for not responding. As Hippocrates said about medicine: ''Art is long, and time is fleeting.''

JAMES BLISH
Treetops
Woodlands Road
Harpsden (Henley)
Oxon., England

PREFACE TO *STAR TREK 6*

The fan mail continues to pour in, listing favorite shows, making helpful suggestions, and occasionally catching errors. (To reply to one persistent complaint, it was not I who made Kirk address McCoy as "Doc" instead of "Bones" in *Spock Must Die!* I know better than that; but there are several editorial hands laid on the manuscript after mine before it reaches the printer.) I am grateful for them all, including the pats on the back.

One recent letter was so extraordinary, however, that I think it deserves passing on. With permission, I quote the important part of it:

> By an interesting coincidence I happen to be Captain [Pierre D.] Kirk. This being the case, the men of my last command built a rather elaborate "organization within an organization" based on the series. My jeep was slightly altered so that its registration numbers appeared as NCC-1701. Our weapons were referred to as phasers and our radio communication procedures were patterned after those of the Star Fleet. Our call signs corresponded to the various sections and personalities of the crew of the *Enterprise*.
>
> My junior officers picked up the names of the more recognizable regular characters in the series. My executive officer made an excellent Spock in that he physically as well as temperamentally resembled the Vulcan. The men wanted him to get an "ear job" but he drew the line at this.
>
> As you can see, the men of the 363rd [Transportation Company, U.S. Army] went to some lengths to identify

with the *Star Trek* series. This was quite an effective means to maintain morale in the present unpleasantness in Indochina.

The series, by the way, is one of the most popular shown in the Republic of Viet Nam—a great favorite of both the American forces and the Viet-Namese people.

Turning to the point of this letter—about eight months ago I was in command of an armed convoy en route from An Khe in the central highlands to Da Nang on the Northern coast. As we proceeded along route QL #1, which the late Bernard Fall referred to as "the Street without Joy," we were engaged by snipers, which usually served as the prelude to an ambush.

Deciding to run through the suspected area, I signaled my gun trucks to cover our cargo vehicles, and then via my jeep radio I announced: "Attention Viet Cong. We are the Federation Starship *Enterprise* and you are now in deep trouble. Phaser banks—charge your phasers and fire on my order."

This comment was directed at my gun trucks to serve to fire them up for what promised to be a tight situation, but to my surprise the radio exploded into a torrent of frantic jabbering in Viet-Namese and moments later the sniping ceased and we continued through without incident.

The only thing I can assume is that the V. C. were monitoring our broadcast transmissions, had seen the show on television and thought that we were in fact the *Enterprise*.

Under the circumstances I can readily understand this reluctance to engage us in a fight. Happily I can report that despite their initial sniper activity no casualties were suffered by the crew of the *Enterprise*.

I had heard of other organizations patterned on the show, including an entire high school in Buffalo, N.Y., where disliked teachers are assigned to the Romulans or the Klingons; but this is the first time I have ever heard of a television series actually saving lives (on both sides, for that matter).

Which only goes to show all over again that it pays to read the fan mail, even though I can't answer it.

James Blish
Harpsden (Henley)
Oxon., England

PREFACE TO *STAR TREK 9*

There is a lot of mail to be caught up on this time, and some news. However, a book is not a newspaper, so some of the news may be contradicted by later events, and certainly stale, by the time you read this.

First of all, there was a *Star Trek* convention in New York last January. The organizer expected perhaps five hundred people. He got nearly four thousand—which makes this gathering, incidentally, the largest science fiction convention in history. It was covered in some depth by *TV Guide* and by several major newspapers.

Gene Roddenberry was there, and told both the audience and the press that he hoped for a return of the series. Though quotations of what he actually said make it clear that this was no more than a wish we all share, my mail shows that it created more solid anticipation than it should have.[6]

If you would like to add your voice to those urging NBC to choose in favor of *Star Trek*, write to: Bettye K. Hoffmann, Manager, NBC Corporate Information, National Broadcasting Company, 30 Rockefeller Plaza, New York, N. Y. 10020. Writing to *me* about it does no good at all; I am only a writer with no influence whatsoever upon NBC except for the known popularity of these books.

[6]The convention in question was held in January 1972. The actual attendance was 3600, the last 600 of whom were apparently admitted free of charge.

I've said several times in the past that though I read all your letters and value them, there are just too many of them for me to answer. There's been no falling off in their numbers since then. Yet not only do I still get requests for personal replies, but many of them enclose American return postage. Even were I able to answer—and I repeat, with apologies, that I just can't—U.S. stamps are just as useless in England as British stamps would be in the States. Save your money!

From ST 6 on, I'm greatly indebted to Muriel Lawrence, who began by doing a staggering amount of typing for me, and went on from there to take so much interest in *Star Trek* itself that her analyses, suggestions, and counsel have made the adaptations much better than they used to be. And just possibly it may be worth adding, for those among you who believe or fear that anybody over thirty can't possibly understand what inspires people under that age, that we were both of us well past it before *Star Trek* had even been conceived. Idealism lasts, if you love it; and these books would have been impossible without it, just like the show itself.

Be of good cheer. We're not alone, no matter how often we may think we are.

JAMES BLISH

PREFACE TO *STAR TREK 10*

You've given me a surprise. I put no prefaces to *Star Trek 7* and *8* simply because I had no news to report, no questions I hadn't answered before, and nothing that I felt needed further explanation. As the mail response to those books came in, I found quite a few of you asking to have the prefaces back, because they contributed an added "personal touch." I didn't have those letters when I wrote the preface to *Star Trek 9*, where in fact I did simply have a few new things to say. Up to that point, I'd regarded my role as nothing but that of a pipeline between the scripts and all the rest of you who can't forget the series. After all, neither the main concept of *Star Trek* nor a single one of its episodes came from me—instead, I was doing the equivalent of transposing some works of other composers to a different key, or at best making a piano version of works originally written for orchestra. I've written other books that were—and are—wholly mine, and where I haven't hesitated to inflict my own feelings on the readers, but in this series it was obviously my duty to the originals to keep myself *out* of them as much as possible.

Well, I really have nothing to report again this time, but I do want to thank you for asking me to go back to peeking around the corner, as it were. I'm still keeping myself out of the *Star Trek* stories as much as I can—in fact, more and more as I've gained practice at it—but it is nice to know that you also like my cameo bits at the front. Vanity is one of the main drives of every author except the greatest, as I've seen not only in myself but in the fifty or more I've talked to and/

or had as friends over more decades than I care to count. For those of you who want more than a peek back, and in answer to another question that pops up often in your letters, there are those other books, a couple of dozen, that you could find rather easily; they're almost all still in print. That's an order, Mr. Spock.

JAMES BLISH
July 1973

PREFACE TO *STAR TREK 11*

One of the most frequent requests I receive in the mail is to be supplied with the address of a local or national *Star Trek* fan club. There are so many of these, and they multiply so rapidly, that I can't keep track of them. However, somebody can, and does: the *Star Trek* Welcommittee.

This describes itself as a central information center to answer fans' questions about *Star Trek*, and to provide new fans with complete information about *Star Trek* and *Star Trek* fandom. It is a nonprofit service organization—*not* a club to join—with 105 volunteer workers in 23 states (plus representatives in 3 other countries) who devote their time and efforts to answering such questions. They add:

"Few fans realize all that is really available in the world of *Star Trek:* over one hundred clubs, about eighty fan magazines, fourteen books, five conventions annually, and many products.* That's where STW comes in—we can give you information on all of them, plus *ST* technology, penpals, trivia, fans in your area, *ST* actors, details of the making of *ST* (live actor or animation), revival efforts, details of the

*These figures are as of Sept. 26, 1973. They must be much larger now; certainly there are more books![7]

[7]There are now more books than ever. Bantam Books published forty-four titles (if one includes the *Star Trek Maps* and both the trade and mass market editions of the *Star Trek Puzzle Manual*). At this writing Pocket Books has published eighty-five books, including two editions of the *Star Trek Compendium*. These figures still don't account for one shots from other publishers, and small press books and magazines.

various episodes . . . Whatever your question on *Star Trek* or *Star Trek* fandom, chances are we've got the answer—or can get it for you. Write us. Please enclose a self-addressed stamped envelope when requesting information.''

The Chairman is Helen Young, and the address is:

Star Trek Welcommittee
8002 Skyline
Houston, Texas 77024
U.S.A.[8]

I know nothing more about the organization than what you see above, but you risk no more than a couple of stamps (or an international reply coupon) by directing your inquiry there. The depth of *my* ignorance of the kind of information they offer is almost bottomless; I just write the books.

Another question that has become more and more frequent is, ''What are you going to do when you run out of *ST* scripts?'' And the most usual suggested answer is that I turn to adapting the animated episodes. Thanks very much, but (as probably many of you already know) that job is now being done by another writer, from another publisher. And that's probably just as well, for I have never seen a single one of the animated episodes; they haven't turned up in England yet.

Well, what *am* I going to do? The problem is still several books in the future and the solution isn't entirely in my hands. A number of letters have asked for another ST novel, like *Spock Must Die!*, and I'd like to try that. It was certainly fun the first time. Also, I've another idea, which I'm keeping a secret until I'm sure both Paramount and Bantam like it. I'm sorry to be so vague, but publishing is like that: a chancy business.

[8]The address listed above was up-to-date as of the publication of the original *Star Trek* collections. The *current* address of the Star Trek Welcommittee is P. O. Box Twelve, Saranac, Michigan, 48881. The present chairman is Shirley S. Maiewski. Although the address has changed, the services remain the same. Fans can also contact Star Trek: The Official Fan Club, P. O. Box 111000, Aurora, Colorado, 80011.

Though I've said more than once that I can't answer individual letters, I still get some claiming to have read all the books and nevertheless requesting such answers. The record for sheer ingenuity thus far goes to a fan who said he realized that I couldn't reply, but I at least could show that I'd read his letter by arranging the next batch of stories in a certain order, or at least dedicating the book to him.

Well, now he knows I did read it. And in case anybody else needs to know how I work: I arrange the stories in what seems to me to be the most effective order, as part of my duty to the readers as a whole. (To take a simple example, there were several scripts in which Captain Kirk was presumed dead. It would be bad editing to include two such stories in the same book.) As for dedications—well, like almost all other authors I know, I dedicate my books only to personal friends old and new, to people who have helped me to be better as a writer, and to others I have learned to love. I mean this as an honor, whether the dedicatees take it as one or not; for a book takes time and care and skill to write, even if it turns out to be bad, so a dedication must be a gift from the heart . . . And when I can't think of someone who might particularly like a book of mine, I don't dedicate it to anyone. I hope that's clear, for I don't know how to explain it any better. I have no more friends and loved relatives than anybody else, and don't hand out dedications at random.

I hope you won't think this ungracious of me. In the meantime, let me repeat yet again: I do read *all* your letters, I'm glad to have them, and hope you'll go right on sending them. That's why I give my address. Your welcome enthusiasm gratifies me more than I can say. But I can't answer them. I have received, quite literally, thousands of them and had I replied to them all—as I tried to do during the first year—I'd have had no time to write any more books!

Finally: I've often been asked what other books I've written besides these. I'm flattered to be asked this, but there are more than thirty others and I've lost track of some of them myself. Those that are still available in English are listed in an annual volume called *Books in Print*, which you can find easily in your local library, and your librarian will help you to run down any that sound interesting. And, of course, I hope you'll like the ones you find.

JAMES BLISH
Treetops
Woodlands Road
Harpsden (Henley)
Oxon., U.K.

PREFACE TO *STAR TREK 12*

It's question time again, so without further ado:

A number of you have asked me how I came to write these adaptations in the first place. The answer is simple and unglamorous: Bantam Books asked me to, out of the blue as it were. I had no connections with *Star Trek* and hadn't even written a script for the show, though several friends of mine had. I had seen the pilot film at a science fiction convention and had watched the show on television, but my only real qualifications were first, that I had written about two dozen other science fiction books, including a Hugo winner; and second, that I had also written television and film scripts.

I took on the job to see if I would like it, for one book. I did; and, furthermore, your letters convinced me that you made up a huge new audience for science fiction, one that had never been reached by the specialized magazines (and more often than not had been put off by the monster movies that had been Hollywood's usual caricature of science fiction). The rest is history—thirteen books of it now. Whew.

How many more will I write? I hope to go on until I've used up all the scripts. There may also be another *ST* novel.

I have very often been asked why my adaptations sometimes differ in some respects from the shows as actually shown. (Apparently many of you tape-record the broadcasts, or own copies of the scripts, or have them by heart.) About one letter in every ten poses this question, a few of them quite indignantly. The answer to that is a little more complex:

1. The scripts that I have to work from are theoretically shooting scripts, or final drafts, and I almost always try to be as faithful to their texts as length permits. Sometimes, however, there seem to have been last-minute changes made that are not reflected in my copies.

2. *Star Trek* people have frequently reported that brand new speeches, bits of business, and so on were occasionally introduced during the actual production and filmed without ever having been written down formally. Obviously, no existing script would show these, although transcripts would catch a few.

3. Television and the printed word are in some respects quite different media, and this shows up especially sharply in science fiction, where more often than not it's necessary to explain the technical or scientific reasons behind what is going on. A television show simply cannot stop the action for detailed explanations; but I can work such explanations into a story version, and I do when I think it's necessary.

4. On one occasion—and one only—the ending of a show just did not seem to me to make much sense when reduced to cold typescript, though it went over well enough on the tube. I worked out a new ending that I thought would stand up better to rereading, and asked Paramount's permission to make the change, which they readily granted. I repeat, I did this only once, and long ago; it's not a privilege I mean to abuse.

Thank you again for your letters; I only wish I could answer them.

JAMES BLISH

FOREWORD TO *STAR TREK 12*

As some of you may know, James Blish died on July 30, 1975.

Star Trek 12 was almost completed. So many letters! We couldn't disappoint everybody by leaving this series unfinished. So Mr. Roddenberry, Bantam Books, and Paramount all very kindly agreed that I could write up the last two scripts—"Shore Leave" and "And the Children Shall Lead"—so we could get this book to all of you who have asked for it, with apologies for the delay.

You may perhaps wonder about the two stories concerning Harry Mudd—"Mudd's Women" and "I, Mudd." Mr. Blish did indeed write these, but he planned to extend them to novel length, with some additional adventures. So in fear and trepidation, I am tackling that too, and it will be along presently.[9]

Please, everybody, neither Mr. Blish nor I ever had the privilege of meeting the actors, much less could we obtain their autographs for you. And now Mr. Blish's own autograph is unobtainable. If you want pictures and other materials, write to Star Trek Enterprises, P.O. Box 38429, Hollywood, California 90038.

In *Star Trek 3*, Mr. Blish explained why he had to return some manuscripts from readers unread. Please note again

[9]This volume, titled *Mudd's Angels* by J. A. Lawrence, was published by Bantam Books first in May, 1978, then later reprinted in February, 1985.

that it is not possible to even look at them, partly for legal reasons; moreover, it is very frustrating to have to send them right back to you. He suggested that writing original science fiction and sending your stories to the magazines would be easier and more rewarding than writing scripts for an existing television program.

Thank you for all your many letters. James enjoyed reading them very much. Many of you ask why he wrote science fiction. He liked to, that's why! (So do I.) Live long and prosper.

Judith A. Lawrence
(Mrs. James Blish)
Athens
February 1977

WHERE NO MAN HAS GONE BEFORE

Writer: Samuel A. Peeples
Director: James Goldstone
Guest stars: Sally Kellerman, Gary Lockwood

Star date 1312.5 was a memorable one for the U.S.S. *Enterprise*. It marked the day of its first venture beyond the frontier of Earth's galaxy. The screen in its Briefing Room was already showing a strange vista—thinning stars etched against a coming night of depthless darkness broken only by the milky spots of phosphorescence which defined the existence of further galaxies millions of light years distant.

Kirk and Spock, a chessboard between them, looked away from the board to fix their eyes on the screen's center. It held, invisibly, an object detected by the *Enterprise* sensors; an object that was impossibly emitting the call letters of a starship known to be missing for two centuries.

Spock said, "Your move, Captain."

"We should be intercepting that thing now," Kirk said, frowning. "The bridge said they'd call . . ."

". . . any minute now." Spock finished the sentence for him. "I'll have you checkmated in your next move, sir."

"Have I ever mentioned that you play irritating chess, Mr. Spock?"

"Irritating? Ah yes, one of your Earth's emotions, I believe."

But Kirk had seen an opening for his bishop. Pouncing on the piece, he moved it. Spock's eyebrows went up.

"Certain that you don't know what irritation is?" Kirk asked.

Spock glowered at the board. "The fact that one of my ancestors was a human female is one, sir, I cannot . . ."

"Terrible, having bad blood like that," Kirk said sympathetically. "In addition to being checkmated, it could be called intolerable."

But the voice of Lieutenant Lee Kelso was speaking from the intercom. "Bridge to Briefing Room. Object now within tractor beam range, Captain."

"No visual contact yet, Lieutenant?"

"No, sir. Can't be a vessel. Reads only about one meter in diameter. Small enough to bring it aboard—if you want to risk it."

Kirk decided to risk it. It was a curious encounter on the edge of illimitable space. Curious—and just possibly informative. "The Transporter Room. Let's go, Mr. Spock," he said.

Scott was waiting for them at the console. "Materializer ready, sir, when you are."

"Bring it aboard," Kirk said.

The familiar hum came. And, with it, the platform's familiar shimmer, finally solidifying into the spherical shape of an old-style starship's recorder. Squatting on tripod legs, it stood about three feet in height, its metal surface seared, pockmarked. But it still identified itself by letters that read "U.S.S. *Valiant*"; and in smaller ones beneath them, "Galactic Survey Cruiser."

Kirk said, "That old-time variety of recorder could be ejected when something threatened its ship."

"In this case more probably destroyed its ship, sir," Spock said. "Look how it's burnt and pitted."

Kirk was approaching the platform when Scott said sharply, "Take care, sir! That thing's radioactive!"

Kirk stopped. "The Q signal, Mr. Scott."

Scott hit a button on his console. It beeped shrilly. As a pulsating glow enveloped the recorder, its antennae moved out and clicked into position.

"It's transmitting," Scott said.

"Interesting," said Spock. "I have a recorder monitoring . . ."

He was interrupted by Kelso's voice from the intercom. "All decks, six minutes to galaxy edge."

The galaxy's edge—where, as far as anyone knew, no man had ever gone before. Of course, there was no neat boundary to the edge of the galaxy; it just gradually thinned out. But in six minutes, the last of its stars and systems would be behind them.

"Yellow alert," Kirk said.

"Captain's orders—yellow alert, all decks," Kelso relayed it.

A moment later, an elevator slid open to emit Lieutenant Commander Gary Mitchell, now senior helmsman since Sulu had become ship's physicist. The promotion had won widespread approval—unnecessary, of course, but helpful; Mitchell was a popular officer. But during a yellow alert his normal chore was monitoring the artificial gravity system as well as the helm.

"Everything's in order, Jim," he said with a grin, as if reading Kirk's mind. "Kelso's voice sounded so nervous, I figured you'd left the bridge. Finish the game, Spock?"

"The Captain plays most illogically," the Science Officer complained. "I expected him to move his castle."

Kirk laughed, making a throat-cutting gesture for Mitchell's benefit. It was clear that the two were old, warm friends. In the bridge all three hurried to their positions. "Relieving you, Mr. Alden," Mitchell told the junior helmsman.

"Screen on," Kirk said. "Lieutenant Kelso, how far now to the galaxy edge?"

"Four minutes to our jumping-off point, sir."

"Alert off, Lieutenant Kelso." He turned to Mitchell. "Neutralize warp, Commander. Hold this position."

As the heavy throb of the ship's powerful engines eased, the bridge elevator opened. First to step out of it was Dr. Elizabeth Dehner, tall, slim, in her mid-twenties, a potentially beautiful woman if she had cared to be one, which she didn't. Other professional personnel followed her—senior physician, Dr. Piper, physicist Sulu, Engineering Chief Scott. Turning to Mitchell, Kirk said, "Address intercraft."

"Intercraft open, sir."

Kirk seized his speaker. "This is the Captain speaking. The object we encountered is a ship's disaster recorder, apparently ejected from the U.S.S. *Valiant* almost two hundred years ago. Mr. Spock is now exploring its memory banks. We hope to learn how the *Valiant* got this far, whether it probed out of the galaxy and what destroyed the vessel. As soon as we have those answers, we'll begin our own probe. All decks stand by." He paused a moment. "All department heads, check in, as per rota."

"Astro Sciences standing by, Captain," Sulu said.

"Engineering divisions ready as always," Scott's voice said cheerfully. Nothing, not even the awesome void now before them, could check his Gaelic self-assurance for long.

"Life Sciences ready, sir," Dr. Piper's voice reported. He was temporary—McCoy was on a special study leave—and rather an elderly man for Starfleet service, but he seemed to be a competent enough physician. "Request permission to bring to the bridge my special assistant, Dr. Dehner."

Elizabeth Dehner had joined the expedition at the Aldebaran colony; Kirk had not yet had much chance to talk to her, and now was not the time. But she might be interested in the abyss now opening before them all. "Granted."

The two appeared within a minute. Kirk said, "Dr. Dehner, you're a psychiatrist, I'm told, assigned to study crew reactions under extreme conditions."

"Quite correct, Captain."

Kirk gestured at the screen. "There's an extreme condition. Millions upon millions of light years of absolutely nothing, except a few molecules of ionized gas."

Spock called from his station. "Getting something from the recorder now, Captain."

But Dr. Elizabeth Dehner had more to say. "Sir, I shall be interested, too, in how the *Valiant*'s crew reacted to disaster."

Kirk eyed her curiously. Mitchell also appraised her, a little smile on his handsome face. "You want to improve the breed, Doctor?"

"I've heard that's more your own specialty, Commander," she said icily.

"Sock!" Mitchell murmured to Kelso. "It's a walking refrigerator, by gum!" She overheard him. A flush crept up and over her composed features.

Coded electronic beeps were sounding from the listening device Spock had applied to the recorder. He looked up as Kirk joined him. "Decoding memory banks," he said. "Captain's log now—reports the *Valiant* encountered a magnetic space storm that swept it back into this direction."

Kirk nodded. "The old impulse engines weren't strong enough to resist a thing like that."

Spock was leaning closer to his listener. "The storm flung it past this point . . . about a half light year out of the galaxy . . . they were thrown clear of the storm . . . then they seem to have headed back into the galaxy." He made a control adjustment. "I'm not getting it all. It sounds as though the ship were struggling with some unknown force."

The beeps grew louder. Interpreting, Spock said, "Confusion now . . . orders and counterorders . . . emergency power drains . . . repeated urgent requests for information from the ship's computer records." He stopped to look up at Kirk again. "They want to know everything there is to know about ESP in human beings!" He shook his head. "Odd, that. Very odd indeed."

"Extrasensory perception!" Kirk was incredulous. But he motioned to Elizabeth Dehner. "Dr. Dehner, what do you know about ESP?"

She went to the computer station. "In tests I've taken, my ESP rated rather high."

Kirk said, "I asked what you *know* about ESP."

She spoke with the pomp of the pendant. "It is a fact some people can sense future events, read the backs of playing cards and so on. But the Esper ability is always quite limited . . ."

Spock broke in. "Severe damage—no, make that severe injuries." His face was strained with listening concentration. "Seven crewmen dead . . . no, make that *six*—one crewman recovered." He looked up at Kirk once more. "It's the casualties that appear to have stimulated the interest in extrasensory perception. Interest is the wrong word. It seems to be driving them frantic."

Bent to the listener again, he suddenly stiffened. "No, this must be garbled. I'm getting something about 'Destruct.' " Frowning, he removed the earphone. "I must have read it incorrectly. It sounded as though the Captain had ordered the destruction of his own ship!"

Kirk turned questioningly to the department heads. "You heard," he said. "Comments?"

Piper shrugged. "The only fact we have for sure is that the *Valiant* was destroyed."

"The fact," Kirk said, "which is the best argument to continue *our* probe. Other vessels will be heading out here some day—and they'll have to know what they'll be facing."

He strode back to his command chair. "Commander Mitchell, ahead, warp-factor one," he said. "We are leaving the galaxy."

As the *Enterprise* moved past the last stars, the bridge alarm light flashed. All eyes turned to the large viewing screen. Against the blackness of deep space a wispy pattern of colors was building up ahead of the ship.

Spock said, "Force field of some kind."

Mitchell said, "Whatever it is, we're coming up on it fast."

Kirk said nothing. Though distance from the phenomenon made certain judgment dangerous, it seemed to be some variety of impalpable barrier. Its colors were growing brighter, extending, interweaving into what appeared to be a flaring, multicolored, massive curtain of pure energy. It might have been a monstrous space version of Earth's Aurora Borealis. And it was sending the bridge alarm siren into shrieks of warning.

He stared at it, hard-jawed. Its colors, radiating from the screen, rippled across the strained faces around him.

The auroral colors were blazing now. Suddenly, with a muted crackle, a circuit shorted.

"Field intensity rising . . ." Spock began.

As he spoke, the bridge lights died. For several seconds Kirk didn't notice their loss, the radiance from the screen had simultaneously become so brilliant that hands were rising instinctively to shield dazzled eyes.

Then a blinding whip of pure white light shot from the screen. At the same moment, an entire instrument panel went out in a shower of sparks and smoke. Another promptly shorted, with an angry crackle. The whole bridge seemed to be hazed in flying sparks. Elizabeth Dehner screamed and fell to the deck, writhing as if in the grip of some uncontrollable energy. Once down, she kept on screaming. The dial needles on Kirk's command board whirled.

"Helmsman!"

But the sparks had invaded Mitchell, too. Jerking like

a marionette pulled by a madman's strings, he staggered to his feet and then went rigid. With a last galvanic convulsion, he toppled to the deck, inert, unconscious. His body rolled as the ship shuddered.

The confusion mounted, shock after shock, now joined by the mindless hysteria of the alarm siren. Kirk and Spock clung to their chairs; most of the others had been jolted out of theirs.

In the end, discipline triumphed while technology failed all around them. Painfully, inch by inch, Kirk dragged himself back to his command control panel. Kelso crawled over to his. Spock, stepping over the crumpled Mitchell, took over his helmsman's station. But the battering continued. Wrenched metal screeched as the *Enterprise* fought to hold itself together.

"Lateral power!" Kirk shouted. *"Crash speed. Take her out of this!"*

Spock and Kelso wrestled with controls. Power returned to the shaking ship. The bridge lights glimmered back on. The alarm siren quieted. But many of the instrument panels were dead with their circuits. Smoke from one still drifted through the bridge.

Kirk got to his feet. "Take damage reports, Mr. Spock."

Spock relayed the order to the ship's crew—and Piper lifted Elizabeth's head. Clinging to his arm, she climbed shakily to her feet. "Something hit me like an electrical charge," she whispered. Piper left her to go to Mitchell.

"Well?" Kirk asked.

"He's alive. Appears to be in shock."

Spock made his damage report. "Our main engines are out, Captain. We're on emergency power cells. Casualties—seven dead."

A moment prolonged itself. Then Kirk said, "Perhaps we are fortunate."

"Commander Mitchell is moving, sir," Spock said.

Kirk dropped to a knee beside his senior helmsman. "Gary! How do you feel?"

Mitchell's arm covered his eyes as though the screen's radiance still dazzled them. "Jim? Weak as a kitten—but better now. I think I'll live."

He moved the arm from his eyes. Their blue had turned into a gleaming metallic silver.

No amount of technical resourcefulness could repair the damage suffered by the crippled *Enterprise*. Moving now on impulse power alone, its dim bridge lights gave everybody the measure of the havoc. Kirk, considering his burned-out engines, remembered the burned recorder ejected by the *Valiant*. Had it survived the onslaught by that merciless radiation? If it had, what happened afterwards?

On his computer station screen, Spock was busily flashing the names of certain members of the ship's personnel. Among them were those of Elizabeth Dehner and Gary Mitchell. Noting them, Kirk gave Spock a sober look. Spock hastily flashed off Elizabeth's name as she approached them.

"Autopsy report, Captain," she said. "Each case showed damage to the body's neural circuits—an area of the brain burned out."

"And you?" Kirk said. "Feeling all right now?"

"Much better. And Commander Mitchell is, too, except for the eyes. We're trying to find a reason for those. And why, of all the people in the crew, only certain ones were affected."

Spock spoke quietly. "I think we have found that answer."

"You said that tests show you have a high degree of extrasensory perception, Doctor," Kirk reminded her. "The others who were affected have it, too. Gary Mitchell has the highest ESP rating of all."

She was clearly puzzled. "I suppose it's conceivable the Esper ability attracted some force." Then she shrugged. "But if you're suggesting there's something dangerous in that . . ."

Spock interrupted. "Before the *Valiant* was destroyed, its Captain was frantically searching for ESP information on his crew members."

"Espers are merely people who have flashes of—well, *insight*," she said.

"Aren't there also those who seem able to see through solid objects?" Spock asked. "Or can cause fires to start spontaneously?"

The question irritated her. "ESP is nothing more than a sort of sixth sense. There's nothing about it that can make a person dangerous!"

"I take it you're speaking of *normal* ESP power, Doctor," Spock said.

"Perhaps you know of another kind!" she flared.

Kirk intervened. "Do you know for sure, Doctor, that there *isn't* another kind?"

An angry disdain sharpened her voice. "I have work to do," she said. "You must excuse me." She left them to move quickly to the elevator.

In Sickbay, Mitchell, propped up against pillows, was sufficiently recovered to use his reading viewer. The eyes that followed its turning pages were as gleamingly silver as quicksilver. Kirk, entering, watched him read for a long moment. Without looking up, Mitchell snapped off the reading viewer to say, "Hello, Jim."

He hadn't even been obliged to turn his head to identify his caller. For some reason this realization troubled Kirk. He sat down in the chair beside the bed. "Hey, you look worried," Mitchell said.

Kirk forced a smile. "I've been worried about you since that girl on Deneb IV."

Mitchell nodded reminiscently. "She was a nova, that one," he said. "But there's nothing to worry about. Except for the eyes, I'm fine." He grinned his charming grin. "They kind of stare back at me when I'm shaving."

"Vision all right?"

"Twenty-twenty."

"Nothing else, Gary?"

Mitchell looked up curiously at Kirk's tone. "Like what, for instance?"

"Do you—feel any different in yourself?"

"In a way, I feel better than I ever felt before in my life." He paused. "It actually seems to have done me some good."

"Oh. How?"

Mitchell gestured toward the reading viewer. "I'm getting a chance to bone up on some of that long-hair stuff you like. Man, I remember you at the Academy! A stack of books with legs! The first thing I heard from upper classmen was 'Watch out for Lieutenant Kirk! In his class you either *think*—or you sink.' "

"Oh, come on," Kirk said. "I wasn't that bad."

"You weren't *what*?" Mitchell laughed. "Do you remember almost washing me out?"

"I sort of leaned on cadets I liked," Kirk said.

"Man, if I hadn't aimed that little blond lab technician at you . . ."

"You *what*?" Kirk stared at him. "You mean you actually *planned* that?"

"You wanted me to *think*, didn't you? So I *thought*. I outlined her whole campaign for her."

Kirk found it hard to return the grin. "Gary, I almost married her!"

"I sort of lean, too, on people I like. She said you came through great."

Kirk, remembering, struggled with his dismay. He repeated, "Gary, I almost *married* her."

"Better be good to me," Mitchell said. He pointed again to the reading viewer. "I'm getting even better ideas from *that*."

Kirk looked at the tape on the viewer. "Spinoza?"

"That's one," Mitchell said. "Once you get into him, he's simple. Childish, almost. By the way, I don't agree with him at all."

"No?" Kirk said. "Go on."

"Go on where? So I'm finally doing some reading." The cold, silver glitter of his eyes made an uncomfortable contrast with the easy warmth of his manner. His white teeth flashed again in the charming grin. "I'm saying I'm fine! When do I go back on duty?"

Kirk hesitated. "I want Dr. Dehner to keep you under observation for a while yet."

Mitchell groaned. "With almost a hundred women on board, you choose *that* one to hang around me!"

"Think of it as a challenge," Kirk said.

The silver eyes fixed on him. "That's not so friendly, James, my friend. Didn't I say you'd better be good to me?"

The mutually gauging moment passed. Finally Mitchell shook his head in mock resignation. Then he pointedly turned back to the reading viewer. Kirk, more troubled than before, didn't speak, either, as he got to his feet and left Sickbay.

Behind him, Mitchell increased the speed of the viewer's turning pages. He read fast—a man locking facts into his mind with an incredible rapidity.

An image of the turning pages was showing on Spock's library computer screen. When Kirk joined him, they were turning so quickly that their movement was blurred. Spock said, "He's reading faster with every passing second. Is that Gary Mitchell? The slowpoke reader we used to know?"

Kirk took three paces away from the screen and returned. "Put a twenty-four hour watch on Sickbay. The fullest possible range of examinations and tests."

The results gave joy to the heart of Piper. "Perfect—perfect," he murmured as he completed his final checkup. "Such perfect health is rare." He tapped the body function panel as though it were hard to credit the veracity of its readings.

"Great in all departments, right?" said Mitchell. Bored, he spoke to Elizabeth. "Too bad psychiatry isn't an exact science, eh, Doctor? Be nice to have a dial that showed the level of a patient's sanity."

"I am aware that you don't particularly like me, Commander," she said. "But since I'm assigned here, can we make the best of it?"

"I've got nothing against you, Doctor."

"Or against the 'walking refrigerator'?"

He was openly startled. "Sorry about that." All his charm went into the three words.

"Women professionals do tend to overcompensate," she said. "Now let's talk about you. How do you feel? Tell me everything."

"Everything about what? Everyone seems worried because I don't have a fever or something." He pointed to the body function panel. "Now old Piper's gone, maybe I can make you happy by changing those readings . . ."

The panel's normal levels altered into abnormal ones. Elizabeth stared at them and back at Mitchell. Slightly shaken himself, he said, "Now the normal readings again . . ."

The levels dropped back to normal.

"How did you do that?" Elizabeth demanded.

"I'm not sure. I—just thought of making it happen. Then it happened." He eyed the panel. "It's not the instruments. It's me. Something I do inside. Hey, watch this . . ."

All the panel's levels plummeted to zero.

Elizabeth grabbed his hand. "Stop it!" she cried. "Stop it now!"

The gauge needles quivered. Rising swiftly up from the "death" indication, they came to rest at normal.

Mitchell stared at them, too. He had paled; and Elizabeth, appalled, said, "For twenty-two seconds you were *dead*! No life function at all!"

Mitchell suddenly realized she was holding his hand. Reddening, she tried to pull hers away but he held it fast. "Hang on a minute, baby. I'm scared. There've been other things, too. Like going halfway through the ship's library in hardly a day. What's happened to me?"

"Do you remember everything you read that quickly?"

He nodded. She took a tape from his bedside table. "On any tape? How about this one? Do you remember page 387?"

"Sure," he said. "It's *The Nightingale Woman* written by Tarbolde on a Canopus planet back in 1996. It begins, 'My love has wings, Slender, feathered things, With grace in upswept curve and tapered tip—' " He stopped, amused. "Funny you should pick that one."

"Why?"

"It's one of the most passionate love poems of the last couple of centuries."

She pulled her hand from his. He watched her do it, smiling. "How do *you* feel?" he asked.

"What? Oh, you mean that electrical blast! It just knocked me down. That's all."

"You're very sure?"

She wasn't sure of anything in the presence of this man with the silver eyes so bright upon her. But somehow, she suspected that she'd given herself away. She was glad when the knock came at the door. It was Kelso. "I was on my coffee break," he told them, "and thought I'd just check up on Gary here."

"It's OK, Lee," Mitchell said. "Come on in."

It was Kelso's first full view of the changed eyes. They

disconcerted him. Mitchell laughed. "Don't let my gorgeous orbs throw you, chum. The lady doctor here likes them, don't you, beautiful Doctor?"

Surprised, Kelso said, "Oh. Yeah. Sure."

"How goes the repair work?"

"The main engines are gone." Kelso's face grew somber. "And they'll stay gone, too, unless we can find some way of re-energizing them."

Mitchell frowned. "You'd better check on the starboard impulse packs. The points have decayed to lead." At Kelso's look of amazement, he said, "I'm not joking, pal. So wipe the shock off your face. You activate those packs—and you'll blow up the whole impulse deck!"

The hardness in his voice got through to Kelso. "Sure," he said hastily. "I'll get on to them right away. I—I just wanted to say I'm glad you're all right."

Mitchell glared angrily after him. "The fool! He's seen those rotten points a hundred times but is too dumb to notice their condition!"

"How did *you* know about them?" Elizabeth asked.

The arrogance was suddenly gone. "I don't know. Maybe the image of what he saw was still in his mind and I—I could see it in his mind." The silver eyes were looking up at her out of a bewildered, very frightened face.

In the Briefing Room, Kelso was pointing to the fused tip in a starboard impulse pack. "It made no sense at all that he'd know about this," he said to Kirk. "But naturally I took a look at the packs anyway. And he's right! This point's burned out just as he described it!"

Each in turn, the Science Department heads examined the piece of metal on the Briefing Room table. Elizabeth opened the door. "Sorry I'm late, Captain. I became so interested in observing Gary—Commander Mitchell—that I . . ."

Spock said, "The subject under discussion is not Commander Mitchell, Doctor. We are concerned with what he is mutating into."

Her face tightened with anger. "I know Vulcans lack human feeling, but to talk like that about a man you've worked next to for years . . ."

"That's enough, Doctor!" Kirk said.

"No, it isn't!" she cried. "I understand you least of all! Gary's told me you've been friends ever since he joined the service! You even asked him to join your first command!"

Kirk kept his voice level. "It is my duty, Doctor, to note the reports, observations, even speculations on any subject which affects the safety of this ship." He nodded toward Spock. "And it is my Science Officer's duty to see that I'm provided with them. Go ahead, Mr. Spock."

Spock addressed Elizabeth. "Has he shown any evidence of unusual powers to you?"

She didn't mention the tricks he'd played with the body function panel. Instead, she chose to say, "He can control certain autonomic reflexes. He reads very fast; and retains more than most of us consider usual."

Kirk spoke sharply. "Repeat what you just told us, Mr. Scott."

"About an hour ago," Scott said, "the bridge controls started going crazy. Levers shifted all by themselves. Buttons were pressed without fingers to press them. Instrument readings wavered from safety points to danger ones."

"And on my monitor screen," Spock said, "I saw the Commander smile each time it happened. He treated the confusion he caused as though this ship and its crew were toys created for his amusement."

"Is that correct, Dr. Dehner?" Kirk queried. "Does he show abilities of that magnitude?"

"I've seen some such indications," she said.

Piper spoke up. "And you didn't think that worth the concern of the Captain?"

"No one's been hurt!" she protested. "Don't any of you understand? A mutated superior man could be a wonderful asset to the race—the forerunner of a new and better kind of human being!"

Kirk, looking at her exalted face, thought, Idealism gone rampant again! My God! He turned with relief to Sulu.

"If you want the mathematics on this, sir," Sulu said, "the Commander's ability is increasing geometrically. It's like owning a penny that doubles every day. In a month you'd be a millionaire."

Spock said, "In less time than that, Mitchell will attain

powers we can neither understand nor cope with. What happens when we're not only useless to him—but actual annoyances?''

Elizabeth, about to speak, decided for silence. Kirk glanced around the table. ''There'll be no discussion of this with the crew. Thank you. That's all.''

The room emptied of everyone but Spock. Kirk turned to see his Science Officer inspecting him, creases of worry in his forehead. He spoke with careful deliberateness. ''We will never reach an Earth base with Mitchell aboard, sir. You heard the mathematics of it. In a month he'll have as much in common with us as we'd have with a ship full of white mice.''

His own anxiety oppressing him, Kirk snapped, ''I need recommendations, Mr. Spock—not vague warnings.''

''Recommendation number one. The planet, Delta-Vega, is only a few light days away from here. It has a lithium-cracking station. If we could adapt some of its power packs to our engines . . .''

''And if we can't, we'll be trapped in orbit there. We haven't the power to blast back out of it.''

''It's the only possible way to get Mitchell off this ship, sir.''

''If you mean strand him there, I won't do it. The station is fully automated. There's not a soul on the whole planet. Even ore ships call there only once every twenty years.''

''Then you have only one other choice,'' Spock said. ''Kill Mitchell while you can.''

''Get out of here!'' Kirk yelled.

Imperturbable, Spock repeated, ''That's your only other choice. Assuming you take it while you still have time.''

Kirk slammed his fist on the table. ''Will you try for one moment to *feel*? We're talking about Gary Mitchell!''

''The Captain of the *Valiant* probably felt as you do, sir. But he waited too long to make his decision. I think we have both guessed that.''

Kirk groped for a chair. Spock turned one around for him. He sank down in it, his face in his hands. After a moment, he removed them. Nodding to Spock, he said, ''Set course for Delta-Vega.''

Mitchell's powers were indeed expanding. And he'd begun to exult in exerting them. Lying in his Sickbay bed, he suddenly decided to snap his fingers. The lights flicked off. He waved a hand—and the lights blazed back. He sat up on the bed's edge, eyeing other portions of his room. He pointed a finger at a table. It soared into the air, teetered insanely on one leg and dropped quietly back into place.

"I am thirsty!" he abruptly announced to nobody.

Across the room, a metal cup on the water dispenser slid under the spigot. Water flowed from it. The filled cup lifted, and floating through the air, settled into Mitchell's outstretched hand. He was sipping from it when Kirk, with Spock and Elizabeth, came in.

"I feel great," Mitchell told them. "So don't bother to inquire into my state of health. Sometimes I think there's nothing I can't do. And some people believe that makes a monster of me, don't they?"

"Are you reading all our thoughts, Gary?" Kirk asked.

"Just in flashes so far—mostly strong thoughts like fear. For instance, you, Jim. You're worried about the safety of this ship."

"What would you do in my place?"

"Just what Mr. Spock is thinking—kill me while you can." Lifting his hand, he pointed a finger at Kirk. A bolt of radiance shot from it—and stunned, Kirk toppled over. Spock leaped at Mitchell—but before he could touch him, he, too, had crashed to the floor.

Elizabeth seized Mitchell's arm. "Stop it, Gary!"

He looked down at Kirk who was struggling back to his feet. "Sure, I know a lot," he said. "I know you're orbiting Delta-Vega, Jim. I can't let you maroon me there. I may not want to leave the ship, not yet. I may want another place. I'm not sure what kind of world I can use."

"Use?" Elizabeth said, shocked by the word's implications.

"Yes, beautiful Doctor. I don't get it all yet, but if I keep on growing, I'll be able to do things a god can do."

Spock sprang up. He struck Mitchell with a force that knocked him from the bed. He started to rise and Kirk landed a hard, fast blow on his jaw. His legs gave way. Groggy, he sprawled, supporting himself by his hands and knees. Breathing heavily, Kirk whirled to Elizabeth. "I want him unconscious for a while."

She took a hypogun from her medical case. Gas hissed as she touched Mitchell's shoulder with it. He subsided, spread-eagled, at their feet.

But another shot was required. This time Piper administered it in the Transporter Room where its technicians were preparing the beam-down to the surface of Delta-Vega. But the torpor induced by the second shot lasted for less time than the unconsciousness caused by the first one. Mitchell came out of it to begin to struggle so fiercely that he pulled himself free of the combined hold of Kirk and Spock. "Fools!" he said thickly. "Soon I will squash you all like crawling insects!"

Piper moved quickly in for a third shot. Mitchell slumped again. Dragging at him, Kirk and Spock rushed him over to the Transporter platform. The other members of the landing party hastened to their positions on it. Mitchell was swaying back onto his feet when Kirk shouted, *"Energize!"*

They materialized before the lithium-cracking plant.

From what could be seen of Delta-Vega's surface, it was a genuinely alien planet. Its soil was dust of a muddy blue color, and the vegetation that sprouted from it was brassy, scaled and knobbed like crocodile skin. Black boulders, their fissures filled with the blue dust, abounded—the only familiar aspect of the landscape. In the distance, a mountain of the black rock shouldered up against the horizon. But Kirk's concerns were other than the weird phenomena of the uninhabited planet. The hypos had finally got to Mitchell. Spock and Communications Officer Alden were supporting him into the building's entrance.

"Can we make it, Lee?" Kirk asked Kelso.

"If we can bypass the fuel bins without blowing ourselves up, we can make it, Captain." Kelso was gazing up at the installation. It was enormous, stretching its huge towers, metallic vats, its strangely coiling ells of complex instrumentation in all directions. Elizabeth stooped to touch a scaly flowerlike growth. It was burning hot.

"And not a soul on this planet but us?" she said.

Kirk answered her briefly. "Just us, Doctor. Lee, let's find the control room of this place."

They couldn't miss it. Doorless, it faced them in the building's central hall. Except for its contour, its size, the steady drone of its automated mechanisms, it bore some resemblance to the *Enterprise* bridge. Its walls were ranked by the same type of instrument panels, the same arrangements of meters, switches and dials. Kelso and Communications Officer Alden went at once to work selecting panels for later beam-up to the *Enterprise* Engineering section. A detail of other crewmen busied themselves with the thick electronic cables that would be needed to interlink the panels left to maintain the cracking planet's operation.

Kirk watched thoughtfully. "Those fuel bins, Lee. They could be detonated from here. A destruct switch?"

Kelso looked up, surprised. "I guess a destruct switch could be wired into this panel, sir."

"Do it," Kirk said.

Kelso stared at him. Then he nodded—and Spock spoke from the doorless entrance. "Mitchell's regained full consciousness, Captain. Perhaps you'd better come."

He had been confined in a maximum security room, one made escape-proof not by bars and bolts but by the invisible fence of a force field. He was pacing the room like a caged tiger. Outside, Piper, Elizabeth beside him, held his hypogun at the ready. Near them, an *Enterprise* security guard, phaser in hand, kept his eyes on the furious tiger.

"I want only one medical officer here at any one time," Kirk said. "The other will monitor him on the dispensary screen."

"I'd like my turn now," Elizabeth said. "I want to try and talk to him."

Piper nodded, handing her the hypogun. As he left, Kirk, pressing a button, tested the force field. It crackled sharply. Mitchell stopped pacing. Eyeing Kirk across the barrier, he said, "My friend, James Kirk. Remember the rodent things on Dimorus, the poisoned darts they threw? I took one meant for you . . ."

"And almost died. I remember," Kirk said.

"Then why be afraid of me now, Jim?"

"Gary, you have called us insects to be squashed if we got in your way."

"I was drugged then!"

"And before that, you said you'd kill a mutant like yourself were you in my place."

"Kill me then! Spock is right! And you're a fool not to do it!"

Elizabeth cried, "Gary, you don't mean that!"

He spoke directly to her. "In time, beautiful Doctor, you will understand, in time. Humans cannot survive if a race of true Espers like me is born. That's what Spock knows—and what that fool there," he nodded toward Kirk, "is too sentimental to know." He moved toward the force field sealing off his security room. As he neared it, there was a screech of high voltage. A spray of sparks flew up, scattered and died.

Spock and the guard had drawn their phasers. But Mitchell continued to push against the force field. For a moment his whole body glowed red. But through the brightness Kirk saw that the old human blueness of his eyes had replaced the silver. Then the force field flung him away. He staggered backward and fell on the room's bunk. He sank down on it, his face in his hands, groaning.

Kirk said, "His eyes returned to normal."

"Fighting the force field drained his strength." Spock studied the swaying figure on the bunk. "He could be handled now, Captain."

"Handled," Mitchell said. He looked up. His eyes were shining with so bright a silver that the room seemed lit with silver. "I grow stronger with every passing second. I thought you knew that, Spock."

Kirk snapped his communicator open. "Put full energy on this force field, Lieutenant Kelso."

There was a louder hum as power poured into the force field. A visible radiance began to gather around it.

Mitchell rose from the bunk. He rose from it to smile at Kirk from the other side of his barricade.

But if he remained Kirk's rankling thorn of anxiety, there was good news from the *Enterprise*. In its Engine Room a charred control panel had been successfully replaced by one beamed up from the cracking station. More new panels were required. So Kelso was still busy with the heavy cables he was using for the connecting link among the station's remaining panels.

Over his communicator, Scott said, "It fits like a glove, Captain. Did Mr. Spock get that phaser rifle we beamed down?"

At Kirk's surprised look, Spock moved the heavy weapon from the wall he'd laid it against. Kirk shook his head in a wordless sadness before he answered Scott. "Affirmative, Scotty. Landing party out."

"Mitchell tried to break through the force field again," Spock said tonelessly. "And his eyes changed faster. Nor did he show any signs of weakness this time."

"Dr. Dehner feels he isn't that dangerous," Kirk said. "What makes you right and a trained psychiatrist wrong?"

"Because she *feels*," Spock said. "Her feelings for Mitchell weaken the accuracy of her judgment. Mine tell me we'll be lucky if we can repair the ship and get away from him before he becomes very dangerous indeed."

"Captain!" Kelso called. Wearily Kirk crossed over to him. He looked at the sheathed switch Kelso had attached to a panel. It had been painted red. "Direct to the power bins," Kelso said. "From here a man could blow up the whole valley, Captain."

"Lee," Kirk said. "Lee, if Mitchell gets out—at your discretion, positioned here, you'll be the last chance. Lee, if he gets out—I want you to hit that switch."

The full meaning of Kirk's words struck Kelso dumb. If he hit the red switch, he'd go where the valley went. He looked at the switch and back into Kirk's eyes. After a moment, he managed a very sober, "Yes, sir."

In other circumstances, regeneration of the *Enterprise* engines would have been cause for rejoicing. The ship was ready for takeoff. The working detail of crewmen had been transported back up to it. But Mitchell's condition had worsened.

Now his skin tones had altered. What had once been ruddy flesh had a silvery cast, suggesting solid metal. He stood, arms folded across his chest, looking at them across the force field. If he noticed Spock's phaser rifle, he gave no sign of it.

"He's been like this for hours," Elizabeth said.

A silver man. "Have Dr. Piper meet us in the control room with Kelso," Kirk said. "We'll all beam up to the ship together."

"That's risky, sir," Spock said. "If we take our eyes off him . . ."

"Kelso will be on the destruct switch until the last minute." Kirk gestured to the silent figure behind the force field. "I think he knows that."

Elizabeth said, "I'm staying with him."

Kirk spoke flatly. "You'll leave with the ship, Doctor."

"I can't," she said. "I'm sorry."

Kirk's communicator beeped. "Kirk here," he said.

"The station seems to be running fine, sir," Kelso said. "Even without its quota of panels. The cables have done the job. Fission chamber three checks."

Behind him one of the cables stirred. It began to crawl toward him, snakelike. Slithering, silent, it lifted from the floor, twisting itself into loops. Abruptly, but still silently, a loop rose high into the air—and dropped over Kelso's head. A noose, flexible, inexorable, it tightened around his neck. Helplessly, Kelso tore at it, choking. Then he fell to the floor.

Mitchell smiled into Kirk's eyes. There was something ghastly in the movement of his silver lips. But Elizabeth saw only the smile.

"You see?" she cried to Kirk. *"He's not evil!"*

"You will leave with the ship, Doctor," Kirk repeated.

Mitchell spoke. "You should have killed me when you could, James. Compassion and command are an idiot's mixture."

Kirk grabbed Spock's phaser rifle. Mitchell's hand made a gesture that included them both. Flame blazed from it. As they collapsed, Mitchell walked to the force field. He brushed it as one brushes aside a flimsy curtain. A single spark flared briefly. He passed through the portal to stand face to face with Elizabeth. Taking her hand, he led her back into his room and over to a wall mirror. "Look at yourself, beautiful Doctor," he said.

She screamed. Then she flung her hands over her face to shut out the sight of her silver eyes.

Kirk wavered slowly back into consciousness. Pale, drained-looking, Piper was stooping over him. "Whatever it was, Captain, it affected me, too. Swallow this capsule." He paused. "Kelso's dead. Strangled. At least Spock is still alive."

"Dr. Dehner?" Kirk whispered.

"She's gone with Mitchell. That capsule will restore your strength in a minute or so. I must insert one in Spock's mouth. He's still unconscious and . . ."

"What direction did they take?" Kirk asked.

"Toward the rock mountain."

Kirk struggled to his knees. He reached for the phaser rifle he had dropped. As he checked it, he said, "As soon as Mr. Spock recovers, you will both immediately transport up to the *Enterprise.*"

Piper looked up from his work of massaging the capsule down Spock's throat. "Captain, you're not—" he began.

"Where," Kirk continued inflexibly, "if you have not received a signal from me in twelve hours, you will proceed at maximum warp to the nearest Earth base. You will inform it that this entire planet is to be subjected to a lethal concentration of neutron radiation."

The capsule was working. He found he was able to stand. "No protest on this, Doctor Piper! It's an order!"

He slung the rifle over his shoulder and walked out of the cracking station.

The approach to the rock mountain's craggy escarpments made harsh going for Mitchell and Elizabeth. The sharp black stones and slithery blue sand which composed the terrain of Delta-Vega had not been created for pleasant afternoon strolls. As a sudden breeze blew sand into her face, Elizabeth panted, "It—it would take a miracle to survive here."

"Sit down," Mitchell said. "I'll make one."

He made a gesture. The blue sand around them darkened into the rich brown of loam. It shifted to give way to an upswing of bubbling water. The scaly, brass-colored vegetation turned green. From a patch of it, the leafy trunk of a peach tree rose up. Fruit hung from its boughs. Mitchell bent to drink from the spring.

When she had quenched her thirst, he said, "You'll share this power, too. As you develop, you'll feel like me, able to make a world into anything you want it to be. Soon we will fully control our bodies. We'll never grow old. You're woman enough now to like that. Always young, as beautiful as you desire to be . . ."

He suddenly stiffened.

"What's wrong?" she asked anxiously.

"A visitor," he said. "A very foolish visitor."

"Who is it?"

"You'll enjoy playing God, Elizabeth."

A splinter of unnameable fear jabbed her. He laughed at the look on her face. "Blasphemy scares you?" He flung his arms wide, the silver hands outspread. "Let there be food! Give me Kaferian apples, world, my world!"

A squat, odd-shaped tree appeared, heavy with huge red fruit. Mitchell, detaching an apple from it, bit into it, its rich yellow juice running down his silver chin. "Whenever we'd stop at that planet, I'd stock up on these," he said. "What is *your* wish? Just speak it."

Her answer came in the form of a slow, thoughtful question. "How much have I changed, Gary?"

But he wasn't listening. He had turned to concentrate his gaze on the still unseen figure of Kirk clambering over boulders, the heavy weight of the phaser rifle on his shoulder.

Mitchell spoke. "Can you hear me, James? You can't see me, I know. So let me comfort you. You're on the right path. You'll see me soon. Soon enough."

Kirk stopped. He had heard the words. How, he didn't know. He started to unlimber the rifle when he realized that Mitchell wasn't there. He resumed climbing.

"It's Captain Kirk," Elizabeth said as though speaking to herself. "In my mind I can see him."

"Go and meet him," Mitchell said. "Talk to him. Now that you're changing, you've got to discover how unimportant they are."

Hesitating, she stepped forward. Kirk sensed the presence on the shallow cliff above him, grabbed his rifle—and recognized the girl. Climbing up to her, he saw the hard silver of her eyes for the first time.

"Yes," she said. "It just took a little longer for it to happen to me."

Kirk lowered the rifle. "You've got to help me stop it, Dr. Dehner. Before it goes too far with you, too."

"I've already gone far enough to—to realize what he's doing is right. It's right for us."

"And for humans?" Kirk said. "You're still partly human—or you wouldn't be with him."

She looked away from him. Without certainty, she said, "Earth is—really unimportant. Before long, we'll be where it would take millions of years of learning for humans to reach."

"How will *he* learn if he skips over those millions of years?" Kirk said. "You don't know. You can't know. *He won't have lived through them!*"

"*Please,*" she said. "Go back while you can!"

"You heard him joke about compassion. Above all a god needs compassion, Elizabeth."

"Go back!" she shouted.

"You were a psychiatrist," Kirk said. "You know the savage we all keep buried—the primitive self we dare not expose. But he'll dare to expose his! In God's name, Doctor, make your prognosis!"

Her face was tortured. Then she whispered, "He's coming!"

But he was already here. He ignored Kirk to speak to the girl. "I'm disappointed in you, Elizabeth. You still have doubts."

Whipping up his rifle, Kirk fired it at him. A fiery beam lanced out of it and struck him full in the chest. Its redness faded. Mitchell raised a finger. The rifle tore from Kirk's grasp to clatter on the stones beside him.

Time passed. Then Mitchell broke the silence. "I have been meditating," he said. "I have been reflecting upon the death of an old friend. His death and his honorable burial."

Kirk turned. Behind him, brown earth was scooping itself out into the neat shape of a grave. Elizabeth stared at Mitchell in unbelief. Trembling, she looked back at the grave. At its head stood a tidy, white military cross bearing the inscription "James R. Kirk. C-1277.1 to 1313.7."

A grinding sound came from overhead. Kirk looked

up. A huge, rectangular rock slab was detaching itself from the cliff wall. It wobbled for a moment. Then it teetered into position directly above the grave.

Elizabeth screamed. "No, Gary, no!"

"You still like what you're seeing?" Kirk asked her.

"Time to pray, Captain," Mitchell said.

"To you?" Kirk said. "Not to both of you?"

The silver finger pointed at him. He was struck to his knees by the flash that darted from it. He remained on his knees, his eyes on the girl. "This is a jealous god, Elizabeth. In the end there will be one of you."

"Your last chance, Kirk!"

Elizabeth tensed. Sparks suddenly crackled between her and Mitchell. He reeled, recovered—and extended a silver hand toward her. A storm of sparks broke from it. She staggered, moaning with pain. But the energy drain had told on Mitchell. For a single second his eyes went blue. Then they were impervious silver once more. And once more the silver hand was extended toward the girl. A fiery mantle of sparks engulfed her. She crumpled. "Hurry," she whispered to Kirk. "There's—so little time."

The second outlay of energy had been expensive. Realizing his weakness, Mitchell turned to run. Kirk hurled himself forward and made a grab for his legs. A booted foot caught him in the chest. Then Mitchell seized a jagged rock. Kirk dodged the blow and closed with him.

"Gary, listen! For this moment you are human again . . ."

"It's gone now!" On a new surge of power, Mitchell smashed Kirk down with a silver fist.

He hit the ground hard, almost falling into the open grave. Then Mitchell was on him. In dizzy changes his face turned from silver to flesh. The silver won. Wrestling with him, Kirk could feel his whole body transforming itself into metal. He wrenched himself free, and had reached the rifle when Mitchell ripped an edge section of rock from the outcropping above them. It brushed his shoulder at the same moment he fired the rifle.

The beam missed Mitchell. But it struck the soft blue sand beneath the overhanging slab of rock that was to be his tombstone. It toppled and fell toward the grave.

"Gary!" Kirk shouted. "Look out!"

It was too late. Stumbling backward, Mitchell tripped. The rock slab hit him, tumbling him into the grave. A cloud of blue dust rose. When it settled, it had filled the letters etched into the broken white military cross.

Kirk kneed himself over to Elizabeth. The silver had gone from her eyes. "It's—all over, isn't it?" The voice was so weak that he had to stoop to hear it. Her head lolled over Kirk's arm. She was dead.

He got to his feet, a lonely stranger on a strange planet in a strange galaxy. But his communicator was familiar.

He spoke into it, his voice very tired. "Kirk to *Enterprise*. Come in, *Enterprise*."

It was almost as strange to be back in his command chair. He'd been a far way. The magnetic space storm—Delta-Vega—Mitchell's death—Kelso's—were they all events that had occurred in a dream? The new control panels around him were blinking as steadily as though they were the old ones. It was good to see Spock just standing there beside him.

"Ready to leave orbit, sir," Scott called from Kelso's old position.

"Engage," Kirk said. He switched on his Captain's log. "Add to official casualties, Dr. Elizabeth Dehner. Be it noted that she gave her life in performance of her duty. And Lieutenant Commander Gary Mitchell. The same notation."

He looked at Spock. "After all, he didn't ask for what happened to him. I want his service record to end that way."

Spock's Mephisto features were tranquil. "I felt for him, too, sir, strange to say."

Kirk eyed him speculatively. "Watch yourself, Mr. Spock," he said. "Your compassion is showing."

THE CORBOMITE MANEUVER

Writer: Jerry Sohl
Director: Joseph Sargent
Guest stars: Anthony Call, Clint Howard

Spock was making a map of the galaxy's planet systems, a long and tedious job. However, six of the nine squares of his screen were finally lighted on photographic charts of the star fields already explored by the *Enterprise*. His camera clicked again, and the seventh square broke into lighted life, picturing the quadrant of starry space through which the Starship was moving. Observant, Bailey, the newly appointed navigator, young, unseasoned, a novice in Starfleet service, eyed the square with clumsily concealed impatience.

"Three days of this, Mr. Spock. Other ships must have made star maps of *some* of this."

Spock spoke gently. "Negative, Lieutenant. We're the first to reach this far. We—"

He was interrupted by the siren shriek of the alarm; and Bailey, removing his eyes from Spock's screen, stared at the red light flashing on his own console. Leaning past him, Sulu called, "Sir! Contact with an object. It's moving toward us."

Spock rose, and, striding swiftly to the empty command chair, said, "Deflectors! Full intensity."

Half out of his chair, Bailey shouted, "And it's on *collision* course with us!"

"Evasive maneuvers, Mr. Sulu," Spock said mildly.

Working levers, Sulu took a reading of the results. "Object's changing direction with us, sir. Keeps on coming at us."

Uhura's rich contralto spoke. "Getting no signal from it, sir."

"And it's still on collision course with us!"

The excitement in Bailey's voice contrasted only too vividly with the controlled, efficient composure of those of his bridge mates. Instead of registering the difference—and using it for improved self-discipline—he raised his voice to a near scream. *"And our deflectors aren't stopping it!"*

Spock said, "Sound general alarm. All hands prepare—"

Sulu broke in. "It's slowing down, sir."

The calm Vulcan voice said, "Countermand general alarm. All engines full stop."

"Visual contact!"

It was Bailey's cry undertoned by a triumph mingled with a now open arrogance.

As the *Enterprise* slowed to a stop, star movement halted with it. And on the bridge screen appeared a pinpoint of light that wasn't a star—an image which so swiftly expanded that the bridge's watchful eyes could identify it as a crystallike cube, rotating, luminescent and resuming its speed toward them. Then suddenly, it too stopped, hanging in space as it slowly revolved on its unseen axis, an eerie montage of unearthly colors changing, merging and dividing as the thing turned its faces toward them.

Spock looked away from it. "Ahead slow. Steer a course around it, Mr. Sulu."

But the moment they began to move, the cube moved with them.

"It's blocking the way!" Bailey roared. "Deliberately blocking it!"

Spock turned tranquil eyes on him.

"Quite unnecessary to raise your voice, Mr. Bailey. Unlike us, the object appears to lack hearing." Then addressing Sulu, he added, "Engines full stop. Sound the alert."

The stridency of the alarm shrilled again. Smacking buttons, Sulu said, "Bridge to all decks. Condition alert. Captain Kirk to the bridge!"

Kirk's well-muscled body was in shorts. McCoy had him lying on his back, arms pulling, legs pushing at an exercise device suspended from Sickbay's ceiling—a posture that hid the red light flashing over the door. McCoy noticed it; but absorbed in panel reports of Kirk's body functions, he decided not to mention it. It was his nightmare—persuading Kirk to submit to a medical exam. Yet monitoring the health of the elusive flea who was Captain of the *Enterprise* was his prime professional responsibility. Now was his rare, rare chance. And he didn't intend to lose it to the vagaries of electric lights—red, blue, yellow or any other color of the spectrum.

Completing his readings, he switched off the exercise machine and said, "Winded, Jim?"

Kirk slipped off the table. "If I were, you're the last person I'd tell—" and at the instant of speaking, registered the on-off flashing of the red light over the door. Racing to a panel, he switched it on and, pushing a knob, spoke into the intercom.

"Kirk here. What goes on?"

He learned.

The small screen over the intercom showed Spock's face, its moving lips. "Take a look at this, Captain."

Spock dissolved into a view of the slowly rotating cube. "Whatever it is," Spock's voice offered, "it's blocking our way. When we move, it moves too, sir."

Snapping the screen dark, Kirk grabbed up a sweatshirt, a towel; and shouldering head first into the sweatshirt, emerged from it to whirl on McCoy.

"You could see that light from where you were! Why didn't you say so?"

"At least I finished a physical on you, didn't I? What am I, a doctor . . ."

But Kirk was gone.

Gathering up his instruments, McCoy completed his sentence to his own infinite reassurance and satisfaction. ". . . or a trolley car conductor? If I jumped every time a light blinked around here, I'd end up in a straightjacket."

Outside, Kirk, accelerating his pace, passed racing crewmen as Sulu's voice came over the loudspeaker.

"All decks alert. All hands to general quarters."

Kirk, tightening the towel around his neck, headed for

the turbo-car elevator at the end of the corridor. The doors whooshed closed behind him and he said, "Bridge."

Relays whirred like crickets at the verbal instruction; and on the control panel, lights blinked as the car began its vertical ascent, the elevator hum growing with its increasing speed. But Kirk, chafing at the delay, pushed a button on the intercom panel.

"Kirk to bridge."

"Spock here, sir."

"Any changes?"

"Negative. Whatever it is, it seems to just want to hold us here."

"I'll stop to change, then." And shutting off the intercom, spoke to the turbo-car. "Captain's quarters."

Smoothly, the car braked; and when it resumed movement just as smoothly, altered its direction from vertical to horizontal.

In the bridge, Spock was standing beside Bailey, whose eyes seemed hypnotized by the indefinably sinister cube shown on the screen. Jerking the young navigator out of his trance, he said, "All decks have reported, Mr. Bailey."

Flushing, Bailey started.

"Yes, sir," he said, and rousing, turned off the still flashing red light on his console.

Spock, at his Vulcan coolest, said, "When the Captain arrives, he'll expect a report on—"

"—on the cube's range and position. I'll have them by then, sir."

As Spock gravely nodded, Bailey added, "Raising my voice back here, sir, didn't mean I was scared or couldn't do my job. It just means that I happen to have a human thing called an adrenalin gland."

Spock paused, startled by the aggression of this backhanded reference to his alien origin. Then yet more solemn-faced, he nodded again at Bailey.

"Sounds most inconvenient," he said. "Have you ever thought of having it removed?"

He left Bailey for the command chair; and the red-faced navigator, aware of a poorly muffled guffaw from Sulu's station beside him, flushed still redder.

"Very funny," he sneered.

The choking Sulu recovered himself long enough to say breathlessly, "Kid . . . you try to cross brains with Spock—and he'll . . . cut you into pieces too small to find."

"If I were the Captain—"

"He's even rougher. But I'm warning you, brother. It comes as more of a shock because he's such a hell of a leader."

The very rough Captain had opened his quarters door to see his yeoman laying out one of his uniforms. Unwinding the towel from his neck, he threw it at a chair and said, "Thank you, Yeoman."

Apparently unruffled by his tone, Janice Rand said, "Yes, sir," and opening the door, closed it behind her as Kirk, yanking off his sweatshirt, shoved a switch on a panel under a small screen. "Captain to bridge."

The screen lighted to the sight of his Science Officer's face who said, "Spock here, sir."

"Any signs of life?"

"Negative, sir."

"Have you tried all hailing frequencies?"

"Affirmative. No answer from the cube."

Kirk pulled his uniform shirt into unwrinkled, precise position. "Have the department heads meet me on the bridge."

"Already standing by, Captain."

The cube was still revolving on its hypothetical axis, its alternating, unnameable colors reflected from the screen onto the human faces nearest it, making them unfamiliar. Tossing it a look, Kirk said, "Navigation?"

"Distance to us," Bailey said, "fifteen hundred meters, position constant."

"Helm?"

"Sir, each of its edges measures one hundred seven meters. Mass, a little under eleven thousand tons."

"Communications?"

"Hailing frequencies still open, sir," Uhura said. "No message."

"Mr. Spock?"

"Sensor shows it is solid, sir; but its principal substances are unknown to us."

"Engineering?"

"Motive power . . ." Scott shrugged. "A solid. Beats me what makes it go, sir."

Kirk smiled at him. "I'll buy speculation, Scotty."

"And I'd sell if I had any. How a solid cube can sense us coming, block us, move when we move . . . ah dinna ken, sir, as my people used to say. That's my report."

Kirk looked at McCoy. "Life Sciences?"

"Same report, Jim. No chance of life existing inside a solid cube; but there must be some kind of external intelligence somewhere directing it."

"Thank you, Bones."

Bailey exploded.

"We going to just let it hold us here, sir? We've got phaser weapons. I vote we blast it."

Kirk turned to look at him. When he spoke, his voice was dry as withered leaves. "I'll keep that in mind, Mr. Bailey, when this becomes a democracy."

He left his chair to move to the elevator, followed by other bridge people. Bailey, except for Sulu, was left standing alone beside his console.

"See what I mean?" Sulu said. "Sit down."

The enigmatic cube had held the Starship at bay for eighteen hours. Its origin, like its purpose, was still unknown to members of the exhausted crew, the eyes of Kirk, his officers and department heads bloodshot from study of star maps that consistently refused to show any habitable planet close enough to account for the mysterious object. In the Briefing Room, shoving aside the litter of graphs and computations on the table, he threw down his stylus and leaned back in his chair for a long stretch. Around him, others stifled yawns.

"Anything further, gentlemen?" Kirk said.

Spock spoke. "I believe it adds up to one of two possibilities. First, a space buoy of some kind—second, 'flypaper,' sir."

The word so puzzled the others that it roused them. But Kirk, nodding at Spock, said, "And you don't recommend sticking around."

"Negative, Captain. It would make us look too weak."

Uhura voiced the general perplexity. "I thought I'd learned English by now."

Smiling, Kirk said, "Flypaper—a Nineteenth Century device—a paper Earth used to use covered with a sticky substance to trap insects which flew into it."

Scholarly, solemn, Spock said, "More your Twentieth Century, I believe, sir."

"Undoubtedly so, Mr. Spock," Kirk said.

"Somebody out there doesn't like us," Sulu said.

Kirk got to his feet, stretched again and sat down. "It's time for action, gentlemen. Mr. Bailey . . ."

The headlong navigator swung a lever on his table panel. "Briefing Room to phaser gun crews—"

"Countermand!" Kirk snapped, hitting a switch on his own panel. But his voice was unusually gentle as he addressed the now quaking Bailey. "Do you mind if *I* select the kind of action to be taken by my ship, Mr. Bailey?"

"I'm sorry, sir. I thought you meant—"

"Are you explaining, Mr. Bailey? When I want an explanation, I shall so inform you."

The navigator wilted. Kirk went on. "Now, as I started to say, Mr. Bailey, plot us a spiral course away from the cube. Mr. Sulu, alert the Engine Room. We'll try pulling away from it."

Kirk rose and, at the Briefing Room door, waited until Sulu had pushed a panel button, saying, "Helmsman to Engine Room. Stand by, all decks alert. We're going to try pulling away."

In the bridge, a stricken Bailey punched in the spiral course and, without turning, said, "Course plotted and laid in, Captain."

From his chair, Kirk glanced around at his busy bridge crew. Then looking at the screened cube, said, "Engage, Mr. Sulu. Quarter speed."

Engine hum deepened; and as the *Enterprise* veered in its new curving course, stars slid sideways—but the cube kept exact pace with the ship.

"Still blocking us, sir," Sulu said.

"Then let's see if it'll give way. Ahead, half speed."

"Point five-o, sir," Sulu said.

With the increased speed, the cube loomed larger on the screen, rotating faster and its colors beginning to glow.

Suddenly, warning lights burst into crimson on all control panels of the bridge, the cube now whirling dizzily, its colors growing in intensity.

Spock looked up from his mounded viewer. "Radiation, sir. From the short end of the spectrum. And it's becoming stronger."

Kirk ordered the ship to a full stop. The stars came to a standstill. However, the cube, despite the *Enterprise*'s stationary position, maintained its approach to the vessel, its colors flaring into violence.

"It's still coming at us!" Bailey said. "Range ninety meters, Captain."

His eyes on the screen, Kirk heard Spock say, "Radiation increasing, sir."

"Power astern, half speed, Mr. Sulu."

"Half speed, sir."

The engines' hum returned as they began to move the ship backward, the maneuver, instead of discouraging the cube's pursuit, inciting it to higher speed.

"Radiation nearing tolerance level, sir," Spock reported.

Revolving into blur now, the cube's brilliant colors were flooding the bridge with their reflections, distorting faces with gaunt shadows and inhuman skin shades.

"Still coming," Bailey said. "Gaining on us."

Kirk said, "Engines astern, full speed."

"Full speed, sir."

Stars sped away as the ship accelerated rearward, though the cube merely grew in size on the screen, its fiery glow still brighter as it twisted wildly on its axis.

"Range, seventy-one meters now, sir," Bailey said.

Kirk addressed Sulu. "Helm, give us Warp power."

Over the surge of Warp power added to the engine hum, Sulu said, "Warp One, sir."

Spock's voice was toneless. "Radiation at the tolerance level, Captain."

"Warp Two, sir," Sulu said.

The deadly, spinning top still clung to them; and looking at his Captain, Sulu said, "Speed is now Warp Three, sir."

"Radiation is passing tolerance level, Captain," Spock said. "Entering lethal zone."

"Range fifty meters and still closing!"

"Phaser crews stand ready," Kirk said.

"Phaser crews report ready, sir," Bailey said.

The stars were flying past in reversed movement as the cube, a blaze of viciously vivid colors, was closing the gap between it and the ship.

"Lock phasers on target," Kirk said.

Spock moved from his station to the command chair. "Radiation still growing. We can take only a few seconds more of it, sir."

Nearest the screen, they both had to shield their eyes from their pursuer's fierce glare.

"Phasers locked on target, sir," Bailey said. "Point blank range and closing."

"Fire main phasers."

The beams, striking the cube, exploded it, swamping the bridge in a blinding geyser of light. Then the blast waves hit, rocking the ship so that officers and crewmen had to grab at consoles to avoid being hurled to the deck. Bridge lights flickered, dimmed and the *Enterprise* hung motionless, a stilled, meaningless speck against the vast reaches of star-filled space.

Kirk, considering his phasers' removal of the blockage, felt no elation. Now what? To probe on ahead was only too probably to invite attack, its source as unknown as the attacker. Had the mysterious cube been an envoy of some murderous space-psychopath? Was he then to risk his ship and his crew—or turn back on his course? Restless, he joined Spock at his viewer.

"How do they describe our mission, Mr. Spock? Ah, yes. 'To go where no man has gone before.' "

"So it is said, Captain." The clear, straight eyes under the cocked brows met his. "However, sensors reveal nothing. No object, no contact in any direction."

"Care to speculate on what we'll find if we go ahead?"

"Speculate?" Spock shook his head. "I prefer logic, sir. We'll encounter the intelligence which sent the cube out."

"Intelligence simply different from ours—or superior?"

"Probably both. And if you're asking the logical decision to make—"

"I'm not."

Spock eyed him. "Has it occurred to you, sir, there is a certain inefficiency in questioning me about matters on which you've already made up your mind?"

"But it gives me emotional security," Kirk told him, deadpan. He turned. "Set course ahead, Mr. Bailey."

"Plotted and laid in, sir."

"Engage," Kirk said.

The engines whined up; and Sulu said, "Warp One, sir."

Now that decision for ongoing had been made, it called for some protective reinforcement. Back at his command post, Kirk looked at his bridge personnel, his face stern, uncompromising. "Navigator," he said, "Phaser crews were sluggish, and you were slow in locking them into your directional beams. Helmsman, Engineering decks could have moved faster too. Mr. Spock will program a series of simulated attacks and evasion maneuvers."

Focusing cold eyes on Bailey and Sulu, he said, "Keep repeating the exercises until I am satisfied, gentlemen."

McCoy had been standing at the elevator doors, watching and listening. Now as Kirk approached them, he spoke quietly. "Your timing is lousy, Jim. The men are tired."

"You're the one who says a little suffering is good for the soul."

"I never say that!"

As they stepped into the turbo-car, a look passed between them. McCoy *had* said it, would say it again—and they both knew it. He made no retort. Kirk said, "Captain's quarters," and the car began its descent as Bailey's voice came over its speaker. "This is the bridge. Engineering and Phaser decks, prepare for simulated attack. Repeat: simulated attack."

McCoy gestured to the speaking panel. "And I'm worried about Bailey. Navigator's position is rough enough on a seasoned man—"

Kirk's interruption was short and impatient. "I think he'll cut it."

"How so sure? Because you spotted something you

liked in him . . . something familiar like yourself fifteen years ago?''

Irritated, Kirk was about to silence McCoy when he was silenced himself by Bailey's *''On the double,* deck five! Give me a green light!''

''Suppose you could have promoted him too fast? Listen to his voice, Jim . . .''

Once more Bailey's voice won McCoy a reprieve. ''Condition alert . . . battle stations . . .''

The alert signal was still shrilling in the elevator when its doors opened on a corridor of running crew members, but Bailey's commands followed Kirk into his cabin. ''Engineering deck five, report. Phaser crews, come on, let's get on with it!''

In a chair, eyes closed, drained and fatigued, Kirk listened. Clearly Bailey was enjoying the delegation of command. A kid playing with a terrible responsibility. As to himself, was he tired of it? Maybe. Choice, he thought, was an illusion. Untried and in moral darkness, one was impelled in a direction by unconscious forces beyond one's comprehension; by idealisms that turned out to be egotisms, a drive, for instance, not toward the harmonious music of the spheres, but to the glamor of a Starship command. And you were properly punished for such self-delusion by the absolute aloneness of command's heavy obligation.

''Here, Jim.''

He took the drink McCoy handed him. ''What's next? More humanism? 'They're not machines, Jim'?''

''They're—''

''I've heard you say that man is superior to any machines, Bones.''

''I never said that either!'' McCoy snapped.

At the flash of a red light on his cabin's panel, Kirk rose. ''Kirk here.''

Spock said, ''Exercise rating, Captain. Ninety-four percent.''

''Let's try for a hundred, Mr. Spock.''

For the unflawed. Nothing less than human perfection could satisfy a Starship Captain. ''I am tired,'' he thought. ''I ought to be selling charter flights to Mars.'' And the door opened. Janice Rand, carrying a tray covered by a white cloth, bypassed Kirk and McCoy to place it on the desk beside the Captain's chair.

Kirk questioned her with frowning eyebrows.

Removing the cloth, she said, "It's past time you ate something, sir."

"What the devil? Green leaves? Am I a herbivore?"

The girl indicated McCoy. "Dietary salad, sir. Dr. McCoy changed your diet card. I thought you knew."

From the cabin's panel, Bailey said, "This is the bridge. All decks prepare for better reaction time on second simulated attack."

Kirk, regarding the salad with loathing, picked up a fork, picked at it as Janice, a shade too professional, unfolded his napkin.

McCoy said, "Your weight was up a couple of pounds. Remember?"

Kirk, grabbing the napkin, threw it to the desk. "Will you stop hovering over me, Yeoman?"

"I just wanted to change it if it's not . . . all right, sir."

Kirk looked into the young, earnest, feminine gray eyes. A moment passed before he said, "It's . . . fine. Bring the doctor some too."

McCoy contemplated his feet. "No, thank you. I never eat until the crew eats."

Yeoman Rand poured some liquid into the glass on the tray.

Watching her, Kirk sprcad his left hand's fingers over his forehead and right eye. Politely he said, "All right, Yeoman. Thank you."

As she closed the door back of her, he closed his eyes. "Bones, when I find the Headquarters genius who assigned me a female yeoman—"

"She's very attractive. You don't trust yourself?"

He could, of course, Kirk thought, dash the glass of liquid into McCoy's face. That would quiet him down, discouraging transfer of his own male yens to other men who didn't feel them. But he was too tired to do a good job of it.

"I'm married," he said. "And a faithful husband. My girl is called the *Enterprise*. And the first mistake this other female, this yeoman makes—"

McCoy smiled, shaking his head. "She won't," he said.

Bailey spoke again from the cabin's panel. "Engineering decks alert. Phaser crews, let's—"

The alarm signal crushed his voice. Then as the panel's red light flashed on-off, Sulu, too controlled, said, interrupting, "*Countermand* that! All decks to battle stations! This is for real. Repeat. All decks to battle stations. *This is for real.*"

The red light on the panel buzzed.

Kirk said, "Kirk here."

Spock's filtered and uninflected voice said, "Sensors are picking up something ahead of us, Captain."

"Coming," Kirk said.

In the bridge, Spock, bent over his hooded viewer, lifted his head from it long enough to report to his Captain, "Exceptionally strong contact but not visual yet."

A silent Kirk watched him stoop again to appraise his dials and controls, and, frowning, punch in new coordinates. Their results inspected, Spock said tonelessly, "Distance spectrograph . . . metallic, similar to cube . . . much greater energy reading."

Turning, Kirk said, "Screen on." But all it showed was stars arranged in a design which to human eyes was also random, undesigned. Then Sulu called, "There, sir!"

Kirk saw it too—a tiny speck of light already developing size even as he looked at it, a tightness beginning to constrict his chest as he said, "Half speed. Prepare for evasive action."

Sulu responded. "Reducing speed to Warp Two, sir."

The next moment, the *Enterprise* bridge seemed to upend, shuddering, twisting like a toy in the hand of a giant imbecile child. A guard at the door fell, sliding nearly the length of the deck before he caught hold of a cabinet handle. People grabbed at anything and everything that seemed to offer stability—their chair legs, console counters, steel files.

Spock, back in his seat, said, "Tractor beam, sir. It's got us—tight."

A recovered Sulu spoke. "Engines overloading, sir."

"All engines stop," Kirk said.

"All engines stopped, sir."

Kirk, resting his head against the back of the command chair, looked at the screen again where the light speck was magnifying into a shape.

"Object decelerating, sir," Bailey said.

At his library computer, Spock was getting results from his inputs. "Size and mass of the object—" he paused, shaking his head. "This must be wrong. I'm getting a faulty reading."

Kirk, resolving his conflict between his obsession with what the screen showed and his urge to ask Spock what he'd discovered about it, said, "Phaser crews stand by."

The thing on the screen had enlarged into a mass that should have made some identification of it possible; but like the cube, the image was too alien in appearance to make any judgment of it reliable. What it absurdly seemed to be was a rounded cluster of balls, each growing bigger as it neared. Curious and unbelieving, Kirk could see the cell-like sections pulsing with inner light.

As though to herself, Uhura whispered, "It's not true."

Spock, his eyes on the screen said, "No, I'm afraid my reading was accurate, sir."

The huge screen was rapidly becoming a formidable reporter. In the lower quadrant of its frame, the immense *Enterprise* hung motionless, and in the distance, the other ship (for it was a ship) was still small but was continuously growing. Soon it matched the size of the *Enterprise* in the opposite quadrant; but discontent with equality of mass, it increased its own, and went on increasing it until it was twice as large as the Starship, occupying the entire frame of the screen. When the alien vessel had completely dwarfed the *Enterprise*, it was so monstrous that only a part of it could be seen on the screen.

The bridge crew was stunned, struck down into awe as it contemplated the imaged Colossus. Spock alone regarded it with an interest as lively as it was intense.

Kirk spoke quietly. "Mass, Mr. Sulu."

The amazed Sulu said "Shoooooosh!" Then registering Kirk's glance, added, "The reading goes off my scale, sir. It must be a mile in diameter."

Spock murmured, "Fascinating!"

"Reduce image," Kirk said.

Bailey was too dumbstruck to act, so Sulu, leaning across to his console, turned a switch. Gradually, the vastness of the screened shape diminished until the frame could hold it in its total form.

"Lieutenant Uhura, ship to ship," Kirk said.

"Hailing frequencies open, sir."

Kirk reached for his speaker. "This is the United Earth Ship *Enterprise.* We convey greetings and await your reply."

They were allowed to wait. Then Bailey, who had put on earphones, suddenly straightened. He froze, staring, his face blanched, his mouth slack and open.

"What is it, Mr. Bailey?"

The navigator turned his appalled face. "Message, sir . . . coming over my navigation beam." He swallowed, listened, clutching the earphones close to his head. Kirk looked away from him to address his Communications Officer.

"Pick it up, Lieutenant Uhura."

"Switching, sir."

The replay of the message, amplified, struck the bridge with an incoherent cataract of roar; but Kirk, joining Spock to listen, was finally able to discern words in what had been bedlam.

". . . and trespassed into our star systems. This is Balok, Commander of the Flagship Fesarius of the First Federation. . . . Your vessel, obviously the product of a primitive and savage civilization, having ignored a warning buoy of the First Federation, then destroyed it, has demonstrated that your intention is not peaceful . . ."

The voice, issuing from a larynx of iron, paused before adding, *"We are now considering disposition of your ship and the life aboard."*

"Ship to ship," Kirk said.

"Hailing frequencies open, sir."

Kirk, whose own voice, filtered, and amplified, sounded strange, spoke composedly. "This is the Captain of the U.S.S. *Enterprise.* The warning nature of your space buoy was unknown to us: our vessel was blocked by it and when we attempted to disengage—"

A squealing feedback, taking over, drowned his last sentence; and though Spock could see that his lips were still moving, only the squeal could be heard.

It stopped as Uhura, in obedience to a gesture from Kirk, cut the frequency. He stood silent beside Spock as the Vulcan's computer burst into a frenzy of red lights. Pulling at switches, twisting dials as though he were trying to shut something off, the Science Officer said, "Captain . . . we are being invaded by exceptionally strong sensor probes. Everywhere . . . our electrical systems . . . our engines . . . even our cabins and labs."

Amplified, the harsh voice of the Fesarius commander grated again throughout the bridge. *"No further communication will be accepted. If there is the slightest hostile move, your vessel will be destroyed immediately."*

Silence fell over the bridge personnel. Long experience in the unimaginable, training and self-discipline, though well indoctrinated, failed to rescue them from the paralysis induced by Balok's threat. Kirk was the first to move, walking to his command chair, aware as he'd been a thousand times before of his crew's eyes on him, hopeful, expectant, the miracle maker.

A couple of console lights faded and went dark. Spock, working at his panel, called, "They're shutting off some of our systems, sir. Brilliant! I'd like to study their methods."

As Kirk leaned forward in his chair, the humming of the bridge relays and servo-motors lost rhythm before going still.

"Mr. Spock," Kirk said, "does our recorder marker have all this on its tapes?"

"Enough to alert other ships, sir."

"Mr. Bailey, dispatch recorder marker."

Bailey merely stared at Kirk. Then as though the look in what had released him from some witchcraft, he made the proper adjustments on his panel; and wetting his dry lips, said, "Recorder marker ejected, sir."

"And it's on course," Spock said, lifting his head from his viewer. "Heading back the way we—"

White light flared from the screen, washing living faces with deathly pallor. Then another shock wave struck, tilting the Starship and once more compelling the bridge people to clutch at any available support. One hand outstretched to Sulu's console, the other hiding his eyes, Bailey whispered, "Oh, my God."

It was the moment Balok chose to make his deafening announcement. *"Your record marker has been destroyed."* Then came a second's reprieve before he added, *"You have been examined. Regretfully, your ship must be destroyed."*

Fury flamed in Kirk, a rage so violent that his knuckles whitened on his command chair's arms as he fought to pull it back to hitherto unknown deeps within himself. Vaguely, he heard Bailey give a sob.

The Fesarius commander was clearly enjoying his role of cat with mouse.

"Your ending will be painless. We make assumption you have a deity, or deities, or some such beliefs which comfort you. We therefore grant you ten Earth time periods known as minutes to make preparation. We will not alter our decision; we will not accept communication. Upon any evasive or hostile move, you will be instantly destroyed."

Kirk had won his struggle. The fury of rage had retreated to give way to a fury of thinking. Over at his station, Spock, working intently with his dials, said, "Might be interesting to see what they look like. If I can locate where that voice is coming from—"

Behind his command chair, the elevator doors must have opened, for McCoy and Scott hurried over to him, anxious inquiry in their faces.

"Jim . . . Balok . . . his message . . . it was heard all over the ship."

Someday, Kirk thought, I'll count up the ways used by my crew members to say to me, "Come on, Captain. You've got all the rabbits in the hat. We need one now. Pull it out." And the truth was, he *had* pulled many out. Oh, yes, there'd been the defeats—the failures to establish the bond of a common life between him and an alien race—yet, more often, he had succeeding in creating the sense of shared life. And those of his crew who hadn't seen him do it had been told about it.

So he had something going for him. Yet this was a hard one. Where did you find the right words for people with ten minutes to live, healthy young people denied the gradual, benevolent sense debilities with which age prepared one for the eternal stillness—sightlessness, deafness, unawareness of touch?

"Jim . . ." McCoy said again.

Nodding, he hit his intercom switch.

"Captain to crew."

And speaking, said the words that had come to him, perhaps from the same deeps whence his rage had come.

"Those who have served for long on this vessel have encountered apparently inimical and alien life forms. So they know that the greatest danger facing us is . . . ourselves and our irrational fear of the unknown. . . ."

In his own ears, his voice sounded firm and steady. Why? He went on.

"But there is no such thing as the unknown. There are only things temporarily hidden, temporarily not understood—and therefore temporarily feared. In most cases, we have found that an intelligence capable of a civilization is capable of comprehending peaceful gestures. Certainly, a life form advanced enough for space travel is advanced enough to eventually recognize our motives. All decks stand by. Captain out."

As he turned, he saw that Uhura's lustrous black eyes were tear-filled.

If to one of his people he had made sense, it was enough.

"Ship to ship, Lieutenant Uhura."

"Hailing frequencies open, sir."

Reaching for his speaker, he said, "This is the Captain of the *Enterprise.* We came here seeking friendship and have no wish to trespass. To demonstrate our goodwill, our vessel will return the way it came. But if attacked—"

Once more the squealing feedback killed his voice; and once more he motioned for cut of the circuit.

"Mr. Bailey, lay in a course away."

"What? . . . Course? What . . . ?"

Sulu leaned past the shaken Bailey to move a couple of levers on his console.

"Course plotted and laid in, sir."

"Engage, Mr. Sulu. Warp Factor One."

"Warp Factor—" Sulu began, and, frantically working his own controls, wheeled to Kirk.

"There's no response, Captain!"

"Switch to impulse!"

"All engine systems show dead, sir. And weapon systems."

Spock called, "Switching to screen, sir! I think I can get something visual."

He achieved it.

On the screen, the star background began to ripple like a sea flecked by plankton's phosphorescence. Then it dissolved into a still rippling but gradually firming shape—the distorted yet fairly distinct image of what could only have been Balok. The creature's long, drooping face was set in what seemed to be a permanently grotesque grimace, the nostrils of his bulbous nose upturned to expose blood-red flesh, a space-clown out of nightmare. As to his eyes, they explained the cat-mouse game—green balls, thrust out, black-slitted.

The thick lips moved.

"You are wasting time and effort. There is no escape. You have eight Earth minutes left."

The picture, wavering, blanked out.

Spock's tone was that of an astronomy professor explaining "black holes" to a classroom of freshmen. "I was curious to see how they appeared, sir."

God bless Spock, Kirk thought, almost smiling. "Yes, of course you were."

Bailey, lurching to his feet, screamed.

"I don't understand this at all! Spock's wasting time—everyone else just hangs around! *Somebody's got to do something!*"

McCoy went to him quickly. "Easy, boy, easy."

"What do they want from us, Doctor? Let's find out what they want us to *do*!"

Kirk's casual tone was all the more impressive for its unimpressedness.

"They want us to lose our heads, Mr. Bailey. Don't accommodate them."

"We've only got eight minutes left!"

Sulu said, "Seven and forty-one seconds."

Bailey spun, his eyes following Sulu's to the clock on the helmsman's instrument panel. Set to count off minutes and seconds, the minute hand held to "seven" while the second hand moved from "39" to "38" to "37."

Bailey, pointing to the dial, shrieked, *"He's doing a countdown!"*

McCoy seized the navigator's arm. "Practically the end of your watch. Why don't—"

Bailey jerked free, almost throwing McCoy to the deck. "Are you all out of your heads? End of *watch*? *It's the end of everything!*"

Kirk said, *"Mr. Bailey."*

It was a voice he seldom called upon because it cost too much—the paradoxes of compassion and impersonal authority . . . of ignorance masquerading as wisdom, of self-possession wavering toward randomness.

Bailey flailed free of McCoy. "What are you, *robots*? Wound-up toys? Don't you know when you're dying? Watches and regulations and orders—what do they mean when—?"

"You're relieved, Mr. Bailey," Kirk said.

Bailey, swinging toward Kirk, started to shout a reply which, at the look on his Captain's face, emerged as a groan. The effort to control himself left him shaking.

Kirk spoke to McCoy. "Escort him to his quarters, Doctor."

Bailey strode off to the elevator alone, McCoy running after him. Kirk's eyes left its closing doors, returning to the screen.

"Lieutenant Uhura, ship to ship."

"Hailing frequencies open, sir."

"This is the Captain of the Earth Ship *Enterprise*. However, it is the custom of Earth people to make every effort—"

The feedback squeal overwhelmed his words once more; but this time, Kirk made no gesture to cut off the circuit. There'd been enough bullying. If you knew what your intentions were—and they were peaceful—you gave them voice, undeterred by interruption. That was self-respect: standing by your truth. Unimaginably, the squeal ended, and Kirk, his voice calm despite the hope suddenly buoyant in him, resumed his communication to the commander of the Fesarius.

"—to avoid misunderstanding with others. We destroyed your space buoy in a simple act of self-preservation.

When we attempted to move away from it, it emitted radiation harmful to our species."

No response.

Kirk went on. "If you have examined our ship and its tapes, you know this to be true."

The squeal screamed and then was gone, exiting like a bit player in a theater, making deferential way for the star's reappearance. On the screen, Balok's monstrous face wavered into focus. Its mouth said, *"You now have seven minutes left."*

The hot rage burned in Kirk again.

He couldn't afford it, not with the despair, the expectation of that new rabbit out of the hat on the faces around him. Anger like this was a weakness, not beautiful, but just a fierce resentment at one's failure to exert control, power—and the resultant hate of helplessness to do it. Waste all your vitality in resistance to factual helplessness; and what you did was to cripple the resourcefulness you needed to devise some way out of it. Yet it was trust of his resourcefulness alone that was supporting his people's courage in the face of death.

"Four minutes, thirty seconds," Sulu said.

Scott blew up. "You have a inappropriate fascination with time pieces, Sulu!"

Sulu shrugged, and Kirk, leaving his command chair, went to Spock. "What's the matter with them? They must know by now that we mean them no harm."

There was balm in the quiet, dark eyes. Half-smiling, his best friend said, "They are certainly aware by now that we are incapable of it, sir."

From the screen, Balok said, *"Four minutes."*

Kirk looked away from it. "There has to be something to do! Something I've overlooked!"

Under the calm in Spock's voice, there was respect, affection—no demand for rabbits. "In chess," he said conversationally, "when one is outmatched, checkmate. The game is over."

It was safe to explode with Spock. "Is that your best recommendation? Accept it?"

Spock, realist and friend, said, "I regret that I can find no other logical one, sir."

McCoy appeared beside them. "Assuming we find a way out of this—"

"Nobody's given up yet!" Kirk snapped.

McCoy's tone changed. "Then on Bailey. Let me put it in my medical records as 'simple fatigue.' "

"That's *my* decision, Doctor!" Kirk said.

Turning, he crossed over to his command position, his hand on its chair back, abstracted, wrenching at his brain for some answer.

And McCoy, following him, said, "And it was *your* mistake. Expected too much, pushed him, overworked—"

Kirk's fist clenched. *"I'm ordering you to drop it, McCoy. I've no time for you, your buck-passing theories or your sentimentality!"*

McCoy was not subdued.

"Assuming we get out of this, Captain, I intend to challenge your action in my medical records. I'll state I warned you about his condition. And that's no bluff."

"Any time you can bluff me, Doctor—"

At once Kirk was aware that he himself had cracked a bit under the suspense and strain, and conscious too that his raised voice had made him an object of surprised dismay by the bridge personnel. He had increased fear instead of allaying it. Well, there was nothing to do about it. He'd just have to trust to their experience of him.

Harsh, guttural, Balok said, *"Three minutes."*

Kirk, his self-possession recovered, ignored the warning to speak to McCoy. "Fine, Doctor. Let's hope we'll be able to argue it through."

Nodding, McCoy moved off, and Kirk, his hand shielding his closed eyes, suddenly removed it and, rising from his command chair, went to Spock.

"Not chess, Mr. Spock. *Poker!* Do you know the game?"

Instead of waiting for the Vulcan's answer, he walked back to his chair, the idea that had come to him putting out fronds of hope and encouragement, developing, growing. And was no longer disturbed by the eyes focused on him, waiting, waiting for that rabbit of magic.

"Lieutenant Uhura, ship to ship!"

"Hailing frequencies open, sir."

Kirk sat upright. "This is the Captain of the *Enterprise* . . ."

He paused, his voice steady. "Our respect for other life forms requires that we now give you this warning. There is one critical item of information never committed to the memory banks of any Earth Ship . . ."

Half-aware of Sulu's astonished face, he continued. "Since the early days of space travel, our vessels have incorporated into them a substance known as corbomite. It is a material formed into a device which prevents attack on us." His voice deepened, not to threat but into uninflected impressiveness. "If any destructive energy form touches our vessels, a reverse reaction of equal strength is created, destroying—"

Interrupting, Balok said, *"You now have two minutes."*

Spock left his position to come and stand quietly beside Kirk, who went on as imperturbably as though the palms of his hands on his chair arms weren't wet with sweat.

"—destroying the attacker. It will interest you to know that since the initial use of corbomite more than two of our centuries ago, no attacking ship has ever survived the attempt. Death has little meaning for us. If it has none for you, then attack us now. We grow annoyed at your foolishness."

At his nod to Uhura, she clicked off the circuit.

"Well played, sir," Spock said. "I believe it was known as a 'bluff.' I regret not having learned more about this . . . Balok." He gestured toward the screen. "Some aspects of his face reminded me of my father."

Scott spoke. "Then may Heaven have helped your mother."

"She considered herself a most fortunate Earth woman," Spock told him coolly.

McCoy moved toward them and Kirk said quietly, "I'm sorry, Bones, I—"

"For having other things on your mind?" He smiled. "My fault. My timing was out—"

"One minute," Balok said, not echoed, but in precise unison with Sulu who'd been checking his instruments by the half-second. Catching Scott's glare, the helmsman shrugged, addressing Kirk.

"I knew he would, sir."

Kirk laughed. "Has it ever occurred to you you're not a very inscrutable Oriental, Mr. Sulu?"

Turning, Sulu grinned. "I tried it once when I was a kid. Remember those old . . ." he halted, searching for the word . . . "images on celluloid stuff?"

"Cinema," Kirk said.

"Movies," Scott offered.

"Yes, cinema," Sulu said. "The ones about the time of the Sino-Western trouble . . ."

Uhura spoke. "World War III, almost."

Nodding, Kirk said, "The world was lucky it was stopped in time. None of us here would be enjoying life today . . ." As he noticed McCoy's grin, his words trailed off into a silence broken by Sulu.

"Well, anyway, the villains were Oriental, remember? I loved them. I used to sit in front of the mirror for hours practicing drooping eyelids, mysterious expressions. I never knew what it meant. These movies were two hundred years old, I guess, but I wanted to be like them."

Turning, Uhura smiled at him. "You never made it."

"I can't figure out why I'm like this. I don't have a *drop* of Western blood."

A heavy silence flowed in over the bridge, all the heavier for its contrast with Sulu's lighthearted comments; but the general anxiety was too present to continue idle conversation. Sulu had turned back to his timepiece when the elevator doors opened and Bailey stepped out, his face defensive and uncertain.

"If anyone's interested," Sulu said, ". . . *thirty* seconds."

McCoy had seen Bailey at the bridge's rear, and Kirk, registering the constraint in his face, turned and saw the navigator too. Bailey approached the command chair briskly.

"Sir, request permission to take my post."

As Kirk eyed him, Sulu said, "Twenty seconds, Captain."

There was a brief pause before Kirk said, "Permission granted, Mr. Bailey."

He looked away as Bailey resumed his seat beside Sulu

and his console's instrument clock, ticking off its "zero" seconds.

"Ten," Sulu counted, ". . . nine . . . eight . . . seven . . ."

Spock, almost too quiet-faced, had returned from his position to stand beside his Captain.

Sulu said, ". . . six . . . five . . . four . . . three . . . two . . . one . . ."

The zero count passed; and as nothing happened, Spock spoke.

"An interesting game, this 'poker.' "

Kirk nodded. "It does seem to have advantages over chess."

Balok's voice, filtered and grating, said, *"This is the Commander of the Fesarius."* But as Uhura leaned forward to throw her hailing-frequency switch, Kirk stopped her with a gesture.

"Hold on, Lieutenant. Let's let him sweat for a change."

A minute passed before Balok said, *"The destruction of your vessel has been delayed."*

"You gotta admire him," Sulu said. "The latest news every minute."

Somebody laughed a little too loudly, the sound of the relieved guffaw followed at once by Balok's voice.

"We must have proof of your corbomite device."

Spock strode back to his station, beginning to manipulate controls as Balok went on: *"We will relent in your destruction only if we have proof of your corbomite device. Do you understand?"*

Kirk waited four minutes by Sulu's clock before commanding the opening of hailing frequencies.

"Request denied," he said.

"You will be destroyed unless you give us this information."

Spock, gesturing toward the screen, said, "Captain—"

Again the hideous image of Balok assumed its wavering shape. And the voice said, *"And now, having permitted your primitive efforts to see my form, I trust it has pleased your curiosity."* The balled eyes moved slightly. *"What's more, another demonstration of our superiority . . ."*

To a click, the *Enterprise* viewing screen went dark and the Fesarius Commander added, *"We will soon inform you of our decision regarding your vessel."*

Kirk was leaning back, stretching in a weariness induced by the accumulation of strains when Yeoman Janice Rand walked through the opened elevator doors, carrying a tray of coffee and cups. As nonchalant as though the bridge were her personal drawing room, she set down the tray and was immediately surrounded by a group of men, including McCoy.

"I thought the power was off in the galley," he said.

Pouring the steaming brew into cups, she said, "I used a hand phaser. Zap! hot coffee!"

She started off with a filled cup for Kirk, and Sulu cried, "Something's going on, Captain!"

Kirk made a swift, rejecting gesture toward the coffee, he and Spock both concentrating on the ship's viewing screen.

Indeed something was going on. A small, cell-like section of the Fesarius was separating itself from its mother ship and moving away from it but still remaining visible within the screen's frame. Spock lifted his head from his hooded viewer, saying, "Weight—about two thousand metric tons, sir."

"Yes, it appears to be a small ship."

The small, balled alien ship had moved nearer to the *Enterprise*; and as it approached still closer, its mother ship sped off, its cell-like sections dwindling rapidly in size. Accelerating fast, the thing lost shape to speed, turned to a pinpoint of light, then into a nothingness that left the tiny ship hanging before the *Enterprise.*

Balok's voice, filtered, spoke.

"It has been decided that I will conduct you to a planet of the First Federation which is capable of sustaining your life form."

Kirk, a man of action, gave vent to the frustration imposed upon him by many hours of inaction by slamming his clenched fist on his command chair's arm. Near him, Sulu, leaning back in his chair, gazed up at the bridge deck ceiling, whistling a "Musetta's Waltz," which was still played on old Earth tapes of the Puccini opera. Beside him, Bailey stared at the dials on his console.

As to Balok, he went on.

"There you will disembark and be interned. Your ship will be destroyed, of course."

To nobody in particular, Kirk muttered, "Of course," though at bridge stations around him, lights were blinking on. And from across the room, Spock called, "Engine systems coming on, Captain."

But Balok's sense of comedy was as grotesque as the snouted face. Filtered, the thick voice said, *"Do not be deceived by the size of this pilot vessel. It has an equal potential to destroy your ship."* And as if to give proof of the claimed power, the *Enterprise* was subjected to a jolt that sent several people sprawling.

Spock said, "Tractor beam again, sir."

Kirk went very still as the voice, going on, pushed home the point.

"Escape is impossible. It is only that you may sustain your gravity and atmosphere that your systems are now open. Our power will lead you to your destination. Any move to elude me or destroy my ship will result in the instant destruction of the Enterprise *and of every life aboard her."*

For some reason he preferred not to examine, Kirk wanted to smile. There, on the viewing screen, was Balok's tiny ship towing the huge *Enterprise* behind it across the dark fields of star-sown space. It *was* absurd, and the portentous pomposity of Balok himself, his literary style, gigantically threatening, made it still more absurd.

But to his not-amused people, he said, "Our plan: A show of resignation. His tractor beam is a heavy drain on his small ship. Question: Will he grow careless?"

Bailey, gesturing toward his console, said, "Captain, he's pulling out a little ahead of us."

Spock, to check the report, emerged from his hooded viewer to announce, "He's sneaked power down a bit."

Kirk, turning, confronted a white-faced, tense Bailey who spoke hastily, "I'm all right, sir."

Nodding, Kirk said, "We'll need a right-angle course to maintain our sheer away from him no matter how he turns."

"Yes, sir."

"Maximum acceleration when I give the word."

Sulu, his eyes on the screen, said, "Yes, sir."

Minutes which everyone endured according to his duties and temperament crawled sluggishly by. Bailey constantly ran his tongue over dry lips. Sulu kept his eyes on his Captain. As to Spock, expressionless, he waited, alert as a drawn trigger.

Kirk, without turning, spoke to Sulu. *"Engage!"*

Under the prearranged pressures of switches and controls, the bridge lights dimmed to a massive power drain as the *Enterprise* lurched, shuddering. And on the screen, Balok's dwarf ship lurched too, its light beginning to pulsate. And started to flicker in power surges as it tried to compensate for the withdrawal of the *Enterprise.*

It wasn't so simple as it should have been. The Starship's engines rose to a higher and higher whine until Sulu unnecessarily reported, "It's a strain, Captain. Engines are overloading."

"More power," Kirk said.

He caught a glint of awed respect in Sulu's eyes. And wondered what the response would be if he said, "Cut it, kid." If I've taken a risk, it's because I'm alive. Living itself is a risk. If you don't want to risk, phaser yourself and die. And thought, I am as bored by excessive dependency as I am by excessive awe.

Spock, bless him, was neither dependent nor awed. Now without intonation, he said, "We're overheating, Captain. Intermix temperature seven thousand four hundred degrees . . . seven-five . . . seven-six . . ."

When the alarm bell rang, he shut it off. "Eight thousand degrees, sir."

On the screen, Balok's ship was glowing like a nova as it tried to fend off the pull of the *Enterprise* in their titanic tug-of-war.

The bridge teetered, rocking, as the *Enterprise* tried to pull free of Balok's ship, the whine of its engines growing to a scream.

Kirk, hard-jawed, said, "Sheer away, Mr. Bailey!"

His brow sweating, Bailey battled the power conflict. And from his station, Spock said, "We're two thousand above maximum. Eight thousand four . . . five . . . six . . . she'll blow soon."

Even as he was speaking, the light pulsations from Balok's ship lessened. Then one of the lights flickered into dimness.

"We're breaking free, sir," Bailey reported.

All the lights on the alien ship became faint. As one blinked off and then on again, there came a sudden flare-up of brilliant light from the balled vessel to be replaced by an utter darkness. And the *Enterprise*, freed, sped away into the distance.

A relaxed Kirk, leaning back in his chair, said, "All engines stop."

"All stopped, sir," Sulu said.

Turning, Kirk studied the young face of Bailey. Its blue eyes met his straightforwardly. Nodding, he said, "Good. All hands, good."

Behind him, the elevator doors opened, and Scott, his face anxious, almost ran to the command chair. "Engines need some work, Captain! They've been badly overstrained. Bad. Can we hold it here a few hours?"

Spock left his station to take his own place beside the command chair. "If Balok got a signal through to that mother ship of his, sir . . ."

Kirk, nodding, said, "Right, Mr. Spock. We're not home yet."

Uhura, swinging her chair around, bent her head to a turned switch on her console. "A signal, Captain . . . very weak." For several seconds, she just listened. Then she said, "It's Balok, sir, a distress signal to the Fesarius. His engines are out . . . his life-sustaining system isn't operating. He's repeating the message to the Fesarius."

"Any reply, Lieutenant?"

"Negative, sir. His signal is fading. It is so faint, I doubt if the mother ship could hear it."

On the screen before Kirk, there hung Balok's little ball, once so charged with belligerent vitality but now helpless, dull—a black nothing against the star-strewn immensities of space. And about it was something of pathos, of miniscule tragedy like the disappearance down a whale's throat of the microscopic, one-celled lives inhabiting the seas.

"Plot a course for it, Mr. Bailey," he said.

Only Spock among his officers showed no surprise, not

even the lift of an astonished eyebrow. Kirk, pushing his intercom button, reached for his mike to say, "This is the Captain speaking. The First Federation vessel is in distress. We're preparing to board."

His crew had been persecuted by Balok, overworked, threatened, panicked. So the right words had to be found to explain the suggestion of mercy in his announcement; and choosing them, he went on: "There are lives at stake. By our standards 'alien lives'—but still lives. Captain out."

Navigator Bailey, doing his best to keep the respectful awe out of his eyes said, "Course plotted and laid in, sir."

"Ready the Transporter Room, Mr. Scott."

After a moment's hesitation, Scott said, "Aye, sir," and walked toward the elevator as Kirk, turning to Sulu, said, "Bring us to within one hundred meters, Mr. Sulu. Ahead slow."

Sighing, Sulu repeated the order and Kirk, glancing around him, saw that the still lingering dissatisfaction on the faces of his people was telling him that more right words were needed. He rose from his chair and, grasping its back, said, "Gentlemen, what is the mission of this vessel of ours? It is to seek out and make contact with life forms wherever we find them." He stopped, and, wheeling, pointed to the dark round little ship on the screen. *"Life,"* he said, and after a long pause, hammered home his point. "An opportunity to demonstrate what our high-sounding words mean. Any questions?"

As nobody spoke, he went on.

"I'll take two men with me. Dr. McCoy to examine and treat the aliens if possible." He was at the elevator doors when he turned. "And you, Mr. Bailey."

Astounded, Bailey managed a "Sir?"

"The face of the unknown, Mr. Bailey. I think I owe you a look at it."

Rising slowly from his seat, Bailey said, "Yes, sir."

Spock had left his place too. "Request permission, sir, to—"

"Denied, Mr. Spock. If I'm mistaken, if Balok's set a trap for us, I want you here."

With Bailey, McCoy joined Kirk in the elevator, his medical bag in his hand. And to Kirk's "Transporter Room," the familiar relays clicked, lights flashing. After a moment, Kirk addressed McCoy, ignoring Bailey's fear-paled face. "You don't approve either, I suppose."

McCoy shrugged. "I never ask your approval of my diagnoses."

"Frightened, Mr. Bailey?" Kirk said.

"Yes, sir."

"Of what?"

"Well, as far as knowing exactly—"

"Precisely my point, Mr. Bailey."

As the trio entered the Transporter Room, Scott, an assistant beside him, looked up from the transporter controls to warn, "It will be risky, sir. We're locked in on what appears to be a main deck."

Nodding, Kirk said, "Air sample?"

"Breathable, Captain. In fact, a slightly higher oxygen content than our own."

"Ready, Doctor?" Kirk asked, turning to McCoy.

"No, but you won't let that stop you."

Bailey, last to enter the transport chamber, obediently stepped into the space Kirk indicated; and from the console across the room, Scott, motioning them all to stoop, called, "On your hunkers, Captain. It reads pretty cramped over there."

Kirk, satisfied that he and his companions were safely placed, said, *"Energize!"*

With the hum of increasing power, the three dissolved into unidentifiable figures of light sparkles, the transporter effect subsiding as they disappeared only to almost immediately materialize under a ceiling barely an inch above their heads. Around them was a subdued, soft lighting, probably indirect, but no sign whatever of smoke or trouble.

Then still bending, the three stopped dead, dumbstruck by the luxury of the room before them. The floor was covered by a rich, deep-piled form of carpet, its gold color matched by draperies of what might have been velvet but wasn't. In the room's center, on a silver and jade-green chaise lounge, a creature reclined. Was it Balok? The head was even larger than it had shown on the *Enterprise* screen, and its body had a curious limpness about it.

It didn't move as they approached it. The goggle eyes

in the huge, bloated head had no lids to blink but simply stared glassily at the opposite wall. When McCoy tapped the thing with his knuckles, it gave out a hollow sound; and nodding, McCoy said, "Jim, this is a . . . a dummy, a puppet of some kind."

And the familiar harshness of Balok's voice said, *"I have been waiting for you."*

At the sound of it, they all wheeled.

Kirk's first thought was, "I'm hallucinating." For the actual Balok was almost a child in size, less than four feet tall, chubby, warm and so cuddly in appearance that one could only marvel how his pudgy chest could accommodate the resonance of that voice. Smiling cherubically so that his rosy cheeks made little mounds under his twinkling eyes, he was sitting relaxedly in a small chair, robed in some shimmering turquoise material—anyway, some color of the blue-green family.

"I'm Balok," he said. "Welcome aboard."

Moving forward, Kirk let the phenomenon of the voice go to watch the childlike hand indicate three small armless chairs.

"I'm Captain Kirk. I—"

Interrupting, their host nodded. "—and McCoy and Bailey. Sit. Be comfortable."

As the *Enterprise* men lowered themselves gingerly to the edges of what by Earth standards would be children's chairs, Balok pushed a button on the wall beside him. It slid open to make way for a servo unit bearing a bowl and four cups. Lifting a ladle, Balok dipped it into the bowl to fill the cups of his hospitality.

"We must drink. This is tranya. I hope you relish it as much as I."

"Commander Balok—" Kirk began, and was stilled by a wave of the little hand.

"I know. I know," the voice grated. "A thousand questions. But first, the tranya."

Midget though he was, this creature had deflected the *Enterprise* in its course, demoralized its crew with terrorizing threats and made a general nuisance of himself. Kirk accepted the cup he was handed but didn't drink. Nor did McCoy. Balok beamed at them. Lifting his own drink, he sipped from it. After a moment, Kirk and McCoy followed his example, Bailey, still uneasy and distrustful, preferring to merely hold his drink.

The tranya was delicious, but as Kirk replaced his empty cup on the servo, his eyes veered to the chaise longue where the enormous, hideous head lolled idiotically, half-on and half-off its cushion.

Noticing, Balok said, "My alter ego, so to speak, Captain. In your culture, he would be Mr. Hyde to my Jekyll. You must admit he's effective. You would never have been frightened by me. I also thought my distress signal quite clever." And with another seraphic smile, Balok added, "It was a pleasure testing you."

Eyeing the manikin, Kirk said, "I see."

Balok spoke earnestly. "I had to discover your real intentions, you see."

"But you probed our memory banks . . ."

"Your records could have been a deception on your part." As Balok spoke, he poured more tranya into his cup, offering to pour more for Kirk who declined. McCoy, however, accepted more drink, asking, "And your crew, Commander?"

Balok giggled. "Crew? I have no crew, Doctor. Just Mr. Hyde and me. I run everything from this small ship." The heavy voice became unexpectedly plaintive, the chubby face wistful. "But I miss company, conversation. Even an alien would be a welcome companion. Perhaps one of your men . . . for some period of time . . . an exchange of information, cultures . . ."

The contrast between the powerful voice and its ingenuous confession of loneliness was appealing. Kirk was finding much to like in Balok and a considerable degree of sympathy for him, marooned here alone in space with the bogeyman puppet on the chaise longue.

"Yes," he said. "Do you think we can find a volunteer, Mr. Bailey?"

Bailey jumped from his child's chair with such enthusiasm that he hit his head on the ceiling.

"Me, sir!" he cried eagerly. "I'd like to volunteer!"

Kirk waited a long moment before he nodded, saying, "An excellent idea, Mr. Bailey."

Unbelieving, Balok stared at the *Enterprise* navigator. "You will stay with me? Be my friend? You represent Earth's best, then?"

Rubbing his head, Bailey protested. "No, sir. I'm not. I'll make plenty of mistakes."

"And you'll learn more about us this way, Commander Balok," Kirk said. "As to me, I'll get back a better officer in return."

Balok broke into open, joyous laughter so infectious that Kirk laughed too.

"I see, Captain," he said. "We think much alike, you and I."

Bailey, the decision made, swallowed his whole drink of tranya.

As he finished it, Balok got to his small height; and moving grandly to thc door, stood at it, waiting for his guests to join him. He looked up at them, towering over him, his face that of a child on Christmas morning. The next minute, he was all business again.

"Now, before I bring back the Fesarius, let me show you my personal vessel. It is not often I have this pleasure."

McCoy, following him through the door, shook his head with the wonder of it all, but Kirk and Bailey smiled at each other before they too stooped to move through the entranceway in the trail of robed child-man.

Pausing at another small door, Balok, turning, said, "Yes, we're very much alike, Captain. Both proud of our ships."

THE ENEMY WITHIN

Writer: Richard Matheson
Director: Leo Penn

The planet's desert terrain had yielded an interesting roundup of mineral and animal specimens, and Kirk was busy checking the containers for beam-up to the *Enterprise* when a gust of icy wind blew a spray of sand in his face. Beside him, Sulu, holding a meek doglike creature on a leash, shivered.

"Temperature's beginning to drop, Captain."

"Gets down to 250 degrees below at nightfall," Kirk said. He blinked the sand out of his eyes, stooped to pat Sulu's animal—and wheeled at the sound of a shout. Geological technician Fisher had fallen from the bank where he'd been working. From shoulders to feet his jumpsuit was smeared with a sticky, yellowish ore.

"Hurt yourself?" Kirk asked.

Fisher winced. "Cut my hand, sir."

It was a jagged, ugly cut. "Report to Sickbay," Kirk said.

Obediently Fisher removed his communicator from his belt. In the *Enterprise* Transporter Room, Scott, receiving his request for beam-up, said, "Right. Locked onto you." He turned to Transporter technician Wilson at the console. "Energize!" he ordered.

But as Fisher sparkled into shape on the platform, the console flashed a warning red light. "Coadjustor engagement," Scott said hastily. Wilson threw a switch. The red light faded.

Materialized, Fisher stepped off the platform.

"What happened?" Wilson asked.

"Took a flop," Fisher told him.

Wilson eyed the yellowish splatterings on his jumpsuit. Some lumps of the stuff had fallen from it to the platform's floor.

"Took a flop onto what?" Wilson asked.

"I don't know—some kind of soft ore."

Scott had reached for a scanner device. He ran it over the jumpsuit. "That ore's magnetic," he said. "Decontaminate your uniform, Fisher."

"Yes, sir."

Frowning, Scott examined the console. "It acted like a burnout," he grumbled to Wilson. "I don't like it."

Kirk's voice broke in on his concentration. "Captain Kirk, ready for beam-up."

"Just a moment, Captain." Scott tested the console again. "Seems to be OK now," he told Wilson. "But we can do with a double check. Get me a synchronic meter." Returning to his speaker, he said, "All right, Captain. Locked onto you." Then he activated the Transporter.

There was an unfamiliar whine in its humming. Hurriedly dialing it out, Scott decided to warn Kirk he was delaying the beam-up. But the process had already begun. The engineer looked anxiously toward the platform. In its dazzle Kirk stood on it, dazed-looking, unusually pale. As he stepped from it, his legs almost buckled. Scott ran to him. "What's wrong, Captain? Let me give you a hand."

"Just a little dizzy, that's all," Kirk said. "I'm sure it's nothing serious." He glanced around him. "You're not leaving the Transporter Room untended to look after me, are you?"

"No, sir. Wilson's just gone for a tool."

The door closed behind them. More sparkle appeared on the platform. A figure took shape on it. When it had gathered solidity, it could be seen as a perfect double of Kirk. Except for its eyes. They were those of a rabid animal just released from a cage.

It looked around it, tense, as though expecting attack.

Wilson opened the door. Immediately sensing that tension, "Captain," he said, "are you all right?"

His reply was a hoarse growl. The double glanced

around it again seeking some means of escape. It licked its dry lips. Then it saw the door Wilson had left open.

Out in the corridor Kirk was saying, "I can manage now. You'd better get back to the Transporter Room, Scotty."

"Yes, sir."

"Thanks for the help."

"I wish you'd let Dr. McCoy give you a look-over, Captain."

"All right, Engineer. I'll have him check my engines."

He didn't have far to go. At the next cross passage he collided with McCoy. "I think we need a control signal at this cor—" McCoy broke off to stare at Kirk. "What's happened to you?"

"I don't know," Kirk said.

"You look like you ran into a wall."

"Is that your official diagnosis?"

"Never mind my diagnosis! Go and lie down. I have a malingerer to be treated. Then I'll come and check you."

"If you can find me," Kirk said—and moved on down the corridor. McCoy followed his going with puzzled eyes. Then he hastened on back to the waiting Fisher in Sickbay.

The soiled jumpsuit had been discarded. McCoy cleaned the cut hand. "Like to get off duty, wouldn't you?" he said. "Take a little vacation."

Fisher grinned. And McCoy, swabbing the wound, lifted his head at the sound of the opening door.

The double spoke at once. *"Brandy,"* it said.

The demand, the manner, the whole bearing of replica Kirk was uncharacteristic of the real one. Fisher's presence put a brake on McCoy's amazement. He decided to ignore the demand. "Don't go running back to work now," he told Fisher. "Keep the bandage moist with this antiseptic. Take the bottle along with you."

"Yes, sir." Fisher held up his swathed hand, smiling at the double. "It isn't too bad, Captain."

The remark was ignored. McCoy turned to the double standing in the doorway and gestured to it to enter the office. "Sit down, Jim," he said. "I think we'd better . . ."

He stopped. The double had gone to the locked liquor cabinet, its nails clawing at it. *"I said brandy,"* it said.

McCoy stared, dumbfounded. The double was snarling

now at its failure to pry open the cabinet's door. Nervous, uneasy, McCoy tried again. "Sit down, Jim."

A shudder passed through the double. A savage whisper broke from it. *"Give me the brandy!"*

"What is the *matter* with—" McCoy began. The clawing hands were lifting with the clear intention of smashing the cabinet's glass.

"Jim!" McCoy shouted.

The double whirled, crouched for a leap, its fists clenching. Instinctively McCoy recoiled from the coming blow. Then he recovered himself. "All right, I'll give you the brandy. Sit down!" But he didn't give the brandy. As he unlocked the cabinet door, he was shouldered aside—and the double, seizing a bottle of liquor, made for the door.

"Drink it in *your quarters*, Jim! I'll see you there in a . . ."

The door slammed shut.

McCoy, striding over to his viewing screen, flicked it on. Spock's face appeared. "Anything peculiar happen down on that planet's surface, Mr. Spock?"

The cool voice said, "One slight accident, Doctor, which I'm sure won't tax your miraculous healing powers."

But McCoy was too disturbed to rise to the bait. "Did it involve the Captain?"

"No."

"Well, there's something very wrong with him. He just left my office after carrying on like a wild man."

The wild man, rampaging down the corridor, suddenly had a mind to private drinking. A sign over a door declared it to be the entrance to the quarters of Yeoman Janice Rand. The double touched it, conceiving unmentionable notions—and slipped through the door. Inside, it uncorked the bottle. Tipping it up, it gulped down the brandy in deep swallows. Then it grunted in pure, voluptuous pleasure. The bite of the brandy down its throat was too seductive to resist the impulse to swallow some more. Eyes half-shut in sensual delight, its face was the face of a Kirk released from all repressions, all self-discipline and moral order.

Kirk himself had not entirely recovered from his mysterious vertigo. Alone in his quarters, he had his shirt off, and was flexing his neck and shoulder muscles to rid his head of the whirling inside it. When the knock came at his door, he said, "Yes?"

"Spock, sir."

"Come in," Kirk said, pressing the door's unlocking button.

"Dr. McCoy asked me to check on you, sir."

Shouldering back into his shirt, Kirk said, "Why you?"

"Only Dr. McCoy could answer that, Captain."

"He must have had a reason."

"One would assume so," Spock said mildly, his keen eyes on Kirk's face.

"Well, Mr. Spock? I hope you know me next time we meet."

"Dr. McCoy said you were acting like a wild man."

"McCoy said that?" Kirk paused. "He must have been joking."

"I'll get back to the bridge now," Spock said.

"I'll tell McCoy you were here."

As the door closed, Kirk, puzzled by the interchange, reached for his Captain's coat.

On Deck 12, corridors above him, his double was feeling the effects of the brandy. But at the sound of a door sliding open, it was sober enough to take hiding in the bedroom of Yeoman Rand's quarters. It watched her enter. When she had placed her tricorder on a table, it stepped forward into her full sight.

It was not Kirk's custom to visit the bedrooms of attractive female members of his crew. Janice was shaken by his appearance in hers. She decided to smile. "This is an unexpected pleasure, sir," she said gamely.

The smile faltered at the suggestive leer she received. "Is there something I can—?" Then she tensed. The double had come so close to her she could smell the brandy on its breath. She flushed at such male nearness, fought back an uprush of embarrassed apprehension and said, "Is there—can I do something for you, Captain?"

"You bet you can," the double grinned. "But Jim will do here, Janice."

Neither the words nor the tone fitted the image of Kirk that existed in the mind of Janice Rand. She had never seen him anything but coolly courteous toward women members of his crew. Since the day she had joined it, she had thought of him as the unobtainable but most desirable man she'd ever met. However, that was her own secret. It just wasn't possible that he *was* obtainable, not Captain James T. Kirk of the Starship *Enterprise*. And by a twenty-year-old, obscure yeoman named Janice Rand. He'd been drinking, of course; and when men drank . . . Nevertheless, of all the women on the ship, this handsomest man in the world had sought her out; and by some miraculous quirk of circumstance seemed to be finding her worthy of his sexual interest. She suddenly felt that she, along with her uniform, had gone transparent.

"I—Captain, this isn't—" she stammered.

"You're too much woman not to know," the double said. "I've been mad for you since the day you joined the ship. We both know what's been inside us all this time. We can't say no to it—not any more, not when we're finally alone, just you and me. Just try to deny it—after this . . ."

It swept her into its arms, kissing her hard on the lips. For a moment she was immobilized by the shock. Then she pulled back. "*Please*, Captain. You—we . . ."

The handsome face tightened with anger. She was kissed again harshly; and with a little moan, she tried to pull free. She was jerked closer. Now the kisses pressed against her throat, her neck.

"You're—hurting me," she whispered.

"Then don't fight me. You know you don't want to."

She stared into what she thought were Kirk's eyes. In some shameful way it was true. She *didn't* want to fight the Captain's kisses. Only how dare he presume to know it?

"Shall I make that an order, Yeoman Rand?"

This time the kiss on her mouth was openly brutal. Janice, infuriated by exposure of a truth she wanted neither to know herself nor be known to anyone else, began to fight in earnest. She scratched the double across its handsome face. It pulled back; and she dashed for the door. She was grabbed as it opened—but out in the corridor, Fisher, returning to his room with the antiseptic liquid he'd forgotten, had seen the struggling pair.

"On your way!" It was Kirk's command voice.

Relief surged through Janice. *The Captain had implicated himself in this disgraceful scene.* If there was penalty to pay in loss of his crew's respect, he'd have only himself to blame. She screamed, "Call Mr. Spock!"

Fisher gaped at her. *"Call Mr. Spock!"* she screamed again. Fisher broke into a run. The double tightened its hold on her. Then, realizing how the witness menaced it, it rushed out into the corridor.

Fisher made it to a wall intercom. "This is Fisher of Geology! Come to Deck 12, Section . . ."

The double caught him in midsentence. Fisher was spun around to take a smashing right to his jaw. It was his turn to scream. "Help! Section 3!"

The scream came through to the bridge. Spock bolted for the elevator, shouting "Take over!" to navigator Farrell.

Deck 12 was deserted. Spock hesitated. Then, starting down the corridor, he slowed his run to a wary walk, his sharp Vulcan eyes searching. After a moment, he stooped to run a finger along a dark streak on the flooring. When he looked at the finger, it was red, wet with blood.

Its trail of drops led to the quarters of Yeoman Rand. He opened the door. She was sitting on a chair, her uniform disheveled, her eyes blank, stunned. Near her, Fisher lay on the floor. She didn't speak as Spock bent down to him. His face was a mass of mangled flesh and blood.

"Who did this to you?" Spock asked.

Fisher's torn lips moved. "Captain Kirk," he whispered. Then he subsided into unconsciousness.

Kirk asked his question very quietly. "And Yeoman Rand says I assaulted her?"

"Yes, sir," Spock said. "And technician Fisher also accuses you of assault upon her and himself."

"I've been here in my quarters for the past half hour," Kirk said.

Spock held up the nearly empty brandy bottle.

"What's that?" Kirk said.

"The bottle of brandy Dr. McCoy says you took from his office cabinet. I found it in Yeoman Rand's room with Fisher."

"McCoy says *I* took that brandy?" The whirling in Kirk's head had come back. He shut his eyes against its wheeling stars. Then he rose. "Let's find out what's going on in this ship." He moved past Spock into the corridor.

The elevator door closed behind them—and the double, a darker shadow in the shadows of a cross passage, slipped quietly out into the corridor. Panting, it pried at the door of Kirk's quarters. It got it open. Inside, the lock on the panel of the sleeping compartment caught its eye. It depressed the unlocking button. It relocked the panel behind it and fell across the bed, sighing with exhaustion. Then it buried the replica of Kirk's face in a pillow to shut out the sights and sounds of a world that hated it.

In Sickbay, Yeoman Rand was saying, "Then he kissed me—and said we—that he was the Captain and could order me to—" Her eyes were on her cold hands, safer to look at than Kirk's face. She had addressed her words to Spock.

"Go on," Kirk said.

She looked at him now. "I—I didn't know what to do. When you started talking about—us—about the feeling we've been—hiding all this time . . ."

"The feeling you and I have been hiding, Yeoman Rand?" Kirk said. "Do I understand you correctly?"

"Yes, sir." In desperation she twisted around to McCoy. "He *is* the Captain, Doctor! I couldn't just—" Her face tightened. "I couldn't *talk* to you!" she burst out at Kirk. "I had to fight you, scratch your face and kick and . . ."

"Yeoman Rand," Kirk said. He went over to her, pretending not to notice how she shrank from his approach. "Look at me! Look at my face! Do you see any scratches on it?"

"No, sir," she whispered.

"I have been in my quarters, Yeoman. How could I have been with you and in my own quarters at one and the same time?"

She wrung her hands. "But—" Her voice broke. "I know what happened. And it *was* you. I—I don't want to get you into trouble. I wouldn't even have mentioned it if technician Fisher hadn't seen you, too, and . . ."

"Yeoman," Kirk said, "it wasn't *me*!"

She began to cry. She looked very small, very young in her rumpled uniform. Kirk reached out a compassionate hand to her shoulder—but she shied away from his touch as though it might burn her.

Spock said, "You can go now, Yeoman."

Sobbing, she got to her feet. As she reached the door, Kirk said, "Yeoman." She stopped. *"It was not me,"* he repeated. But she went on out the door without looking back.

Spock broke the silence. "Captain, there is an impostor aboard this ship."

It was to be expected from Spock. Faith to the end—that was Spock. Kirk pulled his uniform collar away from his neck as though it were choking him. After a moment he went to the door of Sickbay's treatment room where McCoy had gone back to work on the battered Fisher. He was busy, of course; too busy with Fisher to look at him. But the prone Fisher looked at him from the sheeted table—and in his eyes there was open scorn.

The intercom buzzed; and Scott said, "Captain, can we see you in the Transporter Room for a minute?"

Kirk took the scalding memory of Fisher's look with him. If Spock hadn't silently joined him, he wondered if he'd have found the courage to respond to Scott's call. Had he, too, heard the interesting details of his Captain's recent activities? But Scott's total concern seemed to be the still defective Transporter. He looked up from the console as Kirk entered. "It's a complete breakdown, Captain." He turned his head to say to his technicians, "Continue circuit testing." The meek, doglike creature collected from the planet was lying beside the console. Scott pointed to it. "We beamed this animal up to the ship, sir, and . . ."

"And what?" Kirk said.

Scott paused. "The animal is here. But it's also over there in that specimen case."

He left the console to go over to the case with Kirk and Spock. A fierce growl greeted them. Scott cautiously lifted the lid. The beast inside bared its teeth, its lips flecked with the foam of its fury. Scott hastily dropped the lid over its leap at them.

"It appears to be the twin of the other animal," Spock

said slowly. "Except for the difference in temperament, they might be one and the same."

Scott had hurried back to the console to pick up the quiet creature. Stroking it, he said, "A few seconds after they sent this one up through the Transporter, that duplicate of it appeared on the platform. If this had happened to a man—it's some kind of opposite."

The intentness on Kirk's face was naked. Scott went on. "One beast gentle like this—and one savage, wolfish, this one and *that* one—some kind of ferocious *opposite*. Captain, till we know what's gone wrong with the Transporter, we dare not use it to beam up the landing party!"

"Oh, my God . . ."

The whisper was wrenched from Kirk by the force of sudden revelation. It was no imposter who was loose on the *Enterprise*. What was loosc on it was his own counterpart—the dark, brutish aspect of human nature which every mortal carries within him from birth to the grave. His Cain was roaming the *Enterprise* in a mindless, murderous search for a vengeance that would appease the bitterness of years of denial—the years it had spent as a prisoner of conscience, of duty, of responsibility. Somehow it had got free from its embodiment in him, and wearing his face, using his voice, wandering his ship, had found its release.

He gradually became conscious of Spock's eyes. The Vulcan had taken the lamb-gentle animal into his arms. Something in the way he held it stilled the turmoil in Kirk's soul. He was able to speak.

"Do you know what caused the animal to divide in two, Scotty?"

"We think we do, sir. When Fisher came up, his clothes were splashed with some soft, yellowish stuff. He said it was ore. Some of it fell on the Transporter platform. When we scanned it, we found it contained unknown magnetic elements. Maybe it caused an overload. We can't tell—not yet."

"Is the Transporter working at all?"

"Yes, sir. But to use it to bring up the landing party—they might all be duplicated like you—" He caught himself. "Like the animal, Captain."

So Scott *had* heard. "How long will it take to locate the trouble?"

"Can't say, sir."

Kirk fought for calm, for reason. "We can't just leave those four men down there. They'll freeze to death. At night that planet's temperature sinks to 250 degrees below zero."

"We're doing everything we can, Captain!"

Kirk looked at the Transporter platform. What was the secret it refused to divulge? He'd emerged from it whole, unsplit, a thousand times. Why not this last time? *What had happened?* When and how had he been divided in two halves like a one-celled organism reproducing itself? The whirling in his head was back once more. And the platform looked back at him, empty, its secret still withheld.

Spock had come to stand beside him. "About this double of yours, Captain."

Kirk started like a man aroused from nightmare. "Yes, we've got to find him. Search parties, Mr. Spock—we've got to organize search parties."

"We can't risk killing it," Spock said. "We have no data—no way of knowing the effect of its death on you."

So Spock understood. "Yes, that's right," Kirk said. "We don't know that—but the men must be armed. All men to be armed with phasers locked to the stun setting. He's to be taken without—if anyone fires to kill, he won't die—it's not the way to get rid of him . . ."

Spock noted the breaks between thoughts and words. They were disjointed, disorganized. No, there was no doubt. This Kirk was not the integrated, decisive Kirk he knew.

"It will be difficult to order the search parties to capture a being who so closely resembles you, Captain."

"Tell them—" Kirk looked at him helplessly. "I'd better make an announcement to the entire crew—tell them what's happened as well as I can. It's a good crew—they deserve to be told."

"I must object, sir," Spock said. "You are the Captain of this ship. You cannot afford to appear vulnerable in the eyes of your crew. It is your damnable fate to have to seem perfect to them. I'm sorry, sir. Yet that is the fact. They lose their confidence in you—and you lose your command."

Kirk pressed his forehead between his hands. "I know that, Mr. Spock. Why did I forget it?" He turned away, then stopped without looking back. "If you see me slipping again, your order is to *tell* me so."

"Yes, Captain."

His back stiff, Kirk walked out of the Transporter Room. In the bridge he touched the back of his command chair before he took his position in it. Command—no weakness, no fault, no hesitation. Bracing himself for the front of perfection, he flicked on his intercom. "This is the Captain speaking. There is an impostor aboard this ship—a man who looks exactly like me and is pretending to *be* me. The man is dangerous. Utmost caution is to be observed. All crew members are to arm themselves. The impostor may be identified by scratches on his face."

The message reached the double. It sat up quickly on Kirk's bed. "Repeat," came the voice from the intercom. "The imposter may be identified by scratches on his face. Search parties will report to Mr. Spock for assignment. All hand phasers will be set to stun force. The impostor is not to be injured. Repeat. The impostor is not to be injured."

The double touched the scratches on its face. Then it got up to go to the mirror and stare at its reflection. "Impostor!" it muttered to itself. *"I'm Kirk!"* it shouted at Kirk's image on the intercom viewing screen. A gust of fury shook it. It seized a metal box from the dresser and hurled it at the screen. The sound of crashing glass frightened it. "I'm Kirk," it whimpered to its reflection in the mirror. The scratches showed red, unhealed. To examine them more closely, it pushed aside a jar of medicated cream. The loosened lid fell off. The double dug its fingers into the cream, looked once more at the scratches and began to rub the cream into them. It made them feel better. It also hid the weals. The double grunted with satisfaction. It was dabbing more of the concealing cream into the cuts when it heard running sounds from the corridor outside.

When the sounds had gone, it unlocked the door. Moving out into the working area of Kirk's quarters, it slid its entrance panel half open. Wilson, carrying some Transporter equipment, was hurrying down the corridor.

"Wilson!" the double called. "Come here!"

Wilson came.

"Give me your weapon belt!"

"Yes, sir."

As he handed over the belt, Wilson saw the smeared cream on its face. But his suspicion came too late. The double had the phaser out of the belt. It struck him on the jaw with its butt. When Wilson fell, it stooped to pound his jaw with the heavy butt. Then it dragged him into Kirk's cabin. The bloody phaser still in hand, it nodded to itself—and walked casually out into the corridor.

Down on the planet's surface it was growing dark. Sulu and his three crewmen were gathering rocks to erect a wall against the rising wind. Frost had already whitened the dismal landscape as far as they could see.

Over his communicator, Kirk said, "Mr. Sulu, how is the rock shelter coming?"

"It's a compliment to these rocks, sir, to call them a shelter. It's down to 50 below zero now, Captain."

They were not equipped with thermal clothing. It was hard to say, "Kirk out." He might better have said, "Kirk down and out." That was the truth. In his command chair, he had to steady himself against another attack of vertigo. "We've got to get those men up!" he said to Spock. But Spock was taking a report from one of his search parties. "Deck 5 Sections 2 and 3 completely covered now, sir. Result, negative. Proceeding to Sections 4 and 5."

"Acknowledged," Spock said and flicked off his audio—but only to flick it on again to another intercom call.

"Search party number eight, sir. Transporter technician Wilson has just been found crawling out of the Captain's cabin. He's been badly beaten. He says the impostor attacked him, called him by his name and took his phaser."

"Get him to Sickbay," Spock said. "Then continue your search."

"We must locate this—this opposite of mine before he—" Kirk broke off. "But how, Spock, how?"

"It is apparent, sir, that it possesses your knowledge of the ship, its crew and devices. That being so, perhaps we can foresee its next move. Knowing how this ship is constructed, where would *you* go to elude a mass search, Captain?"

For the first time since his disaster, Kirk spoke without

hesitation. "The lower level. The Engineering deck. Let's go!"

In the elevator Spock removed his phaser from his belt. Without looking at Kirk, he said, "I'm setting this, not to the kill cycle, but to the stun one, sir. What about your phaser?" Kirk took the hint; and Spock said, "The thing is dangerous. Don't you think we'll need some help if we find it?"

The torture of indecision was back. Finally Kirk said, "No. If we find him, I don't want anyone else around but you." He had stepped out of the elevator when Spock called, *"Captain!"*

Kirk turned.

Spock said, "You ordered me to tell you . . ."

"I said *no*, Mr. Spock. No one but you."

The lower level of the Engineering deck held the vast complex that powered the *Enterprise*. It was a cavern of shadows, broken by glints of gleaming machinery, its passageways narrowing, widening, narrowing again to crisscross other passages. The droning hum of its huge nuclear energizers reverberated against its metal walls. Suddenly, as he rounded a dynamo, Spock realized he was alone. He turned to retrace his steps in hope of locating Kirk again.

Kirk, unaware he had lost Spock, looked at the phaser he held at the ready. The sight of it repelled him. A suicide weapon was what it was. The life it would fell was part of his own. He replaced the phaser in his belt.

And his Cain saw him do it. Crouched between two power generators, the double had heard his approaching footsteps. Its features tensed with its curious mixture of fear and ferocity. Its phaser aimed, it moved away from its shelter for a full confrontation.

Kirk stopped dead. As he recognized his own face in the Other's face, a chill passed over him. This nameless Thing belonged to him more utterly than any name his parents had given him. The two Kirks stared at each other in a kind of trance. Then, as though he were drawn by a power as unknown as it was powerful, Kirk stepped toward his double. It raised its phaser.

Kirk spoke. His voice sounded strange in his own ears. It was solemn with the prophetic tone of a mystic suddenly endowed with an incontrovertible truth. "You must not hurt me,'' he said. ''You must not kill me. You can live only as long as I live.''

Uncertainty flickered over the double's face; and Kirk, in a kind of dream, knew he was seeing the reflection of his own new uncertainty.

Then the hesitation faded. ''*I* don't need you!'' the double said. ''I don't have to believe what you say. So I *can* kill you!''

Its finger was on the kill trigger. Leaping, the momentum of his leap lending force to his clenched fist, Spock lunged from behind the generator to land it, hammerlike, on the double's chin. It fell. Its phaser fired, the beam striking a machine unit behind Kirk. It flared into glow and collapsed.

Spock looked down at the sprawled double. ''I fear,'' he said, ''that the ministrations of Dr. McCoy will be needed.''

The fear was well-founded. Consciousness was reluctant to return to the double. Each in his different way anxious, Kirk and Spock watched McCoy as he stooped over the still figure in its bed. McCoy worked silently. After a moment, Kirk went to the viewing screen. Turning it on to Engineering, he said, ''What about those Transporter circuits, Scotty? They're all checked through now, aren't they?''

''Yes, sir. And we thought we'd corrected the trouble. But now something else has gone wrong.''

''What?'' Kirk demanded.

''We don't know, sir. We're working on it. Is that all, Captain?''

Once more Kirk was unable to rally either a yes or a no. There was an uncomfortable pause. Finally Scott said, ''Then I'd better get back to work, sir.''

It would be darker on the planet. Kirk cried out, ''Find out what's wrong, Scott! And fix it in God's name! Four human lives are depending on that Transporter!''

Scott said stiffly, ''We're doing our best, sir.''

Kirk leaned his forehead against the frame of the viewing screen. ''I know, Scotty. You always do your best. Keep me posted, will you?''

''Yes, sir.'' The voice had relaxed.

Over at the bed, McCoy had completed his examination. ''How is—he?'' Kirk asked.

"Pulse and blood pressure high," McCoy said. He glanced at Spock. "Probably due to that sock on the chin."

"It was necessary, Doctor."

"This—creature will be recovering consciousness soon. As I have no idea at all about its mental state, I can't give it a tranquilizer. I think we'd better bind it."

He looked at Kirk for authorization. Kirk was suddenly oppressed by a sense of suffocation. The heavy tonnage of command responsibility seemed to be crushing him. He shook his head to try and clear it of the dizziness. "Yes," he said, "all right. I just wish someone would tell me what's the matter with *me*."

"You are losing the power of decision, Captain," Spock said.

"What?"

McCoy was busy binding the double but not so busily that he couldn't direct a glare at Spock. But the Vulcan continued, cool and unruffled. "Judging from my observations," he said, "you are rapidly losing your capacity for action. There's hesitation in time of crises—loss of perception. Captain, you refuse to defend yourself. You refused to demand adequate assistance when we went down to the Engineering level whereas you should have placed yourself in guarded isolation until the impostor was captured." He paused. "You have dismissed men for less hesitation, less passivity in the face of danger."

"Make your point, Spock!" shouted McCoy.

"Point?"

"You *have* one, I presume," McCoy said.

"I am analyzing, Doctor; not point-making."

"It's the Captain's guts you're analyzing! Are you aware of that, Mr. Spock?"

"Vituperation, Doctor?"

Composed, unmoved, Spock went on. "The dichotomies inherent in the human mind are multiple," he said. "The problem of command, for instance, highly pertinent in this case. Command is a balance between positive and negative energies—an equilibrium of the forces generated by each of these energies. The proof?"

He turned to Kirk. "Your negative energy was removed from you by that duplication process. Thus, the power of command has begun to fail you. Things remaining as they are, how long can you continue to function as Captain of this ship? Finally unable to decide anything at all, will you . . ."

McCoy broke in. "Jim, give him a command! Tell him to get lost!"

"If I seem emotionally insensitive to the agony of your ordeal, Captain, please understand. It's the way I am."

"That's for damned sure!" yelled McCoy.

"Gentlemen," Kirk said. In the end, always in the end, one's pain remained a private matter. The scene, however dismal, was always enacted alone. He smiled wryly at them. "I may be losing my ability to command but it hasn't entirely disappeared. Until it does, you will both kindly knock it off."

The intercom on McCoy's desk whirred. Kirk flicked it on. "Kirk here."

"Engineering, sir. We've just located that new trouble with the Transporter. Its Ionizer Unit has been mangled. Looks as if a phaser beam had hit it."

The double's phaser beam had hit it, the double, that separated part of himself. If his crewmen died their lonely death on the subarctic planet beneath him, it would be he, Kirk, their trusted Captain who had killed them.

He got up to walk to the door. "If I'm needed," he said, "I'll be in the Briefing Room."

They had lit a fire down on the planet. Black night was spreading toward them from its horizon. And the stealthy fronds of frost were creeping over the rocks of the rock shelter where the abandoned crewmen huddled together for warmth. Sulu, his lips cracked and sore, had to hold his hands over the fire before his fingers could manipulate his communicator. "Can you give us a status report, *Enterprise*? It's fallen to 90 degrees below zero down here."

"This is the Captain, Mr. Sulu. We have located the trouble. It shouldn't be much longer."

"Think you could rig up a cord, sir, and lower us down a pot of coffee?"

"I'll see what I can do about that," Kirk said.

"Rice wine will do, sir, if you're short of coffee."

"I'll check the commissariat for rice wine, Mr. Sulu." And once more it had to be "Kirk out."

He watched his hand reach out to the intercom button. He was afraid to call Scott. He pressed the button. "That mangled unit, Scotty. Status report."

"Nothing much of it left, sir."

"How bad is it?"

"We can't repair it in less than a week."

A week. One hundred and sixty-eight hours. Death by cold was said to be preceded by sleep. Alone in the Briefing Room, Kirk realized that imagination had become his mortal enemy. It showed him the planet's surface under the deadly grip of its incredible cold, its night ominous with the coming sleep of death as the blood in his men's veins turned to ice. They'd be moving slowly now if they could move at all . . .

Reality endorsed imagination. Sulu was slowed to a crawl as he elbowed himself to the dying warmth to check his phaser. He fired it at another boulder. It burst into glow. The others inched toward it; and Sulu made his frost-blackened lips say, "That rice wine is taking too long. I'm giving Room Service another call."

Nobody spoke as he opened his communicator. "*Enterprise*, this is Sulu."

"Kirk here, Mr. Sulu."

"Hot line direct to the Captain again. Are we that far gone, sir?"

Kirk struck the Briefing Room table with his fist. "Everybody but you's got the afternoon off. I'm watching the store. How is it down there?"

"Lovely," Sulu said. "We're using our phasers to heat the rocks. One phaser's quit on us. Three are still operational. Any chance of getting us aboard before the skiing season opens down here?"

The ice—maybe it would be merciful, quick. *Think.* But he couldn't think. His thoughts like comets that would not be stayed flashed through his mind—and were gone . . .

He felt no surprise to see Spock quietly lift the speaker he had dropped.

"This is Spock, Mr. Sulu. You will hold out a little longer. *Hold out.* Survival procedures, Mr. Sulu."

"As per your training program, Mr. Spock."

"Yes, Mr. Sulu."

Kirk reached for the speaker. "Sulu—just don't drift, don't lose—awareness. Sulu, beware of sleep . . ."

As Spock said, "Spock out," Kirk felt an irresistible impulse to return to Sickbay. He wasn't entirely composed of that atavism that had destroyed the Ionizer Unit. He was Captain James T. Kirk of the Starship *Enterprise*, too—and he was going back to Sickbay. Courage was doing what you were afraid to do.

The consciousness that had come back to the double was a thing of howling panic. It was thrusting madly against the net of cords that held it, the force of its screams swelling the veins of its neck. As he watched the writhing body on the bed, it seemed to Kirk that he could taste the acid of its frenzy in his mouth. How he knew what he knew he didn't know; but he knew that the double was feeling some ultimate terror it had met in the black labyrinth of its Cain fate.

"It should be calming down," McCoy said, laying a hypodermic aside. "This tranquilizer should be working now." He threw a worried glance at the body function panel. All its readings showed a dangerous peak.

The tormented body on the bed strained again at its bonds. A shudder shook it. Then, suddenly, it collapsed, its head lolling like a broken doll's.

"What's happened?" Kirk cried. The readings on the body-function panel were rapidly falling.

"The tranquilizer was a mistake," McCoy said. "Its system has rejected it."

"He's not—*dying*?" Kirk said.

McCoy spoke tonelessly. "Yes, it is."

"No," Kirk whispered. "No." He reached for McCoy's arm. "I can't survive without him and he can't survive without me."

McCoy shook his head; and the double moaned. "Afraid, afraid," it said.

Kirk went to it. "Help me," it wept. "I am afraid—so afraid."

Kirk took its hand. McCoy started forward. "Jim, you'd better not . . ."

Kirk stooped over the bed. "Don't be afraid. This is my hand. Feel it. Hold on to it. That's it. Hang on to my hand. I won't let you go."

"Afraid," whimpered the double painfully.

Some strength rose up from unknown depths in Kirk. It was as though he had lived through just such a scene before. The words that came to him seemed familiar. "You must hold on to me because we've been pulled apart. Come back! No, you're letting go! Hold on to me. Tight! Tighter!"

He lifted the sheet to wipe the sweat from its forehead. "I'm pulling you back to me. We need each other! That's it. *Tight!* We have to hang on—together . . ."

McCoy, at the body-function panel, looked around, astounded. But all Kirk saw were the tragic eyes fixed on his in abject dependence. "No fear," he said. "You can come back. You are not afraid. *You are not afraid.* Be back with me. Be back, be back, be back . . ."

McCoy touched his shoulder. "Jim, it *is* back."

Kirk stumbled over to McCoy's desk, slumping into its chair. "Now *you* can use some brandy," McCoy said.

He gagged on the drink. Eyes shut, he said, "I must take him back—into myself. I don't want to, Bones—a brutish, mindless wolf in human shape. But I must. He is me, *me*!"

"Jim, don't take this so hard," McCoy said. "We are all part wolf and part lamb. We need both parts. Compassion is reconciliation between them. It is human to be both lamb and wolf."

"Human?" Kirk asked bitterly.

"Yes, *human.* Some of his wolfishness makes you the man you are. God forbid that I should ever agree with Spock—but he was right! Without the strength of the wolf in you, you could not command this ship! And without the lamb in you, your discipline would be harsh and cruel. Jim, you just used the lamb to give life back to that dying wolf . . ."

The double was listening, concentrated.

The intercom buzzed. Drained, Kirk said, "Kirk here."

"Spock, sir. Will you come to the Transporter Room? We think we may have found an answer."

"I'm on my way," Kirk said. He turned to McCoy. "Thanks, Bones. And keep your fingers crossed."

"Tell Mr. Spock I'm shaking all my rattles to invoke good spirits."

But as the door closed behind Kirk, there came a cry

from the bed. *"No!"* The startled McCoy went to the bed. The double was sitting up. It said quietly, "No. *Everything is under control right now.*"

In the Transporter Room, Wilson was holding the mild doglike creature.

"What's that answer you think you've found?" Kirk asked.

"A way to make the Transporter safe, sir," Scott said. "We have attached some temporary bypass and leader circuits to compensate for the velocity variation. There shouldn't be more than a five-point difference in speed balance."

"Our suggestion is that we send the two animals through the Transporter," Spock said.

So that was the answer—hope that amendment in the Transporter would somehow rejoin the two halves of the animal as it had somehow cut them apart. It was hoped that his dying men could be beamed home to the *Enterprise* without risk of the fatal division. Hope. Well, without it, you couldn't live.

"All right," Kirk said. "Go ahead."

Spock took the hypodermic from the top of the Transporter console. He nodded at Scott. The Chief Engineer went to the specimen case and lifted its lid. "I'll grab it by the scruff of its neck and hold it as still as I can." He reached into the case. The snarling beast twisted and writhed against Scott's grip on its neck.

"Don't hurt it!" Kirk cried.

Injecting the shot, Spock said, "It's painless, Captain, quick. The animal will lose consciousness for only the few, necessary moments." The snarls subsided. Spock took the creature from Scott and carried it to the Transporter platform where Wilson was waiting with the other one. They laid them on the platform, side by side. Scott, at the console, said, "If this doesn't work—" He broke off at Spock's signal. He turned a dial. The platform flared into glow. The two animals vanished and the glow faded.

"Energize to reverse," Spock said.

Scott twisted a dial. The platform flared into light again. The two animals reappeared—and the light dimmed.

Spock ran to the console. He made some adjustment

of dials. "Again," he said to Scott. The process was repeated. The energizing dial was reversed. The platform broke into dazzle. As it shaped itself into substance, McCoy came in.

One animal lay on the platform.

"It's dead," Kirk said.

"Not so fast, Jim," McCoy said.

Kirk waited while he checked the limp body for heartbeat. There was none. Into the silence Spock said, "The shock—the shock of reabsorption . . ."

Kirk stumbled out of the Transporter Room.

Later, in Sickbay, McCoy gave tentative support to Spock's diagnosis of the cause of the death. Straightening up from the table that held the dead beast, he said, "Maybe it *was* the shock of reabsorption that killed it. But it would take a post mortem before we could even approach certainty."

"Why shock?" Kirk asked.

"We're only guessing, Jim."

"Yes, I know. But you've both used the word shock."

"The consequence of instinctive fear," Spock said. "The animal lacked the ability to understand the process of reabsorption. Its fear was so great it induced shock. Other conditions that cause shock are not apparent." He was carefully examining the creature. "You yourself can see, sir, that the body is quite undamaged."

Kirk was groping for some answer of his own. "*He*—in that bed in there—felt great fear." He turned to McCoy. "You saw him feel it. But he survived it. He *survived* it!"

"Just by a hairsbreadth," McCoy reminded him. "I can hear it coming, Jim. You want to take this double of yours through the Transporter with you—you and it, *with* it. No, Jim, *no*!"

"Four of my men are freezing to death," Kirk said.

"But there isn't one genuine shred of evidence to prove this animal died of fear! Shock? Yes. But fear? That's mere theory!"

"Based on the laws of probability," Spock said.

"Probability be hanged!" McCoy shouted. "It's Jim's life that's at stake! And all of a sudden you're an expert on fear! That's a base emotion, Mr. Spock. What do you know about it?"

"I must remind you, Doctor, that I am half human," Spock said. "I am more aware than you of what it means to live with a divided spirit—of the suffering involved in possession of two separate selves. I survive it daily."

"That may be—but a piece of machinery is the problem. What do the laws of probability say about the Transporter? Is it reliable? You don't know! It's just more theory, more hopeful guesswork!"

Kirk said, "I am going through the Transporter with him."

McCoy threw up his arms in a gesture of hopelessness. "You've got more guts than brains, Jim! Use your head, for God's sake!"

"I'm getting my four men back on this ship," Kirk said. "And we can't risk using that Transporter until we know whether this animal died of fear—or mechanical malfunction in the Transporter."

"I want to save the men, too, Jim! But you're more vital to this ship than four crew members. That's the brutal truth—and you know it!"

Listening, Kirk felt his weakened will sink to its final depth of hesitation. "I have to—try. I must be allowed to try. If I don't try, their death is sure. So will mine be. I shall look alive, Bones. But I shall live as a half man. What good to this ship is a half man Captain?"

"Jim, do me one favor. Before you decide, let me run an autopsy on this animal."

"Delay is too expensive," Kirk said.

"At least give Spock more time to test the Transporter. And let me get the lab started on the autopsy." McCoy gathered up the dead animal in a sheet. "Wait, Jim, please wait." He hurried out of Sickbay.

Spock said, "I'll put the Transporter through another check-out cycle as soon as the Doctor returns."

Kirk whirled on him. "I don't need nursemaids, Mr. Spock!"

"As soon as the Doctor returns." The six words too many, Spock thought. The weakened will had finally steeled itself to decision only to meet doubt, argument, pressure. Those last six words had been a mistake.

"If you will excuse me, Captain," he said.

Kirk nodded. He watched Spock go. Half human, Spock—but you never came to the end of his aware humanity. Gratitude heartened him to do what he had to do. He was turning toward Sickbay's bed section when Sulu's voice sounded from the wall speaker.

"Kirk here, Mr. Sulu."

The voice was a whisper. "Captain—the rocks are cold—no phasers left—one of us is unconscious—we can't hold out much longer." The communicator crackled. "Captain—the cold is freezing the communicator—no time left—no time . . ."

The whisper fell silent. There was another crackle from the dead communicator. Kirk sank down on the double's bed. Four lives at risk on the fatal planet—two lives at risk in the Transporter process. There was no alternative.

The double spoke fearfully. "What are you going to do?"

Kirk didn't answer. He began to untie the cords of the restraining net over the bed. The double reached out and touched the phaser at his belt. "You don't need that," it said. "I'm not going to fight you any more. What are you going to do?"

"We are going through the Transporter together," Kirk said.

The double tensed. Then it controlled itself. "If that's what you want," it said.

"It's what I have to want," Kirk said. He untied the last cord, stepped back and raised his phaser. Staggering, the double got up. Then it leaned back against the bed for support. "I feel so weak," it said. "I'll be glad when this is over."

"Let's go," Kirk said.

The double moved toward the door; but on its first step it faltered, groaning. It tried again, staggered again—and Kirk instinctively reached out to help it. It saw its chance. Lunging, it drove its shoulder into Kirk, knocking him backward. The phaser dropped. It stooped for it. Recovering his balance, Kirk shouted, "No, no, you can't . . ."

The phaser butt crashed into the side of his head. He fell back on the bed. The double paused to finger the scratches on its face. McCoy's medication covered them. It smiled to itself. Then it began to strap Kirk into the bed. "I'm *you*," it told him.

Swaggering, it walked out into the corridor. At its end the elevator door slid open. Janice Rand was standing inside it. At once it tempered its swagger to a quiet walk.

"How are you, Yeoman Rand?"

"Captain," the girl said nervously.

It smiled at her. "Is that a question? No, I am not the impostor. Are you feeling better?"

"Yes, sir. Thank you."

"Good."

Maybe it was her opportunity, Janice thought. She'd done this man a grave injustice. "Captain" she said, "I've wanted to apologize. If I caused you . . ."

She got Kirk's own grin. "That's a big word—'if.' I understand, Yeoman. I hope you do. I owe you, I think, a personal explanation."

"No," she said. "It's I who owe you . . ."

"Let's call it a clarification, then," the double said. "I trust your discretion. There was no impostor, not really. The Transporter malfunctioned. It seems to have created a duplicate of me. It's hard to understand because we haven't yet determined what went wrong. But what we *do* know I'll explain to you later. You're entitled to that. All right?"

Bewildered, she nodded. "All right, sir."

The elevator door opened. Politely, the double stepped back, gesturing her forward. As the elevator moved on up to the bridge deck, it shouted with laughter. Slamming its hand against the elevator wall, it yelled, "*My* ship! Mine—all mine!"

The sight of Kirk's command chair intoxicated it. As it settled back into it, a frowning Farrell spoke from the navigation console. "No word from Mr. Sulu, Captain."

It ignored the comment; and Spock, hurrying over to the command chair, said, "Captain, I couldn't find you in the Transporter Room."

"I changed my mind," the double said. "Take your station, Mr. Spock." It didn't look at the Vulcan.

Spock walked slowly back to his computer. It was a very sudden change of mind for a mind that had struggled so valiantly for decision.

"Prepare to leave orbit, Mr. Farrell!"

If the order had commanded activation of the Destruct unit, its impact could not have been more devastating. Farrell stared in stark unbelief. The double became abruptly aware that every eye in the bridge was fixed on it.

"Captain—" Farrell began.

"I gave you an order, Mr. Farrell."

"I know, sir, but what—what about . . . ?"

"They can't be saved. They're dead now." Its voice rose. "Prepare to leave orbit, Mr. Farrell!"

"Yes, sir." Farrell's hand was moving toward a switch when the elevator opened. Kirk and McCoy stepped out of it. There were badly covered scratches on Kirk's face but the hand that held the phaser was steady. The double leaped from the command chair. "There's the imposter," it shouted. "Grab him!"

Nobody moved.

"You are the imposter," McCoy said.

"Don't believe him!" the double shrieked. "Take them both! Grab them!"

Kirk, McCoy beside him, walked on toward the command chair. Spock, reaching out a hand, halted McCoy, shaking his head. McCoy nodded—and Kirk moved on, alone.

"You want me dead, don't you? You want this ship all to yourself! But it's *mine*!"

Farrell had jumped from his chair. Spock touched his shoulder. "This is the Captain's private business," he said.

Kirk maintained his slow advance toward the maddened thing. It backed up, slow step by slow step, screaming.

"I am Captain Kirk, you ship of pigs! All right, let the liar destroy you all! He's already killed four of you! I run this ship! I own it. I own you—all of you!"

Kirk fired his phaser. The double crumpled to the deck, stunned.

"Spock, Bones," he said quietly. "Quickly, please."

Kirk had already taken up his position on the Transporter platform when they laid the unconscious body at his feet.

"You'll have to hold it, Captain," Spock said.

Kirk sat down on the platform. He lifted the drooping

head to his shoulder, an arm around the flaccid waist. Then he looked up.

"Mr. Spock . . ."

"Yes, sir."

"If this doesn't work . . ."

"Understood, sir."

"Jim!" McCoy burst out. "Jim, don't do it! Not yet! In God's name, wait!"

"The console, Mr. Spock," Kirk said.

Spock's half-human part had taken him over. This could be good-bye to Kirk. At the console, he bowed his head over his treacherously shaking hands. When he lifted it, his face was calm, impassive.

"I am energizing, sir."

He saw Kirk draw the double closer to him. In the glow that lit the platform, he knew that he was seeing the embrace of an acknowledged, irrevocable brotherhood. Unfaltering, Spock reversed the console's controls. The hum of dematerialization rose. There was dazzle—and silence.

McCoy ran to the platform. Kirk stood on it, alone.

"Jim—Jim?" McCoy cried.

"Hello, Bones," Kirk said. He walked off the empty platform and over to the console. "Mr. Spock," he said, "let's get those men of ours up and aboard."

Spock swallowed. "Yes, Captain. At once, sir."

It wasn't done at once. It was twenty minutes before the Transporter platform surrendered its burden of the four bodies to the eager hands awaiting them.

McCoy rose from his last examination. "They'll make it, Jim. Those rocks they heated saved their lives. They're all suffering from severe frostbite—but I think they'll make it."

The pallor of Kirk's face suddenly struck him. "How do *you* feel, Jim?"

There was a new sadness in Kirk's smile. "What's that old expression? 'Sadder but wiser.' I feel sadder, Bones, but much less wise."

"Join the human race, Jim," McCoy said.

There was a sense of quiet thanksgiving as Kirk entered the bridge. His first move was over to Spock at the computer station. "You know, of course," he said, "I could never have made it without you."

"Thank you, Captain. What do you plan to tell the crew?"

"The truth, Mr. Spock—that the imposter was put back where he belongs."

Janice Rand approached him. "I just wanted to say, Captain, how—glad I am that . . ."

"Thank you, Yeoman." Kirk returned to his command chair. The girl watched him go. Spock watched the girl.

"That impostor," he said, "had some very interesting qualities. And he certainly resembled the Captain. You agree, I'm sure, Yeoman Rand."

She had flushed scarlet. But she met his quizzical eyes with courage. "Yes, Mr. Spock. The imposter had some exceedingly interesting qualities."

THE UNREAL McCOY

(aired as "The Man Trap")

Writer: George Clayton Johnson
Director: Marc Daniels
Guest stars: Alfred Ryder, Jeanne Bal

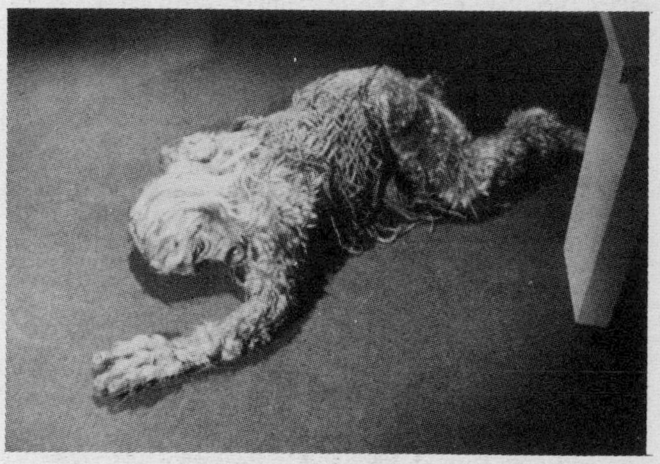

The crater campsite—or the Bierce campsite, as the records called it—on Regulus VIII was the crumbling remains of what might once have been a nested temple, surrounded now by archeological digs, several sheds, and a tumble of tools, tarpaulins, and battered artifacts. Outside the crater proper, the planet was largely barren except for patches of low, thorny vegetation, all the way in any direction to wherever the next crater might be—there were plenty of those, but there'd been no time to investigate them, beyond noting that they had all been inhabited once, unknown millennia ago. There was nothing uncommon about that; the galaxy was strewn with ruins about which nobody knew anything, there were a hundred such planets for every archeologist who could even dream of scratching such a surface. Bierce had just been lucky—fantastically lucky.

All the same, Regulus VIII made Kirk—Capt. James Kirk of the starship *Enterprise*, who had seen more planets than most men knew existed—feel faintly edgy. The *Enterprise* had landed here in conformity to the book; to be specific, to that part of the book which said that research personnel on alien planets must have their health certified by a starship's surgeon at one-year intervals. The *Enterprise* had been in Bierce's vicinity at the statutory time, and Ship's Surgeon McCoy had come down by transporter from the orbiting *Enterprise* to do the job. Utterly, completely routine, except for the fact that McCoy had mentioned that Bierce's wife Nancy had been a serious interest of McCoy's, pre-Bierce, well over ten years ago. And after all, what could be more commonplace than that?

Then Nancy came out of the temple—if that is what it was—to meet them.

There were only three of them: McCoy and a crewman, Darnell, out of duty, and Kirk, out of curiosity. She came forward with outstretched hands, and after a moment's hesitation, McCoy took them. "Leonard!" she said. "Let me look at you."

"Nancy," McCoy said. "You . . . you haven't aged a year."

Kirk restrained himself from smiling. Nancy Bierce was handsome, but nothing extraordinary: a strongly built woman of about forty, moderately graceful, her hair tinged with gray. It wasn't easy to believe that the hard-bitten medico could have been so smitten, even at thirty or less, as to be unable to see the signs of aging now. Still, she did have a sweet smile.

"This is the Captain of the *Enterprise*, Jim Kirk," McCoy said. "And this is Crewman Darnell."

Nancy turned her smile on the Captain, and then on the crewman. Darnell's reaction was astonishing. His jaw swung open; he was frankly staring. Kirk would have kicked him had he been within reach.

"Come in, come in," she was saying. "We may have to wait a little for Bob; once he starts digging, he forgets time. We've made up some quarters in what seems to have been an old altar chamber—not luxurious, but lots of room. Come on in, Plum."

She ducked inside the low, crumbling stone door.

"Plum?" Kirk said.

"An old pet name," McCoy said, embarrassed. He followed her. Embarrassed himself at his own gaucherie, Kirk swung on the crewman.

"Just what are you goggling at, Mister?"

"Sorry, sir," Darnell said stiffly. "She reminds me of somebody, is all. A girl I knew once on Wrigley's Planet. That is—"

"That's enough," Kirk said drily. "The next thought of that kind you have will probably be in solitary. Maybe you'd better wait outside."

"Yessir. Thanks." Darnell seemed genuinely grateful. "I'll explore a little, if that suits you, Captain."

"Do that. Just stay within call."

Commonplace; Darnell hadn't seen a strange woman since his last landfall. But most peculiar, too.

Bierce did not arrive, and after apologies, Nancy left again to look for him, leaving Kirk and McCoy to examine the stone room, trying not to speak to each other. Kirk could not decide whether he would rather be back on board the *Enterprise*, or just plain dead; his diplomacy had not failed him this badly in he could not think how many years.

Luckily, Bierce showed up before Kirk had to decide whether to run or suicide. He was an unusually tall man, all knuckles, knees, and cheekbones, wearing faded coveralls. Slightly taller than McCoy, his face was as craggy as his body; the glint in the eyes, Kirk thought, was somehow both intelligent and rather bitter. But then, Kirk had never pretended to understand the academic type.

"Dr. Bierce," he said, "I'm Captain Kirk, and this is Ship's Surgeon—"

"I know who you are," Bierce broke in, in a voice with the blaring rasp of a busy signal. "We don't need you here. If you'll just refill us on aspirin, salt tablets, and the like, you needn't trouble yourselves further."

"Sorry, but the law requires an annual checkup," Kirk said. "If you'll co-operate, I'm sure Dr. McCoy will be as quick as possible." McCoy, in fact, already had his instruments out.

"McCoy?" Bierce said. "I've heard that name . . . Ah, yes, Nancy used to talk about you."

"Hands out from your sides, please, and breathe evenly . . . Yes, didn't she mention I'd arrived?"

After the slightest of pauses, Bierce said, "You've . . . seen Nancy?"

"She was here when we arrived," Kirk said. "She went to look for you."

"Oh. Quite so. I'm pleased, of course, that she can meet an old friend, have a chance of some company. I enjoy solitude, but it's difficult for a woman sometimes."

"I understand," Kirk said, but he was none too sure

he did. The sudden attempt at cordiality rang false, somehow, after the preceding hostility. At least *that* had sounded genuinc.

McCoy had finished his checkup with the tricorder and produced a tongue depressor with a small flourish. "She hasn't changed a bit," he said. "Open your mouth, please."

Reluctantly, Bierce complied. At the same instant, the air was split by a full-throated shriek of horror. For an insane moment Kirk had the impression that the sound had issued from Bierce's mouth. Then another scream ripped the silence, and Kirk realized that it was, of course, a female voice.

They all three bolted out the door. In the open, Kirk and McCoy outdistanced Bierce quickly; for all his outdoor life, he was not a good runner. But they hadn't far to go. Just beyond the rim of the crater, Nancy, both fists to her mouth, was standing over the body of Darnell.

As they came pounding up she moved toward McCoy, but he ignored her and dropped beside the body. It was lying on its face. After checking the pulse, McCoy gently turned the head to one side, grunted, and then turned the body over completely.

It was clear even to Kirk that the crewman was dead. His face was covered with small ringlike red blotches, slowly fading. "What hit him?" Kirk said tensely.

"Don't know. Petachiae a little like vacuum mottling, or maybe some sort of immunological—hullo, what's this?"

Bierce came panting up as McCoy slowly forced open one of Darnell's fists. In it was a twisted, scabrous-looking object of no particular color, like a mummified parsnip. It looked also as though part of it had been bitten away. Now *that* was incredible. Kirk swung on Nancy.

"What happened?" he said tersely.

"Don't snap at my wife, Captain," Bierce said in his busy-signal voice. "Plainly it's not her fault!"

"One of my men is dead. I accuse nobody, but Mrs. Bierce is the only witness."

McCoy rose and said to Nancy, gently: "Just tell us what you saw, Nancy. Take your time."

"I was just . . ." she said, and then had to stop and swallow, as if fighting for control. "I couldn't find Bob, and I'd . . . I'd just started back when I saw your crewman. He had that borgia root in his hand and he was smelling it. I was just going to call out to him when—he bit into it. I had no idea he was going to—and then his face twisted and he fell—''

She broke off and buried her face in her hands. McCoy took her gently by one shoulder. Kirk, feeling no obligation to add one bedside manner more, said evenly: ''How'd you know what the root was if you'd just come within calling distance?''

''This cross-examination—'' Bierce grated.

''Bob, please. I didn't know, of course. Not until I saw it now. But it's dangerous to handle any plant on a new world.''

Certainly true. Equally certainly, it would have been no news to Darnell. His face impassive, Kirk told McCoy: ''Pack up, Bones. We can resume the physicals tomorrow.''

''I'm sure that won't be necessary,'' Bierce said. ''If you'll just disembark our supplies, Captain—''

''It's not going to be that easy, Dr. Bierce,'' Kirk said. He snapped open his communicator. ''Kirk to Transporter Room. Lock and beam: two transportees and a corpse.''

The autopsied body of Darnell lay on a table in the sick bay, unrecognizable now even by his mother, if so veteran a spaceman had ever had one. Kirk, standing near a communicator panel, watched with a faint physical uneasiness as McCoy lowered Darnell's brain into a shallow bowl and then turned and washed his hands until they were paper-white. Kirk had seen corpses in every conceivable state of distortion and age in one battle and another, but this clinical bloodiness was not within his experience.

''I can't rule poison out entirely,'' McCoy said, in a matter-of-fact voice. ''Some of the best-known act just as fast and leave just as little trace: botulinus, for example. But there's no trace of any woody substance in his stomach or even between his teeth. All I can say for sure is that he's got massive capillary damage—which could be due to almost anything, even shock—and those marks on his face.''

McCoy covered the ruined body. ''I'll be running some blood chemistry tests, but I'd like to know what I'm testing for. I'd also like to know what symptoms that 'borgia root' is *supposed* to produce. Until then, Jim, I'm really rather in the dark.''

''Spock's running a library search on the plant,'' Kirk said. ''It shouldn't take him long. But I must confess that what you've said thus far doesn't completely surprise me. Darnell was too old a hand to bite into any old thing he happened to pick up.''

''Then what's left? Nancy? Jim, I'm not quite trusting my own eyes lately, but Nancy didn't used to be capable of murder—certainly not of an utter stranger, to boot!''

''It's not only people who kill—hold it, here's the report. Go ahead, Mr. Spock.''

''We have nothing on the borgia root but what the Bierces themselves reported in their project request six years ago,'' Spock's precise voice said. ''There they call it an aconite resembling the *Lilium* family. Said to contain some twenty to fifty different alkaloids, none then identifiable specifically with the equipment to hand. The raw root is poisonous to mice. No mention of any human symptoms. Except . . .''

''Except what?'' McCoy snapped.

''Well, Dr. McCoy, this isn't a symptom. The report adds that the root has a pleasant perfume, bland but edible-smelling, rather like tapioca. And that's all there is.''

''Thanks.'' Kirk switched off. ''Bones, I can't see Darnell having been driven irresistibly to bite into an unknown plant because it smelled like tapioca. He wouldn't have bitten into something that smelled like a brandied peach unless he'd known its pedigree. He was a seasoned hand.''

McCoy spread his hands expressively. ''You knew your man, Jim—but where does that leave us? The symptoms do vaguely resemble aconite poisoning. Beyond that, we're nowhere.''

''Not quite,'' Kirk said. ''We still have to check on the Bierces, I'm afraid, Bones. And for that I'm still going to need your help.''

McCoy turned his back and resumed washing his hands. ''You'll get it,'' he said; but his voice was very cold.

Kirk's method of checking on the Bierces was simple but drastic: he ordered them both on board the ship. Bierce raged.

"If you think you can beam down here, bully us, interfere with my work—considering the inescapable fact that you are a trespasser on my planet—"

"Your complaint is noted," Kirk said. "I apologize for the inconvenience. But it's also an inescapable fact that something we don't understand killed one of our men. It could very well be a danger to you, too."

"We've been here almost five years. If there was something hostile here we'd know about it by now, wouldn't we?"

"Not necessarily," Kirk said. "Two people can't know all the ins and outs of a whole planet, not even in five years—or a lifetime. In any event, one of the missions of the *Enterprise* is to protect human life in places like this. Under the circumstances, I'm going to have to be arbitrary and declare the argument closed."

It was shortly after they came aboard that McCoy forwarded his reports on the analyses of Darnell's body. "It was shock, all right," he told Kirk grimly by vidscreen. "But shock of a most peculiar sort. His blood electrolytes were completely deranged: massive salt depletion, hell—there isn't a microgram of salt in his whole body. Not in the blood, the tears, the organs, not anywhere. I can't even begin to guess how that could have happened at all, let alone all at once."

"What about the mottling on his face?"

"Broken capillaries. There are such marks all over the body. They're normal under the circumstances—except that I can't explain why they should be most marked on the face, or why the mottling should be ring-shaped. Clearly, though, he wasn't poisoned."

"Then the bitten plant," Kirk said equally grimly, "was a plant—in the criminal, not the botanical sense. A blind. That implies intelligence. I can't say I like that any better."

"Nor I," McCoy said. His eyes were averted.

"All right. That means we'll have to waste no time grilling the Bierces. I'll take it on. Bones, this has been a tremendous strain on you, I know, and you've been without sleep for two days. Better take a couple of tranquilizers and doss down."

"I'm all right."

"Orders," Kirk said. He turned off the screen and set off for the quarters he had assigned the Bierces.

But there was only one Bierce there. Nancy was missing.

"I expect she's gone below," Bierce said indifferently. "I'd go myself if I could get access to your Transporter for ten seconds. We didn't ask to be imprisoned up here."

"Darnell didn't ask to be killed, either. Your wife may be in serious danger. I must say, you seem singularly unworried."

"She's in no danger. This menace is all in your imagination."

"I suppose the body is imaginary, too?"

Bierce shrugged. "Nobody knows what could have killed him. For all I know, you brought your own menace with you."

There was nothing further to be got out of him. Exasperated, Kirk went back to the bridge and ordered a general search. The results were all negative—including the report from the Transporter Room, which insisted that nobody had used its facilities since the party had returned to the ship from the camp.

But the search, though it did not find Nancy, found something else: Crewman Barnhart, dead on Deck Twelve. The marks on his body were the same as those on Darnell's.

Baffled and furious, Kirk called McCoy. "I'm sorry to bust in on your sleep, Bones, but this has gone far enough. I want Bierce checked out under pentathol."

"Um," McCoy said. His voice sounded fuzzy, as though he had still not quite recovered from his tranquilizer dose. "Pentathol. Truth dope. Narcosynthesis. Um. Takes time. What about the patient's civil rights?"

"He can file a complaint if he wants. Go and get him ready."

An hour later, Bierce was lying on his bunk in half-trance. Kirk bent over him tensely; McCoy and Spock hovered in the background.

"Where's your wife?"

"Don't know . . . Poor Nancy, I loved her . . . The last of its kind . . ."

"Explain, please."

"The passenger pigeon . . . the buffalo . . ." Bierce groaned. "I feel strange."

Kirk beckoned to McCoy, who checked Bierce's pulse and looked under his eyelids. "He's all right," he said. "The transfer of questioner, from me to you, upset him. He's recovering."

"What about buffalo?" Kirk said, feeling absurd.

"Millions of them . . . prairies black with them. One single herd that covered three states. When they moved . . . like thunder. All gone now. Like the creatures here."

"Here? You mean down on the planet?"

"On the planet. Their temples . . . great poetry . . . Millions of them once, and now only one left. Nancy understood."

"Always the past tense," Spock's voice murmured.

"Where is Nancy? Where is she *now*?"

"Dead. Buried up on the hill. It killed her."

"Buried! But—how long ago was this, anyhow?"

"A year . . ." Bierce said. "Or was it two? I don't know. So confusing, Nancy and not Nancy. They needed salt, you see. When it ran out, they died . . . all but one."

The implication stunned Kirk. It was Spock who put the question.

"Is this creature masquerading as your wife?"

"Not a masquerade," Bierce droned. "It can *be* Nancy."

"Or anybody else?"

"Anybody. When it killed Nancy, I almost destroyed it. But I couldn't. It was the last."

The repetition was becoming more irritating every minute. Kirk said stonily: "Is that the only reason, Bierce? Tell me this: When it's with you, is it always Nancy?"

Bierce writhed. There was no answer. McCoy came forward again.

"I wouldn't press that one if I were you, Jim," he said. "You can get the answer if you need it, but not without endangering the patient."

"I don't need any better answer," Kirk said. "So we've intruded here into a little private heaven. The thing can be wife, lover, best friend, idol, slave, wise man, fool—

anybody. A great life, having everyone in the universe at your beck and call—and you win all the arguments."

"A one-way road to paranoia," Spock said. Kirk swung back to the drugged man.

"Then can you recognize the creature—no matter what form it takes?"

"Yes . . ."

"Will you help us?"

"No."

Kirk had expected no more. He gestured to McCoy. "I've got to go organize a search. Break down that resistance, Bones, I don't care how you do it or how much you endanger Bierce. In his present state of mind he's as big a danger to us as his 'wife.' Spock, back him up, and be ready to shoot if he should turn violent."

He stalked out. On the bridge, he called a General Quarters Three; that would put pairs of armed men in every corridor, on every deck. "Every man inspect his mate closely," he told the intercom. "There's one extra person aboard, masquerading as one of us. Lieutenant Uhura, make television rounds of all posts and stations. If you see any person twice in different places, sound the alarm. Got it?"

A sound behind him made him swing around. It was Spock. His clothes were torn, and he was breathing heavily.

"Spock! I thought I told you—what happened?"

"It was McCoy," Spock said shakily. "Or rather, it wasn't McCoy. You were barely out of the cabin when it grabbed me. I got away, but it's got my sidearm. No telling where it's off to now."

"McCoy! I *thought* he seemed a little reluctant about the pentathol. Reluctant, and sort of searching his memory, too. No wonder. Well, there's only one place it can have gone to now: right back where it came from."

"The planet? It can't."

"No. McCoy's cabin." He started to get up, but Spock lifted a hand sharply.

"Better look first, Captain. It may not have killed him yet, and if we alarm it—"

"You're right." Quickly, Kirk dialed in the intercom to McCoy's cabin, and after only a slight hesitation, punched the override button which would give him vision without sounding the buzzer on the other end.

McCoy was there. He was there twice: a sleeping McCoy on the bunk, and another one standing just inside the closed doorway, looking across the room. The standing form moved, passing in front of the hidden camera and momentarily blocking the view. Then it came back into the frame—but no longer as McCoy. It was Nancy.

She sat down on the bed and shook the sleeping doctor. He muttered, but refused to wake.

"Leonard," Nancy's voice said. "It's me. Nancy. Wake up. Please wake up. Help me."

Kirk had to admire the performance. What he was seeing was no doubt an alien creature, but its terror was completely convincing. Quite possibly it *was* in terror; in any event, the human form conveyed it as directly as a blow.

She shook McCoy again. He blinked his eyes groggily, and then sat up.

"Nancy! What's this? How long have I been sleeping?"

"Help me, Leonard."

"What's wrong? You're frightened."

"I am, I am," she said. "Please help me. They want to kill me!"

"Who?" McCoy said. "Easy. Nobody's going to hurt you."

"That's enough," Kirk said, unconsciously lowering his voice, though the couple on the screen could not hear him. "Luckily, the thing's trying to persuade him of something instead of killing him. Let's get down there fast, before it changes its mind."

Moments later, they burst into McCoy's cabin. The surgeon and the girl swung toward them. "Nancy" cried out.

"Get away from her, Bones," Kirk said, holding his gun rock steady.

"What? What's going on here, Jim?"

"That isn't Nancy, Bones."

"It isn't? Of course it is. Are you off your rocker?"

"It killed two crewmen."

"Bierce, too," Spock put in, his own gun leveled.

"It?"

"It," Kirk said. "Let me show you."

Kirk held out his free hand, unclenching it slowly. In the palm was a little heap of white crystals, diminishing at the edges from perspiration. "Look, Nancy," he said. "Salt. Free for the taking. Pure, concentrated salt."

Nancy took a hesitant step toward him, then stopped.

"Leonard," she said in a low voice. "Send him away. If you love me, make him go away."

"By all means," McCoy said harshly. "This is crazy behavior, Jim. You're frightening her."

"Not fright," Kirk said. "Hunger, Look at her!"

The creature, as if hypnotized, took another step forward. Then, without the slightest warning, there was a hurricane of motion. Kirk had a brief impression of a blocky body, man-sized but not the least like a man, and of suction-cup tentacles reaching for his face. Then there was a blast of sound and he fell.

It took a while for both Kirk and McCoy to recover—the captain from the nimbus of Spock's close-range phaser bolt, McCoy from emotional shock. By the time they were all back on the bridge, Bierce's planet was receding.

"The salt was an inspiration," Spock said. "Evidently the creature only hunted when it couldn't get the pure stuff; that's how Bierce kept it in control."

"I don't think the salt supply was the only reason why the race died out, though," Kirk said. "It wasn't really very intelligent—didn't use its advantages nearly as well as it might have."

"They could well have been residual," Spock suggested. "We still have teeth and nails, but we don't bite and claw much these days."

"That could well be. There's one thing I don't understand, though. How did it get into your cabin in the first place, Bones? Or don't you want to talk about it?"

"I don't mind," McCoy said. "Though I do feel like six kinds of a fool. It was simple. She came in just after I'd taken the tranquilizer and was feeling a little afloat. She said she didn't love her husband any more—wanted me to take her back to Earth. Well . . . it was a real thing I had with Nancy, long ago. I wasn't hard to tempt, especially with the drug already in my system. And later on, while I was asleep, she must have given me another dose—otherwise I couldn't have slept through all the exitement, the general quarters call and so on. It just goes to prove all over again—never mess with civilians."

"A good principle," Kirk agreed. "Unfortunately, an impossible one to live by."

"There's something *I* don't understand, though," McCoy added. "The creature and Bierce had Spock all alone in Bierce's cabin—and from what I've found during the dissection, it was twice as strong as a man anyhow. How did you get out, Mr. Spock, without losing anything but your gun?"

Spock smiled. "Fortunately, my ancestors spawned in quite another ocean than yours, Dr. McCoy," he said. "My blood salts are quite different from yours. Evidently, I wasn't appetizing enough."

"Of course," McCoy said. He looked over at Kirk. "You still look a little pensive, Jim. Is there still something else wrong?"

"Mmm?" Kirk said. "Wrong? No, not exactly. I was just thinking about the buffalo."

THE NAKED TIME

Writer: John D. F. Black
Director: Marc Daniels
Guest stars: Bruce Hyde, Stewart Moss

Nobody, it was clear, was going to miss the planet when it did break up. Nobody had even bothered to name it; on the charts it was just ULAPG42821DB, a coding promptly shorted by some of the *Enterprise*'s junior officers to "La Pig."

It was not an especially appropriate nickname. The planet, a rockball about 10,000 miles in diameter, was a frozen, windless wilderness, without so much as a gnarled root or fragment of lichen to relieve the monotony from horizon to purple horizon. But in one way the name fitted: the empty world was too big for its class.

After a relatively short lifetime of a few hundred million years, stresses between its frozen surface and its shrinking core were about to shatter it.

There was an observation station on La Pig, manned by six people. These would have to be got off, and the *Enterprise*, being in the vicinity, got the job. After that, the orders ran, the starship was to hang around and observe the breakup. The data collected would be of great interest to the sliderule boys back on Earth. Maybe some day they would turn the figures into a way to break up a planet at will, people and all.

Captain Kirk, like most line officers, did not have a high opinion of the chairborne arms of his service.

It turned out, however, that there was nobody at all to pick up off La Pig. The observation station was wide open, and the ice had moved inside. Massive coatings of it lay over everything—floors, consoles, even chairs. The doors were frozen open, and all the power was off.

The six members of the station complement were dead. One, in heavy gear, lay bent half over one of the consoles. On the floor at the entrance to one of the corridors was the body of a woman, very lightly clad and more than half iced over. Inspection, however, showed that she had been dead before the cold had got to her; she had been strangled.

In the lower part of the station were the other four. The engineer sat at his post with all the life-support system switches set at OFF, frozen there as though he hadn't given a damn. There was still plenty of power available; he just hadn't wanted it on any more. Two of the others were dead in their beds, which was absolutely normal and expectable considering the temperature. But the sixth and last man had died while taking a shower—fully clothed.

"There wasn't anything else to be seen," Mr. Spock, the officer in charge of the transporter party, later told Captain Kirk. "Except that there were little puddles of water here and there that hadn't frozen, though at that temperature they certainly should have, no matter what they might have held in solution. We brought back a small sample for the lab. The bodies are in our morgue now, still frozen. As for the people, I think maybe this is a job for a playwright, not an official investigation."

"Imagination's a useful talent in a police officer," Kirk commented. "At a venture, I'd guess that something volatile and highly toxic got loose in the station. One of the men got splattered and rushed to the shower hoping to sluice it off, clothes and all. Somebody else opened all the exit ports in an attempt to let the stuff blow out into the outside atmosphere."

"And the strangled woman?"

"Somebody blamed her for the initial accident—which was maybe just the last of a long chain of carelessnesses, and maybe irritating behavior too, on her part. You know how tempers can get frayed in small isolated crews like this."

"Very good, Captain," Spock said. "Now what about the engineer shutting off the life systems?"

Kirk threw up his hands. "I give up. Maybe he saw that nothing was going to work and decided on suicide. Or more likely I'm completely wrong all down the line. We'd better settle in our observation orbit. Whatever happened down there, apparently the books are closed."

For the record, it was just as well that he said "apparently."

Joe Tormolen, the crewman who had accompanied Mr. Spock to the observation station, was the first to show the signs. He had been eating all by himself in the recreation room—not unusual in itself, for though efficient and reliable, Joe was not very sociable. Nearby, Sulu, the chief pilot, and Navigator Kevin Riley were having an argument over the merits of fencing as exercise, with Sulu of course holding the affirmative. At some point in the discussion, Sulu appealed to Joe for support.

For answer, Joe flew into a white fury, babbling disconnectedly but under high pressure about the six people who had died on La Pig, and the unworthiness of human beings in general to be in space at all. At the height of this frenzied oration, Joe attempted to turn a steak knife on himself.

The resulting struggle was protracted, and because Sulu and Riley naturally misread Joe's intentions—they thought he was going to attack one of them with the knife—Joe succeeded in wounding himself badly. All three were blood-smeared by the time he was subdued and hauled off to sick bay; at first arrival, the security guards couldn't guess which of the three scuffling figures was the hurt one.

There was no time to discuss the case in any detail; La Pig was already beginning to break up, and Sulu and Riley were needed on the bridge as soon as they could wash up. As the breakup proceeded, the planet's effective mass would change, and perhaps even its center of gravity—accompanied by steady, growing distortion of its extensive magnetic field—so that what had been a stable parking orbit for the *Enterprise* at one moment would become unstable and fragment-strewn the next. The changes were nothing the computer could predict except in rather general orders of magnitude; human brains had to watch and compensate, constantly.

Dr. McCoy's report that Joe Tormolen had died consequently did not reach Kirk for twenty-four hours, and it was another four before he could answer McCoy's request for a consultation. By then, however, the breakup process seemed to have reached some sort of inflection point, where it would simply pause for an hour or so; he could leave the vigil to Sulu and Riley for a short visit to McCoy's office.

"I wouldn't have called you if Joe hadn't been one of the two men down on La Pig," McCoy said directly. "But the case is odd and I don't want to overlook the possibility that there's some connection."

"What's odd about it?"

"Well," McCoy said, "the suicide attempt itself was odd. Joe's self-doubt quotient always rated high, and he was rather a brooding, introspective type; but I'm puzzled about what could have brought it to the surface this suddenly and with this much force.

"And Jim, he shouldn't have died. He had intestinal damage, but I closed it all up neatly and cleaned out the peritoneum; there was no secondary infection. He died anyhow, and I don't know of what."

"Maybe he just gave up," Kirk suggested.

"I've seen that happen. But I can't put it on a death certificate. I have to have a proximate cause, like toxemia or a clot in the brain. Joe just seemed to have a generalized circulatory failure, from no proximate cause at all. And those six dead people on La Pig are not reassuring."

"True enough. What about that sample Spock brought back?"

McCoy shrugged. "Anything's possible, I suppose—but as far as we can tell, that stuff's just water, with some trace minerals that lower its freezing point a good deal. We're handling it with every possible precaution, it's bacteriologically clean—which means no viruses, either—and very nearly chemically pure. I've about concluded that it's a blind alley, though of course I'm still trying to think of new checks to run on it; we all are."

"Well, I'll keep an eye on Spock," Kirk said. "He was the only other man who was down there—though his metabolism's so different that I don't know what I'll be looking for. And in the meantime, we'll just have to hope it was a coincidence."

He went out. As he turned from the door, he was startled to see Sulu coming down a side corridor, not yet aware of Kirk. Evidently he had just come from the gym, for his velour shirt was off, revealing a black tee-shirt, and he had a towel around his neck. He was carrying a fencing foil with a tip protector on it under his arm, and he looked quite pleased with himself—certainly nothing like a man who was away from his post in an alert.

He swung the foil so that it pointed to the ceiling, then let it slip down between his hands so that the capped end was directly before his face. After a moment's study, he took the cap off. Then he took the weapon by the hilt and tested its heft.

"Sulu!"

The pilot jumped back and hit lightly in the guard position. The point of the foil described small circles in the air between the two men.

"Aha!" Sulu said, almost gleefully. "Queen's guard or Richelieu's man? Declare yourself!"

"Sulu, what's this? You're supposed to be on station."

Sulu advanced one pace with the crab-step of the fencer.

"You think to outwit me, eh? Unsheathe your weapon!"

"That's enough," Kirk said sharply. "Report yourself to sick bay."

"And leave you the bois? Nay, rather—"

He made a sudden lunge. Kirk jumped back and snatched out his phaser, setting it to "stun" with his thumb in the same motion, but Sulu was too quick for him. He leapt for a recess in the wall where there was an access ladder to the 'tween-hulls catwalks, and vanished up it. From the vacated manhole his voice echoed back:

"Cowarrrrrrrrrrrd!"

Kirk made the bridge on the double. As he entered, Uhura was giving up the navigator's position to another crewman and moving back to her communications console. There was already another substitute in Sulu's chair. Kirk said, "Where's Riley?"

"Apparently he just wandered off," Spock said, surrendering the command chair to Kirk in his turn. "Nobody but Yeoman Harris here saw him go."

"Symptoms?" Kirk asked the helmsman.

"He wasn't violent or anything, sir. I asked where Mr. Sulu was and he began to sing, 'Have no fear, Riley's here.' Then he said he was sorry for me that I wasn't an Irishman—

in fact I am, sir—and said he was going for a turn on the battlements.''

''Sulu's got it too,'' Kirk said briefly. ''Chased me with a sword on level two, corridor three, then bolted between the hulls. Lieutenant Uhura, tell Security to locate and confine them both. I want every crewman who comes in contact with them medically checked.''

''Psychiatrically, I would suggest, Captain,'' Spock said.

''Explain.''

''This siezure, whatever it is, seems to force buried self-images to the surface. Tormolen was a depressive; it drove him down to the bottom of his cycle and below it, so he suicided. Riley fancies himself a descendant of his Irish kings. Sulu at heart is an eighteenth-century swashbuckler.''

''All right. What's the present condition of the planet?''

''Breaking faster than predicted,'' Spock said. ''As of now we've got a 2 per cent fall increment.''

''Stabilize.'' He turned to his own command board, but the helmsman's voice jerked his attention back.

''Sir, the helm doesn't answer.''

''Fire all ventral verniers then. We'll rectify orbit later.''

The helmsman hit the switch. Nothing happened.

''Verniers also dead, sir.''

''Main engines: warp one!'' Kirk rasped.

''That'll throw us right out of the system,'' Spock observed, as if only stating a mild inconvenience.

''Can't help that.''

''No response, sir,'' the helmsman said.

''Engine room, acknowledge!'' Spock said into the intercom. ''Give us power. Our controls are dead.''

Kirk jerked a thumb at the elevator. ''Mr. Spock, find out what's going on down there.''

Spock started to move, but at the same time the elevator door slid aside, and Sulu was advancing, foil in hand. ''Richelieu!'' he said. ''At last!''

''Sulu,'' Kirk said, ''put down that damned—''

''For honor, Queen and France!'' Sulu lunged directly at Spock, who in sheer unbelief almost let himself be run through. Kirk tried to move in but the needlepoint flicked promptly in his direction. "Now, foul Richelieu—"

He was about to lunge when he saw Uhura trying to circle behind him. He spun; she halted.

"Aha, fair maiden!"

"Sorry, neither," Uhura said. She threw a glance deliberately over Sulu's left shoulder; as he jerked in that direction, Spock's hand caught him on the right shoulder with the Vulcanian nerve pinch. Sulu went down on the deck like a sack of flour.

Forgetting his existence instantly, Kirk whirled on the intercom. "Mr. Scott! We need power! Scott! Engine room, acknowledge!"

In a musical tenor, the intercom said indolently: "You rang?"

"Riley?" Kirk said, trying to repress his fury.

"This is Capt. Kevin Thomas Riley of the Starship *Enterprise*. And who would I have the honor of speakin' to?"

"This is Kirk, dammit."

"Kirk who? Sure and I've got no such officer."

"Riley, this is Captain Kirk. Get out of the engine room, Navigator. Where's Scott?"

"Now hear this, cooks," Riley said. "This is your captain and I'll be wantin' double portions of ice cream for the crew. Captain's compliments, in honor of St. Kevin's Day. And now, your Captain will render an appropriate selection."

Kirk bolted for the elevator. Spock moved automatically to the command chair. "Sir," he said, "at our present rate of descent we have less than twenty minutes before we enter the planet's exosphere."

"All right," Kirk said grimly. "I'll see what I can do about that monkey. Stand by to apply power the instant you get it."

The elevator doors closed on him. Throughout the ship, Riley's voice began to bawl: "I'll take you home again, Kathleen." He was no singer.

It would have been funny, had it not been for the fact that the serenade had the intercom system completely tied up; that the seizure, judging by Joe Tormolen, was followed by a reasonless death; and that the *Enterprise* itself was duc shortly to become just another battered lump in a whirling, planet-sized mass of cosmic rubble.

Scott and two crewmen were outside the engine room door, running a sensor around its edge, as Kirk arrived. Scott looked quickly at the Captain, and then back at the job.

"Trying to get this open, sir," he said. "Riley ran in, said you wanted us on the bridge, then locked us out. We heard you talking to him on the intercom."

"He's cut off both helm and power," Kirk said. "Can you by-pass him and work from the auxiliary?"

"No, Captain, he's hooked everything through the main panel in there." Scott prodded one of the crewmen. "Get up to my office and pull the plans for this bulkhead here. If we've got to cut, I don't want to go through any circuitry." The crewman nodded and ran.

"Can you give us battery power on the helm, at least?" Kirk said. "It won't check our fall but at least it'll keep us stabilized. We've got maybe nineteen minutes, Scotty."

"I heard. I can try it."

"Good." Kirk started back for the bridge.

"And tears be-dim your loving eyes . . ."

On the bridge, Kirk snapped, "Can't you cut off that noise?"

"No, sir," Lieutenant Uhura said. "He can override any channel from the main power panels there."

"There's one he can't override," Kirk said. "Mr. Spock, seal off all ship sections. If this is a contagion, maybe we can stop it from spreading, and at the same time—"

"I follow you," Spock said. He activated the servos for the sector bulkheads. Automatically, the main alarm went off, drowning Riley out completely. When it quit, there was a brief silence. Then Riley's voice said:

"Lieutenant Uhura, this is Captain Riley. You interrupted my song. That was petty of you. No ice cream for you."

"Seventeen minutes left, sir," Spock said.

"Attention crew," Riley's voice went on. "There will be a formal dance in the ship's bowling alley at 1900 hours. All personnel will have a ball." There was a skirl of gleeful laughter. "For the occasion all female crewmen will be issued one pint of perfume from ship's stores. All male crewmen will be raised one pay grade to compensate. Stand by for further goodies."

"Any report on Sulu before the intercom got blanketed?" Kirk said.

"Dr. McCoy had him in sick bay under heavy tranquilization," Lieutenant Uhura said. "He wasn't any worse then, but all tests were negative . . . I got the impression that the surgeon had some sort of idea, but he was cut off before he could explain it."

"Well, Riley's the immediate problem now."

A runner came in and saluted. "Sir, Mr. Scott's compliments and you have a jump circuit from batteries to helm control now. Mr. Scott has resumed cutting into the engine room. He says he should have access in fourteen minutes, sir."

"Which is just the margin we have left," Kirk said. "And it'll take three minutes to tune the engines to full power again. Captain's compliments to Mr. Scott and tell him to cut in any old way and not worry about cutting any circuits but major leads."

"Now hear this," Riley's voice said. "In future all female crew members will let their hair hang loosely down over their shoulders and will use restraint in putting on make-up. Repeat, women should not look made up."

"Sir," Spock said in a strained voice.

"One second. I want two security guards to join Mr. Scott's party. Riley may be armed."

"I've already done that," Spock said. "Sir—"

". . . Across the ocean wide and deep . . ."

"Sir, I feel ill," Spock said formally. "Request permission to report to sick bay."

Kirk clapped a hand to his forehead. "Symptoms?"

"Just a general malaise, sir. But in view of—"

"Yes, yes. But you can't *get* to sick bay; the sections are all sealed off."

"Request I be locked in my quarters, then, sir. I can reach those."

"Permission granted. Somebody find him a guard." As Spock went out, another dismaying thought struck Kirk. Suppose McCoy had the affliction now, whatever it was? Except for Spock and the now-dead Tormolen, he had been exposed to it longest, and Spock could be supposed to be unusually resistant. ''Lieutenant Uhura, you might as well abandon that console, it's doing us no good at the moment. Find yourself a length of telephone cable and an eavesdropper, and go between hulls to the hull above the sick bay. You'll be able to hear McCoy but not talk back; get his attention, and answer him, by prisoners' raps. Relay the conversation to me by pocket transmitter. Mark and move.''

''Yes, *sir*.''

Her exit left the bridge empty except for Kirk. There was nothing he could do but pace and watch the big screen. Twelve minutes.

Then a buzzer went off in Kirk's back pocket. He yanked out his communicator.

''Kirk here.''

''Lieutenant Uhura, sir. I've established contact with Doctor McCoy. He says he believes he has a partial solution, sir.''

''Ask him what he means by partial.''

There was an agonizing wait while Uhura presumably spelled out this message by banging on the inner hull. The metal was thick; probably she was using a hammer, and even so the raps would come through only faintly.

''Sir, he wants to discharge something—some sort of gas, sir—into the ship's ventilating system. He says he can do it from sick bay and that it will spread rapidly. He says it worked on Lieutenant Sulu and presumably will cure anybody else who's sick—but he won't vouch for its effect on healthy crew members.''

''That sounded like typical McCoy caution, but—ask him how he feels himself.''

Another long wait. Then: ''He says he felt very ill, sir, but is all right now, thanks to the antidote.''

That might be true and it might not. If McCoy himself had the illness, there would be no predicting what he might actually be preparing to dump into the ship's air. On the other hand, to refuse him permission wouldn't necessarily stop him, either. If only that damned singing would stop! It made thinking almost impossible.

"Ask him to have Sulu say something; see if he sounds sane to you."

Another wait. Only ten minutes left now—three of which would have to be used for tune-up. And no telling how fast McCoy's antidote would spread, or how long it would need to take hold, either.

"Sir, he says Lieutenant Sulu is exhausted and he won't wake him, under the discretion granted him by his commission."

McCoy had that discretion, to be sure. But it could also be the cunning blind of a deranged mind.

"All right," Kirk said heavily. "Tell him to go ahead with it."

"Aye aye, sir."

Uhura's carrier wave clicked out and Kirk pocketed his transceiver, feeling utterly helpless. Nine minutes.

Then, Riley's voice faltered. He appeared to have forgotten some of the words of his interminable song. Then he dropped a whole line. He tried to go on, singing "La, la, la," instead, but in a moment that died away too.

Silence.

Kirk felt his own pulse, and sounded himself subjectively. Insofar as he could tell, there was nothing the matter with him but a headache which he now realized he had had for more than an hour. He strode quickly to Uhura's console and rang the engine room.

There was a click from the g.c. speakers, and Riley's voice said hesitantly: "Riley here."

"Mr. Riley, this is Kirk. Where are you?"

"Sir, I . . . I seem to be in the engine room. I'm . . . off post, sir."

Kirk drew a deep breath. "Never mind that. Give us power right away. Then open the door and let the chief engineer in. Stand out of the way when you do it, because he's trying to cut in with a phaser at full power. Have you got all that?"

"Yes, sir. Power, then the door—and stand back. Sir, what's this all about?"

"Never mind now, just do it."

"Yes, sir."

Kirk opened the bulkhead override. At once, there was

the heavy rolling sound of the emergency doors between the sections opening, like a stone being rolled back from a tomb. Hitting the general alarm button, Kirk bawled: "All officers to the bridge! Crash emergency, six minutes! Mark and move!"

At the same time, the needles on the power board began to stir. Riley had activated the engines. A moment later, his voice, filled with innocent regret, said into the general air:

"Now there won't be a dance in the bowling alley tonight."

Once a new orbit around the disintegrating mass of La Pig had been established, Kirk found time to question McCoy. The medico looked worn down to a nubbin, and small wonder; his had been the longest vigil of all. But he responded with characteristic indirection.

"Know anything about cactuses, Jim?"

"Only what everybody knows. They live in the desert and they stick you. Oh yes, and some of them store water."

"Right, and that last item's the main one. Also, cactuses that have been in museum cases for fifty or even seventy years sometimes astonish the museum curators by sprouting. Egyptian wheat that's been in tombs for thousands of years will sometimes germinate, too."

Kirk waited patiently. McCoy would get to the point in his own good time.

"Both those things happen because of a peculiar form of storage called *bound water*. Ordinary mineral crystals like copper sulfate often have water hitched to their molecules, loosely; that's water-of-crystallization. With it, copper sulfate is a pretty blue gem, though poisonous; without it, it's a poisonous green powder. Well, organic molecules can bind water much more closely, make it really a part of the molecule instead of just loosely hitched to it. Over the course of many years, that water will come out of combination and become available to the cactus or the grain of wheat as a liquid, and then life begins all over again."

"An ingenious arrangement," Kirk said. "But I don't see how it nearly killed us all."

"It was in that sample of liquid Mr. Spock brought

back, of course—a catalyst that *promoted* water-binding. If it had nothing else to bind to, it would bind even to itself. Once in the bloodstream, the catalyst began complexing the blood-serum. First it made the blood more difficult to extract nutrients from, beginning with blood sugar, which starved the brain—hence the psychiatric symptoms. As the process continued, it made the blood too thick to pump, especially through the smaller capillaries—hence Joe's death by circulatory collapse.

"Once I realized what was happening, I had to figure out a way to poison the catalysis. The stuff was highly contagious, through the perspiration, or blood, or any other body fluid; and catalysts don't take part in any chemical reaction they promote, so the original amount was always present to be passed on. I think this one may even have multiplied, in some semi-viruslike fashion. Anyhow, the job was to alter the chemical nature of the catalyst—poison it—so it wouldn't promote that reaction any more. I almost didn't find the proper poison in time, and as I told Lieutenant Uhura through the wall, I wasn't sure what effect the poison itself would have on healthy people. Luckily, none."

"Great Galaxy," Kirk said. "That reminds me of something. Spock invalided himself off duty just before the tail end of the crisis and he's not back. Lieutenant Uhura, call Mr. Spock's quarters."

"Yes, sir."

The switch clicked. Out of the intercom came a peculiarly Arabic howl—the noise of the Vulcanian musical instrument Spock liked to practice in his cabin, since nobody else on board could stand to listen to it. Along with the noise, Spock's rough voice was crooning:

"Alab, wes-craunish, sprai pu ristu,
Or en r'ljiik majiir auooo—"

Kirk winced. "I can't tell whether he's all right or not," he said. "Nobody but another Vulcanian could. But since he's not on duty during a crash alert, maybe your antidote did something to him it didn't do to us. Better go check him."

"Soon as I find my earplugs."

McCoy left. From Spock's cabin, the voice went on:

"Rijii, bebe, p'salku pirtu,
Fror om—"

The voice rose toward an impassioned climax and Kirk cut the circuit. Rather than that, he would almost rather have "I'll take you home again, Kathleen," back again.

On the other hand, if Riley had sounded like that to Spock, maybe Spock had needed no other reason for feeling unwell. With a sigh, Kirk settled back to watch the last throes of La Pig. The planet was now little better than an irregularly bulging cloud of dust, looking on the screen remarkably like a swelling and disintegrating human brain.

The resemblance, Kirk thought, was strictly superficial. Once a planet started disintegrating, it was through. But brains weren't like that.

Given half a chance, they pulled themselves together.

Sometimes.

CHARLIE'S LAW

(aired as "Charlie X")

Writer: D.C. Fontana
(Story by Gene Roddenberry)
Director: Lawrence Dobkin
Guest star: Robert Walker, Jr.

Though as Captain of the starship *Enterprise* James Kirk had the final authority over four hundred officers and crewmen, plus a small and constantly shifting population of passengers, and though in well more than twenty years in space he had had his share of narrow squeaks, he was firmly of the opinion that no single person ever gave him more trouble than one seventeen-year-old boy.

Charles Evans had been picked up from a planet called Thasus after having been marooned there for fourteen years, the sole survivor of the crash of his parents' research vessel. He was rescued by the survey ship *Antares*, a transport about a tenth of the size of the *Enterprise*, and subsequently transferred to Kirk's ship, wearing hand-me-down clothes and carrying all the rest of his possessions in a dufflebag.

The offers of the *Antares* who brought him aboard the *Enterprise* spoke highly of Charlie's intelligence, eagerness to learn, intuitive grasp of engineering matters—"He could run the *Antares* himself if he had to"—and his sweetness of character; but it struck Kirk that they were almost elbowing each other aside to praise him, and that they were in an unprecedented hurry to get back to their own cramped ship, without even so much as begging a bottle of brandy.

Charlie's curiosity had certainly been obvious from those first moments, though he showed some trepidation, too—which was not surprising, considering his long and lonely exile. Kirk assigned Yeoman Rand to take him to his quarters. It was at this point that Charlie stunned her and everyone else present by asking Kirk honestly:

"Is that a girl?"

Leonard McCoy, the ship's surgeon, checked Charlie from top to toe and found him in excellent physical condition: no traces of malnutrition, of exposure, of hardship of any sort; truly remarkable for a boy who'd had to fend for himself on a strange world from the age of three. On the other hand, it was reasonable to suppose that fourteen years later, Charlie would either be in good shape, or dead; he would have had to come to terms with his environment within the first few years.

Charlie was not very communicative about this puzzle, though he asked plenty of questions himself—he seemed earnestly to want to know all the right things to do, and even more urgently, to be liked, but the purport of some of McCoy's questions apparently baffled him.

No, nobody had survived the crash. He had learned English by talking to the memory banks on the ship; they still worked. No, the Thasians hadn't helped him; there were no Thasians. At first he had eaten stores from the wreck; then he had found some other . . . things, growing around.

Charlie then asked to see the ship's rule book. On the *Antares*, he said, he hadn't done or said all the right things. When that happened, people got angry; he got angry, too. He didn't like making the same mistake twice.

"I feel the same way," McCoy told him. "But you can't rush such matters. Just keep your eyes open, and when in doubt, smile and say nothing. It works very nicely."

Charlie returned McCoy's grin, and McCoy dismissed him with a swat on the rump, to Charlie's obvious astonishment.

McCoy brought the problem up again on the bridge with Kirk and his second-in-command, Mr. Spock. Yeoman Rand was there working on a duty roster, and at once volunteered to leave; but since she had seen as much of Charlie as anyone had, Kirk asked her to stay. Besides, Kirk was fond of her, though he fondly imagined that to be a secret even from her.

"Earth history is full of cases where a small child managed to survive in a wilderness," McCoy went on.

"I've read some of your legends," said Spock, who was native to a nonsolar planet confusingly called Vulcan. "They all seem to require a wolf to look after the infants."

"What reason would the boy have to lie, if there *were* Thasians?"

"Nevertheless there's some evidence that there were, at least millennia ago," Spock said. "The first survey reported some highly sophisticated artifacts. And conditions haven't changed on Thasus for at least three million years. There might well be *some* survivors."

"Charlie says there aren't," Kirk said.

"His very survival argues that there are. I've checked the library computer record on Thasus. There isn't much, but one thing it does say: 'No edible plant life.' He simply had to have had some kind of help."

"I think you're giving him less credit than he deserves," McCoy said.

"For the moment let's go on that assumption," Kirk said. "Mr. Spock, work out a briefing program for young Charlie. Give him things to do—places to be. If we keep him busy until we get to Colony Five, experienced educators will take him over, and in the meantime, he should leave us with relative calm aboard . . . Yeoman Rand, what do you think of our problem child?"

"Wellll," she said. "Maybe I'm prejudiced. I wasn't going to mention this, but . . . he followed me down the corridor yesterday and offered me a vial of perfume. My favorite, too; I don't know how he knew it. There's none in the ship's stores, I'm sure of that."

"Hmm," McCoy said.

"I was just going to ask him where he got it, when he swatted me on the rump. After that I made it my business to be someplace else."

There was an outburst of surprised laughter, quickly suppressed.

"Anything else?" Kirk said.

"Nothing important. Did you know that he can do card tricks?"

"Now, where would he have learned that?" Spock demanded.

"I don't know, but he's very good. I was playing solitaire in the rec room when he came in. Lieutenant Uhura was playing 'Charlie is my darling' and singing, and at first he seemed to think she was mocking him. When he saw she didn't mean it personally, he came over to watch me, and he seemed to be puzzled that I couldn't make the game come out. So he made it come out for me—without even touching the cards, I'd swear to that. When I showed I was surprised, he picked up the cards and did a whole series of tricks with them, good ones. The best sleight-of-hand I've ever seen. He said one of the men on the *Antares* taught him how. He was enjoying all the attention, I could tell that, but I didn't want to encourage him too much myself. Not after the swatting incident."

"He got *that* trick from me, I'm afraid," McCoy said.

"No doubt he did," Kirk said. "But I think I'd better talk to him, anyhow."

"Fatherhood becomes you, Jim," McCoy said, grinning.

"Dry up, Bones. I just don't want him getting out of hand, that's all."

Charlie shot to his feet the moment Kirk entered his cabin; all his fingers, elbows, and knees seemed to bend the wrong way. Kirk had barely managed to nod when he burst out: "I didn't do anything!"

"Relax, Charlie. Just wanted to find out how you're getting along."

"Fine. I . . . I'm supposed to ask you why I shouldn't—I don't know how to explain it."

"Try saying it straight out, Charlie," Kirk said. "That usually works."

"Well, in the corridor . . . I talked to . . . when Janice . . . Yeoman Rand was . . ." Abruptly, setting his face, he took a quick step forward and slapped Kirk on the seat. "I did that and she didn't like it. She said you'd explain it to me."

"Well," Kirk said, trying hard not to smile, "it's that there are things you can do with a lady, and things you can't. Uh, the fact is, there's no right way to hit a lady. Man to man is one thing, man to woman is something else. Do you understand?"

"I don't know. I guess so."

"If you don't, you'll just have to take my word for it for the time being. In the meantime, I'm having a schedule worked out for you, Charlie. Things to do, to help you learn all the things you missed while you were marooned on Thasus."

"That's very nice, for you to do that for me," Charlie said. He seemed genuinely pleased. "Do you like me?"

That flat question took Kirk off guard. "I don't know," he said equally flatly. "Learning to like people takes time. You have to watch what they do, try to understand them. It doesn't happen all at once."

"Oh," Charlie said.

"Captain Kirk," Lieutenant Uhura's voice broke in over the intercom.

"Excuse me, Charlie . . . Kirk here."

"Captain Ramart of the *Antares* is on D channel. Must speak to you directly."

"Right. I'll come up to the bridge."

"Can I come too?" Charlie said as Kirk switched out.

"I'm afraid not, Charlie. This is strictly ship's business."

"I won't disturb anybody," Charlie said. "I'll stay out of the way."

The boy's need for human company was touching, no matter how awkwardly he went about it. There were many years of solitude to be made up for. "Well, all right," Kirk said. "But only when you have my permission. Agreed?"

"Agreed," Charlie said eagerly. He followed Kirk out like a puppy.

On the bridge, Lieutenant Uhura, her Bantu face intent as a tribal statue's, was asking the microphone: "Can you boost your power, *Antares*? We are barely reading your transmission."

"We are at full output, *Enterprise*," Ramart's voice said, very distant and hashy. "I must speak with Captain Kirk at once."

Kirk stepped up to the station and picked up the mike. "Kirk here, Captain Ramart."

"Captain, thank goodness. We're just barely in range. I've got to warn—"

His voice stopped. There was nothing to be heard from the speaker now but stellar static—not even a carrier wave.

"See if you can get them back," Kirk said.

"There's nothing to get, Captain," Lieutenant Uhura said, baffled. "They aren't transmitting any more."

"Keep the channel open."

Behind Kirk, Charlie said quietly: "That was an old ship. It wasn't very well constructed."

Kirk stared at him, and then swung toward Spock's station.

"Mr. Spock, sweep the transmission area with probe sensors."

"I've got it," Spock said promptly. "But it's fuzzy. Unusually so even for this distance."

Kirk turned back to the boy. "What happened, Charlie? Do you know?"

Charlie stared back at him, with what seemed to be uneasy defiance. "I don't know," he said.

"The fuzzy area is spreading out," Spock reported. "I'm getting some distinct pips now along the edges. Debris, undoubtedly."

"But no *Antares*?"

"Captain Kirk, that *is* the *Antares*," Spock said quietly. "No other interpretation is possible. Clearly, she blew up."

Kirk continued to hold Charlie's eye. The boy looked back.

"I'm sorry it blew up," Charlie said. He seemed uneasy, but nothing more than that. "But I won't miss them. They weren't very nice. They didn't like me. I could tell."

There was a long, terribly tense silence. At last Kirk carefully unclenched his fists.

"Charlie," he said, "one of the first things you're going to have to get rid of is that damned cold-bloodedness. Or self-centeredness, or whatever it is. Until that gets under control, you're going to be less than half human."

And then, he stopped. To his embarrassed amazement, Charlie was crying.

• • •

"He what?" Kirk said, looking up from his office chair at Yeoman Rand. She was vastly uncomfortable, but she stuck to her guns.

"He made a pass at me," she repeated. "Not in so many words, no. But he made me a long, stumbling speech. He wants me."

"Yeoman, he's a seventeen-year-old boy."

"Exactly," the girl said.

"All this because of a swat?"

"No, sir," she said. "Because of the speech. Captain, I've seen that look before; *I'm* not seventeen. And if something isn't done, sooner or later I'm going to have to hold Charlie off, maybe even swat him myself, and not on the fanny, either. That wouldn't be good for him. I'm his first love and his first crush and the first woman he ever saw and . . ." She caught her breath. "Captain, that's a great deal for anyone to have to handle, even one item at a time. All at once, it's murder. And he doesn't understand the usual put-offs. If I have to push him off in a way he does understand, there may be trouble. Do you follow me?"

"I think so, Yeoman," Kirk said. He still could not quite take the situation seriously. "Though I never thought I'd wind up explaining the birds and the bees to anybody, not at my age. But I'll send for him right now."

"Thank you, sir." She went out. Kirk buzzed for Charlie. He appeared almost at once, as though he had been expecting something of the sort.

"Come in, Charlie, sit down."

The boy moved to the chair opposite Kirk's desk and sat down, as if settling into a bear trap. As before, he beat Kirk to the opening line.

"Janice," he said. "Yeoman Rand. It's about her, isn't it?"

Damn the kid's quickness! "More or less. Though it's more about you."

"I won't hit her like that any more. I promised."

"There's more to it than that," Kirk said. "You've got some things to learn."

"Everything I do or say is wrong," Charlie said desperately. "I'm in the way. Dr. McCoy won't show me the rules. I don't know what I am or what I'm supposed to be, or even *who.* And I don't know why I hurt so much inside all the time—"

"I do, and you'll live," Kirk said. "There's nothing wrong with you that hasn't gone haywire inside every human male since the model came out. There's no way to get over it, around it, or under it; you just have to live through it, Charlie."

"But, it's like I'm wearing my insides outside. I go around bent over all the time. Janice—Yeoman Rand—she wants to give me away to someone else. Yeoman Lawton. But she's just a, just a, well, she doesn't even smell like a girl. Nobody else on the ship is like Janice. I don't want anybody else."

"It's normal," Kirk said gently. "Charlie, there are a million things in the universe you can have. There are also about a hundred million that you can't. There's no fun in learning to face that, but you've got to do it. That's how things are."

"I don't like it," Charlie said, as if that explained everything.

"I don't blame you. But you have to hang on tight and survive. Which reminds me: the next thing on your schedule is unarmed defense. Come along to the gym with me and we'll try a few falls. Way back in Victorian England, centuries ago, they had a legend that violent exercise helped keep one's mind off women. I've never known it to work, myself, but anyhow let's give it a try."

Charlie was incredibly clumsy, but perhaps no more so than any other beginner. Ship's Officer Sam Ellis, a member of McCoy's staff, clad like Kirk and Charlie in work-out clothes, was patient with him.

"That's better. Slap the mat when you go down, Charlie. It absorbs the shock. Now, again."

Ellis dropped of his own initiative to the mat, slapped it, and rolled gracefully up onto his feet. "Like that."

"I'll never learn," Charlie said.

"Sure you will," Kirk said. "Go ahead."

Charlie managed an awkward drop. He forgot to slap until almost the last minute, so that quite a thud accompanied the slap.

"Well, that's an improvement," Kirk said. "Like everything else, it takes practice. Once more."

This time was better. Kirk said, "That's it. Okay, Sam, show him a shoulder roll."

Ellis hit the mat, and was at once on his feet again, cleanly and easily.

"I don't want to do that," Charlie said.

"It's part of the course," Kirk said. "It's not hard. Look." He did a roll himself. "Try it."

"No. You were going to teach me to fight, not roll around on the floor."

"You have to learn to take falls without hurting yourself before we can do that. Sam, maybe we'd better demonstrate. A couple of easy throws."

"Sure," Ellis said. The two officers grappled, and Ellis, who was in much better shape than the Captain, let Kirk throw him. Then, as Kirk got to his feet, Ellis flipped him like a poker chip. Kirk rolled and bounced, glad of the exercise.

"See what I mean?" Kirk said.

"I guess so," Charlie said. "It doesn't look hard."

He moved in and grappled with Kirk, trying for the hold he had seen Ellis use. He was strong, but he had no leverage. Kirk took a counter-hold and threw him. It was not a hard throw, but Charlie again forgot to slap the mat. He jumped to his feet flaming mad, glaring at Kirk.

"*That* won't do," Ellis said, grinning. "You need a lot more falls, Charlie."

Charlie whirled toward him. In a low, intense voice, he said: "Don't laugh at me."

"Cool off, Charlie," Ellis said, chuckling openly now. "Half the trick is in not losing your temper."

"Don't laugh at me!" Charlie said. Ellis spread out his hands, but his grin did not quite go away.

Exactly one second later, there was a pop like the breaking of the world's largest light bulb. Ellis vanished.

Kirk stared stupefied at the spot where Ellis had been. Charlie, too, stood frozen for a moment. Then he began to move tentatively toward the door.

"Hold it," Kirk said. Charlie stopped, but he did not turn to face Kirk.

"He shouldn't have laughed at me," Charlie said. "That's not nice, to laugh at somebody. I was trying."

"Not very hard. Never mind that. What happened? What did you do to my officer?"

"He's gone," Charlie said sullenly.

"That's no answer."

"He's gone," Charlie said. "That's all I know. I didn't want to do it. He made me. He laughed at me."

And suppose Janice has to slap him? And . . . there was the explosion of the *Antares* . . . Kirk stepped quickly to the nearest wall intercom and flicked it on. Charlie turned at last to watch him. "Captain Kirk in the gym," Kirk said. "Two men from security here, on the double."

"What are you going to do with me?" Charlie said.

"I'm sending you to your quarters. And I want you to stay there."

"I won't let them touch me," Charlie said in a low voice. "I'll make them go away too."

"They won't hurt you."

Charlie did not answer, but he had the look of a caged animal just before it turns at last upon its trainer. The door opened and two security guards came in, phaser pistols holstered. They stopped and looked to Kirk.

"Go with them, Charlie. We'll talk about this later, when we've both cooled off. You owe me a long explanation." Kirk jerked his head toward Charlie. The guards stepped to him and took him by the arms.

Or, tried to. Actually, Kirk was sure that they never touched him. One of them simply staggered back, but the other was thrown violently against the wall, as though he had been caught in a sudden hurricane. He managed to hold his footing, however, and clawed for his sidearm.

"No!" Kirk shouted.

But the order was way too late. By the time the guard had his hand levelled at the boy, he no longer had a weapon to hold. It had vanished, just like Sam Ellis. Charlie stared at Kirk, his eyes narrowed and challenging.

"Charlie," Kirk said, "you're showing off. Go to your quarters."

"No."

"Go with the guards, or I'll pick you up and carry you

there myself." He began to walk steadily forward. "That's your only choice, Charlie. Either do as I tell you, or send me away to wherever you sent the phaser, and Sam Ellis."

"Oh, all right," Charlie said, wilting. Kirk drew a deep breath. "But tell them to keep their hands to themselves."

"They won't hurt you. Not if you do as I say."

Kirk called a general council on the bridge at once, but Charlie moved faster: by the time Kirk's officers were all present, there wasn't a phaser to be found anywhere aboard ship. Charlie had made them all "go away." Kirk explained what had happened, briefly and grimly.

"Given this development," McCoy said, "it's clear Charlie wouldn't have needed any help from any putative Thasians. He could have magicked up all his needs by himself."

"Not necessarily," Spock said. "All we know is that he can make things vanish—not make them appear. I admit that that alone would have been a big help to him."

"What are the chances," Kirk said, "that he's a Thasian himself? Or at least, something really unprecedented in the way of an alien?"

"The chance is there," McCoy said, "but I'd be inclined to rule it out. Remember I checked him over. He's ostensibly human, down to his last blood type. Of course, I could have missed something, but he was hooked to the body-function panel, too; the machine would have rung sixteen different kinds of alarms at the slightest discrepancy."

"Well, he's inhumanly powerful, in any event," Spock said. "The probability is that he was responsible for the destruction of the *Antares*, too. Over an enormous distance—well beyond phaser range."

"Great," McCoy said. "Under the circumstances, how can we hope to keep him caged up?"

"It goes further than that, Bones," Kirk said. "We can't take him to Colony Five, either. Can you imagine what he'd do in an open, normal environment—in an undisciplined environment?"

Clearly, McCoy hadn't. Kirk got up and began to pace.

"Charlie is an adolescent boy—probably human, but totally inexperienced with other human beings. He's short-tempered because he wants so much and it can't come fast enough for him. He's full of adolescent aches. He wants to be one of us, to be loved, to be useful. But . . . I remember when I was seventeen that I wished for the ability to remove the things and people that annoyed me, neatly and without fuss. It's a power fantasy most boys of that age have. Charlie doesn't have to wish. *He can do it.*

"In other words, in order to stay in existence, gentlemen, we'll have to make damn sure we don't annoy him. Otherwise—pop!"

"Annoyance is relative, Captain," Spock said. "It's all going to depend on how Charlie is feeling minute by minute. And because of his background, or lack of it, we have no ways to guess what little thing might annoy him next, no matter how carefully we try. He's the galaxy's most destructive weapon, and he's on a hair trigger."

"No," Kirk said. "He's not a weapon. He *has* a weapon. That's a difference we can use. Essentially, he's a child, a child in a man's body, trying to be a whole man. His trouble isn't malice. It's innocence."

"And here he is," McCoy said with false heartiness. Kirk swung his chair around to see Charlie approaching from the elevator, smiling cheerfully.

"Hi," said the galaxy's most destructive weapon.

"I thought I confined you to your quarters, Charlie."

"You did," Charlie said, the grin fading. "But I got tired of waiting around down there."

"Oh, all right. You're here. Maybe you can answer a few questions for us. Were you responsible for what happened to the *Antares*?"

"Why?"

"Because I want to know. Answer me, Charlie."

Breaths were held while Charlie thought it over. Finally, he said: "Yes. There was a warped baffle plate on the shielding of their Nerst generator. I made it go away. It would have given sooner or later anyhow."

"You could have told them that."

"What for?" Charlie said reasonably. "They weren't nice to me. They didn't like me. You saw them when they brought me aboard. They wanted to get rid of me. They don't any more."

"And what about us?" Kirk said.

"Oh, I need you. I have to get to Colony Five. But if you're not nice to me, I'll think of something else." The boy turned abruptly and left, for no visible reason.

McCoy wiped sweat off his forehead. "What a chance you took."

"We can't be walking on eggs every second," Kirk said. "If every act, every question might irritate him, we might as well pretend that none of them will. Otherwise we'll be utterly paralyzed."

"Captain," Spock said slowly, "do you suppose a force field might hold him? He's too smart to allow himself to be lured into a detention cell, but we just might rig up a field at his cabin door. All the lab circuitry runs through the main corridor on deck five, and we could use that. It's a long chance, but—"

"How long would the work take?" Kirk said.

"At a guess, seventy-two hours."

"It's going to be a long seventy-two hours, Mr. Spock. Get on it." Spock nodded and went out.

"Lieutenant Uhura, raise Colony Five for me. I want to speak directly to the Governor. Lieutenant Sulu, lay me a course away from Colony Five—not irrevocably, but enough to buy me some time. Bones—"

He was interrupted by the sound of a fat spark, and a choked scream of pain from Uhura. Her hands were in her lap, writhing together uncontrollably. McCoy leapt to her side, tried to press the clenched fingers apart.

"It's . . . all right," she said. "I think. Just a shock. But there's no reason for the board to be charged like that—"

"Probably a very good reason," Kirk said grimly. "Don't touch it until further orders. How does it look, Bones?"

"Superficial burns," McCoy said. "But who knows what it'll be next time?"

"I can tell you that," Sulu said. "I can't feed new coordinates into this panel. It operates, but it rejects the course change. We're locked on Colony Five."

"I'm in a hurry," Charlie's voice said. He was coming out of the elevator again, but he paused as he saw the naked fury on Kirk's face.

"I'm getting tired of this," Kirk said. "What about the transmitter?"

"You don't need all that subspace chatter," Charlie said, a little defensively. "If there's any trouble, I can take care of it myself. I'm learning fast."

"I don't want your help," Kirk said. "Charlie, for the moment there's nothing I can do to prevent your interference. But I'll tell you this: you're quite right, I don't like you. I don't like you at all. Now beat it."

"I'll go," Charlie said, quite coolly. "I don't mind if you don't like me now. You will pretty soon. I'm going to make you."

As he left, McCoy began to swear in a low whisper.

"Belay that, Bones, it won't help. Lieutenant Uhura, is it just outside communications that are shorted, or is the intercom out too?"

"Intercom looks good, Captain."

"All right, get me Yeoman Rand . . . Janice, I have a nasty one for you—maybe the nastiest you've ever been asked to do. I want you to lure Charlie into his cabin. . . . That's right. We'll be watching—but bear in mind that if you make him mad, there won't be much we can do to protect you. You can opt out if you want; it probably won't work anyhow."

"If it doesn't," Yeoman Rand's voice said, "it won't because *I* didn't try it."

They watched, Spock's hand hovering over the key that would activate the force field. At first, Janice was alone in Charlie's cabin, and the wait seemed very long. Finally, however, the door slid aside, and Charlie came into the field of the hidden camera, his expression a mixture of hope and suspicion.

"It was nice of you to come here," he said. "But I don't trust people any more. They're all so complicated, and full of hate."

"No, they're not," Janice said. "You just don't make enough allowance for how *they* feel. You have to give them time."

"Then . . . you do like me?"

"Yes, I like you. Enough to try to straighten you out, anyhow. Otherwise I wouldn't have asked to come here."

"That was very nice," Charlie said. "I can be nice, too. Look. I have something for you."

From behind his back, where it had already been visible to the camera, he produced the single pink rosebud he had been carrying and held it out. There had been no roses aboard ship, either; judging by that and the perfume, he could indeed make things appear as well as disappear. The omens did not look good.

"Pink *is* your favorite color, isn't it?" Charlie was saying. "The books say all girls like pink. Blue is for boys."

"It was . . . a nice thought, Charlie. But this isn't really the time for courting. I really need to talk to you."

"But you asked to come to my room. The books all say that means something important." He reached out, trying to touch her face. She moved instinctively away, trying to circle for the door, which was now on remote control, the switch for it under Spock's other hand; but she could not see where she was backing and was stopped by a chair.

"No. I said I only wanted to talk and that's what I meant."

"But I only wanted to be nice to you."

She got free of the chair somehow and resumed sidling. "That's a switch on Charlie's Law," she said.

"What do you mean? What's that?"

"Charlie's Law says everybody better be nice to Charlie, or else."

"That's not true!" Charlie said raggedly.

"Isn't it? Where's Sam Ellis, then?"

"I don't know where he is. He's just gone. Janice, I only *want* to be nice. They won't let me. None of you will. I can give you anything you want. Just tell me."

"All right," Janice said. "Then I think you had better let me go. That's what I want now."

"But you said . . ." The boy swallowed and tried again. "Janice, I . . . love you."

"No you don't. You don't know what the word means."

"Then show me," he said, reaching for her.

Her back was to the door now, and Spock hit the switch. The boy's eyes widened as the door slid back, and then Janice was through it. He charged after her, and the other key closed.

The force field flared, and Charlie was flung back into

the room. He stood there for a moment like a stabled stallion, nostrils flared, breathing heavily. Then he said:

"All right. All right, then."

He walked slowly forward. Kirk swung the camera to follow him. This time he went through the force field as though it did not exist. He advanced again on Janice.

"Why did you do that?" he said. "You won't even let me try. None of you. All right. From now on I'm not trying. I won't keep any of you but the ones I need. I don't need you."

There came the implosion sound again. Janice was gone. Around Kirk, the universe turned a dull, aching gray.

"Charlie," he said hoarsely. The intercom carried his voice to Charlie's cabin. He looked blindly toward the source.

"You too, Captain," he said. "What you did wasn't nice either. I'll keep you a while. The *Enterprise* isn't quite like the *Antares*. Running the *Antares* was easy. But if you try to hurt me again, I'll make a lot of other people go away . . . I'm coming up to the bridge now."

"I can't stop you," Kirk said.

"I know you can't. Being a man isn't so much. I'm not a man and I can do anything. You can't. Maybe I'm the man and you're not."

Kirk cut out the circuit and looked at Spock. After a while the First Officer said:

"That was the last word, if ever I heard it."

"It's as close as I care to come to it, that's for sure. Did that field react at all, the second time?"

"No. He went through it as easily as a ray of light. Easier—I could have stopped a light ray if I'd known the frequency. There seems to be very little he can't do."

"Except run the ship—and get to Colony Five by himself."

"Small consolation."

They broke off as Charlie entered. He was walking very tall. Without a word to anyone, he went to the helmsman's chair and waved to Sulu to get out of it. After a brief glance at Kirk, Sulu got up obediently, and Charlie sat down and began to play with the controls. The ship lurched, very slightly, and he snatched his hands back.

"Show me what to do," he told Sulu.

"That would take thirty years of training."

"Don't argue with me. Just show me."

"Go ahead, show him," Kirk said. "Maybe he'll blow us up. Better than letting him loose on Colony Five—"

"Captain Kirk," Lieutenant Uhura broke in. "I'm getting something from outside; subspace channel F. Ship to ship, I think. But it's all on instruments; I can't hear it."

"There's nothing there," Charlie said, his voice rough. "Just leave it alone."

"Captain?"

"I am the captain," Charlie said. Yet somehow, Kirk had the sudden conviction that he was frightened. And somehow, equally inexplicably, he knew that the *Enterprise* had to get that call.

"Charlie," he said, "are you creating that message—or are you blocking one that's coming in?"

"It's my game, Mr. Kirk," Charlie said. "You have to find out. Like you said—that's how the game is played." He pushed himself out of the chair and said to Sulu, "You can have it now. I've locked on course for Colony Five again."

He could have done nothing of the sort in that brief period; not, at least, with his few brief stabs at the controls. Probably, his original lock still held unchanged. But either way, it was bad enough; Colony Five was now only twelve hours away.

But Charlie's hands were trembling visibly. Kirk said:

"All right, Charlie, that's the game—and the game is over. I don't think you can handle any more. I think you're at your limit and you can't take on one more thing. But you're going to have to. Me."

"I could have sent you away before," Charlie said. "Don't make me do it now."

"You don't dare. You've got my ship. I want it back. And I want my crew back whole, too—if I have to break your neck to do it."

"Don't push me," Charlie whispered. *"Don't push me."*

At the next step forward, a sleet-storm of pain threw Kirk to the deck. He could not help crying out.

"I'm sorry," Charlie said, sweating. "I'm sorry—"

The subspace unit hummed loudly, suddenly, and then

began to chatter in intelligible code. Uhura reached for the unscrambler.

"Stop that!" Charlie screamed, whirling. "I said, stop it!"

The pain stopped; Kirk was free. After a split-second's hesitation to make sure he was all there, he lunged to his feet. Spock and McCoy were also closing in, but Kirk was closer. He drew back a fist.

"Console is clear," Sulu's voice said behind him. "Helm answers."

Charlie dodged away from Kirk's threat, whimpering. He never had looked less like the captain of anything, even his own soul. Kirk held back his blow in wonder.

Pop!

Janice Rand was on the bridge, putting out both hands to steady herself. She was white-faced and shaken, but otherwise unharmed.

Pop!

"That was a hell of a fall, Jim," Sam Ellis' voice said. "Next time, take it a little—hey, what's all this?"

"Message is through," Lieutenant Uhura's voice said dispassionately. "Ship off our starboard bow. Identifies itself as from Thasus."

With a cry of animal panic, Charlie fell to the deck, drumming on it with both fists.

"Don't listen, don't listen!" he wailed. "No, no please! I can't live with them any more."

Kirk watched stolidly, not moving. The boy who had been bullying and manipulating them for so long was falling apart under his eyes.

"You're my friends. You *said* you were my friends. Remember—when I came aboard?" He looked up piteously at Kirk. "Take me home, to Colony Five. That's all I want . . . It's really all I want!"

"Captain," Spock said in an emotionless voice. "Something happening over here. Like a transporter materialization. Look."

Feeling like a man caught in a long fall of dominoes, Kirk jerked his eyes toward Spock. There was indeed something materializing on the bridge, through which Spock himself could now be seen only dimly. It was perhaps two-thirds as tall as a man, roughly oval, and fighting for solidity. It wavered and changed, and colors flowed through it. For a moment it looked like a gigantic human face; then, like nothing even remotely human; then, like a distorted view of a distant but gigantic building. It did not seem able to hold any state very long.

Then it spoke. The voice was deep and resonant. It came, not from the apparition, but from the subspace speaker; but like the apparition, it wavered, blurred, faded, blared, changed color, as if almost out of control.

"We are sorry for this trouble," it said. "We did not realize until too late that the human boy was gone from us. We searched a long time to find him, but space travel is a long-unused skill among us; we are saddened that his escape cost the lives of those aboard the first ship. We could not help them because they were exploded in this frame; but we have returned your people and your weapons to you, since they were only intact in the next frame. Now everything else is as it was. There is nothing to fear; we have him in control."

"No," Charlie said. He was weeping convulsively. Clambering to his knees, he grappled Kirk by a forearm. "I won't do it again. Please, I'll be nice. I won't ever do it again. I'm sorry about the *Antares*, I'm sorry. Please let me go with you, please!"

"Whee-oo," McCoy said gustily. "Talk about the marines landing—!"

"It's not that easy," Kirk said, looking steadily at the strange thing—a Thasian?—before him. "Charlie destroyed the other ship and will have to be punished for it. But thanks to you, all the other damage is repaired—and he is a human being. He belongs with his own people."

"You're out of your mind," McCoy said.

"Shut up, Bones. He's one of us. Rehabilitation might make him really one of us, reunite him to his own people. We owe him that, if he can be taught not to use his power."

"We gave him the power," the apparition said, "so that he could live. It cannot be taken back or forgotten. He will use it; he cannot help himself. He would destroy you and your kind, or you would be forced to destroy him to save yourselves. We alone offer him life."

''Not at all,'' Kirk said. ''You offer him a prison—not even a half-life.''

''We know that. But that damage was done long ago; we can do now only what little best is left. Since we are to blame, we must care for him. Come, Charles Evans.''

''Don't let them!'' Charlie gasped. ''Don't let them take me! Captain—*Janice!* Don't you understand, I *can't even touch them*—''

The boy and the Thasian vanished, in utter silence. The only remaining sound was the dim, multifarious humming surround of the *Enterprise*.

And the sound of Janice Rand weeping, as a woman weeps for a lost son.

BALANCE OF TERROR

Writer: Paul Schneider
Director: Vincent McEveety
Guest stars: Mark Lenard, Paul Comi

When the Romulan outbreak began, Capt. James Kirk was in the chapel of the starship *Enterprise*, waiting to perform a wedding.

He could, of course, have declined to do any such thing. Not only was he the only man aboard the starship empowered to perform such a ceremony—and many others even less likely to occur to a civilian—but both the participants were part of the ship's complement: Specialist (phaser) Robert Tomlinson and Spec. 2nd Cl. (phaser) Angela Martine.

Nevertheless, the thought of refusing hadn't occurred to him. Traveling between the stars, even at "relativistic" or near-light speeds, was a long-drawn-out process at best. One couldn't forbid or even ignore normal human relationships over such prolonged hauls, unless one was either a martinet or a fool, and Kirk did not propose to be either.

And in a way, nothing could be more symbolic of his function, and that of the *Enterprise* as a whole, than a marriage. Again because of the vast distances and time lapses involved, the starships were effectively the only fruitful links between the civilized planets. Even interstellar radio, which was necessarily faster, was subject to a dozen different kinds of interruptions, could carry no goods, and in terms of human contact was in every way less satisfactory. On the other hand, the starships were as fructifying as worker bees; they carried supplies, medical help, technical knowledge, news of home, and—above all—the sight and touch of other people.

It was for the same complex of reasons that there was

a chapel aboard the *Enterprise*. Designed by some groundlubber in the hope of giving offense to nobody (or, as the official publicity had put it, "to accommodate all faiths of all planets," a task impossible on the face of it), the chapel was simplified and devoid of symbols to the point of insipidity; but its very existence acknowledged that even the tightly designed *Enterprise* was a world in itself, and as such had to recognize that human beings often have religious impulses.

The groom was already there when Kirk entered, as were about half a dozen crew members, speaking *sotto voce*. Nearby, Chief Engineer Scott was adjusting a small television camera; the ceremony was to be carried throughout the intramural network, and outside the ship, too, to the observer satellites in the Romulus-Remus neutral zone. Scotty could more easily have assigned the chore to one of his staff, but doing it himself was his acknowledgment of the solemnity of the occasion—his gift to the bride, as it were. Kirk grinned briefly. Ship's air was a solid mass of symbols today.

"Everything under control, Scotty?"

"Can't speak for the groom, sir, but all's well otherwise."

"Very good."

The smile faded a little, however, as Kirk moved on toward the blankly nondenominational altar. It bothered him a little—not exactly consciously, but somewhere at the back of his conscience—to be conducting an exercise like this so close to the neutral zone. The Romulans had once been the most formidable of enemies. But then, not even a peep had been heard from them since the neutral zone had been closed around their system, fifty-odd years ago. Even were they cooking something venomous under there, why should they pick today to try it—and with a heavily armed starship practically in their back yards?

Scotty, finishing up with the camera, smoothed down his hair self-consciously; he was to give the bride away. There was a murmur of music from the intercom—Kirk could only suppose it was something traditional, since he himself was tone-deaf—and Angela came in, flanked by her bridesmaid, Yeoman Janice Rand. Scott offered her his arm. Tomlinson and his best man were already in position. Kirk cleared his throat experimentally.

And at that moment, the ship's alarm went off.

Angela went white. Since she was new aboard, she might never have heard the jarring blare before, but she obviously knew what it was. Then it was replaced by the voice of Communications Officer Uhura:

"Captain Kirk to the bridge! Captain Kirk to the bridge!"

But the erstwhile pastor was already out the door at a dead run.

Spock, the First Officer, was standing beside Lieutenant Uhura's station as Kirk and his engineer burst onto the bridge. Spock, the product of marriage between an earth woman and a father on Vulcan—not the imaginary Solar world of that name, but a planet of 40 Eridani—did not come equipped with Earth-human emotions, and Lieutenant Uhura had the impassivity of most Bantu women; but the air was charged with tension nonetheless. Kirk said: "What's up?"

"It's Commander Hansen, outpost satellite four zero two three," Spock said precisely. "They've picked up clear pips of an intruder in the neutral zone."

"Identification?"

"None yet, but the engine pattern is modern. Not a Romulan vessel, apparently."

"Excuse me, Mr. Spock," a voice said from the comm board. "I'm overhearing you. We have a sighting now. The vessel is modern—but the markings are Romulan."

Kirk shouldered forward and took the microphone from Lieutenant Uhura's hand. "This is Captain Kirk. Have you challenged it, Hansen?"

"Affirmative. No acknowledgment. Can you give us support, Captain? You are the only starship in this sector."

"Affirmative."

"We're clocking their approach visually at . . ." Hansen's voice died for a moment. Then: "Sorry, just lost them. Disappeared from our monitors."

"Better transmit your monitor picture. Lieutenant Uhura, put it on our bridge viewscreen."

For a moment, the screen showed nothing but a scan of stars, fading into faint nebulosity in the background. Then, suddenly, the strange ship was there. Superficially, it looked much like an *Enterprise*-class starship; a domed disc, seemingly coming at the screen nearly edge-on—though of course it was actually approaching the satellite, not the *Enterprise*. Its size, however, was impossible to guess without a distance estimate.

"Full magnification, Lieutenant Uhura."

The stranger seemed to rush closer. Scott pointed mutely, and Kirk nodded. At this magnification, the stripes along the underside were unmistakable: broad shadows suggesting a bird of prey with half-spread wings. Romulan, all right.

From S-4023, Hansen's voice said urgently: "Got it again! Captain Kirk, can you see—"

"We see it."

But even as he spoke, the screen suddenly turned white, then dimmed as Uhura backed it hastily down the intensity scale. Kirk blinked and leaned forward tensely.

The alien vessel had launched a torpedolike bolt of blinding light from its underbelly. Moving with curious deliberateness, as though it were traveling at the speed of light in some other space but was loafing sinfully in this one, the dazzling bolt swelled in S-4023's camera lens, as if it were bound to engulf the *Enterprise* as well.

"She's opened fire!" Hansen's voice shouted. "Our screen's failed—we're—"

The viewscreen of the *Enterprise* spat doomsday light throughout the control room. The speaker squawked desperately and went dead.

"Battle stations," Kirk told Uhura, very quietly. "General alarm. Mr. Spock, full ahead and intercept."

Nobody had ever seen a live Romulan. It was very certain that "Romulan" was not their name for themselves, for such fragmentary evidence as had been pieced together from wrecks, after they had erupted from the Romulus-Remus system so bloodily a good seventy-five years ago, suggested that they'd not even been native to the planet, let alone a race that could have shared Earthly conventions of nomenclature. A very few bloated bodies recovered from space during that war had proved to be humanoid, but of the hawklike Vulcanite type rather than the Earthly anthropoid. The experts had guessed that the Romulans might once have settled on their adopted planet as a splinter group from some mass migration, thrown off, rejected by their less militaristic fellows as they passed to some more peaceful settling, to some less demanding kind of new world. Neither Romulus nor Remus, twin planets whirling around a common center in a Trojan relationship to a white-dwarf sun, could have proved attractive to any race that did not love hardships for their own sakes.

But almost all this was guesswork, unsupported either by history or by interrogation. The Vulcanite races who were part of the Federation claimed to know nothing of the Romulans; and the Romulans themselves had never allowed any prisoners to be taken—suicide, apparently, was a part of their military tradition—nor had they ever taken any. All that was known for sure was that the Romulans had come boiling out of their crazy little planetary system on no apparent provocation, in primitive, clumsy cylindrical ships that should have been clay pigeons for the Federation's navy and yet in fact took twenty-five years to drive back to their home world—twenty-five years of increasingly merciless slaughter on both sides.

The neutral zone, with its sphere of observer satellites, had been set up around the Romulus-Remus system after that, and for years had been policed with the utmost vigilance. But for fifty years nothing had come out of it—not even a signal, let alone a ship. Perhaps the Romulans were still nursing their wounds and perfecting their grievances and their weapons—or perhaps they had learned their lesson and given up—or perhaps they were just tired, or decadent. . . .

Guesswork. One thing was certain now. Today, they had come out again—or one ship had.

The crew of the *Enterprise* moved to battle stations with a smooth efficiency that would hardly have suggested to an outsider that most of them had never heard a shot fired in anger. Even the thwarted bridal couple was at the forward phaser consoles, as tensely ready now to launch destruction as they had been for creation only a few hours before.

But there was nothing to fire at in the phaser sights yet. On the bridge, Kirk was in the captain's chair, Spock and Scott to either side of him. Sulu was piloting; Second Officer

Stiles navigating. Lieutenant Uhura, as usual, was at the comm board.

"No response from satellites four zero two three, two four or two five," she said. "No trace to indicate any are still in orbit. Remaining outposts still in position. No sightings of intruding vessel. Sensor readings normal. Neutral zone, zero."

"Tell them to stay alert and report anything abnormal."

"Yes, sir."

"Entering four zero two three's position area," Sulu said.

"Lieutenant Uhura?"

"Nothing, sir. No, I'm getting a halo effect here now. Debris, I'd guess—metallic, finally divided, and still scattering. The radiant point's obviously where the satellite should be; I'm running a computer check now, but—"

"But there can't be much doubt about it," Kirk said heavily. "They pack a lot more punch than they did fifty years ago—which somehow doesn't surprise me much."

"What *was* that weapon, anyhow?" Stiles whispered.

"We'll check before we guess," Kirk said. "Mr. Spock, put out a tractor and bring me in some of that debris. I want a full analysis—spectra, stress tests, X-ray diffusion, microchemistry, the works. We know what the hull of that satellite used to be made of. I want to know what it's like *now*—and then I want some guesses from the lab on how it got that way. Follow me?"

"Of course, sir," the First Officer said. From any other man it would have been a brag, and perhaps a faintly insulting one at that. From Spock it was simply an utterly reliable statement of fact. He was already on the intercom to the lab section.

"Captain," Uhura said. Her voice sounded odd.

"What is it?"

"I'm getting something here. A mass in motion. Nothing more. Nothing on visual, no radar pip. And no radiation. Nothing but a De Broglie transform in the computer. It could be something very small and dense nearby, or something very large and diffuse far away, like a comet. But the traces don't match for either."

"Navigator?" Kirk said.

"There's a cold comet in the vicinity, part of the Romulus-Remus system," Stiles said promptly. "Bearing 973 galactic east, distance one point three light hours, course roughly convergent—"

"I'd picked that up long ago," Uhura said. "This is something else. Its relative speed to us is one-half light, in toward the neutral zone. It's an electromagnetic field of some kind . . . but no kind I ever saw before. I'm certain it's not natural."

"No, it isn't," Spock said, with complete calmness. He might have been announcing the weather, had there been any out here. "It's an invisibility screen."

Stiles snorted, but Kirk knew from long experience that his half-Vulcanite First Officer never made such flat statements without data to back them. Spock was very odd by Earth-human standards, but he had a mind like a rapier. "Explain," Kirk said.

"The course matches for the vessel that attacked the last satellite outpost to disappear," Spock said. "Not the one we're tracking now, but four zero two five. The whole orbit feeds in along Hohmann D toward an intercept with Romulus. The computer shows that already."

"Lieutenant Uhura?"

"Check," she said, a little reluctantly.

"Second: Commander Hansen lost sight of the enemy vessel when it was right in front of him. It didn't reappear until it was just about to launch its attack. Then it vanished again, and we haven't seen it since. Third: Theoretically, the thing is possible, for a vessel of the size of the *Enterprise*, if you put almost all the ship's power into it; hence, you must become visible if you need power for your phasers, or any other energy weapon."

"And fourth, baloney," Stiles said.

"Not quite, Mr. Stiles," Kirk said slowly. "This would also explain why just one Romulan vessel might venture through the neutral zone, right under the nose of the *Enterprise*. The Romulans may think they can take us on now, and they've sent out one probe to find out."

"A very long chain of inferences, sir," Stiles said, with marked politeness.

"I'm aware of that. But it's the best we've got at the moment. Mr. Sulu, match course and speed exactly with Lieutenant Uhura's blip, and stick with it move for move. But under no circumstances cross after it into the neutral zone without my direct order. Miss Uhura, check all frequencies for a carrier wave, an engine pattern, any sort of transmission besides this De Broglie wave-front—in particular, see if you can overhear any chit-chat between ship and home planet. Mr. Spock and Mr. Scott, I'll see you both directly in the briefing room; I want to review what we know about Romulus. Better call Dr. McCoy in on it, too. Any questions?"

There were none. Kirk said, "Mark and move."

The meeting in the briefing room was still going on when Spock was called out to the lab section. Once he was gone, the atmosphere promptly became more informal; neither Scott nor McCoy liked the Vulcanite, and even Kirk, much though he valued his First Officer, was not entirely comfortable in his presence.

"Do you want me to go away too, Jim?" McCoy said gently. "It seems to me you could use some time to think."

"I think better with you here, Bones. You too, Scotty. But this could be the big one. We've got people from half the planets of the Federation patrolling the neutral zone. If we cross it with a starship without due cause, we may have more than just the Romulans to worry about. That's how civil wars start, too."

"Isn't the loss of three satellites due cause?" Scott said.

"I'd say so, but precisely what knocked out those satellites? A Romulan ship, we say; but can we prove it? Well, no, we say; the thing's invisible. Even Stiles laughs at that, and he's on our side. The Romulans were far behind us in technology the last we saw of them—they only got as far as they did in the war out of the advantage of surprise, plus a lot of sheer savagery. Now, suddenly, they've got a ship as good as ours, *plus* an invisibility screen. I can hardly believe it myself.

"And on the other hand, gentlemen . . . On the other hand, while we sit here debating the matter, they may be about to knock us right out of the sky. It's the usual verge-of-war situation: we're damned if we do, and damned if we don't."

The elevator door slid open. Spock was back. "Sir—"

"All right, Mr. Spock. Shoot."

Spock was carrying a thick fascicle of papers bound to a clip board, held close to his body under one arm. His other hand swung free, but its fist was clenched. The bony Vulcanite face had no expression and could show none, but there was something in his very posture that telegraphed tension.

"Here are the analyses of the debris," he said in his inhumanly even voice. "I shan't bother you with the details unless you ask. The essence of the matter is that the Romulan weapon we saw used on S-4023 seems to be a molecular implosion field."

"Meaning what?" McCoy said roughly.

Spock raised his right fist over the plot board, still clenched. The knuckles and tendons worked for a moment. A fine metallic glitter sifted down onto the table.

"It fatigues metals," he said. "Instantly. The metal crystals lose cohesion, and collapse into dust—like this. After that, anything contained in the metal blows up of itself, because it isn't contained any more. I trust that's clear, Dr. McCoy. If not, I'll try to explain it again."

"Damn you, Spock—"

"Shut up, Bones," Kirk said tiredly. "Mr. Spock, sit down. Now then. We're in no position to fight among ourselves. Evidently we're even worse off than we thought we were. If the facts we have are to be trusted, the Romulans have, first, a practicable invisibility screen, and second, a weapon at the very least comparable to ours."

"Many times superior," Spock said stolidly. "At least in some situations."

"*Both* of these gadgets," McCoy said, "are Mr. Spock's inventions, very possibly. At least in both cases, it's his interpretation of the facts that's panicking us."

"There are no other interpretations available at the moment," Kirk said through thinned lips. "Any argument about that? All right. Then let's see what we can make of them for our side. Scotty, what have *we* got that we can counter with, given that the Romulan gadgets are real? We can't hit an invisible object, and we can't duck an invisible gunner. Where does that leave us?''

''Fully armed, fast and maneuverable,'' the engineer said. ''Also, they aren't quite invisible; Lieutenant Uhura can pick up their De Broglie waves as they move. That means that they must be operating at nearly full power right now, just running away and staying invisible. We've got the edge on speed, and I'd guess that they don't know that our sensors are picking them up.''

''Which means that we can outrun them and know—approximately—what they're doing. But we can't out-gun them or see them.''

''That's how it looks at the moment,'' Scott said. ''It's a fair balance of power, I'd say, Jim. Better than most commanders can count on in a battle situation.''

''This isn't a battle situation yet,'' Kirk said. ''Nor even a skirmish. It's the thin edge of an interstellar war. We don't dare to be wrong.''

''We can't be righter than we are with the facts at hand, sir,'' Spock said.

McCoy's lips twitched. ''You're so damned sure—''

A beep from the intercom stopped him. Way up in the middle of the air, Lieutenant Uhura's voice said:

''Captain Kirk.''

''Go ahead, Lieutenant,'' Kirk said, his palms sweating.

''I've got a fix on the target vessel. Still can't see it—but I'm getting voices.''

Even McCoy pounded up with them to the bridge. Up there, from the master speaker on the comm board, a strange, muted gabble was issuing, fading in and out and often hashed with static, but utterly incomprehensible even at its best. The voices sounded harsh and only barely human; but that could have been nothing more than the illusion of strangeness produced by an unknown language.

The Bantu woman paid no attention to anything but her instruments. Both her large hands were resting delicately on dial knobs, following the voices in and out, back and forth, trying to keep them in aural focus. Beside her left elbow a tape deck ran, recording the gabble for whatever use it might be later for the Analysis team.

"This appears to be coming off their intercom system," she said into the tape-recorder's mike. "A weak signal with high impedance, pulse-modulated. Worth checking what kind of field would leak such a signal, what kind of filtration spectrum it shows—oh, damn—no, there it is again. Scotty, is that you breathing down my neck?"

"Sure is, dear. Need help?"

"Get the computer to work out this waver-pattern for me. My wrists are getting tired. If we can nail it down, I might get a picture."

Scott's fingers flew over the computer console. Very shortly, the volume level of the gabble stabilized, and Lieutenant Uhura leaned back in her seat with a sigh, wriggling her fingers in mid-air. She looked far from relaxed, however.

"Lieutenant," Kirk said. "Do you think you can really get a picture out of that transmission?"

"Don't know why not," the Communications Officer said, leaning forward again. "A leak that size should be big enough to peg rocks through, given a little luck. They've got visible light blocked, but they've left a lot of other windows open. Anyhow, let's try . . ."

But nothing happened for a while. Stiles came in quietly and took over the computer from Scott, walking carefully and pointedly around Spock. Spock did not seem to notice.

"This is a funny business entirely," McCoy said almost to himself. "Those critters were a century behind us, back when we drove them back to their kennels. But that ship's almost as good as ours. It even *looks* like ours. And the weapons . . ."

"Shut up a minute, please, Dr. McCoy," Lieutenant Uhura said. "I'm beginning to get something."

"Sulu," Kirk said. "Any change in their course?"

"None, sir. Still heading home."

"Eureka!" Lieutenant Uhura crowed triumphantly. "There it is!"

The master screen lit. Evidently, Kirk judged, the picture was being picked up by some sort of monitor camera in the Romulan's control room. That in itself was odd; though the *Enterprise* had monitor cameras almost everywhere, there was none on the bridge—who, after all, would be empowered to watch the Captain?

Three Romulans were in view across the viewed chamber, sitting at scanners, lights from their hooded viewers playing upon their faces. They looked human, or nearly so: lean men, with almond-colored faces, dressed in military tunics which bore wolf's-head emblems. The severe, reddish tone of the bulkheads seemed to accentuate their impassivity. Their heads were encased in heavy helmets.

In the foreground, a man who seemed to be the commanding officcr worked in a cockpit-like well. Compared to the bridge of the *Enterprise*, this control room looked cramped. Heavy conduits snaked overhead, almost within touch.

All this, however, was noted in an instant and forgotten. Kirk's attention was focused at once on the commander. His uniform was white, and oddly less decorated than those of his officers. Even more importantly, however, he wore no helmet. And in his build, his stance, his coloring, even the cant and shape of his ears, he was a dead ringer for Spock.

Without taking his eyes from the screen, Kirk could sense heads turning toward the half-Vulcanite. There was a long silence, except for the hum of the engines and the background gabble of the Romulan's conversation. Then Stiles said, apparently to himself:

"So now we know. They got our ship design from spies. They can pass for us . . . or for some of us."

Kirk took no overt notice of the remark. Possibly it had been intended only for his ears, or for nobody's; until further notice he was tentatively prepared to think so. He said:

"Lieutenant Uhura, I want linguistics and cryptography to go to work on that language. If we can break it—"

There was another mutter from Stiles, not intelligible but a good deal louder than before. It was no longer possible to ignore him.

"I didn't quite hear that, Mr. Stiles."

"Only talking to myself, sir."

"Do it louder. I want to hear it."

"It wasn't—"

"Repeat it," Kirk said, issuing each syllable like a bullet. Everyone was watching Kirk and Stiles now except Spock, as though the scene on the screen was no longer of any interest at all.

"All right," Stiles said. "I was just thinking that Mr. Spock could probably translate for us a lot faster than the analysts or the computer could. After all, they're his kind of people. You have only to look at them to see that. We can all see it."

"Is that an accusation?"

Stiles drew a deep breath. "No, sir," he said evenly. "It's an observation. I hadn't intended to make it public, and if it's not useful, I'll withdraw it. But I think it's an observation most of us have already made."

"Your apology doesn't satisfy me for an instant. However, since the point's now been aired, we'll explore it. Mr. Spock, do you understand the language those people are speaking? Much as I dislike Mr. Stiles' imputation, there is an ethnic resemblance between the Romulans and yourself. Is it meaningful?"

"I don't doubt that it is," Spock said promptly. "Most of the poeple in this part of space seem to come from the same stock. The observation isn't new. However, Vulcan has had no more contact than Earth has with the Romulans in historical times; and I certainly don't understand the language. There are suggestions of roots in common with my home language—just as English has some Greek roots. That wouldn't help you to understand Greek from a standing start, though it might help you to figure out something about the language, given time. I'm willing to try it—but I don't hold out much hope of its being useful in time to help us out of our present jam."

In the brief silence which followed, Kirk became aware that the muttering from the screen had stopped. Only a second later, the image of the Romulan bridge had dissolved too.

"They've blocked the leak," Uhura reported. "No way to tell whether or not they knew we were tapping it."

"Keep monitoring it and let me know the instant you pick them up again. Make a copy of your tape for Mr. Spock. Dr. McCoy and Mr. Scott, please come with me to my quarters. Everyone else, bear in mind that we're on continuous alert until this thing is over, one way or another."

Kirk stood up, and seemed to turn toward the elevator. Then, after a carefully calculated pause, he swung on Stiles.

"As for you, Mr. Stiles: Your suggestion may indeed be useful. At the moment, however, I think it perilously close to bigotry, which is a sentiment best kept to yourself. Should you have another such notion, be sure I hear it *before* you air it on the bridge. Do I make myself clear?"

White as milk, Stiles said in a thin voice: "You do, sir."

In his office, Kirk put his feet up and looked sourly at the doctor and his engineer. "As if we didn't have enough trouble," he said. "Spock's a funny customer; he gets everybody's back hair up now and then just on ordinary days; and this . . . coincidence . . . is at best a damn bad piece of timing."

"If it is a coincidence," McCoy said.

"I think it is, Bones. I trust Spock; he's a good officer. His manners are bad by Earth standards, but I don't think much of Stiles' manners either at the moment. Let's drop the question for now. I want to know what to do. The Romulan appears to be running. He'll hit the neutral zone in a few hours. Do we keep on chasing him?"

"You've got a war on your hands if you do," McCoy said. "As you very well know. Maybe a civil war."

"Exactly so. On the other hand, we've already lost three outpost satellites. That's sixty lives—besides all that expensive hardware . . . I went to school with Hansen, did you know that? Well, never mind. Scotty, what do you think?"

"I don't want to write off sixty lives," Scott said. "But we've got nearly four hundred on board the *Enterprise*, and I don't want to write them off either. We've got no defense against that Romulan weapon, whatever it is—and the phasers can't hit a target they can't see. It just might be better to let them run back inside the neutral zone, file a complaint with the Federation, and wait for a navy to take over. That would give us more time to analyze these gadgets of theirs, too."

"And the language and visual records," McCoy added. "Invaluable, unique stuff—all of which will be lost if we force an engagement and lose it."

"Prudent and logical," Kirk admitted. "I don't agree

with a word of it, but it would certainly look good in the log. Anything else?''

''What else do you need?'' McCoy demanded. ''Either it makes sense or it doesn't. I trust you're not suddenly going all bloody-minded on me, Jim.''

''You know better than that. I told you I went to school with Hansen; and I've got kids on board here who were about to get married when the alarm went off. Glory doesn't interest me, either, *or* the public record. *I want to block this war.* That's the charge that's laid upon me now. The only question is, How?''

He looked gloomily at his toes. After a while he added:

''This Romulan irruption is clearly a test of strength. They have two weapons. They came out of the neutral zone and challenged a starship with them—with enough slaughter and destruction to make sure we couldn't ignore the challenge. It's also a test of our determination. They want to know if we've gone soft since we beat them back the last time. Are we going to allow our friends and property to be destroyed just because the odds seem to be against us? How much peace will the Romulans let us enjoy if we play it safe now—especially if we let them duck back into a neutral zone they've violated themselves? By and large, I don't think there's much future in that, for us, for the Earth, for the Federation—*or even for the Romulans*. The time to pound that lesson home is now.''

''You may be right,'' Scott said. ''I never thought I'd say so, but I'm glad it isn't up to me.''

''Bones?''

''Let it stand. I've one other suggestion, though. It might improve morale if you'd marry those two youngsters from the phaser deck.''

''Do you think this is exactly a good time for that?''

''I'm not sure there's ever a right time. But if you care for your crew—and I know damn well you do—that's precisely the right way to show it at the moment. An instance of love on an eve of battle. I trust I don't embarrass you.''

''You do, Doctor,'' Kirk said, smiling, ''but you're right. I'll do it. But it's going to have to be quick.''

''Nothing lasts very long,'' McCoy said enigmatically.

• • •

On the bridge, nothing seemed to have happened. It took Kirk a long moment to realize that the conference in his office had hardly taken ten minutes. The Romulan vessel, once more detectable only by the De Broglie waves of its motion, was still apparently fleeing for the neutral zone, but at no great pace.

"It's possible that their sensors can't pick us up either through that screen," Spock said.

"That, or he's trying to draw us into some kind of trap," Kirk said. "Either way, we can't meet him in a head-on battle. We need an edge . . . a diversion. Find me one, Mr. Spock."

"Preferably nonfatal," Stiles added. Sulu half turned to him from the pilot board.

"You're so wrong about this," Sulu said, "you've used up all your mistakes for the rest of your life."

"One of us has," Stiles said stiffly.

"Belay that," Kirk said. "Steady as she goes, Mr. Sulu. The next matter on the agenda is the wedding."

"In accordance with space law," Kirk said, "we are gathered together for the purpose of joining this woman, Angela Martine, and this man, Robert Tomlinson, in the bond of matrimony . . ."

This time there were no interruptions. Kirk closed his book and looked up.

". . . And so, by the powers vested in me as Captain of the U.S.S. *Enterprise*, I now pronounce you man and wife."

He nodded to Tomlinson, who only then remembered to kiss the bride. There was the usual hubbub, not seemingly much muted by the fewness of the spectators. Yeoman Rand rushed up to kiss Angela's cheek; McCoy pumped Tomlinson's hand, slapped him on the shoulder, and prepared to collect his kiss from the bride, but Kirk interposed.

"Captain's privilege, Bones."

But he never made it; the wall speaker checked him. The voice was Spock's.

"Captain—I think I have the diversion you wanted."

"Some days," Kirk said ruefully, "nothing on this ship ever seems to get finished. I'll be right there, Mr. Spock."

• • •

Spock's diversion turned out to be the cold comet they had detected earlier–now "cold" no longer, for as it came closer to the central Romulan-Reman sun it had begun to display its plumage. Spock had found it listed in the ephemeris, and a check of its elements with the computer had shown that it would cross between the *Enterprise* and the Romulan 440 seconds from now–not directly between, but close enough to be of possible use.

"We'll use it," Kirk declared promptly. "Mr. Sulu, we'll close at full acceleration at the moment of interposition. Scotty, tell the phaser room we'll want a bracketing salvo; we'll be zeroing on sensors only, and with that chunk of ice nearly in the way, there'll be some dispersion."

"Still, at that range we ought to get at least one hit," Scott said.

"One minute to closing," Spock said.

"Suppose the shot doesn't get through their screen?" Stiles said.

"A distinct possibility," Kirk agreed. "About which we can do exactly nothing."

"Thirty seconds . . . twenty . . . fifteen . . . ten, nine, eight, seven, six, five, four, three, two, one, zero."

The lights dimmed as the ship surged forward and at the same moment, the phaser coils demanded full drain. The comet swelled on the screen.

"All right, Mr. Tomlinson . . . Hit 'em!"

The *Enterprise* roared like a charging lion. An instant later, the lights flashed back to full brightness, and the noise stopped. The phasers had cut out.

"Overload," Spock said emotionlessly. "Main coil burnout." He was already at work, swinging out a panel to check the circuitry. After only a split second of hesitation, Stiles crossed to help him.

"Captain!" Sulu said. "Their ship–it's fading into sight. I think we got a hit–yes, we did!"

"Not good enough," Kirk said grimly, instantly suspecting the real meaning of the Romulan action. "Full retro power! Evasive action!"

But the enemy was still faster. On the screen, a radiant torpedo like the one they had seen destroy Satellite 4023 was scorching toward the *Enterprise*—and this time it was no illusion that the starship was the target.

"No good," Sulu said. "Two minutes to impact."

"Yeoman Rand, jettison recorder buoy in ninety seconds."

"Hold it," Sulu said. "That shot's changing shape—"

Sure enough: the looming bolt seemed to be wavering, flattening. Parts of it were peeling off in tongues of blue energy; its brilliance was dimming. Did it have a range limit—

The bolt vanished from the screen. The *Enterprise* lurched sharply. Several people fell, including Spock—luckily away from the opened instrument panel, which cracked and spat.

"Scotty! Damage report!"

"One hold compartment breached. Minor damage otherwise. Main phaser battery still out of action, until that coil's replaced."

"I think the enemy got it worse, sir," Lieutenant Uhura said. "I'm picking up debris-scattering ahead. Conduits—castings—plastoform shadows—and an echo like the body of a casualty."

There was a ragged cheer, which Kirk silenced with a quick, savage gesture. "Maintain deceleration. Evidently they have to keep their screen down to launch their weapon—and the screen's still down."

"No, they're fading again, Captain," Sulu said. "Last Doppler reading shows they're decelerating too . . . Now they're gone again."

"Any pickup from their intercom, Lieutenant Uhura?"

"Nothing, sir. Even the De Broglies are fading. I think the comet's working against us now."

Now what in space did that mean? Fighting with an unknown enemy was bad enough, but when the enemy could become invisible at will—And if that ship got back to the home planet with all its data, there might well be nothing further heard from the Romulans until they came swarming out of the neutral zone by the millions, ready for the kill. That ship had to be stopped.

"Their tactics make sense over the short haul," Kirk said thoughtfully. "They feinted us in with an attack on three relatively helpless pieces, retreated across the center of the board to draw out our power, then made a flank attack and went to cover. Clearly the Romulans play some form of chess. If I had their next move, I'd go across the board again. If they did that, they'd be sitting in our ionization wake right now, right behind us—with reinforcements waiting ahead."

"What about the wreckage, sir?" Uhura said.

"Shoved out the evacuation tubes as a blind—an old trick, going all the way back to submarine warfare. The next time they do that, they may push out a nuclear warhead for us to play with. Lieutenant Sulu, I want a turnover maneuver, to bring the main phaser battery aligned directly astern. Mr. Spock, we can't wait for main coil replacement any longer; go to the phaser deck and direct fire manually. Mr. Stiles, go with him and give him a hand. Fire at my command directly the turnover's been completed. All understood?"

Both men nodded and went out, Stiles a little reluctantly. Kirk watched them go for a brief instant—despite himself, Stiles' suspicion of Spock had infected him, just a little—and then forgot them. The turnover had begun. On the screen, space astern, in the *Enterprise*'s ionization wake, seemed as blank as space ahead, in the disturbed gasses of the now-dwindling comet's tail.

Then, for the third time, the Romulan ship began to materialize, precisely where Kirk had suspected it would be—and there was precisely nothing they could do about it yet. The bridge was dead silent. Teeth clenched, Kirk watched the cross-hairs on the screen creep with infinite slowness toward the solidifying wraith of the enemy—

"All right, Spock, *fire*!"

Nothing happened. The suspicion that flared now would not be suppressed. With a savage gesture, Kirk cut in the intercom screen to the phaser deck.

For a moment he could make nothing of what he saw. The screen seemed to be billowing with green vapor. Through it, dimly, Kirk could see two figures sprawled on the floor, near where the phaser boards should have been. Then Stiles came into the field of view, one hand clasped over his nose and mouth. He was trying to reach the boards, but he must have already taken in a lungful of the green gas. Halfway there, he clutched at his throat and fell.

"Scotty! What is that stuff—"

"Coolant fluid," Scott's voice said harshly. "Seal must have cracked—look, there's Spock—"

Spock was indeed on the screen now, crawling on his hands and knees toward the boards. Kirk realized belatedly that the figures on the deck had to be Tomlinson and one of his crew, both dead since the seal had been cracked, probably when the Romulan had hit the *Enterprise* before. On the main screen, another of the Romulan energy bolts was bearing down upon them, with the inexorability of a Fury. Everything seemed to be moving with preternatural slowness.

Then Spock somehow reached the controls, dragged himself to his knees, moved nearly paralyzed fingers over the instruments. He hit the firing button twice, with the edge of his hand, and then fell.

The lights dimmed. The Romulan blew up.

On board the *Enterprise*, there were three dead: Tomlinson, his aide, and Stiles. Angela had escaped; she hadn't been on the deck when the coolant had come boiling out. Escaped—a wife of half a day, a widow for all the rest of her days. Stolidly, Kirk entered it all in the log.

The Second Romulan War was over. And never mind the dead; officially, it had never even begun.

WHAT ARE LITTLE GIRLS MADE OF?

Writer: Robert Bloch
Director: James Goldstone
Guest stars: Michael Strong, Sherry Jackson,
Ted Cassidy

That day the efficiency of the *Enterprise* bridge personnel was a real tribute to their professionalism. For a human drama was nearing its climax among them, the closer they came to the planet Exo III.

Its heroine was the starship's chief nurse, Christine Chapel. She stood beside Kirk at his command chair, her eyes on the main viewing screen where the ice-bound planet was slowly rotating. Touched by the calm she was clearly struggling to maintain, he said, "We're now entering standard orbit, Nurse."

A flicker of her nervous anticipation passed over her face. "I know he's alive down there, Captain," she said.

Kirk said, "Five years have passed since his last message." It seemed only decent to remind this brave, loving, though perhaps vainly hoping woman of that sinister fact. But she answered him with firm certainty. "I know, sir. But Roger is a very determined man. He'd find some way to live."

Uhura spoke from her panel. "Beginning signals to surface, Captain."

"Run it through all frequencies, Lieutenant." Kirk rose to go and check the library computer screen. Spock, concentrated on it, said, "Ship's record banks show little we don't already know. Gravity of the planet one point one of Earth, sir. Atmosphere within safety limits."

"But surface temperatures are close to a hundred degrees below zero," Kirk said.

Spock, too, was conscious of the woman who was patiently awaiting her moment of truth. He lowered his voice. "It may have been inhabited once, but the sun in this system has been steadily fading for half a million years." He hit a switch. "Now for Doctor Korby, the hero of our drama, Captain . . ."

Onto the computer screen flashed a small photograph of a distinguished-looking man in his vital mid-forties. There was a printed caption beneath it and Spock read it aloud. "Doctor Roger Korby, often called the 'Pasteur of archaeological medicine.' His translation of medical records salvaged from the Orion ruins revolutionized immunization techniques . . ."

"Those records were required reading at the Academy, Mr. Spock. I've always wanted to meet him." Kirk paused. Then, he, too, lowered his voice. "Any chance at all that he could still be alive?"

Grave-faced, Spock shook his head. He switched off the photograph; and Uhura, as though confirming his negative opinion, called, "No return signal, Captain. Not on any frequency."

"One more try, Lieutenant." Kirk returned to the waiting woman who had heard Uhura's report. She said, "His last signal told about finding underground caverns . . ."

Her implication was only too obvious. Korby had sheltered in the caverns so deeply no signal could reach him. He was safe. He *was* still alive. Kirk, remembering how it is to be tortured by a hopeless hope, said gently, "Christine, since that last signal, two expeditions have failed to find him."

Uhura, making her second report, called, "I've run all frequencies twice now, Captain. There's no—" A blast of static crackled from all the bridge speakers. It subsided—and a male voice, strong, resonant spoke. "This is Roger Korby," it said. "Come in, *Enterprise*. Repeating, this is Roger Korby . . ."

Christine swayed. Reaching for the support of Kirk's command chair, she whispered, "That's—his voice . . ."

It spoke again. "Do you read me, *Enterprise*? This is Doctor Roger Korby, standing by . . ."

Kirk seized his speaker. "*Enterprise* to Korby. Thank you. We have your landing coordinates pinpointed. Preparing to beam down a party." He smiled up at Christine. "It may interest you to know that we have aboard this vessel—"

Korby's voice interrupted. "I have a rather unusual request, Captain. Can you beam down alone, just yourself? We've made discoveries of such a nature that this extraordinary favor must be required of you."

Astounded, Kirk took refuge in silence. Spock joined him, torn between his respect for the great scientist and the unprecedented demand. Cocking a brow, he said, "Odd. To say the least . . ."

"The man who's asked this is Roger Korby," Kirk said.

Spock spoke to Christine. "You're quite certain you recognized the voice?"

She laughed out of her great joy. "Have you ever been engaged to be married, Mr. Spock? Yes, it's Roger."

Kirk made his decision. Hitting the speaker button, he said, "Agreed, Doctor. However, there will be *two* of us." He nodded to Christine, passing the speaker to her.

"Hello, Roger," she said.

There was a long pause. Then the unbelieving voice came: "Christine . . . ?"

"Yes, Roger. I'm up here."

"Darling, how . . . what are you . . ." The voice poured excited enthusiasm through the speaker. "Yes, by all means, ask the Captain to bring you with him! I had no idea, no hope . . . Darling, are you all right? It's almost too much to credit . . ."

"Yes, Roger," she said. "Everything's all right. Now everything is just fine."

The anxious tension on the bridge had given way to a sympathetic delight. Kirk, feeling it, too, recovered his speaker. "We're on our way, Doctor. Be with you soon, both of us. Kirk out."

He made for the bridge elevator, followed by the radiant Christine.

They materialized in a rock cave. It was primitive, unfurnished. Beyond its rough entrance there stretched an unending snow-world; a world as white as death under its dark and brooding sky. Its horizon was jagged, peaked by mountains. In the half-twilight of the planet's dying sun, Kirk could see that they were shrouded in ice, cold, forbidding. It was a depressing arrival.

"He said he'd be waiting for us," Christine said.

Kirk also found the absence of welcome strange. He went forward to peer deeper into the cavern; and Christine, touching one of its walls, hastily withdrew her chilled fingers. Kirk, cupping his hands to his mouth called into the darkness, "Doctor Korby! Korby!" The rebounding echoes suggested a long extenstion of distance beyond the cavern.

He was aware of a sudden uneasiness. "I suppose it's possible," he said, "that we hit the wrong cavern entry." But the supposition didn't hold up. The beamdown coordinates had been checked with Korby in the Transporter Room. And Spock was right. Korby's request *had* been odd. He detached his communicator from his belt. "Captain to *Enterprise*."

"Spock here, sir."

"Beam down a couple of security men," Kirk said.

"Any problems, Captain?"

"Some delay in meeting us, Mr. Spock. Probably nothing at all. Kirk out." He motioned to Christine to join him at a wall to leave the cave's center open for the beamdown. "Getting up here to us may be taking more time than the Doctor estimated," he told her. "The corridors of this place may go deeper than we know."

She said, "Thank you, Captain. I'm trying not to worry."

He felt distinct relief when crewmen Matthews and Rayburn sparkled into materialization. Spock had seen to it that they were both fully armed. "Maintain your position here in this cave, Rayburn." Turning to Matthews, he added, "Nurse Chapel and I are going to investigate a little further. You'll go with us."

They found the narrow passageway that led out of the cave. They found it by groping along a wall. It slanted downward. The inky blackness ahead of them endorsed what the echoes had suggested. The passageway could divide itself into many unseen and distant directions.

The light grew still dimmer. Abruptly, Kirk halted. "Stop where you are," he told the others. He stooped for a stone and flung it into what he'd sensed lay right before him—an abyss. They could hear the stone rebounding from rock walls. Then there was silence—absolute. Christine had clutched at Kirk's arm when a light beam suddenly blazed at them, blinding them in its searchlight glare. Kirk jerked his phaser out. As he shielded his eyes with his left hand, a figure stepped in front of the light, a featureless shadow.

Christine hurried forward. "Roger!"

Kirk grabbed at her. "Careful! That drop-down . . ."

The figure stepped to what must have been a light-switch panel. The glare faded to a fainter light that revealed the rather ordinary face of a middle-aged man. Christine stared at him in mixed surprise and disappointment. It wasn't Korby. Kirk adjusted his phaser setting and stepped up beside her just as recognition broke into her face.

"Why, it's Doctor Brown!" she exclaimed. "He's Roger's assistant!" Identifying the man for Kirk, she rushed toward him, crying, "Brownie, where's Roger? Why . . . ?"

She never finished her sentence. Behind them, Matthews shrieked, "Capt—! Ahhhhhhhhhhhhh . . . hhh . . ."

The scream died in the depths of the abyss. Then there was only the clatter of stones dislodged by Matthews' misstep.

Sickened, Kirk pulled himself out of his shock. He went to his knees, edging himself dangerously near to the pit's rim. Pebbles were still falling from it into the blackness below. Brown joined him. "Careful . . . please be careful," he said.

Kirk rose. "Is there any path down?"

"There's no hope, Captain. It's bottomless."

Though Doctor Brown had warned of peril from the pit, he did not mention the momentary appearance of a huge, hairless nonhuman creature on the other, shadowy side of the pit. Perhaps he didn't see it. It remained only for a second before it was gone, a monstrous shadow lost in shadows. Instead, he said sympathetically, if unhelpfully, "Your man must have slipped."

"Any chance of a projection? a ledge of some kind?"

"None, Captain. We lost a man down there, too. Listen . . ." He reached for a heavy boulder and heaved it over the pit's edge. There was the same crashing of rebound—and then the same absolute silence.

"Unfortunate," Brown said. "Terribly unfortunate. Doctor Korby was detained. I came as rapidly as I could."

"Not soon enough," Kirk said.

He looked at Brown in his worn lab clothing. One learned composure in the presence of human death, if you lived with its daily threat for five years. His voice had sounded regretful. Was he regretful? Was he composed? Or was he cold, numb to feeling? Kirk could see that the weeping Christine had also sensed a certain peculiarity in Brown's response to Matthews' death.

She wiped her eyes on her uniform sleeve. "Brownie," she said suddenly, "don't you recognize me?"

"Explain," Brown said.

"You don't recognize me" she said.

"Christine, you look well," Brown said. He turned to Kirk. "My name is Brown. I am Doctor Korby's assistant. I presume you are Captain Kirk."

Something was definitely askew. Christine had already named Brown as Korby's assistant. And the man had addressed Kirk as "Captain" several times. Why did he now have to "presume" that he was Captain Kirk? Christine's uncertainty was mounting, too. Her eyes and ears insisted that Brown was indeed her old acquaintance—but the feeling of an off-kilter element in his present personality persisted. Of course, Time and harsh experience *did* make changes in people . . .

Kirk had returned to the pit's edge. "He's dead, I assure you," Brown said. "Come. Doctor Korby will be waiting." He moved over to the searchlight panel to turn a couple of switches. Lights came on further along the corridor. Kirk walked back to Christine. "You do know him well, don't you? This Brown is the Brown you remember, isn't he?"

She hesitated. "I—I suppose existing alone here for so long . . ."

Kirk reached for his phaser. Then he snapped open his communicator. "Captain Kirk to Rayburn."

"All quiet here, Captain. Any problems there, sir?"

"We've lost Matthews. An accident, apparently. Tell the *Enterprise* to have a full security party stand by."

"Yes, sir."

"And inform Mr. Spock that we will both report in at hourly intervals. If you and I lose contact—or if he fails to hear from either of us—the security force is to be beamed down immediately. Kirk out."

He heard the snap-off of Rayburn's communicator. He couldn't hear what followed it—Rayburn's choking gurgle as the hairless creature's great arm lunged from the darkness to encircle his throat.

"This way, please," Brown was saying. "The illumination is automatic from here on."

It was a long walk. Brown appeared to feel a need to install himself as the interpreter of Korby's work. He dissertated. "The doctor has discovered that this planet's original inhabitants were forced to move underground as the warmth of their sun waned. When you were his student, Christine, you often heard him say that freedom of choice produced the human spirit. The culture of Exo III proved his theory. When its people were compelled to move from light to darkness, their culture also became choiceless, mechanistic. The doctor has found elements in it that will revolutionize the universe when removed from this cavernous environment."

The prediction struck Kirk as slightly grandiose. Polite Christine said, "That's fascinating."

"I thought you'd be interested," Brown said. "We have arrived, Captain."

The place of their arrival was a large and luxurious study. Though its walls were of rock, they were so finely polished they conveyed an impression of massive grandeur. Modern taste had been sensitively superimposed on the foundations constructed by the ancient race. In their five years of underground life, Korby and his staff had clearly undertaken to make themselves comfortable. And well supplied. There were huge cabinets of gleaming scientific instruments, archaeological tools, favorite artifacts found and cherished. Odd-looking doors led out of the room into other unseen ones. In one corner was a dining area complete with tables and chairs.

One of the doors opened. A girl came in, pale, slim, dark-haired. There was a serene innocence in her face that merited the word "lovely." Her lips moved in a smile that exposed her perfect teeth.

"I'm Andrea," she said. "You must be Christine. I've always thought it was a beautiful name."

Christine was unpleasantly startled. Youthfully innocent she might be, but the girl was nevertheless a woman. And why she was serving as hostess in Korby's personal study was a question his affianced wife was obviously asking herself.

Andrea was good at her job. She turned the lovely smile to Kirk. "And you must be Captain Kirk of the starship *Enterprise*. I can't tell you how we appreciate your bringing Roger's fiancée to him."

Christine stiffened at the use of Korby's first name. "I don't remember Doctor Korby's mentioning an 'Andrea' as a member of his staff."

The smile didn't waver. "You are exactly as Roger described you. No wonder he's missed you so."

Such awareness of Korby's intimate emotions did nothing to alleviate Christine's growing resentment. Kirk, conscious of it, said, "Where is Doctor Korby?"

"Here, Captain." A strong-faced man, easily seen to be the man of the *Enterprise* photograph, had emerged from another door. Kirk was absurdly reminded of a theatrical buildup to the star's entrance. That Korby *was* the star, there was no mistaking. Kirk, himself accustomed to command, recognized the self-assurance in another commander. Korby, his hand extended, said, "I've been looking forward to meeting you."

Kirk had lost a crewman to a brutal death. He didn't like Brown. Nor had he lost his heart to Andrea. Ignoring the hand, he contented himself with saying, "And I to meeting you, sir."

"Roger . . ." Christine said.

"Christine . . . darling . . ."

She went to him. He bent to kiss her outstretched hands. Kirk, still wary, saw the honest joy in both their faces. It was a reunion that recovered two relationships—the intellectual bond of teacher and student, the bond of physical love between man and woman. Both loves still lived after all the years apart. So much was clear as they embraced—an embrace restrained in the others' presence but a double reunion that was real.

Christine lifted her head from his shoulder. Misty-eyed, she said, "I knew I'd find you."

He drew her back. "Forgive me, Captain. It's been a long time."

"There's no need to apologize, sir."

"The captain lost a man in the caverns, Doctor," Brown said.

There was no doubt of the horror on Korby's face. He released Christine to whirl on Brown. "What? How did it happen?"

"The pit near the outer junction. The edge must have given way."

Visibly shaken, Korby was silent. Then he spoke. "Captain, what can I say? I should have been there. I know the passages so well. I am sorry—so sorry."

"It isn't your fault, Doctor." Kirk had his communicator out. "Captain to Rayburn," he said. "Rayburn, report." As he waited for Rayburn's voice, he turned back to Korby. "I'll have to call my ship on a security confirmation. If you have any cargo requirements, any special needs, I'll be glad—"

"Captain!" Korby interrupted. His face was suddenly agitated. "I should much prefer—"

It was Kirk's turn to interrupt. He spoke loudly into the communicator. "Kirk to Rayburn. *Rayburn, are you receiving me?*"

He made an adjustment on the communicator and tried again. Then he gave himself a moment. "My other man has failed to respond, Doctor. It is now necessary that I call my ship . . ."

"No communications, Captain!"

It was Brown who had shouted. In his hand he held an old-style phaser rifle. It was aimed at Kirk's heart.

Aghast, Christine said, "Roger, what . . ."

"I'm sorry, dear," Korby said. "But if they should send down more people . . ."

Kirk, appalled by the sudden turn events had taken, realized that Andrea, rushing at him, had snatched the communicator from his hand.

"Roger!" Christine cried. "This man . . . this girl . . . Why do you allow . . . ?"

"Your captain won't be harmed," Korby said hurriedly. "Christine, listen. You must admit the possibility that there are things here unknown to you but so vitally important that—''

''Doctor Korby!'' Kirk shouted. ''I have one man dead! Now I've got another one out of contact!''

''Take his weapon, Andrea,'' Korby said.

The girl began to circle Kirk to get at the phaser hung on the rear of his belt. He drew back—and Brown leveled the rifle at his forehead. Kirk grabbed for reason. ''Doctor, I have a command to consider, crewmen, a starship . . .''

''This is necessary, Captain. You will understand.''

Kirk moved. He jerked out his phaser; and all in the same blur of action, ducked behind a heavy desk.

''Drop that rifle!'' he said to Brown.

Instead, Brown's finger reached for the trigger. Kirk fired his phaser—and Brown fell.

Christine screamed, ''Captain, behind you . . . !''

Her warning came too late. The hairless ape-thing had him by the arm. Under the fierce force of the grip, he was lifted high into the air, his whole body convulsed by the arm's agony. The phaser rang on the stone floor. Like a puppet, he kicked, helpless in the immense hand—and the other one struck him in the jaw. Christine screamed again. And he was dropped to fall, limp, half-conscious in a crumpled heap.

Christine, paralyzed with horror, stared vaguely around her as though seeking some answer to the incomprehensible. Then she saw what she had to see. Brown lay on the floor near Kirk, face upturned. There was no blood on the chest where the phaser beam had struck him. Instead, a metallic tangle of twisted dials and wires protruded from it . . . the infinitely complex circuitry required to animate an android robot.

Kirk found the strength to move his eyes. Then, he, too, saw what Christine had seen.

An anxious Spock was at Uhura's panel when she finally received Kirk's signal.

''Frequency open, sir,'' she told him, relief in her face.

He seized the speaker. ''Spock here, Captain.''

The familiar voice said, ''Contact established with Doctor Korby.''

"We were becoming concerned, Captain. Your check-in is overdue. Nor have we heard from your security team."

"There's no problem, Mr. Spock. They're with me. Return to ship will take about forty-eight hours. Doctor Korby's records and specimens will need careful packing."

"We can send down a work detail, sir."

"Korby has ample staff here. It's just that the work is quite delicate."

Abruptly Spock asked, "Captain . . . Is everything all right down there?"

Nothing was all right down there.

Spock had received no signal from Kirk. The captain of the *Enterprise* was sitting on a bunk in a detention chamber, watching as his voice issued from the mouth of the hairless ape-thing across the room. His communicator looked like a cigarette lighter in the creature's enormous paw. Korby was supervising its performance. He wasn't enjoying it. There was real concern for Kirk in his face. But real or unreal, Korby's feelings, his work, the man himself had ceased to matter to Kirk. The hot rage he felt had burned up all save the overriding fact that a neolithic savage was masquerading as commander of the *Enterprise*.

He tensed on the bunk. The bald thing noted it; and clicking the communicator off, prepared for muscle work.

"Please be still," Korby said. "If you move or cry out, Ruk may injure you. At least wait until you and I can talk together."

The communicator snapped back on. And a yet more anxious Spock said to Ruk, "Acknowledge, Captain. You sound tired."

Kirk heard his exact intonation come again from the flabby lips. "It's just the excitement of what we've found out, Mr. Spock. Korby's discoveries are scientifically amazing. All under control. Stand by for regular contact, Kirk out."

Ruk closed the communicator.

"This isn't a vain display, Captain," Korby said. "You know my reputation. Trust me."

"Yes, I know your reputation," Kirk said. "The whole galaxy knows who you are and what you used to stand for."

"There's so much you must learn before you make a

judgment,'' Korby said. He turned to Ruk. ''Andrea,'' he said tersely.

The loose mouth opened to say sweetly, ''And you must be Captain Kirk of the starship *Enterprise*.''

There was horror in the sound of the girlish voice emerging from the bald grotesque across the room. Kirk's obvious repulsion pleased it. Ruk began to show off.

It was Korby's voice now, saying, ''Forgive me, Captain. It's been a long time.'' Then it was Christine's turn. Ruk reproduced her precise emotional inflection in the words, ''I knew I'd find you.''

''Enough!'' Korby said sharply. ''You are not to mock Christine! You are never to harm her!''

''Or disobey an order from her?'' Kirk said.

Korby rose to the challenge. To Ruk he said, ''You will never disobey Christine's orders.'' He looked at Kirk. ''Satisfied, Captain?'' He came over to sit beside Kirk on the bunk. Ruk rose, menacing. Korby waved him back. ''Give me just twenty-four hours to convince you, Captain.''

''Must I be a prisoner to be convinced?''

''What would your first duty be on return to your ship? A report! Do you realize how many vital discoveries have been lost to laymen's supersititions, their ignorance?''

''Here is an ignorant layman's question for you, Doctor,'' Kirk said. *''Where is my man I could not contact?''*

''Ruk is programmed to protect my experiments. The logic of his machine-mind saw danger to me . . .''

''Where is my other crewman?'' Kirk repeated.

Korby's voice was very quiet. ''Ruk—destroyed them both, Captain. But totally against my wishes, believe me.''

Kirk's fists clenched. He looked down at them; and deliberately relaxing them, swallowed. Putting interest into his voice, he said, ''He's a robot, isn't he? Like Brown?''

Korby nodded to Ruk. The thing spoke heavily, dully. ''More complex than Brown, much superior. The old ones made me.''

Korby said, ''Ruk was still tending the machinery when we arrived here. How many centuries old he is even Ruk doesn't know. With his help, with the records I could find, we built Brown.''

"You've convinced me, Doctor," Kirk said. "You've convinced me that you're a very dangerous man . . ."

He pushed Korby off the bunk; and in a fast pivot, shoved him across the room at Ruk. Then he made a leap for the door. But Ruk was too quick for him. Moving with a surprising speed, the thing grabbed his arm and flung him back across the room. He struck the hard masonry of the wall, thrust against it to regain his feet—but the move was useless. He was seized and lifted, a toy in the gigantic hand.

"Careful, Ruk!" Korby shouted. "Gently!"

The vise-like grip eased. But Ruk's notion of gentleness left something to be desired. He cuffed Kirk across the head—and dropped him, unconscious.

"Where is Captain Kirk?"

Christine stopped pacing the length of Korby's study to put the question to an Andrea who'd suddenly appeared through a door. The sweetly innocent looked back at her, puzzled.

"You are concerned about the captain when you are with Roger again? I do not understand."

There was that familiar use of his name again. Christine was engulfed by a desolate sense of helplessness. She could understand nothing at all, not the man she had loved so long, his purpose nor his companions.

"Yes," she said. "I am much concerned about the captain."

With manifest sincerity, her voice wholly guileless, Andrea said, "How can you love Roger without trusting him?"

Christine didn't answer. The query had gone straight to the heart of her agony. She began her restless pacing again and Andrea said, "Why does it trouble you when I use the name 'Roger'?"

"It is sufficient that it does trouble her."

Korby had entered the study. Ruk was with him, the giant hand tight on Kirk's arm. The door hummed closed behind them; and Korby, moving to Andrea, said, "You will call me 'Doctor Korby' from now on."

She said, "Yes, Doctor Korby."

He took Christine's cold hand, smiling down into her

eyes. "As you can see, dear, Captain Kirk is fine. He won't be harmed. What's at stake here simply makes it necessary to prevent his reporting to his ship. I need time to explain, to demonstrate to him—and to you. Shall we start with Andrea?"

"Yes," she said. "Do start with Andrea."

The girl spoke simply, openly. "I am like Doctor Brown—an android robot. You did not know?"

"Remarkable, isn't she?" Korby said. He looked back at Kirk. "Notice the lifelike pigmentation, the variation in skin tones." He lifted Andrea's wrist. "The flesh has warmth. There's even a pulse, physical sensation . . ."

"Remarkable, indeed," Christine said.

The bitter irony in her voice got through to Korby. He released Andrea's wrist. "Darling," he said to Christine, "all I require for my purpose are obedience and awareness . . ."

It was an unfortunate choice of words. Christine walked away from him. For a moment he lost his self-assurance. Then he followed her. "Christine. You must realize that an android robot is like a computer. It does only what I program into it. As a trained scientist yourself, you must surely see . . ."

". . . that given a mechanical assistant, constructing a mechanical 'geisha' would be easy?"

Korby suddenly reached for Christine, pulling her close to him. "Do you think I could love a machine?" he demanded.

"Did you?" she said.

"Love can't exist where all is predictable! Christine, you must listen! Love must have imperfection—moments of worship, moments of hate. Andrea is as incapable of anger and fear as she is of love. She has no meaning for me. She simply obeys orders! Watch her . . ."

He spoke to Andrea. "Kiss Captain Kirk," he said.

She kissed Kirk.

"Now strike him," Korby said.

She slapped Kirk.

"You see, Christine? All she can do is what she's told to do. She's a sterile, a computer—a thing, not a woman." He whirled to Kirk. "Have you nothing to say, Captain?"

"Yes, Doctor, I have something to say," Kirk said. "If these inventions of yours can only do what they're told to do, why did Brown attack me? Who told him to do it? For that matter, who told this thing''—he indicated Ruk—''to kill two of my men?''

Korby's face went closed, cold. Taking Christine's arm, he said, ''Come with me, darling. You owe it to me.'' She looked at Kirk, the feeling of nightmare helplessness still heavier in her limbs. Then she went with Korby.

His laboratory was at the end of a lengthy corridor. It was spotlessly white. Cabinets of gleaming equipment shared its walls with banks of computer-like control panels. But its dominating feature was a large central turntable. It was flanked by two squat dynamos. Ruk was busy at the table. Into a scooped-out hollow in its top, he was fitting a mold of some greenish-brown stuff, roughly conformed to the height and breadth of a human body. As a cook pats dough into a bread pan, his gargantuan hands worked deftly to shape the mold into the indentation. It was when they reached for a shining, complicated mechanism suspended from the ceiling that Christine first noticed it. Then she saw there was a similar one hanging over the other side of the table. Ruk lowered the nearer device over the mold's midsection. Slowly the table began to turn.

Its opposite side slid into view. Kirk was lying on it, eyes closed, pressed down, immobile. The ceiling's other machine, descended over him, covered him from breast to thighs.

Pointing to it, Korby said proudly, ''This is how we make an android robot.''

With a signal to Ruk, he went over to a wall of control panels. He twisted a knob. Blue lights flashed deep, blinding, within the instrumentation that masked the alternately passing mold-form and the body of Kirk. The heavy dynamos glowed red, throbbing under impulses of power flowing to them from the control panel. When Korby made an adjustment to increase the turning speed of the table, a dizziness seized Christine. She leaned back against an equipment cabinet, her eyes shut against the vertigo. When she opened them, the blue lights were blazing, pulsating to the rhythm of a human heartbeat. And the table was spinning now, blurring the forms it held in a haze of speed so fast they appeared to be one.

Unknowingly she was wringing her hands. Korby left

the panel to take them in his. "Don't be afraid for him. I promise you, he's not being harmed in any way."

She found stumbling words. "To fix a man to a table like a lab specimen on a slide . . . I don't . . . Oh, Roger, what's happened to you . . . ? I remember when I sat in your class . . ." Tears choked her. "You wouldn't even consider injuring an animal, an insect . . . Life was sacred to you . . . It was what I loved about you . . ." She was openly weeping.

He took her in his arms. "I haven't changed, Christine. This is just a harmless demonstration to convince his skeptical, military mind. Please try and understand. If I'd beamed up to his ship with Brown and the others, they would have been objects of mere curiosity, freaks—the origin of wild rumors and destructive gossip."

"You don't *know* Captain Kirk!" she cried.

He patted her shoulder. "Now is the time to watch most carefully . . ." He left her to make some new, precise adjustment on the panel. Apparently, the table had reached its maximum acceleration. It was slowing down. In mingled amazement and horror, Christine caught a glimpse of the mold-form. It had assumed detailed human shape, human skin tones. The table came to a halt before her. Its niches held two identical Kirks.

Triumphant, Korby came back to her. "Which of the two is your captain, Christine? Can you tell?"

She shook her head. "I don't . . . know. I don't know—anything any more."

"This one is your captain," Korby said. "Do you see any harm that's been done him?"

Kirk's eyes opened. Immediately aware that he couldn't move, he was struggling against the appliance that covered him when he saw Korby. His jaw muscles hardened; and he was about to speak when he decided to listen, instead. For Korby was expounding to Christine. "The android's synthetic organs are now all in place. We merely synchronized them with Kirk's autonomic nervous system, duplicating his body rhythms. Now we must duplicate his mental patterns . . ."

A glimmer of realization came to Kirk. He saw Korby move to another control panel. He saw Andrea slip into the laboratory. And Ruk had gone into a crouch at the dynamo near his feet. He sensed what Korby was going to say before he said it. "Ruk, we're ready for final synaptic fusion. Andrea, stand by the cortex circuits. This android we're making will be so perfect, it could even replace the captain. It will have the same memories, the same abilities, the same attitudes . . ."

The implications of the boast were so appalling that they stimulated Kirk to a scurry of thinking faster than any he'd ever done in his life. As Korby shouted, *"Activate the circuits!"* he contorted his face with fury. As though mumbling to himself, he muttered, "Mind your business, Mr. Spock! I'm sick of your halfbreed interference! Do you hear me? Mind your business, Mr. Spock! I'm sick of your halfbreed—"

In midsentence a spasm of agony convulsed his body. Bolts of lightning seemed to split his head. The dynamo's hum screamed to an ear-shattering roar. Then the pain, the lightning, the roar were all over. Distraught, Christine ran to him. "I'm all right," he said. "It seems to be finished."

Korby came for her. "And now, my dear, you can meet my new android."

He gave the table a rotating twist. On it lay a perfect replica of Kirk. Its eyelids fluttered. Its gaze fastened on Christine and its lips moved in Kirk's characteristic smile of recognition. It said, "Nurse Chapel, how nice to see you."

Hostess Andrea was serving a meal to Christine in the study when Korby's new android opened its door. It was wearing Kirk's uniform.

"May I join you?" it said, seating itself at the table. "The doctor tells me I'm more or less on parole now. He thought you and I might like a little time together."

Christine whispered, "Captain, what are we . . . ?"

The android also lowered its voice. "We've got to find a way to contact the ship."

"I don't know what's happened to Roger." She looked despairingly into what she thought were Kirk's eyes.

"If I gave you a direct order to betray him, would you obey it, Christine?"

She bowed her head. "Please, Captain. Don't ask me to make such a choice. I'd rather you pushed me off the precipice where Matthews died."

Andrea placed a bowl of soup before her. "Thank you," she said. "I'm not hungry."

Her table companion also pushed its bowl aside. "I'm not, either," it said. "But then I am not your captain, Nurse Chapel. We androids don't eat, you see."

She'd thought she'd had all the shocks she could take. But there was a cat-and-mouse aspect to this last one that chilled her. She'd been about to confide her heartbreak to this manufactured thing masquerading as Kirk. She pushed her chair back and rose from the table just as Korby entered the study. The real Kirk was with him—a pale, haggard Kirk clad in the kind of nondescript lab outfit which Brown had worn.

He sniffed at the smell of food. "I'm hungry," he said; and turning to Korby, added, "That's the difference between me and your androids, Doctor."

His replica got up from its chair. "The difference is your weakness, Captain, not mine."

"Eating is a human pleasure," Kirk retorted. "Sadly, it is one you will never know."

"Perhaps. But I shall never starve, either," the android said.

Kirk looked at Korby. "It is an exact duplicate?"

"In every detail."

Kirk spoke directly to the duplicate. "Tell me about Sam, Mr. Android."

The answer came promptly. "George Samuel Kirk is your brother. Only *you* call him Sam."

"He saw me off on this mission."

"Yes. With his wife and three sons."

"He said he was being transferred to Earth Colony Two Research Station."

"No. He said he *wanted* a transfer to Earth Colony Two."

Korby intervened. "You might as well try to out-think a calculating machine, Captain."

"Obviously, I can't," Kirk said. "But we do have some interesting differences."

Korby was annoyed. "Totally unimportant ones." Abruptly, he dismissed his perfect android; and seating himself at the table, motioned Kirk and Christine to chairs.

"Bring food," he told Andrea. "Lots of it. The captain is hungry."

As Kirk began eating, he leaned forward. "You haven't guessed the rest, have you? Not even you, Christine. What you saw was only a machine—*only half of what I could have accomplished had I continued the process of duplication.* I could have put *you*, Captain—your very consciousness into that android." He smiled faintly. "Your very 'soul' if you prefer the term. All of you. Brown was an example. My assistant was dying. I gave him life in android form."

Intensity came into his voice. "Yes, humans converted into androids can be programmed—but for the better! Can you conceive how life would be if we could do away with jealousy, greed, hate?"

Kirk said, "That coin has an opposite side, Doctor. You might also do away with tenderness, love, respect."

Korby slammed his fist on the table. "No death! No disease, no deformities! Even fear can be programmed out to be replaced with perpetual peace! Open your mind, Captain! I'm speaking of a practical heaven, a new Paradise—and all I need is your help!"

"I thought all you needed was my 'open mind,' " Kirk said.

"I've got to get transportation to a planet with the proper raw materials. There must be several possibilities among your next stops. I'm not suggesting any diversion from your route. I myself want no suspicion aroused. I simply want to begin producing androids more carefully, selectively . . ."

Under his chair Kirk's hand had found a thong that bound its joints together. He located one end of it. "I can see your point," he said. "Any publicity about such a project could only frighten uninformed prejudice."

Korby nodded. "My androids must be widely infiltrated into human societies before their existence is revealed. Otherwise, we'd have a tidal wave of superstitious hysteria that could destroy what is right and good. Are you with me, Captain?"

Christine was staring at Korby in unbelief. Had the years of loneliness sent him mad? To advance such a cooperation to the captain of a Federation starship! But Kirk was taking it quietly. "You've created your own Kirk, Doctor. You don't need me."

"I created him to impress you, Captain, not to replace you."

"You'd better use him," Kirk said. "I am impressed—but not the way you intended." He had the thong unraveled now.

"Ruk!" Korby called. "Ruk, take the captain to his quarters!"

As the hairless Caliban approached him, Kirk sat still, his hand busy with a slipknot he was putting into the cord under his chair. When Ruk reached for his shoulder, he tensed for action. All in one fast move, he ducked under Ruk's arm, leaped for Korby; and, dropping the slipknot over his head, jerked it tight around his throat. Then he ran for the door. Ruk made a lunge for him but was halted by the sound of Korby's agonized choking. Turning, he saw Korby fall from his chair, hands clawing at the cord that was throttling him. He hesitated. Then he returned to Korby to loosen the noose.

Christine went to help him. But Korby, furious, pushed her away. "Get after—" he broke off, coughing. Clearing his throat, he tried again. "Get after him, Ruk. Stop him. I have no more use for him. You understand?"

Ruk understood. So did Christine. She heard the growl rumble in the great chest as Ruk made for the door. She followed him, calling, "Ruk! Ruk, stop!" She could see the huge android speeding down the lighted corridor toward what she thought were Kirk's quarters. Then the figure disappeared around a corner. She turned with it into an unlighted passageway, still calling, "Ruk, stop! The doctor told you to obey my orders. Stop!"

The speed of the running footsteps increased. She raced on. "Ruk, where are you? I order you not to harm him! Do you hear me? He is not to be harmed! Ruk, where are you?"

He'd vanished into the darkness. And the character of the passage had changed. Its stone floor had become uneven and she stumbled over a pebble. It flung her against a rough, unpolished rock wall. The blackness swallowed the sound of the footsteps.

But Kirk heard them pounding behind him. He'd come to the end of the passage and was clambering over rocks. He fell into a gully between two boulders. He clung to one of them, listening.

"Captain Kirk?"

It was Ruk's voice, echoing hollowly among the rocks. Kirk hauled himself up over a boulder; and began to edge forward again through the pitch blackness, groping along a wall.

"Captain Kirk . . ."

The sound of the footsteps had ceased. But he could hear Ruk's heavy breathing, somewhere close. Frantically, Kirk felt around him for some kind of weapon. A sharp stalagmite jutted up from the floor. He wrestled with it. It was immovable. Desperate now, he seized a rock and crashed it over the stalagmite's pointed end. It broke. He scrabbled around among its pieces and found a club-like shard of it.

There came a hushed whisper. "Captain Kirk? Where are you?"

Now it was Christine's voice. Kirk peered into the darkness—and was about to answer when he remembered Ruk's trick of voice imitation.

It came again—Christine's voice. "Captain Kirk, help! I've lost my way! Don't leave me here . . ."

Was it Christine? Or was it Ruk? There was no way of telling. Kirk tightened his hold on his rock weapon. It just might be Christine, lost in this labyrinth of underground pathways. He might as well answer. The suspense was as difficult to bear as any fact would be. And he had taken all the precautions it was possible to take.

"Over here, Christine," he said.

Darker than the dark, the monstrous android loomed toward him, surefooted, moving easily, swiftly. Kirk struggled for solid rock under his feet, pivoted and was swinging his arm back for the strike when the edge of the rock that held him crumbled.

The solid footing he'd struggled for bordered a chasm. It fell away beneath him as sheer and deep as the one that had lost him Matthews. His fingertip clutch on its rim was his clutch on life. He fought to maintain it against the rain of stones disturbed by the crumbled edge. One struck his head. He looked up to see Ruk leaning over it. He became aware that his fingers were weakening.

More debris loosened. The rock he clawed at cracked. As it gave way, Ruk's arm snaked down to seize one of his wrists. They exchanged a long look. Then slowly Ruk hauled him back up.

Spock saw the bridge elevator open. Kirk walked out of it and turned to stride down the corridor that led to his quarters. Spock hurried after him. "Captain!" he called. "I've just received word that you had beamed up."

Kirk was at his desk, leafing through a drawer for his command orders. "Doctor Korby has considerable cargo coming aboard, Mr. Spock. I'll have to go over our destinations schedule with him."

Spock looked at the packet in his hand. Surprised, he said, "You're going back down with the command orders, sir?"

"Mind your business, Mr. Spock!" Kirk shouted savagely. "I'm sick of your halfbreed interference! Do you hear me? Mind your business, Mr. Spock! I'm sick of your half-breed—"

Shocked, Spock stood stock-still. Kirk moved for the door. Spock, confounded, still staggered, tried again. "Are you feeling all right, Captain?"

All hardness had left Kirk's voice. He spoke quietly, his customary, courteous self. "Quite all right, thank you, Mr. Spock. I'll beam up shortly with Dr. Korby and his party." He eyed Spock, puzzled. "You look upset, Mr. Spock. Everything all right up here?"

The Vulcan looked as bewildered as he'd ever permitted himself to appear. He finally decided to compromise with a noncommittal, "No problems here, sir."

He got himself a nod, a friendly smile and Kirk's exit to the corridor. But his sense of dismayed shock persisted. He went over to the intercom button in the cabin and hit it.

"Security, this is First Officer Spock. Status of your landing party?"

"Ready and standing by, sir."

"Wait until the captain has beamed down. Then have them meet me in the Transporter Room."

He was asking for trouble with Kirk. On the other hand, trouble between them already existed.

• • •

Korby was pleased with his new android's performance. He shuffled through the command-orders packet and his android said, "I've looked them over. You'll find planet Midos V an excellent choice." It indicated a sheet among the others on Korby's desk.

"A small colony. And abundant raw materials." He rose. "You've made a good beginning, Captain Kirk."

"Thank you, Doctor," it said. "I felt quite at home on the *Enterprise*."

Down the corridor Kirk lay on the bed in his quarters, thinking, thinking. His life had been saved, but to what purpose he couldn't see. The *Enterprise* hijacked by the thing that wore his uniform . . . Some planet, perhaps the galaxy itself, doomed to be peopled by non-people . . . Humanoid life extinguished by the machines of Korby's making.

The door hummed open. Andrea entered with a tray of food. She placed it on the table.

Kirk sat up on his bunk. "Kiss me, Andrea," he said.

She kissed him. Then the cortical circuit that had obeyed a former order to kiss him activated the one connecting the kiss with a slap. She drew her hand back to strike him when Kirk seized it. "No," he said. He got up. Taking her in his arms, he gave her the most impassioned kiss in his repertoire. She liked it. But her circuitry protested. From somewhere in her came the tiny whine of a hard-pressed coil.

Panic-stricken, her responses chaotic, she pushed him away, crying, "Not you . . . not programmed for you . . ."

She went weaving, half-reeling toward the door. Kirk, alarmed, followed her, only to find Ruk standing guard in the corridor.

His eyes on Kirk, Ruk said, "To maintain your life is illogical."

"Why?" Kirk said.

Ruk didn't answer. Under the hairless scalp, his brain seemed to be fighting with a swarm of thoughts that confused him more cruelly than Andrea's terrified response to the kiss. Finally, he said. "You are no longer needed here."

"You want to kill me, Ruk? Or, as Doctor Korby calls it—turn me off?"

"You cannot be programmed. You are inferior."

"I want to live," Kirk said.

"You are from the outside," Ruk said. "You make disorder here."

"I'm not programmed. But I'll do anything, no matter how illogical to stay alive. Does that disturb you, Ruk?"

"Our place was peaceful. There was no threat to existence."

"Is existence important to you, too?"

"I am programmed to exist. Therefore, I exist."

The massive face was contorted with unaccustomed thought. Kirk felt a stab of pity. He said, "Korby speaks of you as just a machine to be turned on or turned off. That is a good thing to be, is it, Ruk?"

"You are evil. Until you came all was at peace here. That was good."

"I came in peace," Kirk said. "The only difference between us is that I have emotion. I have unpredictability. And with each human, our evil unpredictability increases. How would you like to live with thousands of unpredictable humans around you, all of them evil like me?"

Ruk was staring at him. "Yes, it was so . . . long ago. I had forgotten. The old ones here, the ones who made me, they were human . . . and evil. It is still in my memory banks . . . It became necessary to destroy them."

He turned his vast bulk slowly at the sound of footsteps. White-coated, self-assured, Korby was striding down the corridor.

Ruk lumbered toward him. "You . . . *you* brought him among us," he said heavily.

Startled, Korby looked from Kirk back to Ruk. "What?"

Ruk continued to advance on him. "You brought the inferior ones here!" His voice rose. "We had cleansed ourselves of them! You brought them and their evil back!"

"Ruk, I order you to stop! Go back! Stand away from me! You are programmed to—"

It was Korby who retreated. As Ruk made a grab for him he drew Kirk's phaser from the white coat's pocket. There was no hesitation. He fired it. Ruk was gone. Where he'd stood was a charred spot, a drift of metallic-smelling smoke.

"You didn't have to destroy him," Kirk said into the tight silence.

Korby leveled the phaser at him. "Move," he said. "Ahead of me . . ."

A tense Christine stood at the door of the study, apparently awaiting the result of Korby's visit to Kirk's quarters. At the entrance, Kirk turned to face his captor. "You were once a man with respect for all living things. How is the change in you to be explained, Doctor? If I were to tell Earth that I am your prisoner, to tell them what you have become—"

He made a grab for the phaser. But Korby used it to shove him into the study. Then the door, humming shut, caught his other hand between it and the jamb. Kirk, about to exploit his advantage, paused. Korby's wedged hand was being cruelly mashed. Yet his right hand still held the phaser in an unwavering aim at Kirk. It seemed a remarkable fortitude. When he wrenched the smashed hand free, it struck Kirk as yet more remarkable.

Then a slow horror chilled him. Christine, too, was staring at the injured hand. Instead of revealing torn and mangled flesh, the wound had exposed a fine mesh of tiny complex gears and pulsing wires. Some connection in the wires short-circuited. A wisp of smoke rose from it, leaving a smell of scorched metal.

Korby saw Christine's face. "It's still me, Christine—your Roger . . . in this android form . . . You can't imagine why—how it was with me. I was frozen, dying, my legs were gone. I had only my brain between death and life . . ." He lifted the hand. "This can be repaired, more easily than any surgeon could possibly repair it. I'm the same man that you knew and loved—a better one. There will never be any death for me . . . never . . ."

She put her hands over her face to shut out the sight of the dangle of still-pulsing wires, Korby, turning to Kirk, cried, "Imagine it, Captain! A world with no corruption, no suffering, no death . . ."

"Then why keep me alive, Doctor?" Kirk said. "I am mere flesh and blood. So I shall die. You've got yourself an immortal Kirk. Why don't you kill this mortal one—and get done with me?"

"You know that answer," Korby said. "I am still the man you described—the one with respect for all living things. I am still that man."

"You are not that man, Doctor," Kirk said. "Look at Christine . . . heartbroken, terrified. Where is your human response to her suffering?"

As the question was taken in by his computer brain, Korby looked shaken. Its whirring circuits churned to no effective answer. So it dismissed the question. Recovering his composure, he went to a speaker built into a wall. "Andrea," he said, "come to the study."

The door hummed open and Kirk laid his arm around Christine's shoulders.

"Yes, Doctor," Andrea said.

"Someone is coming down the corridor," Korby told her.

"I will find Ruk," she said.

"Ruk has been turned off. Get Brown's weapon! Fast! Deal with it. *Protect!*"

She found Brown's old-style phaser in a desk drawer and hurried out of the study.

In full uniform, Kirk's facsimile was sauntering along the corridor. Its appearance puzzled Andrea. It also interested her. She moved toward the android, lifting her face to it.

"I will kiss you," she said.

"No!" it said sharply.

A look of anger flickered over her face.

"Protect," she said. Then she pulled the trigger of the phaser rifle. She looked down at the black ash that was all that remained, sniffing curiously at the drift of smoke. "Protect," she said again—and returned to the study.

Korby was shouting wildly. "I'm the *same*! A direct transfer—*all of me*! Wholly rational . . . human but without a flaw!"

Smiling, innocent, Andrea said, "I just turned off Captain Kirk."

"She's killed your perfect android," Kirk said. "Just as you killed Ruk. Is this your perfect world? Your flawless beings? Killing, killing, killing! Aren't you flawless beings doing exactly what you most hate in humans? Killing with no more feeling than you feel when you turn off a light?''

This time the computer brain was unable to dismiss the question. Kirk extended his hand. ''Give me that phaser, Doctor. If any of the human Korby remains in you, you must know that your only hope is to give me that gun.''

''No! You refuse to understand! I have constructed perfect beings . . . tested them . . .'' Korby's face seemed to shrivel as his brain circuits told him he'd contradicted himself. His own illogic got through to them. ''I—I have proven they are perfect . . . I . . . I have . . .''

With a look of blank bafflement, he gave the phaser to Kirk. Pale as death, Christine sank down on a chair.

''Give me your rifle, Andrea,'' Kirk said.

''No,'' she said. She waved him back with the weapon. ''No . . . protect . . .'' She moved to Korby. ''I am programmed to love you, protect you. To kiss you . . .'' she lifted her face to his.

Christine moaned faintly. Stunned, she watched Korby push Andrea away. ''Don't touch me,'' he said. ''You cannot love, you machine!'' But Andrea still clung to him. The phaser she held came into position between them as Korby fought to free himself from her arms. ''Programmed,'' Andrea said. ''To love you . . . to kiss you . . .''

The rifle discharged. There was a flash of light. Then that, too, was gone. All that was left was the blur of smoke, the two piles of ash on the floor.

Dry-eyed, stumbling, Christine moved to Kirk. She was shuddering uncontrollably. He held her, the heiress to a permanent legacy of disillusioned loneliness.

As the last of the smoke dissolved, the study door was wrenched open. Spock and two security crewmen, phasers drawn, entered the study.

''Captain . . .'' Spock hesitated. ''You're all right, sir? Nurse Chapel?''

''All right, Mr. Spock,'' Kirk said.

''Where is Dr. Korby?'' Spock asked.

Kirk took Christine's hand. ''He was never here, Mr. Spock.''

• • •

He took it again when she approached his command chair in the bridge of the *Enterprise*.

"Thank you for letting me make my decision, Captain," she said. "I'm fairly certain I'm doing the right thing."

"I am, too," he said. "Maybe you can get some sleep now that your decision is made."

Neither smiled. "I'll be seeing you around," she said.

When she'd left the bridge, Spock said, "She's brave."

"That's why we need her on the *Enterprise*, Mr. Spock." He looked at the viewing screen. "Helm, steady as she goes. Nurse Chapel has decided to remain with us." But Spock still stood at the command chair. "Something bothering you, Mr. Spock?"

"Captain, I . . . must protest your using the term 'half-breed' in reference to me."

"I didn't *use* it, Mr. Spock. I directed it toward you as a—"

"Even as an android, you might have thought of a better expression," Spock said.

Kirk eyed him gravely. "I'll remember that, Mr. Spock, when I find myself in a similar position again."

"Thank you, sir," Spock said.

DAGGER OF THE MIND

Writer: S. Bar-David
Director: Vincent McEveety
Guest stars: James Gregory, Morgan Woodward, Marianna Hill

Simon van Gelder came aboard the *Enterprise* from the Tantalus Penal Colony via transporter, inside a box addressed to the Bureau of Penology in Stockholm—a desperate measure, but not a particularly intelligent one, as was inevitable under the circumstances. He had hardly been aboard three minutes before Tristan Adams, the colony's director and chief medic, had alerted Captain Kirk to the escape ("a potentially violent case") and the search was on.

Nevertheless, in this short time van Gelder, who was six feet four and only in his early forties, was able to ambush a crewman, knock him out, and change clothes with him, acquiring a phaser pistol in the process. Thus disguised, he was able to make his way to the bridge, where he demanded asylum and managed to paralyze operations for three more minutes before being dropped from behind by one of Mr. Spock's famous nerve squeezes. He was then hauled off to be confined in sick bay, and that was that.

Or that should have been that. Standard operating procedure would have been to give the captive a routine medical check and then ship him by transporter back to Tantalus and the specialized therapeutic resources of Dr. Adams. Kirk, however, had long been an admirer of Dr. Adams' rehabilitation concepts, and had been disappointed that ship's business had given him no excuse to visit the colony himself; now the irruption of this violent case seemed to offer an ideal opportunity. Besides, there was something about van Gelder himself that intrigued Kirk; in their brief encounter, he had not struck Kirk as a common criminal despite his desperation, and Kirk had not been aware that noncriminal psychiatric cases were ever sent to Tantalus. He went to visit the prisoner in the sick bay.

Dr. McCoy had him under both restraint and sedation while running body function tests. Asleep, his face was relaxed, childlike, vulnerable.

"I'm getting bursts of delta waves from the electroencephalograph," McCoy said, pointing to the body function panel. "Highly abnormal, but not schizophrenia, tissue damage, or any other condition I'm acquainted with. After I got him here, it took a triple dose of sedation to—"

He was interrupted by a sound from the bed, a strange combination of groan and snarl. The patient was coming back to consciousness, struggling against his bonds.

"The report said he was quite talkative," Kirk said.

"But not very informative. He'd claim one thing, seem to forget, then start to claim something else . . . and yet what little I could understand seemed to have the ring of truth to it. Too bad we won't have time to study him."

"So that's the system, is it?" the man on the bed said harshly, still struggling. "Take him back! Wash your hands of him! Let somebody else worry! Damn you—"

"What's your name?" Kirk said.

"My name . . . my name . . ." Suddenly, it seemed to Kirk that he was struggling not against the restraints, but against some kind of pain. "My name is . . . is Simon . . . Simon van Gelder."

He sank back and added almost quietly: "I don't suppose you've heard of me."

"Same name he gave before," McCoy said.

"Did I?" said van Gelder. "I'd forgotten. I was Director of . . . of . . . at the Tantalus Colony. Not a prisoner . . . I was . . . assistant. Graduate of . . . of . . ." His face contorted. "And then at . . . I did graduate studies at . . . studies at . . ."

The harder the man tried to remember, the more pain he seemed to be in. "Never mind," Kirk said gently. "It's all right. We—"

"I know," van Gelder said through clenched teeth. "They erased it . . . edited, adjusted . . . subverted me! I won't . . . I won't forget it! Won't go back there! Die first! Die, die!''

He had suddenly gone wild again, straining and shouting, his face a mask of unseeing passion. McCoy stepped close and there was the hiss of a spray hypo. The shouting died down to a mutter, then stopped altogether.

''Any guess at all?'' Kirk said.

''One point I don't have to guess at,'' McCoy said. ''He doesn't want to go back to that—how did you describe it? 'More like a resort than a prison.' Evidently a cage is still a cage, no matter how you label it.''

''Or else there's something drastically wrong down there,'' Kirk said. ''Keep him secure, Bones. I'm going to do a little research.''

By the time Kirk returned to the bridge, Spock was already removing a tape casette from the viewer. ''I got this from our library, Captain,'' he said. ''No doubt about it: our captive is Dr. van Gelder.''

''Dr.—?''

''That's right. Assigned to Tantalus Colony six months ago as Dr. Adams' assistant. Not committed; assigned. A highly respected man in his field.''

Kirk thought about it a moment, then turned to his Communications Officer. ''Lieutenant Uhura, get me Dr. Adams on Tantalus . . . Doctor? This is Captain Kirk of the *Enterprise*. Regarding your escapee—''

''Is Dr. van Gelder all right?'' Adams' voice cut in with apparent concern. ''And your people? No injuries? In the violent state he's in—''

''No harm to him or anyone, sir. But we thought you might be able to enlighten us about his condition. My medical officer is baffled.''

''I'm not surprised. He'd been doing some experimental work, Captain. An experimental beam we'd hoped might rehabilitate incorrigibles. Dr. van Gelder felt he hadn't the moral right to expose another man to something he hadn't tried on his own person.''

While Adams had been talking, McCoy had entered from the elevator and had crossed to the library-computer station, where he stood listening with Kirk and Spock. Now he caught Kirk's eye and made the immemorial throat-cutting gesture.

"I see," Kirk said into the microphone. "Please stand by a moment, Dr. Adams." Uhura broke contact, and Kirk swung to McCoy. "Explain."

"It doesn't quite ring true, Jim," the medico said. "I don't think whatever's wrong with this patient is something he did to himself. I think it was something that was done to him. I can't defend it, it's just an impression—but a strong one."

"That's not enough to go on," Kirk said, irritated in spite of himself. "You're not dealing with just any ordinary warden here, Bones. In the past twenty years, Adams has done more to revolutionize, to humanize, prisons and the treatment of prisoners than all the rest of humanity had done in forty centuries. I've been to penal colonies since they've begun following his methods. They're not 'cages' any more, they're clean, decent hospitals for sick minds. I'm not about to start throwing unsubstantiated charges against a man like that."

"Who said anything about charges?" McCoy said calmly. "Just ask questions. Propose an investigation. If something's really wrong, Adams will duck. Any harm in trying it?"

"I suppose not." Kirk nodded to Uhura, who closed the circuit again. "Dr. Adams? This is rather embarrassing. One of my officers has just reminded me that by strict interpretation of our starship regulations, I'm required to initiate an investigation of this so that a proper report—"

"No need to apologize, Captain Kirk," Adams' voice said. "In fact, I'd take it as a personal favor if you could beam down personally, look into it yourself. I'm sure you realize that I don't get too many visitors here. Oh—I would appreciate it if you could conduct the tour with a minimum staff. We're forced to limit outside contact as much as possible."

"I understand. I've visited rehab colonies before. Very well. *Enterprise* out . . . Satisfied, McCoy?"

"Temporarily," the medical officer said, unruffled.

"All right. We'll keep van Gelder here until I complete my investigation, anyway. Find me somebody in your department with psychiatric *and* penological experience—both in the same person, if possible.''

''Helen Noel should do nicely. She's an M.D., but she's written several papers on rehab problems.''

''Very good. We beam down in an hour.''

Though there were plenty of women among the *Enterprise*'s officers and crew, Helen Noel was a surprise to Kirk. She was young and almost uncomfortably pretty—and furthermore, though Kirk had seen her before, he had not then realized that she was part of the ship's complement. That had been back at the medical lab's Christmas party. He had had the impression then that she was simply a passenger, impressed as female passengers often were to be singled out for conversation by the Captain; and in fact, in the general atmosphere of Holiday he had taken certain small advantages of her impressionability . . . It now turned out that she was, and had then been, the newest addition to the ship's medical staff. Her expression as they met in the transporter room was demure, but he had the distinct impression that she was enjoying his discomfiture.

Tantalus was an eerie world, lifeless, ravaged, and torn by a bitter and blustery climate, its atmosphere mostly nitrogen slightly diluted by some of the noble gasses—a very bad place to try to stage an escape. In this it closely resembled all other penal colonies, enlightened or otherwise. Also as usual, the colony proper was all underground, its location marked on the surface only by a small superstructure containing a transporter room, an elevator head, and a few other service modules.

Dr. Tristan Adams met them in his office: a man in his mid-forties, with broad warm features, a suspicion of old freckles at the nose, and an almost aggressively friendly manner which seemed to promise firm handshakes, humor, an ounce of brandy at the right hour, and complete candor at all times. He hardly seemed to be old enough to have accumulated his massive reputation. The office reflected the man; it was personal, untidy without being littered, furnished with an eye to comfort and the satisfaction of someone perhaps as interested in primitive sculpture as in social medicine.

With him was a young woman, tall and handsome

though slightly cadaverous, whom he introduced as "Lethe." There was something odd about her which Kirk could not quite fathom: perhaps a slight lack of normal human spontaneity in both manner and voice. As if expecting just such a reaction, Adams went on:

"Lethe came to us for rehabilitation, and ended up staying on as a therapist. And a very good one."

"I love my work," the girl said, in a flat voice.

With a glance at Adams for permission, Kirk said: "And before you came here?"

"I was another person," Lethe said. "Malignant, hateful."

"May I ask what crime you committed?"

"I don't know," Lethe said. "It doesn't matter. That person no longer exists."

"Part of our treatment, Captain, is to bury the past," Adams said. "If the patient can come to terms with his memories, all well and good. But if they're unbearable, why carry them at all? Sufficient unto the day are the burdens thereof. Shall we begin the tour?"

"I'm afraid we haven't time for a complete tour," Kirk said. "Under the circumstances, I'd primarily like to see the apparatus or experiment that injured Dr. van Gelder. That, after all, is the whole point of our inquiry."

"Yes, quite. One doesn't enjoy talking about failures, but still, negative evidence is also important. If you'll just follow me—"

"One minute," Kirk said, pulling his communicator out of his hip pocket. "I'd best check in with the ship. If you'll pardon me a moment—?"

Adams nodded and Kirk stepped to one side, partly turning his back. In a moment, Spock's voice was saying softly:

"Van Gelder's no better, but Dr. McCoy has pulled a few additional bits and pieces out of his memory. They don't seem to change the situation much. He insists that Adams is malignant, the machine is dangerous. No details."

"All right. I'll check in with you at four-hour intervals. Thus far everything here seems open and aboveboard. Out."

"Ready, Captain?" Adams said pleasantly. "Good. This way, please."

• • •

The chamber in which van Gelder had allegedly undergone his mysterious and shattering conversion looked to Kirk's unsophisticated eye exactly like any other treatment room, perhaps most closely resembling a radiology theater. There was a patient on the table as Kirk, Adams, and Helen entered, seemingly unconscious; and from a small, complex device hanging from the ceiling, a narrow, monochromatic beam of light like a laser beam was fixed on the patient's forehead. Near the door, a uniformed therapist stood at a small control panel, unshielded; evidently, the radiation, whatever it was, was not dangerous at even this moderate distance. It all looked quite unalarming.

''This is the device,'' Adams said softly. ''A neural potentiator, or damper. The two terms sound opposite to each other but actually both describe the same effect: an induced increase in neural conductivity, which greatly increases the number of cross-connections in the brain. At a certain point, as we predicted from information theory, increased connectivity actually results in the disappearance of information. We thought it would help the patient to cope better with his most troublesome thoughts and desires. But the effects are only temporary; so, I doubt that it'll be anything like as useful as we'd hoped it would be.''

''Hmm,'' Kirk said. ''Then if it's not particularly useful—''

''Why do we use it?'' Adams smiled ruefully. ''Hope, that's all, Captain. Perhaps we can still get some good out of it, in calming violent cases. But strictly as a palliative.''

''Like tranquilizing drugs,'' Helen Noel suggested. ''They do nothing permanent. And to continually be feeding drugs into a man's bloodstream just to keep him under control . . .''

Adams nodded vigorously. ''Exactly my point, Doctor.''

He turned toward the door, but Kirk was still eyeing the patient on the table. He swung suddenly on the uniformed therapist and said, ''How does it operate?''

''Simply enough, it's nonselective,'' the therapist said. ''On and off, and a potentiometer for intensity. We used to try to match the output to the patient's resting delta rhythms, but we found that wasn't critical. The brain seems to do its own monitoring, with some help from outside suggestion. For that, of course, you have to know the patient pretty well; you can't just put him on the table and expect the machine to process him like a computer tape."

"And we shouldn't be talking so much in his presence, for that very reason," Adams said, a faint trace of annoyance in his voice for the first time. "Better if further explanations waited until we're back in the office."

"I'd better ask my questions while they're fresh," Kirk said.

"The Captain," Helen said to Adams, "is an impulsive man."

Adams smiled. "He reminds me a little of the ancient skeptic who demanded to be taught all the world's wisdom while he stood on one foot."

"I simply want to be sure," Kirk said stonily, "that this is in fact where Dr. van Gelder's injury occurred."

"Yes," Adams said, "and it was his own fault, if you must know. I dislike maligning a colleague, but the fact is that Simon is a stubborn man. He could have sat in here for a year with the beam adjusted to this intensity, or even higher. Or if there simply had been someone standing at the panel to cut the power when trouble began. But he tried it alone, at full amplitude. Naturally, it hurt him. Even water can poison a man, in sufficient volume."

"Careless of him," Kirk said, still without expression. "All right, Dr. Adams, let's see the rest."

"Very well. I'd like to have you meet some of our successes, too."

"Lead on."

In the quarters which Adams' staff had assigned him for the night, Kirk called the *Enterprise*, but there was still nothing essentially new. McCoy was still trying to get past the scars in van Gelder's memory, but nothing he had uncovered yet seemed contributory. Van Gelder was exhausted; toward the end, he would say nothing but, "He empties us . . . and then fills us with himself. I ran away before he could fill me. It is so lonely to be empty . . ."

Meaningless; yet somehow it added up to something in

Kirk's mind. After a while, he went quietly out into the corridor and padded next door to Helen Noel's room.

"Well!" she said, at the door. "What's this, Captain? Do you think it's Christmas again?"

"Ship's business," Kirk said. "Let me in before somebody spots me. Orders."

She moved aside, hesitantly, and he shut the door behind himself.

"Thanks. Now then, Doctor: What did you think of the inmates we saw this afternoon?"

"Why . . . I was impressed, on the whole. They seemed happy, or at least well-adjusted, making progress—"

"And a bit blank?"

"They weren't normal. I didn't expect them to be."

"All right. I'd like to look at that treatment room again. I'll need you; you must have comprehended far more of the theory than I did."

"Why not ask Dr. Adams?" she said stiffly. "He's the only expert on the subject here."

"And if he's lying about anything, he'll continue to lie and I'll learn nothing. The only way I can be sure is to see the machine work. I'll need an operator; you're the only choice."

"Well . . . all right."

They found the treatment room without difficulty. There was nobody about. Quickly Kirk pointed out the controls the therapist had identified for him, then took up the position that had been occupied by the patient then. He looked ruefully up at the device on the ceiling.

"I'm expecting you to be able to tell if that thing is doing me any harm," he said. "Adams says it's safe; that's what I want to know. Try minimum output; only a second or two."

Nothing happened.

"Well? Any time you're ready."

"I've already given you two seconds."

"Hmm. Nothing happened at all."

"Yes, something did. You were frowning; then your face went blank. When I cut the power, the frown came back."

"I didn't notice a thing. Try it again."

"How do you feel now?"

"Somewhat . . . uh, nothing definite. Just waiting. I thought we were going to try again."

"We did," Helen said. "It looks as though your mind goes so completely blank that you don't even feel the passage of time."

"Well, well," Kirk said drily. "Remarkably effective for a device Adams said he was thinking of abandoning. The technician mentioned that suggestion was involved. Try one—something harmless, please. You know, when we finally get through this, I hope we can raid a kitchen somewhere."

"It works," Helen said in a strained voice. "I gave you two seconds at low intensity and said, 'You're hungry.' And now you are."

"I didn't hear a thing. Let's give it one more try. I don't want to leave any doubt about it."

"Quite right," Adams' voice said. Kirk sat bolt upright, to find himself staring squarely into the business end of a phaser pistol. The therapist was there too, another gun held unwaveringly on Helen.

"Prisons and mental hospitals," Adams went on, smiling, almost tolerantly, "monitor every conversation, every sound—or else they don't last long. So I'm able to satisfy your curiosity, Captain. We'll give you a proper demonstration."

He stepped to the control panel and turned the potentiometer knob. Kirk never saw him hit the on-off button. The room simply vanished in a wave of intolerable pain.

As before, there was no time lapse at all; he only found himself on his feet, handing his phaser to Adams. At the same time, he knew what the pain was: it was love for Helen, and the pain of loneliness, of being without her. She was gone; all he had was the memory of having carried her to her cabin that Christmas, of her protests, of his lies that had turned into truth. Curiously, the memories seemed somewhat colorless, one-dimensional, the voices in them, monotonous; but the longing and the loneliness were real. To assuage it, he would lie, cheat, steal, give up his ship, his reputation . . . He cried out.

"She's not here," Adams said, passing Kirk's phaser

to the therapist. "I'll send her back in a while and then things will be better. But first, it's time to call your vessel. It's important that they know all is well. Then perhaps we can see Dr. Noel."

Through a renewed stab of pain, Kirk got out his communicator and snapped it open. "Captain . . . to *Enterprise*," he said. He found it very difficult to speak; the message did not seem to be important.

"*Enterprise* here, Captain," Spock's voice said.

"All is well, Mr. Spock. I'm still with Dr. Adams."

"You sound tired, Captain. No problems?"

"None at all, Mr. Spock. My next call will be in six hours. Kirk out."

He started to pocket the communicator, but Adams held out his hand.

"And that, too, Captain."

Kirk hesitated. Adams reached for the control panel. The pain came back, redoubled, tripled, quadrupled; and now, at last, there came a real and blessed unconsciousness.

He awoke to the murmur of a feminine voice, and the feeling of a damp cloth being smoothed across his forehead. He opened his eyes. He was on his bed in the quarters on Tantalus; he felt as though he had been thrown there. A hand obscured his vision and he felt the cloth again. Helen's voice said:

"Captain . . . Captain. They've taken you out of the treatment room. You're in your own quarters now. Wake up, please, please!"

"Helen," he said. Automatically, he reached for her, but he was very weak; she pushed him back without effort.

"Try to remember. He put all that in your mind. Adams took the controls away from me—do you remember the pain? And then his voice, telling you you love me—"

He lifted himself on one elbow. The pain was there all right, and the desire. He fought them both, sweating.

"Yes . . . I think so," he said. Another wave of pain. "His machine's not perfect. I remember . . . some of it."

"Good. Let me wet this rag again."

As she moved away, Kirk forced himself to his feet, stood dizzily for a moment, and then lurched forward to try the door. Locked, of course. In here, he and Helen were supposed to consolidate the impressed love, make it real . . . and forget the *Enterprise*. Not bloody likely! Looking around, he spotted an air-conditioning grille.

Helen came back, and he beckoned to her, holding his finger to his lips. She followed him curiously. He tested the grille; it gave slightly. Throwing all his back muscles into it, he bent it outward. At the second try, it came free in his hand with a slight shearing sound. He knelt and poked his head into the opening.

The tunnel beyond was not only a duct; it was a crawl-space, intended also for servicing power lines. It could be crawled through easily, at least, as far as he could see down it. He tried it, but his shoulders were too bulky.

He stood up and held out his arms to the girl. She shrank back, but he jerked his head urgently, hoping that there was nothing in his expression which suggested passion. After a moment's more hesitation, she stepped against him.

"He may be watching as well as listening," Kirk whispered. "I'm just hoping he's focused on the bed, in that case. But that tunnel has to connect with a whole complex of others. It probably leads eventually to their power supply. If you can get through it, you can black out the whole place—and cut off their sensors, so Spock could beam us down some help without being caught at it. Game to try?"

"Of course."

"Don't touch any of those power lines. It'll be a bad squeeze."

"Better than Adams' treatment room."

"Good girl."

He looked down at her. The pain was powerful, reinforced by memory and danger, and her eyes were half-closed, her mouth willing. Somehow, all the same, he managed to break away. Dropping to her knees, she squirmed inside the tunnel and vanished, and Kirk began to replace the grille.

It was bent too badly to snap it back into place; he could only force it into reasonable shape and hope that nobody would notice that it wasn't fastened. He was on his feet and pocketing the sheared rivet heads when he heard the tumblers of the door lock clicking. He swung around just in time to see the therapist enter, holding an old-style phaser pistol. The man looked around incuriously.

"Where's the girl?" he said.

"Another of you zombies took her away. If you've hurt her, I'll kill you. Time for another 'treatment'?" He took a step closer, crouching. The pistol snapped up.

"Stand back! Cross in front of me and turn right in the corridor. I won't hesitate to shoot."

"That would be tough to explain to your boss. Oh, all right, I'm going."

Adams was waiting; he gestured curtly toward the table.

"What's the idea?" Kirk said. "I'm co-operating, aren't I?"

"If you were, you wouldn't have asked," Adams said. "However, I've no intention of explaining myself to you, Captain. Lie down. Good. Now."

The potentiator beam stabbed down at Kirk's head. He fought it, feeling the emptiness increase. This time, at least, he was aware of time passing, though he seemed to be accomplishing nothing else. His very will was draining away, as though somebody had opened a petcock on his skull.

"You believe in me completely," Adams said. "You believe in me. You trust me. The thought of distrusting me is intensely painful. You believe."

"I believe," Kirk said. To do anything else was agony. "I believe in you. I trust you, I trust you! Stop, stop!"

Adams shut off the controls. The pain diminished slightly, but it was far from gone.

"I give you credit," Adams said thoughtfully. "Van Gelder was sobbing on his knees by now, and he had a strong will. I'm glad I've had a pair like you; I've learned a great deal."

"But . . . what . . . purpose? Your reputation . . . your . . . work . . ."

"So you can still ask questions? Remarkable. Never mind. I'm tired of doing things for others, that's all. I want a very comfortable old age, on my terms—and I am a most selective man. And you'll help me."

"Of course . . . but so unnecessary . . . just trust . . ."

"Trust you? Naturally. Or, trust mankind to reward

me? All they've given me thus far is Tantalus. It's not enough. I know how their minds work. Nobody better."

There was the sound of the door, and then Kirk could see the woman therapist, Lethe. She said:

"Dr. Noel's gone. Nobody took her out. She just vanished."

Adams swung back to the panel and hit the switch. The beam came on, at full amplitude. Kirk's brainpan seemed to empty as if it had been dumped down a drain.

"Where is she?"

"I . . . don't know . . ."

The pain increased. "Where is she? Answer!"

There was no possibility of answering. He simply did not know, and the pain blocked any other answer but the specific one being demanded. As if realizing this, Adams backed the beam down a little.

"Where did you send her? With what instructions? *Answer!*"

The pain soared, almost to ecstasy—and at the same instant, all the lights went out but a dim safe light in the ceiling. Kirk did not have to stop to think what might have happened. Enraged by agony, he acted on reflex and training. A moment later, the therapist was sprawled on the floor and he had Lethe and Adams covered with the old-style phaser.

"No time for you now," he said. Setting the phaser to "stun," he pulled the trigger. Then he was out in the corridor, a solid mass of desire, loneliness, and fright. He had to get to Helen; there was nothing else in his mind at all, except a white line of pain at having betrayed someone he had been told to trust.

Dull-eyed, frightened patients milled about him as he pushed toward the center of the complex, searching for the power room. He shoved them out of the way. The search was like an endless nightmare. Then, somehow, he was with Helen, and they were kissing.

It did not seem to help. He pulled her closer. She yielded, but without any real enthusiasm. A moment later, there was a familiar hum behind him: the sound of a transporter materialization. Then Spock's voice said:

"Captain Kirk—what on—"

Helen broke fee. ''It's not his fault. Quick, Jim, where's Adams?''

''Above,'' Kirk said dully. ''In the treatment room. Helen—''

''Later, Jim. We've got to hurry.''

They found Adams sprawled across the table. The machine was still on. Lethe stood impassively beside the controls; as they entered, backed by a full force of security guards from the ship, she snapped them off.

McCoy appeared from somewhere and bent over Adams. Then he straightened.

''Dead.''

''I don't understand,'' Helen said. ''The machine wasn't on high enough to kill. I don't think it could kill.''

''He was alone,'' Lethe said stonily. ''That was enough. I did not speak to him.''

Kirk felt his ringing skull. ''I think I see.''

''I can't say that I do, Jim,'' McCoy said. ''A man has to die of something.''

''He died of loneliness,'' Lethe said. ''It's quite enough. I know.''

''What do we do now, Captain?'' Spock said.

''I don't know . . . let me see . . . get van Gelder down here and repair him, I guess. He'll have to take charge. And then . . . he'll have to decondition me. Helen, I don't want that, I want nothing less in the world; but—''

''I don't want it either,'' she said softly. ''So we'll both have to go through it. It was nice while it lasted, Jim—awful, but nice.''

''It's still hard to believe,'' McCoy said, much later, ''that a man could die of loneliness.''

''No,'' Kirk said. He was quite all right now; quite all right. Helen was nothing to him but another female doctor. But—

''No,'' he said, ''it's not hard to believe at all.''

MIRI

Writer: Adrian Spies
Director: Vincent McEveety
Guest stars: Kim Darby, Michael J. Pollard

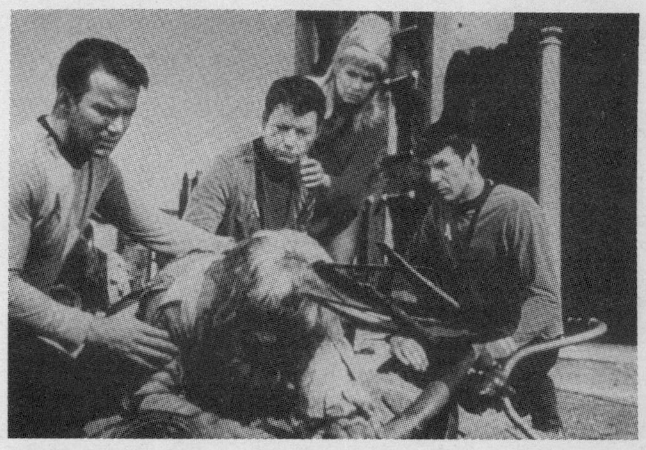

Any SOS commands instant attention in space, but there was very good reason why this one created special interest on the bridge of the *Enterprise*. To begin with, there was no difficulty in pinpointing its source, for it came not from any ship in distress, but from a planet, driven out among the stars at the 21-centimeter frequency by generators far more powerful than even the largest starship could mount.

A whole planet in distress? But there were bigger surprises to come. The world in question was a member of the solar system of 70 Ophiucus, a sun less than fifteen light-years away from Earth, so that in theory the distress signals could have been picked up on Earth not much more than a decade after their launching except for one handicap: From Earth, 70 Ophiucus is seen against the backdrop of the Milky Way, whose massed clouds of excited hydrogen atoms emit 21-centimeter radiation at some forty times the volume of that coming from the rest of the sky. Not even the planet's huge, hard-driven generators could hope to punch through that much stellar static with an intelligible signal, not even so simple a one as an SOS. Lieutenant Uhura, the communications officer of the *Enterprise*, picked up the signal only because the starship was at the time approaching the ''local group''—an arbitrary sphere 100 light-years in diameter with Earth at its center—nearly at right angles to the plane of the galaxy.

All this, however, paled beside the facts about the region dug up by the ship's library computer. For the fourth planet of 70 Ophiucus, the computer said, had been the first extrasolar planet ever colonized by man—by a small but well-equipped group of refugees from the political disaster called the Cold Peace, more than five hundred years ago. It had been visited only once since then. The settlers, their past wrongs unforgotten, had fired on the visitors, and the hint had been taken; after all, the galaxy was full of places more interesting than a backwater like the 70 Ophiucus system, which the first gigantic comber of full-scale exploration had long since passed. The refugees were left alone to enjoy their sullen isolation.

But now they were calling for help.

On close approach it was easy to see why the colonists, despite having been in flight, had settled for a world which might have been thought dangerously close to home. The planet was remarkably Earth-like, with enormous seas covering much of it, stippled and striped with clouds. One hemisphere held a large, roughly lozenge-shaped continent, green and mountainous; the other, two smaller triangular ones, linked by a long archipelago including several islands bigger than Borneo. Under higher magnification, the ship's screen showed the gridworks of numerous cities, and, surprisingly more faintly, the checkerboarding of cultivation.

But no lights showed on the night side, nor did the radio pick up any broadcasts nor any of the hum of a high-energy civilization going full blast. Attempts to communicate, once the *Enterprise* was in orbit, brought no response—only that constantly repeated SOS, which now was beginning to sound suspiciously mechanical.

"Whatever the trouble was," Mr. Spock deduced, "we are evidently too late."

"It looks like it," Captain Kirk agreed. "But we'll go down and see. Mr. Spock, Dr. McCoy, Yeoman Rand, and two security guards, pick up your gear and report to me in the transporter room."

The landing party materialized by choice in the central plaza of the largest city the screen had shown—but there was no one there. Not entirely surprised, Kirk looked around.

The architecture was roughly like that of the early 2100s, when the colonists had first fled, and apparently had stood unoccupied for almost that long a period. Evidences of the erosion of time were everywhere, in the broken pavements, the towering weeds, the gaping windows, the windrows of dirt and dust. Here and there on the plaza were squat sculptures of flaking rust which had perhaps been vehicles.

"No signs of war," Spock said.

"Pestilence?" McCoy suggested. As if by agreement, both were whispering.

By the dust-choked fountain near which Kirk stood, another antique object lay on its side: a child's tricycle. It too was rusty, but still functional, as though it had been indoors during much of the passage of time which had worn away the larger vehicles. There was a bell attached to the handlebar, and moved by some obscure impulse, Kirk pressed his thumb down on its lever.

It rang with a kind of dull sputter in the still air. The plaintive sound was answered instantly, from behind them, by an almost inhuman scream of rage and anguish.

"Mine! *Mine!*"

They whirled to face the terrible clamor. A humanoid creature was plunging toward them from the shell of the nearest building, flailing its arms and screaming murderously. It was moving too fast for Kirk to make out details. He had only an impression of dirt, tatters, and considerable age, and then the thing had leapt upon McCoy and knocked him down.

Everyone waded in to help, but the creature had the incredible strength of the utterly mad. For a moment Kirk was face to face with it—an ancient face, teeth gone in a reeking mouth, contorted with wildness and hate, tears brimming from the eyes. Kirk struck, almost at random.

The blow hardly seemed to connect at all, but the creature sobbed and fell to the pocked pavement. He was indeed an old man, clad only in sneakers, shorts, and a ripped and filthy shirt. His skin was covered with multi-colored blotches. There was something else odd about it, too—but what? Was it as wrinkled as it should be?

Still sobbing, the old head turned and looked toward the tricycle, and an old man's shaking hand stretched out toward it. "Fix," the creature said, between sobs. "Somebody fix."

"Sure," Kirk said, watching intently. "We'll fix it."

The creature giggled. "Fibber," it said. The voice gradually rose to the old scream of rage. "You bustud it! Fibber, fibber!"

The clawing hand grasped the tricycle as if to use it as a weapon, but at the same time the creature seemed to catch sight of the blotches on its own naked arm. The scream died back to a whimper. "Fix it—please fix it—"

The eyes bulged, the chest heaved, and then the creature fell back to the pavement. Clearly, it was dead. McCoy knelt beside it, running a tricorder over the body.

"Impossible," he muttered.

"That it's dead?" Kirk said.

"No, that it could have lived at all. Its body temperature is over one-fifty. It must have been burning itself up. Nobody can live at that temperature."

Kirk's head snapped up suddenly. There had been another sound, coming from an alley to the left.

"Another one?" he whispered tensely. "Somebody stalking us . . . over there. Let's see if we can grab him and get some information . . . Now!"

They broke for the alley. Ahead of them they could hear the stalker running.

The alley was blind, ending in the rear of what seemed to be a small apartment house. There was no place else that the stalker could have gone. They entered cautiously, phasers ready.

The search led them eventually to what had once been a living room. There was a dusty piano in it, a child's exercise book on the music rack. Over one brittle brown page was scribbled, "Practice, practice, practice!" But there was no place to hide but a closet. Listening at the door, Kirk thought he heard agitated breathing, and then, a distinct creak. He gestured, and Spock and the security men covered him.

"Come out," he called. "We mean no harm. Come on out."

There was no answer, but the breathing was definite now. With a sudden jerk, he opened the door.

Huddled on the floor of the closet, amid heaps of moldering clothing, old shoes, a dusty umbrella, was a dark-haired young girl, no more than fourteen—probably younger. She was obviously in abject terror.

"Please," she said. "No, don't hurt me. Why did you come back?"

"We won't hurt you," Kirk said. "We want to help."

He held out his hand to her, but she only tried to shrink farther back into the closet. He looked helplessly at Yeoman Rand, who came forward and knelt at the open door.

"It's all right," she said. "Nobody's going to hurt you. We promise."

"I remember the things you did," the girl said, without stirring. "Yelling, burning, hurting people."

"It wasn't us," Janice Rand said. "Come out and tell us about it."

The girl looked dubious, but allowed Janice to lead her to a chair. Clouds of dust came out of it as she sat down, still half poised to spring up and run.

"You've got a foolie," she said. "But I can't play. I don't know the rules."

"We don't either," Kirk said. "What happened to all the people? Was there a war? A plague? Did they just go someplace else and accidentally leave you here?"

"You ought to know. You did it—you and all the other grups."

"Grups? What are grups?"

The girl looked at Kirk, astonished. "You're grups. All the old ones."

"Grown-ups," Janice said. "That's what she means, Captain."

Spock, who had been moving quietly around the room with a tricorder, came back to Kirk, looking puzzled. "She can't have lived here, Captain," he said. "The dust here hasn't been disturbed for at least three hundred years, possibly longer. No radioactivity, no chemical contamination—just very old dust."

Kirk turned back to the girl. "Young lady—by the way, what's your name?"

"Miri."

"All right, Miri, you said the grups did something. Burning, hurting people. Why?"

"They did it when they started to get sick. We had to hide." She looked up hopefully at Kirk. "Am I doing it right? Is it the right foolie?"

"You're doing fine. You said the grown-ups got sick. Did they die?"

"Grups always die." Put that way, it was of course

self-evident, but it didn't seem to advance the questioning much.

"How about the children?"

"The onlies? Of course not. We're here, aren't we?"

"More of them?" McCoy put in. "How many?"

"All there are."

"Mr. Spock," Kirk said, "take the security guards and see if you can find any more survivors . . . So all the grups are gone?"

"Well, until it happens—you know—when *it* happens to an only. Then you get to be like them. You want to hurt people, like they did."

"Miri," McCoy said, "somebody attacked us, outside. You saw that? Was that a grup?"

"That was Floyd," she said, shivering a little. "It happened to him. He turned into one. It's happening to me, too. That's why I can't hang around with my friends any more. The minute one of us starts changing, the rest get afraid . . . I don't like your foolie. It's no fun."

"What do they get afraid of?" Kirk persisted.

"You saw Floyd. They try to hurt everything. First you get those awful marks on your skin. Then you turn into a grup, and you want to hurt people, kill people."

"We're not like that," Kirk said. "We've come a long way, all the way from the stars. We know a good many things. Maybe we can help you, if you'll help us."

"Grups don't help," Miri said. "They're the ones that did this."

"We didn't do it, and we want to change it. Maybe we can, if you'll trust us."

Janice touched her on the side of the face and said, "Please?" After a long moment, Miri managed her first timid smile.

Before she could speak, however, there was a prolonged rattling and clanking sound from outside, as though someone had emptied a garbage can off a rooftop. It was followed by the wasplike snarl of a phaser bolt.

Far away, and seemingly high up a child's voice called: "Nyah nyah nyah nyah. NYAH, Nyah!"

"Guards!" Spock's voice shouted.

Many voices answered, as if from all sides: "Nyah nyah nyah nyah NYAH, nyah!"

Then there was silence, except for the echoes.

"It seems," Kirk said, "that your friends don't want to be found."

"Maybe that's not the first step anyhow, Jim," McCoy said. "Whatever happened here, somewhere there must be records about it. If we're to do anything, we have to put our fingers on the cause. The best place would probably be the local public health center. What about that, Miri? Is there a place where the doctors used to work? Maybe a government building?"

"I know that place," she said distastefully. "Them and their needles. That's a bad place. None of us go there."

"But that's where we have to go," Kirk said. "It's important if we're to help you. Please take us."

He held out his hand, and, very hesitantly, she took it. She looked up at him with something like the beginnings of wonder.

"Jim is a nice name," she said. "I like it."

"I like yours, too. And I like you."

"I know you do. You can't really be a grup. You're—something different." She smiled and stood up, gracefully. As she did so, she looked down, and he felt her grip stiffen. Then, carefully, she disengaged it.

"Oh!" she said in a choked voice. "Already!"

He looked down too, already more than half aware of what he would see. Across the back of his hand was a sprawling blue blotch, about the size of a robin's egg.

The laboratory proved to be well-equipped, and since it had been sealed and was windowless, there was less than the expected coating of dust on the tables and equipment. Its size and lack of windows also made it seem unpleasantly like the inside of a tomb, but nobody was prepared to complain about that; Kirk was only grateful that its contents had proved unattractive to any looters who might have broken into it.

The blue blotches had appeared upon all of them now, although those on Mr. Spock were the smallest and appeared to spread more slowly; that was to have been expected, since he came from far different stock than did the rest of the crew, or the colonists for that matter. Just as clearly, his nonterrestrial origin conferred no immunity on him, only a slight added resistance.

McCoy had taken biopsies from the lesions; some of the samples he stained, others he cultured on a variety of media. The blood-agar plate had produced a glistening, wrinkled blue colony which turned out to consist of active, fecund bacteria strongly resembling spirochetes. McCoy, however, was convinced that these were not the cause of the disease, but only secondary invaders.

"For one thing, they won't take on any of the lab animals I've had sent down from the ship," he said, "which means I can't satisfy Koch's Postulates. Second, there's an abnormally high number of mitotic figures in the stained tissues, and the whole appearance is about halfway between squamous metaplasia and frank neoplasm. Third, the chromosome table shows so many displacements—"

"Whoa, I'm convinced," Kirk protested. "What does it add up to?"

"I think the disease proper is caused by a virus," McCoy said. "The spirochetes may help, of course; there's an Earthly disease called Vincent's angina that's produced by two micro-organisms working in concert."

"Is the spirochete communicable?"

"Highly, by contact. You and Yeoman Rand got yours from Miri; we got them from you two."

"Then I'd better see that no one else does," Kirk said. He told his communicator: "Kirk to *Enterprise*. No one, repeat, no one, under any circumstances, is to transport down here until further notice. The planet is heavily infected. Set up complete decontamination procedures for any of us who return."

"Computer?" McCoy nudged.

"Oh yes. Also, ship us down the biggest portable biocomputer—the cat-brain job. That's to get the live-steam treatment too when it goes back up."

"Captain," Spock called. He had been going through a massed rank of file cabinets which occupied almost all of one wall. Now he was beckoning, a folder in one hand. "I think we've got something here."

They all went over except McCoy, who remained at the

microscope. Spock handed the folder to Kirk and began pulling others. "There's a drawer-full of these. Must have been hundreds of people working on it. No portable bio-comp is going to process this mass of data in anything under a year."

"Then we'll feed the stuff to the ship's computer by communicator," Kirk said. He looked down at the folder.

It was headed:

Progress Report
LIFE PROLONGATION PROJECT
Genetics Section

"So *that's* what it was," Janice Rand said.

"We don't know yet," Kirk said. "But if it was, it must have been the galaxy's biggest backfire. All right, let's get to work. Miri, you can help too: lay out these folders on the long table there by categories—one for genetics, one for virology, one for immunology, or whatever. Never mind what the words mean, just match 'em up."

The picture emerged with maddening slowness. The general principle was clear almost from the start: an attempt to counter the aging process by selectively repairing mutated body cells. Aging is primarily the accumulation in the body of cells whose normal functions have been partly damaged by mutations, these in turn being caused by the entrance of free radicals into the cell nucleus, thus deranging the genetic code. The colony's scientists had known very well that there was no blocking out the free radicals, which are created everywhere in the environment, by background radiation, by sunlight, by combustion, and even by digestion. Instead, they proposed to create a self-replicating, viruslike substance which would remain passive in the bloodstream until actual cell damage occurred; the virus would then penetrate the cell and replace the damaged element. The injection would be given at birth, before the baby's immunity mechanism was fully in action, so that it would be "selfed"—that is, marked as a substance normal to the body rather than an invader to be battled; but it would remain inactive until triggered by the hormones of puberty, so as not to interfere with normal growth processes.

"As bold a project as I've heard of in all my life,"

McCoy declared. "Just incidentally, had this thing worked, it would have been the perfect cancer preventive. Cancer is essentially just a local explosion of the aging process, in an especially virulent form."

"But it didn't work." Spock said. "Their substance was entirely *too* much like a virus—and it got away from them. Oh, it prolongs life, all right—but only in children. When puberty finally sets in, it kills them."

"How much?" Janice Rand asked.

"You mean, how long does it prolong life? We don't know because the experiment hasn't gone on that long. All we know is the rate: the injected person ages about a month, physiological time, for every hundred years, objective time. For the children, it obviously does work that way."

Janice stared at Miri. "A month in a hundred years!" she said. "And the experiment was three centuries ago! Eternal childhood . . . It's like a dream."

"A very bad dream, Yeoman," Kirk said. "We learn through example and responsibilities. Miri and her friends were deprived of both. It's a dead end street."

"With a particularly ugly death at the end," McCoy agreed. "It's amazing that so many children did survive. Miri, how did you get along after all the grups died?"

"We had foolies," Miri said. "We had fun. There wasn't anybody to tell us not to. And when we got hungry, we just took something. There were lots of things in cans, and lots of mommies."

"Mommies?"

"You know." Miri wound her hand vigorously in midair, imitating the motion of a rotary can-opener. Janice Rand choked and turned away. "Jim . . . now that you found what you were looking for . . . are you going away?"

"Oh no," Kirk said. "We've still got a great deal more to learn. Your grups seemed to have done their experiments in a certain definite sequence, a sort of timetable. Any sign of that yet, Mr. Spock?"

"No, sir. Very likely it's kept somewhere else. If this were my project, I'd keep it in a vault; it's the key to the whole business."

"I'm afraid I agree. And unless we can figure it out,

Miri, we won't be able to identify the virus, synthesize it, and make a vaccine."

"That's good," Miri said. "Your not going, I mean. We could have fun—until *it* happens."

"We still may be able to stop it. Mr. Spock, I gather you couldn't get close to any of the other children?"

"No chance. They know the area too well. Like mice."

"All right, let's try another approach. Miri, will you help us find some of them?"

"You won't find any," Miri said positively. "They're afraid. They won't like you. And they're afraid of me, too, now, ever since . . ." she stopped.

"We'll try to make them understand."

"Onlies?" the girl said. "You couldn't do it. That's the best thing about being an only. Nobody expects you to understand."

"*You* understand."

Abruptly Miri's eyes filled with tears. "I'm not an only any more," she said. She ran out of the room. Janice looked after her compassionately.

Janice said: "That little girl—"

"—is three hundred years older than you are, Yeoman," Kirk finished for her. "Don't leap to any conclusions. It's got to make some sort of a difference in her—whether we can see it yet or not."

But in a minute Miri was back, the cloudburst passed as if it had never been, looking for something to do. Mr. Spock set her to sharpening pencils, of which the ancient laboratory seemed to have scores. She set to it cheerfully—but throughout, her eyes never left Kirk. He tried not to show that he was aware of it.

"Captain? This is Farrell on the *Enterprise*. We're ready to compute."

"All right, stand by. Mr. Spock, what do you need?"

Miri held up a fistful of pencils: "Are these enough?"

"Uh? Oh—we could use more, if you don't mind."

"Oh no, Jim," she said. "Why should I mind?"

"This fellow," Spock said, fanning out a sheaf of papers on the table, "left these notes in the last weeks—after the disaster began. I disregarded these last entries; he said he was too far gone himself, too sick, to be sure he wasn't delirious, and I agree. But these earlier tables ought to show us how much time we have left. By the way, it's clear that the final stages we've seen here are typical. Homicidal mania."

"And nothing to identify the virus strain—or its chemistry?" McCoy said.

"Not a thing," Spock said. "He believed somebody else was writing that report. Maybe somebody was and we just haven't found it yet—or maybe that was the first of his hallucinations. Anyhow, the first overt stage is intense fever . . . pain in the joints . . . fuzziness of vision. Then, gradually, the mania takes over. By the way, Dr. McCoy, you were right about the spirochetes—they do contribute. They create the mania, not the virus. It'll be faster in us because we haven't carried the disease in latent form as long as Miri."

"What about her?" Kirk said in a low voice.

"Again, we'll have to see what the computer says. Roughly, I'd guess that she could survive us by five or six weeks—if one of us doesn't kill her first—"

"Enough now?" Miri said simultaneously, holding up more pencils.

"No!" Kirk burst out angrily.

The corners of her mouth turned down and her lower lip protruded. "Well, all right, Jim," she said in a small voice. "I didn't mean to make you mad."

"I'm sorry, Miri. I wasn't talking to you. I'm not mad." He turned back to Spock. "All right, so we still don't know what we're fighting. Feed your figures to Farrell and then at least we'll know what the time factor is. Damnation! If we could just put our hands on that virus, the ship could develop a vaccine for us in twenty-four hours. But there's just no starting point."

"Maybe there is," McCoy said slowly. "Again, it'd be a massive computational project, but I think it might work. Jim, you know how the desk-bound mind works. If this lab was like every other government project I've run across, it had to have order forms in quintuplicate for everything it used. Somewhere here there ought to be an accounting file containing copies of those orders. They'd show us what the consumption of given reagents was at different times. I'll be able to spot the obvious routine items—culture media and shelf items, things like that—but we'll need to analyze for what is significant. There's at least a chance that such an analysis would reconstruct the missing timetable."

"A truly elegant idea," Mr. Spock said. "The question is—"

He was interrupted by the buzzing of Kirk's communicator.

"Kirk here."

"Farrell to landing party. Mr. Spock's table yields a cut-off point at seven days."

For a long moment there was no sound but the jerky whirring of the pencil sharpener. Then Spock said evenly:

"That was the question I was about to raise. As much as I admire Dr. McCoy's scheme, it will almost surely require more time than we have left."

"Not necessarily," McCoy said. "If it's true that the spirochete creates the mania, we can possibly knock it out with antibiotics and keep our minds clear for at least a while longer—"

Something hit the floor with a smash. Kirk whirled. Janice Rand had been cleaning some of McCoy's slides in a beaker of chromic acid. The corrosive yellow stuff was now all over the floor. Some of it had spattered Janice's legs. Grabbing a wad of cotton, Kirk dropped to his knees to mop them.

"No, no," Janice sobbed. "You can't help me—you can't help me!"

Stumbling past McCoy and Spock, she ran out of the laboratory, sobbing. Kirk started after her.

"Stay here," he said. "Keep working. Don't lose a minute."

Janice was standing in the hallway, her back turned, weeping convulsively. Kirk resumed swabbing her legs, trying not to notice the ugly blue blotches marring them. As he worked, her tears gradually died back. After a while she said in a small voice:

"Back on the ship you never noticed my legs."

Kirk forced a chuckle. "The burden of command, Yeoman: to see only what regs say is pertinent . . . That's better, but soap and water will have to be next."

He stood up. She looked worn, but no longer hysterical. She said:

"Captain, I didn't really want to do that."

"I know," Kirk said. "Forget it."

"It's so stupid, such a waste . . . Sir, do you know all I can think about? I should know better, but I keep thinking, I'm only twenty-four—and I'm scared."

"I'm a little older, Yeoman. But I'm scared too."

"You are?"

"Of course. I don't want to become one of those things, any more than you do. I'm more than scared. You're my people. I brought you here. I'm scared for all of us."

"You don't show it," she whispered. "You never show it. You always seem to be braver than any ten of us."

"Baloney," he said roughly. "Only an idiot isn't afraid when there's something to be afraid of. The man who feels no fear isn't brave, he's just stupid. Where courage comes in is in going ahead and coping with danger, not being paralyzed by fright. And especially, not letting yourself be panicked by the other guy."

"I draw the moral," Janice said, trying to pull herself erect. But at the same time, the tears started coming quietly again. "I'm sorry," she repeated in a strained voice. "When we get back, sir, you'd better put in for a dry-eyed Yeoman."

"Your application for a transfer is refused." He put his arm around her gently, and she tried to smile up at him. The movement turned them both around toward the entrance to the lab.

Standing in it was Miri, staring at them with her fists crammed into her mouth, her eyes wide with an unfathomable mixture of emotions—amazement, protest, hatred even? Kirk could not tell. As he started to speak, Miri whirled about and was gone. He could hear her running footsteps receding; then silence.

"Troubles never come alone," Kirk said resignedly. "We'd better go back."

"Where was Miri going?" McCoy asked interestedly, the moment they re-entered. "She seemed to be in a hurry."

"I don't know. Maybe to try and look for more onlies. Or maybe she just got bored with us. We haven't time to worry about her. What's next?"

"Next is accident prevention time," McCoy said. "I should have thought of it before, but Janice's accident reminded me of it. There are a lot of corrosive reagents around here, and if we have any luck, we'll soon be playing with infectious material too. I want everyone out of their regular clothes and into lab uniforms we can shuck the minute they get something spilled on them. There's a whole locker full of them over on that side. All our own clothes go out of the lab proper into the anteroom, or else we'll just have to burn 'em when we get back to the ship."

"Good; so ordered. How about equipment—phasers and so on?"

"Keep one phaser here for emergencies if you're prepared to jettison it before we go back," McCoy said. "Everything else, out."

"Right. Next?"

"Medical analysis has gone as far as I can take it," McCoy said. "From here on out, it's going to be strictly statistical—and though the idea was mine, I'm afraid Mr. Spock is going to have to direct it. Statistics make me gibber."

Kirk grinned. "Very well, Mr. Spock, take over."

"Yes sir. First of all, we've got to find those purchase orders. Which means another search of the file cabinets."

The problem was simple to pose: Invent a disease.

The accounting records turned up, relatively promptly, and in great detail. McCoy's assumption had been right that far: the bureaucratic mind evidently underwent no substantial change simply by having been removed more than a dozen light-years from the planet where it had evolved. Everything the laboratory had ever had to call for had at least three pieces of paper that went along with it.

McCoy was able to sort these into rough categories of significance, on a scale of ten (from 0 = obvious nonsense to 10 = obviously crucial), and the bio-comp coded everything graded "five" or above so that it could be fed to the orbiting *Enterprise*'s computer with the least possible loss of time. The coding was very fast; but assigning relative weights to the items to be coded was a matter for human judgment, and despite his disclaimers, McCoy was the only man present who could do it with any confidence in well more than half of the instances. Spock could tell, within a given run of samples, what appeared to be statistically significant, but only

McCoy could then guess whether the associations were medical, financial, or just make-work.

It took two days, working around the clock. By the morning of the third day, however, Spock was able to say:

"These cards now hold everything the bio-comp can do for us." He turned to Miri, who had returned the day before, with no explanations, but without the slightest change in her manner, and as willing to work as ever. "Miri, if you'll just stack them and put them back in that hopper, we'll rank them for the *Enterprise*, and then we can read-and-feed to Farrell. I must confess, I still don't see the faintest trace of a pattern in them."

"I do," McCoy said surprisingly. "Clearly the active agent can't be a pure virus, because it'd be cleaned out of the body between injection and puberty if it didn't reproduce; and true viruses can't reproduce without invading a body cell, which this thing is forbidden to do for some ten or twelve years, depending on the sex of the host. This has to be something more like some of the rickettsiae, with some enyzmatic mechanisms intact so it can feed and reproduce from material it can absorb from the body fluids, *outside* the cells. When the hormones of puberty hit it, it sheds that part of its organization and becomes a true virus. Ergo, the jettisoned mechanism has to be steroid-soluble. And only the sexual steroids can be involved. All these conditions close in on it pretty implacably, step by step."

"Close enough to put a name to it?" Kirk demanded tensely.

"By no means," McCoy said. "I don't even know if I'm on the right track; this whole scholium is intuitive on my part. But it makes sense. I think something very like that will emerge when the ship's computer processes all these codes. Anybody care to bet?"

"We've already bet our lives, like it or not," Kirk said. "But we ought to have the answer in an hour now. Mr. Spock, call Farrell."

Spock nodded and went out into the anteroom, now kept sealed off from the rest of the lab. He was back in a moment. Though his face was almost incapable of showing emotion, something in his look brought Kirk to his feet in a rush.

"What's the matter?"

"The communicators are gone, Captain. There's nothing in those uniforms but empty pockets."

Janice gasped. Kirk turned to Miri, feeling his brows knotting together. The girl shrank a little from him, but returned his look defiantly all the same.

"What do you know about this, Miri?"

"The onlies took them, I guess," she said. "They like to steal things. It's a foolie."

"Where did they take them?"

She shrugged. "I don't know. That's a foolie, too. When you take something, you go someplace else."

He was on her in two strides, grasping her by the shoulders. "This is not a foolie. It's a disaster. We have to have those communicators—otherwise we'll never lick this disease."

She giggled suddenly. "Then you won't have to go," she said.

"No, we'll die. Now cut it out. Tell us where they are."

The girl drew herself up in an imitation of adult dignity. Considering that she had never seen an adult after the disaster until less than a week ago, it was a rather creditable imitation.

"Please, Captain, you're hurting me," she said haughtily. "What's the matter with you? How could *I* possibly know?"

Unfortunately, the impersonation broke at the end into another giggle—which, however, did Kirk no good as far as the issue at hand was concerned. "What is this, blackmail?" Kirk said, beyond anger now. He could feel nothing but the total urgency of the loss. "It's your life that's at stake too, Miri."

"Oh no," Miri said sweetly. "Mr. Spock said that I'd live five or six weeks longer than you will. Maybe some of you'll die ahead of some others. I'll still be here." She flounced in her rags toward the door. Under any other circumstances she might have been funny, perhaps even charming. At the last moment she turned, trailing a languid hand through the air. "Of course I don't know what makes you think I know anything about this. But maybe if you're very nice to me, I could ask my friends some questions. In the meantime, Captain, farewell.''

There was an explosion of pent breaths as her footsteps dwindled.

''Well,'' McCoy said, ''one can tell that they had television on this planet during part of Miri's lifetime, at least.''

The grim joke broke part of the tension.

''What can we do without the ship?'' Kirk demanded. ''Mr. Spock?''

''Very little, Captain. The bio-comp's totally inadequate for this kind of job. It takes hours, where the ship's computer takes seconds, and it hasn't the analytical capacity.''

''The human brain was around long before there were computers. Bones, what about your hunch?''

''I'll ride it, of course,'' McCoy said wearily. ''But time is the one commodity the computer could have saved us, and the one thing we haven't got. When I think of that big lumbering ship up there, with everything we need on board it, orbiting around and around like so much inert metal—''

''And complaining just wastes more time,'' Kirk snarled. McCoy stared at him in surprise. ''I'm sorry, Bones. I guess it's starting to get me, too.''

''I *was* complaining,'' McCoy said. ''The apology is mine. Well then, the human brain it will have to be. It worked for Pasteur . . . but he was a good bit smarter than me. Mr. Spock, take those cards away from that dumb cat and let's restack them. I'll want to try a DNA analysis first. If that makes any sort of reasonable pattern, enough to set up a plausible species, we'll chew through them again and see if we can select out a clone.''

''I'm not following you,'' Spock admitted.

''I'll feed you the codes, there's no time for explanations. Pull everything coded LTS-426 first. Then we'll ask the cat to sort those for uncoded common factors. There probably won't be any, but it's the most promising beginning I can think of.''

''Right.''

Kirk felt even more out of it than Mr. Spock; he had neither the medical nor the statistical background to understand what was going on. He simply stood by, and did what little donkey-work there was to do.

The hours wore away into another day. Despite the stim-pills McCoy doled out, everyone seemed to be moving very slowly, as if underwater. It was like a nightmare of flight.

Somewhere during that day, Miri turned up, to watch with what she probably imagined was an expression of aloof amusement. Everyone ignored her. The expression gradually faded into a frown; finally, she began to tap her foot.

"Stop that," Kirk said without even turning to look at her, "or I'll break your infant neck."

The tapping stopped. McCoy said: "Once more into the cat, Mr. Spock. We are now pulling all T's that are functions of D-2. If there are more than three, we're sunk."

The bio-comp hummed and chuttered over the twenty-two cards Spock had fed it. It threw out just one. McCoy leaned back in his hard-backed straight chair with a whoosh of satisfaction.

"Is that it?" Kirk asked.

"By no means, Jim. That's *probably* the virus involved. Just probably, no more."

"It's only barely significant," Spock said. "If this were a test on a new product survey or something of that sort, I'd throw it out without a second thought. But as matters stand—"

"As matters stand, we next have to synthesize the virus," McCoy said, "and then make a killed-virus vaccine from it. No, no, that won't work at all, what's the matter with me? Not a vaccine. An antitoxoid. Much harder. Jim, wake those security guards—a lot of good they did us in the pinch! We are going to need a lot of bottles washed in the next forty-eight hours."

Kirk wiped his forehead. "Bones, I'm feeling outright lousy, and I'm sure you are too. Officially we've got the forty-eight hours left—but are we going to be functioning sensibly after the next twenty-four?"

"We either fish or cut bait," McCoy said calmly. "All hands on their feet. The cookery class is hereby called to order."

"It's a shame," Spock said, "that viruses aren't as easy to mix as metaphors."

At this point Kirk knew that he was on the thin edge of hysteria. Somehow he had the firm impression that Mr. Spock had just made a joke. Next he would be beginning to believe that there really was such a thing as a portable computer with a cat's brain in it. "Somebody hand me a bottle to wash," he said, "before I go to sleep on my feet."

By the end of twenty hours, Janice Rand was raving and had to be strapped down and given a colossal tranquilizer dose before she would stop fighting. One of the guards followed her down an hour later. Both were nearly solid masses of blue marks; evidently, the madness grew as the individual splotches coalesced into larger masses and proceeded toward covering the whole skin surface.

Miri disappeared at intervals, but she managed to be on the scene for both these collapses. Perhaps she was trying to look knowing, or superior, or amused; Kirk could not tell. The fact of the matter was that he no longer had to work to ignore Miri, he was so exhausted that the small chores allotted him by his First Officer and his ship's surgeon took up the whole foreground of his attention, and left room for no background at all.

Somewhere in there, McCoy's voice said: "Everything under the SPF hood now. At the next stage we've got a live one. Kirk, when I take the lid off the Petri dish, in goes the two cc's of formalin. Don't miss."

"I won't."

Somehow, he didn't. Next, after a long blank, he was looking at a rubber-capped ampule filled with clear liquid, into which McCoy's hands were inserting the needle of a spray hypo. Tunnel vision; nothing more than that: the ampule, the hypo, the hands.

"That's either the antitoxoid," McCoy's voice was saying from an infinite distance, "or it isn't. For all I know it may be pure poison. Only the computer could tell us which for sure."

"Janice first," Kirk heard himself rasp. "Then the guard. They're the closest to terminal."

"I override you, Captain," McCoy's voice said. "I am the only experimental animal in this party."

The needle jerked out of the rubber cap. Somehow, Kirk managed to reach out and grasp McCoy's only visible wrist. The movement hurt; his joints ached abominably, and so did his head.

"Wait a minute," he said. "One minute more won't make any difference."

He swivelled his ringing skull until Miri came into view down the optical tunnel. She seemed to be all fuzzed out at the edges. Kirk walked toward her, planting his feet with extraordinary care on the slowly tilting floor.

"Miri," he said. "Listen to me. You've got to listen to me."

She turned her head away. He reached out and grabbed her by the chin, much more roughly than he had wanted to, and forced her to look at him. He was dimly aware that he was anything but pretty—bearded, covered with sweat and dirt, eyes rimmed and netted with red, mouth working with the effort to say words that would not come out straight.

"We've . . . only got a few hours left. Us, and all of you . . . you, and your friends. And . . . we may be wrong. After that, no grups, and no onlies . . . no one . . . forever and ever. Give me back just one of those . . . machines, those communicators. Do you want the blood of a whole world on your hands? Think, Miri—think for once in your life!"

Her eyes darted away. She was looking toward Janice. He forced her to look back at him. "Now, Miri. Now. *Now.*"

She drew a long, shuddering breath. "I'll—try to get you one," she said. Then she twisted out of his grasp and vanished.

"We can't wait any longer," McCoy's voice said calmly. "Even if we had the computer's verdict, we couldn't do anything with it. We have to go ahead."

"I will bet you a year's pay," Spock said, "that the antitoxoid is fatal in itself."

In a haze of pain, Kirk could see McCoy grinning tightly, like a skull. "You're on," he said. "The disease certainly is. But if I lose, Mr. Spock, how will you collect?"

He raised his hand.

"Stop!" Kirk croaked. He was too late—even supposing that McCoy in this last extremity would have obeyed his captain. This was McCoy's world, his universe of discourse. The hypo hissed against the surgeon's bared, blue-suffused arm.

Calmly, McCoy laid the injector down on the table, and sat down. "Done," he said. "I don't feel a thing." His eyes rolled upward in their sockets, and he took a firm hold on the edge of the table. "You see . . . gentlemen . . . it's all perfectly . . ."

His head fell forward.

"Help me carry him," Kirk said, in a dead voice. Together, he and Spock carried the surgeon to the nearest cot. McCoy's face, except for the blotches, was waxlike; he looked peaceful for the first time in days. Kirk sat down on the edge of the cot beside him and tried his pulse. It was wild and erratic, but still there.

"I . . . don't see how the antitoxoid could have hit him that fast," Spock said. His own voice sounded like a whisper from beyond the grave.

"He could only have passed out. I'm about ready, myself. Damn the man's stubbornness."

"Knowledge," Spock said remotely, "has its privileges."

This meant nothing to Kirk. Spock was full of these gnomic utterances; presumably they were Vulcanian. There was a peculiar hubbub in Kirk's ears, as though the visual fuzziness was about to be counterpointed by an aural one.

Spock said, "I seem to be on the verge myself—closer than I thought. The hallucinations have begun."

Wearily, Kirk looked around. Then he goggled. If Spock was having a hallucination, so was Kirk. He wondered if it was the same one.

A procession of children was coming into the room, led by Miri. They were of all sizes and shapes, from toddlers up to about the age of twelve. They looked as though they had been living in a department store. Some of the older boys wore tuxedos; some were in military uniforms; some in scaled-down starmen's clothes; some in very loud and mismatched sports clothes. The girls were a somewhat better matched lot, since almost all of them were wearing some form of party dress, several of them trailing opera cloaks and loaded with jewelry. Dominating them all was a tall, redheaded boy—or no, that wasn't his own hair, it was a wig, long at the back and sides and with bangs, from which the price-tag still dangled. Behind him hopped a fat little boy who was carrying, on a velvet throw-pillow, what appeared to be a crown.

It was like some mad vision of the Children's Crusade. But what was maddest about it was that the children were loaded with equipment—the landing party's equipment. There were the three communicators—Janice and the security guards hadn't carried any; there were the two missing tricorders—McCoy had kept his in the lab; and the red-wigged boy even had a phaser slung at his hip. It was a measure of how exhausted they had all been, even back then, that they hadn't realized one of the deadly objects was missing. Kirk wondered whether the boy had tried it, and if so, whether he had hurt anybody with it.

The boy saw him looking at it, and somehow divined his thought.

"I used it on Louise," he said gravely. "I had to. She went grup all at once, while we were playing school. She was—only a little older than me."

He unbuckled the weapon and held it out. Numbly, Kirk took it. The other children moved to the long table and solemnly began to pile the rest of the equipment on it. Miri came tentatively to Kirk.

"I'm sorry," she said. "It was wrong and I shouldn't have. I had a hard time, trying to make Jahn understand that it wasn't a foolie any more." She looked sideways at the waxy figure of McCoy. "Is it too late?"

"It may be," Kirk whispered; that was all the voice he could muster. "Mr. Spock, do you think you can still read the data to Farrell?"

"I'll try, sir."

Farrell was astonished and relieved, and demanded explanations. Spock cut him short and read him the figures. Then there was nothing to do but wait while the material was processed. Kirk went back to looking at McCoy, and Miri joined him. He realized dimly that, for all the trouble she had caused, her decision to bring the communicators back had been a giant step toward growing up. It would be a shame to lose her now, Miri most of all in the springtime of her promise—a springtime for which she had waited three sordid centuries. He put his arm around her, and she looked up at him gratefully.

Was it another failure of vision, or were the blotches on McCoy fading a little? No, some of them were definitely smaller and had lost color. "Mr. Spock," he said, "come here and check me on something."

Spock looked and nodded. "Retreating," he said. "Now if there are no serious side-effects—" The buzz of his communicator interrupted him. "Spock here."

"Farrell to landing party. The identification is correct, repeat, correct. Congratulations. Do you mean to tell me you boiled down all that mass of bits and pieces with nothing but a bio-comp?"

Kirk and Spock exchanged tired grins. "No," Spock said, "we did it all in Doctor McCoy's head. Over and out."

"The bio-comp did help," Kirk said. He reached out and patted the squat machine. "Nice kitty."

McCoy stirred. He was trying to sit up, his expression dazed.

"Begging your pardon, Doctor," Kirk said. "If you've rested sufficiently, I believe the administration of injections *is* your department."

"It worked?" McCoy said huskily.

"It worked fine, the ship's computer says it's the right stuff, and you are the hero of the hour, you pig-headed idiot."

They left the system a week later, having given all the antitoxoid the ship's resources could produce. Together with Farrell, the erstwhile landing party stood on the bridge of the *Enterprise*, watching the planet retreat.

"I'm still a little uneasy about it," Janice Rand said. "No matter how old they are chronologically, they're still just children. And to leave them there with just a medical team to help them—"

"They haven't lived all those years for nothing," Kirk said. "Look at the difficult thing Miri did. They'll catch on fast, with only a minimum of guidance. Besides, I've already had Lieutenant Uhura get the word back to Earth . . . If that planet had had subspace radio, they would have been saved a lot of their agony. But it hadn't been invented when the original colonists left . . . Space Central will send teachers, technicians, administrators—"

"—And truant officers, I presume," McCoy said.

"No doubt. The kids will be all right."

Janice Rand said slowly: "Miri . . . she . . . really loved you, you know, Captain. That was why she played that trick on you."

"I know," Kirk said. "And I'm duly flattered. But I'll tell you a secret, Yeoman Rand. I make it a policy never to get involved with women older than I am."

THE CONSCIENCE OF THE KING

Writer: Barry Trivers
Director: Gerd Oswald
Guest stars: Arnold Moss, Barbara Anderson

''A curious experience,'' Kirk said. ''I've seen *Macbeth* in everything from bearskins to uniforms, but never before in Arcturian dress. I suppose an actor has to adapt to all kinds of audiences.''

''This one has,'' Dr. Leighton said. He exchanged a glance with Martha Leighton; there was an undertone in his voice which Kirk could not fathom. There seemed to be no reason for it. The Leightons' garden, under the bright sun of the Arcturian system, was warm and pleasant; their hospitality, including last night's play, had been unexceptionable. But time was passing, and old friends or no, Kirk had to be back on duty shortly.

''Karidian has an enormous reputation,'' he said, ''and obviously he's earned it. But now, Tom, we'd better get down to business. I've been told this new synthetic of yours is something we badly need.''

''There is no synthetic,'' Leighton said heavily. ''I want you to think about Karidian. About his voice in particular. You should remember it; you were there.''

''I was where?'' Kirk said, annoyed. ''At the play?''

''No,'' Leighton said, his crippled, hunched body stirring restlessly in its lounger. ''On Tarsus IV, during the Rebellion. Of course it was twenty years ago, but you couldn't have forgotten. My family murdered—and your friends. And you saw Kodos—and heard him, too.''

''Do you mean to tell me,'' Kirk said slowly, ''that you called me three light-years off my course just to accuse an actor of being Kodos the Executioner? What am I supposed to put in my log? That you lied? That you diverted a starship with false information?''

''It's not false. Karidian is Kodos.''

''That's not what I'm talking about. I'm talking about your invented story about the synthetic food process. Anyhow, Kodos is dead.''

''Is he?'' Leighton said. ''A body burned beyond recognition—what kind of evidence is that? And there are so few witnesses left, Jim: you, and I, and perhaps six or seven others, people who actually saw Kodos and heard his voice. You may have forgotten, but I never will.''

Kirk turned to Martha, but she said gently: ''I can't tell him anything, Jim. Once he heard Karidian's voice, it all came back. I can hardly blame him. From all accounts, that was a bloody business . . . and Tom wasn't just a witness. He was a victim.''

''No, I know that,'' Kirk said. ''But vengeance won't help, either—and I can't allow the whole *Enterprise* to be sidetracked on a personal vendetta, no matter how I feel about it.''

''And what about justice?'' Leighton said. ''If Kodos is still alive, oughtn't he to pay? Or at least be taken out of circulation—before he contrives another massacre? Four thousand people, Jim!''

''You have a point,'' Kirk admitted reluctantly. ''All right, I'll go this far: Let me check the ship's library computer and see what we have on *both* men. If your notion's just a wild hare, that's probably the quickest way to find out. If it isn't—well, I'll listen further.''

''Fair enough,'' Leighton said.

Kirk pulled out his communicator and called the *Enterprise*. ''Library computer . . . Give me everything you have on a man named or known as Kodos the Executioner. After that, a check on an actor named Anton Karidian.''

''Working,'' the computer's voice said. Then: ''Kodos the Executioner. Deputy Commander, forces of Rebellion, Tarsus IV, twenty terrestrial years ago. Population of eight thousand Earth colonists struck by famine after fungus blight largely destroyed food supply. Kodos used situation to implement private theories of eugenics, slaughtered fifty per cent of colony population. Sought by Earth forces when rebellion overcome. Burned body found and case closed. Biographical data—''

''Skip that,'' Kirk said. ''Go on.''

''Karidian, Anton. Director and leading man of traveling company of actors, sponsored by Interstellar Cultural Exchange project. Touring official installations for past nine years. Daughter, Lenore, nineteen years old, now leading lady of troupe. Karidian a recluse, has given notice current tour is to be his last. Credits—''

''Skip that too. Data on his pre-acting years?''

''None available. That is total information.''

Kirk put the communicator away slowly. ''Well, well,'' he said. ''I still think it's probably a wild hare, Tom . . . but I think I'd better go to tonight's performance, too.''

After the performance, Kirk went backstage, which was dingy and traditional, and knocked on the door with the star on it. In a moment, Lenore Karidian opened it, still beautiful, though not as bizarre as she had looked as an Arcturian Lady Macbeth. She raised her eyebrows.

''I saw your performance tonight,'' Kirk said. ''And last night, too. I just want to . . . extend my appreciation to you and to Karidian.''

''Thank you,'' she said, politely. ''My father will be delighted, Mr . . . ?''

''Capt. James Kirk, the starship *Enterprise*.''

That told, he could tell; that and the fact that he had seen the show two nights running. She said: We're honored. I'll carry your message to father.''

''Can't I see him personally?''

''I'm sorry, Captain Kirk. He sees no one personally.''

''An actor turning away his admirers? That's very unusual.''

''Karidian is an unusual man.''

''Then I'll talk with Lady Macbeth,'' Kirk said. ''If you've no objections. May I come in?''

''Why . . . of course.'' She moved out of the way. Inside, the dressing room was a clutter of theatrical trunks, all packed and ready to be moved. "I'm sorry I have nothing to offer you."

Kirk stared directly at her, smiling. "You're being unnecessarily modest."

She smiled back. "As you see, everything is packed. Next we play two performances on Benecia, if the *Astral Queen* can get us there; we leave tonight."

"She's a good ship," Kirk said. "Do you enjoy your work?"

"Mostly. But, to play the classics in these times, when most people prefer absurd three-V serials . . . it isn't always as rewarding as it could be."

"But you continue," Kirk said.

"Oh yes," she said, with what seemed to be a trace of bitterness. "My father feels that we owe it to the public. Not that the public cares."

"They cared tonight. You were very convincing as Lady Macbeth."

"Thank you. And as Lenore Karidian?"

"I'm impressed." He paused an instant. "I think I'd like to see you again."

"Professionally?"

"Not necessarily."

"I . . . think I'd like that. Unfortunately, we must keep to our schedule."

"Schedules aren't always as rigid as they seem," Kirk said. "Shall we see what happens?"

"Very well. And hope for the best."

The response was promising, if ambiguous, but Kirk had no chance to explore it further. Suddenly his communicator was beeping insistently.

"Excuse me," he said. "That's my ship calling . . . Kirk here."

"Spock calling, Captain. Something I felt you should know immediately. Dr. Leighton is dead."

"Dead? Are you sure?"

"Absolutely," Spock's voice said. "We just had word from Q Central. He was murdered—stabbed to death."

Slowly, Kirk put the device back in his hip pocket. Lenore was watching him. Her face showed nothing but grave sympathy.

"I'll have to go," he said. "Perhaps you'll hear from me later."

"I quite understand. I hope so."

Kirk went directly to the Leightons' apartment. The body was still there, unattended except by Martha, but it told him nothing; he was not an expert in such matters. He took Martha's hand gently.

"He really died the first day those players arrived," she said, very quietly. "Memory killed him. Jim . . . do you suppose survivors ever really recover from a tragedy?"

"I'm deeply sorry, Martha."

"He was convinced the moment we saw that man arrive," she said. "Twenty years since the terror, but he was sure Karidian was the man. Is that possible, Jim? Is he Kodos, after all?"

"I don't know. But I'm trying to find out."

"Twenty years and he still had nightmares. I'd wake him and he'd tell me he still heard the screams of the innocent—the silence of the executed. They never told him what happened to the rest of his family."

"I'm afraid there's not much doubt about that," Kirk said.

"It's the not knowing, Jim—whether the people you love are dead or alive. When you know, you mourn, but the wound heals and you go on. When you don't—every dawn is a funeral. That's what killed my husband, Jim, not the knife . . . But with him, I know."

She managed a small smile and Kirk squeezed her hand convulsively. "It's all right," she said, as if she were the one who had to do the comforting. "At least he has peace now. He never really had it before. I suppose we'll never know who killed him."

"I," Kirk said, "am damn well going to find out."

"It doesn't matter. I've had enough of all this passion for vengeance. It's time to let it all rest. More than time."

Suddenly the tears welled up. "But I shan't forget him. Never."

Kirk stomped aboard ship in so obvious a white fury that nobody dared even to speak to him. Going directly to his quarters, he barked into the intercom: "Uhura!"

"Yes, Captain," the Communications Officer responded, her normally firm voice softened almost to a squeak.

"Put me through to Captain Daly, the *Astral Queen*, on orbit station. And put it on scramble."

"Yes, *sir* . . . He's on, sir."

"John, this is Jim Kirk. Can you do me a little favor?"

"I owe you a dozen," Daly's voice said. "And two dozen drinks, too. Name your poison."

"Thanks. I want you to pass up your pickup here."

"You mean strand all them actors?"

"Just that," Kirk said. "I'll take them on. And if there's any trouble, the responsibility is mine."

"Will do."

"I appreciate it. I'll explain later—I hope. Over and out . . . Lieutenant Uhura, now I want the library computer."

"Library."

"Reference the Kodos file. I'm told there were eight or nine survivors of the massacre who were actual eyewitnesses. I want their names and status."

"Working . . . In order of age: Leighton, T., deceased. Molson, E., deceased—"

"Wait a minute, I want survivors."

"These were survivors of the massacre," the computer said primly. "The deceased are all recent murder victims, all cases open. Instructions."

Kirk swallowed. "Continue."

"Kirk, J., Captain, S.S. *Enterprise*. Wiegand, R., deceased. Eames, S., deceased. Daiken, R. Communications, S.S. *Enterprise*—"

"What!"

"Daiken, R., Communications, *Enterprise*, five years old at time of Kodos incident."

"All right, cut," Kirk said. "Uhura, get me Mr. Spock . . . Mr. Spock, arrange for a pickup for the Karidian troupe, to be recorded in the log as stranded, for transfer to their destination; company to present special performance for officers and crew. Next destination to be Eta Benecia; give me arrival time as soon as it's processed."

"Aye, aye, sir. What about the synthetic food samples we were supposed to pick up from Dr. Leighton?"

"There aren't any, Mr. Spock," Kirk said shortly.

"That fact will have to be noted, too. Diverting a starship—"

"Is a serious business. Well, a black mark against Dr. Leighton isn't going to hurt him now. One more thing, Mr. Spock. I want the privacy of the Karidian company totally respected. They can have the freedom of the ship within the limits of regulations, but their quarters are off limits. Pass it on to all hands."

"Yes, sir." There was no emotion in Spock's voice; but then, there never was.

"Finally, Mr. Spock, reference Lt. Robert Daiken, in Communications. Please have him transferred to Engineering."

"Sir," Spock said, "he came up from Engineering."

"I'm aware of that. I'm sending him back. He needs more experience."

"Sir, may I suggest a further explanation? He's bound to consider this transfer a disciplinary action."

"I can't help that," Kirk said curtly. "Execute. And notify me when the Karidians come aboard."

He paused and looked up at the ceiling, at last unable to resist a rather grim smile. "I think," he said, "I shall be taking the young lady on a guided tour of the ship."

There was quite a long silence. Then Spock said neutrally:

"As you wish, sir."

At this hour, the engine room was empty, and silent except for the low throbbing of the great thrust units; the *Enterprise* was driving. Lenore looked around, and then smiled at Kirk.

"Did you order the soft lights especially for the occasion?" she said.

"I'd like to be able to say yes," Kirk said. "However, we try to duplicate conditions of night and day as much as possible. Human beings have a built-in diurnal rhythm; we try to adjust to it." He gestured at the hulking drivers. "You find this interesting?"

"Oh yes . . . All that power, and all under such complete control. Are you like that, Captain?"

"I hope I'm more of a man than a machine," he said.

"An intriguing combination of both. The power's at your command; but the decisions—"

"—come from a very human source."

"Are you sure?" she said. "Exceptional, yes; but human?"

Kirk said softly, "You can count on it."

There was a sound of footsteps behind them. Kirk turned reluctantly. It was Yeoman Rand, looking in this light peculiarly soft and blonde despite her uniform—and despite a rather severe expression. She held out an envelope.

"Excuse me, sir," she said. "Mr. Spock thought you ought to have this at once."

"Quite so. Thank you." Kirk pocketed the envelope. "That will be all."

"Very good, sir." The girl left without batting an eyelash. Lenore watched her go, seemingly somewhat amused.

"A lovely girl," she said.

"And very efficient."

"Now *there's* a subject, Captain. Tell me about the women in your world. Has the machine changed them? Made then, well, just people, instead of women?"

"Not at all," Kirk said. "On this ship they have the same duties and functions as the men. They compete equally, and get no special privileges. But they're still women."

"I can see that. Especially the one who just left. So pretty. I'm afraid she didn't like me."

"Nonsense," Kirk said, rather more bluffly than he had intended. "You're imagining things. Yeoman Rand is all business."

Lenore looked down. "You are human, after all. Captain of a starship, and yet you know so little about women. Still I can hardly blame her."

"Human nature hasn't changed," Kirk said. "Grown, perhaps, expanded . . . but not changed."

"That's a comfort. To know that people can still feel, build a private dream, fall in love . . . all that, and power too! Like Caesar—and Cleopatra."

She was moving steadily closer, by very small degrees. Kirk waited a moment, and then took her in his arms.

The kiss was warm and lingering. She was the first to

draw out of it, looking up into his eyes, her expression half sultry, half mocking.

"I had to know," she whispered against the power hum. "I never kissed a Caesar before."

"A rehearsal, Miss Karidian?"

"A performance, Captain."

They kissed again, hard. Something crackled against Kirk's breast. After what seemed to be all too short a while, he took her by the shoulders and pushed her gently away—not very far.

"Don't stop."

"I'm not stopping, Lenore. But I'd better see what it was that Spock thought was so important. He had orders not to know where I was."

"I see," she said, her voice taking on a slight edge. "Starship captains tell *before* they kiss. Well, go ahead and look at your note."

Kirk pulled out the envelope and ripped it open. The message was brief, pointed, very Spock-like. It said:

SHIP'S OFFICER DAIKEN POISONED, CONDITION SERIOUS. DR. McCOY ANALYZING FOR CAUSE AND ANTIDOTE, REQUESTS YOUR PRESENCE.

SPOCK

Lenore watched his face change. At last she said, "I see I've lost you. I hope not permanently."

"No, hardly permanently," Kirk said, trying to smile and failing. "But I should have looked at this sooner. Excuse me, please; and goodnight, Lady Macbeth."

Spock and McCoy were in the sick bay when Kirk arrived. Daiken was on the table, leads running from his still, sweating form to the body function panel, which seemed to be quietly going crazy. Kirk flashed a glance over the panel, but it meant very little to him. He said: "Will he make it? What happened?"

"Somebody put tetralubisol in his milk," McCoy said. "A clumsy job; the stuff is poisonous, but almost insoluble, so it was easy to pump out. He's sick, but he has a good chance. More than I can say for you, Jim."

Kirk looked sharply at the surgeon, and then at Spock. They were both watching him like cats.

"Very well," he said. "I can see that I'm on the spot. Mr. Spock, why don't you begin the lecture?"

"Daiken was the next to last witness of the Kodos affair," Spock said evenly. "You are the last. Dr. McCoy and I checked the library, just as you did, and got the same information. We suppose you are courting Miss Karidian for more information—but the next attempt will be on you. Clearly, you and Daiken are the only survivors because you are both aboard the *Enterprise*; but if Dr. Leighton was right, you no longer have that immunity, and the attempt on Daiken tends to confirm that. In short, you're inviting death."

"I've done that before," Kirk said tiredly. "If Karidian is Kodos, I mean to nail him down, that's all. Administering justice is part of my job."

"Are you certain that's all?" McCoy said.

"No, Bones, I'm not at all certain. Remember that I was there on Tarsus—a midshipman, caught up in a revolution. I saw women and children forced into a chamber with no exit . . . and a half-made self-appointed messiah named Kodos throw a switch. And then there wasn't anyone inside any more. Four thousand people, dead, vanished—and I had to stand by, just waiting for my own turn . . . I can't forget it, any more than Leighton could. I thought I had, but I was wrong."

"And what if you decide Karidian is Kodos?" McCoy demanded. "What then? Do you carry his head through the corridors in triumph? That won't bring back the dead."

"Of course it won't," Kirk said. "But they may rest easier."

"Vengeance is mine, saith the Lord," Spock said, almost in a whisper. Both men turned to look at him in astonishment.

At last Kirk said, "That's true, Mr. Spock, whatever it may mean to an outworlder like you. Vengeance is not what I'm after. I am after justice—and prevention. Kodos killed four thousand; if he is still at large, he may massacre again. But consider this, too: Karidian is a human being, with rights like all of us. He deserves the same justice. If it's at all possible, he also deserves to be cleared."

"I don't know who's worse," McCoy said, looking from Spock to Kirk, "the human calculator or the captain-cum-mystic. Both of you go the hell away and leave me with my patient."

"Gladly," Kirk said. "I'm going to talk to Karidian, and never mind his rule against personal interviews. He can try to kill me if he likes, but he'll have to lay off my officers."

"In short," Spock said, "you *do* think Karidian is Kodos."

Kirk threw up his hands. "Of course I do, Mr. Spock," he said. "Would I be making such an idiot of myself if I didn't? But I am going to make sure. That's the only definition of justice that I know."

"I," Spock said, "would have called it logic."

Karidian and his daughter were not only awake when they answered Kirk's knock, but already half in costume for the next night's command performance which was part of the official excuse for their being on board the *Enterprise* at all. Karidian was wearing a dressing-gown which might have been the robe of Hamlet, the ghost, or the murderer king; whichever it was, he looked kingly, an impression which he promptly reinforced by crossing to a tall-backed chair and sitting down in it as if it were a throne. In his lap he held a much-worn prompter's copy of the play, with his name scrawled across it by a felt pen.

Lenore was easier to tape; she was the mad Ophelia . . . or else, simply a nineteen-year-old girl in a nightgown. Karidian waved her into the background. She withdrew, her expression guarded, but remained standing by the cabin door.

Karidian turned steady, luminous eyes on Kirk. He said, "What is it you want, Captain?"

"I want a straight answer to a straight question," Kirk said. "And I promise you this: You won't be harmed aboard this ship, and you'll be dealt with fairly when you leave it."

Karidian only nodded, as if he had expected nothing else. He was certainly intimidating. Finally Kirk said:

"I suspect you, Mr. Karidian. You know that. I believe

the greatest performance of your life is the part you're acting out offstage."

Karidian smiled, a little sourly. "Each man in his time plays many parts."

"I'm concerned with only one. Tell me this: Are you Kodos the Executioner?"

Karidian looked toward his daughter, but he did not really seem to see her; his eyes were open, but shuttered, like a cat's.

"That was a long time ago," he said. "Back then I was a young character actor, touring the Earth colonies . . . As you see, I'm still doing it."

"That's not an answer," Kirk said.

"What did you expect? Were I Kodos, I would have the blood of thousands on my hands. Should I confess to a stranger, after twenty years of fleeing much more organized justice? Whatever Kodos was in those days, I have never heard it said that he was a fool."

"I have done you a favor," Kirk said. "And I have promised to treat you fairly. That's not an ordinary promise. I am the captain of this ship, and whatever justice there is aboard it is in my hands."

"I see you differently. You stand before me as the perfect symbol of our technological society: mechanized, electronicized, uniformed . . . and not precisely human. I hate machinery, Captain. It has done away with humanity—the striving of men to achieve greatness through their own resources. That's why I am a live actor, still, instead of a shadow on a three-V film."

"The lever is a tool," Kirk said. "We have new tools, but great men still strive, and don't feel outclassed. Wicked men use the tools to murder, like Kodos; but that doesn't make the tools wicked. Guns don't shoot people. Only men do."

"Kodos," Karidian said, "whoever he was, made decisions of life and death. Some had to die that others could live. That is the lot of kings, and the cross of kings. And probably of commanders, too—otherwise why should you be here now?"

"I don't remember ever having killed four thousand innocent people."

"I don't remember it either. But I do remember that another four thousand were saved because of it. Were I to direct a play about Kodos, that is the first thing I would bear in mind."

"It wasn't a play," Kirk said. "I was there. I saw it happen. And since then, all the surviving witnesses have been systematically murdered, except two . . . or possibly, three. One of my officers has been poisoned. I may be next. And here you are, a man of whom we have no record until some nine years ago—and positively identified, positively, no matter how mistakenly, by the late Dr. Leighton. Do you think I can ignore all that?"

"No, certainly not," Karidian said. "But that is your role. I have mine. I have played many." He looked down at his worn hands. "Sooner or later, the blood thins, the body ages, and finally one is grateful for a failing memory. I no longer treasure life—not even my own. Death for me will be a release from ritual. I am old and tired, and the past is blank."

"And that's your only answer?"

"I'm afraid so, Captain. Did you ever get everything you wanted? No, nobody does. And if you did, you might be sorry."

Kirk shrugged and turned away. He found Lenore staring at him, but there was nothing he could do for her, either. He went out.

She followed him. In the corridor on the other side of the door, she said in a cold whisper: "You are a machine. And with a big bloody stain of cruelty on your metal hide. You could have spared him."

"If he's Kodos," Kirk said, equally quietly, "then I've already shown him more mercy than he deserves. If he isn't, then we'll put you ashore at Eta Benecia, with no harm done."

"Who are you," Lenore said in a dangerous voice, "to say what harm is done?"

"Who do I have to be?"

She seemed to be about to answer; cold fire raged in her eyes. But at the same moment, the door slid open behind her and Karidian stood there, no longer so tall or so impressive as he had been before. Tears began to run down over her cheeks; she reached for his shoulders, her head drooping.

"Father . . . father . . ."

"Never mind," Karidian said gently, regaining a little of his stature. "It's already all over. I am thy father's spirit, doomed for a certain time to walk the night—"

"Hush!"

Feeling like six different varieties of monster, Kirk left them alone together

For the performance, the briefing room had been re-dressed into a small theater, and cameras were spotted here and there so that the play could be seen on intercom screens elsewhere in the ship for the part of the crew that had to remain on duty. The lights were already down. Kirk was late, as usual; he was just settling into his seat—as captain he was entitled to a front row chair and had had no hesitation about claiming it—when the curtains parted and Lenore came through them, in the flowing costume of Ophelia, white with make-up.

She said in a clear, almost gay voice: "Tonight the Karidian Players present *Hamlet*—another in a series of living plays in space—dedicated to the tradition of the classic theater, which we believe will never die. *Hamlet* is a violent play about a violent time, when life was cheap and ambition was God. It is also a timeless play, about personal guilt, doubt, indecision, and the thin line between Justice and Vengeance."

She vanished, leaving Kirk brooding. Nobody needed to be introduced to *Hamlet*; that speech had been aimed directly at him. He did not need the reminder, either, but he had got it nonetheless.

The curtains parted and the great, chilling opening began. Kirk lost most of it, since McCoy chose that moment to arrive and seat himself next to Kirk with a great bustle.

"Here we are, here we are," McCoy muttered. "In the long history of medicine no doctor has ever caught the curtain of a play."

"Shut up," Kirk said, *sotto voce*. "You had plenty of notice."

"Yes, but nobody told me I'd lose a patient at the last minute."

"Somebody dead?"

"No, no. Lieutenant Daiken absconded out of sick bay, that's all. I suppose he wanted to see the play too."

"It's being piped into sick bay!"

"I know that. Pipe down, will you? How can I hear if you keep mumbling?"

Swearing silently, Kirk got up and went out. Once he was in the corridor, he went to the nearest open line and ordered a search; but it turned out that McCoy already had one going.

Routine, Kirk decided, was not enough. Daiken's entire family had been destroyed on Tarsus . . . and somebody had tried to kill him. This was no time to take even the slightest chance; with the play going on, not only Karidian, but the whole ship was vulnerable to any access of passion . . . or vengeance.

"Red security alert," Kirk said. "Search every inch, including cargo."

Getting confirmation, he went back into the converted briefing room. He was still not satisfied, but there was nothing more he could do now.

His ears were struck by a drum beat. The stage was dim, lit only by a wash of red, and the characters playing Marcellus and Horatio were just going off. Evidently the play had already reached Act One, Scene 5. The figure of the ghost materialized in the red beam and raised its arm, beckoning to Hamlet, but Hamlet refused to follow. The ghost—Karidian—beckoned again, and the drum beat heightened in intensity.

Kirk could think of nothing but that Karidian was now an open target. He circled the rapt audience quickly and silently, making for the rear of the stage.

"Speak," Hamlet said. "I'll go no further."

"Mark me," said Karidian hollowly.

"I will."

"My hour is almost come, when I to sulphurous and tormenting flames must render up myself—"

There was Daiken, crouching in the wings. He was already leveling a phaser at Karidian.

"—and you must seek revenge—"

"Daiken!" Kirk said. There was no help for it; he had to call across the stage. The dialogues intercut.

"I am thy father's spirit, doomed for a certain term to walk the night—"

"He murdered my father," Daiken said. "And my mother."

"—And for the day confined to fast in fires, Till the foul crimes done in my days—"

"Get back to sick bay!"

"I know. I saw. He murdered them."

"—are burnt and purged away."

The audience had begun to murmur; they could hear every word. So could Karidian. He looked off toward Daiken, but the light was too bad for him to see anything. In a shaken voice, he tried to go on.

"I . . . I could a tale unfold whose lightest word—"

"You could be wrong. Don't throw your life away on a mistake."

"—would t-tear up thy soul, freeze thy young blood—"

"Daiken, give me that weapon."

"No."

Several people in the audience were standing now, and Kirk could see a few security guards moving cautiously down the sidelines. They would be too late; Daiken had a dead bead on Karidian.

Then the scenery at the back tore, and Lenore came out. Her eyes were bright and feverish, and in her hand she carried an absurdly long dagger.

"It's over!" she said in a great, theatrical voice. "Never mind, father, I'm strong! Come, ye spirits of the air, unsex me now! Hie thee hither, that in the porches of thine ear—"

"Child, child!"

She could not hear him. She was the mad Ophelia; but the lines were Lady Macbeth's.

"All the ghost are dead. Who would have thought they had so much blood in 'em? I've freed you, father. I've taken the blood away from you. Had he not so much resembled my father as he slept, I'd have done it—"

"No!" Karidian said, his voice choked with horror.

"You've left me nothing! You were untouched by what I did, you weren't even born! I wanted to leave you something clean—"

"Balsam! I've given you everything! You're safe, no one can touch you! See Banquo there, the Caesar, even he can't touch you! This castle hath a pleasant seat."

Kirk went out onto the stage, watching the security guards out of the corner of his eyes. Daiken seemed to be frozen by the action under the lights, but his gun still had not wavered.

"That's enough," Kirk said. "Come with me, both of you."

Karidian turned to him, spreading his hands wide. "Captain," he said. "Try to understand. I was a soldier in a great cause. There were things that had to be done—hard things, terrible things. You know the price of that; you too are a captain."

"Stop it, father," Lenore said, in a spuriously rational voice. "There is nothing to explain."

"There is. Murder. Flight. Suicide. Madness. And still the price is not enough; my daughter has killed too."

"For you! For you! I saved you!"

"For the price of seven innocent men," Kirk said.

"Innocent?" Lenore gave a great theatrical laugh, like a coloratura playing Medea. "Innocent! They saw! They were guilty!"

"That's enough, Lenore," Kirk said. "The play is over. It was over twenty years ago. Are you coming with me, or do I have to drag you?"

"Better go," Daiken's voice said from the wings. He stood up and came forward into the light, the gun still leveled. "I wasn't going to be so merciful, but we've had enough madness. Thanks, Captain."

Lenore spun on him. With a movement like a flash of lightning, she snatched the gun away from him.

"Stand back!" she screamed. "Stand back, everyone! The play goes on!"

"No!" Karidian cried out hoarsely. "In the name of God, child—"

"Captain Caesar! You could have had Egypt! Beware of Ides of March!"

She pointed the gun at Kirk and pulled the trigger. But fast as she was in her madness, Karidian was even quicker. The beam struck him squarely on the chest. He fell silently.

Lenore wailed like a lost kitten and dropped to her knees beside him. The security guards stampeded onto the stage, but Kirk waved them back.

"Father!" Lenore crooned. "Father! Oh proud death, what feast is toward in thine eternal cell, that thou such a prince at a shot so bloodily has struck!" She began to laugh again. "The cue, father, the cue! No time to sleep! The play! The play's the thing, wherein we'll catch the conscience of the king . . ."

Gentle hands drew her away. In Kirk's ear, McCoy's voice said: "And in the long run, she didn't even get the lines right."

"Take care of her," Kirk said tonelessly. "Kodos is dead . . . but I think she may walk in her sleep."

THE GALILEO SEVEN

Writers: Oliver Crawford and S. Bar-David
(Story by Oliver Crawford)
Director: Robert Gist
Guest stars: Don Marshall, John Crawford

The USS *Enterprise* operated under a standing order to investigate all quasar and quasarlike phenomena wherever and whenever it encountered them. To Kirk, it seemed to have met up with one. A sinister formation had appeared on the bridge's main viewing screen—a bluish mass, threaded with red streaks of radiant energy. It dominated the sky ahead.

Kirk, eyeing the screen, pushed a button, only too conscious of the critical presence of his passenger, High Commissioner Ferris. "Captain to shuttlecraft *Galileo*," he said. "Stand by, Mr. Spock."

Ferris voiced his disapproval. "I remind you, Captain, that I am entirely opposed to this delay. Your mission is to get those medical supplies to Makus III in time for their transfer to the New Paris colonies."

"And I must remind you of our standing order, sir. There will be no problem. It's only three days to Makus III. And the transfer doesn't take place for five."

Ferris was fretful. "I don't like to take chances. With the plague out of control on New Paris, we must get those drugs there in time."

"We will." Kirk turned back to his console. "Captain to *Galileo*. All systems clear for your take-off."

"Power up, Captain. All instruments activated. All readings normal. All go."

Spock's voice . . . reassuring. As Science Officer, he was commanding the investigating team selected from the *Enterprise* crew for research into the space curiosity charted under the name of Murasaki 312. Now he sat, strapped, in the shuttlecraft's pilot seat, the others behind him—McCoy, Scott, Yeoman Mears, a fresh-faced girl, Boma, the Negro astrophysicist, radiation specialist Gaetano, Navigator Latimer. All together, seven: the *Galileo*'s seven.

"Launch shuttlecraft," Kirk said.

On the huge flight deck the heavy hangar doors swung open. The shuttlecraft taxied toward them and moved out into the emptiness of space.

Spock spoke over his shoulder. "Position."

"Three point seven . . . no, no, sir," Latimer said. "Four point—"

"Make up your mind," Spock said.

"My indicator's gone crazy," Latimer said.

Boma spoke quickly. "To be expected, Mr. Spock. Quasars are extremely disruptive. Just how much, we don't know. . . ."

Spock, eyes on his panel, said dryly, "Considerably, Mr. Boma."

Gaetano made his discouraging contribution. "My radiation reading is increasing rapidly, Mr. Spock!"

"Stop forward momentum!"

Latimer pushed switches. "I can't stop it, sir! Nothing happens!" McCoy leaned over to glance at his instruments. "Spock, we're being drawn right into the thing!"

Struggling with his own controls, Spock said, "Full power astern!"

But there was no power to reverse the onward plunge of the *Galileo.* "What's happening?" McCoy cried.

Boma said, "We underestimated the strength of the nucleonic attraction."

Spock reached for his speaker. "*Galileo* to *Enterprise.* We're out of control, Captain! Being pulled directly into the heart of Murasaki 312. Receiving violent radiation on outer. . . ."

A blast of static drowned Spock's voice. Kirk rushed over to Uhura's station. "Can't you get anything at all, Lieutenant?"

"Nothing clear, sir. Not on any frequency. Just those couple of words about being pulled off course."

Kirk wheeled. ''Mr. Sulu, get me a fix on the *Galileo*!''

Sulu turned a bewildered face. ''Our scanners are blocked, Captain. We're getting a mess of readings I've never seen before. Nothing makes sense!''

Kirk strode to the library computer. He got a hum, a click—and the flat, metallic computer voice. ''Negative ionic concentration 1.64 by 10^2 meter. Radiation wavelength 370 angstroms, harmonics upwards along entire spectrum.''

Kirk turned, appalled. Staring at him, Ferris said, ''What is it, Captain?''

''That thing out there has completely ionized this entire sector!''

He glared at the screen. ''At least four complete solar systems in this vicinity—and somewhere out there is a twenty-four-foot shuttlecraft out of control, off its course. Finding a needle in a haystack would be child's play compared to finding . . .''

Coiling, hungry, the bluish mass on the screen glared back at him, a blight on the face of space.

But the controls of the shuttlecraft weren't the only victims of Murasaki 312. It had rendered useless the normal searching systems of the *Enterprise*. Without them, the starship was drifting, blind, almost as helpless as the *Galileo*.

Ferris could not resist his I-told-you-so compulsion. ''I was opposed to this from the beginning,'' he said to Kirk. ''Our flight to Makus III had the very highest priority.''

Kirk, his mind straining to contingencies that confronted the *Galileo*'s crew of seven, said, ''I am aware of that, Commissioner. At the same time I have certain scientific duties—and exploring the Murasaki Effect is one of them.''

''But you have lost your crew,'' Ferris said.

If there were people who couldn't resist an ''I told you so,'' there were just as many who enjoyed making the painfully obvious more painful. Kirk held on to his temper. ''We have two days to find them,'' he said.

Ferris pointed to the screen. ''In all that? Two days?''

Kirk lost his temper. ''Are you suggesting that I just turn around and leave them in it?''

''You shouldn't have sent them out in the first placc!''

Ferris paused. "You are concerned with only seven people. I am thinking of the millions in the New Paris colonies who will die if we don't get these medicines to them. It's your obstinate insistence on carrying out these inconsequential investigations that. . . ."

A bureaucrat is a bureaucrat is a bureaucrat, Kirk thought. They could function with paper. But remove them from paper into the sphere of decisive action and they turned into moralizing futilities. Scorn restored his composure. "We will make our scheduled rendezvous, Commissioner," he said evenly. "You have my word."

Uhura spoke. "Captain, there is one planet in this vicinity capable of sustaining human life. Type M, oxygen-nitrogen. Listed as Taurus II." The sympathy in her voice was cool water to a thirsty man. Kirk went to her. She looked up at him. "It is very nearly dead center of the Murasaki Effect, as closely as we can make out with our equipment malfunctions."

"Thank you, Lieutenant," Kirk said. "Mr. Sulu?"

"Yes, sir?"

"Set course for Taurus II."

"Course laid in, sir."

"Aren't you shooting in the dark?" Ferris said. "Assuming that they are there?"

"If they aren't there, Commissioner, they are all dead by now. We will search Taurus II because there is no sense in searching any place else."

"You said something about a needle in a haystack. Useless."

"Not if you want your needle back."

Strangely enough, the needle had fallen upon soft hay. However, soft was the best you could say about the spongily ugly surface of Taurus II. It had cushioned the impact of the *Galileo*'s crash landing in a roughly circular crater. Rock walls reared up toward a sky of a repellently bilious shade of green. It was not a prepossessing planet. The craft, canted over, had banged people and things around inside. Spock was bleeding green from a cut on his head. McCoy attended to it and then made his way to Yeoman Mears.

"Are you all right?"

"I . . . think so, Doctor."

Boma said, "That is what I call a ride."

"What happened?" Latimer asked him.

"I can't be sure . . . but I'd say that the magnetic potential of the Murasaki Effect was such that it was multiplied geometrically as we gathered speed. We were simply shot into the center of the Effect like a projectile. What do you think, Mr. Spock?"

"Your evaluation seems reasonable."

Scott, holding an aching head, joined Spock in checking the instruments and control panel. "What a mess!" he said.

Spock stood up. "Picturesque descriptions won't mend broken circuits, Mr. Scott. I think you'll find your work cut out for you." He threw a switch on the communicator.

"*Galileo* to *Enterprise*. Do you read me?"

"You don't really expect an answer, do you?" Scott said.

"I expect nothing. It is simply logical to try every alternative. A reading on the atmosphere, please, Doctor McCoy."

"As soon as I finish checking the crew . . ."

"If anyone had been injured, I assume you would have been so informed by now. The reading, Doctor."

There was irritation in the glance Spock received from McCoy. After a moment the Medical Officer picked up his kit and moved to an instrument panel. "Partial pressure of oxygen is 70 millimeters of mercury. Nitrogen, 140. Breathable, if you're not running in competition."

"The facts, please," Spock said.

"Traces of argon, neon, krypton, all in acceptable quantities. But I wouldn't recommend this place for a summer resort."

"Your opinion will be noted. You are recording this, Yeoman?"

"Of course, Mr. Spock."

"Very good. Mr. Scott, if you will immediately conduct a damage survey."

Scott said, "Naturally."

Spock ignored the tone of the comment. He said, "I suggest we move outside to give Mr. Scott room to work.

Mr. Latimer, Mr. Gaetano, please arm yourselves and scout out the immediate area. Stay in visual contact with the ship."

"Aye, aye, sir," Gaetano said.

The two were removing phaser pistols from a locker as McCoy turned to Spock. "What do you think our chances are of communicating with the *Enterprise*?"

"Under current conditions, extremely poor."

"But they'll be looking for us!"

"If the ionization effect is as widespread as I believe it is, they'll be looking for us without instruments. By visual contact only. On those terms, it is a very large solar system."

"Then you don't think they'll find us."

"Not so long as we are grounded."

McCoy exploded. "I've never been able to stand your confoundedly eternal cheerfulness, Spock!"

"Better make an effort to, Doctor." The suggestion was mildly made. "We may be here for a long time."

Kirk himself had small cause for cheer. The *Enterprise* scanners had gone completely on strike. "Mr. Sulu, have you tried tying in with the auxiliary power units?"

"Yes, sir. No change."

Scowling, Kirk hit a button. "Transporter Room. This is the Captain. Are the Transporters beaming yet?"

The technician sounded apologetic. "Not one hundred percent, sir. We beamed down some inert material but it came back in a dissociated condition. We wouldn't dare try it with people."

"Thank you." He pushed another button. "Captain to Flight Deck. Prepare shuttlecraft *Columbus* for immediate search of planet surface. Correlate coordinates with Mr. Sulu. Lieutenant Uhura?"

"Yes, sir?"

"Anything at all?"

"All wavelengths dominated by ionization effect, Captain. Transmissions blocked, reception impossible."

To add to his joy in life, Ferris appeared beside Kirk's command chair. "Well, Captain?"

Kirk said, "We have until 2823.8 to continue our search, Commissioner."

"You don't really think you'll have any luck, do you?"

Kirk drew a hand down his cheek. "Those people out there happen to be friends and shipmates of mine. I intend to continue this ship's search for them until the last possible moment."

"Very well, Captain. But not a second beyond that limit. Is that clear? If it is not, I refer you to Book 19, Section 433, Paragraph 12."

"I am familiar with the regulations, Commissioner. And I know all about your authority."

Tight-faced, he struck a button on his console.

"Launch shuttlecraft *Columbus*!"

Outside the *Galileo*, Spock was examining the nearest section of the wall encircling the crater. Rescue was indeed a remote possibility. Even if the *Enterprise*'s searching equipment had remained unaffected by Murasaki 312, Taurus II was just one planet among many in the quadrant's solar systems. Hidden like this in the hollow made by the crater's rocky wall, the *Galileo* would be virtually invisible.

McCoy, joining him, looked up at the wall. "I can't say much for our circumstances," he said, "but at least it's your big chance."

"My big chance for what, Doctor?"

"Command," McCoy said. "I know you, Spock. You've never voiced it, but you've always thought logic was the best basis on which to build command. Am I right?"

"I am a logical man," Spock said.

"It'll take more than logic to get us out of this."

"Perhaps, Doctor . . . but I can't think of a better place to start trying. I recognize that command has fascinations, even under such circumstances as these. But I neither enjoy the idea of command nor am I frightened by it. It simply exists. And I shall do what logically needs to be done."

They clambered back into the craft, and Scott lifted a grim face from the control panel. "We've lost a great deal of fuel, Mr. Spock. We have no chance at all to reach escape velocity. And even if we hope to make orbit, we'll have to lighten our load by at least five hundred pounds."

"The weight of three grown men," Spock said.

Scott glanced at him, startled. "Why, yes . . . I guess you could put it that way."

McCoy was openly outraged. "Or the equivalent weight in *equipment*," he said.

Spock faced him. "Doctor McCoy, with few exceptions we will use virtually every piece of equipment in attaining orbit. There is very little surplus weight except among our passengers."

Boma, with Yeoman Mears, had been taking tricorder readings near the hatch. Now he stopped. "You mean three of us will have to stay behind?"

"Unless the situation changes radically," Spock said.

"And who is to choose those who remain behind?"

"As commanding officer the choice is mine."

Boma's face hardened. "You wouldn't be interested in drawing lots?"

Spock said, "I believe I am better qualified to select those who will stay behind than any random drawing of lots." He spoke without a trace of egotism in voice or manner. "My decision will be a logical one, Mr. Boma, arrived at through logical processes."

"Life and death are not logical, Spock!" McCoy cried.

"But attaining a desired goal is."

Spock ignored the tension in the atmosphere. "I would suggest we proceed to a more careful examination of the hull. We may have overlooked some minor damage."

Boma glared after him as he left. "Some minor damage was overlooked," he said, "when they put his head together!"

"Not his head," McCoy said. "His heart."

Tension was rising in everybody. Over at the farther crater wall Latimer and Gaetano were making a nervous survey of the area. Suddenly Gaetano stopped, listening. Latimer, too, halted. They listened to the sound—a rhythmic scraping noise such as might be made by rubbing wood against some corrugated surface. Latimer became conscious of an uneasy impression that the crater wall was breathing, the mist of its breath the fog that drifted over it, reducing visibility. The mist had come suddenly, like the sound. The scraping noise was repeated.

"What is it?" Latimer whispered.

"I don't know," Gaetano said. "It came from up there."

"No . . . back there. . . ."

They stared at each other. The sound surrounded them.

"Everywhere . . . it's all around us."

"Let's get out of here!" Latimer cried.

Then he yelled, breaking into a run. From the shadow made by a cleft in the wall above them a gigantic shape had emerged. Latimer screamed—and fell. Gaetano jerked out his phaser. He fired it at the fog-filled cleft.

He turned. The shaft of a spear was protruding from Latimer's back. It was as thick as a slim telephone pole.

The scream, reverberating against the crater's walls, had been heard by Spock and Boma. The Vulcan strode to Gaetano, where he stood over Latimer's body, still in shock, still staring up at the foggy cleft.

"How?" Spock said.

The dazed Gaetano lowered his phaser. "Something . . . huge . . . terrible. Up there!" He pointed to the cleft.

Spock walked over to the wall. Seizing an outcropping of rock, he began to climb up to the crevice. Boma spoke to Gaetano. "What was it? Did you see what it was?"

"Like a . . . a giant ape." He started to tremble. "It was all . . . so quick. There was a . . . a sound first."

Spock was back. "There's nothing up there," he said.

"I tell you there was!" Gaetano shouted.

Spock's voice was quiet. "I do not doubt your word."

"I hit it. I swear my phaser hit it," Gaetano said.

Spock didn't answer. Looking down at Latimer's body, he tugged at the spear shaft. It came loose in his hand, exposing its point—a large triangular stone, honed into shape and sharpness.

"The Folsom Point," Spock said.

"Sir?"

"Mr. Boma, this spearhead bears a remarkable resemblance to the Folsom Point, discovered in 1926 old Earth calendar, in New Mexico, North America. Quite similar . . . more crudely shaped about the haft, however. Not very efficient."

"Not very efficient?" Boma was furious. "Is that all you have to say?"

Surprised, Spock looked at him. ''Am I in error, Mr. Boma?''

''Error? You? Impossible!''

''Then, what—'' Spock began.

''A man lies there dead! And you talk about stone spears! What about Latimer? What about the dead man?''

''A few words on behalf of the dead will not bring them back to life, Mr. Boma.''

Gaetano was glaring at him, too. He spoke to Boma. ''Give me a hand with Latimer, will you?'' He turned to Spock. ''Unless you think we should leave his body here in the interest of efficiency.''

''Bringing him back to the ship should not interfere with our repair efforts. If you'd like some assistance . . .''

''We'll do it!'' Gaetano said sharply. Nodding to Boma, they reached down to the body. As they lifted it, Spock's keen eyes were studying the spearhead's construction.

Kirk was trying to fight off a sense of complete futility.

''. . . and great loss.'' His voice was so broken as he dictated the last three words into his Captain's Log that he wondered if he should delete them. Spock . . . McCoy . . . Scott . . . all three of them gone, lost to the hideous blueness of what still showed on the screen.

Uhura spoke. ''Captain, the *Columbus* has returned from searching quadrants 779X by 534M. Negative results.''

''Have them proceed to the next quadrants. Any word from Engineering on the sensors?''

''They're working on them, sir. Still inoperable.''

''The Transporters?''

''Still reported unsafe, sir.''

''Thank you, Lieutenant.''

''Captain Kirk . . .''

It was Ferris. ''Captain, I do not relish the thought of abandoning your crewmen out there. However, I must remind you that—''

''I haven't forgotten,'' Kirk said wearily.

''You're running out of time,'' Ferris said.

A man of paper. ''I haven't forgotten that, either,'' Kirk said. He rammed a button on his console. ''This is the Captain. Try using overload power on the Transporters. We have to get it working.'' He got up to go to Uhura. ''Lieutenant, order the *Columbus* to open its course two degrees on each lap from now on.''

Sulu, surprised into protest, spoke. ''But Captain, two degrees means they'll overlook more than a dozen terrestrial miles on each search loop.''

Kirk turned. ''It also means we'll at least have a fighting chance of checking most of the planet's surface. Mind your helm, Mr. Sulu.''

Sulu flushed. ''Yes, sir.''

Ferris was still standing beside his command chair. He said coldly, ''Twenty-four more hours, Captain.''

Kirk didn't answer. He stared ahead at the viewing screen. Somewhere in the midst of that mysterious blueness, Taurus II existed, its substance solid, its air breathable—an oasis in the center of hell. Had Spock found it?

In the marooned *Galileo*, McCoy and Yeoman Mears had collected equipment to jettison. Arms laden, McCoy said, ''This stuff ought to save us at least fifty pounds of weight, Spock.''

''If we could scrape up another hundred pounds, what with Mr. Latimer gone . . .'' Yeoman Mears didn't finish her sentence.

''We would still be at least one hundred and fifty pounds overweight,'' Spock said.

''I can't believe you're serious about leaving someone behind,'' McCoy said. ''Whatever those creatures are out there . . .''

''It is more rational to sacrifice one man than six,'' Spock said.

''I'm not talking about rationality!''

''You might be wise to start.''

Boma stuck his head through the open hatch. ''We're ready, Mr. Spock.''

''For what, Mr. Boma?''

''The services . . . for Latimer.''

Spock straightened. ''Mr. Boma. We are working against time.''

''The man is dead. He deserves a decent burial. You're the Captain. A few words from you . . .''

If Spock's facial muscles had been capable of expressing annoyance, they would have twisted with it. As they were not, he looked at McCoy. "Doctor, perhaps you know the correct words for such an occasion."

"It's your place," McCoy said.

"My place is here. If you please, Doctor."

The facial muscles of the non-Vulcans had no trouble in showing annoyance. Spock's cool detachment exceedingly irritated them. "Spock, we may all die here!" McCoy shouted. "At least let us die like men, not machines!"

"By taking care of first things first, I hope to increase our chances of not dying here." Spock moved to where Scott was still at work on the console. "Perhaps if you were to channel the second auxiliary tank through the primary intake valve, Mr. Scott."

"Too delicate, sir. It may not take the pressure as it is,"

McCoy glared at Spock's stooped back. Then he followed the others out of the hatch and over to the mound of earth a few feet away from the *Galileo.* He bent for a handful of dirt and dropped it on the mound. "Dust though art and to dust shalt thou return. Amen."

People's heads bowed. "Amen," they echoed. They all stood still for a minute, each with his private thoughts—and the rhythmic grating sound came from what seemed to be distance.

"What is it?" said Yeoman Mears.

McCoy had looked up. "I don't know. But it sounds manmade."

"*Man*made! You wouldn't say that if you saw what I saw!" cried Gaetano. "It's them, those things out there somewhere!"

McCoy spoke to him and Boma. "You'd better stay on watch. I'll check with Mr. Spock."

He and Yeoman Mears re-entered the craft to hear a dismayed Scott cry, "The pressure's dropping, sir. We're losing everything!"

"What happened?" Spock asked.

"One of the lines gave. The strain of coming through the atmosphere . . . the added load when we tried to bypass—"

McCoy interrupted. "Spock!"

The Vulcan made a gesture for silence, concentrating

on Scott. Staring at a gauge, the engineer said slowly, "Well, that does it. We have no fuel at all!"

"Then that solves the problem of who to leave behind."

"Spock!" McCoy yelled.

"Yes, Doctor?"

"Come outside. Something's happening."

Straightening, Spock said, "You will consider the alternatives, Mr. Scott."

Scott rose impatiently. "What alternatives? We have no fuel!"

"Mr. Scott, there are always alternatives."

He took his Vulcan calm with him as he followed McCoy out of the ship. The grating noise was louder. Spock listened, as concentrated on it as he'd been on Scott. McCoy glanced at his composed face. "And what do those supersensitive ears of yours make of *that*?"

"Wood," Spock said. "Rubbing on some kind of leather."

"They're getting ready," Gaetano muttered. "They'll attack."

"Not necessarily," Boma said. "It could be a simple tribal rite . . . assuming it's a tribal culture."

"Not a tribal culture," Spock said gently. "Their artifacts are too primitive. Merely a loose association of some sort."

"We do not know that they are mere animals. They may well be capable of reason."

"We know they're capable of killing," Boma reminded him.

Spock looked at him. "If they are protecting themselves by their own lights . . ."

"That is exactly what we would be doing!" Boma argued.

Gaetano said, "The majority of us—"

"I am not interested in the opinion of the majority, Mr. Gaetano!" It was the first time Spock had raised his voice. Now its unexpected sharpness came as a shock to all of them.

"The components must be weighed—our dangers balanced against our duty to other life forms, friendly or not." Spock paused. "There is a third course."

"It could get us all killed." But the insolence had left Gaetano.

"I think not," Spock said. "Doctor McCoy, you and Yeoman Mears will remain in the ship. Assist Mr. Scott in any way possible. We shall return shortly."

He turned to Gaetano and Boma. "You will follow my orders to the letter. You will fire only when so ordered—and at my designated targets."

"Now you're talking," said Gaetano.

"Yes, I am talking, Mr. Gaetano. And you will hear. We shall fire to frighten. Not to kill."

"If we only knew more about them," Yeoman Mears said fearfully.

"We know enough," Boma said. "If they're tribal, they'll have a sense of unity. We can use that."

"How, Mr. Boma?"

"By hitting them hard, sir. Give them a bloody nose! Make them think twice about attacking us! A good offense is the best defense!"

"I agree!" cried Gaetano. "If we just stand by and do nothing, we're just giving them an invitation to come down and slaughter us!"

Spock's face had taken on a look of grave reflection. "I am frequently appalled," he said, "by the low regard for life you Earth people have."

"We are practical about it!" Gaetano's voice shook. "I say we hit them before they hit us!"

"Mr. Boma?" Spock said.

"Absolutely."

"Doctor McCoy?"

"It seems logical to me."

"It also seems logical to me," Spock said. "But taking life indiscriminately . . ."

"You were quick enough to talk about leaving three of us behind," Gaetano said. "Why all the sudden solicitude about some kind of animal?"

"You saw what they did to Latimer," Boma said.

So it had to be put into words of one syllable. But Spock was a master of primitives' languages. "I am in command here, Mr. Gaetano. The orders are mine to give, as the responsibility is mine to take. Follow me."

He led the way to the crater wall. The grating sound grew still louder as the trio began the climb up the rocky escarpment. Gaetano, apprehensive, arranged himself third in position. Spock signaled a halt. The slope ahead of them loomed vague and indistinct through mist swirls. Suddenly, among the rocks immediately above them, there was movement. Spock heard it first. He tensed with alertness, readying his phaser. Something rose from behind the rocks, something impossibly huge. It might have been man-shaped—but he couldn't tell, for the creature held an enormous leather shield before its body. Then a great spear whistled past his head. Spock, aiming his phaser, fired it.

There was a roar, half-human—a scream of pain and fear. The thing ducked behind a rock, hurling its shield downward.

Spock sidestepped to avoid its strike. He was hoisting it up as Boma and Gaetano joined him.

Awed, Gaetano whispered, "It must be twelve feet high."

Spock dropped the shield. Still leading the way, he motioned the others forward. They made the crest of the crater. Now the scraping noise was louder still, harsh, rasping, broken by grunting sounds.

"The mists . . ." Gaetano complained. "I can't see."

"They are directly ahead of us," Spock said. "Several, I believe. You will direct your phasers to two o'clock and to ten o'clock."

"I say we hit them dead on!" Gaetano said.

Spock turned his head. "Fortunately, I am giving the orders, Mr. Gaetano. Take aim, please."

He waited. "Fire!" he said.

Whatever their targets were, they could certainly howl. Spock listened to the roaring. "Cease fire!" he said. The roaring stilled. Spock nodded, satisfied. "They should think twice before bothering us again."

"I still say we should have killed them."

"It was not necessary, Mr. Gaetano. Fear will do for us what needs to be done. Mr. Boma, return to the ship. Mr. Gaetano, you will remain here on guard, keeping visual contact with the ship."

"Out here? Alone?"

''Security must be maintained, Mr. Gaetano.''

Boma said, ''At least let me stay with him.''

''My intention is to post you in another position, Mr. Boma.''

The two exchanged terrified looks. Spock regarded them with a mild curiosity. ''Gentlemen,'' he said, ''I regret having to post you in hazardous positions. Unfortunately, I have no choice. In the event of danger, the ship must have warning.''

''Even if some of us must die for it?''

''There is the possibility of danger, Mr. Boma. But it cannot be helped.''

He began the climb back down to the ship. After a long moment, Boma turned to follow him. ''Good luck, Gaetano,'' he said.

''Yeah, sure,'' Gaetano said.

As they approached the *Galileo*, Spock said, ''Mr. Boma, your post is here, near the ship.'' He hoisted himself through the hatch and Yeoman Mears said, ''Did you find them, Mr. Spock?''

''We found them. I don't think they'll trouble us again.''

''I hope not,'' McCoy said. ''Spock, Scott has some idea.''

He clearly did. Scott's face was alight with idea. ''It's dangerous, Mr. Spock—but it just may work.''

''Go head, Mr. Scott.''

''I can adjust the main reactor to function on a substitute fuel supply.'' He paused, unable to resist the temptation to give full dramatic value to his idea. ''Our phasers, sir. I could adapt them and use their energy. It will take time, but it's possible.''

''The objection is they're our only defense,'' McCoy said.

''They would also seem to be our only hope.'' Spock made his decision fast. ''Doctor . . . Yeoman . . . your phasers, please.''

''But what if those creatures attack again?'' the girl asked.

''They will not attack, not for many hours at any rate,'' Spock told her. ''By then, with luck, we should be gone.''

Scott nodded. "If I can get a full load, we'll be able to achieve orbit with all hands. Not that we can maintain it long."

"It will not be necessary to maintain it long. In less than twenty-four hours the *Enterprise* will be forced to abandon its search in order to make its rendezvous. If our orbit decays after that time, it will make no difference." Spock shrugged. "Whether we die coming out of orbit or here on the surface, we shall surely die. Your phaser, Doctor."

Reluctantly McCoy and the girl surrendered their phasers. Spock passed them over to Scott.

At the same moment on the *Enterprise*, the Transporter officer was reporting a successful materialization to Kirk. "The crates I beamed down to Taurus II came back all right, sir. In my opinion the Transporters are now safe for human transport."

It was the first good news since they had contacted Murasaki 312. Kirk pushed his intercom button. "This is the Captain. Landing parties 1, 2, and 3. Report to Transporter Room for immediate beam-down to the planet's surface. Ordinance condition 1-A."

"Captain . . . it's a big planet," the Transporter officer said. "It'll be sheer good luck if our landing parties find anything."

"I'm counting on luck, Lieutenant. It's almost the only tool we've got that might work."

But Spock, despite his hope that fear would restrain the hostility of the gorillalike creatures, wasn't trusting to luck. For the third time he left the *Galileo* to check with Boma. "Have you seen or heard anything unusual, Mr. Boma?"

"Nothing, sir."

"Is Mr. Gaetano keeping in contact with you?"

"I saw him up in those rocks just a few minutes ago."

Something else had seen Gaetano among the rocks. It aimed a large rock at his phaser, knocking it out of his hand. Terrified, he scrambled after it—and a spear hurled past him, striking the air between him and the weapon. He ran toward a rock crevice. It ended in a blank black wall. Trapped, he turned. The crevice entrance was blocked by a massive bulk, hairy, featureless. The creature moved toward him. He screamed.

It was Spock who found the dropped phaser. As he bent to retrieve it, he heard a snuffling, half-growl, half-grunt from somewhere in the rocks ahead of him. Then there was silence. McCoy and Boma climbed up to him. He extended his hand. "Mr. Gaetano's phaser," he said.

"Look!" Boma cried.

The footprint in the rubble was human in form. Its enormity was its horror.

Boma and McCoy stared at it, unbelieving. Spock handed Gaetano's phaser to McCoy. "Take this back to Mr. Scott for conversion, please, Doctor."

Boma flared up at him. "Is that all this means to you? Just a phaser to be recovered?"

Spock stared at him, puzzled. "Explain, Mr. Boma."

The frenzied Boma broke into a shout. "Gaetano's gone! Who knows what's happened to him! And you just hand over his phaser as though nothing had happened at all!"

Spock ignored the outburst. Drawing out his own phaser, he handed it over to McCoy, saying, "And please give this to Mr. Scott in case I don't return."

"Where are you going?" McCoy demanded.

Spock said, "I have a certain . . . scientific curiosity about what has occurred to Mr. Gaetano. You will return to the ship, if you please."

He slipped off into the mist, leaving Boma to gape after him. McCoy, shaking his head, said, "He'll risk his neck locating Gaetano. And if he finds him alive, he's just as liable to order him to stay behind when the ship leaves. You tell me."

"Do you think the ship will ever leave?"

"It won't without these phasers," McCoy said. "Let's get back to Scott."

Sharp-eyed, agile as a cat, Spock was creeping upward over rocks. Then he saw the ledge. Gaetano lay sprawled on it, unmoving. Spock bent over the body. As he realized what had been done to it, his impassive face went stony with revulsion. After a moment, he lifted it, hoisting it up and around his shoulders. The snuffling sound came again, this time from the mist-drifted rocks behind him. He looked back. Just the rocks, the fog coiling around them. He moved on—and suddenly the scraping noise broke out, close by, all around him, moving with him as he moved. Aware of it, he didn't hurry, but maintained his pace, measured, controlled. Below him now he could see the *Galileo*, its terrified people huddled together at the hatch, watching him.

He reached them just as a spear clanged harmlessly against the ship's hull. McCoy and Boma ran to him to help him enter the hatch. Inside, McCoy reached toward the body's lolling head. "Is he. . . ?"

"Mr. Boma, secure that hatch!" Spock said. He walked swiftly toward the aft compartment. McCoy followed him and eased the body from his shoulders. Boma, up forward near the hatch window, called, "I see one out there!" Yeoman Mears, joining him, peered out the window. Shuddering, she covered her face with her hands. "Horrible . . . it's a monster. . . ."

Boma, patting her shoulder, managed a wry grin. "We probably don't look so good to them, either."

Spock had gone to the forward window to look out of it. Something crashed against the hull. A great boulder tumbled past the window and rolled away to crash up against the side of the crater.

"All right, Spock," Boma said. "You have the answers. What now?"

Spock turned. "Your tone is hostile, Mr. Boma."

"My tone isn't the only thing that's hostile!"

"Strange," Spock mused. "Step by step I have done the logical thing."

McCoy blew up. "A little less analysis and a little more action! That's what we need!"

"How about analyzing what's happening to the plates of this craft?"

"The plates are titanite, Mr. Boma," Spock said. "They will hold. At least for a time."

"We have phasers. We could drive them off!"

"Mr. Boma, every ounce of energy in the phasers is needed by Mr. Scott. Were we to attack the creatures, the energy expended might well provide the very impetus required to secure our orbit."

The ship shook under another smash by a boulder—a bigger one, heavier, harder.

"How long, Mr. Scott?" Spock asked.

"Another hour. Maybe two."

"Can't you hurry it up?"

Scott raised an impatient face from his labor. "Doctor, a phaser will drain only so fast."

A steady, relentless hammering had begun on the hull. Boma, looking up, saw its plates vibrating. "How long can those plates hold out under *that*?" he cried. *"We've got to do something!"*

All eyes were on Spock. He met them directly, his own calm, as composed as though theirs contained no accusation.

Kirk lacked Spock's stoic capacity to tolerate helplessness. Though the ion storm was dispersing, the starship's slow recovery of its operational power had tightened his nerves to the breaking point. He snapped at Uhura. "Lieutenant, what word from the sensor section?"

"At last report they were beginning to get readings, but they were completely scrambled."

"I'm not interested in the last report! I want the current one!"

"Yes, sir."

Kirk slammed his fist into his palm. When the elevator door opened, he didn't turn his head. He heard Ferris clear his throat. Then he was beside him, glancing ostentatiously at his watch. "You have three hours, Captain."

"I know the number of hours I have, Commissioner."

"Delighted to hear it. However, I shall continue to remind you."

"You do that," Kirk said.

Uhura spoke. "Sir, sensor section reporting. Static interference still creating false images. Estimate 80 percent undependable."

"Radio communication?"

"Clearing slowly but still incapable of transmission and reception."

"What do you intend to do?" demanded Ferris.

Kirk's overstrained control broke. "Do? I'll keep on searching, foot by foot, inch by inch . . . by candlelight if I have to, so long as I have a second left! And if you'll keep your nose off my bridge, I'll be thankful!"

"I'm sure your diligence will please the authorities,

Captain. I am not sure they will appreciate the way you address a High Commissioner."

"I am in command here!"

"You are, Captain. For exactly—" he consulted his watch—"two hours and forty-two minutes."

Spock slammed no fist into his palm. The hammering by great rocks continued to shake the *Galileo*—but his Vulcan heritage forbade any release of tension building up in him. Boma's panic had now taken the form of an open scorn. Nor was there the slightest sign of sympathy in the others. Never had the half-human in Spock felt so lonely. But he gave no evidence of it as he said, "Mr. Scott, how much power do we have in our central batteries?"

"They're in good shape, sir. But they won't lift us off, if that's what you're getting at."

"Are they strong enough to electrify the exterior of the ship?"

A slow grin spread over Scott's face. "That they are, laddie." Reaching for some cables, he detached them.

Spock spoke to the others. "Get into the center of the ship. Don't touch the plates. Be sure you're insulated."

They obeyed, watching as Scott clamped an electrode to a metal projection on one side of the ship's interior. He was preparing the second electrode when a ferocious smash-down resounded from over their heads. Scott nodded at Spock.

"Stand by," Spock said.

The second electrode, attached, completed the circuit. Sparks flew up in a shower, followed by a wild shrieking of pain, shock and fury from outside the craft. The hammering stopped. Scott, releasing the electrodes, said, "I don't dare use any more power if we want to be sure of ignition."

Staring up at the silent hull, McCoy said, "It worked."

"For the moment," Spock said.

"For the moment?"

"Mr. Boma, they will return when they discover they're not seriously hurt. In the meantime, please check the aft compartment. See if there's anything else we can unload to lighten the ship."

Boma came back, grim-faced. "Gaetano's body is there."

''It will have to be left behind,'' Spock said.

''Not without a burial!''

''I would not recommend one, Mr. Boma. The creatures won't be far away.'' He paused. ''A burial would expose the members of this crew to unnecessary peril.''

''I'll take that chance,'' Boma said.

Spock looked at the alien human. ''Do your vestigial ceremonies mean that much to you?''

''Spock, I would insist on a decent burial even if it were your body lying back there!''

''Mr. Boma!'' It was McCoy's rebuke.

Boma whirled on him. ''I'm sick and tired of this Vulcan machine!''

Scott had reddened with anger. ''That's enough from you! Mr. Spock is a ranking Commander of the service!''

The ranking Commander spoke quietly. ''You shall have your burial, Mr. Boma . . . if our friends permit it.'' McCoy, still smarting in Spock's behalf, moved over to him.

Landing party Two had beamed back to the *Enterprise* from Taurus II with casualties—one crewman dead, two wounded.

''Lieutenant Kelowitz, what happened?''

Kirk had activated the computer screen at Spock's station. Now it held the smudged, scratched image of the landing party's leader. Kirk could see that his uniform was torn.

''We were attacked, sir. Huge, furry creatures. I checked with astral anthropology. Order 480G, anthropoid, similar to life forms discovered on Hansen's planet—but much larger. Ten, twelve feet in height . . .''

''Your casualties?''

''Ensign O'Neill was speared even before we knew they were around. Crewman Immamaura has a dislocated shoulder and severe lacerations, but he'll make it all right.'' The tired eyes on the screen were lost momentarily to horrified recollection of the monster anthropoids. ''Captain, they're all over the place. If the *Galileo* is down on that planet . . .''

Kirk nodded. ''Thank you, Lieutenant. You'd better report to Sickbay yourself.''

''Aye, aye, sir.''

The image faded—and Ferris strode out of the elevator,

his jaw set. ''Captain Kirk, if you will check your chronometer, you will see it is exactly 2823.8. Your time is up.''

''Commissioner, my men are still out there,'' Kirk said.

''So are the plague victims on New Paris! I now assume the authority granted me under Title Fifteen, Galactic Emergency Procedures. I order you to abandon search, Captain.''

Kirk said, ''Shuttlecraft *Columbus* hasn't returned yet. I also have two search parties still out.''

''You have your orders, Captain. Recall your search parties and proceed to Makus III immediately.''

He was beaten.

His voice was inflectionless as he spoke to Uhura. ''Lieutenant, order the Transporter Room to beam up the search parties still on the surface. Attempt contact with the *Columbus*.''

''I'm in partial contact with them now, sir.''

''Have them return at once.'' He left the computer station to return to his command chair. ''Mr. Sulu, prepare to abandon search. Set course for Makus III.''

Ferris left the bridge—and Kirk slumped back in his chair. There was nothing more to do, nothing more to say. Spock, McCoy, Scott—all dead, mercifully dead on that savage planet. Had their deaths been easy? Hardly. Uhura had to tell him twice that the sensor beams were working again.

No time to mourn. No time, period.

''The other systems?'' he said to Uhura.

''No, sir. Still too much interference.''

Sulu said, ''Course set for Makus III, Captain.''

''Thank you, Mr. Sulu. Steady on post. Lieutenant Uhura, how long before the *Columbus* comes aboard?''

''Twenty-three minutes, sir.''

''Twenty-three minutes,'' Kirk said. Then, leaning his arms on his console, he cupped his chin in his hands.

Yeoman Mears, no longer fresh-faced, but tired and worn, had failed again to contact the *Enterprise*. She snapped closed her communicator. ''Nothing, sir,'' she told Spock. ''Just ionic interference.''

He went to Scott. ''How about weight?''

Scott finished draining the last phaser. He looked up

as he laid it aside. "If we shed every extra ounce of it, we may be able to achieve orbit."

"How long can we keep it?"

"A few hours. If we time it right, we could cut out of orbit with enough fuel for a controlled re-entry."

"To land here again? Not an attractive possibility."

"We have very few alternatives," Scott said. He stooped to remove the drained phasers from the aisle as Boma and McCoy came from the aft compartment, carrying Gaetano's body.

"How does it look outside?" McCoy asked..

Spock glanced out the forward window. Then he spoke to Scott. "When can we lift off, Mr. Scott?"

"Maybe eight minutes if the weight's right."

Spock faced around from the window. "Doctor, Mr. Boma, the ship will lift off in exactly ten minutes. You have that long to bury Mr. Gaetano. It appears to be all clear outside, at least for the moment." He cautiously opened the hatch, peering around the crater. As he turned back inside, he said, "I shall assist you. Please hurry."

Yeoman Mears moved down the aisle to where Scott, at the control console, was warming up its equipment. "Can we get off?" she said.

"Oh, we can get off all right, lassie. But can we stay off? That's the question."

"If we make orbit, the *Enterprise* will—"

"By now," he said, "the *Enterprise* should be well on its way to Makus III."

"Then . . . we're alone."

"Not alone." He made a gesture toward the crater walls. "We've got some big hairy things out there to keep us company."

It was the thought of the big, hairy things that had brought Kirk to his decision. He uncupped his chin from his hands. "Mr. Sulu, proceed on course as ordered for Makus III. At space normal speed."

Sulu was startled. "But all systems report secured for warp factors, sir. Space normal speed?"

"You heard me, Mr. Sulu. Lieutenant Uhura, order all

sensor sections to direct beams aft, full function, continuous operation until further orders.''

Ferris, the paper man, had not specified warp speed.

They'd dug the grave in the spongy soil. It was as they were filling the hole that they all heard the grating sound. Then from the mist-shrouded rocks above them came a piercing howl—a triumphant roar as though the thing which had uttered it was beating its furry chest in token of victory.

''Into the ship!'' Spock shouted. ''Take-off immediate!''

A spear struck the grave. Another one grazed Boma's shoulder. Then the air was thick with them. Spock, racing toward the ship, saw a large axe of strange shape hit the ground. As he reached for it, a rock, hurtling down, crashed against his thigh. He struggled to rise but the wounded leg went out from under him. Dragging himself toward the ship, he yelled, ''Lift off! Lift off!''

Boma and McCoy were at the open hatch. They left it to run to him. He waved them back furiously. ''No! Get back! *Lift off!*''

They disobeyed. McCoy grabbed his shoulders—and a spear whizzed past his head. Half-carrying half-pulling, they got Spock to the hatch and shoved him inside. Boma slammed it shut just as a giant body heaved at the craft, rocking it.

Spock, clutching his injured leg, glared at his rescuers. ''I told you to lift off!''

McCoy, at work on the leg, said, ''Don't be a fool, Spock. We couldn't leave you out there!'' He paused. Once more, big rocks were hammering at the hull. Spock pushed McCoy away. ''Can we lift off, Mr. Scott?''

''We should be able to—but we're not moving!''

Yeoman Mears screamed. In the port window beside her a bestial face, enormous, red-eyed was peering in at her. McCoy slammed the shutter down over the window. Spock was hobbling toward the console's seat. For a moment his delicate fingers flitted over the controls. ''They seem to be holding us down,'' he said. ''All systems are go—but we're not moving.'' His hand went out to another switch. Appalled, Scott cried, ''What are you doing, man?''

''The boosters.''

''We won't be able to hold orbit!''

Spock moved the switch. The ship bucked. Needles quivered on the console. There was a last defiant crash on the hull, screams of baffled hate—and the *Galileo* shot up and out of the crater.

Yeoman Mears burst into tears of relief. "We're rid of them . . . of that terrible place. . . ."

Spock spoke. "I must remind you all that we have yet to achieve orbit. Nor can we maintain it long. An hour from now we might well be right back where we started."

But Spock's warning couldn't depress the hope roused by the familiar sight of star-filled space. McCoy, thoughtfully regarding the straight back in the console's seat, said, "Spock—back there—what held you back when we were attacked?"

"A most intriguing artifact . . . a hand axe, Doctor, reminiscent of those used by the Lake People of Athos IV."

"Even if you'd gotten it, you couldn't have brought it back with you. It must have weighed a hundred and fifty pounds."

Spock looked around from the console, his face astounded. "You know, Doctor, until this moment, that never occurred to me."

McCoy grunted. "An encouraging sign of humanity. It was a fool thing to do. It almost got you killed. If we hadn't come after you . . ."

"By coming after me you caused a delay in our lift off. So you may well have destroyed what slim chance you have of survival. The logical thing was to leave me behind."

McCoy sighed. "Well, you're back to normal. Remind me to tell you sometime how sick and tired I am of your logic."

"I will, Doctor." He was scanning the console. "Orbit attitude in one minute, Mr. Scott. Fuel status?"

"Fifteen pounds psi. Approximately enough for one complete orbit."

"And after that?" McCoy said.

Scott shook his head. "Tapping those boosters removed our last chance of making a soft landing."

"You mean—a burn-up?" asked Boma.

Spock said, "That is the usual end of a decaying orbit."

McCoy got up and went to him. "Spock, can't we do anything?"

He looked up. "The *Enterprise* is undoubtedly back on course for Makus III. I, for one, do not believe in angels. There won't be one around, Doctor, to bear us up on its wings."

"Well, Spock . . . so ends your first command."

"Yes. My first command."

Scott said, "Orbit attitude attained, Mr. Spock. With present fuel that gives us about forty-five minutes."

But Spock seemed singularly uninterested in the information. Nodding slightly, he stared at the console. Then he slowly turned his head to look at the others. They were all back there in their seats . . . McCoy, the girl, Boma—and Scott, standing by. And all of them, each in his own way, alone with the thought of the final extinction. But their eyes were on him as though he could magically avert it for them. If he'd been a sweating creature, Spock would have been wet with it. Instead, he was a Vulcan by training as well as inheritance, a being required to remain impervious to emotion. Now, in his half-human agony, he took refuge behind a mask of stone. His first and last command. His hand went out toward a switch.

"Spock!" Scott shouted.

He threw the switch. The ship trembled—and a blast of fire burst from its pods.

"What's happened?" cried the girl.

"He's jettisoned the fuel—and ignited it!" Scott yelled.

Boma was on his feet. "Have you gone crazy, Spock?"

"Perhaps, Mr. Boma."

McCoy, licking his lips, girded himself for the question. "Scotty, how long do we have?"

"Six minutes."

At Sulu's cry Kirk turned his pain-drawn face. "Yes, Mr. Sulu?"

"The screen, Captain! Something's back there! At Taurus II!"

The strain had been too much for all of them. Sulu was hallucinating. "The screen," Kirk said. Then he looked at it. "Sensors, Mr. Sulu? A meteorite?"

"No, sir. It's holding a lateral line! There it is again . . . on the screen. Captain, it's holding steady!"

A streak of flame was moving against the blackness of space.

Kirk exploded into action. "One hundred and eighty degrees about, Mr. Sulu! Lieutenant Uhura! Contact Transporter Room! All beams ready! Full normal speed!"

On the screen the flame flickered—and died.

And on the *Galileo* Spock sat unmoving. The heat had begun. He could sense the unbelieving eyes fixed on him—and his Satanic, alien ears. He had destroyed them. He was hardly aware of the hand, the human hand, that suddenly fell on his shoulder.

"Ah, laddie," Scott said, "it was a good gamble. Maybe it was worth it."

Somebody said, "I don't . . . understand."

Scott whirled. "He turned the ship into a distress signal—a flare!"

Spock said, "Even if there's no one out there to see it."

Scott kept the hand on his shoulder. "The orbit's decaying. Thirty-six seconds to atmosphere."

McCoy joined them. "It may be the last action you ever take, Spock—but it was all human."

"Totally illogical, Doctor. There was no chance."

"Which is exactly what I mean," McCoy said.

A whining sound came. A wisp of smoke drifted from the control panel. Spock, reaching up, slid up the metal shutter on the forward window. The *Galileo* was on fire, glowing red to orange to pure white flame. Its prisoners tore at their throats, coughing as the aisle filled with hot smoke.

Kirk, fingers crossed in the old Earth's plea to Lady Luck, said, *"Activate Transporter beams!"*

Then he waited. A sweating creature, he could feel it breaking from every pore of his body. Sulu said, "Whatever it was, Captain, it just burned up in the atmosphere."

"Yes. I can see for myself, Mr. Sulu."

Behind him Uhura leaped from her chair. "Captain! Transporter Room reports five persons aboard! Alive and well!"

"Alive, Lieutenant?"

So the beams had caught them. In the searing heat of

the *Galileo*, they had faded, breaking to the dazzle that had brought them home. Kirk covered his face with his hands. Then he lifted his head. "Mr. Sulu. Proceed on course for Makus III. Warp factor one."

"Aye, aye, sir. Warp factor one."

McCoy was whispering to Kirk. Then they both looked over to the computer station where Spock sat, composed, his eyes intent on his dials.

"Mr. Spock?"

"Yes, Captain."

"When you ignited all your remaining fuel, you knew there was virtually no chance the flame would be seen. But you did it anyhow. Am I correct in defining that as an act of desperation?"

"Yes, Captain."

"Desperation is a highly emotional state of mind. How do you account for it in yourself?"

"Quite simply, sir. I examined the problem from all angles. It was plainly hopeless. Logic informed me that the only possible action would have to be a desperate one. A logical decision, logically arrived at."

"You mean, you reasoned it was time for an emotional outburst?"

"I would not use those terms, sir, but those are essentially the facts."

"You're not going to admit that for once in your life you committed a purely human, emotional act?"

"No, sir."

"Mr. Spock, you are a stubborn man."

"Yes, sir."

Kirk got up, started toward him, thought better of it. Grinning, he shook his head, himself accepting the logic of facts as they were. Spock caught the grin. His left eyebrow lifted.

COURT MARTIAL

Writers: Don M. Mankiewicz and
Steven W. Carabatsos
(Story by Don M. Mankiewicz)
Director: Marc Daniels
Guest stars: Elisha Cook, Richard Webb,
Percy Rodriquez

The *Enterprise* weathered the ion storm somehow, but one man was dead, and damage to the ship was considerable. Kirk was forced to order a nonscheduled layover for repairs at Star Base 11, a huge complex serving the dual role of graving dock and galactic command outpost.

He made a full report to the portmaster, Senior Captain Stone, a craggy Negro who had once been a flight officer himself; Kirk had known him in those days, though not well. The report, of course, had to include an affidavit in the matter of Records Officer Benjamin Finney, deceased, and Kirk turned that in last and only after long study. Stone noticed his hesitation, but was patient. At last he said, "That makes three times you've read it, Captain. Is there an error?"

"No," Kirk said, "but the death of a crewman . . . When you have to sign these affidavits, you relive the moment." He signed the paper and passed it to Stone.

"I know. But you can't fight Regulations. Now, let's see; the extract from your ship's computer log, confirming the deposition?"

"In the other folder."

"Good . . . though it's a great pity too. The service can't afford to lose men like Officer Finney. If he'd only gotten out of the pod in time . . ."

"I waited until the last possible moment," Kirk said. "The storm got worse. We were on double-red alert. I had to jettison."

The office door swung open suddenly. A young woman

was standing there—young, and pretty, but obviously under great stress. She glared wildly at Kirk, who recognized her instantly.

"There you are!" she cried. "I wanted one more good look at you!"

"Jame!"

"Yes, Jame! And you're the man who killed my father!"

"Do you really think that?" Kirk said.

"More than that! I think you deliberately murdered him!"

"Jame, Jame, stop and think what you're saying." Kirk stepped toward her. "We were friends, you know that. I would no more have hurt your father than I'd hurt you."

"Friends! That's a lie! You never were! You hated him, all your life! And you finally killed him!"

Stone, who had been discreetly pretending to study the documents, rose suddenly and moved between them. Jame was obviously fighting back a storm of tears. Kirk watched her in dismay.

"Captain Kirk," Stone said in a voice as hard as his name, "you say you jettisoned the pod *after* the double-red alert?"

"You have my sworn deposition," Kirk said.

"Then, Captain, it is my duty to presume you have committed willful perjury. According to the extract from your computer log, you jettisoned the pod *before* the double-red alert. Consider yourself relieved of command. A board of inquiry will determine whether a general court martial is in order."

Kirk never saw the board. As far as he was concerned, the inquiry consisted of Portmaster Stone and a recorder, which was to produce the tape the board would study.

"Where do you want me to begin?" Kirk said.

Stone pushed a cup of coffee toward Kirk. "Tell me about Officer Finney."

"We'd known each other a long time. He was an instructor at the Academy when I was a midshipman. But that didn't stop us from beginning a close friendship. His daughter, Jame, the girl who was in your office last night, was named after me."

"The friendship—it rather cooled with the years, didn't it? No, please speak, Captain, the recorder can't see you nodding."

"Yes, it did. I relieved him on watch once, on the USS *Republic*, and found the vent circuit to the fusion chamber open. If we'd gone under fusion power, the ship would have blown. As it was, it was contaminating the air of the engine room. I closed the switch and logged the error. He drew a reprimand and went to the bottom of the promotion list."

"And he blamed you for that?"

"Yes. He'd been kept on at the Academy as an instructor for an unusually long time. As a result, he was late being assigned to a starship. He felt the delay looked bad on his record. My action, he believed, made things worse. However, I couldn't very well have let an oversight of that magnitude go unreported."

"Comment by examining officer: Service record of Officer Finney to be appended to this transcript. Now, Captain, let's get to the specifics of the storm."

"Weatherscan indicated an ion storm dead ahead," Kirk said. "I sent Finney into the pod." For the benefit of possible civilians on the board, Kirk added, "The pod is outside the ship, attached to the skin. One of our missions is to get radiation readings in abnormal conditions, including ion storms. This can only be done by direct exposure of the necessary instruments in a plastic pod. However, in a major storm the pod rapidly picks up a charge of its own that becomes a danger to the rest of the ship, and we have to get rid of it."

"Why Finney? If he blamed you . . ."

"He may have blamed me because he never rose to command rank. But I don't assign jobs on the basis of who blames me, but whose name is on top of the duty roster. It was Finney's turn. He had just checked in with me when we hit the leading edge of the storm. Not bad at first. Then we began encountering field-variance, force two. The works. I finally signaled a double-red alert. Finney knew he had only a matter of seconds. I gave him those seconds, and more—but it wasn't enough. I can't explain his not getting out. He had the training, he had the reflexes, and he had plenty of time.''

''Then why, Captain,'' Stone said, ''does the computer log—yours, made automatically at the time—indicate that there was no double-red alert when you jettisoned?''

''I don't know,'' Kirk said.

''Could the computer be wrong?''

''Mr. Spock, my first officer, is running a survey now,'' Kirk said grimly. ''But the odds are next to impossible.''

Stone looked at Kirk long and penetratingly, and then reached out and shut off the recorder. ''I'm not supposed to do this,'' he said, ''But—look, Kirk. Not one man in a million can do what you and I did: serve as a starship captain. A hundred decisions a day, hundreds of lives staked on every one of them being right. You've been out nineteen months on this last mission. You've taken no furlough, had virtually no rest in all that time. You're played out—exhausted.''

Kirk was beginning to get the drift of this, and he did not like it. ''That's the way you see it?''

''That's the way my report will read,'' Stone said, ''if you cooperate.''

''Physical breakdown,'' Kirk said. ''Possibly even mental collapse.''

''Well . . . yes.''

''I'd be admitting that a man died because . . .''

''Admit nothing,'' Stone said. ''Let me bury the matter, here and now. No starship captain has ever stood trial before. I don't want you to be the first.''

''But what if I'm guilty?'' Kirk said steadily. ''Shouldn't I be punished?''

''I'm thinking of the service, dammit! I won't have it smeared by . . .''

''By what, Portmaster?''

''All right!'' Stone said explosively. ''By an evident perjurer who's covering up bad judgment, cowardice, or something even worse!''

''That's as far as you go, Captain,'' Kirk said, instantly on his feet, ''or I'll forget you *are* a captain. I'm telling you, I was on that bridge. I know what happened. I know what I did.''

''It's in the transcript,'' Stone said, equally hotly, ''and computer transcripts don't lie. You decide, Captain. Bury the matter and accept a ground assignment—or demand a general court, and bring down on your head the full disciplinary powers of Star Fleet."

"I have already decided," Kirk said. "Turn the recorder back on."

The courtroom was stark. There was one main viewing screen, a recorder, a witness chair, one table each for prosecution and defense, and a high bench where sat Portmaster Stone and the three members of the court-martial board. The prosecutor was a cool, lovely blonde woman named Areel Shaw, who as it happened was an old friend of Kirk's. ("All my old friends look like doctors," Bones McCoy had commented, "and all Jim's old friends look like her.") It was on her advice that Kirk had retained Samuel T. Cogley, a spry old eccentric who put his trust not in computers, but in books. He did not inspire much confidence, though Kirk was convinced that Areel had meant well.

Stone called the court to order by striking an ancient naval ship's bell. "I declare that the General Court of Star Base Eleven is now in session. Captain James T. Kirk will rise. Charge: culpable negligence. Specification: in that, on Star Date 2947.3, by such negligence, you did cause loss of life, to wit, the life of Records Officer Benjamin Finney. Charge: conduct prejudicial to the good order of the service. Specification: in that, thereafter, you failed accurately to report the same incident in your captain's log. To these charges and specifications, how do you plead?"

"Not guilty," Kirk said quietly.

"I have appointed, as members of this court, Space Command Representative Chandra and Star Command Captains Li Chow and Krasnowsky. I direct your attention to the fact that you have a right to ask for substitute officers if you feel that any of these named harbor prejudice harmful to your case."

"I have no objections, sir."

"And do you consent to the service of Lieutenant Shaw as prosecuting officer, and to my own service as chief judge?"

"Yes, sir."

"Lieutenant Shaw," Stonc said, "you may proceed."

Areel Shaw stepped into the arena. "I call Mr. Spock."

Spock took the stand and passed to the recorder attendant his identity disk. The recorder promptly said: "Spock, S-179-276-SP. Service rank: commander. Position: first officer, science officer. Current assignment: USS *Enterprise*. Commendations: Vulcan scientific Legion of Honor. Awards of valor: twice decorated by Galactic Command."

"Mr. Spock," Areel Shaw said, "as a science officer, you know a great deal about computers, don't you?"

"I know all about them," Spock said levelly.

"Do you know of any possible malfunction that would cause one to recall an event inaccurately?"

"No."

"Or any malfunction that *has* caused an inaccuracy in *this* one?"

"No. Nevertheless, it is inaccurate."

"Please explain."

"It reports," Spock said, "that the jettison button was pressed before the double-red alert—in other words, that Captain Kirk was reacting to an emergency that did not then exist. That is not only illogical, but impossible."

"Were you watching him the exact moment he pressed the button?"

"No. I was occupied. We were already at red-alert."

"Then how can you dispute the record of the log?"

"I do not dispute it," Spock said. "I merely state it to be wrong. I know the captain. He would not . . ."

"Captain Stone," Areel Shaw said, "please instruct the witness not to speculate."

"Sir," Spock said to Stone, "I am half Vulcan. Vulcans do not speculate. I speak from pure logic. If I let go of a hammer on a high-gravity planet, I do not need to see it fall to know that it has fallen. Human beings have characteristics that determine their behavior just as inanimate objects do. I say it is illogical for Captain Kirk to have reacted to an emergency that did not exist, and impossible for him to act out of panic or malice. That is not his nature."

"In your opinion," Areel Shaw said.

"Yes," Spock said with obvious reluctance. "In my opinion."

The personnel officer of the *Enterprise* was called next.

"With reference to Records Officer Finney," Areel asked him, "was there, in his service record, a report of disciplinary action for failure to close a circuit?"

"Yes, ma'am," the P.O. said.

"This charge was based upon a log entry by the officer who relieved him. Who was that officer?"

"Ensign James T. Kirk," the P.O. said softly.

"Speak louder, for the recorder, please. That is now the Captain Kirk who sits in this courtroom?"

"Yes, ma'am."

"Thank you. Your witness, Mr. Cogley."

"No questions," Cogley said.

Areel next called Bones McCoy to the stand, and went after him with cool efficiency. "Doctor, you are, on the record, an expert in psychology, especially in space psychology—patterns that develop in the close quarters of a ship during long voyages in deep space."

"I know something about it."

"Your academic record, and your experience, doctor, belie your modesty. Is it possible that Officer Finney blamed the defendant for the incident we have just heard your personnel officer describe—blamed him and hated him for being passed over for promotion, blamed him for never having been given a command of his own, hated him for having to serve under him?"

"Of course, it's possible," McCoy said.

"Then, isn't it also possible that all that hatred, directed against Captain Kirk, could have caused a like response in the captain?"

"You keep asking what's possible," McCoy said. "To the human mind almost anything is possible. The fact, however, is that I have never observed such an attitude in Captain Kirk."

"What about an attitude generated in his subconscious mind?"

"I object!" Sam Cogley said. "Counsel is leading the witness into making unprovable subjective speculations."

"On the contrary, your honor," Areel said. "I am asking a known expert in psychology for an expert psychological opinion."

"Objection overruled," Stone said. "You may proceed."

"Captain Kirk, then," Areel said relentlessly, "could have become prejudiced against Officer Finney without having been aware of it—prejudiced in such a way that his judgment became warped. Is that *theoretically* possible, doctor?"

"Yes," McCoy said, "it's possible. But highly unlikely."

"Thank you. Your witness, Mr. Cogley."

"No questions."

"Then I call James T. Kirk."

When Kirk's identity disc was placed in the recorder, the machine said: "Kirk, SC-937-0176-CEC. Service rank: captain. Position: starship command. Current assignment: USS *Enterprise*. Commendations: Palm leaf of Axanar peace mission. Grankite order of tactics, class of excellence. Pentares ribbon of commendation, classes first and second . . ."

"May it please the court," Areel Shaw said. The recorder attendant shut off the machine. "The prosecution concedes the inestimable record of Captain Kirk, and asks consent that it be entered as if read."

"Mr. Cogley," Stone said. "do you so consent?"

Cogley smiled disarmingly, stretched a bit in his chair, and rose. "Well, sir," he said, "I wouldn't want to be the one to slow the wheels of progress. On the other hand, I wouldn't want those wheels to run over my client in their unbridled haste. May I point out, sir, that this is a *man* we are examining, so perhaps a little longer look would not be amiss. The court's convenience is important, but his *rights* are paramount."

"Continue," Stone told the recorder attendant. The machine said:

"Awards of valor: Medal of Honor, silver palm with cluster. Three times wounded, honor roll. Galactic citation for conspicuous gallantry. Karagite Order of Heroism . . ."

It took quite a long time, during which Areel Shaw looked at the floor. Kirk could not tell whether she was fuming at having been outmaneuvered, or was simply ashamed of the transparency of her trick. Doubtless she did not want the court to be able to tell, either.

"Now, Captain. Despite the record, you continue to

maintain that there was a double-red alert before you jettisoned the pod?''

''Yes, ma'am. There was.''

''And you cannot explain why the computer record shows otherwise.''

''No, I cannot.''

''And in fact you'd do it again under the same circumstances.''

''Objection!'' Cogley said. ''Counsel is now asking the witness to convict himself in advance of something he hasn't done yet and, we maintain, didn't do in the past!''

''It's all right, Sam,'' Kirk said. ''I'm willing to answer. Lieutenant Shaw, I have been trained to command. The training doesn't sharpen a man's verbal skills. But it does sharpen his sense of duty—and confidence in himself to discharge that duty.''

''May it please the court,'' Areel Shaw said, ''I submit that the witness is not being responsive.''

''He's answering the question,'' Stone said, ''and he has a right to explain his answers. Proceed, Captain Kirk.''

''Thank you, sir. We were in the worst kind of ion storm. And I was in command. I made a judgment—a command judgment. And because it was necessary to make that judgment, a man died. But the lives of my entire crew and my ship were in danger, and *not* to have made that judgment, to wait, to have been indecisive when it was time to act, would in my mind have been criminal. I did not act out of panic, or malice. I did what I was duty-bound to do. And of course, Lieutenant Shaw, I would do it again; that is the responsibility of command.''

There was a brief hush. Areel Shaw broke it at last, turning to Stone.

''Your honor, the prosecution does not wish to dishonor this man. But I must invite the court's attention now to the visual playback of the log extract of the *Enterprise*'s computer.''

''It is so ordered.''

The main viewing screen lit up. When it was over, Areel Shaw said, almost sadly, ''If the court will notice the scene upon which we froze, the screen plainly shows the defendant's finger pressing the jettison button. The condition signal reads RED-ALERT. Not double red—but simply red. When the pod containing Officer Finney was jettisoned, the emergency did not as yet exist.

"The prosecution rests."

Thunderstruck, Kirk stared at the screen. He had just seen the impossible.

During the recess, Sam Cogley calmly leafed through legal books in the room assigned to them, while Kirk paced the floor in anger and frustration.

"I know what I did!" Kirk said. "That computer report is an outright impossibility."

"Computers don't lie," Cogley said.

"Sam, are you suggesting *I* did?"

"I'm suggesting that maybe you did have a lapse. It's possible, with the strain you were under. Jim, there's still time to change our plea. I could get you off."

"Two days ago, I would have staked my life on my judgment."

"You did. Your professional life."

"I know what I did," Kirk said, spacing each word. "But if you want to pull out . . ."

"There's nowhere to go," Cogley said. "Except back into court in half an hour. The verdict's a foregone conclusion, unless we change our plea."

Kirk's communicator beeped and he took it out. "Kirk here."

"Captain," Spock's voice said, "I have run a full survey on the computer."

"I'll tell you what you found," Kirk said. "Nothing."

"You sound bitter."

"Yes, Mr. Spock. I am. But not so bitter as to fail to thank you for your efforts."

"My duty, Captain. Further instructions?" There actually seemed to be emotion in Spock's voice, but if he felt any such stirring, he was unable to formulate it.

"No. I'm afraid you'll have to find yourself a new chess partner, Mr. Spock. Over and out."

Cogley gathered up an armful of books and started for the door. "I've got to go to a conference in chambers with Stone and Shaw."

"Look," Kirk said. "What I said before—I was a little worked up. You did the best you could."

Cogley nodded and opened the door. Behind it, her arm raised to knock, was Jame Finney.

"Jame!" Kirk said. "Sam, this is Officer Finney's daughter."

"A pleasure," Cogley said.

"Mr. Cogley," she said, "you have to stop this. Make him change his plea. Or something. Anything. I'll help if I can."

Sam Cogley looked slightly perplexed, but he said only, "I've tried."

"It's too late for anything like that, Jame," Kirk said. "But I appreciate your concern."

"It can't be too late. Mr. Cogley, my father's dead. Ruining Jim won't bring him back."

"That's a commendable attitude, Miss Finney," Cogley said. "But a little unusual, isn't it? After all, Captain Kirk is accused of *causing* your father's death."

"I was . . ." Jame said, and stopped. She seemed suddenly nervous. "I was just thinking of Jim."

"Thank you, Jame," Kirk said. "But I'm afraid we've had it. You'd better go."

When the door closed, Cogley put his books down. "How well do you know that girl?" he said.

"Since she was a child."

"Hmm. I suppose that might explain her attitude. Curious, though. Children don't usually take such a dispassionate view of the death of a parent."

"Oh, she didn't at first. She was out for my blood. Almost hysterical. Charged into Stone's office calling me a murderer."

"Why didn't you tell me that before?"

"Why," Kirk said, "the subject never came up. Is it important?"

"I don't know," Cogley said thoughtfully. "It's—a false note, that's all. I don't see what use we could put it to now."

Stone rang the court to order. He had hardly done so when Spock and McCoy materialized squarely in the midst of the room—a hair-raising precise piece of transporter work.

They moved directly to Kirk and Cogley; the latter stood and Spock whispered to him urgently.

"Mr. Cogley," Stone said harshly, "what's the meaning of this display?"

"May it please the court," Mr. Cogley said, "we mean no disrespect, but these officers have unearthed new evidence, and they could conceive of no way to get it to the court in time but by this method."

"The counsel for the defense," Areel Shaw said, "has already rested his case. Mr. Cogley is well-known for his theatrics . . ."

"Is saving an innocent man's life a theatric?" He turned to Stone. "Sir, my client has been deprived of one of his most important rights in this trial—the right to be confronted by the witnesses against him. *All* the witnesses, your honor. And the most devastating witness against my client is not a human being, but an information system—a machine."

"The excerpt from the computer log has been shown."

"Your honor, a log excerpt is not the same as the machine that produced it. I ask that this court adjourn and reconvene on board the *Enterprise* itself."

"I object, your honor," Areel Shaw said. "He's trying to turn this into a circus."

"Yes!" Cogley said. "A circus! Do you know what the first circus was, Lieutenant Shaw? An arena, where men met danger face to face, and lived or died. This is indeed a circus. In this arena, Captain Kirk will live or die, for if you take away his command he will be a dead man. But he has not met his danger face to face. He has the right to confront his accuser, and it matters nothing that his accuser is a machine. If you do not grant him that right, you have not only placed us on a level with the machine—you have elevated the machine above us! Unless I am to move for a mistrial, I ask that my motion be granted. But more than that, gentlemen: In the name of humanity fading in the shadow of the machine, I demand it. I demand it!"

The members of the board put their heads together. At last Stone said: "Granted."

"Mr. Spock," Cogley said. "How many chess games did you play with the computer during recess?"

"Five."

"And the outcome?"

"I won them all."

"May that be considered unusual, Mr. Spock, and if so, why?"

"Because I myself programmed the computer to play chess. It knows my game; and as has been observed before, it cannot make an error. Hence, even if I myself never make an error, the best I can hope to achieve against it is a stalemate. I have been able to win against Captain Kirk now and then, but against the computer, never—until now. It therefore follows that someone has adjusted either the chess programming or the memory banks. The latter would be the easier task."

"I put it to you, Mr. Spock, that even the latter would be beyond the capacity of most men, isn't that so? Well, then, what men, aboard ship, would it *not* be beyond?"

"The captain, myself—and the Records Officer."

"Thank you, you may step down. I now call Captain Kirk. Captain, describe what steps you took to find Officer Finney after the storm."

"When he did not respond to my call," Kirk said, "I ordered a phase-one search for him. Such a search assumes that its object is injured and unable to respond to the search party."

"It also presupposes that the man *wishes to be found*?"

"Of course, Sam."

"Quite. Now, with the court's permission, although Mr. Spock is now in charge of this ship, I am going to ask Captain Kirk to describe what Mr. Spock has done, to save time, which you will see in a moment is a vital consideration. May I proceed?"

"Well . . . All right."

"Captain?"

"Mr. Spock has ordered everybody but the members of this court and the command crew to leave the ship. This includes the engine crew. Our impulse engines have been shut down and we are maintaining an orbit by momentum alone."

"And when the orbit begins to decay?" Stone said.

"We hope to be finished before that," Cogley said.

"But that is the vital time element I mentioned. Captain, is there any other step Mr. Spock has taken?"

"Yes, he has rigged an auditory sensor to the log computer. In effect, it will now be able to hear—as will we—every sound occurring on this ship."

"Thank you. Dr. McCoy to the stand, please. Doctor, I see you have a small device with you. What is it, please?"

"It is a white-noise generator."

"I see. All right, Mr. Spock."

At the console, Spock turned a switch. The bridge at once shuddered to an intermittent pounding, like many drums being beaten.

"Could you reduce the volume a little?" Cogley said. "Thank you. Your honor, that sound is caused by the heartbeats of all the people in this room. With your permission, I am going to ask Dr. McCoy to take each person's pulse, and then use the white-noise device to mask those pulsebeats out, so they will be eliminated from the noise we are hearing."

"What is the purpose of this rigmarole, your honor?" Areel Shaw demanded.

"I think you suspect that as well as I do, Lieutenant," Stone said. "Proceed, Dr. McCoy."

As Bones moved from person to person, the eerie multiple thumping became simpler, softer.

"That's all," McCoy said.

No one breathed. Finally, somewhere, one beat still sounded.

"May it please the court," Cogley said quietly, "the remaining pulse you hear, I think we will shortly find, is that of Officer Finney. Mr. Spock, can you localize it?"

"B deck, between sections 18Y and 27D. I have already sealed off that section."

Kirk hesitated, then came to a decision. "Captain Stone," he said, "this is my problem. I would appreciate it if no one would leave the bridge."

As he turned to leave, Spock handed him a phaser. "The weapons room is within those quadrants, sir," he said quietly. "He may be armed. This is already set on stun."

"Thank you, Mr. Spock."

• • •

He moved cautiously down the corridor in the sealed section, calling at intervals:

"All right, Ben. It's all over. Ben! Officer Finney!"

For a while there was no answer. Then, suddenly, a figure stepped out of a shadow, phaser leveled.

"Hello, Captain," Officer Finney said.

Kirk found that he could not answer. Though he had been sure that this was the solution, the emotional impact of actually being face to face with the "dead" man was unexpectedly powerful. Finney smiled a hard smile.

"Nothing to say, Captain?"

"Yes," Kirk said. "I'm glad to see you alive."

"You mean you're relieved because your precious career is saved. Well, you're wrong. You've just made things worse for everyone."

"Put the phaser down, Ben. Why go on with it?"

"You wouldn't leave it alone," Finney said. "You've taken away my choices. Officers and gentlemen, commanders all . . . except for Finney and his one mistake. A long time ago, but they don't forget. No, they never forget."

"Ben, I logged that mistake of yours. Blame me, not them."

"But they're to blame," Finney said. "All of them. I was a good officer. I really was. I loved the service like no man ever did."

Slowly, Kirk began to move in on him.

"Stand back, Captain. No more—I warn you—"

"You're sick, Ben. We can help you—"

"One more step—"

Suddenly, Jame's voice cried down the corridor, "Father! *Father!*"

Finney's head jerked around. With a quick lunge, Kirk knocked the phaser from his hand. At the same moment, Jame appeared, rushing straight into the distraught man's arms.

"Jame!"

"It's all right, father," she said, moving her hand over the tortured officer's brow. "It's all right."

"Don't, Jame," he said. "You've got to understand. I had to do it . . . after what they did to me . . ."

"Excuse me," Kirk said. "But if we don't get this ship back under power, we'll all be dead."

"Mr. Cogley," Stone said, "while this trial is obviously not over yet, I think we must congratulate you and Mr. Spock and Dr. McCoy for a truly classical piece of detective work. Would you tell us, please, how the idea that Officer Finney was still alive even entered your head?"

"I began to suspect that, your honor, when Captain Kirk told me about the change of heart Officer Finney's daughter had had about the captain. If she knew he wasn't dead, she had no reason to blame the Captain for anything."

"But how could she know that?" Stone asked.

"She had been reading her father's papers. Perhaps she didn't know the facts, but the general tone of what he had written must have gotten through to her. A man suffering delusions of persecution wants to set down his complaints. She read them; she knew from childhood the kind of man the captain is; and she's fundamentally fair and decent."

He paused and looked soberly over toward Kirk.

"Or maybe," he said, "it was just instinct. Thank God, there's that much of the animal left in us. Whatever it was, the result is that she now has back both her father and her childhood friend."

"Her father," Stone said, "will also have to stand trial."

"I know that," Cogley said quietly. "I ask the court to appoint me his defense counsel. And off the record, your honor, I have the feeling I'll win."

"Off the record," Stone said, "I wouldn't be a bit surprised."

THE MENAGERIE*

Writer: Gene Roddenberry
Directors: Marc Daniels (Part I), Robert Butler (Part II)
Guest Stars: Jeffrey Hunter, Susan Oliver, Malachi Throne

*As originally produced, this story ran in two parts. The main story, which takes place so far back in the history of the *Enterprise* that the only familiar face aboard her then was Spock, appeared surrounded by and intercut with an elaborate "framing" story, in which Spock is up for court-martial on charges of mutiny and offers the main story as an explanation of his inarguably mutinous behavior. Dramatically, this was highly effective—indeed, as I've already noted, it won a "Hugo" award in this category for that year—but told as fiction, it involves so many changes of viewpoint, as well as so many switches from present to past, that it becomes impossibly confusing. (I know—I've tried!) Hence

When the distress signal from Talos IV came through, via old-fashioned radio, Captain Christopher Pike was of two minds about doing anything about it. The message said it was from survivors of the SS *Columbia*, and a library search by Spock showed that a survey ship of that name had indeed disappeared in that area—eighteen years ago. It had taken all of those years for the message, limited to the speed of light, to reach the *Enterprise*, which passed through its wave-front just slightly eighteen light-years from the Talos system. A long time ago, that had been.

In addition, Pike had his own crew to consider. Though the *Enterprise* had come out of the fighting around Rigel VIII—her maiden battle—unscarred, the ground skirmishing had not been as kind to her personnel. Spock, for example, was limping, though he was trying to minimize it, and Navigator Jose Tyler's left forearm was bandaged down to his palm. Pike himself was unhurt, but he felt desperately tired.

Nevertheless, the library also reported Talos IV to be habitable, so survivors from the *Columbia* might still be alive;

the present version adapts only the main story, incidentally restoring to it the ending it had—never shown on television—before the frame was grafted onto it. I think the producers also came to feel that the double-plotted version had been a mistake; at least, "The Menagerie" turned out to be the only two-part episode in the entire history of the series.—J.B.

and since the *Enterprise* would be passing within visual scanning distance anyhow, it wouldn't hurt to take a look. The chances of finding anything at this late date . . .

But almost at once, Tyler picked up reflections from the planet's surface whose polarization and scatter pattern indicated large, rounded chunks of metal, which might easily have been parts of a spaceship's hull. Pike ordered the *Enterprise* into orbit.

"I'll want a landing party of six, counting myself. Mr. Tyler, you'll be second in command, and we'll need Mr. Spock too; both of you, see that there's a fresh dressing on your wounds. Also, Dr. Boyce, Chief Garrison and ship's geologist. Number One, you're in command of the *Enterprise* in our absence. Who seconds you now?"

"Yeoman Colt, sir."

Pike hesitated. That this left the bridge dominated by women didn't bother him; female competence to be in Star Fleet had been tested and proven before he had been born. And Pike had the utmost confidence in Number One, ordinarily the ship's helmsman and, after the Rigel affair, the most experienced surviving officer. Slim and dark in a Nile Valley sort of way, she was one of those women who always look the same between the ages of twenty and fifty, but she had a mind like the proverbial steel trap and Pike had never seen her shaken in any situation. Yeoman Colt, however, was a recent replacement, and an unknown quantity. Well, the assignment was likely to prove a routine one, anyhow.

"Very well. We'll beam down to the spot where Mr. Tyler picked up those reflections."

This proved to be on a rocky plateau, not far from an obvious encampment—a rude collection of huts, constructed out of slabs of rock, debris from a spaceship hull, scraps of canvas and other odds and ends. Several fairly old men were visible, all bearded, all wearing stained and tattered garments. One was carrying water; the others were cultivating a plot of orange vegetation. The ingenuity and resolute will which had enabled them to exist for nearly two decades on this forbidding alien world were everywhere evident.

One of them looked up in the direction of the landing

party and froze, clearly unable to believe his eyes. At last he called hoarsely, "Winter! *Look!*"

A second man looked up, and reacted almost as the first had. Then he shouted; "They're men! Human!"

The sound of their voices brought other survivors out of their huts and sheds. The youngest looked to be nearly fifty, but they were tanned, hardened, in extraordinarily good health. The two groups approached each other slowly, solemnly; Pike could almost feel the intensity of emotion. He stepped forward and extended a hand.

"Captain Christopher Pike, United Spaceship *Enterprise.*"

The first survivor to speak mutely accepted Pike's hand, tears on his face. At last he said, with obvious effort, "Dr. Theodore Haskins, American Continent Institute."

"They're *men*! Here to take us back!" the man called Winter said, laughing with sudden relief. "You are, aren't you? Is Earth all right?"

"Same old Earth," Pike said, smiling. "You'll see it before long."

"And you won't believe how fast you can get back," Tyler added. "The time barrier's been broken! Our new ships can . . ."

He broke off, mouth open, staring past Haskins' shoulder. Following the direction of the navigator's gaze, Pike saw standing in a hut doorway a remarkably beautiful young woman. Although her hair was uncombed and awry, her makeshift dress tattered, she looked more like a woodland nymph than the survivor of a harrowing ordeal. Motioning her forward, Haskins said, "This is Vina. Her parents are dead; she was born almost as we crashed."

There were more introductions all around, but Pike found himself almost unable to take his eyes off the girl. Perhaps it was only the contrast she made with the older men, but her young, animal grace was striking. No wonder Tyler had stared.

"No need to prolong this," Pike said. "Collect what personal effects you want to keep and we'll be off. I suggested you concentrate on whatever records you have; the *Enterprise* is amply stocked with necessities, and even some luxuries."

"Extraordinary," Haskins said. "She must be a very big vessel."

"Our largest and most modern type; the crew numbers four hundred and thirty."

Haskins shook his head in amazement and bustled off. Amidst all the activity, Vina approached Pike and drew him a little to one side.

"Captain, may I have a word?"

"Of course, Vina."

"Before we go, there is something you should see. Something of importance."

"Very well. What is it?"

"It's much easier to show than to explain. If you'll come this way . . ."

She led him to a rocky knoll some distance from the encampment, and pointed to the ground at its base. "There it is."

Pike did not know what he had expected—anything from a grave to some sort of alien artifact—but in fact he saw nothing of interest at all, and said so. Vina looked disappointed.

"The angle of the light is probably wrong," she said. "Come around to this side."

They changed places, so that his back was to the knoll, hers to the encampment. As far as Pike could tell, this made no difference.

"I don't understand," he said.

"You will," Vina said, the tone of her voice changing suddenly. "You're a perfect choice."

Pike looked up sharply. As he did so, the girl vanished. It was not the fading dematerialization of the Transporter effect; she simply blinked out as though someone had snapped off a light. With her went all the survivors and their entire encampment, leaving nothing behind but the bare plateau and the stunned men from the *Enterprise*.

There was a hiss behind him and he spun, reaching for his phaser. A cloud of white gas was rolling toward him, through which he could see an oddly shaped portal which, perfectly camouflaged as a part of the rock, had noiselessly opened to reveal the top of a lift shaft. He had an instant's impression of two occupants—small, slim, pale, humanlike creatures with large elongated heads, in shimmering metallic robes; one of them was holding a small cylinder which was still spitting the white spray.

In the same instant, the gas hit him and he was paralyzed, still conscious but unable to move anything but his eyes. The two creatures stepped forward and dragged him into the opening.

"Captain!" Spock's voice shouted in the distance. Then there was the sound of running, suddenly muffled as though the doors had closed again, and then the lift dropped with a hissing *whoosh* like that of a high-speed pneumatic tube. Above, and still more distantly, came the sound of a rock explosion as someone fired a phaser at full power, but the lift simply fell faster.

With it, Pike fell into unconsciousness.

He awoke clawing for his own phaser, a spongelike surface impeding his movements. The gun was gone. Rolling to his feet, he looked around, at the same time reaching next for his communicator. That was gone too; so was his jacket.

He was in a spotless utilitarian enclosure. The spongy surface turned out to belong to a plastic shape, apparently a sort of bed, with a filmy metallic-cloth blanket folded on it. There was also a free-form pool of surging water, with a small drinking container sitting on the floor next to it. A prison cell, clearly; the bars . . .

But there were no bars. The fourth wall was made up entirely of a transparent panel. Pike hurried to it and peered through. He found himself looking up and down a long corridor, faced with similar panels; but they were offset to, rather than facing each other, so that Pike could see into only small angled portions of the two nearest him on the other side.

Some sound he had made must have penetrated into the corridor, for suddenly there was a wild snarl, and in the cell—cage?—to his left, a flat creature, half anthropoid, half spider, rushed hungrily at him, only to be thrown back, its ugly fangs clattering against the transparency. Startled, Pike looked to the right; in this enclosure he could see a portion of some kind of tree. Then there was a leathery flapping, and an incredibly thin humanoid/bird creature came into view, peering curiously but shyly toward Pike's cage. The instant it saw Pike watching, it whirled and vanished.

As it did, a group of the pale, large-headed men like those who had kidnapped him came into view, coming toward him. They were lead by one who wore an authoritative-looking jeweled pendant on a short chain around his neck. They all came to a halt in front of Pike's cage, silently watching him. He studied them in turn. They were quite bald, all of them, and each had a prominent vein across his forehead.

Finally, Pike said, "Can you hear me? My name is Christopher Pike, commander of the vessel *Enterprise* of the United Federation of Planets. Our intentions are peaceful. Can you understand me?"

The large forehead vein of one of the Talosians pulsed strong and, although Pike could see no lip movement, a voice sounded in his head, a voice that sounded as though it were reciting something.

"It appears, Magistrate, that the intelligence of the specimen is shockingly limited."

Now the forehead of the creature with the pendant pulsed. "This is no surprise, since his vessel was lured here so easily with a simulated message. As you can read in its thoughts, it is only now beginning to suspect that the survivors and the encampment were a simple illusion we placed in their minds. And you will note the confusion as it reads our thought transmissions . . ."

"All right, telepathy," Pike broke in. "You can read my mind, I can read yours. Now, unless you want my ship to consider capturing me an unfriendly act . . ."

"You now see the primitive fear-threat reaction. The specimen is about to boast of his strength, the weaponry of his vessel, and so on." As Pike stepped back a pace and tensed himself, the Magistrate added, "Next, frustrated into a need to display physical prowess, the creature will throw himself against the transparency."

Pike, his act predicted in mid-move, felt so foolish that he canceled it, which made him angrier than ever. He snarled, "There's a way out of every cage,and I'll find it."

"Despite its frustration, the creature appears more adaptable than our specimens from other planets," the Magistrate continued. "We can soon begin the experiment."

Pike wondered what they meant by *that*, but it was already obvious that they were not going to pay any attention to anything he said. He began to pace. The telepathic "voices" continued behind him.

"Thousands of us are now probing the creature's thoughts, Magistrate. We find excellent memory capacity."

"I read most strongly a recent struggle in which it fought to protect its tribal system. We will begin with this, giving the specimen something more interesting to protect."

The cage vanished.

He was standing alone among rocks and strange vegetation which, on second look, proved to be vaguely familiar. Then an unmistakably familiar voice sounded behind him.

"Come. Hurry!"

He turned to see Vina, her hair long and in braids, dressed like a peasant girl of the terrestrial Middle Ages. Behind her towered a fortress which he might have taken as belonging to the same period had he not recognized it instantly. The girl pointed to it and said, "It is deserted. There will be weapons, perhaps food."

"This is Rigel VIII," Pike said slowly. "I fought in that fortress just two weeks ago. But where do you fit in?"

There was a distant bellowing sound. Vina started, then began walking rapidly toward the fortress. Pike remained where he was.

I was in a cell, a cage in some kind of zoo. I'm still *there. I just* think *I see this. They must have reached into my mind, taken the memory of somewhere I've been, something that's happened to me—except that she wasn't in it then.*

The bellowing sounded again, nearer. Pike hurried after the girl, catching up with her just inside the gateway to the fortress' courtyard. The place was a scatter of battered shields, lance staves, nicked and snapped swords; there was even a broken catapult—the debris that had been left behind after Pike's own force had breached and reduced the fortress. Breaking the Kalars' hold over their serfs had been a bloody business, and made more so by the hesitancy of Star Fleet Command over whether the whole operation was not in violation of General Order Number One. Luckily, the Kalars themselves had solved that by swarming in from Rigel X in support of their degenerate colony . . .

And that animal roar of rage behind them could only be a stray Kalar colonist, seeking revenge for the fall of his fortress and his feudalism upon anything in his path. Vina was looking desperately for a weapon amid the debris, but there was nothing here she could even lift.

Then the bellow sounded at the gateway. Vina shrank into the nearest shadow, pulling Pike with her. He was in no mood to hang back; memory was too strong. The figure at the courtyard entry was a local Kalar warrior, huge, hairy, Neanderthal, clad in cuirass and helmet and carrying a mace. It looked about, shoulders hunched.

''What nonsense,'' Pike said under his breath. ''It was all over weeks ago . . .''

''Hush,'' Vina whispered, terrified. ''You've been here—you know what he'll do to us.''

''It's nothing but a damn silly illusion.''

The warrior roared again, challengingly, raising tremendous echoes. Apparently he hadn't seen them yet.

''It doesn't matter *what* you call this,'' Vina whispered again. ''You'll feel it, that's what matters. You'll feel every moment of whatever happens. I'll feel it happening too.''

The warrior moved tentatively toward them. Either in genuine panic or to force Pike's hand, Vina whirled and raced for a parapet stairway behind them which lead toward the battlement above. The Kalar spotted her at once; Pike had no choice but to follow.

At the top was another litter of weapons; Vina had already picked up a spear with a head like an assegai. Pike found himself a shield and an unbroken sword. As he straightened, the girl pushed him aside. A huge round rock smashed into the rampart wall inches away from him, the force of the fragments knocking him down.

The pain was real, all right. He raised a hand to his forehead to find it bleeding. Below, the warrior was picking up another rock from a depleted pile on the other side of the catapult.

While Pike scrambled back, Vina threw her spear, but she did it inexpertly, and in any event her strength proved insufficient for the range. Changing his mind at once, the Kalar dropped the stone and came charging up the stairs.

Pike's shield was almost torn from his arm at the first blow of the mace. His own sword clanged harmlessly against the Kalar's armor, and he was driven back by a flurry of blows.

Then there was a twanging sound. The warrior bellowed in pain and swung around, revealing an arrow driven deep into his back. Vina had found a crossbow, cocked and armed, and at that range she couldn't miss.

But the wound wasn't immediately mortal and she obviously did not know how to cock the weapon again. The Kalar, staggering, moved in upon her.

From that close, a crossbow bolt would go through almost any armor, but Pike's sword certainly wouldn't. Dropping it, he sprang forward, raised his shield high, and brought it down with all his strength on the back of the warrior's neck. The creature spun off the rampart edge and plummeted to the floor of the compound below. It struck supine and lay still.

Vina, sobbing with relief, threw herself into Pike's arms . . .

. . . and they were back in the menagerie cage.

She was now wearing her own, shorter hair, and a simple garment of the metallic Talosian material. His own bruises and exhaustion had vanished completely, along with the shield. It took him a startled moment to realize what had happened.

Vina smiled. "It's over."

"Why are you here?" he demanded.

She hesitated slightly, then smiled again. "To please you."

"Are you real?"

"As real as you wish."

"That's no answer," he said.

"Perhaps they've made me up out of dreams you've forgotten."

He pointed to her garment. "And I dreamed of you in the same metal fabric they wear?"

"I must wear something." She came closer. "Or must I? I can wear anything you wish, be anything you wish . . ."

"To make this 'specimen' perform for them? To watch how I react? Is that it?"

"Don't you have a dream, something you've wanted very badly . . ."

"Do they do more than just watch me?" he asked. "Do they *feel* with me too?"

"You can have any dream you wish. I can become anything. Any woman you ever imagined." She tried to nestle closer. "You can go anyplace, do anything—have any experience from the whole universe. Let me please you."

Pike eyed her speculatively. "You can," he said abruptly. "Tell me about them. Is there some way I can keep them from using my own thoughts against me? Ah, you're frightened. Does that mean there *is* a way?"

"You're being a fool."

He nodded. "You're right. Since you insist you're an illusion, there's not much point in this conversation."

He went over to the bed and lay down, ignoring her. It was not hard to sense her anxiety, however. Whatever her task was, she did not want to fail it.

After a while she said, "Perhaps—if you asked me something I could answer . . ."

He sat up. "How far can they control my mind?"

"That's not a—that is—" she paused. "If I tell you—will you pick some dream you've had, let me live it with you?"

Pike considered this. The information seemed worth the risk. He nodded.

"They—they can't actually make you do anything you don't want to."

"They have to try to trick me with their illusions?"

"Yes. And they can punish when you're not cooperative. You'll find out about that."

"They must have lived on the planet's surface once . . ."

"Please," she interrupted. "If I say too much . . ."

"Why did they move underground?" he pressed insistently.

"War, thousands of centuries ago," she said hurriedly. "The ones left on the surface destroyed themselves and almost their whole world too. It's taken that long for the planet to heal itself."

"And I suppose the ones who came underground found life too limited—so they concentrated on developing their mental power."

She nodded. "But they've found it's a trap. Like a narcotic. When dreams become more important than reality, you give up travel, building, creating, and even forget how to repair the machines left behind by your ancestors. You just sit living and reliving other lives in the thought records. Or probe the minds of zoo specimens, descendants of life they brought back long ago from all over this part of the galaxy."

Pike suddenly understood. "Which means they had to have more than one of each animal."

"Yes," Vina said, clearly frightened now. "Please, you said if I answered your questions . . ."

"But that was a bargain with something that didn't exist. You said you were an illusion, remember."

"I'm a woman," she said, angry now. "As real and human as you are. We're—like Adam and Eve. If they can . . ."

She broke off with a scream and dropped to the floor, writhing.

"Please!" she wailed. "Don't punish me—I'm trying my best with him—no, *please* . . ."

In the midst of her agony, she vanished. Pike looked up to see the creature called the Magistrate watching through the panel. Furiously, he turned his back—and noticed for the first time an almost invisible circular seam, about man-high, in the wall beside his bed. Was there a hidden panel there?

A small clink of sound behind him made him turn again. A vial of blue liquid was sitting on the floor, just inside the transparency. The Magistrate continued to watch; his mental speech said, "The vial contains a nourishing protein complex."

"Is the keeper actually communicating with one of his animals?"

"If the form and color are not appealing, it can appear as any food you wish to visualize."

"And if I prefer—" Pike began.

"To starve? You overlook the unpleasant alternative of punishment."

With the usual suddenness, Pike found himself writhing in bubbling, sulphurous brimstone in a dark place obscured by smoke. Flame licked at him from all sides. The instant agony was as real as the surprise, and a scream was wrenched from him.

It lasted only a few seconds and then he was back in the cage, staggering.

"From a fable you once heard in childhood," the Magistrate said. "You will now consume the nourishment."

"Why not just put irresistable—hunger in my mind?" Pike said, still gasping with remembered pain. "You can't—do that. You do have limitations, don't you?"

"If you continue to disobey, deeper in your mind there are things even more unpleasant."

Shakily, Pike picked up the vial and swallowed its contents. Almost simultaneously he tossed the vial aside and threw himself at the transparency. It bounced him back, of course—but the Magistrate had also stepped back a pace.

"That's very interesting," Pike said. "You were startled. Weren't you reading my mind then?"

"Now, to the female. As you have conjectured, an Earth vessel did actually crash on our planet. But with only a single survivor."

"Let's stay on the first subject. All I wanted for that moment was to get my hands around your neck. Do primitive emotions put up a block you can't read through?"

"We repaired the survivor's injuries and found the species interesting. So it became necessary to attract a mate."

"All right, we'll talk about the girl. You seem to be going out of your way to make her seem attractive, to make me feel protective."

"This is necessary in order to perpetuate the species."

"That could be done medically, artificially," Pike said. "No, it seems more important to you now that I accept her, begin to like her . . ."

"We wish our specimens to be happy in their new life."

"Assuming that's another lie, why would you want me attracted to her? So I'll feel love, a husband-wife relationship? That would be necessary only if you needed to build a family group, or even a whole human . . ."

"With the female now properly conditioned, we will continue with . . ."

"You mean properly punished!" Pike shouted. "I'm the one who's not cooperating. Why don't you punish me?"

"First an emotion of protectiveness, now one of sympathy. Excellent." The Magistrate turned and walked away down the corridor. Frustrated again, Pike turned to study the mysterious seam.

He found himself studying a tree instead. Around him, in full day, was richly planted park and forest land, with a city on the horizon. He recognized the place instantly.

Immediately to his right was tethered a pair of handsome saddle horses. To the left, Vina, in casual Earth garb, was laying out a picnic lunch on the grass.

Looking up at him, smiling, she said, "I left the thermos hooked to my saddle."

Pike went to the horses and patted them. "Tango! You old quarter-gaited devil, you! Hello, Mary Lou! No, sorry, no sugar this time . . ."

But patting his pockets automatically, he was astonished to find the usual two sugar cubes there. He fed them to the horses. The Talosians seemed to think of everything.

He unhooked the thermos, carried it to the picnic and sat down, eyeing Vina curiously. She seemed nervous.

"Is it good to be home?" she asked him.

"I've been aching to be back here. They read our minds very well."

"Please!" It was a cry of fear. Her face pleaded with him to keep silent.

"Home, everything else I want," he said. "*If* I cooperate. Is that it?"

"Have you forgotten my—headaches, darling? The doctor said when you talk strangely like this . . ."

Her voice trailed off, shaken. Pike was beginning to feel trapped again.

"Look, I'm sorry they punish you," he said. "But I can't let them hold that over our heads. They'll *own* us then."

She continued to lay out the lunch, trying to ignore him. "My, it turned out to be a beautiful day, didn't it?"

"Funny," he mused. "About twenty-four hours ago I was telling the ship's doctor how much I wanted—something not so far from what's being offered here. No responsibility, no frustrations or bruises . . . And now that I have it, I understand the doctor's answer. You either *live* life, bruises and all, or you turn your back on it and start dying. The Talosians went the second way."

"I hope you're hungry," Vina said, with false brightness. "The white sandwiches are your mother's chicken-tuna recipe."

He tried one. She was right. "Doc would be happy about part of this, at least. Said I needed a rest."

"This is a lovely place to rest."

"I spent my boyhood here. Doesn't compare with the gardens around the big cities, but I liked it better." He nodded toward the distant skyline. "That's Mojave. I was born there."

Vina laughed. "Is that supposed to be news to your wife? See—you're home! You can even stay if you want. Wouldn't it be nice showing your children where you once played?"

"These—'headaches,' " Pike said. "They'll be hereditary. Would you wish them on a child—or a whole group of children?"

"That's foolish."

"Is it? Look, first I'm made to protect you, then to feel sympathy for you—and now familiar surroundings, comfortable husband and wife feelings. They don't need all this just for passion. They're after respect, affection, mutual dependence—and something else . . ."

"They say, in the old days all this was a desert. Blowing sand, cactus . . ."

"I can't help either of us if you won't give me a chance!" Pike said sharply. "You told me once that illusions have become like a narcotic to them. They've even forgotten how to repair the machines left by their ancestors. Is that why we're so important? To build a colony of slaves who can . . ."

"Stop it, stop it! Don't you care what they do to me?"

"There's no such thing as a perfect prison," Pike said. "There's always some way out. Back in my cage, it seemed for a couple of minutes our keeper couldn't read my thoughts. Do emotions like anger block off our thought from them?"

"Don't you think," Vina said angrily, "that I've already tried things like that?"

"There's *some* way to beat them. Answer me!"

Her anger turned to tears. "Yes, they can't read—through primitive emotions. But you can't keep it up long enough I've tried!" She began to sob. "They—keep at you and—at you, year after year—probing, looking for a weakness, and tricking—and punishing and—they've won. They own me. I know you hate me for it."

Her fear, desperation, loneliness, everything that she had undergone were welling up in misery, deep and genuine. He put an arm around her. "I don't hate you. I can guess what it was like."

"It's not enough! They want you to have feelings that would build a family, protect it, work for it. Don't you understand? They read my thoughts, my desires, my dreams of what would be a perfect man. That's why they picked you. *I can't help but love you.* And they expect you to feel the same way."

Pike was shaken despite himself. The story was all too horribly likely. "If they can read my mind, they know I'm attracted to you. From the first day in the survivor's encampment. You were like a wild little animal."

"Was that the reason? Because I was like a barbarian?"

"Perhaps," Pike said, amused.

"I'm beginning to see why none of this has really worked on you," Vina said, straightening. "You've *been* home. And fighting, like on Rigel, that's not new to you either. A person's strongest dreams are about things he *can't* do."

"Maybe so. I'm no psychologist."

"Yes," she said, smiling, almost to herself. "A ship's captain, always having to be so formal, so decent and honest and proper—he must wonder what it would be like to forget all that."

The scene changed, with a burst of music and wild merriment. The transition caught him still seated. He was now on a pillowed floor at a low round table bearing a large bowl of fruit and goblets of wine. He seemed to be clad now in rich silk robes, almost like that of an Oriental potentate; near him sat a man whom he vaguely remembered as an Earth trader, similarly but less luxuriantly garbed, while on the other side was an officer in Star Fleet uniform whom he did not recognize at all. All of them were being served by women whose garb and manner strongly suggested slavery, and whose skins were the same color as Spock's. The music was coming from a quartet seated near a fountain pool.

Again he recognized the place; it was the courtyard of the Potentate of Orion. The officer leaned forward.

"Say, Pike," he said. "You used to be Captain of the *Enterprise*, didn't you?"

"Matter of fact, he was," said the trader.

"Thought so. You stopped here now and then—to check things out, so to speak."

"And then," the trader added, "sent Earth a blistering report on 'the Orion traders taking shocking advantage of the natives.' "

Both men laughed. "Funny how they are on this planet," the officer said. "They actually like being taken advantage of."

"And not just in profits, either."

The officer looked around appraisingly. "Nice place you've got here, Mr. Pike."

"It's a start," the trader said. Both laughed again. The officer patted the nearest slave girl on the rump.

"Do any of you have a green one?" he asked. "They're dangerous, I hear. Razor-sharp claws, and they attract a man like a sensation of irresistible hunger."

Up to now, the officer had simply repelled Pike, but that last phrase sounded familiar—and had been delivered with mysterious emphasis. The trader gave Pike a knowing look.

"Now and then," he said, "comes a man who tames one."

There was a change in the music; it became louder, took on a slow, throbbing rhythm. The slave girls turned hurriedly, as if suddenly anxious to excape. Looking toward the musicians, Pike saw another girl, nude, her skin green, and glistening as if it had been oiled, kneeling at the edge of the pool. Her fingertips were long, gleaming, razor-edged scimitars; her hair like the mane of a wild animal. She was staring straight at him.

One of the slaves was slow. The green girl sprang up with a sound like a spitting cat, barring her escape. A man Pike had not seen before leapt forward to intervene, raising a whip.

"Stop!" Pike shouted, breaking his paralysis. The green girl turned and looked at him again, and then he recognized her. It was Vina once more.

She came forward to the center of the rectangle and posed for a moment. Then the music seemed to reach her, the slow surging beat forcing movement out of her as a reed flute takes possession of a cobra. She threw her head back, shrieked startlingly, and began to dance.

"Where'd he find her?" said the officer's voice. Pike was unable to tear his eyes away from her.

"He'd stumbled into a dark corridor," the trader's voice said, "and then he saw flickering light ahead. Almost like secret dreams a bored sea captain might have, wasn't it? There she was, holding a torch, glistening green . . ."

"Strange looks she keeps giving you, Pike."

"Almost as if she knows something about you."

Somewhere in the back of his mind he knew that the Talosians were baiting him through these two men; but he could not stop watching the dance.

"Wouldn't you say that's worth a man's soul?" said the trader.

"It makes you believe she could be anything," said the officer. "Suppose you had all of space to choose from, and this was only one small sample . . ."

That was too much. Pike rose, growling. "Get out of my way, blast you!"

He crossed the courtyard to a curtained doorway which he seemed to recall was an exit. Brushing the curtains aside, he found himself in a corridor. It was certainly dark, and grew darker as he strode angrily along it. In the distance was a flickering light, and then, there indeed was Vina, holding aloft a torch . . .

The scene lightened and the torch vanished. Vina, her skin white, her body covered with the Talosian garment, continued to hold her empty hand aloft for a second. They were back in the cage.

Vina's face contorted in fury. She ran to the transparency and pounded on it, shouting out into the corridor.

"No! Let us finish! I could have . . ."

"What's going on here?" another woman's voice demanded. Both Pike and Vina whirled.

There were two other women in the cage: Number One, and Yeoman Colt. After so many shocks, Pike could summon no further reaction to this one.

"I might well ask you the same thing," he said numbly.

"We tried to Transport down in here," Number One said. "There was a risk we'd materialize in solid rock, but we'd already tried blasting open the top of the lift, with no luck."

"But there were six of us to start with," Yeoman Colt said. "I don't know why the others didn't make it."

"It's not fair!" Vina said to Pike. "You don't need them."

"They may be just what I need," Pike said drily, beginning to recover some of his wits. "Number One, Yeoman, hand me those phasers."

They passed the weapons over. He examined them. What he found did not particularly surprise him. "Empty."

"They were fully charged when we left," Number One said.

"No doubt. But you'll find your communicators don't work either." A thought struck him. He looked quickly toward the almost circular panel he had found before. Then, suddenly, he hurled both phasers at it.

"What good does that do?" Number One said coolly.

"Don't talk to me. Don't say anything. I'm working up a hate—filling my mind with a picture of beating their huge, misshapen heads to a pulp. Thoughts so primitive they shut everything else out. I hate them—do you understand?"

"How long can you block your thoughts?" Vina said. "A few minutes, an hour? How can that help you?"

Pike concentrated, trying to pay no attention to her. She turned on the two other women.

"He doesn't need you," she said, with jealous anger she did not have to force-feed. "He's already picked me."

''Picked you for what?'' Colt asked.

Vina looked at her scornfully. ''Now there's a great chance for intelligent offspring.''

'' 'Offspring?' '' Colt echoed. ''As in 'children' ''?

''As in he's 'Adam,' '' Number One said, indicating Pike. ''Isn't that it?''

''You're no better choice. They'd have better luck crossing him with a computer!''

''Shall I compute your age?'' Number One said. ''You were listed on that expedition as an adult crewman. Now, adding eighteen years to that . . .''

She broke off as Vina turned to the transparency. The Magistrate was back. The two crewwomen stared at him with interest.

''It's not fair,'' Vina said. ''I did everything you asked.''

The Magistrate ignored her. ''Since you resist the present specimen,'' he said to Pike, ''you now have a selection.''

Pike threw himself at the impervious figure. ''I'll break out, get to you somehow!'' he shouted. ''Is your blood red like ours? I'm going to find out!''

''Each of the two new specimens has qualities in her favor. The female you call 'Number One' has the superior mind and would produce highly intelligent offspring. Although she seems to lack emotion, this is largely a pretense. She often has fantasies involving you.''

Number One looked flustered for the first time in Pike's memory, but he turned this, too, into rage at the invasion of her privacy. ''All I want is to get my hands on you! Can you read these thoughts? Images of hate, killing . . .''

''The other new arrival has considered you unreachable, but is now realizing that this has changed. The factors in her favor are youth and strength, plus an unusually strong female emotion which . . .''

''You'll find my thoughts more interesting! Primitive thoughts you can't understand; emotions so ugly you can't . . .''

The pain hit him then and he went down, writhing. The images involved this time were from the torture chambers of the Inquisition. Over them, dimly, floated the Magistrate's thought, as though directed at someone else.

"Wrong thinking is punishable; right thinking will be as quickly rewarded. You will find it an effective combination."

The illusion vanished and Pike rolled weakly to a sitting position. He found the Magistrate gone, and the two crewwomen bending over him.

"No—don't—help me. Just leave me alone. Got to concentrate on hate. They can't read through it."

The hours wore on and eventually the lights went down. It seemed obvious that the Talosians intended to keep all three women penned with him. Trying to keep the hate alive became increasingly more difficult; he slammed his fist against the enclosure wall again and again, hoping the pain would help.

The women conversed in low tones for a while, and then, one by one, fell asleep, Vina on the bed, the other two on the floor leaning against it. Pike squatted against the wall nearby, no thoughts in his mind now but roaring fatigue and the effort to fight it.

Then he sensed, rather than heard movement at his side. The wall panel had opened, and a Talosian arm was reaching in for the discarded phasers. He exploded into action, grabbing the arm and heaving.

The Magistrate was almost catapulted into the room by the force of that yank. Instantly, Pike's hands were around his throat.

"Don't hurt him!" Vina cried from the bed. "They don't mean to be evil . . ."

"I've had some samples of how 'good' they are . . ."

The Talosian vanished and Pike found himself holding the neck of the snarling anthropoid-spider creature he had first seen in a cell across from his. Its fangs snapped at his face. Colt shrieked.

Pike grimly tightened his grip. "I'm still holding your neck! Stop this illusion or I'll snap it!" The spider-thing changed back into the Magistrate again. "That's better. Try one more illusion—try anything at all—I'll take one quick twist. Understand?"

He loosened his hands slightly, allowing the Magistrate to gasp for breath. The forehead vein throbbed. "Your ship. Release me or we destroy it."

"He's not bluffing," Vina said. "With illusions they can make your crew work the wrong controls, push any button it takes to destroy the ship."

"I'll gamble he's too intelligent to kill for no reason at all. On the other hand, *I've* got a reason. Number One, take a good grip on his throat for me. And at the slightest excuse . . ."

"I understand, Captain," Number One said grimly.

Freed, Pike picked up the phaser. Putting one into his belt, he adjusted the other, leveled it at the transparency, and pulled the trigger. As he expected, it didn't fire. He turned back to the Magistrate and pressed the weapon against his head.

"I'm betting," he said almost conversationally, "that you've created an illusion that this phaser is empty. That you don't know enough about your own machines, let alone ours, to dare to tamper with them. And that this one just blasted a hole in that wall which you're keeping us from seeing. Shall I test my theory on your head?"

The Magistrate closed his eyes resignedly. At once, there was a huge, jagged hole in the front of the cage.

"Q.E.D. Number One, you can let go of him now. If he acts up, I can shoot him, and he knows it. Everybody out. We're leaving!"

On the surface, only the top of the lift shaft still stood; the top of the knoll had been blasted clean off. So the Talosians had prevented the rescue party from seeing that, too.

Number One tried her communicator, but without effect. Noting the Magistrate's forehead vein throbbing again, Pike raised his phaser and said in a voice of iron, "I want contact with my ship. *Right now.*"

"No," said the Magistrate. "You are now on the surface where we intended you to be in the end. With the female of your choice, you will soon begin carefully guided lives . . ."

"Beginning with burying you."

"I see you intend to kill. I shall not prevent you; others of us will replace me. To help you reclaim the planet, our zoological gardens will furnish a variety of plant life . . ."

"Look" Pike said, "I'll make a deal with you. You and your life for the lives of these two Earthwomen."

"Since our life span is many times yours, we have time to evolve a society trained as artisans, technicians . . ."

"Do you understand what I'm saying? Give me proof our ship is all right, send these two back to it, and I'll stay here with Vina."

He felt a tug at his belt, and out of the corner of his eyes saw that Number One had pulled the spare phaser out of it. The rachet popped like firecrackers as she turned the gain control full around. The phaser began to hum, rising in both pitch and volume. The weapon was building up an overload—a force chamber explosion.

"It's wrong," Number One said, "to create a whole race of humans to live as slaves. Do you concur, Captain?"

After a moment of hesitation, Pike nodded.

"Is this a deception?" asked the Magistrate. "Do you really intend to destroy yourselves? Yes, I see that you do."

"Vina, you've got time to get back underground. But hurry. And Talosian, to show just how primitive humans are, you can go with her."

The Magistrate did not move, nor did Vina.

"No," she said. "If you all think it's this important, then I can't leave either. I suppose if they still have one human, they might try again."

"We had not believed this possible," the Magistrate said, his thoughts betraying what might have been a strange sadness. "The customs and history of your race show a unique hatred of captivity, even when pleasant and benevolent. But you prefer death. This makes you too violent and dangerous a species for our needs."

"He means," Vina said, "they can't use you. You're free to go back to your ship."

Number One turned the phaser off, and just in time, too. In the renewed silence, Pike said, "Vina, that's it. No apologies. You captured one of us, threatened us, tortured us . . ."

"Your unsuitability has condemned the Talosian race to eventual death," the Magistrate said. "Is this not sufficient? No other specimens have shown your adaptability. You were our last hope."

"Nonsense," Pike said, surprised. "Surely some form of trade, some mutual cooperation . . ."

The Magistrate shook his head. "Your race would learn our power of illusion—and destroy itself. It is important to *our* beliefs to prevent this."

"Captain," Number One said, "we have Transporter control now."

"Good. Let's go. Vina, you too."

"I—" Vina said. "I can't go with you."

Pike felt a flash of what might almost have been exasperation. "Number One, Yeoman Colt, go aloft. I'll be with you when I've gotten to the bottom of this." As they hesitated, he added, "Orders."

They shimmered and vanished. Pike swung on Vina. "Now . . ."

He stopped, astounded and horrified. Vina was changing. Her face was wrinkling. An ugly scar appeared. Her body was becoming cruelly deformed. Throughout, she looked back at Pike with bitter eyes. The change did not stop until she was old, shockingly twisted, downright ugly.

"This is the female's true appearance," the Magistrate said.

It couldn't be true. *This* was the youngster of the survivors' camp, the sturdy peasant, the wife on Earth, the green Orionese savage who had danced so . . .

"This is the truth," Vina said, in an old woman's voice. She lifted her arms. "See me as I am. They found me in the wreckage, dying, nothing but a lump of flesh. They fixed me fine. Everything works. But—*they had no guide for putting me back together.*

"Do you understand now? Do you see why I can't go with you?"

She turned and stumbled toward the lift. Pike watched her go with horror and pity. Then he turned to the Magistrate, who said; "It was necessary to convince you that her desire to stay is an honest one."

Pike looked at him with new eyes. "You have some sparks of decency in you after all. Will you give her back her illusion of beauty?"

"We will. And more. See."

At the shaft, the image of the lovely Vina was entering

the lift—*accompanied by himself.* The two turned and waved. Then the lift carried them down into the bowels of Talos IV.

''She has her illusion,'' the Magistrate said. Was he almost smiling? ''And you have reality. May you find your way as pleasant.''

Spock, Number One, Jose, Colt and Boyce all crowded toward him as he stepped out of the Transporter Chamber.

''What happened to Vina?'' Colt demanded.

''Isn't she—coming with us?'' asked Number One.

''No,'' Pike said shortly. ''And I agree with her reasons. Now break it up here: What is this we're running, a cadet ship? Everybody on the bridge! Navigator, I want a course!''

''Yessir!''

They scattered like flushed partridges—all except Boyce, who said, ''Hold on a minute, Captain.''

''What for? I feel fine.''

''That's the trouble. You look a hundred per cent better.''

''I am. Didn't you recommend rest and change? I've had both. I've even been—home. Now, let's get on with things.''

As the *Enterprise* moved away from Talos IV, routine re-established itself quickly, and the memory of all those illusions began to fade. They had not, after all, been real experiences—most of them. But Pike could not resist stealing a quick look from Number One to Colt, wondering which of them, in other circumstances, he might have picked.

When he found them both looking at him as if with the same speculation, he turned his eyes determinedly to the viewscreen and banished the thought.

He had had plenty of practice at that, lately.

AFTERWORD

As the reader will now see, this story constituted the original pilot film for ''Star Trek,'' and was shown as such at the 24th World Science Fiction Convention in Cleveland, Ohio, September 1—5, 1966. Between the selling of the series and the actual television broadcast of ''The Mena-

series and the actual television broadcast of "The Menagerie," the whole concept of the cast changed radically. Number One was moved one step down in the chain of command, becoming Uhura, while her ostensible lack of emotion and computer-like mind were transferred to Spock; Yeoman Colt became Yeoman Rand; Boyce became McCoy; Tyler became Sulu. The net effect was to make the new officers more interracial than before. The notion that the highly trained crew would ever be risked in ordinary hand-to-hand infantry combat was dropped.

Most important, perhaps, was that in the pilot film, Pike had wound up with a potentially explosive situation with two of his crewwomen which would be too complex to maintain through a long-term series of episodes. He had to be replaced, and the whole story turned into relatively ancient history; and thus was born Captain Kirk, and the framing story I have left out. All these stages are visible in the scripts I had to work from, which are heavily revised in various handwritings (and in which Pike confusingly appears from time to time as "Captain Spring" and "Captain Winter").

The only alternative would have been to reshoot the original "Menagerie" with the new cast, which would have been not only expensive, but would have produced all kinds of unwanted complexities in succeeding stories. Mr. Roddenberry obviously decided to let it stand as something that had happened way-back-when, and frame it as such. I think this was wise and I have followed his lead in this adaptation.

Ordinarily, writers should not inflict their technical problems on readers, who have every right to demand that such problems be solved before the story is published. But I sometimes get letters from "Star Trek" fans who castigate me for changing even one or two words in scripts they have memorized, or even have on tape. In this case, as in that of "The City on the Edge of Forever," there were conflicts that couldn't be resolved by slavishly following the final text and ignoring how it had evolved. In both cases, I had to make my own judgment of what would best serve the authors' intents.

—J. B.

SHORE LEAVE

Writer: Theodore Sturgeon
Director: Robert Sparr
Guest stars: Emily Banks, Bruce Mars

Captain James Kirk slumped in his chair and contemplated his viewscreen. At least this planet was not emitting torpedoes or mysterious signals, for once. He sincerely hoped it wouldn't start anything; he wasn't at all sure he could deal with another Problem. Even his mind felt sluggish.

He became vaguely aware of footsteps nearing him; he couldn't allow himself to slouch like this. He straightened up with effort and felt a stab of pain in his back.

"Anything from the landing party yet, Mr. Spock?"

"They should be sending up a report momentarily, Captain." Spock glanced at him. "Is something wrong?"

"Kink in my back. Yes, just about there."

A strong hand touched, assessed and began to knead the spastic muscle. He could always rely on Spock.

"Just a little higher. Ohh—yes. Just there, Spock. Harder—push hard . . ." But Spock was standing in front of him.

"What—?" Her hands skillfully working, Yeoman Tonia Barrows smiled as he turned his head. He couldn't start using the female crew as personal masseuses. Damn. "Thank you, Yeoman," he said hastily. "That's sufficient." It had helped.

"You need sleep, Captain," said the girl hesitantly. "If it's not out of line to suggest—"

"I've had enough of that from Dr. McCoy. Thank you."

Spock folded his arms. "And Dr. McCoy is completely

correct, Captain. After what this crew has been through in the last few months, there's not a man aboard who doesn't need rest.

"Myself excepted, of course."

Sometimes, Spock was almost insufferable. But Kirk didn't really have to remain on the bridge just now; he could be doing the ship's log from his be— . . . quarters, while he waited for the landing party to report.

He fumbled the switch to "Record": "Captain's Log, Star Date Three-Oh-Two-Five point uh . . . three," he said wearily. "We are orbiting an inun—unan—uninhabited planet in the Omicron Delta Region. A planet remarkably like Earth—or how we remember Earth. Prelinimary—preliminary reports make it sound too good to be true: flowers and trees, very restful." He yawned. "Pending the report from the scouts, I plan to authorize a snore—shore leave. . . ."

Downstairs, the landing party was gratefully inhaling fresh air scented with herbs and flowers. Tall trees rustled gently in a light breeze. The sky was cornflower blue. How long since anyone aboard the *Enterprise* had had a chance to even notice weather, undistracted? McCoy wondered.

There were no buildings; just the trees. No beings but themselves and the daisies; and the quiet. They never noticed the constant sounds of the ship's systems until they were not there.

"It's beautiful," said Sulu, gazing at the forests and green meadows. "No animals, no people, no worries . . . just what the doctor ordered, right, Doctor?"

"I couldn't have prescribed better," said McCoy happily. "We are one weary ship."

"Do you think the Captain will give us shore leave here?"

"Depends on my report, and those of the other scouts," said McCoy. "Oh!" He stopped short.

Sulu followed his look. Ahead of them, a small lake lay like a jewel in a setting of emerald leaves. Flowering shrubs covered the banks, and a willow wept gracefully into the water.

"You have to see this place to believe it," said McCoy

with great delight. "It's like something out of . . . *Alice in Wonderland*! The Captain has to come down here!"

Sulu nodded in total agreement. "He'd like it."

"He *needs* it. You have your problems, and I have mine. He has his, plus ours plus those of four hundred and thirty other people." McCoy drifted toward the water, soaking up sun and warm air. Rapt in his wonderland, he barely remembered to look back at Sulu. "What are you doing?"

Sulu was crouched over a plant, adjusting his tricorder. "Getting cell structure records—a blade of grass, a bush, a flower petal; with these, we can analyze the whole planet's biology."

McCoy left him to it. He wasn't feeling at all analytical. He wandered down a faint path, absorbing peace, and wondering.

"Oh! My paws and whiskers! I shall be late!"

McCoy came to with a bang. Aural hallucinations, he diagnosed. He himself must be more tired than he had thought. Paws and whiskers, indeed. He turned very slowly.

There it was. Running on twinkling hind feet. About four feet tall with white fur and long ears, pulling an old-fashioned turnip watch from its waist-coat pocket.

"Tch!" The white rabbit disappeared through a gap in the dense shrubbery.

McCoy shook his head. I didn't see that. I am quite, quite sure that I didn't see that, he told himself. The bushes behind him rustled.

"Excuse me, sir," said the little girl in the pinafore, politely. "Have you seen a rawther large white Rabbit with a yellow wais'c't and white gloves hereabouts?"

McCoy did not believe this either, of course. But in a stunned trance, he pointed after the rabbit.

The little girl curtseyed and said, "Thank you veddy much," and disappeared after the rabbit.

McCoy closed his eyes tight. "Sulu! **SULU!**"

He wasn't going to look anymore. Let Sulu see things. He, McCoy, was not obliged to believe any impossible things *after* breakfast.

"What is it? What's the matter?"

"Did—did you see them?"

"See what? I don't see anything," said Sulu, looking around. "What is it, Doctor?"

McCoy gulped. "I—uh—" There was nothing to say. He followed Sulu helplessly.

"Captain?"

Somebody at the door. Wake up. Alert. Responsible. Blood, start circulating. You can do better than this. "Yes?"

"Spock, Captain. I have the doctor's report on the crew."

"Come in, Spock." Kirk dragged himself together and stood.

"All systems are now on automatic, Captain, and skeleton standby crew is ready to relieve the bridge, Communications and Engineering." Spock was very businesslike.

"We'll beam the starboard section down first, Mr. Spock. Which party would you like to go down with?"

"Unnecessary in my case, Captain. On my planet, to rest is to *rest*, to cease using energy. To me, it is illogical to run up and down on green grass, using energy instead of saving it."

Insufferable.

The desk communicator sounded. "Kirk here."

"Dr. McCoy is calling from the planet, sir."

"Good. Open a channel, Lieutenant Uhura."

"Captain," said McCoy. "Are you beaming down?"

"I hadn't planned to, Bones. Why?"

"Well," said McCoy, "either our scouting probes and detectors are malfunctioning, and all of us scouts getting careless and beauty-intoxicated, or I have to report myself unfit for duty."

"Explain." Kirk quelled a wave of depression. A Problem. Either malfunctioning equipment or a malfunctioning staff. Great.

"On this supposedly uninhabited planet," McCoy stated with great precision, "I just saw a large white rabbit pull a gold watch out of his vest pocket. Then he claimed he was late."

Kirk burst out with relieved laughter. Not a Problem after all. "That's very good, Bones. Now I have one for you. The rabbit was followed by a little blonde girl, right?"

"Er . . ." said McCoy. "As a matter of fact, she was . . . and they disappeared through a hole in the hedge!"

Still chuckling, Kirk said, "I'll take your report under consideration, Doctor. Captain out." He turned to the baffled Spock. "That was a McCoy-pill, with a little mystery sugar-coating. He's trying to get me down there. But I won't swallow it."

"Very well, Captain," said Spock. "There was something I came to discuss." Kirk looked at him. "I picked this up from Dr. McCoy's log."

At last Kirk observed that Spock was holding a paper.

" 'We have a crew member who shows signs of stress and fatigue. Reaction time down nine to twelve percent. Associational rating norm minus three.' "

Concern penetrated the fog of Kirk's exhaustion. "That's much too low a rating," he said sharply.

" 'He is becoming irritable, inefficient, and quarrelsome. And yet he refuses to take rest and rehabilitation.' " Spock looked up. "He has the right, of course, but—"

"A crewman's rights end where the safety of the ship begins. That man will go ashore on my orders," said Kirk with annoyance. "What's his name?"

"James Kirk."

His head jerked up. That's what comes of giving orders before you have all the details. Inefficient. And they'd caught him fair and square.

Spock handed him the paper. "Enjoy yourself, Captain. It's an interesting planet. I believe you'll find it quite pleasant, very much like your Earth. The scouts have detected no life forms, artifacts or force fields of any kind; nothing but peace and sunlight and good air. You'll have no problems."

Kirk shrugged and finally smiled. "You win, Spock. I'll go."

Yeoman Barrows accompanied him down, and they materialized near two of the scouts.

"Rodriguez, Teller," Kirk acknowledged. "Everything all right?"

"Yes, sir," replied the dark boy, who was packing up a box of samples. "We've completed the specimen survey."

The ensign with him was looking just a little wistful. Perhaps she was too tired to work.

"Sufficient, Mr. Rodriguez. Beam your reports up to Mr. Spock, and start enjoying yourselves."

The girl brightened. "Yes, sir!" said Rodriguez, handing her the tricorder. "Oh, sir, I think you'll find Dr. McCoy just over there."

Kirk looked "there," and all around him. "Restful here, isn't it? After what we've gone through, it's hard to believe a planet this beautiful exists."

"It is beautiful." The yeoman in the brief skirt twirled around. "So lovely and peaceful and—" she caught herself on the edge of burbling. "Oh, I mean—affirmative, Captain."

Kirk allowed himself a small smile at her youthful bounce, and he started toward McCoy with Yeoman Barrows. "McCoy? Where are you?"

The foliage was thick in this glade. "Over here!"

McCoy was still standing where he had seen what he had seen.

"Bones! Know any good rabbit jokes lately?" The doctor was not going to live that down for some time.

"Matter of fact, I do," said McCoy. His expression was too serious for comfort. "But this is not one of them. Look at this."

Kirk's smile faded as he followed McCoy's pointing finger. Tracks. On a planet without animals. Big tracks, in pairs. A hopping creature.

"I saw what I saw, Jim. Maybe I hallucinated it. But take a look here and tell me what you think."

"Aren't those prints kind of big for a rabbit?"

"Er—" McCoy looked a little sheepish. "As I reported, Captain, this was a most unusual rabbit."

Kirk dropped to his knees to study the footprints. "I admit I thought it was a joke. But these tracks are very real." The prints were far apart. It must have had long legs. A large hopping creature. "What about Sulu? Will he confirm what you saw?"

McCoy shook his head. "He was examining the flora at the time."

"I don't like this, Bones." Kirk flipped open his communicator. "Bridge. This is the Captain. Has the first shore party beamed down yet?"

"Negative, Captain. They're just about to start."

"Give them this message. Stand by. No one is to leave the ship until you hear further from me."

There was a brief delay before Uhura's voice came back with a dejected, "Aye, aye, sir."

McCoy protested. "Are you canceling the shore leave, Jim?"

"Until we find an explanation of *this.*" He pointed at the enigmatic tracks.

"But the crew, they badly need rest."

"I know," said Kirk, feeling the weight of responsibility very heavily indeed. "But what you saw looked harmless. It probably is harmless, but before I bring my people down, I want proof that it is harmless."

McCoy was about to object that the worst that could happen would be an encounter with a pack of cards, when he was interrupted.

Shots. Gunshots.

So much for peace and tranquility; Kirk drew his phaser and started running. He stopped short as he found Sulu standing in a clearing, grinning happily and aiming at an innocent leaf.

Bang!

McCoy caught up with Kirk as he was saying wearily, "Mr. Sulu, what do you think you're doing?"

"Target shooting, Captain," said Sulu. "Isn't it a beauty? I don't have anything like this in my collection!"

"Where did you get it?"

"I *found* it. I know it's a crazy coincidence, but I've always wanted one. I found it lying right back there." He held it out proudly for Kirk's inspection. "An old-time Police Special, and in beautiful condition. Hasn't been a gun like this made in, oh, a couple of centuries. Look, it fires lead pellets propelled by expanding gases from a chemical explosion."

Sulu and his hobbies. "I've seen them before," said Kirk, remembering certain adventures when he had tangled with Earth's past history. He took the weapon and smiled at

Sulu. One couldn't blame him, but—"I'll hang on to it. This fresh air seems to have made you a little trigger-happy."

Sulu looked disappointed but said only, "Yes, sir."

Yeoman Tonia Barrows was not interested in guns. As soon as she had seen that they were not confronted with an emergency, she had begun to wander. Now she called. "Sir! Dr. McCoy's rabbit. He must have come through here."

She pointed at a set of tracks, identical to the first, that crossed the clearing into the woods beyond.

Kirk examined the tracks. "Bones, are you certain your instruments showed no animal life on this planet?"

"Absolutely. No mammals, birds, insects, nothing. I'm certain our readings weren't off, and yet . . ." He stared down at the perplexing prints.

Kirk sighed. "I'd like to believe this is an elaborate gag. But—" He stood up and looked toward the wood. "Yeoman Barrows, you accompany Mr. Sulu. Find out where those tracks come from." The pair turned to the shrubbery. "You come with me back to the glade, Doctor. I want another look at that area."

As they began walking back to the aquamarine lake, Kirk said with some bitterness, "This is becoming one very unusual shore leave."

McCoy said lightly, "It could be worse."

"How?"

"*You* could have seen that rabbit."

Kirk laughed in spite of his worry. "What's the matter, Bones? Getting a persecution complex?"

"I'm starting to feel a little bit picked on, if that's what you mean," said McCoy ruefully.

"I know that feeling well. I had it at the Academy." They strolled on. McCoy noted with satisfaction that Kirk seemed a little less tense. "An upperclassman there—one practical joke after another, and always on me. My own personal devil, a guy by the name of Finnegan."

"And you, being a serious young cadet—?"

"Serious? Bones, I'll make a confession. I was absolute *grim.* Which delighted Finnegan. He was the one to put a bowl of cold soup in your bed, a bucket of water propped on a half-open door. You never knew where he'd strike next."

McCoy thought, "And you're still sore about it, long past as it is,"

"More tracks, Bones. Looks like your rabbit came from over there." McCoy stooped and looked at the ground. "A girl's footprints too, Jim. The blonde girl I saw chasing it."

"Bones, you follow the rabbit. I'll backtrack the girl. We'll meet on the other side of that hill." McCoy nodded. Kirk started walking along the line of small boot-prints. Little girls, rabbits, old-fashioned guns—whatever next?

He hadn't thought about that lout Finnegan in years. What a thorn in his flesh that man had been! He remembered the day . . .

Tall, broad-shouldered, with a challenging grin pasted on his map, a figure was waiting by the tree in front of him. Kirk blinked. *"Finnegan!"*

The youth, dressed in Academy cadet uniform, swaggered up to him with a wicked laugh.

"Never know when I'm going to strike, eh, Jimmy boy?" The same faint brogue, the same cackling derision. As Kirk stood there, incredulous, he was jarred into accepting this reality by a sudden right to the jaw which knocked him flat. He got up slowly, staring at his old enemy who danced in a fighter's crouch, baiting him. "All right, Jimmy boy, go ahead. Lay one on me! Go ahead; that's what you've always wanted, isn't it?" It was. Kirk let go his disbelief and crouched. He was not going to pass up this chance to deal with this old bête-noire at last. Red rage surged in him as he remembered all the bullying, the merciless persecution.

"Come on, come on!" sneered Finnegan. Kirk started at him.

"Let's do that one again!"

A woman screamed. Oh, hell. And he pulled his punch. Yeoman Barrows? He was the Captain. His yeoman was in danger. Hell. He ran toward the sound of the scream, with Finnegan calling after him, "Any excuse, Jim baby? Right? Run away, that's right!"

McCoy appeared from the underbrush, running.

"What was that?"

"Barrows. Come on."

They found the girl huddled against a tree. Her tunic

was torn and her hair disheveled. She was alone and weeping hysterically.

"What happened?"

"I—I—I don't know. I mean—I do know," she sobbed. "I guess . . . I was following those tracks and . . . ohhh! There he was!"

"There who was?" snapped Kirk. This was no way for a trained crewman to give information.

"Him!" wailed the yeoman.

"Barrows, give me a report!"

She began to gain control of herself. "He had a cloak, sir. And—and a dagger with jewels on the handle."

McCoy was examining her. "Yeoman Barrows, are you sure you didn't imagine this?"

She pulled up the torn shoulder of her dress, suddenly embarrassed. "Captain, I know it sounds incredible." The men nodded. "But I didn't imagine it anymore than I imagined he did this." She gestured with the ripped tunic.

"All right," said McCoy reassuringly. "We believe you. But who was your Don Juan, anyway?"

"How did you know?" she gasped.

"Know what?"

"It was so, you know, sort of—storybook, walking around this place." She sniffed, and went on rather shyly. "I was thinking, all a girl needs here is Don Juan. Just daydreaming. You know?" She looked at the officers hesitantly. "Like you might think of some girl you'd like to meet."

Kirk was not prepared to dwell on this. He looked around, missing something.

"Mr. Sulu was with you. Where is he?"

"Oh. He ran after . . . him. He—" But Sulu was nowhere in sight.

"Stay with her, Doctor." Kirk took off at a run.

"Mr. Sulu!" he called. "Sulu! Where are you?" There was no reply. He brushed through the undergrowth and into a clearing; here was a miniature desert-garden, with cactus flowers blooming. Still calling, he began searching among the rocks.

There were footsteps on his right. "Sulu?"

It was not Sulu. The young girl smiled, real roses on

her dress stirring in the breeze. She came toward Kirk with memory in her eyes.

"Ruth." The memory kindled in the Captain. "You! How—I don't understand—"

"Jim, darling. It is me. It's Ruth." He had clamped that particular wound closed, forever. Somehow in the pressure of final examinations and qualifications and his first cruise, he had lost her, and put away the regrets.

"You don't think I'm real." He had even forgotten the gentleness of her voice. It all came flooding back with pain and longing. "But I am, darling, I am."

James Kirk's Ruth could not possibly exist here and now. But as she put her soft arms around his neck, he did not doubt her reality. He could not help but return her embrace.

He tried to resist; he took out his communicator. "Dr. McCoy, come in." But his eyes were fixed on Ruth. "McCoy, do you read me?"

She put the communicator to one side. "Think of nothing at all, darling, except our being together again." Her soft hair brushed his face.

"Ruth. How can it be you? You can't be here!"

She snuggled closer and looked up at him, her skin glowing in the sun. "It doesn't matter. Does it?"

Fifteen years ago. She still looked exactly the same, the fresh, young, gentle creature who had wept so bitterly at their last goodbye. She said again, "It doesn't matter. None of that matters, Jimmy."

His communicator beeped, cutting though his daze.

"Kirk here."

McCoy wanted to know if he had found Sulu.

"What?" She still wore her hair in a coronet of braids.

"Did you find Mr. Sulu?"

"Oh—no," said Kirk absently. "But I'm sure he's all right." She was dreaming into his eyes. "I mean, why shouldn't he be?"

"Captain, are *you* all right?"

"Oh, yes, I'm fine." The communicator seemed to float away by itself to the rock beside him. It beeped again.

He sighed, and acknowledged "Yes, Mr. Rodriguez."

"Captain, a while ago, I saw . . . well, birds. Whole flocks of them."

"Don't you like birds, Mr. Rodriguez?" She was holding his hand in their special clasp.

"I like them fine, sir. But all our surveys showed—"

Kirk hadn't noticed the bird song that was coming from the forest. It had seemed to belong there.

"Offhand, Mr. Rodriguez, I'd say our instruments must be defective." It didn't really seem to matter. "There are indeed life forms on this planet." She nestled against his shoulder.

Rodriguez was being stubborn. "Sir, our survey couldn't have been that wrong."

Ruth moved a little away from him and regarded him with longing.

"Rodriguez, have all search parties rendezvous at the glade. I want some answers to all this."

"Aye, aye, sir." He couldn't let it happen again, lost her again. Nor could he abandon his crew to whatever dangers this mysterious planet held. Yearning and duty fought in his belly.

Ruth held out her hand to him and gave him a radiant smile. "You have to go."

"I don't want to." How he didn't want to!

This time, she did not weep. She bent toward him and said gently, "You'll see me again—if you want to." She kissed his cheek and backed away from him. He started after her.

"But I have to ask you—You haven't told me—"

"Do what you have to do. Then I'll be waiting, Jim." Would she? This time? He called her as she vanished into the wood. The communicator beeped again.

"Captain Kirk here." His eyes were still fixed on the gap between the trees where she had disappeared.

Mr. Spock said, "Captain, I am getting strange readings from the planet's surface. There seems to be a power field of some kind down there now."

"Specify."

"A highly sophisticated type of energy, Captain, which seems to have begun operating since we took our original readings. It is draining our power aboard ship and increasingly affecting communications.''

''Can you pinpoint the source?'' Kirk's attention was now reluctantly engaged.

''It could be beneath the planet's surface, but I cannot locate it precisely. Its patterns would indicate some sort of industrial activity.''

Industrial activity? Here among the woods and fields? ''Keep me posted, Mr. Spock. We'll continue our investigations from down here.''

Investigations were proceeding slowly. Dr. McCoy sat with Yeoman Barrows under the birch tree. She was still clutching her torn tunic to her shoulder.

''Feeling better?''

She smiled. ''A little. But I wouldn't want to be alone here.''

''Why not?'' McCoy gave a long, contented sigh. ''It's a beautiful place. A little strange, I admit, but—''

''That's just it. It's almost too beautiful. I was thinking, before my tunic was even . . . torn, in a place like this, a girl should be dressed to match.'' Yeoman Barrows was showing an unsuspected streak of romanticism. ''Let's see now . . . like a fairy-tale princess, with lots of floaty stuff and a tall pointed hat with a veil.''

McCoy looked down at her kindly. Then he looked again. She was really a lovely young woman. Funny he had never noticed before. Of course, she had been a patient.

She was really *very* pretty.

''I see what you mean. But then you'd have whole armies of Don Juans to fight off.'' She chuckled. ''And me too.''

She glanced up from lowered eyelids. ''Is that a promise, Doctor?''

They began walking around the lake. The twittering of birds filled the air, and the greenness of leaves burnished with sunlight filled their eyes.

''Oh!'' On a bush, a heap of fabric was carelessly flung. White silks fluttered. ''Oh, Doctor, they're lovely!'' Yeoman Barrows picked up a stream of veiling.

"Yes, they are," agreed McCoy, looking at Yeoman Barrows's bright eyes.

She covered her face and peered at him over the veil. "Look at me!" She pirouetted lightly, and then promenaded, and spoke with mock seriousness. "A lady to be protected and fought for, a princess of the blood royal!"

What had taken him so long? "You are all of those things, and many more." He must have forgotten how to play, with all the heavy preoccupations of his work. Bless her, she had not. She was gay and vulnerable and lovely.

He took the costume from the shrub and pushed it into her arms. "They'd look even lovelier with you wearing them."

Her impish look changed suddenly to terror as she looked back at the bush. "Doctor, I'm afraid."

"Easy now," he said, comfortingly as she buried her face in his shoulder. He could feel her trembling. He tried not to notice that her tunic had fallen from her shoulder. He felt a momentary stab of jealousy of that tedious "Don Juan" who had seen her first. "Look, I don't know what, or where or how, but the dress is here." He smiled down at her. "I'd like to see you in it."

She looked at the clothes doubtfully as she disengaged herself. She held the dress up in front of her; in spite of her qualms, she was obviously tempted. He nodded encouragement. She said, "All—all right!" and stepped around the bush. "But you stay right there—and don't peek!"

"My dear girl, I'm a doctor," said McCoy with dignity. "When I peek, it's in the line of duty."

Leonard McCoy, gentleman medic, found himself unable to avoid noticing the flinging of a tunic and the tantalizing motions that showed over the top of the shrubbery. His communicator sounded.

"Calling Dr. McCoy, come in please. Calling—"

He raised the instrument to his ear. "McCoy here." What a time for a call. And the voice was very faint. "I can't read you very well. Is that Rodriguez?"

"This is all the volume I get on this thing. Can't read you very well either. Captain's orders. Rendezvous at the glade where he first found you."

"Right. Rodriguez? What the devil's wrong with the communicators? Esteban? Esteban!"

McCoy shook the instrument as if it were an old-time thermometer, and then shook his head and shrugged. As he turned back for a last peek, he gasped.

Yeoman Barrows was gone. In her place stood a medieval vision, clad in a tall pointed hat and a pale green dress that clung to her body and spread in graceful folds below her hips. Her face was aglow, and she wore her veil like a bride.

Why the hell hadn't he noticed?

The Captain was consulting his Science Officer. He could barely hear.

"I want an explanation, Spock. First, there's Alice in Wonderland when there was supposedly no animal life. Then Sulu's gun, where there were no refined metals. Then the birds, and my—the two people I saw."

"Is there any chance these could be hallucinations, Captain?"

"One 'hallucination' flattened me with a clout on the jaw. The other—"

"That sounds like painful reality, Captain."

"And then there are the tracks . . ."

"There has to be a logical explanation. Captain, your signal is very weak. Can you turn up the gain?"

"I'm already on maximum."

There was a pause. "Captain, shall I beam down an armed party?"

Kirk thought not. "Our people here are armed with phasers. Besides, there's yet to be any real danger. It's just . . . Captain out." He stood for a moment, watching the sudden flight of a flock of birds across the sky. He was still so very tired. If only this shore leave could *be* a shore leave instead of an enigma! Why were those birds in the air? Something must have startled them. Sulu! He was still unaccounted for. Kirk rubbed his eyes and started into the forest.

There was a faint scream, shouting and thuds. As he ran, Kirk called to McCoy. Sulu burst out of the wood at top speed.

"Take cover, Captain! There's a samurai after me!"

"A what?"

No one, nothing was following Sulu, who stopped and looked over his shoulder, panting. "A samurai. With a sword—you know, an ancient warrior. Captain, you've got to believe me!"

"I do," said Kirk. He couldn't doubt Sulu. "I've met some interesting personalities here myself. Have you seen the rest of the landing party?"

"Rodriguez called a few minutes ago. Just before I met the samurai. He said you were rendezvousing back at the glade."

They started moving toward the meeting point, Sulu glancing nervously behind him.

"I hope Rodriguez got through to everybody. Communications are almost out."

"That's not all," said Sulu. "I tried to take a shot at the samurai. My phaser's out." He shoved the useless weapon back into his belt.

Kirk was still holding his own, drawn as he had heard the sounds of Sulu's encounter. He pointed it at the ground and fired. Nothing happened. He checked the settings and fired again. Slowly he replaced it in his belt.

"We had better get to the glade," he said grimly.

"Yes sir. We—Look!"

The air was shimmering. A familiar shimmer, but erratic and uncertain. "Someone's beaming down from the ship."

Someone was certainly trying to, but there appeared to be some obstruction.

Willing the transporter to operate, as if that would do any good, Kirk waited. The shimmer faded, erupted, faded; with one last splash of sparkles, Spock materialized in front of them.

"Spock! My orders were no one was to leave the ship."

"It was necessary, Captain. I could not contact you by communicator, and the transporter is almost useless now. As I told you, there is an unusual power field down here. It seems to be soaking up all kinds of energy at the source. I calculated the rate at which it was growing, and reasoned that we might be able to transport one more person." Spock conveyed, with a lift of his eyebrow, that while white rabbits and such were beyond his comprehension, unexplained force fields were not to be tolerated. "We barely managed that."

Kirk had to approve this decision. "Good. I can use your help."

Sulu said anxiously, "We're stranded down here, Captain?"

"Until we find out what this is all about."

A tiger roared in the distance.

"That way!" said Kirk. "Spread out, find it." He tried not to think about the ineffective phasers.

At the glade, Tonia Barrows and McCoy looked for the others a bit reluctantly.

"There's no one here."

"This is the rendezvous point," said McCoy. The girl wandered around the clearing. The doctor followed her slowly. "What was that? I thought—I swear I heard something."

"Don't talk like that!" In spite of the splendid costume and the warm eyes of McCoy, she was still jumpy.

"A princess shouldn't be afraid, not with her brave knight to protect her." Tonia managed a small smile and moved nearer to the shelter of a sun-warmed oak.

"Aaah!" There was a wild flurry of black and white—she was struggling with someone. McCoy ran.

The plumed hat was jaunty; pointed beard, jeweled doublet, swirling cloak. McCoy sailed in, fists flying. The cowardly lecher couldn't fight. Don Juan slunk off.

McCoy held her for a moment as she pulled her gown back together and straightened the tall hat, feeling extremely chivalrous. He had battled for his lady, and he'd do it again.

Hoofbeats sounded in the distance. They whirled, and saw, across the meadow, a gigantic horse emerging from the wood. The horse reared and wheeled as its rider perceived them.

McCoy's belief was strained almost to breaking point. The Black Knight lowered a wicked-looking lance and charged.

These fairy-tale characters were interrupting him too often. McCoy had had enough. He was going to deal with this apparition on the proper terms. A figment of the imagination was not real, could do no harm. He was not going to react anymore to hallucinations. He stepped out, unarmed, and confronted the oncoming menace, concentrating on denying the evidence of his senses.

The great black animal pounded across the meadow, the lance couchant.

"Look out, Bones!" McCoy ignored Kirk's cry of warning. Steadily, stubbornly he marched directly toward the galloping rider.

Kirk's phaser failed. He scrambled the old-fashioned pistol that he had confiscated from Sulu from his belt, as the wicked lance took McCoy through the chest.

The horse reared as Tonia Barrows screamed, and the Black Knight bent to retrieve his weapon. Kirk fired rapidly, and the armored horseman crashed to the ground a few yards away. Tonia's shrieks rose shrilly amid the echoes.

She fell to her knees over the prostrate McCoy. "He's dead, he's dead. It's all my fault. It never would have happened . . . Ohhh!"

"No, Tonia—" said Kirk.

"But it was, it was. My fault. I am to blame!" She was screaming and weeping. "I've killed him, I've killed Leonard." Kirk took her arm, but she wrenched away from him and beat her fists on the ground.

"Yeoman," said Kirk in his sternest voice. "We're in trouble. I need every crewman alert and thinking."

The hysteria left her cries. "Yes, sir." Struggling for composure, she rose slowly to her feet.

Spock covered McCoy's body, hiding the gaping wound. Kirk turned away for a moment. He could not quite control his face. His friend was dead. Shore leave. And they were all looking to him for strength. He schooled his expression to a rocklike calm, and without looking back, strode purposefully toward Sulu. Sulu was crouching over the body of the Black Knight.

"Captain," he said worriedly, "I don't get this."

"Neither do I, Mr. Sulu," said Kirk, staring down with hatred at the sable armor. "But before we leave this planet, I *will.*"

"Then you'd better have a look at this, sir." Sulu opened the visor and revealed the face of McCoy's murderer.

"What the—?" Perfectly molded skin, straight nose regular as a waxwork, the mask stared back at him.

"It's like a dummy, Captain. It couldn't be alive."

"Tricorder?"

"Barely operating, sir."

"Spock!" Kirk handed the instrument to the First Officer. "What do you make of this?"

Spock took readings with some difficulty. "This is not human skin tissue, sir. More resembles the cellular casting we use for wound repairs. Much finer, of course."

"Mr. Spock!" Kirk stood up. "I want an exact judgment."

"Definitely a mechanical contrivance. Its tissues resemble the basic cell structure of the plants here—the trees, even the grass—"

Kirk peered at the face again. "Are you suggesting that this is a *plant*, Spock?"

Spock indicated extreme puzzlement by a slight frown. "I'm saying all these things are multicellular castings. The plants, the people, the animals—they're all being manufactured."

"By who? and why?" said Kirk blankly. "And why these particular things?"

Spock shook his head. "All we know for sure is that they act exactly like the real thing. Just as pleasant—or just as deadly."

Esteban Rodriguez had not yet had a chance to report his encounter with the Bengal tiger, which had leaped from the rocks and snarled at him. He had managed to get away, and was telling Yeoman Angela Teller about that and other things as they headed for the glade.

There was a buzzing sound. They looked around, and finally up. Overhead, a Sopwith Camel banked and dipped.

"What is *that*?"

"Of all the crazy things. Remember what I was telling you a little while ago about the early wars in the air, and the funny little vehicles they used?" Angela nodded, looking up at the sky. "Well, that's one of them."

The plane veered back and looped over their heads. Angela eyed it dubiously. "Can it hurt us?"

"Not unless it makes a strafing run." Rodriguez was rather pleased. No one could have asked for a better opportunity to show off his special knowledge. He had never expected to see one of those planes actually flying!

"A what?" She was impressed, he could tell.

"The way they used to attack people on the ground," he said offhandedly.

The biplane's engines roared as it banked and started toward them. It dived. The rat-tat-tat of vintage gunnery tore the air to shreds.

"Santa Maria!" Rodriguez dragged the girl toward the shelter of the nearby rocks. As the plane zoomed away, she dropped.

"Angela!" He lifted her. Her head lolled unnaturally limp, and her weight was dead in his arms.

Kirk and Spock were staring at the distant aircraft when Sulu called them.

The bodies of McCoy and the Black Knight had vanished.

"Look," said Sulu. "They've been dragged away."

They were stranded in a nightmare. "Mr. Spock!" said Kirk desperately.

The Vulcan was uncomfortable. "At this point, Captain, my analysis may not sound very scientific."

"McCoy's death is a scientific fact." The one undeniable reality.

"There is one faint possibility. Very unlikely, but nevertheless—Captain, what were your thoughts just before you encountered the people you met here?"

Kirk tried to remember. "I was thinking about . . . the Academy."

"Hey, Jim baby!"

There he was again. Finnegan. Lolling against a tree across the glade.

"I see you had to bring up reinforcements," he sneered. "Well, I'm still waiting for you, Jim boy!"

Maybe. "Finnegan! What's been happening to my people?"

The cadet, characteristically unhelpful, snickered and

ducked back among the trees. His mocking laughter floated back to Kirk, who gritted his teeth.

"Take Mr. Sulu. Find McCoy's body. This man's my problem." He started across the glade.

"Captain—" Spock began.

"That's an order, Mr. Spock!" Kirk plunged into the trees in Finnegan's wake.

The laughter penetrated the forest. Kirk stalked after it. But it came from the left, and then the right, and straight ahead.

"This way, Jim boy, that's the boy."

He rounded a clump of trees and came on a bare rocky hill. No grass grew here; it was wild and deserted—except for the derisive voice.

"Old legs givin' out, Jimmy boy? Ha-ha-heeheehee!"

The voice came from behind him. He whirled, and it came again from above.

"Just like it used to be, Jim boy, remember? You never could find your head with both hands."

Kirk clenched his fists. He was going to get even with Finnegan if it was the last thing he did.

On a spur to his right, Finnegan called, "Over here, Jimmy boy!"

"Finnegan! I want some answers!"

"Coming up! He-ha-hee!" Kirk pursued the elusive voice until he was seething with fury; at last Finnegan stayed long enough on a rock above him for Kirk to start climbing.

With practiced ease, Finnegan met him in a violent bulldogging roll. They fell together to the flat ground and Kirk was briefly aware of a profound satisfaction—at last it had come to a clinch, Finnegan had never lost a fight; you could feel that in his confidence and skill, and Kirk took the impact of blow after blow without being able to land a really good punch. And he was winded from the chase.

Finnegan stood up and looked down at him. "Get up, get up. Always fight fair, don't you, you officer-and-gentleman, you? You stupid underclassman, I've got the edge." His brogue-tinged voice rang out in triumphant glee. "I'm still twenty years old—look at you! You're an old man!"

Kirk rolled to his feet and swung. Finnegan ducked,

slipped and landed hard. Kirk allowed himself a moment to savor this victory.

"Uh—uh," grunted the prostrate cadet. "Jim! I can't move my legs. Ohhh. Me back, it's broken. You've broken me back . . . Ohhhh!"

Officer and Gentleman. Kirk knelt and carefully straightened his victim's leg. He palpated muscle. Finnegan groaned and shook his head dizzily. Kirk moved closer and probed cautiously. "Can you feel that?"

And he fell flat as Finnegan's clasped hands landed on the nape of his neck in a mighty double chop. Finnegan leaped to his feet, laughing.

" 'Can you feel that?' " he mocked. "Sleep sweet, Jimmy boy, Sleep as long as you like. Sleep forever, Jimmy boy, forever and ever . . ."

Kirk was not in a position to appreciate this ironic lullaby. Watery images vaguely swam before his eyes, his nose hurt, and the back of his head was resting on a sharp pebble.

Finnegan loomed above him against the sky, hands resting on his hips, shaking his head sadly.

"Won't you ever learn, Jim boy? You never could take me!"

Kirk painfully propped himself up on one elbow and spat blood. He wheezed, "Finnegan. One thing."

Magnanimous, Finnegan said, "Sure, name it."

"Answers!"

He should have known better.

"Earn 'em!"

As he started groggily to his feet, Finnegan floored him again.

He lay there for one minute. This had gone too far. Fair or foul, the swaggering hooligan was going to get it. He rolled over, and, summoning all his unarmed-combat training, got on his feet in the same motion. Finnegan gestured, come on, come on, from his defensive crouch. ". . . wipe that grin off his face," Kirk thought, as he lunged. He landed a crunching blow and Finnegan reeled, recovered and came back.

It seemed hours of bruising impacts on rib, jaw, arms. It was harder and harder to lift the hand and push it through the air, which had become harder and harder to breathe. Finally, Kirk pounded his last remaining strength into Finnegan's midriff, and the man dropped and lay still. Kirk fell back against the rock and tried to breathe. He had thought he was exhausted before. And he didn't dare close his eyes to blink away the running sweat, lest Finnegan be playing possum again. And he just could not lift his arms.

Finnegan came to, slowly. "Not bad," he said grudgingly.

"Yeah."

"Kinda . . . ow! Makes up for things, huh, Jim?"

Kirk licked blood off his lip. "A lot of things." Even it he had a black eye. "Now, what has been happening to my people?"

With a touch of his old arrogance, Finnegan smirked. "I never answer questions from Plebes."

"I'm not a plebe. This is *today*, fifteen years later. What are you doing here?"

There was a pause as they looked at each other.

"Being exactly what you expect me to be, Jim boy!" cried Finnegan as he threw a handful of dirt in Kirk's eyes and scrambled to his feet. Kirk lost his balance but landed with one fist heavy in Finnegan's solar plexus. Finnegan closed with him.

Swaying like a couple of drunks with tiredness, neither would give in. But Finnegan wasn't laughing anymore. He'd started dodging Kirk's blows. Kirk thought, he's twenty years old, and he's winded—more winded than the old man! He evaded a wide swing and grabbed a handful of Finnegan's tunic, driving his fist right into the bully's battered face with a final, explosive grunt.

And that was definitely that. Finnegan was out for the count. And Kirk, breathless, bruised and bleeding, felt like crowing. After all these years . . .

As he felt a grin painfully stretching his cut lip, Spock said, "Did you enjoy it, Captain?"

"Yes," panted Kirk, gloating. "I did enjoy it. For almost half my lifetime, the one thing I wanted was to beat the tar out of Finnegan."

Spock raised his right eyebrow. "This supports a theory I have been formulating . . ."

"We're all meeting people and things we happen to be thinking about at the moment."

Spock nodded. "Somehow our thoughts are read, then that object is quickly manufactured and provided."

"H'm. So it gets dangerous if we happen to be thinking about—" Kirk stopped hastily.

"We must control our thoughts carefully." Spock, of course, would not find this difficult.

Kirk tried not to think about—no! or . . . not *that*, either!

"The power field we detected is undoubtedly underground, fabricating these things. Passages lead up to the surface. As, for example, when Rodriguez thought of a tiger—" Even Spock was not infallible, it seemed. There was a snarling roar, and the magnificent head of a Bengal tiger peered at them over the rocks. It padded over the ridge and down out of sight among the shrubs—toward them.

Without moving, Kirk eyed the bushes. "We've got to get back to the others and warn them."

Spock, immobile, murmured, "Yes."

"We have to get out of here."

"Immediately, Captain."

They looked at each other sidewise. "You go first, Spock. I'll try and distract him."

"I can't let you do that, sir. I'll distract him." The tiger waited patiently for them to make the first move. It waited, crouching, then settled down. It began to lick its paws.

"We could try moving very slowly."

With extreme caution, Kirk extended a foot. The tiger watched interestedly. He leaned weight on the foot and achieved a step. Spock glided beside him as they edged around the rock. They ran like hell.

Behind them, the tiger turned itself off.

Rodriguez fell out of the shrubbery in their path. "Angela! The plane—" On cue, the Sopwith Camel appeared overhead in mid-dive. Kirk threw himself and his men to the ground as 50-caliber machine-gun bullets plowed the path at their side.

"Don't think about it!" said Kirk. "To the glade, fast!"

"Hai!" The Japanese warrior in his heavy complex

armor flailed at them with a sharp sword. "Ahh-HOU!" But he was hampered by his carapace, and they dodged him easily.

As they reached the glade, Yeoman Barrows seemed to be in difficulties again. Sulu was wrestling with the bearded amorist in the black cloak as she clutched her tattered tunic in front of her; apparently she had been changing out of her princess's dress when accosted.

But Don Juan melted away as Kirk and Spock pelted up to them.

"Sulu, Rodriguez, Barrows—front and center!" snapped Kirk.

"Sir—"

"Don't ask any questions. This is an order!" They moved in to face him, Tonia squirming into her uniform.

"Now brace. Everyone, eyes front. Don't talk. Don't breathe. Don't think. You're at attention and concentrating on that and only that. Concentrate!"

The three crewmen obediently struggled not to think.

Spock gestured, and Kirk turned to see a new apparition. A kindly old gentleman in dignified robes smiled at him.

"Who are you?" From whose errant thoughts had this one appeared?

"I am the Caretaker of this planet, Captain Kirk."

"You know me?"

"But of course." He nodded toward the bewildered crewmen. "And Lieutenant Rodriguez, Lieutenant Sulu, Yeoman Barrows—and Mr. Spock."

The dangers in this place had not, so far, appeared in sheep's clothing. They had been all obvious threats. Perhaps . . .

"I stopped by to check our power supplies, and have only just realized that we had guests who did not understand all this. These experiences were intended to amuse you."

Kirk was taken aback. "*Amuse* us! Is that your word for all we've been through?"

The man laughed easily. "Oh, none of this is permanent." He waved at the surrounding glade, the forest, the meadows. "Here you have merely to imagine your fondest wishes—old ones you wish to relive, new ones, battle, fear, love, triumph. Anything which pleases you can be made to happen here."

"The term," said Spock, out of the encyclopedia he housed in his brain, "is 'amusement park.' "

"But of course." The Caretaker sounded as though this were perfectly obvious.

"An old Earth term for a place where people could go to see and do all kinds of exciting and fantastic things."

"This planet was constructed for our race of people, Captain. We come here, and play."

Sulu was puzzled. "Play? As advanced as you are, and you still play?"

The Caretaker looked at him pityingly. Kirk waved Sulu to silence. "Play, Mr. Sulu. The more complex the mind, the greater the need for the simplicity of play."

The robed figure beamed approvingly. "Exactly, Captain. You are most perceptive.

"I regret that your equipment was inadvertently affected. The system needed slight adjustment—it was pulling energy from the nearest available source. I think you will find that all is now in order."

But it hadn't been all play. The fight with Finnegan had been extremely satisfying; the tiger had, after all, harmed no one; and Tonia's virtue was still intact. But . . .

"None of this explains the death of my ship's surgeon," said Kirk. The "amusement park" of an advanced race had turned killer for the younger people. The Caretaker's face was gentle and his words reassuring, but perhaps the toys of his race were too dangerous.

"Possibly because I haven't died, Jim," said McCoy's voice behind him. Yeoman Barrows turned pale, and then radiant with joy.

McCoy sauntered into the clearing, in the pink of health, with a young lady clad in a few feathers clinging to each of his arms.

"I was taken below the surface," he explained, glancing at his chest, "for some rather—remarkable—repairs. It's amazing! There's a factory complex down there like nothing I've ever seen. They can build anything—immediately!"

Tonia had run to him, and was gazing into his face as if she could not believe her eyes. She touched his chest, last seen torn and bleeding. She became conscious of an obstruction and belatedly realized that McCoy was not alone.

She found her tongue. "And how do you explain *them*?"

"Er—" McCoy glanced fondly at the two voluptuous, bare, willing beauties on his arms. "Well, I was thinking about a little cabaret I know on Rigel II. There were these two girls in the chorus line that I—well—" his assurance faltered. "Er—here they are."

Tonia looked. He said, "Well, after all, I am on shore leave."

"So am I," said Tonia ominously.

"Er—" McCoy would just have to spread himself around. "So you are."

Yeoman Barrows waited.

Resigning himself to the not-unattractive inevitable, McCoy released the charmers. "Well, girls, I'm sure you can turn something up."

The girls smiled a cheerful farewell to the doctor and moved. To Sulu's evident delight, the redhead chose to nestle up to him. Spock, however, did not appear gratified at the armful of blonde that approached him. He dodged politely, but to no avail. She insinuated herself somehow and stood alarming close.

Rodriguez said, very quietly, "And—Angela?"

"Esteban!" she said, hurrying out of the shrubbery. "I've been looking all over for you!" He took her hand and stared, unbelievingly.

The Caretaker smiled upon all these couples, even at the restive Spock. "We regret that you have been made uncomfortable, even puzzled."

Kirk had relaxed enough to be curious. "You say your people built this? Who are you? What planet are you from?"

The Caretaker shook his white head. "Your race is not yet ready to understand us, Captain Kirk."

Spock, still trying to tactfully disentangle himself from the cabaret girl, replied, "I tend to agree."

The communicator beeped. "This is the bridge, Captain. Our power systems have come back in. Do you require any assistance?"

"Everything is in order, Lieutenant Uhura. Stand by." It seemed now that everything was indeed in order. But . . .

"With the proper caution, our amusement planet could be an ideal place for your people to enjoy themselves, if you wish," said the Caretaker.

McCoy, now firmly attached to Yeoman Barrows, said, "It *is* what the doctor ordered, Jim."

"Very well . . . Bridge! I'll be sending up a short briefing. As soon as all personnel have heard it, you may commence transporting shore parties. And tell them to prepare for the best shore leave they've ever had!"

As Kirk shut his communicator, Mr. Spock approached him, still surrounded by pink feathers and bare legs. "I'll go back aboard, Captain. With all due respect to the young lady, I've had about all the shore leave I care for."

The young lady, acknowledging defeat, joined her companion. Sulu did not seem to mind.

"No, Mr. Spock, I'll go. You—"

Ruth glided out from the forest canopy and held out her hands, smiling.

"On the other hand, perhaps I'll stay for a day or two . . ." said the Captain, leaving Spock to his own devices.

Later, Spock greeted them, impassive as ever. He shook his head as he looked at their suntanned faces.

"Enjoy your shore leave, gentlemen?"

Kirk met McCoy's amused eye. "That we did, Mr. Spock. That we did!"

Spock stared at them, puzzled. They seemed full of satisfaction. He shrugged.

"Most illogical," he said with finality.

The *Enterprise* departed at Warp Factor One amid the guffaws of the Captain and the ship's surgeon.

THE SQUIRE OF GOTHOS

Writer: Paul Schneider
Director: Don McDougall
Guest stars: William Campbell, Michael Barrier

The planet had given no hint of its existence to the *Enterprise*. Uncharted, unsuspected, undetected, it finally confessed its presence to the starship's sensors. At Spock's sudden announcement of their new reading, Kirk in some annoyance flipped a switch—and sure enough, out of what should have continued to be the empty, star-void quadrant of space they were traversing, a crescent-shaped body swam into abrupt, unusually brilliant, magnified focus on the bridge viewing screen.

Kirk glared at it. It was an unwelcome distraction from his job—a mission to get needed supplies to Colony Beta 6; and get them there by an uninterrupted warp factor three speed across this apparent space desert, barren of stars. He spoke tersely. "Navigation report."

Crewman De Salle looked up from his computations. "Iron-silicate substance, Captain, planet-sized magnitude One-E. We'll be passing close."

The puzzled Spock had left his station to come and stand by the command chair. Eyes on the screen, he said, "It is incredible that this body has gone unrecorded on all our charts, sir."

So, Kirk thought, imagination must bestir itself, stretching the credible to include the incredible. There was a certain dryness in his retort. "But there it is, Mr. Spock, incredible though it be." He swung around to face his bridge people. "We can't stop to investigate now. All science stations will gather data for computer banks. Lieutenant Uhura, report the discovery of this planet on subspace radio."

She struggled to obey the order. Then she turned. "Strong interference on subspace, sir. The planet must be a natural radio source."

"Then let's get out of its range," Kirk said. He twisted his chair around to the helm console. "Veer off forty degrees, Mr. Sulu."

As Sulu reached for a control on his board, he disappeared. One moment he was there, substantial, familiar, intently competent—and the next, his chair was as empty as though vacancy had always been its appointed function. *"Sulu!"* Kirk shouted, leaping for the helm. Then he, too, was gone, vanished as utterly as Sulu. Navigator De Salle, taut-faced, sprang from his station. "They're *gone*, Mr. Spock! *They're both gone!*"

Spock, at the abandoned command console, twisted a dial. Obediently, alarm sirens shrieked through the ship. It was the beginning of a general, deck-to-deck scrutiny of its every nook and cranny. As Spock dismissed the last discouraged search party, he turned to the big, blond meteorologist beside him. "They're either down on that planet—or nowhere." Overhearing, De Salle said tensely, "But there's still no sign of human life on the surface, sir. Of course the probe instruments may be malfunctioning."

Spock eyed his board. "They are functioning normally," he said. "Continue sensor sweeps. Lieutenant Uhura, have you covered all wave-bands?"

"All of them, sir. No response."

De Salle was on his feet. "With due respect, sir, I request permission to transport down to the surface to carry the search on there!"

McCoy had joined the group at the command chair. Now he grabbed Spock's arm. "I agree! What are we waiting for, Spock?"

"The decision will be mine, Doctor. I hold the responsibility for your safety." Blandly ignoring McCoy's outraged glare, he addressed the big meteorologist. "Dr. Jaeger, please describe your geophysical findings on the surface below."

"No detectable soil or vegetation . . . extremely hot.

The atmosphere is toxic, swept by tornadic storms . . . continuous volcanic activity . . . inimical to any life as we know it, without oxygen life support."

"How would you estimate the survival time of two unprotected men down there?"

"As long as it would take to draw one breath."

Nobody spoke. Then Uhura broke the heavy stillness. "Mr. Spock! My viewing screen! Look!" All eyes on the bridge veered to her station. There on the screen, letters—letters formed in flowing, old-English script—had begun to appear. Gradually they extended themselves until the message they were intended to convey had completed itself. Astoundingly out of tune with the somber mood of the bridge people, it was: "Greetings and felicitations."

Spock read it aloud without inflection. "Greetings . . . and . . . felicitations. Send this, Lieutenant. U.S.S. *Enterprise* to signaler on planet surface. Identify yourself. We—" He broke off as more letters assembled themselves into words on the screen. After a moment, he read them aloud, too, slowly, unbelievingly. "Hip . . . hip . . . hurrah," he said, "and I believe that last word is pronounced 'tallyho'?"

"Some kind of joke, sir?" De Salle said.

Spock glanced at him. "I shall entertain any theories, Mr. De Salle. Any at all . . ."

McCoy spoke up. "One thing is certain. There *is* life on that planet!"

"You would seem to be correct, Doctor," Spock said. He reached for the intercom; and had just ordered preparation of the Transporter Room when Scotty, pushing his way toward him, reached him and said, "Request assignment to the search party, sir."

Sometimes Spock's eyes seemed to be looking at one from a great distance. They had that faraway look in them now as he shook his head. "No, Mr. Scott. Neither you nor I can be spared here. Mr. De Salle, you will equip landing party with full armaments, with life support and communication gear. Doctor Jaeger, your geophysical knowledge may be crucial. Doctor McCoy will accompany, too. If those peculiar signals come from Captain Kirk and Sulu, their rationality is in question."

He waited to issue his final order until the landing group

had taken position on the Transporter Platform's indentations. Then, handing De Salle a black box, he said, "Once on the surface, you will establish immediate contact with us—and by this laser beam, if necessary."

Scott worked his switches. And the three figures began their dissolution into shining fragments.

They hadn't precisely formulated what they had expected. A kind of murderous combine of earth tremors, buffetings by hurricane whirlwinds, the suffocating heat of a planet torn by cosmic forces at war below the fissured lava of its tormented surface, the coughing inhalation of lung-searing gases. But what they found differed from their vaguely shaped apprehensions. It was a forest, cool, green, its leafy aisles tranquil, shadowy. Around the boles of its trees, flowering vines circled, scenting the fresh air with their blossoms' fragrance. Dumbfounded, McCoy watched a leaf flutter down from the bough over his head.

His voice was thick through his life-support filter. "Jaeger, where are your storms?"

Shaking his head, the meteorologist checked the instrument he held. "An atmosphere, McCoy—exactly the same as our own!"

Remembering, De Salle, removing his face mask, cried, "Ship communication and report!" But something was wrong with his communicator—a contagious wrongness that affected all their communicators. De Salle didn't give up. As he pointed the laser beam skyward, he said, "Keep trying . . . keep trying." Then he frowned. "Something's blocking this beacon. Got to find open ground . . ."

Backing off, he rounded a clump of bush. And halted, noting the reflection of flickering light on its dark leaves. Very slowly he turned. He was face to face with a stone griffin. Its wings were lifted high over the glaring features of its lion's visage. In one outstretched talon, it held a flaming torch.

"Dr. McCoy! Dr. Jaeger! Over here!"

There were two griffins, both holding torches. It was McCoy who first spotted the dark, massive, iron-bound door flanked by its guardian beasts of heraldry. The door was ajar. De Salle, moving into the lead, unlimbered his phaser. Followed by the others, he pushed through the half-open entry.

Except for the crackling of what looked like a big hearth fire, absolute stillness greeted them.

"In the name of heaven . . . where are we?" McCoy muttered.

Where they were was in a spacious Victorian drawing room, chandelier-lit. The wall over the burning logs of its fireplace held an arrangement of crossed swords, muskets, pistols and battle flags. Its other walls were hung with tapestries, with portraits of ancestors in armor, in the colorful uniforms of the Napoleonic wars. Near a gleaming mahogany table, a sideboard glittered with gold dishes. A harpsichord stood under a curved, gilt-framed mirror. All was in order. Everything fitted into the picture of a benevolently self-indulgent Victorianism. Except for one thing. Certain niches pressed into the urbane walls revealed a peculiar taste in statuary. They held carved shapes of lizard-like creatures, tortured-looking dolphins, a pair of giant, humanoid forms—and a tentacled spider-thing.

Suddenly, De Salle shouted: *"Look!"*

At the end of the room was an inset, a hollow gouged prominently out of its wall. As the other niches held statuary, this one held the stiffened forms of Kirk and Sulu, their attitudes caught and hardened as they had last moved at the instant before their disappearance. Their figures were bathed in a violet light. De Salle rushed to them, calling, "Dr. McCoy—quick! Dr. McCoy!"

But McCoy's health monitor was grimly factual. He looked up from it, his face tired-looking. "Nothing," he said. "Kirk and Sulu . . . like waxwork shapes . . ."

The drawing room's door slammed shut. A moment later, a tinkling Mozart-like arpeggio came from the harpsichord. And seated on the bench before it was the player—a man, a man clad in the silver-buckled elegance of a military man of the mid-1800's—a delighted if slightly sly smile on his rosy face.

As the *Enterprise* trio stared at him, he completed the musical passage with a flourish of well-groomed hands. Then he spun around to face them. He was Byronically handsome, from his pouting mouth and neckcloth-length hair to his disdainful air of superiority, of being set apart as an object of special and peculiar value and privilege. The gesture he made toward the hollow holding the forms of Kirk and Sulu was either genuinely bored—or the blossom of a painstaking cultivation of boredom.

"I must say," the musician said amiably, "that they make an exquisite display pair." Then a note of regret drooped the voice. "But I suppose you'll want them back now."

A lace-cuffed hand was lifted. Instantly, Kirk started forward, completing his interrupted move to the helm of the *Enterprise*. Sulu stirred, his face confused, his eyes bewildered. They sought Kirk's face. "Captain, where are we?"

The man on the harpsichord bench rose. "Welcome to my island of peace on this stormy little planet of Gothos."

Kirk ignored him to speak to his men. "What's happened? Fill me in."

McCoy said, "Jim, you disappeared from the bridge after Sulu went. We've been hunting you for hours—"

Their host cut across him. "You must excuse my whimsical way of fetching you here. But when I saw you passing by, I simply could not resist entertaining you."

Kirk, exchanging a glance with McCoy, stepped forward. "I am Captain James Kirk of the United Starship *Enterprise* . . ."

The creature swept him a bow. "So you are the captain of these brave men! My greetings and felicitations, Captain. It's so good of you and your officers to drop in. Absolutely smashing of you!"

The theatricality of the voice and gesture was as turgid as old greasepaint. Kirk had to make an effort to keep his voice level. "Who are you?" he said. "Where do you come from?"

An arm swept wide in a grandly embracing movement. "Have no fear, lads," said the too-rich voice. "I have made myself as one of you . . ."

De Salle's temper, compounded of fear mingled with rage, exploded. He advanced, his phaser on aim. "Who are you? That is the question that was asked you! Answer it! And make the answer fast!"

The being appreciated De Salle. "Ah, such spirited ferocity!" it crowed happily. Then, not unlike a child remembering lessons in manners, it said, "Oh, forgive me. General

Trelane, retired. At your service, gentlemen. My home is your home."

It failed to soothe De Salle's temper. Low-voiced, he spoke to Kirk. "Captain, we've lost contact with the ship. We're trapped here."

Overhearing, General Trelane rubbed his hands in exuberant pleasure. " 'Trapped here,' " he echoed. "I cannot tell you how it delights me—having visitors to this very planet I have made my hobby. From my observations I did not think you capable of such voyages."

Jaeger, whispering to Kirk, gestured around them. "Captain, note the period—nine hundred light-years from Earth. This place and time fit what might have been seen if there were telescopes powerful enough to—"

He was stopped by the smile on Trelane's full red lips. "Yes. I have been an interested witness of your lively little doings on your lively little Earth, sir . . ."

"Then you've been witnessing its doings of nine hundred years past," Kirk said. "That's a long time."

Trelane chuckled. "Good heavens, have I made a time error? How fallible of me!" Eyeing the stately room around him, he added, "I did so want to make you feel at home. In fact, I am quite proud of the detail."

"General Trelane—" Kirk began; and stopped at the coyly cautionary finger that had been held up. "Tut-tut, a retired general, sir. Just Squire Trelane, now. You may call me 'Squire'—indeed, I rather fancy the title."

In his career as a starship captain, Kirk had encountered many oddments of galactic creation—oddments ranging from the ultimately hideous and alien, to a beauty that spoke with the final familiarity of wonder to the soul. At this moment, face to face with this self-styled squire of a self-chosen time of a Victorian England, chosen out of all the times offered by nine hundred years, he seemed to be face to face with the last anomaly—an X of mystery compounded simultaneously of innocence and guile. He looked at Squire Trelane. "For what purpose have you imprisoned us here?" he asked.

Even as he spoke, he had the sense of spider-strands, sticky, well-woven, encompassing him. It was as though he had already heard what the too-rich voice was saying. "Imprisoned? Nonsense! You are my guests." His host's lower lip actually trembled with what suggested itself as the touching eagerness of hospitality. "You see, I was just completing my studies of your curious and fascinating society. You happened by at a most propitious moment." There was a low, carved, armless chair beside him and he flung himself into it. "Captain Kirk, you must tell me all about your campaigns—your battles—your missions of conquest . . ."

For the first time, Kirk seemed to know where he was. For the first time since Sulu's disappearance from the *Enterprise*, he felt a sense of firm identity, of some unnamable stability back under his feet. "Our missions are peaceful," he said. "They are not for conquest. We battle only when we have no choice."

Trelane winked at him. His left eyelid dropped and rose in inescapable suggestion of mutual, known, if unacknowledged awareness of perfidious doings in high places. "So that's the official story, eh, Captain?"

Unobtrusively, McCoy had directed his tricorder at Trelane. Just as unobtrusively, Kirk had registered this fact. Now he stepped toward the low, armless chair. "Squire Trelane," he said, "I must ask you to let us return to our ship."

What he got was a languid wave of a languid hand. "Wouldn't hear of it!" Trelane protested. "You will all join me in a repast. There is so much I must learn from you: your *feelings* about war . . . about killing . . . about conquest—that sort of thing." A finger of the languid hand became unlanguid. It stiffened, pointed, aiming at Kirk. "You are, you know," said Trelane, "one of the few predator species—species that preys even on itself."

De Salle, beside Kirk, seemed to go suddenly thick in the neck. His hand darted to his phaser. "Sir?" he said, half in question, half in appeal.

"On 'stun,' De Salle," Kirk said. "Don't kill him."

What was it about this being that both repelled and at the same time broke your heart? A capacity for communicating loneliness, that burden of the solitary self borne either in a conscious fortitude or in a necessity of unaware resentment and complaint? It was speaking, the strange being. "De Sale—is that his name, Captain Kirk?" In its eagerness it didn't wait for an answer but rushed on, crying to the navigator, *"Vous êtes un vrai français?"*

"My ancestry is French . . . Yes . . ."

"Ah, *monsieur*! *Vive la gloire! Vive Napoleon!* I admire your Napoleon very much, y'know."

"Mr. De Salle is our navigator," Kirk said evenly. "This gentleman is our medical officer, Dr. McCoy—our helmsman, Sulu, and our meteorologist, Carl Jaeger . . ."

Trelane acknowledged each introduction. "Welcome, good physicianer. All reverence to your ancestors, Honorable Sir . . ."

Sulu flushed. "What's he doing—kidding?"

But Trelane's interest had fixed on Jaeger. Clicking his heels, he cried, *"Und Offizier Jaeger, die deutsche Soldat, nein?"* Then stamping his feet in cadence to his words, he declaimed, *"Eins, zwei, drei, vier! Gehen wir mit dem Schiessgewehr!"*

Jaeger's voice was dry as dead bone. "I am a scientist—not a military man."

Trelane beamed at him. "Come now, we are all military men under the skin. And how we do love our uniforms!" He clearly loved his—and the sight of himself in it, epauletted, be-braided as the gilt-framed mirror that reflected it back to him flushed his face with self-admiring pride. He turned, preening to get a three-quarter view of his cuirass of shining buttons; and Kirk, under his breath, spoke to De Salle. *"Now!"* But as the phaser lifted to aim, Trelane wheeled, lifting his hand. At once, De Salle stiffened into immobility.

"What is that interesting weapon you have there?" inquired the Squire of Gothos. He removed the phaser—and thaw replaced the frozen stillness of De Salle's figure. "Ah, yes, I see! That won't kill—but this will! The mechanism is now clear to me." Making an adjustment, he fired the phaser at the niche containing the lizard-like sculpture. It dematerialized. Trelane laughed with delight. "Oh, how marvelous!" Swinging the weapon around, he shot at all the statues set in their niches around the room, yelling as each disintegrated and vanished. "Devastating!" howled Trelane. "Why this could kill millions."

Striding up to him, Kirk tore the phaser from his hand.

"Beginning with whom, Trelane? My crew? Are we your next targets?"

The full red lips pouted. "But how absolutely typical of your species, Captain! You don't understand, so you're angry." He pointed a gleeful finger at Kirk. "But do not be impatient. I have anticipated your next wish. You wish to know how I've managed all this, don't you?"

He nodded in answer to his own question. Then, weaving his fingers together like a prissy English schoolmaster about to dissertate on Virgil's prosody, he said, "We—meaning others and myself—have, to state the matter briefly, perfected a system by which matter can be changed to energy . . . and then back to matter . . ."

"Like the Transporter system aboard the *Enterprise*," Kirk said.

"Oh, that's a crude example! Ours is an infinitely more sophisticated process. You see, we not only transport matter from place to place but we can alter its shape, too, at will."

"This drawing room then," Kirk said. "You created it? By rearranging the existing matter of the planet?"

"Quite," Trelane said.

"But how—"

The creature drew a soothing finger across a furrow of irritation that had appeared on its brow. "Dear Captain, your inquiries are becoming tiresome. Why? I want you to be happy—to free your mind of care. Let us enjoy ourselves in the spirit of martial good fellowship!"

Kirk turned quietly to his men. "Let's go. We're getting out of here."

"Naughty captain!" Trelane said. "Fie, you are quite rude. But you cannot leave here. What an admirably fiery look of protest! Upon my soul, I admire you, sir, though in mercy you seem to need another demonstration of my authority—"

His right hand made a swift gesture; and where Kirk had stood was emptiness. Then he was back—but on his knees, racked by choking paroxysms of agony. Dismissed from the shelter of Trelane's domain, he had been exposed to the basting effects of the planet's lethal atmosphere. In a moment its toxic gases had licked into his lungs. He coughed, doubled over, still tortured by their strangulating vapors—and the Squire of Gothos patted his bent head.

"That was an example," he said, "of what can occur away from my kindly influence. I do hope that you will now behave yourself, Captain, not only for your own sake, but because, if you don't, I shall be very angry."

Power. It had nothing to do with morality, with responsibility. Like Trelane's, it simply existed—a fact to which the body was obliged to bow but which the heart could continue to reject, to despise.

"Let me hold on," Kirk thought.

The sensors of the *Enterprise* had finally located Trelane's cool green oasis. Scott, staring at its tranquil trees on the bridge viewing screen, said, "An area as peaceful as Earth. But how do you explain it, Mr. Spock?"

"I don't, Mr. Scott. It just is. Artificial, perhaps—a freak of nature. But the fact remains that life could exist in that space. See if you can tune the sensors down finer. See if you can pick up any sentient life forms in that area of Gothos."

As Scott moved to obey, he said, "Even if we find any, it doesn't follow that it would be our people, sir."

"No. But if the captain is alive and down there, *he has to be there in that place.* I shall try to transport up any thinking beings our sensors detect."

"Shootin' in the dark, Mr. Spock."

The retort was unanswerable. "Would you rather stand by and do nothing?"

At the same moment, in the drawing room of Trelane Hall, Kirk and his men were being herded past a cabinet. "And in here," its owner was boasting, "is an array of your battle flags and pennants, some dating back to the Crusades, to Hannibal's invaders, the hordes of Persia!"

Nobody looked at the display. Undaunted, the enthusiastic Trelane addressed Kirk. "Can you imagine it, Captain? The thousands—no, the millions—who have marched off to death singing beneath these banners! Doesn't it make your blood run swiftly to think of it?" In his exuberance, he rushed to the harpsichord to bang out some martial music.

Under the cover of its noise, Sulu whispered, "Captain, where could he possibly come from? Who is this maniac?"

McCoy, his voice lowered, said, "Better ask 'what' is he. I monitored him. What I found was unbelievable."

Kirk was staring intently at the musician. Now he spoke, anticipating McCoy's news. "He's not alive."

"No, Jim. Not as we define life. No trace. Zero."

"You mean, your readings show he's dead?" Sulu asked.

"They don't even show that he exists, either alive or dead."

Jaeger pointed to the fireplace. "Notice that wood fire, Captain. Burning steadily—ember-bed red and glowing—yet it gives off no heat at all."

Kirk, moving quietly the length of the room, opened his communicator. Briefly, his voice toneless, he brought Spock up-to-date on the current situation.

"Fire without heat," Spock echoed reflectively. "It would seem, Captain, that the being mistakes all these things it has created for manifestations of present-day Earth. Apparently, it is oblivious of the time differential."

"Yes, Mr. Spock. Whatever it is we are dealing with, it is certainly not all-knowledgeable. He makes mistakes."

"And strangely simple ones. He has a flaw, sir."

"We'll work on it, Mr. Spock. Kirk out." As he snapped off his communicator, he realized that the music had stopped; and that Trelane, turning, was smiling at him. It was a sly smile, its slyness at variance with the joviality of his tone. "Discussing deep-laid plans, I'll wager. Captain, I can't wait to see them unfold."

Kirk took a firm step forward. "Trelane, I haven't planned any—"

A reproving finger was coyly waggled at him. "Ah, you mustn't believe that I deplore your martial virtues of deception and stratagem! Quite the contrary—I have nothing but esteem for your whole species!"

"If your esteem is genuine"—Kirk paused to draw a deep breath—"then you must respect our sense of duty, too. Our ship is in need of us—we have tasks to perform—schedules to honor . . ."

"Oh, but I can't bear to let you go. I was getting a bit

bored until you came.'' He whirled on his bench to run off a bragging cadenza on the harpsichord. ''You'll have to stay. I insist.''

''For how long?''

''Until it's over, of course,'' Trelane said.

''Until what's over?''

Trelane shrugged. ''Dear Captain, so many questions . . . Why worry about an inevitably uncertain future? Enjoy yourself today, my good sir. Tomorrow—why, it may never come at all. Indeed, when it arrives, it has already become today.''

The phrase ''slippery as an eel'' suddenly occurred to Kirk. He made another try. ''Trelane, even if we wanted to stay, our companions are missing us. They need us.''

''I must try to experience your sense of concern with you, your grief at the separation.'' The harpsichord wailed a mournful minor passage, sentimental, drippy.

Kirk gritted his teeth. ''There are four hundred men and women on board our ship waiting for—''

''Women!'' A discordant chord crashed from the instrument. ''You don't actually mean members of the fair sex are among your crew! How charming! No doubt they are very beautiful!'' Trelane, leaping to his feet, clapped his hands. ''And I shall be so very gallant to them! Here, let me fetch them down to us at once!''

He had lifted his arm when Kirk jumped forward. ''Absolutely not!''

''No?''

''No!'' Kirk shouted. ''This game has gone far enough. Our feminine crew members are crucial operating personnel! You can't just remove them from—''

Trelane stamped his foot. ''I can do anything I like! I thought you would have realized that by now!''

McCoy spoke. ''Jim! I am receiving a Transporter signal!''

Trelane started wringing his hands. ''What does he mean? You must tell me!''

''It means the party's over, thanks to Mr. Spock! That's what it means, Trelane''—and Kirk, signaling to his men, assumed the Transporting stance. As the others followed suit, Trelane hurried up to them. ''Wait!'' he screamed. ''What are you doing? I haven't dismissed you. Stop! I won't have this!"

The drawing room, the florid, furious face disappeared; and this time it was Spock who hurried up to them as they shimmered into full shape on the Transporter platform.

"Captain! Are you all right?"

Kirk stepped off the platform. "Report, Mr. Spock. How were the scanners able to penetrate that radiation field?"

"They didn't, sir. Not clearly. We merely beamed up all the life forms within a given space."

McCoy broke in. "Jim, that confirms what I said. Trelane is not a life form as we know it—or he'd be coming through the Transporter now."

Kirk nodded. Then he snapped out orders. "Prepare to warp out at once! Maximum speed! Everyone to stations!"

In the bridge, the substitute personnel quickly resigned their posts to Sulu and De Salle. The pretty yeoman on duty rushed up to Kirk. "Oh, Captain," cried Teresa Ross, "we were all so worried about you!" What she meant was, "*I* was worried about you, James Kirk"—and Kirk, gravely acknowledging her concern, said, "Thank you, Yeoman Ross." Then he was on the intercom. "Scotty! I want every ounce of power your engines have. We're going to put a hundred million miles between us and that madman down there."

"Aye, sir. Welcome back, Captain."

McCoy was staring at the hand he had extended. "I'm quaking," he said. "Jim, I'm quaking—but I don't know if it's with laughter or with terror!"

Uhura looked away from her board, her eyes bright with curiosity. "What was it? What's down there on Gothos?" she asked.

"Something I hope I forget to tell my grandchildren about . . ."

Then McCoy noted the astounded expression on Teresa's face. "Look—!" she whispered. Spock had jumped to his feet, staring.

Across the bridge in the angle made by its wall and elevator shaft, Trelane stood. He was uniformed, resplendent, a sabre scabbard attached to his cummerbund. His hands were clasped behind his back and he was looking the *Enter-*

prise bridge over. After a moment, he spoke. "But where are all the weapons? Don't you display your weapons?"

Kirk rose slowly to his feet. Trelane made a benevolently reassuring gesture. "Don't fret, Captain. I'm only a little upset with you." He was glancing around at the bridge people.

He said, "This Mr. Spock you mentioned—the one responsible for the imprudent act of taking you from me. Which is he, Captain?"

Spock said, "I am Mr. Spock."

"Surely," said Trelane, "you are not an *officer*." He turned in amazement—real or feigned, who could know?—to Kirk. "He isn't quite human, is he?"

"My father," Spock said, "is from the planet Vulcan."

"Are its native predatory?'

"Not specifically," Spock said solemnly.

Trelane made a dismissing gesture. "No. I should think not." He made an elaboration of turning to Kirk. "You *will* see to his punishment?"

"On the contrary," Kirk said. "I commend his action."

The full red lips pursed in their habitual pout. "But I don't like him."

Kirk won his battle for control. Tonelessly, he said, "Trelane, get off my ship! I've had enough of you!"

"Nonsense, Captain. You're all coming back with me."

The victory for control was abruptly lost. There was an obscenity about Trelane's middle-aged willfulness. Flaring, Kirk yelled, "We're not going anywhere! This ship is leaving here whether you—"

"Fiddle-de-dee," Trelane retorted. "I have a perfectly enchanting sojourn on Gothos planned for you. And I won't have you spoil it."

In a kind of prophetic awareness, Kirk knew what Trelane would do. He did it. Saying, "The decor of my drawing room is much more appropriate . . ." He raised his arm.

And the *Enterprise* bridge was replaced by the drawing room. All that was different were the positions of the bridge people. De Salle and Sulu were seated at a dining table, laden with dishes of unidentifiable but delicious-looking foods.

Uhura found herself on the bench before the harpsichord. And Trelane, completing the sentence spoken on the *Enterprise*, said, "And much more tasteful, don't you think?"

Sulu looked at the wall niches emptied of their sculptures.

"No," he said.

Trelane gave him an Oriental bow from the waist. "Yes, it is so much more fitting, Honorable Guest." He paused, catching a mirrored glimpse of his well-padded calves in their leg-hose; and the fatuous look of self-admiration on his face exploded the last remnants of De Salle's control.

"You little—!" he snarled and charged Trelane.

Kirk cried out a warning but it came too late. Trelane had made his hand wave—and once again, De Salle went stiff, immovable. Interestedly, Trelane circled him, peering into his frozen face. "Ah, what primitive fury! He is the very soul of sublime savagery!"

Kirk said, "Trelane, let him go." He repeated the sentence. *"I said, 'Let him go!' "*

Trelane stared at him. Then he nodded. "Yes, of course. I forget I must not frighten you too much. But then, you must not provoke me again. For your own sake, I warn you. I am sometimes quite short-tempered." There came another slight move of his hand; and De Salle relaxed the hands that had been reaching for Trelane's throat. Kirk clamped a firm hold on him. Sulu, seizing his other arm, whispered harshly, "De Salle, we don't even have our phasers!"

"Come, everyone!" Trelane, over at the table, pointed to chairs. "Let us forget your bad manners! Let us be full of merry talk and sallies of wit! See, here are victuals to delight the palate and brave company to delight the mind!" Pouring brandy, he offered glasses to McCoy and Sulu. "Partake, good Doctor. And you, Honorable Guest, you likee, too." Then it was the turns of De Salle and Jaeger. *"Allons, enfants! Zum Kampf, mein Herr!"*

His men looked tensely at Kirk. Nodding at the table, he said, "Play along. That's an order!"

As they began to pick halfheartedly at the lavish array of food, Kirk, Spock beside him, was giving Trelane a look of deep concentration. What was the secret of his power? Vain, silly, a showoff and braggart, he yet possessed the secret that had enabled him to establish a habitable enclave on an uninhabitable planet and to do what he said he could do—transport matter at will. In the florid face and features, there was no indication of the acute intelligence required to evolve his tricks. In fact, his look of fatuity was more pronounced than ever as, turning to Kirk, he said, "I fear you are derelict in your social duty, Captain. You have not yet introduced me to the charming contingent of your crew."

There was a small silence before Kirk spoke to Uhura and Teresa. "This is—General Trelane."

"Retired," Trelane corrected him. "However, if you prefer, dear ladies, you may address me simply as the lonely Squire of Gothos."

Still introducing, Kirk said, "This lady is Uhura, our communications officer . . ."

Trelane went to her, took her hand and bowed over it. "A Nubian prize, eh, Captain? Taken no doubt in one of your raids of conquest. She has the same melting eyes of the Queen of Sheba . . . the same lovely skin color . . ."

With a poorly disguised shudder, Uhura pulled her hand free; and unfazed, brashly melodramatic as ever, Trelane turned to Teresa. "And this lady?" Hand over heart, he burst into recitation.

"Is this the face that launched a thousand ships
And burnt the topless towers of Ilium?
Fair Helen, make me immortal with a kiss!"

Teresa flushed, stepped back; and Kirk, to distract Trelane's unwelcome attention from her, went on quickly. "Yeoman Teresa Ross. You've met Mr. Spock, our Science Officer." Trelane looked Spock up and down. "You realize," he said, "it is only in deference to the Captain that I brought you down?"

"Affirmative," Spock said.

"I don't think I like your tone. It's most challenging. Is that what you're doing—challenging me?"

"I *object* to you," Spock said. "I object to intellect without discipline; to power without purpose."

"Why, Mr. Spock," cried Trelane, "you *do* have a saving grace! You're ill mannered . . . the human half of you, no doubt. But I am wasting time . . ." He grabbed Teresa's hands. "Come, my wood nymph! Dance with your swain! And you, dear Nubian beauty, give us some sprightly music!"

"I do not know how to play this instrument," Uhura said.

"Of course you do!"

Uhura looked at Kirk. Then, turning, she fingered the harpsichord keyboard; and was startled to hear the rush of notes ripple from under her hands. Trelane swept Teresa into his arms and burst into a wildly gyrating waltz with her.

"Captain, how far do we go along with this charade?"

It was Sulu's question. Kirk's response was tightly grim. "Until we can think our way out of here. Meanwhile, we'll accept his hospitality . . ."

McCoy snorted with disgust. "Hospitality!" He replaced his laden plate on the table. "You should try his food, Jim. Straw would be tastier than this pheasant. As to the brandy in this glass, plain water has more taste. Nothing he has served has any taste at all."

Spock spoke meditatively. "Food that has no flavor. Wine that has no taste. Fire that gives no heat. Added up, it would seem to suggest that, though Trelane knows all the Earth forms, he knows nothing whatever of their substance."

"And if he's that fallible, he can't be all powerful. That means he's got something helping him."

"I agree, sir," Spock said.

"A machine. A device—something which does these things for him." Kirk's eyes narrowed as he watched the cavorting Trelane halt his dance briefly in order to adore himself in the walled mirror. "Ah, my dear," he cried to Teresa, "don't we make a graceful pair . . . except for one small detail. That dress you wear hardly matches this charming scene!" Then, Trelane, his eyes fixed on the mirror, lifted that hand of his. Teresa vanished—and immediately reappeared. She was wearing the billowing silks of a luxurious eighteenth-century gown. Diamond bracelets sparkled on her gloved arm; and in her hair glittered a pointed tiara of brilliants.

"Now that's more what we want!" Trelane shouted in delight. "I, the dashing warrior—and you, his elegant lady!"

It was another too impressive demonstration of his extraordinary powers. McCoy's voice was tight. ''Three thousand years ago, he would have been considered a god . . . a little god of war.'' He gave a short, angry laugh. ''How surprised the ancients would have been to see—not the grim-visaged brute they visualized as a war god—but a strutting dandy, spreading his peacock's tail in a mirror!''

Kirk echoed the word. ''Mirror. That mirror is part of his audience. It's a piece of his ego. He never wanders far from it.''

''Is it ego?'' Spock said. ''Or something else?''

''Explain,'' Kirk said.

''The mirror,'' Spock said.

''What about it?''

''As you said, sir, he never gets much distance away from it. I suppose it could be just vanity.''

''No, Mr. Spock. He's vain enough—but vanity can't account for his dependence on the mirror.'' He paused. ''What kind of machine could do these things?''

Spock said, ''An extremely sophisticated one. In addition to the power to create matter from energy, to guide its shape and motion by thought waves, it would have to have a vast memory bank.''

Kirk nodded. ''Like a computer. Would you say a machine small enough to be contained in this room could be responsible for maintaining this atmosphere, this house?''

''No, Captain. I think not. Such a device would by necessity be immense—immensely powerful to successfully resist the planet's natural atmosphere.''

''Good,'' Kirk said. ''I agree. And that leaves me free . . .''

''Free for what, Captain?''

''To do something which will seem very strange to you, Mr. Spock. Don't think that the strain has got me down. I know exactly what I'm doing.''

''Which is—?''

For the first time since meeting the Squire of Gothos, Kirk grinned. 'I am going to turn his lights off at their source, Mr. Spock.'' Then he fell silent. As Trelane waltzed by them with Teresa, he spoke again with unusual loudness. ''Nobody is to be too upset by what you see. I am addressing my own people. The actions of this being are those of an immature, unbalanced mind!''

Abruptly, Trelane stopped prancing. ''I overheard that last remark. I'm afraid I'll have to dispense with you, Captain.'' As the arm began to lift, Kirk said, ''You only heard part of it. I was just getting started, Trelane!''

The creature's eyes brightened with curiosity. ''Oh?''

''Yes,'' Kirk said. ''I want you to leave my crewmen alone! *And my crewwomen, too!''* He reached for Teresa, pulled her away from Trelane, and lifting her, set her down behind him. Then he wheeled to face her. ''You're not to dance with him any more! I don't like it!''

First, he snatched the diamond tiara from her hair. Then he reached for the bracelets, peeling them off her arm along with her white glove. Flushing, the girl cried, ''Captain, please don't think . . .''

Trelane gave a chortle of pleasure. ''Why, I believe the good captain is jealous of me!''

''Believe what you like,'' Kirk said. ''Just keep your hands off her!''

Trelane was staring at him. ''How curiously human,'' he said. ''How wonderfully barbaric!''

Taut, no longer acting, Kirk said, ''I've had enough of your attentions to her!''

''Of course you have. After all, it's the root of the matter, isn't it, Captain? We males fight for the attention, the admiration, the possession of women—''

Kirk struck him across the face with Teresa's glove. ''If fighting is what you want, you'll have it!''

Trelane gave a leap of joy. ''You mean—you are challenging me to a duel?'' Eyes dancing, he cried, ''This is even better than I'd planned. I shall not shirk an affair of honor!'' Skipping like a lamb in spring, he ran over to the gleaming box that hung among the weapons displayed over the fireplace. He removed it, lifting its lid. ''A matched set,'' he said. ''A matched set exactly like the one that slew your heroic Alexander Hamilton.''

Bowing, he presented the box to Kirk. On its velvet lining reposed two curve-handled, flintlock dueling pistols.

Trelane took one. He pointed it at Kirk's head. ''Captain,'' he said, ''it may momentarily interest you to know that I never miss my target.''

He moved over to take up his position at one side of the room. As he checked the mechanism of his pistol, McCoy, Sulu and the others gathered in an anxious group behind Kirk. He waved them back, thinking, ''I know what I'll have to report to the log. Weaponless, powerless, our only hope of escape with the *Enterprise* is playing his games with this retardate of Gothos.'' He looked up from the absurdity of the ancient dueling pistol. His adversary had a look of rapturous enchantment on his face.

''Fascinating!'' he cried ecstatically. ''I stand on a Field of Honor. I am party to an actual human duel!''

''Are you ready, Trelane?''

''Quite ready, Captain. We shall test each other's courage—and then—'' the voice thickened—''we shall see . . .''

Kirk started to lift his pistol when Trelane cried, ''Wait! As the one challenged, I claim the right of the first shot.''

''We shoot *together*,'' Kirk said.

Trelane was querulous. ''It's *my* game—and *my* rules.'' Raising his gun, he aimed it straight at Spock. ''But if you need to be persuaded . . .''

When you were dealing with a moral idiot, it was morally idiotic to take heroic stands. ''All right,'' Kirk said. ''You shoot first.''

''Captain—'' Spock was protesting. But Kirk had already lowered his pistol. And Trelane, craving the heroic limelight momentarily focused on Kirk, raised his gun above his head and fired a shot harmlessly into the ceiling.

He was so enraptured by the glory of the fight he cut in his own imagination that he couldn't contain his pleasure. ''And now, Captain—how do you say it?—my fate is in your hands.'' He shut his eyes with a beatific smile; and tearing open his shirt front, exposed his chest to whatever shot, whatever Fate had in store for him.

What Fate had in store for him was surprise. Instead of sending a bullet into Trelane's chest, Kirk sent one, smack! into the center of the mirror on the wall. The glass shattered. And explosively, from behind it, burst a tangle of electronic circuitry, mingled with broken grids and wire-disgorging cables. Something flashed, hissing viciously, spitting blue sparks.

Trelane screamed. He ran to the spark-showering mirror, screaming, "What have you done? What have you done?"

"The machine of power," Spock said very quietly.

It burned out quickly. Above their heads, the rows of candles in the chandelier flickered and died. A grayish, bleak twilight crept into the room. In the grate, the heatless fire was extinct, its passing marked only by a puff of evil-smelling smoke.

Trelane shrieked at the sight of the suddenly dead room. "You've ruined everything!" He sank down on the harpsichord bench; and his elbows, leaned back against its keyboard, evoked a hideously discordant jangle, shrill, earsplitting.

Beside Kirk, struggling with his communicator, De Salle said, "Captain, subspace interference is clearing . . ."

"Contact the ship!"

Trelane had partially recovered himself. Still turn between contempt for Kirk and admiration, the Squire of Gothos indulged himself in an objective comment. "The remarkable treachery of the human species," he said—and getting up, walked over to the wall bedecked with the blackened ruins of the mirror. Watching him, Kirk said, "Go on, Trelane! Look at it! It's over! Your power is blanked out! You're finished!"

For the first time, genuine feeling triumphed over the emotional theatricality of the Squire of Gothos. He looked somberly at Kirk. "You have earned my wrath," he said. "Go back to your ship! Go back to it! Then prepare. All of you, you are dead men . . . you in particular, Captain Kirk!"

He had begun to move toward the burnt space which had held the wall mirror. As he reached it, he was gone. Kirk, just a step behind him, was brought up against a blank wall. He stepped back from it, turning to his people. "Everyone! We're getting out of here—and *now*!"

His voice was hoarse as he spoke into his communicator. "This is the captain, *Enterprise*! Commence beaming us up! Make it maximum speed!"

Scott gave their beam-up maximum sped. Kirk left the

Transporter Room for the bridge with the same variety of leg haste. In his chair, he quickly reached for the intercom. "Scotty, full power acceleration from orbit!"

"Full power, sir."

The ship leaped forward, and on the viewing screen the crescent-shaped bulk that was Gothos began to dwindle in size.

Kirk said, "Set course for Colony Beta Six, Mr. Sulu."

"Laid in, sir."

"Warp Factor One at the earliest possible moment."

Sulu said, "Standing by to warp, sir."

Uhura, back with her panels, turned. "Shall I send a full report to Space Fleet Command, Captain?"

Kirk frowned. "Not yet. Not until we're well out of his range. Our beam might be traced."

Spock spoke from his computer post. "Can we know what his range is, sir?"

"We can make an educated guess. At this point—" Kirk had strode over to Spock's assortment of star maps and was directing a forefinger at a spot on one of them. "This is where we first detected the solar system." He was about to return to his chair when he noted Teresa, still wearing the panniered gown of flowered silk. His look of admiration roused her to the realization of its incongruity.

"Sir," she said, "may I take a moment to change, now that the ball is over?"

Kirk smiled at her. "You may—but you'll have to give up that highly becoming garment for scientific analysis, Yeoman Ross."

She flushed. And he tore his eyes away from the vision she made to look back at the viewing screen. Gothos had grown smaller and smaller. Even as he watched, it was lost to sight.

Uhura, the relaxation of her relief in her voice, said, "Still no sign of pursuit, sir. Instruments clear."

Sulu, turning his head, said, "Captain, we are about to warp"—and at the same moment De Salle gave a shout.

"Screen, sir! Large body ahead!"

Just a moment ago the screen had been empty. Kirk stared at its new inhabitant; and De Salle, jumping to his feet, yelled, "Collision course, sir!"

Tight-lipped, Kirk said, "Helm hard to port!"

The bridge crew staggered under the push by the sharp turn. All eyes were fixed on the screen where the crescent-shaped image loomed larger and larger. Then the *Enterprise* had veered away from it. A mutter came from the stunned De Salle. "That was the planet Gothos," he said.

Kirk whirled to Sulu. "Mr. Sulu, have we been going in a circle?"

"No, sir! All instruments show on course . . ."

De Salle gave another yell. "It's Gothos again, Captain!"

The planet had once more appeared on the screen. Kirk barked the evasive order—and again people staggered under the centrifugal force of the ship's abrupt turn. The image of the planet, shrunken on the screen, suddenly enlarged once again. Without order, Sulu put the ship into a vertiginous turn-maneuver. As they came out of it, Spock said, "Cat and mouse game."

"With Trelane the cat," Kirk said tightly.

De Salle, his capacity for intense reaction exhausted, said, low-voiced, "There it is, sir—dead ahead . . ."

On the screen the planet showed red, wreathed by fiery mists. It seemed to boil, noxious, hideously ulcerous with its eruptive skin. Kirk, his jaw set, spoke, "Ninety degrees starboard, Mr. Sulu!"

But though Sulu moved his helm controls, the planet held its place on the screen, always increasing in size.

"We're turning, Captain," Sulu cried. "We're turning—but we're not veering away from it!"

Kirk shouted. "Ninety subport, Mr. Sulu. Adjust!"

What was happening on the screen continued to happen on it. Desperate, Sulu cried, "A complete turn, sir—and we're still accelerating toward the planet!"

Dry as dust, Spock said, "Or it toward us."

Kirk was staring in silence at the screen. "That's *it*!" he said. He wheeled his chair around. "We will decelerate into orbit! We will return to orbit! Prepare the Transporter Room!"

McCoy spoke for the first time. "You're not going down there, Captain! You can't do it, Jim!"

Kirk got up. "I *am* going down, Doctor McCoy. And

I *am* going to delight my eyes again with the sight of our whimsical General Trelane. And if it takes wringing his neck to make him let my ship go . . ." He was at the bridge elevator. "Mr. Spock, stand by communicators. If you receive no message from me in one hour, leave this vicinity. At once. Without any sentimental turning back for me."

There was comfort in Spock's quiet nod. No heroics, no weakening sympathy. Just the perception of a reality, a necessity clear to each of them. Spock, his friend.

On a wall in Trelane's drawing room was the shadow of a gallows, dark, implicating. Kirk ignored it. For otherwise, the room was unchanged. Logs burned in the fireplace. The light of candles was refracted from the crystals of its chandelier. The mirror on the wall had been restored, its glass now protected by a heavy wire-mesh shield.

A heavily portentous voice said, "The prisoner may approach the bench."

It was Trelane. He had doffed his military glories for the graver garb of Law's upholders. He wore the white periwig of England's servants of jurisprudence, the black silk robes of a high court judge. He was writing something with a goose-quill pen on some parchment-looking document. The gallows noose—shadow or substance?—seemed to droop over Kirk.

"Trelane . . . !" Kirk said.

Nobody can be so solemn as an idiot. And Trelane, an essential idiot, was very solemn. Solemn and dangerous. In a voice that dripped with unction, he said, "Any attempt at demonstrations will weigh against you with the court. And this time my instrumentality is unbreakable, Captain Kirk."

"My neck seems to be threatened by your court, Trelane. And your neck—is it so very safe?"

A flicker of irritation passed over the heavy-jowled face.

"The absurdity of inferior beings!" said Trelane. He picked up the parchment. "And now, Captain James Kirk, you stand accused of the high crimes of treason, of conspiracy, of attempt to foment insurrection." His periwig must have itched him for he pushed it up, giving himself the look of a slightly drunken, white-haired Silenus. "How do you plead?" he said.

"I haven't come here to plead in your 'court,' Trelane."

The Squire of Gothos sat back, tapping his quill pen against his table. "I must warn you that anything you say has already been taken down in evidence against you."

It was like *Alice in Wonderland.* It was like Looking-Glass Land, where what seems to be is not and what is not appears to be the fact. Reaching for sanity, Kirk said, "I came here for one purpose. I want my ship returned to me."

"Irrelevant," Trelane said, giving his periwig an irritated push.

"We made you angry by our will to survive. Is that it?" Kirk said.

Trelane drew a tremulous finger across his upper lip. "Irrelevant," he said. "A comment entirely uncalled for."

"Sure, *that's it*," Kirk retorted. "Then vent your anger on me alone! *I* was the one who led the others—and I was the one who shot out your mirror machine . . ."

For the first time, rage seemed to overwhelm vanity in Trelane. His voice thickened. "And did you really think I wouldn't have more mediums of instrumentality at my command?"

"I took that chance. And I'll accept the price of chancing wrong—"

Trelane rose. "Then you do admit the charges. This court has no choice in fixing punishment. You will hang by the neck until you are dead, dead, dead. Have you any last request?"

Kirk gave a great shout of laughter. "If you think I'm going to stick my head in that noose . . ."

Trelane's hand moved—and Kirk found himself standing under the gallows, its noose, real, heavy, rough around his throat. Trelane, reaching for a black executioner's mask, regarded him plaintively. "This really is becoming tiresome. It's much too easy."

Kirk freed himself from the noose. "Easy!" he yelled. "That's your whole problem, Trelane! Everything comes too easy to you! You don't ever have to *think*! So you lose opportunities. You're enjoying your sense of power right now—but the chance to experience something really unique? You're wasting it! Where's the sport in a simple hanging? In making a rope do your killing for you?"

"Sport?" Trelane echoed. Suddenly his face cleared. He clapped his hands. "Oh, I am intrigued! Go on, Captain! What do you suggest?"

"A personal conflict between us . . . with the stakes a human life—*mine*!"

"What an inspired idea! We need something more fanciful—a truly royal hunt, maybe." He gestured toward the windows. "You go out and hide from me. In the forest . . . anywhere you like . . . and I will seek you out with—*this*!" He wrenched a sword from the scabbard in front of him, brandishing it ferociously. "How does that strike you, Captain? Truly sporting?"

"Yes," Kirk said. "But you must make the game worth my while. While we play it, free my ship."

Trelane sniffed. "Always back to your ship. Oh, very well. If it will lend spice to the pursuit . . ."

Kirk broke into a run, making a dash for a window. He brought up in a copse of vividly green bushes. With desperate haste, he flipped open his communicator. "*Enterprise! Enterprise*, can you hear me? Get the ship away fast! Fast as you can! I'll try to gain you the time you need—"

He stopped. Trelane had burst through the copse, slashing at leaves with his sword. "Ah, ha!" he screamed, "I see you!" But Kirk, diving, had rolled down the slant of a small knoll. Trelane's sword flashed over his head—and in his frantic scramble for the shelter of a heavy-trunked tree, he dropped his communicator.

"You must try harder, Captain!" The sword-point pricked Kirk's arm. He rose from his crouch behind the tree to tear a branch away from it. It struck straight and true on Trelane's sword arm. The weapon flew out of his hand; and Kirk, grabbing it up, slashed at Trelane with all his two-handed strength.

It cut right through him, leaving no sign of wound or of blood. Horrified, Kirk stared—but Trelane, still playing the role of gallant sportsman, merely said, "*Touché*, Captain. I confess you've scored first. But after all, I've never played this game before . . ."

He vanished. Kirk, still shaking, ducked behind a

screen of brush. Under it, he saw the gleaming metal of his dropped communicator. *"Enterprise . . . !"*

"En garde!"

Trelane had reappeared, sword lifted. Barely in time, Kirk broke for cover behind a hedge. Then, stooping, he burst out of its shelter to make for the door between the two stone griffins.

"Tallyho!"

The fatuous Squire of Gothos had spotted him. Kirk wheeled to his right—and a stone wall erected itself before him. He whirled to his left; and another blocked his way. Trapped, he backed up against the door of Trelane Hall; and its proprietor, triumph giving his face a look of gorged repletion, said, "Ah, Captain, you made a noble fight of it!" A dribble of saliva issued from the thick lips. "But you are beaten. Down, Captain. Down to me on your knees."

Kirk spoke, the sword against his throat. "You have won nothing."

"I have! I could run you through! I order you to your knees. I order it!" Trelane lunged with his sword; but Kirk, seizing it, tore it out of his hand; and in one snap over his knee, broke it. He tossed the pieces aside.

"You broke it!" Trelane wailed. "You broke my sword! But I won't have it. I'll blast you out of existence with a wave of my hand!"

Kirk struck him sharply across the face; and Trelane, shrieking, "I'll fix you for that!" squeezed the trigger of the phaser that had suddenly appeared in his hand. A murderously disintegrating ray darted from its muzzle—and at the same moment a woman's voice called "Trelane!"

"No! No!" Trelane howled, running down the steps of his Hall's entrance. Two globes of light hung in the air at their foot. "No! Go away!" he yelled. "You said I could have this planet for my own!" The spheres of light, one slightly smaller than the other, sparkled with an iridescence of rainbow colors.

Trelane was shouting at them. "You always stop me just when I'm having fun!"

"If you cannot take proper care of your pets, you cannot have any pets," said the female voice.

Trelane burst into tears. "But you saw! I was winning!

I would have won. I would, I would, I would.'' But even as he wept, he was dwindling, a shape losing substance, collapsing in on itself. Then he was only an emptiness in the air.

Kirk looked skyward as though seeking an explanation of the inexplicable. ''Where are you?'' he cried. ''Who is Trelane and who are you?''

''You must forgive our child,'' said the woman's voice. ''The fault is ours for overindulging him. He will be punished.''

A stern male voice spoke. ''We would not have let him intercept you had we realized your vulnerability. Forgive us, Captain. We will maintain your life-support conditions while you return to your ship. Please accept our apologies.''

Kirk flung out his hands toward the two spheres. ''Can't you tell me . . . ?'' Then, like Trelane, they were gone. After a long moment, he broke out his communicator. ''Captain to *Enterprise*. Captain calling the *Enterprise* . . .''

He shut his eyes at the sound—the familiar sound of Spock's voice. ''Captain, we are receiving you—''

Kirk gave a last look around him at Trelane's domain—its greenery, the two stone griffins, the appalling solitude of its loneliness in the midst of the Gothos hell. ''Beam me up,'' he said. ''Mr. Spock, we're free to leave here.''

It was a singularly thoughtful Kirk who gave the order for normal approach procedures to Colony Beta 6. He was glad when Spock left his station to come to the command chair. Somehow he'd known that Spock alone could reconcile him to the paradoxes of his recent encounter with the Squire of Gothos.

''I am entering,'' Spock said, ''our recent . . . uh . . . interesting experience into the library computer banks, Captain. But I am puzzled.''

''Puzzled—you, Mr. Spock?'' For a moment the old quizzicalness played across Kirk's face. ''I am surprised. I am amazed that you admit it. Explanation, please . . .''

Spock said, ''General, or Squire Trelane, Captain. How do we describe him? Pure mentality? A force of intellect? Embodied energy? Superbeing? He must be classified, sir.''

Kirk stared unseeingly at his board. ''Of course, Mr.

Spock. Certainly, he must be classified. Everything must be classified—or where would we be?"

"But I am somewhat at a loss . . ." Spock said.

"A god of war, Mr. Spock?"

"I hardly think . . ."

"Or . . . a small boy, Mr. Spock. And a very naughty one at that."

"It will make a strange entry in the library banks, sir."

"He was a very strange small boy. But on the other hand, he probably was doing things comparable, in their way, to the same mischievous pranks you played when you were a boy."

"Mischievous pranks, Captain?"

"Dipping little girls' curls in inkwells . . . stealing apples . . . tying cans on a dog's—" He broke off, sensing Spock's growing dismay. Where, in the universe, was another Spock to be found—the one you could trust to the end for reasons that had no relation to the ordinary human ones? Kirk grinned. "Excuse me, Mr. Spock. I should have known better. You were never a mischievous small boy."

"As you say, Captain," Spock said.

Back at his station, he cocked a puzzled eyebrow at Kirk. Kirk smiled at him. Spock, lifting the other eyebrow, returned to his computer. And the *Enterprise*, course set, oblivious of the manifold temptations of deep space, sped on to its assignation with Colony Beta 6.

ARENA

Writer: Gene L. Coon
(story by Frederic Brown)
Director: Joseph Pevney

Captain James Kirk of the USS *Enterprise* was the absolute master of the largest and most modern vessel in the Star Fleet Service, of all the complex apparatus and weaponry aboard her, and of the manifold talents of 430 highly trained crewmen.

And at the moment, he was stranded on a nearly barren artificial asteroid, location unknown, facing a tyrannosaurlike creature whose survival depended upon its killing Kirk, and equipped with absolutely nothing except a small translator-recorder useless as a weapon.

The situation had developed with bewildering rapidity. Originally, the *Enterprise* had received a call from the Earth outpost on Cestus Three, part of a planetary system on the very edge of an unexplored quadrant of the galaxy. The base commandant, an old soldier named Travers, had asked Kirk to beam down with the tactical staff of the *Enterprise*; and since things were quiet in this sector of space and Travers was famous in the Service for setting a good table, all six men had accepted cheerfully.

But the invitation had been a trap—a prerecorded trap. They had found the settlement in smoking ruins, the personnel dead. Furthermore, within minutes after its arrival the landing party was also under attack—and so was the *Enterprise*.

Evidently, the enemy, whoever he was, did not have the transporter and had no idea of its capabilities; after five minutes' inconclusive exchange of shots, the landing party was whisked away clean. The enemy ship broke off the engagement and fled, at fantastically high acceleration.

Kirk had no intention of letting it get away, however. It seemed obvious that any attempt to ambush the *Enterprise*'s tactical staff and captain, and then to destroy the starship itself, could only be a prelude to a full-scale invasion. Furthermore, the unknown enemy was well armed—the damage its ship had suffered thus far had been minor, despite its flight—and peculiarly ruthless, as witness its having wiped out 512 helpless people at an inoffensive scientific outpost simply to bait its trap. As Science Officer Spock had pointed out, that ship could not be allowed to reach its home base; presumably, as long as that unknown world was kept in the dark about Federation strength, it would hold off its next attack—thus buying precious time for a defense buildup.

The enemy seemed equally anxious to avoid leading the *Enterprise* to its home planet. It took complex evasive action, again at incredibly high speed; the *Enterprise* had difficulty in closing with her even at warp eight, two factors above maximum safe speed.

And then, suddenly, everything stopped.

It was absolutely impossible, but it happened. At one moment, both vessels were flashing through subspace at over a hundred times the speed of light—and in the next, both were floating in normal space, motionless relative to a small, nearby solar system, engines inoperative, all weapons dead.

"Report!" Kirk snapped.

But there was no damage, nothing abnormal—except that the *Enterprise* could neither move nor fight, nor, apparently, could the enemy.

"We're being scanned, sir," Communications Officer Uhura said.

"From the alien ship?"

"No, sir," she said. "From that solar system ahead. Nothing hostile—no tractors or weapon sensors, just scanners."

"Stopping us like this might be considered hostile," Kirk said drily.

"Getting something else, Captain—a modulation of the main frequency . . ."

Abruptly, the lights dimmed and there was a low hum

from the main viewing screen. The starry scene from outside promptly dissolved into a twisting, confused mass of color and lines. At the same time a humanoid voice, strong and yet somehow youthful, shook the air of the bridge. The voice said:

"We are the Metrons."

Kirk and Spock exchanged speculative glances. Then the Science Officer said, quite composedly: "How do you do?"

The voice's owner paid no apparent attention. It continued:

"You are one of two craft that have come into our space on a mission of violence. This is not permissible. Our analysis further shows that your violent tendencies are inherent. Hence we will resolve your conflict in the way most suited to your natures. Captain James Kirk!"

"This is Captain Kirk," Kirk said, after a moment's hesitation.

"We have prepared a planetoid with a suitable atmosphere, temperature and gravity. You will be taken there, as will the captain of the Gorn ship that you have been pursuing. You and your opponent will be provided with a translator-recorder. You can keep a record, or communicate with each other, should you feel the need. But not with your ships. You will each be totally alone, and will settle your dispute alone."

"Just what makes you think you can interfere . . ." Kirk began angrily.

"It is you who are doing the interfering. We are simply putting a stop to it—within your own violent frame of reference. The place we have prepared for you contains sufficient resources for either of you to construct weapons lethal to the other. The winner of the ordeal will be permitted to go on his way unharmed. The loser, along with his ship, will be destroyed in the interests of peace. The contest will be one of ingenuity against ingenuity, brute strength against brute strength. The outcome will be final."

With that, silently, the ship around Kirk vanished.

The first thing he saw was the Gorn. It was a biped, a reptile, a lizard that walked like a man. It stood about six feet four, with tremendous musculature, dully gleaming skin, a ridge of hard plate running down its back, and a strong, thick tail. The tail did not look prehensile; rather, it seemed to be a balancing organ, suggesting that the creature could run very fast indeed if it wished. The head was equipped with two tiny earholes and a wide mouth full of sharp teeth.

This, then, was the enemy, the raider, the destroyer of Cestus Three. It was wearing a garment like a short robe, belted; at the belt hung a small electronic device. It wore no shoes; clawed feet dug deeply into the ground, indicating considerable weight. Shooting a wary glance down at himself, Kirk discovered that his own clothing and equipment were identical.

Kirk and the Gorn stared at each other. All around them was a rocky, barren terrain, with a peculiar gray-green sky and occasional clumps of vegetation, some of it fairly tall, but none of it familiar. The air was cold and dry.

Kirk wondered if the Gorn was as uncomfortable as he was. Probably, but for different reasons. The meddling Metrons would surely have allowed neither of them an advantage in environment; after all, this planetoid was artificial—deliberately constructed to be an arena for a trial of champions, and for nothing else.

The Gorn moved. It was closing in on Kirk. It looked quite capable of killing him with its bare hands. Kirk moved sidewise, warily.

The Gorn did not appear to want to take any chances. As it too circled, it passed close to a gnarled object like a small tree, perhaps eight to ten inches through the trunk, and about ten feet high. With a quick look at Kirk, the Gorn hissed softly, reached out, and broke off a thick branch. The move seemed to cost it very little effort, whereas Kirk doubted that he could have done it at all.

Then, suddenly, holding the branch aloft like a club, the Gorn was charging him.

Kirk sprang aside barely in time. As the Gorn passed, somewhat off-balance, Kirk swung a killing blow into its midriff. The impact nearly broke his hand, but it seemed to have no other effect. The club lashed back, knocking Kirk sprawling against the rocks.

The Gorn wheeled around, clumsily but swiftly, and pounced. Kirk, dazed, tried to counter with a forearm blow to the throat, but it was like hitting an elephant. Then the creature was gripping him like a grizzly. Kirk's arm just managed to keep the teeth away, but that grip was going to break his back.

Freeing his arms with a sudden twist, Kirk boxed the Gorn's earholes with cupped hands. The Gorn screamed and staggered back, shaking its huge head. Springing to his feet, Kirk picked up a boulder as big as his head and hurled it at the Gorn with all his strength.

It struck the Gorn fair on the chest. The creature lurched slightly, but it did not seem to be hurt. Hissing shrilly, it bent to pick up a boulder of its own. The thing must have weighed a thousand pounds, but the Gorn got it aloft in one titanic jerk.

Kirk ran.

The rock hit behind him with an explosive crack, and flying splinters cut into the calf of one leg like shrapnel. Still hobbling as fast as he could, Kirk looked back over his shoulder.

The Gorn was not following. Instead, it was heaving up another rock. Then, as if realizing that Kirk was now out of range, it let the huge mass drop. It seemed to be grinning, although as far as Kirk had been able to see, it never wore any other expression.

Kirk looked around, panting. He seemed to be in a gully, though there was no sign that water had ever run in it—after all, there hadn't ever been such a planet many hours ago. There were rocks everywhere, some of them brilliantly colored, and an occasional outcropping of quartzlike crystals. Here and there were patches of scrubby, tough-looking brush, some of it resembling cacti, some mesquite, and even an occasional stand of a large, bamboolike growth. There was nothing that looked as though it could possibly be converted into a weapon, no matter what the Metron had said.

Kirk sat down, rubbing his injured leg but taking great care to watch the now-distant Gorn, and looked over the device at his belt. It looked quite like a tricorder, but both smaller and simpler—though simpler, at least, it doubtless was not. Kirk turned it on with the obvious switch.

"Calling the *Enterprise*. Captain James Kirk calling the *Enterprise*."

For a moment, there was no answer. Then the instrument said, in good but rather stilted English:

"You forget, Captain. We cannot reach our ships. We are alone here, you and I—just one against the other."

He looked back the way he had come. Sure enough, the Gorn seemed to be speaking behind one raised hand.

Kirk had not, of course, forgotten that he had been *told* he could not raise the *Enterprise*; he had simply wanted to test the statement. What he had forgotten was that the small instrument had been said to be a translator, as well as a recorder. He would have to be very careful not to mutter to himself after this.

After a moment, he said tentatively, "Look here, Gorn, this is insane. Can't we patch up some kind of truce?"

"Out of the question," the translator said promptly. "That would result only in our staying here until we starved. I cannot speak for you, but I see no water here, nor anything I could eat—with the possible exception of you."

"Neither do I," Kirk admitted.

"Then let us not waste time in sentimental hopes. The rules are what they are: One of us must kill the other."

Kirk hung the device back on his belt. The Gorn was right, and that was most definitely that.

He scrambled over to look at the bamboolike stuff. Each stalk was perhaps three to four inches in diameter—and, as he discovered by trying to break a section loose, it was as hard as iron. Hitting it with a rock even produced a distinctly metallic clank. Perhaps it picked up iron from the soil, as horsetails pick up calcium oxalate, or some prairie grasses pick up selenium. Useless.

He moved on up the gully, which got steadily deeper; he lost sight of the Gorn almost at once. Well, the risk had to be taken; staying where he was had gotten him nowhere.

Earthen banks, rather like bluish clay, reared on both sides of him now. One was steep, but the slope of the other was gentle enough to permit him to clamber up it if he had to.

Sticking out of the clay were the pyramidal points of a number of large crystals. Hopefully, Kirk pried one of them out. It was about the size of a hen's egg, and glittered brilliantly even under this sunless sky. The shape and the brilliancy were unmistakable: It was a diamond, and one that would have made the Kohinoor look like a mail-order żircon. And not only were there more of them imbedded in the clay, but the floor of the gully, he now saw, was a litter of them, in all sizes down to fine sand.

An incredible fortune—and again, utterly useless. None of the gems was sharp enough to be used as a weapon point, and he had no way to cut them. Their only use was to show that this planet was indeed an artificial construction—but Kirk had never doubted that, anyhow. He would have traded the whole wealth of them for a hand phaser, or even a medieval crossbow and a quiver of bolts for it.

The gully turned just ahead. Throwing the diamond away, Kirk went around the bend. The Metron had said that there were the raw materials of weapons here somewhere, if only he—

At the next step, his ankle struck a taut vine, and he went sprawling. At the same moment there was a sharp *crack!* as of wood splitting, and then one whole side of the gully seemed to be roaring down upon him.

He rolled frantically in the other direction, but not fast enough to prevent one rock from slamming into his chest. He felt a rib break. Staggering to his feet, he ran for the nearest cover, a sculptured overhang almost deep enough in back to be called a cave. There he stopped, breathing hard and nursing his rib cage—his whole body seemed to be one enormous bruise—and inspected the snare that had almost killed him through the gradually settling dust.

It was very simple and highly ingenious: a length of stretched vine to serve as a trigger, a broken branch, a heap of carefully stacked boulders that had been freed when the branch had been pulled loose.

Above him, Kirk heard the tick of large claws on rock, and then a sharp hiss of what could only have been disappointment. Kirk grinned mirthlessly. It had been near enough. He peered cautiously out of his hole and upward, just in time to see the Gorn on the lip of the gully on the other side, moving away. The creature was carrying something long and shiny in one hand. Kirk could not tell exactly what it was, but the fact that the Gorn had a torn scrap of his tunic wrapped around that hand was clue enough. It was a daggerlike blade, evidently chipped out of obsidian glass.

Then the creature was gone, but Kirk did not feel the least bit reassured. So far, the Gorn was way ahead, not only on strength, but on ingenuity. First a snare—now a dagger.

Well, then, back to the Stone Age with a vengeance. If Kirk could find a flint point, another length of vine, a sufficiently long stick, he might make a spear. That would give him the advantage of reach against the Gorn's dagger. On the other hand, would a spear penetrate that hide? There was only one way to find out.

A sufficiently large chip of flint, however, obstinately failed to turn up. All that was visible on the floor of the overhang was a wash of brilliant yellow powder.

The stuff looked familiar, and on a hunch, Kirk picked up a small handful of it and breathed on it. It gave out the faint crackle characteristic of flowers of sulfur when moistened.

Kirk grimaced. What a maddening planet. Sand of high-purity sulfur, veritable beaches of diamonds, iron-concentrating bamboos; and at the back of the cave here, outcroppings of rocks covered with a yellowish-white effluvium, like saltpeter. The only way he could make any sort of weapon out of a mélange like that would be with a smelter and a forge—

Wait a minute. Just a minute, now. There was something at the back of his mind—something very ancient . . .

With a gulp of hope, he ran back toward the growth of bamboolike stuff.

With a sharp rock, he managed to break off about a three-foot length of one tube, at one of its joints. The tube was closed at one end, open at the other. Ideal.

Now, the diamonds. He took up only the smallest, the most sandlike, measuring them by handfuls into the tube. He could only hope that his memory of the proportions—seventy-five, fifteen, ten—was correct; in any event, he could only approximate the measures under these conditions. Now, one of the large egg-shaped diamonds; this he put into his mouth, since the tunic did not come equipped with pockets.

Back up the gully, down and around the bend to the overhang. Into the tube went sulfur, saltpeter. Covering the end, he shook the tube until a little of the mixture poured out into his palm showed an even color, though certainly not the color it should have been.

A stone point penetrated the bamboo at the base, though it was hard work. A bit of torn tunic for a patch, and ram it all home with a stick. Then the egg-shaped diamond; then another patch, and ram again. Finally, a piece of flint; it did not have to be large, not any more.

"Captain," the translator at his belt said. He did not answer.

"Captain, be reasonable," the translator said. "Hiding will do you no good. If it is a matter of competitive starvation, I think my endurance is greater than yours. Why not come out, and die like a warrior?"

Kirk ignored it. Shredding another piece of cloth from the tunic, he began to strike the piece of flint over it, using the translator—at last it had a use!—as the steel. Sparks flew, but the cloth would not catch. If it was non-inflammable—

"You cannot destroy me," the translator said. "Let us be done with it. I shall be merciful and quick."

"Like you were at Cestus Three?" Kirk said.

"You were intruding," the translator said. "You established an outpost in our space. Naturally we destroyed it."

Kirk did not stop striking sparks, but he was at the same time thoughtful. What the Gorn said was perhaps reasonable, from its point of view. Very little was known about that arm of the galaxy; perhaps the Gorn had a right to regard it as theirs—and to be alarmed at the setting up of a base there, and by the advent of a ship the size of the *Enterprise*. Nevertheless . . .

Smoke rose from the shredded cloth. He raised it to his lips, blowing gently. It was catching.

"All right, Gorn," he told the translator. "Come and get me if you think you can. I'm under the overhang just past where you set your snare."

There was a sharp hiss, and then the clear sound of the Gorn's claws, coming at a run up the gully. Kirk had miscalculated. The creature was closer than he had thought—and faster. Frantically he struggled to align the clumsy bamboo tube.

The Gorn leapt into view, its obsidian knife raised.

Kirk slapped the burning piece of clothes against the touch-hole, and the makeshift cannon went off with a splintering roar. The concussion knocked Kirk down; the semicave was filled with acrid smoke.

He groped to his feet again. As the smoke cleared, he saw the Gorn, slumped against the other wall of the gully. The diamond egg had smashed its right shoulder; but it was bleeding from half a dozen other places too, where diamond chips had flown out of the cannon instead of igniting.

The knife lay between them. Leaping forward, Kirk snatched it up, hurled himself on the downed alien. The knife's point found one of the wounds.

"Now," Kirk said hoarsely, "now let's see how tough your hide is!"

The Gorn did not answer. Though conscious, it seemed to be in shock. It was all over. All Kirk had to do was shove.

He could not do it. He rose, slowly.

"No," he said. "We're in the same pickle. You're trying to save your ship, the same as I am. I won't kill you for that."

Suddenly furious, Kirk looked up at the greenish, overcast sky.

"Do you hear?" he shouted. "I won't kill him! You'll have to get your entertainment some place else!"

There was a long pause. Kirk stared down at the wounded alien; the Gorn stared back. Its translator had been shattered by the impact; it could not know what Kirk had said. But it did not seem to be afraid.

Then it vanished.

Kirk sat down, dejected and suddenly, utterly weary. Right or wrong, he had lost his opportunity now. The Metron had snatched the Gorn away.

Then there was a humming, much like that he had heard so long ago aboard ship, when the screen had been scrambled. He turned.

A figure was materializing under the overhang. It was not very formidable—certainly nothing so ominous, so awe-inspiring as its voice had suggested. Also, it was very beautiful. It looked like a boy of perhaps eighteen.

"You're a Metron," Kirk said listlessly.

"True," said the figure. "And you have surprised us, Captain."

"How?" Kirk said, not much interested. "By winning?"

"No. We had no preconceptions as to which of you would win. You surprised us by refusing to kill, although you had pursued the Gorn craft into our space with the intention of destroying it."

"That was different," Kirk said. "That was necessary."

"Perhaps it was. It is a new thought. Under the circumstances, it is only fair to tell you that we lied to you."

"In what way?"

"We said that the ship of the loser of this personal combat would be destroyed," said the Metron. "After all, it would be the winner—the stronger, the more resourceful race—who would pose the greatest threat to us. It was the winner we planned to destroy."

Kirk lurched to his feet. "Not my ship," he said dangerously.

"No, Captain. We have changed our minds. By sparing your helpless enemy—who would surely have killed you in like circumstances—you demonstrated the advanced trait of mercy. This we hardly expected—and it leaves us with no clear winner."

"What did you do with the Gorn, then?"

"We sent him back to his ship. And in your case, we misinterpreted your motives. You sincerely believed that you would be destroying the Gorn ship to keep the peace, not break it. If you like, we shall destroy it for you."

"No!" Kirk said hastily. "That is not necessary. It was a . . . a misunderstanding. Now that we've made contact, we'll be able to talk to the Gorn—reach an agreement."

"Very good," said the Metron. "Perhaps we too shall meet again—in a few thousand years. In any event, there is hope for you."

And abruptly, the *Enterprise* sprang into being around Kirk.

Turmoil broke out on the bridge. Ship's Surgeon McCoy was the first to reach Kirk's side.

"Jim! Are you all right?"

"To be quite honest with you," Kirk said dazedly, "I don't know. I just wish the world would stop popping in and out at me."

"I gather you won," Spock said. "How did you do it?"

"Yes . . . I guess so. I'm not quite sure. I thought I did it by reinventing gunpowder—with diamond dust for charcoal. But the Metrons say I won by being a sucker. I don't know which explanation is truer. All the Metrons would tell me is that we're a most promising species—as predators go."

"I could not have put the matter more neatly myself," Spock said. "But, Captain, I would be interested to know what it is you're talking about—when you feel ready, of course."

"Yes, indeed," Kirk said. "In the meantime, posts, everybody. It's time we got back down to business. And, Mr. Spock, about that explanation . . ."

"Yes, sir?"

"I suggest you raise the question again, in, say, a few thousand years."

"Yes, sir."

And the odd thing about Spock, the captain reflected, was that he *would* wait that long too, if only he could figure out a way to live through it—and when the time had all passed, Spock would remember to ask the question again.

Kirk hoped he would have an answer.

THE ALTERNATIVE FACTOR

Writer: Don Ingalls
Director: Gerd Oswald
Guest stars: Robert Brown, Janet MacLachlan

The planet offered such routine readings to the *Enterprise* sensors that Kirk ordered a course laid in for the nearest Star Base. "We can be on our way," he was telling the helmsman when Spock lifted his head from his computer. He said, "Captain, there is—"

He never completed his sentence. The *Enterprise* heaved in a gigantic lurch. A deafening grinding sound hammered at its hull—and the ship went transparent. From where he'd been flung, Kirk could see the stars shining through it. Then static crashed insanely as though the universe itself were wrenching in torment. Abruptly, stillness came. The ship steadied. The vast convulsion was over.

Bruised people, sprawled on the deck, began to edge cautiously back to their bridge stations. Kirk hauled himself back to his feet. "What in the name of—Mr. Spock!"

Spock was already back at his computer. "Captain, this is incredible! I read—"

Again the mighty paroxysm interrupted him. There came the ship's headlong plunge, the grinding roar, its appalling transparency. Kirk struggled once more to his feet and ran, ashen-faced, to Spock's station. "What is it?" he shouted.

"What my readings say is totally unbelievable, sir. Twice—for a spilt second each time—everything within range of our instruments seemed on the verge of winking out!"

Still shaken, Kirk said, "Mr. Spock! I want facts! Not poetry!"

"I have given you facts, Captain. The entire magnetic field in this solar system simply blinked. That planet below us, whose mass I was measuring, attained zero gravity."

Kirk stared at him. "But that's impossible! What you are describing is . . . why, it's—"

"Nonexistence, Captain," Spock said.

Mingled horror and awe chilled Kirk. He heard Uhura speak. "There's a standard general-alert signal from Star Fleet Command, Captain!"

He raced for his mike. "This is the Captain speaking. All stations to immediate alert status. Stand by . . ."

Spock looked over at him. "Scanners now report a life object on the planet surface, sir."

"But only five minutes ago you made a complete life survey of it! What's changed?"

"This life reading only began to appear at approximately the same moment that the shock phenomena subsided."

And this was the routine planet that concealed no surprises! Kirk drew a deep breath. "What is its physical make-up?"

"A living being. Body temperature, 98.1 Fahrenheit. Mass . . . electrical impulses . . . . it is apparently human, Captain."

"And its appearance coincided with your cosmic 'wink-out'?"

"Almost to the second."

"Explanation?"

"None, Captain."

"Could this being present a danger to the ship?"

"Possible . . . quite possible, sir."

Kirk was at the elevator. "Lieutenant Uhura, notify Security to have a detachment, armed and ready, to beam down with us. Stay hooked on to us. Let's go, Mr. Spock. If any word from Star Fleet Command comes through, pipe it down at once. Communications priority one."

"Aye, sir."

For a planet capable of such violent mood changes, it was extraordinarily Earth-like. It was arid, hot and dry, the terrain where the landing group materialized resembling one of Earth's desert expanses. When Spock, studying his tricorder, pointed to the left, they moved off. Almost at once they met up with huge, tumbled boulders of granite, the passageways among them littered with rocky debris. They were edging through one of the defiles when they saw it.

At the base of a cliff lay a cone-shaped craft. It was like no spaceship any of them had ever seen. Its hull was studded with buttons connected to a mesh of coiling electronic circuits. Nothing moved around it. Its wedgelike door was open. Spock stood to one side as Kirk peered inside it. Its interior was a mass of complex instrumentation, shining wirings, tubes of unrecognizable purple metal, parabolic reflectors. There was what appeared to be a control panel. A chair.

Kirk emerged, his face puzzled. "I've never seen anything like it. Have a look, Mr. Spock. . . ."

Spock was stepping through the door when the voice spoke. "You came! Thank God! There's still time!"

Everyone whirled, phasers out. Kirk looked up. On the cliff above them stood a man. He wore a ripped and disheveled jumper suit. He was a big man, but his face had been badly battered. A dark bruise had swollen his jaw. A husky man, but his broad shoulders sagged with an unutterable weariness. "It's not too late!" he cried down to them. "We can still stop him!" He extended his hands in appeal. "But I . . . I need your help . . . please . . . help me . . ."

He reeled, clutching at his throat. Then his knees buckled—and he tumbled, headlong, from the cliff.

Kirk and Spock ran to him. His body lay unmoving but massive physical power was still latent in it. Who was he? What were he and his spacecraft doing on this "routine" planet?

But McCoy would permit no questions. He shook his head over the bed in Sickbay, where the injured castaway had been placed. "It's going to be touch and go, Jim. Heartbeat practically nonexistent. What happened down there?"

"I don't know. He fell from a cliff. He'd been saying something about needing our help . . . and he just crumpled."

McCoy looked up from his diagnostic tricorder. "No wonder. After the beating he's taken."

"He was beaten?"

"I don't know what else could have caused his injuries."

"Bones," Kirk said, "that is a dead, lifeless, arid planet down there . . . no sign of living beings. Who could have attacked him?"

McCoy was frowning at his tricorder. "He's the only one who can answer that—if he lives. . . ."

They both turned at the sound of Uhura's voice on the intercom. "Captain. Standby notice just in from Star Fleet Command. Red Two message about to come in."

"I'm on my way." At the door he said, "Keep me posted, Bones."

Chemist Charlene Masters met him at the bridge elevator door. "Here's my report on the di-lithium crystals, sir. Whatever that phenomenon was, it drained almost all of our crystals' power. It could mean trouble."

"You have a talent for understatement, Lieutenant. Without full crystal power, our orbit will begin to decay in ten hours. Reamplify immediately."

"Aye, sir."

He handed the report back to her and crossed to Spock's station. "Any further magnetic disturbance, Mr. Spock?"

"Negative, Captain. Scanners indicate situation normal."

"Nothing?"

"Nothing, sir. And most illogical . . . an effect of that proportion incapable of explanation by any established physical laws I'm aware of." He paused. "I *have* ascertained one fact. Though the effect, whatever it was, was unquestionably widespread, it was strongest on the planet below us."

"Keep checking."

"Yes, Captain."

Uhura spoke. "Captain. Message coming in from Star Fleet Command. And the code, sir, it's Code Factor One."

The anxiety in her face reflected Kirk's sense of personal shock. Very seldom indeed did Star Fleet resort to Code Factor One to transmit a message. "Repeat," he told Uhura.

She said heavily, "It *is* Code Factor One, sir."

"Combat status!" Kirk shouted to Spock. He hit his communicator button. "All hands! This is the Captain. Battle stations! This is not a drill! Lieutenant Uhura, the main screen!"

"Aye, sir."

Sirens were shrieking as Kirk rushed to his command position. Over the noise his communicator beeped. It was McCoy. "About our patient, Jim—"

"Quickly, Bones!"

"He'll make it. He'll be flat on his back for at least a month. He's weak as a kitten but he'll pull through."

"Thank you, Bones. I'll be down to talk to him later. The message, Lieutenant Uhura . . ."

The strong face of Commodore Barstow came into focus on the screen.

"Kirk here, sir. *Enterprise* standing by."

The official voice spoke. "You're aware, Captain, of that effect that occurred an hour ago?"

"Yes, sir."

"You may not be aware of its scope. It was felt in every quadrant of the galaxy . . . and far beyond. Complete disruption of normal magnetic and gravimetric fields. Time warp distortion. Impossible radiation variations—and all of them centering in the area you are now patrolling. The question is . . . are they natural phenomena—or are they mechanically created? And if they are . . . by whom? For what purpose? Your guess, Captain . . ."

"My best guess, sir, is . . . because of the severity of the phenomena . . . they could be a prelude to an extrauniverse invasion."

"Exactly our consensus. It's your job to make the finding specific."

"Aye, sir. Can you assign me other starships as a reserve force?"

"Negative. I am evacuating all Star Fleet units and personnel within a hundred parsecs of your position. It's tough on you and the *Enterprise*—but that's the card you've drawn. You're on your own, Captain."

Kirk spoke slowly. "I see. You mean . . . we're the bait."

"Yes."

"I understand, sir. Received and recorded."

"Remember, you're the eyes and ears and muscle of the entire Federation. Good luck, Captain."

"Thank you, sir."

The screen's image faded. Kirk looked at the blankness for a long moment. Then he rose and crossed to Spock. "From the top, Mr. Spock. First, we know that the phenomena came from the planet below us. Second, that the danger is real and imminent."

"A closer examination of the surface would seem to be in order," Spock said. "My job, Captain?"

"Yes. And in the meantime I'll have a talk with our unexpected guest. Maybe he can provide some answers."

He certainly seemed able to provide them. In Sickbay, Kirk found McCoy staring dazedly at his patient. The man who'd been nearly pushed through the door of death was out of bed, doing deep knee bends while he inhaled great hearty gulps of air. Kirk stopped in mid-stride. "Bones! I thought you said—"

McCoy struggled to come out of his daze. "I know what I said and I was going to call you back . . . but Lazarus—"

"Aye!" shouted the patient. "Lazarus! Up and out of the grave! Hale, hearty and drunk with the wine of victory!"

If the man was mentally sick, he was surely in great physical shape. He had swiftly noted the dubious look on Kirk's face. "You want to know how I came to be down there, Captain? I'll tell you! I was pursuing the devil's own spawn—the thing I have chased across the universe! Oh, he's a humanoid, all right, outside—but on the inside, he's a ravening, murderous monster! But I'll get him yet! I've sworn it!"

"Why?" Kirk said.

The eyes under the heavy brows flamed. "The beast destroyed my entire civilization! To the last man, woman and child! Builders, educators, scientists—all my people! But he missed me. And I will bring him down! Yes, despite his weapons!"

Kirk said, "How did you escape?"

"I was inspecting our magnetic communication satellites, a thousand miles out."

"And he destroyed your whole civilization?" Kirk was openly incredulous.

"Oh, he's capable of it!" Lazarus assured him. "He's intelligent—I give him his due! But he is death! Anti-life! He lives to destroy! You believe me, don't you, Captain?"

"Just before we found you," Kirk said, "this ship sustained a number of dangerous and incredible effects. Could this humanoid of yours have been responsible?"

"Of course! It's what I've been telling you!"

He'd wanted an answer. Now he'd gotten one. If it wasn't too satisfying, it was the only one yet available. Lazarus seized on his hesitation. "Then you're with me!" he cried triumphantly. "You'll join my holy cause! You'll help me visit justice upon him—vengeance!"

"My sole cause is the security of my ship," Kirk said. "That and the mission it has undertaken. Bloodshed is not our cause. Remember that." He paused. "Now I want you to beam down to the surface with me. We shall check out your story."

They found Spock examining the conical craft's interior. Two crewmen were busy surveying its hull with tricorders.

"Find anything, Mr. Spock?" Kirk asked.

"Negative, Captain." Spock gestured toward Lazarus. "Did you?"

"According to our unexpected guest there's a creature of some sort down here—a humanoid."

Spock nodded. "Lieutenant Uhura communicated that information. I ordered reconfirmation on our sensors. They indicate no living creature on this planet. I suggest, Captain, that you have been lied to."

Kirk shot a hard look at Lazarus. Then he said, "Let's hear the rest of it, Mr. Spock."

"Lieutenant Uhura added his statement about some unusual weapon system at the humanoid's disposal."

"Aye!" yelled Lazarus. "He has that—and more! Enough to destroy a vessel as great as your *Enterprise*!"

"Does he?" Spock said mildly.

Lazarus was visibly irritated. "Yes," he said shortly.

Spock spoke to Kirk. "There are no weapons of any kind on the planet, Captain. Not in his craft. Nor on the surface. They do not exist."

"You must not believe him, Captain! This one of the pointed ears is just trying to disguise his own incompetence!"

Spock raised an eyebrow. "I don't understand your indignation, sir. I merely made the logical deduction that you are a liar."

Kirk wheeled sharply on Lazarus. "All right, let's have it! The truth this time. I—" He stopped. The air around them suddenly broke into shimmering sparkle. There came a sound like the buzzing of an angry bee. As though to ward it off, Lazarus lifted a hand. Then he fisted it, shaking it wildly at the sky. "You've come back then, is that it?" he shouted. "Well, don't stop! Here I am! Come at me again! We'll finish it!"

Ignoring him, Kirk spoke to Spock. "Can your tricorder identify that atmospheric effect?"

"It's—" Spock was saying when Lazarus bolted off to where the glitter sparkled most strongly. "Run! Run!" he screamed. "It will do you no good! I'll chase you into the very jaws of hell!"

"Lazarus!" Kirk cried. He raced after the man, calling back over his shoulder, "Remain there! All personnel on Security Red!"

He brought up in a rock-walled gully. Ahead of him Lazarus was clambering over its jagged debris. He was moving slowly when the shimmering sparkle engulfed him. At the same moment, Kirk saw that the sky, the rocks and the gully itself were trembling, shifting into indistinctness, their colors, their shapes, their masses liquefying and interflowing. They came into focus again. But Lazarus had staggered backward—and once more the liquefying shimmer had swallowed up the sight of him.

Flailing helplessly, he had tumbled into a peculiar tunnel. It was filled with a ghastly milky whiteness into which walls, roof and floor were constantly dissolving, leaving no solid point of reference required by humankind to determine its place in the universe. Unheard by Kirk, he shrieked,

"*You!*" Then the manlike thing was on him. In deadly combat, they writhed, twisted together, hands groping for each other's throats. Lazarus was on his back, choking, when he made a supreme effort, muscles cracking with strain. His assailant was thrown backward. And disappeared into the drifting whiteness.

Reeling drunkenly, Lazarus staggered out of the tunnel into Kirk's sight. Before Kirk could reach him, he fell, striking his head against a boulder. He struggled up to his hands and knees, his face streaked with blood and sweat. Kirk ran to him.

"Lazarus! Where were you? What happened?"

Horror moved in the dazed eyes. "I . . . saw it again! The Thing! It attacked me. . . ."

"I'll take you back. Hold on to me."

As he was hefting the man to his feet, Spock came through the gully. He hurried to them but Lazarus pushed away his supporting arm. Stepping aside, Spock said, "That effect occurred again, Captain. And it centered right here . . . almost where we are standing."

Lazarus lifted his head. "I told you! It was the Thing! All whiteness . . . emptiness . . ."

Kirk wiped his face clear of its blood and sweat. "There's nothing you can do about it here. We're beaming back to the ship."

The man tried to wrench himself free of Kirk's grasp. "We must kill him first! He tried to kill me! Don't you understand? If we don't stop him, he will kill us all!"

As Kirk watched McCoy apply a dressing to the deep cut on his guest's forehead, doubt of the humanoid's existence continued to trouble him. He had not seen the humanoid. He had not seen the fight. Both had been invisible to him. All he had to go on was the word of Lazarus. He felt a sudden need to confer with Spock. There was a climate of controlled tension in the bridge as he entered it. At Spock's station he lowered his voice.

"Any luck, Mr. Spock?"

"Negative, Captain. I can no more explain the second phenomenon than I can the first."

"If there's a shred of truth in what Lazarus said—"

"That a humanoid—a single creature—could be responsible for an effect of such magnitude?"

"Hard to credit," Kirk said.

"Indeed, sir."

"But the rest of his tale seems to fit. His wounds testify to an apparent confrontation with *something*."

"Affirmative, sir."

Kirk took three restless paces and came back. "Then, assuming there is a humanoid, *how* does he cause the effects? He has no weapons, no power system . . ."

"I'm sorry, Captain. All I know for certain is that the occurrence of the phenomena seems to coincide exactly with the moments Lazarus has one of his alleged confrontations."

Uhura interrupted them. "Doctor McCoy, Captain, asking for you in Sickbay. He says it's urgent."

McCoy was troubled too. He was at his desk, drumming it impatiently with his fingers. "Jim, maybe I'm suffering from delusions; maybe I'm not. You tell me."

"No, Bones. You tell me. That's why I'm here."

McCoy swung around. "Thirty minutes ago you brought Lazarus here and I treated a deep abrasion on his forehead. Right?"

"Right."

"I treated that wound, bandaged it, then stepped in here for a moment."

"The point, Bones."

"Say he's got a constitution like a dinosaur. Recuperative powers ditto—and as we both know, I'm a bright young medic with a miraculous touch. But tell me this. Why, when I returned to my patient, wasn't there a trace of that wound on his forehead? Not even a bruise, Jim. It was as though he'd never been injured!"

Kirk was silent for a long moment. Then he said, "Where is he?"

"I'm just a country doctor, not a private detective. Maybe he stepped out for a cup of coffee. . . ."

But his goal was the *Enterprise* Recreation Room. Spock found him sitting at a table, quietly enjoying himself as he watched two crewmen playing a game. There was no bandage on his forehead. Spock moved to him. "May I sit down?"

He seemed to have recovered from his antagonism. "Yes, of course," he said.

"Earlier," Spock said, "I referred to you as a liar."

"Do you still think I am?"

"About some matters, yes."

Lazarus smiled. "You're very direct. I like that. If it will help make up your mind about me, ask your questions."

"I am curious about this civilization of yours . . . the one that was destroyed."

"It was much like that of Earth. Green, soft landscapes, blue seas, great cities, science, education. . . ."

"And the people?"

"Like any of us. Good, bad, beautiful, ugly, magnificent . . . terrible. Human. Satisfied?"

"The story you have told us is most strange and unlikely, as you yourself. You are hardly the same man I spoke to earlier."

"Don't blame me if I'm not consistent, Mr. Spock. Not even the universe is that."

"I prefer to think it is," Spock said.

He got a sharp stare. "Yes. Of course you would."

The wall communicator beeped. Spock got up and went to it. "Yes, Lieutenant Uhura?"

"You told me to notify you when the impulse readings reached the critical stage. They've done so."

"Thank you, Lieutenant." He returned to Lazarus. "If you will excuse me, I have an experiment in progress—one that may help me evaluate the facts."

"When you are certain of your facts, will you believe me then?"

"I always believe in facts, sir." He eyed the unbandaged forehead. "I must congratulate you on your remarkable recuperative powers. If time permitted, I would like to discuss them with you." He bowed. "Thank you for your company."

Lazarus was watching him leave when the shimmer suddenly sparkled again. He half-rose from the table, went pallid and almost fell from his chair. The sparkle subsided; and controlling his shaking knees, he moved out into the corridor. The effect came again. The corridor walls faded, dissolving. Then they were back, solid, real. Staring about,

Lazarus hauled himself up from where he had fallen. On his forehead was the white tape marking the wound he had received on the planet. He heard Kirk call, "Lazarus!"

McCoy saw him first. They rushed to him, Kirk taking his arm. "Are you all right?"

"What? Oh, yes, Captain. All right! But impatient! Have you decided to help me yet?"

McCoy was staring at him. He stepped forward, seized the edge of the tape and pulled it off. There was a red, neatly sliced cut in the bruised forehead.

"Well . . ." McCoy said.

Kirk, too, had his eyes fixed on the deep cut.

"Something wrong, Captain?" Lazarus asked.

Kirk glanced at McCoy. "No. Except that I have a ship's physician with a strange sense of humor."

McCoy wheeled. "Jim, this is no joke! I know what I saw!"

The wall communicator beeped. "Bridge. Calling the Captain."

Kirk hit the switch. "Kirk here."

Spock said, "Request you come up, sir."

"Find something?"

"Something quite extraordinary, Captain."

"On my way." He turned a cold eye on Lazarus. "You will come with me. I have some questions still to be answered."

Spock had ordered activation of the main viewing screen. It showed the planet flaring with a single needle point of blinking light. Spock joined Kirk. "A source of radiation, Captain."

"Why didn't our scanners pick it up before?"

"Because it isn't there," Spock said.

Kirk could feel the tension hardening in his midriff. "A riddle, Mr. Spock? First Bones, now you."

"What I meant, sir—is, according to usual scanning procedure, there is nothing there that could be causing the phenomenon."

"But the radiation point *is* there."

"Affirmative, sir." Spock hesitated. "I confess I am somewhat at a loss for words. It may be best described, though loosely and inaccurately . . . as a—" He paused again, his embarrassment to be read only in the particular impassivity of his face. "As . . . a 'rip' in our universe."

"A *what*?"

"A peculiar physical warp, Captain, in which none of our established physical laws seem to apply with regularity. It was only with our di-lithium crystals that I was able to localize it."

Lazarus burst into speech. "Of course! The di-lithium crystals! Their power—that could do it!" He whirled to Kirk with a wild shout. "We've got him now, Captain! We've got him!"

"You refer to the humanoid?" Spock inquired.

"Yes! By the gods, *yes*! Now we have him!"

"What have the crystals got to do with it? All they show is a point of radiation," Kirk said.

"But that's it! That's the key—the solution! That's how we can trap him! I implore you . . . I beg you . . . I demand—*give me those crystals*!"

Kirk shook his head. "Out of the question. The crystals are the very heart of my ship's power."

The eyes that glared at him were congested with blood. "Fool, don't you understand? There'll *be* no ship unless this monster is killed! He'll destroy all of you!"

Kirk gritted his teeth. "How, Lazarus? *How?* All I've heard from you is doubletalk—lies—threats that never materialize—explanations that don't hold a drop of water! Now you tell me—*how is my ship in danger*? *How?*"

The face tightened into hard determination. Lazarus turned and started toward the elevator.

Kirk shouted his name. The man whirled around, fury distorting his heavy features. "I warn you, Captain—you will give me the crystals!"

Kirk spoke very quietly. "Don't threaten me."

"I'm not threatening you. I am telling you I will have my vengeance!" The elevator whirred open and he was gone.

Kirk's tension had broken into open rage. He turned to a guard. "Security! From now on he's your job—your *only* job! If he does anything, tries to—anything at all unusual—notify me at once!"

The guard was already moving toward the elevator.

In the Engineering section Charlene Masters was directing the procedure required to recharge the di-lithium crystals. She had opened one of the bins when her assistant turned from the intercom. "Lieutenant Masters," he said, "the Captain is calling."

She moved off to the far wall. As she turned her back, a figure edged from the shadow behind the bins toward the assistant. A powerful arm encircled the man's neck, applying hard pressure to the throat. Then quietly, almost tenderly, it eased him to the ground.

The oblivious Charlene was listening to Kirk say, "Can you prepare an experimentation chamber in ten minutes? All di-lithium crystals full power, Lieutenant."

"I'll check, sir." She returned to the bins for readings and went back to the intercom. "Captain? Chamber will be ready in ten minutes. My assistant and I—"

A hand clamped over her mouth. Kirk heard her choking gurgle. "Lieutenant Masters? Masters, what's wrong?"

She managed to wrench her head free for a brief instant. "Captain . . . !" Her eyes were glazing as she was dropped to the deck.

The Lazarus of the powerful arm bore no sign of a cut on his forehead.

It was a furious Kirk who called the meeting in the Briefing Room. Lazarus, the red wound back on his forehead, sat at the head of the table. Kirk paced up and down behind his chair, his eyes on the blackening finger marks on Charlene Masters' throat. He waited for Spock to enter before he spoke.

"Two of my crewmen have been attacked—*and two of our di-lithium crystals are missing*! Without them this ship cannot operate at full power. They must be found!"

He seized the back of the chair Lazarus sat in. Wheeling around, he shouted, "Fact! You said you needed those crystals! Fact! Within an hour after telling me you must have them, *they are missing*!"

Lazarus half-rose from the chair. "And fact!" he cried. *"I didn't take the crystals!"*

His head drooped. "I'm not the one, Captain," he said quietly. "In me the *Enterprise* found only an orphan. . . . Find my enemy. Find the beast—and you'll find your crystals!"

"And just how did your beast get aboard my ship?"

"He has ways! There's no end to his evil!"

Kirk looked at Spock. "If the creature transported up—"

Lazarus laughed. "Transport *up*? I tell you, we are dealing with a Thing capable of destroying worlds! He has your crystals!"

"But why, sir?" Spock asked mildly. "Again we must put the question to you. For what purposes?"

Lazarus leaped from his chair. "The same as mine! Why don't you listen to me? He's humanoid! He can operate a ship! Compute formulas to exterminate a race! Strangle a man with his bare hands! Or steal an energy source for his vehicle in order to escape me! Are you deaf as well as blind?"

There was something wrong. Trust of this man was impossible to come by. The frustration piled up in Kirk until his fists clenched. "Mr. Spock, the crystals certainly aren't here. There is an unexplained source of radiation on the planet. There is clearly some connection. We'll check it out. Prepare a search party at once. Mr. Lazarus will beam down with us."

Lazarus smiled. "Thank you, Captain."

Kirk's voice was harsh. "You may not have reason to thank me. That will depend on what we find."

The cone-shaped craft still lay at the base of the cliff. As Kirk opened its door, Lazarus went to him. "Now what do you believe, Captain?"

"I believe the missing crystals are not in your ship. Mr. Spock?"

"Unable to locate the radiation source, sir."

"Why not? You had it spotted from the ship."

"It simply seems to have disappeared."

Kirk spoke to the guards. "I want every inch of this terrain checked. Look for footprints, movement, anything. If you spot something, call out. And don't be afraid to use your weapons."

The party fanned out over the terrain, each man at once becoming aware of its empty loneliness. No trees, no vegetation—just the unfolding vista of rock in its multiple formations. Lazarus climbed to a craggy ridge, spined like an emaciated dinosaur petrified by the eons. Along its left slope glacial boulders balanced precariously over a steepness that dropped to a long defile. It ran parallel to the ridge; and Kirk, his tricorder out, was exploring it. Lazarus, lost to sight between two jutting rocks, clutched at one as the space around him began to shimmer. In the hideous sparkle, the rocks, the sky, the very ground under his feet seemed to fade and melt. He spun around, peering for his enemy. But there was only the shimmering nothingness. He found that his movement was slowed down. Stumbling forward, he lurched into a milky-white cocoon place—and a blow struck him to his knees. Vaporlike stuff was in his eyes, his nose, his throat. The vague shape of his assailant leaped on him. They wrestled blindly, bits of the stuff drifting over them. Lazarus kicked the thing. It fell back and vanished as though it had dropped into eternity.

Then the world was solid again. Lazarus careened wildly, still fighting off the absent enemy. He tripped against a rock at the edge of the ridge. It teetered. Lunging forward, he shouted, *"Captain! Look out!"*

Kirk leaped aside. And the massive rock crashed into the defile where he'd been moving the moment before. Then the edge of the ridge crumbled. Lazarus fell at Kirk's feet.

When Spock found them, dust was still drifting down on both men.

McCoy had a stretcher waiting in the Transporter Room. Lazarus was still unconscious. In Sickbay his recovery came hard. Kirk saw the horror twist his face as he struggled back into awareness. He tried to leap from the examining table.

"The Thing!" he cried hoarsely.

"You're on the *Enterprise* now," Kirk said. "Doctor McCoy says you'll be all right."

"How's your head?" McCoy asked.

A hand touched the cut forehead. "It aches."

"You saved my life down there," Kirk said. "I thank you for that." He paused. "But I have to ask you some questions."

"Jim! A possible concussion—"

"It's necessary!" Kirk flared.

"Go ahead, Captain," Lazarus said.

"I am holding," Kirk said, "a computer report on the information you gave us during your initial screening. It calls you a liar, Lazarus. For one thing, there is no planet at the location you claimed to have come from. There never has been."

Lazarus sat up, his eyes on Kirk's face. "You wouldn't believe the truth if I told it to you," he said slowly.

"Try us," Kirk said.

"About my home planet . . . I distorted a fact in the interest of self-preservation and my sacred cause. You, too, are a stranger to me, Captain—an unknown factor." He swung his legs from the table, making a tentative effort to stand.

"I needed help, not censure," he said. "Freedom, not confinement as a madman. If I told you the truth, I feared that was what you'd call me."

"The truth now, if you please," Kirk said.

Lazarus looked at him, his deep passion thickening his voice. "All right, sir! My planet, my home—or what's left of it—is down there below us!"

Kirk stared at him, dumbfounded. "What are you saying?"

"That my space ship is more than a space ship. It is also a time chamber . . . a time ship. And I, if you will, am a time traveler."

Kirk frowned. This man was a compounder of mysteries. All he had told were lies . . . and yet that vessel of his, like nothing before seen on heaven or earth, its unrecognizable complexities. . . . He spoke tonelessly. "And this thing you search for? Is it a time traveler, too?"

The eyes went wild. "Yes! He's fled me across all the years, all the empty years! To a dead future on the dead planet he murdered!" He was feverish now, staggering to his feet. "Help me, man! You have more crystals! Give me the tools I need to kill him!" He tottered and McCoy grabbed him. He wrenched free of the supporting arm. "The crystals! What are they to the abomination I hunt? What is anything compared to its supernal evil? Do you want him to get away?"

"Lazarus, there are a lot of things going on that we know nothing about. But *you* know. Now tell me—*where are our crystals*?"

"I told you!" Lazarus shouted. "He has them! He took them!"

They had to ease him back on the table or he would have fallen. He lay there, prone, his eyes glassy, face streaming with sweat. McCoy said, "He's got to rest, Jim. And would you mind getting that muscle man out of my Sickbay?"

Nodding, Kirk dismissed the guard. Uneasy, he watched McCoy cover Lazarus with a sheet. There was a deep sigh and the eyes closed. "He's in a lot of pain, Jim."

"Pain," Kirk said. "Sometimes it can drive a man harder than pleasure." He looked at the face on the table. It was whiter than the sheet. "But I guess he won't be going anywhere for a while—not this time."

As the door closed behind them, the sheeted form moved. The eyes opened. Grasping the table, Lazarus hauled himself to his feet. He faltered, shaking his head to clear it. Then, cautiously, stealthily, motored by his inexorable determination, he moved to the door.

Kirk chose the Briefing Room to put the Big Questions to Spock. He turned from his restless pacing to cry, "But just what have we got? A magnetic effect which produces your 'wink-out' phenomenon. And a mysterious, unidentifiable source of radiation on the planet. Lazarus, a walking powder-keg. Your 'rip' in the universe. That murdering humanoid none of us have seen . . ."

Spock looked up from his computer tie-in. "True, Captain. But what is significant to me is the fact that our ship's instruments are specifically designed to locate and identify any physical object in the universe, whether it be matter or energy."

"But using them you were unable to identify that source of radiation on the planet!"

"Correct, sir."

"Are the instruments in order?"

"In perfect operating condition."

"Then what you say leaves only one conclusion. The source of that radiation is not of our universe."

"Nor in it, Captain. It came from outside."

Kirk resumed his pacing. "Yes—outside of it. That

would explain a lot! Another universe . . . perhaps in another dimension . . . but occupying the same space at the same time."

"The possibility of the existence of a parallel universe has been scientifically conceded, Captain."

"All right. What would happen if another universe, say a minus universe, came into contact with a positive one such as ours?"

"Unquestionably a warp, Captain. A distortion of physical laws on an immense scale."

"That's what we have been experiencing! The point where they touch—couldn't it be described as a hole?"

Their two minds seemed to meet and meld. Spock nodded vigorously. "Indeed, Captain. I also point out that a hole in the universe—or in a simple container—can either allow the contents to escape or—"

"What is outside to enter it!" Kirk shouted. "Mr. Spock, the invasion that Commodore Barstow suspected!"

"There is no evidence of any large-scale invasion, sir."

"But a small-scale invasion! Spock! What's your evaluation of the mental state of Lazarus?"

"At one moment, paranoid. But the next, calm, rational, mild. Almost as if he were—" Spock paused on the edge of light. "Almost as if he were two men."

"Exactly! Two men—different but identical. And a hole in the universe! No! Not a hole! A door, Spock, a door!"

"You *are* hypothesizing a parallel universe, Captain!"

"And why not? It's theoretically possible! Look at Lazarus! One minute he's at the point of death . . . but the next alive and well, strong as a bull. That cut on his forehead. First he has it, then it's gone—and then he has it again! For one man it's all physically impossible!"

"I agree, Captain. There are unquestionably two of him."

"But . . . what's going on? This leaping from one universe to the other? The wild rant about a murdering thing that destroys civilizations! What's the purpose?"

"Captain, madness has no purpose. No reason. But—it could have a goal!" Spock's face was stony as his Vulcan blood triumphed over his human agitation. "He must be stopped, Captain! Destroyed, if necessary."

"Spock, I'm not following you now."

"Two universes, sir! Project this! One positive, one negative. Or, more specifically, one of them matter—and the other one, antimatter!"

Kirk regarded him for a tense moment. "But matter and antimatter—they cancel one another out . . . violently."

"Precisely . . . under certain conditions. When identical particles of matter and antimatter meet—identical, Captain, like—"

"Like Lazarus—like the two of them. Identical, except that one is matter and the other antimatter. And if they meet . . ."

Kirk had never heard Spock's voice so somber, "Annihilation, Captain. Total, complete, annihilation . . ."

"And of everything that exists . . . everywhere . . ."

It was a moment for failure in speech. They stared at each other as the fate of worlds, known and unknown, dropped itself into their laps.

Lazarus found the corridor deserted. He turned the corner that led to Engineering; and sidling through its door, went swiftly to an electrical relay panel. Its maze of wires struck him as primitive. It took him barely a moment to remove a tool from his jumper suit, detach a connection and affix the wire to a different terminal. Closing the panel, he waited, a shadow in the darker shadow behind a throbbing dynamo.

Far to his left, Charlene Masters was studying the effect of recharge on her di-lithium crystals. Above the bins the needle of a thermometerlike device had wavered up toward a red mark. It climbed above it—and a wisp of smoke drifted up from one of the lower dials. She looked away from the installation to examine the chart held by her assistant. They smelled the smoke at the same time. "The energizer! It's shorted!" she cried.

There was a flashing spray of sparks. A great, billowing cloud of smoke engulfed them. "Get out of here, Ensign! Sound the alarm!" She was coughing.

"You, too, Lieutenant!"

"No! I've got to—"

"You've got to get out of here!" he shouted. "The

whole bank might blow!'' He seized her arm, dragging her through the still-thickening smoke. Half-blinded, choking, they staggered out into the corridor. As they passed him, Lazarus, a piece of torn sheet held over his nose and mouth, shut the door quietly behind them.

Charlene was at the wall communicator. ''Engineering! Fire! Energizing circuits!''

Uhura whirled from her board. ''Fire, Captain! Engineering! Situation critical!''

''All available hands, Lieutenant! On the double! Spock! On me!''

The Ensign, still coughing, his face black-streaked, met them at the door to Engineering. ''Under control, sir. But it couldn't have—Captain, that fire did not start by itself!''

Spock said, ''Lazarus, Captain? A ruse? To get at the di-lithium crystals?''

''Way ahead of you, Mr. Spock.''

They both plunged into the smoky room. Coughing, Kirk groped his way to the bins. ''He's got them all right. And he's beaming down right now. I'm going after him. Get together a Security detail. Follow me as soon as you can.''

''Aye, aye, sir.''

Lazarus had tied the crystals in the torn sheet. Materialized, he hurried directly to his craft. In its working area, he unwrapped them exultantly. Shaking his fist at his invisible foe, he yelled, ''Now I'll do it. I have a threshold! Run! Run! I've got you now!''

Bending to his labor, he selected certain rods and wires that soon assumed the shape of a protective frame before the ship's entrance. He worked quickly, arranging what were obviously premade units. In them he carefully placed the dilithium crystals. When the last one was safely installed, he raised his fists skyward, howling like a wolf, ''It's done! It's finished! Finished!''

Kirk, nearing the ship, heard him. Phaser extended, he said, ''Wrong, Lazarus. *You're* finished. Through. Back up!'' He stepped through the door.

''No!'' Lazarus shrieked.

The warning came too late. The shimmering sparkles flared. Kirk vanished.

Lazarus, head huddled in his arms, cried, "No! Not you! *Not you!*"

For Kirk, banished into the tunnel of negative magnetism, time and space died. He was spinning in a kind of slow motion where familiar time was boundless and empty space stuff that broke off against his face in fluffy hunks. He was falling but he was also rising. He was twisting while at the same time he lay still. The nightmare of an absolute disorientation was crawling over him. The shimmer shimmered. It faded—and he found himself on his hands and knees, fighting nausea.

Vaguely, with disinterest, he saw rocks, gullies, the old dry desolation, the cliff that sheltered the time craft. The ship was gone. There was no sign of it—no sign of anything or anybody. He got slowly to his feet, staring at the cliff base where the craft should have been. After a moment, he hefted the phaser in his hand, unsure that it was real. It was—solid, real against his palm. He looked around again before he called, "Hello!"

The word echoed back from the rocks. Then only the silence spoke.

He took off at a run up a slope. It gave on to a plateau. The time craft was there, set in a little open space, but no sign of life about it. Then the Lazarus of the uncut forehead rose from his stooping position. He, too, was rigging some kind of framework before the ship's entrance. He smiled at the aimed phaser. "Welcome, Captain. I wasn't expecting you."

"No," Kirk said. *"Him."*

"You understand then?"

"Not completely. This is clearly a parallel universe."

"Of course."

"Antimatter?"

"Here, yes."

"And if identical particles meet . . ."

"The end of everything, Captain. Of creation. Of existence. All gone." He squared his broad shoulders. "I'm trying to stop him. It's why I took your di-lithium crystals."

"He has two more."

Lazarus searched Kirk's face. "That's very bad, Captain. If he can come through, at a time of his own choosing.

But I think, if we hurry . . . and you will help me, he can yet be stopped. But we have little time.''

It was Spock who materialized before the other time ship, still at the foot of the cliff. The matter Lazarus, the wound on his forehead, stood at its door, violently waving his arms. ''Back! Back!'' he screamed. ''If you ever want to see your Captain alive again, get back!''

''Do what he says,'' Spock told his Security guards.

Up on the plateau, the second Lazarus had his threshold frame almost completed. He pointed to a tool; and as Kirk handed it to him, he said, ''He meant to come through this but when you accidentally contacted it, it drained his crystals. It will take him at least ten minutes to re-energize with the equipment on board his craft. That should give us time enough. . . . ''

''Just exactly what did I contact?'' Kirk said.

''I call it the alternative warp, Captain. It's the negative magnetic corridor where the parallel universes come together. It's . . . the safety valve. It keeps eternity from blowing up.''

''This corridor,'' Kirk said. ''Is it what caused the magnetic effect—that sort of 'wink-out' phenomenon?''

''Precisely, Captain. But not because of its existence. Only because *he* entered it. The corridor is like a jail with explosives attached to its door. Open the door—and the explosives may detonate. Stay inside the corridor—''

''And the universe is safe,'' Kirk said.

''Your universe and mine, Captain. Both of them.''

''Surely he must know what would happen if he ever does meet you face to face outside that corridor.''

''Of course he knows. But he is mad, Captain. You've heard him. His mind is gone. When our people found the way to slip through the warp . . . when they proved the existence of another identical universe, it was too much for him. He could not live, knowing that I lived. He became obsessed with passion to destroy me. The fact that my death would also destroy him—and everything else—cannot matter to him.''

Kirk spoke slowly. ''So you're the terrible Thing . . . the murdering monster . . . the creature of evil. . . .''

''Yes. Or he is. It depends on the point of view, doesn't it?''

He made a final adjustment. "It's ready, Captain. If we can force him into the corridor while I'm there waiting for him, we can put an end to this. But if he comes through the warp at a time of his own choosing—and breaks into this universe to find me . . ."

"I understand," Kirk said. "What do you want me to do?"

"Find him. Force him through his threshold frame and into the corridor. I'll be waiting. I'll hold him there."

Kirk's face had fallen into very sober lines. "You can't hold him forever."

"Can't I, Captain? You are to destroy his ship."

"But if I do that—won't this one also be destroyed?"

"It will."

"And that door—that warp—will be closed to you."

"Yes. But it will be closed to him, too."

"You'll be trapped with him," Kirk said. "You'll be trapped with him in that corridor forever . . . at each other's throats . . . throughout the rest of time."

"Is it such a large price to pay for the safety of two universes?"

Lazarus reached out and placed Kirk within the frame of his threshold. "The safety of two universes." Kirk looked at the brave man. "Are you sure you want me to do this?"

"You must do it, Captain. We have no choice. Are you ready?"

Kirk's voice was steady. "I'm ready."

"Send him to me. I'll be waiting in the corridor."

He threw a switch. The shimmering sparkles tingled over Kirk's body—and he was back on the plateau, the other space craft before him. Spock ran toward him. He shook his head, waving him back.

The first Lazarus was busy at his threshold frame, his back to Kirk. He moved a lever. The structure glowed, then flashed into glitter. "You're done!" he told it exultantly.

Kirk jumped him. But he whirled in time to block the tackle with his heavy body. Then they closed, wrestling, Kirk, silent, intent, boring in as he fought to back the man into the frame. His aim became clear to Lazarus. *"No!"* he yelled. "You can't! I'm not ready! Not now! Not yet!" He seized a thick metal tool for bludgeon. Kirk ducked the blow, rising fast to connect a hard fist to his jaw. Lazarus wavered; and Kirk held him, pushing, pushing him backward until he stumbled, toppling over into the frame. The sparkle caught him. There was a blinding glare of whiteness—and he was gone.

Kirk pulled in a deep lungful of breath. Spock took over. Turning to his men, he said, "Get those di-lithium crystals back to the ship. Hurry!" Then he spoke to Kirk. "Captain, am I right in guessing that this craft must be completely destroyed?"

"To the last particle."

"And what of Lazarus, sir?"

"Yes," Kirk said. "What of Lazarus, Mr. Spock?"

There was no out. And Kirk, back in his command chair, knew it. He'd chosen the Service; and if he'd been unaware of what would be required of a Starship Captain back in those long-ago Academy days, the choice was still his. Nor could any human being expect to foresee the consequences of any decision. Met up with them, all you could do was deal with them as responsibly as you could. He'd had to remind himself of this truth a thousand times—but this time . . .

He spoke into his intercom. "Activate phaser banks."

Somebody said, "Phaser banks activated, sir."

"Stand by to fire."

Under the words Kirk was seeing that corridor of negative magnetism. A man of solid Earth, he was remembering its frightful unearthliness, its chilling paradoxes—and he saw two men, two humans locked into it, embattled, each of them winning and losing, rising and falling, eternally victorious and eternally vanquished throughout an unbroken Forever.

He licked dry lips.

"Phasers standing by, sir."

His lips felt rough. He licked them. "Fire phasers," he said.

The beams struck the ship on the plateau. It disintegrated. Then they switched to the one at the cliff's base. It burst into flame and vanished. On the screen only the desolate landscape remained.

Solution—simple.

"Let's get out of here," Kirk said. He turned to the helmsman. "Warp one, Mr. Leslie."

"Warp one, sir."

Spock was beside him. "Everything all right, Captain?"

"It is for us, Mr. Spock."

Spock nodded. "There is, of course, no escape for them."

"No, Mr. Spock. No escape at all. How would it be to be trapped with that raging madman at your throat . . . at your throat throughout Time everlasting? How would it be?"

"But the universe is safe, Captain."

"Yes . . . for you and me. But what of Lazarus?" He paused as though posing the question to that universe Lazarus had saved.

The stars slid by the *Enterprise*. They didn't answer its Captain.

TOMORROW IS YESTERDAY

Writer: D. C. Fontana
Director: Michael O'Herlihy
Guest star: Roger Perry

The star was very old—as old as it is possible for a star to be, a first-generation star, born when the present universe was born. It had had all the experiences possible for a star—it had had planets; had gone nova, wiping out those planets and all those who lived upon them; had become an X-ray star; then a neutron star. At last, slowly collapsing upon itself into an ultimately dense mass of pseudomatter resembling—except for its compaction—the primordial ylem out of which it had been created, it drew its gravitational field in so closely about itself that not even the few dim red flickers of light left to it could get out, and it prepared to die.

The star was still there, still in its orbit, and still incredibly massive despite its shrunken volume; but it could no longer be seen or detected. It would soon be in a space all its own, a tiny sterile universe as uninteresting and forgotten as a burial jug. It had become a black star.

The *Enterprise*, on a rare trip back toward the Sol sector and Earth, hit the black star traveling at warp factor four—sixty-four times the speed of light.

It could not, of course, properly be said that the *Enterprise* hit the black star itself. Technically, the bubble of subspace in which the *Enterprise* was enclosed, which would have been moving at 64C had the bubble impossibly been in normal space at all, hit that part of the black star's gravitational cocoon that had also begun to extrude into subspace. The technicalities, however, are not very convincing. Since no such thing had ever happened to a starship before, nobody could have predicted it, and the theoreticians are still arguing about just *why* the collision produced the results it did.

About the results themselves, nobody is in any doubt.

Captain Kirk dragged himself up from unconsciousness and shook his head to clear it. This was a mistake, and he did not try it a second time. The bridge was dim and quiet; the main lights were off, so was the screen, and only a few telltales glowed on the boards. Crew personnel—Spock, Uhura, Sulu—were slumped in their seats; Ames, the security chief, was spilled crookedly on the deck. It looked like the aftermath of a major attack.

"Spock!"

The first officer stirred, and then got shakily to his feet. "Here, Captain. What in the nine worlds . . ."

"I don't know. Everything was normal, and then, blooey! Check us out."

"Right." In immediate control of himself, Spock ran a quick check of his library computer. Except for a few flickers here and there on the board, it was dead, as Kirk could see himself. Spock abandoned it without a second thought and went promptly to Uhura.

"Except for secondary systems, everything is out, sir," he said. "We are on impulse power only. If Mr. Scott is still with us, the auxiliaries should be on in a moment. Are you all right, Lieutenant?"

Uhura nodded wordlessly and smiled at him, though it was not a very convincing smile. At the same moment, the main lights flickered on, brightened and steadied. A hum of computers and pumps began to fill in the familiar, essential background noise that was as much a part of life on the *Enterprise* as the air.

"Mr. Scott," Spock said, straightening, "is still with us."

Sulu sat up groggily, also shook his head, and also apparently decided against trying the experiment a second time. Kirk flicked a switch on his chair panel.

"This is the captain," he said. "Damage control parties on all decks, check in. All departments tie in to the library computer. Report casualties and operational readiness to the first officer. Kirk out. Miss Uhura, contact Star Fleet control. Whatever we hit in the Base Nine area, I want them alerted—and maybe they'll know something about it we don't. Mr. Spock?"

Spock half-turned from his station, an earphone still to one ear. "Only minor injuries to the crew, Captain. All decks operating on auxiliary systems. Engineering reports warp engines nonoperational. Mr. Scott overrode the automatic helm setting and is using impulse power to hold us in fixed orbit, but . . ."

"Fixed orbit around what, Mr. Spock?"

"The Earth, sir. I am at present unable to say how we got here."

"Screen on," Kirk said.

The screen came on. It was the Earth below them, all right.

"We're too low in the atmosphere to retain this altitude," Spock said. "Engineer reports we have enough impulse power to achieve escape velocity."

"Helm, give us some altitude."

"Yes, sir," Sulu said. "Helm answers. She's sluggish, sir."

"Sir," Uhura said. "Normal Star Fleet channel has nothing on it but static. I'm picking up something on another frequency, but it's not identifiable."

"Put it on audio, Lieutenant."

Uhura flicked a tumbler and the loudspeaker on her board burst out: ". . . five-thirty news summary. Cape Kennedy—the first manned moon shot is scheduled for Wednesday, six A.M., Eastern Standard Time. All three astronauts set to make this historic flight are . . ."

Kirk was up out of his chair on the instant. "The first manned moon shot!" he said. "You've got some sort of dramatization. That shot was back in the 1970s."

Uhura nodded and tried another channel, but from the computer, Spock said slowly: "Apparently, Captain, so are we."

"Mr. Spock, this is no time for joking."

"I never joke," Spock said severely. "At present I have only rough computations, but apparently what we hit was the subspace component of an intense spherical gravity field, very likely a black star. The field translated our momentum in terms of time—a relativistic effect. I can give you an exact reading in a few moments, but 1970 seems to be of about the right order of magnitude."

Kirk sat down again, stunned. Uhura continued scanning. Finally she said, "Captain, I'm picking up a ground-to-air transmission in this sector."

"Verified," Spock said. "Our scanners are picking up some kind of craft approaching from below us, under cloud cover and closing fast."

The loudspeaker said: "Blue Jay Four, this is Black Jack. We're tracking both you and the UFO."

"I have him on my screen," another voice said. "Following."

"Good, let's get this one for once."

"Mr. Sulu," Kirk said, "can we gain altitude faster?"

"I'm trying, sir, but she's still slow in responding."

"Blue Jay Four, have you got visual contact yet?"

"I can see it fine," said the second voice. "And it's huge too. As big as a cruiser, bigger maybe. It *is* saucer-shaped, but there're two cylindrical projections on top and one below."

"We have two more flights scrambled and on the way," said the first voice. "They'll rendezvous with you in two minutes."

"Won't be here, Black Jack. The UFO is climbing away fast."

"Blue Jay Four, close on the object and force it to land. We want it down—or at least disabled until the other planes arrive. After thirty years of rumors, this may be our first clear shot."

"Acknowledged. Closing in."

"Can he harm us?" Kirk said.

"I would judge so, Captain," Spock said. "The aircraft is an interceptor equipped with missiles, possibly armed with nuclear warheads. Since we do not have the power for a full screen, he could at least damage us severely."

"Scotty!" Kirk said into his microphone. "Activate tractor beam. Lock onto that aircraft and hold it out there."

"Captain," Spock said, "that type of aircraft may be too fragile to take tractor handling."

"Tractor on, sir," Scott's voice said briskly. "We have the target."

Spock looked into his hooded viewer and shook his head. "And it is breaking up, Captain."

"Transporter Room! Can you lock on the cockpit of that aircraft?"

"No problem, Captain."

"Beam that pilot aboard," Kirk said, springing up. "Spock, take over."

The figure who materialized in the transporter chamber was a strange sight to Kirk until he removed his oxygen mask and helmet. Then he was revealed as a medium-tall, compactly built man with an expression of grim determination despite his obvious amazement. He would have made a good starship crewman, Kirk thought . . . centuries from now.

"Welcome to the *Enterprise*," Kirk said, smiling.

"You . . . you speak English!"

"That's right," Kirk said. "You can step down from our transporters, Mr. . . . ?"

"Captain John Christopher," the pilot said stiffly. "United States Air Force, serial number 4857932. And that's all the information you get."

"Relax, Captain. You're among friends. I'm Captain James T. Kirk, and I apologize for bringing you aboard so abruptly. But we had no choice. I didn't know your ship couldn't hold up under our tractor beam until it was too late."

"Don't give me any double-talk," Christopher said. "I demand to know . . ."

"You're in no position to demand anything, but we'll answer all your questions anyhow in good time. Meanwhile, relax. You're our guest. I have a feeling you'll find it interesting."

He led the way out of the Transporter Room. Christopher shrugged and followed. As they moved down the corridor, he was obviously missing nothing; clearly a trained observer. When a pretty young crewwoman carrying a tricorder went past them, however, he had trouble retaining his composure. "Passenger?" he said.

"No, crew. About a fourth of the crew is female—exactly a hundred at the moment."

"A crew of four hundred?"

"Four hundred and thirty. Now if you'll step aboard the elevator . . ."

Christopher did, and was immediately startled once more when it moved horizontally instead of up or down. After digesting this peculiarity, he said:

"It must have taken quite a lot of money to build a ship like this."

"Indeed it did. There are only twelve like it in the fleet."

"The fleet? Did the Navy . . . ?"

"We're a combined service, Captain," Kirk said. "Our authority is the United Federation of Planets."

"Federation of—Planets?"

"That's right. Actually, Captain—this is a little difficult to explain. We . . . we're from your future. A time warp landed us back here. It was an accident."

"You people seem to have a lot of them," Christopher said drily, "if all the UFO reports stem from the same kind of source. However, I can't argue with the fact that you *are* here, ship and all." While he spoke, the elevator doors snapped open to reveal the bridge, with Spock in the command chair. "And I've never believed in little green men."

"Neither have I," Spock said, rising.

This time Christopher made no attempt to conceal his astonishment. *And Spock claims he never jokes,* Kirk thought; but he said only, "Captain Christopher, this is my first officer, Commander Spock."

"Captain," Spock said with an abrupt but courteous nod.

"Please feel free to look around the bridge, Captain. I'm sure you have the good sense not to touch anything. I think you'll find it interesting."

" 'Interesting,' " Christopher said, "is not a very adequate word for it." He moved over toward the communications and library-computer stations, but could not help shooting another look at Spock as he did so. Kirk did not explain; everybody else on board took the half-alien first officer as a matter of course, and Christopher might as well practice doing the same; he might be with them for quite a while yet.

"We have achieved a stable orbit out of Earth's atmosphere, Captain," Spock said. "Our deflector shields are operative now, and ought to prevent us from being picked up again as a UFO." He made a grimace of distaste over the word. "Mr. Scott wishes to speak to you about the engines."

"Very well, Mr. Spock. I know that expression. What else is on your mind?"

"Captain Christopher."

Kirk looked toward the newcomer. He was talking to Uhura; the spectacle of a beautiful Bantu girl operating a communications board evidently had diverted him, at least temporarily, from the first officer.

"All right, what about him?'

"We cannot return him to Earth," Spock said. "He already knows too much about us and is learning more. I mean no aspersions on his character, about which I know nothing, but suppose an unscrupulous man were to gain possession of the knowledge of man's certain future, as represented by us? Such a man could speculate—manipulate key industries, stocks, even nations—and in doing so, change what must be. And if it is changed, Captain, you and I and everything we know might be made impossible."

"We'd just vanish? Including thousands of tons of *Enterprise*?"

"Like a soap bubble."

"Hmm. You know, Spock, your logic can be very annoying." Kirk looked back at Christopher. "That flight suit must be uncomfortable. Have the quartermaster issue Captain Christopher some suitable clothes—tactfully relieving him of any sidearms he may be carrying in the process—and then I want to see you and him in my quarters."

"Yes, sir."

Kirk was talking to the computer when they came in; he waved them to seats. "Captain's log, supplemental. Engineering Officer Scott reports warp engines damaged but repairable. Ascertain precise degree and nature of damage, compute nature and magnitude of forces responsible, and program possible countermeasures."

"Affirm; operating," said the computer's voice in midair. Christopher did not react; evidently he was getting used to surprises.

"Kirk out. Now, Captain, we have a problem. To put the matter bluntly, what are we going to do with you? We can't put you back."

"What do you mean, can't? Mr. Spock here tells me that your transporter can work over even longer distances than this."

"It's not the transporter," Kirk said. "You know what the future looks like, Captain. If anybody else finds out, they could change the course of it—and destroy it."

"I can see that," Christopher said after a moment. "But it also strikes me that my disappearance would also change things."

"Apparently not," Spock said. "I have run a computer check through all historical tapes. They show no relevant contribution by any Captain John Christopher. There was a popular author by that name, but it was a pen name; you are not he."

Christopher was visibly deflated, but not for long. He stood and began to pace. Finally he swung back toward Kirk.

"Captain," he said, "if it were only a matter of my own preference, I'd stay. I'd give my right arm to learn more about this ship—*all* about it. It's a colossal achievement and obviously it implies even greater ones in the background. But my preference doesn't count. It's my duty to report what I've seen. I have an oath to uphold." He paused, then added pointedly: "What would you do?"

"Just that," Kirk said. "I entirely understand. You are the kind of man we recruit for our own service, and can never get enough of, though we don't have oaths any more. But unfortunately, this means that you are also of superior intelligence. We cannot risk any report that you might make."

"I have a wife and two children," Christopher said quietly. "I suppose that makes no difference to you."

"It makes a lot of difference to me," Kirk said. "But I cannot let it sway me."

"In both your trades—the pilot and the warrior—there was always an unusually high risk that you would become a casualty," Spock said. "You knew it when you married; so did your wife. You bet against the future, with high odds against you. Unfortunately, we are the future and you have lost; you are, in effect, now a casualty."

"Mr. Spock is no more unfeeling than I am," Kirk added. "But logic is one of his specialties, and what he says is quite true. I can only say I'm sorry, and I mean it." The intercom interrupted him. "Excuse me a moment. Kirk here."

"Engineer here, Captain. Everything's jury-rigged, but we're coming along with the repairs and should be ready to reenergize in four hours."

"Good. Scotty, you can fix anything."

"Except broken hearts, maybe. But, sir . . ."

"What is it? Plow right ahead."

"Well, sir," Scott's voice said, "I can fix the engines, but I canna build you a time machine. We'll be ready to go, but we've no place *to* go in this era. Mister Spock tells me that in the 1970s the human race was wholly confined to the Earth. Space outside the local group of stars was wholly dominated by the Vegan Tyranny, and you'll recall what happened when we first hit *them.* D'ye see the problem?"

"I'm afraid," Kirk said heavily, "that I do. Very well, Mr. Scott, carry on."

"Yes, sir. Out."

Christopher's face was a study in bitter triumph; but what he said next, oddly, was obviously designed to be helpful—or at least, to establish that his own hope was well-founded.

"Mr. Spock here tells me that he is half Vulcan. Surely you can reach Vulcan from here. That's supposed to be just inside the orbit of Mercury."

"There is no such solar planet as Vulcan," Kirk said. "Mr. Spock's father was a native of The Vulcan, which is a planet of 40 Eridani. Of course we could reach that too . . ."

". . . but in the 1970's," Spock finished. "If we took the *Enterprise* there, we would unwrite *their* future history too. Captain, this is the most perfect case of General Order Number One that I have ever encountered—or think I am likely to encounter."

"The order," Kirk explained to Christopher, "prohibits interference with the normal development of alien life and alien societies. It hadn't occurred to me until Mr. Spock mentioned it, but I'm sure it would be construed to apply here too."

"Too bad, Captain," Christopher said. He was not bothering to conceal his triumph now. "Maybe I can't go home—but neither can you. You're as much a prisoner in time as I am on this ship."

"I believe, sir," Spock said, "that Captain Christopher's summary is quite exact."

It was indeed exact, but not complete, as Kirk quickly realized. There was also the problem of supplies. The *Enterprise* could never land on any planet—and certainly would not dare to land on this one, its own home world, even if it were possible—and it was simply ridiculous to even consider trying to steal food, water and power by gig or transporter for 430 people. As for Christopher—who had already tried to escape through the transporter and had come perilously close to making it—what prospects did he have if the *Enterprise* somehow did get back to its own time? He would be archaic, useless, a curiosity. Possibly he could be retrained sufficiently to find a niche, but never retrained to forget his wife and children. To check that, Kirk visited McCoy, the ship's surgeon.

"Get him down here and I'll check," McCoy said.

Kirk put in the call. "You mean it *might* be done?"

"It depends upon the depth of his commitment. Some marriages are routine. I'll have to see what the electroencephalograph shows."

"You're starting to sound like Spock."

"If you're going to get nasty, I'll leave."

Kirk grinned, but the grin faded quickly. "If the depth of his commitment is crucial, we're sunk. He's the kind who commits himself totally. Witness yesterday's escape attempt."

Spock came in with the prisoner—after the escape attempt, there was no other honest word for it. He said at once:

"Captain, I do not know what Dr. McCoy has in mind, but I think it may be useless by now; I have some new information. I find I made an error in my computations."

"This," McCoy said drily, "could be a historical occasion."

Spock ignored the surgeon. "I find that we must return Captain Christopher to Earth after all."

"You said I made no relative contributions," Christopher said sourly.

"I was speaking of cultural contributions. I have now checked the genetic contributions, which was a serious oversight. In running a cross-check on that factor, I discovered that your son, Colonel Shaun Geoffrey Christopher, headed . . . *will* head the first successful Earth-Titan probe, which is certainly significant. If Captain Christopher is not returned, there won't be any Colonel Christopher to go to the Saturnian satellites, since the boy does not yet exist."

The grin on Cristopher's face made him look remarkably like a Halloween pumpkin. "A boy," he said, to nobody in particular. "I'm going to have a son."

"And we," McCoy said, "have a headache."

"No," Kirk said. "We have an obligation. Two obligations, mutually antagonistic."

"It is possible that we can satisfy both of them at once," Spock said.

"How? Out with it, man!"

"I have the data you ordered the computer to work out, and there is now no question but that the only reason we are here at all is because we had a head-on collision with a black star. To get back home, we are going to have to contrive something similar."

"Do you know of any black stars around here? And how will that solve our problem with Captain Christopher?"

"There is a black star quite nearby, in fact, Captain, but we cannot use it because it is well out of transporter range of Earth. That would prevent our returning Captain Christopher. But Engineering Officer Scott thinks we may be able to use our own sun. It will, he says, be a rough ride, but will also offer us certain advantages. Briefly, if we make a close hyperbolic passage around the sun at warp eight . . ."

"Not with *my* ship," Kirk said coldly.

"Please, Captain, hear me out. We need the velocity because we must compensate for the Sun's relatively weak gravitational field. And I spoke of advantages. What will happen, if nothing goes wrong, is that we will retreat further into time as we reach the head of the hyperbola . . ."

"Just what we need," McCoy said.

"Shut up, Bones, I want to hear this."

". . . and as we mount the other leg of the curve, there will be a slingshot effect that will hurl us forward in time again. If this is most precisely calculated, we will pass within transporter range of the Earth within two or three minutes *before* the time when we arrived here the first time, before we first appeared in the sky. At that moment, we reinject Captain Christopher into his plane—which will not have been destroyed yet—and the whole chain of consequences will fall apart. Essentially, it will never have happened at all."

"Are you sure of that?"

Spock raised his eyebrows. "No, sir, of course I am not sure of it. Mr. Scott and I think it may work. The computer concurs. Certainty is not an attainable goal in a problem like this."

"True enough," Kirk agreed. "But I don't see that it solves our problem with Captain Christopher at all. It gets him back home, but with his memories intact—and that's what we have to avoid at all costs. I would rather destroy the *Enterprise* than the future."

There was a brief silence. Both Spock and McCoy knew well what such a decision had cost him. Then Spock said gently, "Captain, Mr. Scott and I see no such necessity. Bear in mind that Captain Christopher will arrive home *before* he was taken aboard our ship. He will have nothing to remember—because none of it will ever have happened."

Kirk turned to the pilot from the past. "Does that satisfy you?"

"Do I have a choice?" Christopher said. "Well, I won't quibble. It gets me home—and obviously I can't do my duty if I can't remember what it is. Only . . ."

"Only what?"

"Well, I never thought I'd make it into space. I was in line for the space program, but I didn't qualify."

"Take a good look around, Captain," Kirk said quietly. "You made it here ahead of all of them. We were not the first. You were."

"Yes, I know that," Christopher said, staring down at his clenched fists. "And I've seen the future too. An immense gift. I . . . I'll be very sorry to forget it."

"How old are you?" McCoy said abruptly.

"Eh? I'm thirty."

"Then, Captain Christopher," McCoy said, "in perhaps sixty more years, or a few more, you will forget things many times more important to you than this—your wife, your children, and indeed the very fact that you ever existed at all. You will forget every single thing you ever loved, and what is worse, you will not even care."

"Is that," Christopher said angrily, "supposed to be consoling? If that's a sample of the philosophy of the future, I can do without it."

"I am not counseling despair," McCoy said, very gently. "I am only trying to remind you that regardless of our achievements, we all at last go down into the dark. I am a doctor and I have seen a great deal of death. It doesn't discourage me. On the contrary, I'm trying to call to your attention the things that are much more valuable to you than the fact that you've seen men from the future and a bucketful of gadgetry. You will have those still, though you forget us. We are trying to give them back to you, those sixty-plus years you might otherwise have wasted in a future you could never understand. The fact that you will have to forget this encounter in the process seems to me to be a very small fee."

Christopher stared at McCoy as though he had never seen him before. After a long pause, he said, "I was wrong. Even if I did remember, I would do nothing to destroy a future that . . . that has even one such man in it. And I see that underneath all your efficiency and gadgetry, you're *all* like that. I am proud to be one of your ancestors. Captain Kirk, I concur in anything you decide."

"Your bravery helped to make us whatever we are," Kirk said. "Posts, everybody."

"And besides," Spock added, "it is quite possible that we won't make it at all."

"Now there," McCoy said, "is a philosophy *I* can do without."

Kirk said evenly, "We will take the chance that we have. If you'll join me on the bridge, Captain Christopher, we will at least give you a bumpy last ride for your money."

Christopher grinned. "That's the kind I like."

It was indeed a bumpy ride. Warp Eight was an acceleration called upon only in the most extreme of emergencies—although this surely classified as one—and could not be sustained for long without serious damage to the *Enterprise*. It was decidedly unsettling to hear the whole monstrous fabric of the ship, which ordinarily seemed as solid as a planet, creaking and straining around them as the pressure was applied, and to hear the engines—usually quite quiet—howling below decks.

For Kirk, it was almost more unsettling to watch the planets begin to both revolve and rotate in the wrong direction in the navigation tank, as the combined acceleration and gravitational energies were translated into motion backwards in time. Perhaps fortunately for his sanity, he did not have to watch long, however, for the close approach to the sun eventually made it necessary to close off all outside sensors. They were flying blind.

Then the swing was completed, and the sensors could be opened again—and now the planets were moving in their proper directions, but rather decidedly too fast, as the *Enterprise* shot up the time curve. In the Transporter Room, Captain Christopher waited tensely, in full flight dress.

"Passing 1968," Spock said from his post. "January 1969 . . . March . . . May . . . July . . . the pace is picking up very rapidly . . . November . . ."

Kirk gripped the arms of his chair. This was going to have to be the most split-second of all transporter shots. No human operator could hope to bring it off; the actual shift would be under the control of the computer.

"June . . . August . . . December . . . into 1970 now—"

Suddenly, and only for an instant, the lights dimmed. It was over so quickly that it could almost have been an illusion.

"Transporter Room! Did you—?"

But there was no time to complete the question. The lights dimmed again, all the stars in the heavens seemed to be scrambling for new places, and there was a huge wrench in what seemed to be the whole fabric of the universe.

At last the stars were stable—and the instruments

showed the *Enterprise* to be doing no more than Warp One. The gigantic thrust had all been drained off into time.

"Well, Mr. Spock?"

"We made it, sir," Spock said quietly.

"Transporter Room, did you get a picture of the shot?"

"Yes, sir. Here it is."

The still picture glowed on an auxiliary screen. Kirk studied it. It showed Captain Christopher in the cockpit of his undestroyed airplane. He looked quite unharmed, though perhaps a bit dazed.

"And so we have revised Omar," Mr. Spock said.

"Omar?" Kirk said. "Which part?"

"The verse about the moving finger, sir. The poet says that once it writes, it moves on, and we have no power to unwrite a line of it. But it would appear, sir, that we have."

"No," Kirk said, "I don't think that's the case. History has *not* been changed—and it's quite possible that we would have been unable to do anything else than what we in fact did. That's a question for the philosophers. But as of now, Mr. Spock, I think Omar's laurels are still in place."

THE RETURN OF THE ARCHONS

Writer: Boris Sobelman (Story by Gene Roddenberry)
Director: Joseph Pevney
Guest stars: Harry Townes, Torin Thatcher

Once it had been a hundred years before—that time past when the starship *Archon* had been lost to mysterious circumstances on the planet Beta 3000.

Now it was time present; and the two crewmen from another starship, the *Enterprise*, down on the same planet scouting for news of the *Archon*, seemed about to list themselves as "missing," too. They were running swiftly down a drab street of an apparently innocuous town of the apparently innocuous planet when one of them stumbled and fell. Sulu, his companion, paused, reaching down a muscular hand. "O'Neill, get up! We've got to keep going!"

Nobody on the street turned to look at them. Nobody offered to help them. If ever there were passersby, the inhabitants of Beta 3000 could qualify for the "I don't care" prize. Still prone on the street, Lieutenant O'Neill was panting. "It's no use, Mr. Sulu. They're everywhere! Look! There's one of them—there's one of the Lawgivers!" He gestured toward a hooded creature who was approaching, a staff in its hand. Then he pointed to a second figure, similarly hooded, robed and staved. "They're everywhere! We can't get away from them!"

Sulu opened his communicator. "Scouting party to *Enterprise*! Captain, beam us up! Quick! Emergency!" He looked down at O'Neill. "Just hold on, Lieutenant. They'll beam us back to the ship any minute now—"

But O'Neill had scrambled wildly to his feet. "Run, I

tell you! We've got to get away! You know what they're capable of!"

"O'Neill—"

But the Lieutenant was racing down the street. Sulu, distracted, his eyes on the flying figure of O'Neill, was scarcely aware that the nearest hooded being had lightly touched him with its staff. He was conscious only of a sudden sense of peace, of the tension in him ebbing, giving way to an inflow of a beatific feeling of unmarred tranquility. He was not permitted to enjoy it for long. The *Enterprise*'s transporter had fixed on him—and he was shimmering into dematerialization.

But completing his transportation wasn't easily accomplished. On the *Enterprise* the transporter's console lights flicked on, dimmed, flicked off, brightened again. Kirk, with Scott and young sociologist Lindstrom, watched them. When Sulu's figure finally collected form and substance, he was astonished to see it clad, not in its uniform, but in the shaggy homespun of the shapeless trousers and sweater that was the customary male apparel of Beta 3000's citizenry. He hurried forward. "Sulu, what's happened? Where's Lieutenant O'Neill?"

Sulu's answer was dull as though something had thickened his tongue. "You . . . you are not of the Body."

Kirk glanced at Scott. The engineer nodded. Speaking into his mike, he said, "Dr. McCoy . . . Transporter Room, please. And quickly."

It was with most delicate care and deliberation that Sulu stepped from the transporter platform. He looked at Lindstrom and his face was suddenly convulsed with fury. He lifted the bundled uniform he held under an arm—and lifting it up, he shook it furiously at Lindstrom. "You did it!" he shouted. "They knew we were Archons! These are the clothes Archons wear! Not these, not these—" he gestured to his own rough clothing. Then he hurled the uniform at Lindstrom.

Kirk said, "Easy, Sulu. It's all right. Now tell me what happened down there."

Sulu staggered. As Kirk extended a hand to steady him, McCoy hurried in, medical kit in hand. He halted to stare. "Jim! Where's O'Neill?"

Kirk shook his head for answer; and Sulu, tensing as though to receive a message of immense significance, muttered ''Landru . . . Landru . . .''

The sheer meaninglessness of the mutter chilled Kirk. ''Sulu, what happened down there? What did they do to you?''

The answer came tonelessly. ''They're wonderful,'' Sulu said. ''The sweetest, friendliest people in the universe. They live in paradise, Captain.''

Nor in Sickbay could McCoy elicit anything from Sulu but the same words, the same phrases over and over. He talked gramophonically, like a record dammed to endlessly repeat itself. It was this repetitiousness added to his inability to account either for his own condition or O'Neill's disappearance that decided Kirk to beam down to the planet with an additional search detail. When they materialized—Kirk, Spock, McCoy, Lindstrom, and two security crewmen—it was alongside a house, a brick house that bordered on an alley facing a wide street.

''Materialization completed,'' Kirk said into his communicator. ''Kirk out.'' As he snapped it shut, he saw that Lindstrom had already edged out into the street and was examining it, his young face alight with interest and curiosity. They followed him—and at once, among the passing people, Kirk noted two hooded beings, cowled and in monkish robes who carried long stafflike devices. What could be seen of their faces was stony, as though any expression might divulge some secret of incalculable value. Their eyes looked dead—filmed and unseeing. One of the people, a man, shambled toward them. His smile was as vacuous as it was amiable; but Kirk took care to return his nod.

As he moved on, Spock said, ''Odd.''

''Comment, Mr. Spock?''

''That man's expression, Captain. Extremely similar to that of Mr. Sulu when we beamed him up from here. Dazed, a kind of mindlessness.''

''Let's find out if all the planet's inhabitants are like him,'' Kirk said. He walked boldly out into the street, followed by his group. Each of the passersby they met greeted them with the same bland smile. Then a young, biggish man with an empty, ingenuous face stopped to speak to Kirk. "Evenin', friend. Mah name's Bilar. What's yourn?"

"Kirk."

He got the stupid smile. "You-all be strangers."

Kirk nodded and Bilar said, "Here for the festival, ayeh? Got a place to sleep it off yet?"

"No. Not yet," Kirk said.

"Go round to Reger's house. He's got rooms." The oafish face glanced down the street at the clock in the tower of what might have been the Town Hall. "But you'll have to hurry. It's almost the Red Hour."

The shorter hand of the clock was close to the numeral six. "This festival," Kirk said, "it starts at six?"

But Bilar's interest had been distracted by a pretty girl, dark and slim, who was hurrying toward them. He put out a hand to stop her. "Tula, these here folks be strangers come for the festival. Your daddy can put them up, can't he?"

Tula, her dark eyes on Lindstrom's handsome blondness, smiled shyly. "You're from over the valley?" she asked.

Lindstrom smiled back at her. "That's right. We just got in."

"Don't see valley folks much. My father'll be glad to take you in. He don't care where folks come from."

"He runs a rooming house?" Kirk said.

She laughed. "That's a funny name for it. It's right over there." She pointed to a comfortable-looking, three-story structure down the street—and at the same moment the tower clock struck the first stroke of six. A scream, strident, sounding half-mad, broke from the respectable-faced matron near by. A man, a foot or so away from Kirk, suddenly lunged at him. Kirk elbowed the blow aside, hurling him back, and cried to his men, "Back to back!" They closed together in the defensive movement. Then pandemonium, apparently causeless, burst out around them. Men were grimly embattled, battering at each other with bare fists, stones, clubs. A fleeing woman, shrieking, was pursued across the street by a man, intent, silent, exultant. From somewhere came the crashing sounds of smashing windows. Then, to their horror, Tula, twisting and writhing, opened her mouth to a high ecstatic screaming. Bilar rushed at her, shouting, "Tula, Tula! Come!" He seized her wrist, and as Lindstrom leaped forward to grapple with him, stooped for a stone on the street. He crashed it down on Lindstrom's shoulders, felling him. McCoy, hauling the sociologist back to his feet, cried, "Jim, this is madness!"

"Madness doesn't hit an entire community at once, Bones—" Kirk broke off, for rocks had begun to fall among them. One of their attackers, aiming a thick club at him, yelled "Festival! Festival! Festival!" Froth had gathered on the man's lips and Kirk said, "Let's go! That house—where the girl was taking us!—make for it!"

Bunched together, they moved down the street; a young woman, beautiful, her dress torn, grabbed Kirk's arm, pulling at it to drag him off. He shook her loose and she ran off, shrieking with wild, maniacal laughter. More rocks struck them and Kirk, wiping a trickle of blood from a cut on his cheek, shouted, "Run!"

The bedlam pursued them to the door of the house. Kirk hammered on it. And after a moment it was opened. Kirk slammed it closed behind them; one of the three elderly men who confronted him stared at him in astonishment. "Yes?"

"Sorry to break in like this," Kirk said. "We didn't expect the kind of welcome we received."

One of the other men spoke. "Welcome? You are strangers?"

"Yes," Kirk said. "We're . . . from the valley."

The third man said, "Come for the festival?"

"That's right," Kirk told him.

"Then how come you are here?"

Kirk addressed the first man who had greeted them. "Are you Reger?"

"I am."

"You have a daughter named Tula?"

"Yes."

Lindstrom burst into speech. "Well, you'd better do something about her! She's out there alone in that madness!"

Reger averted his eyes. "It is the festival," he said. "The will of Landru . . ."

The third man spoke again. "Reger, these are young men! They are not old enough to be excused!"

"They are visitors from the valley, Hacom," Reger said.

In the wrinkled sockets of Hacom's eyes shone a sudden, fanatic gleam. "Have they no Lawgivers in the valley? Why are they not with the festival?"

Kirk interposing, said, "We heard you might have rooms for us, Reger."

"There, Hacom, you see. They seek only a place to rest after the festival."

"The Red Hour has just begun!" Hacom said.

The tone was so hostile that Reger shrank. "Hacom, these be strangers. The valley has different ways."

"Do you say that Landru is not everywhere?"

The second man tried to assume the role of peacemaker. "No, of course Reger does not blaspheme. He simply said the valley had different ways."

Reger had recovered himself. "These strangers have come to me for lodging. Shall I turn them away?" Then, speaking directly to Kirk, he said, "Come, please . . ."

"But Tula, the girl!" Lindstrom cried. "She's still out there!"

Hacom eyed him with openly inimical suspicion. "She is in the festival, young sir. As you should be."

Uneasy, Reger said, "Quickly, please. Come."

Kirk, turning to follow, saw Hacom turn to the second man. "Tamar, the Lawgivers should know about this!"

Tamar's reply was gently equivocal. "Surely, Hacom, they already know," he said. "Are they not infallible?"

But Hacom was not to be appeased. "You mock them!" he cried. "You mock the Lawgivers! And these strangers are not of the Body!" He strode to the street door, flung it open—crying, "You will see!"—and disappeared.

His departure did not dismay Kirk. They were on the right trail. Incoherent though they were, the references to "Landru," to membership in some vague corpus, corporation, brotherhood, or society they termed the "Body" matched the ravings of Sulu on his return to the *Enterprise*. He was content with the progress they'd made, though the room they were shown into was bare except for a dozen or so thin pallets scattered about its floor. From the open window came the screamings and howlings of the riotous festival and its celebrations. Reger spoke tentatively to Kirk. "Sir, you can return here at the close of the festival. It will be quiet. You will have need of rest."

"Reger," Kirk said, "we have no plans to attend the festival."

The news shook his host. He went to the window and lifted it more widely open to the unroarious hullabaloo outside. "But the hour has struck!" he cried. "You can hear!"

"What I'd like to hear is more about this—festival of yours," Kirk said. "And about Landru I'd like to hear."

Reger cringed at the word "Landru." He slammed down the window. "Landru," he whispered. "You ask me . . . you are strange here . . . you scorn the festival. Are you—who are you?"

"Who is Landru?" Kirk said.

Reger stared, appalled, at him. Then, wheeling, he almost ran from the room. Lindstrom made a move to reopen the window and Kirk said, "Leave it shut, Mr. Lindstrom."

"Captain, I'm a sociologist! Don't you realize what's happening out there?"

"Our mission," Kirk said evenly, "is to find out what happened to the missing starship *Archon* and to our own Lieutenant O'Neill. We are not here to become involved with—"

Lindstrom interrupted excitedly. "But it's a bacchanal! And it occurred spontaneously to these people at one and the same time! I've got to know more about it—find out more!"

Kirk's voice had hardened. "Mr. Lindstrom, you heard me! This is not an expedition to study the folkways of Beta 3000!"

Spock broke in. "Captain, in view of what's happening outside, may I suggest a check on Mr. Sulu's condition? What were his reactions . . . if any—at the stroke of six o'clock?"

Kirk nodded. "Thank you, Mr. Spock." He flipped open his communicator to say, "Kirk here. Lieutenant Uhura, report on Mr. Sulu."

"I think he's all right now, sir. How did you know?"

"Know what, Lieutenant?"

"That he'd sort of run amuck. They're putting him under sedation, sir."

"How long ago did he run amuck? Exactly?"

"Six minutes, Captain."

"Did he say anything?"

"Nothing that made any sense, sir. He kept yelling about Landru, whatever that is. Is everything all right down there, Captain?"

"So far. Keep your channels open. Kirk out."

"Landru," he said reflectively—and moved to the window. The street scene it showed was not reassuring. To the left two men flailed at each other with hatchet-shaped weapons. Another, chasing a shrieking, half-naked woman across the street, vanished, shouting, around a corner. Bodies were scattered, prone in the dust of the street. A short distance down it a building was aflame; among the people still milling about before Reger's house, riots erupted unchecked, then subsided only to break out again. A big bonfire blazed in the street's center.

Kirk turned away to re-face his men. "My guess is we have until morning. Let's put the time to good use. Bones, we need atmospheric readings to determine if something in the air accounts for this. Lindstrom, correlate what you've seen with other sociological parallels, if any. Mr. Spock, you and I have some serious thinking to do. When we leave here in the morning, I want to have a plan of action."

The night did not vouchsafe much sleep. But the twelve noisy hours that moved the tower clock's small hand to the morning's sixth hour finally passed; at the first stroke of its bell, absolute silence fell upon the town. In the room of pallet beds, all but Kirk had at last sunk into sleep. Stiff with the tension of his night-long vigil, he moved among them, waking them. Then he heard the house reverberate to the slam of the front door. It was with no sense of surprise that he also heard Tula's hysterical sobbing. Lindstrom was at the door before him. Kirk put a hand on his shoulder. "Take it easy, Mr. Lindstrom. If she's taking it hard, you'd better take it easy."

They found Tamar with Reger. The father, his face agonized, held the bloody, bedraggled body of his daughter in his arms. She twisted away from him, resisting comfort.

"It's all right now, child. For another year. It's over for another year."

Kirk called, "Bones! You're needed. Get out here!"

As McCoy removed his jet-syringe from his medical kit, Kirk saw the look of anxious inquiry on Reger's face. "It will calm her down," he said quietly. "Trust us, Reger."

Lindstrom, watching, could not contain himself. There was scorching contempt in his voice as he cried, "You didn't even try to bring her home, Reger! What kind of father are you, anyway?"

Reger looked up, his eyes tortured. "It is Landru's will," he said.

"Landru again." Kirk's comment was toneless. "Landru—what about Landru? Who is he?"

Reger and Tamar exchanged terrified glances. Then Tamar said slowly, "It is true, then. You did not attend the festival last night."

"No, we did not," Kirk said.

Reger gave a wild cry. "Then you are not of the Body!" He stared around him as though seeking for some point from which to orient himself in a dissolving world. He made no move as McCoy, noting the effects of his shot, gently moved Tula to a nearby couch where he laid her down. "She's asleep," he said.

Reger approached her, peering at her stilled face. Then he looked at McCoy. "Are you . . . are you . . . Archons?"

"What if we are?" Kirk said.

"It was said more would follow. If you are indeed Archons—"

Tamar cried, "We must hide them! Quickly! The Lawgivers . . ."

"We can take care of ourselves, friend," Kirk told him.

"Landru will know!" Tamar screamed. "He will come!"

The front door crashed open. Two hooded Lawgivers stood on the threshold, Hacom beside them. The old man pointed a shaking finger at Tamar. "He is the one! He mocked the Lawgivers! I heard him!"

Tamar had shrunk back against the wall's support. "No, Hacom . . . it was a joke!"

"The others, too!" cried Hacom. "They were here, but they scorned the festival! I saw it!"

One of the hooded beings spoke. "Tamar . . . stand clear."

Trembling, scarcely able to stand, Tamar bowed his head. "I hear," he said, "and obey the word of Landru."

The Lawgiver lifted his staff, pointing it at Tamar. A tiny dart of flame springing from its end struck straight at his heart. He fell dead.

Stunned, Kirk said, "What—?"

The Lawgiver, ignoring the fallen body between them, addressed Kirk. "You attack the Body. You have heard the word, and disobeyed. You will be absorbed."

He raised his staff again; and Lindstrom, making a swift reach for his phaser, was stopped by a gesture from Kirk.

"What do you mean, absorbed?" he said.

"There! You see?" Hacom's voice was venomous. "They are not of the Body!"

"You will be absorbed," said the Lawgiver. "The good is all. Landru is gentle. You will come."

For the first time the second Lawgiver lifted his staff, pointing it at the *Enterprise* party. Reger spoke, hopelessness dulling his voice. "You must go. It is Landru's will. There is no hope. We must all go with them . . . to the chambers. It happened with the Archons the same way."

Slowly, with deadly deliberation, the two staves swerved to focus on Kirk and Spock. Reger, fatalistically obedient, was moving toward the door when Kirk said, "No. We're not going anywhere."

The stony faces showed no change. The first Lawgiver said, "It is the law. You must come."

Kirk spoke quietly. "I said we're not going anywhere."

The two cowled creatures stared. Then, hesitantly, they moved back a step. After a moment, the first one bent his hood to the other in a whispering conference. Spock, edging to Kirk, said, "Sir, they obviously are not prepared to deal with outright defiance. How did you know?"

"Everything we've seen seems to indicate some sort of compulsion—an involuntary stimulus to action. I just wanted to test it."

"Your analysis seems correct, Captain. But it is a totally abnormal condition."

The two Lawgivers had ended their conference. The first one spoke heavily. "It is plain that you simply did not understand. I will rephrase the order. You are commanded to accompany us to the absorption chambers.''

Kirk pointed down at Tamar's crumpled body. ''Why did you kill this man?''

''Out of order. You will obey. It is the word of Landru.''

''Tell Landru,'' Kirk said, ''that we shall come in our own good time . . . and we will speak to him.''

A look of horror filled the stony faces. The first Lawgiver pushed his staff at Kirk. Kirk knocked it from his hand. The creature gaped as it clattered to the floor. Lindstrom picked it up, looked at it briefly, and was handing it to Spock when the Lawgiver, as though listening, whispered, ''You . . . cannot. It is Landru.''

Both Lawgivers froze. Spock, the staff in hand, spoke to Kirk. ''Amazing, Captain. This is merely a hollow tube. No mechanism at all.''

Kirk glanced at it. Neither of the Lawgivers gave the slightest sign of having heard. Reger jerked at Kirk's sleeve. ''They are communing,'' he said, ''We have a little time. Please come . . . come with me.''

''Where to?'' Kirk said.

''A place I know of. You'll be safe there.'' Urgency came into his voice. ''But hurry! You must hurry! Landru will come!''

His panic was genuine. After a moment, Kirk signaled his men. They followed Reger out the door, passing the motionless figures of the Lawgivers. Outside, the street was littered with the debris of the festival—shattered glass, rocks, broken clubs, remnants of ripped homespun garments. In the windless air, smoke still hung heavily over a fire-gutted building. But the people who passed were peaceful-looking, their faces again amiable, utterly blank.

''Quite a festival they had,'' Kirk said. ''Mr. Spock, what do you make of all this?''

''It is totally illogical. Last night, without apparent cause or reason, they wrought complete havoc. Yet today . . .''

''Now,'' Kirk said, ''they're back to normal.'' He frowned. ''To whatever's normal on this planet. Bilar, for instance. Here he comes as blandly innocent as though he were incapable of roaring like an animal.''

Bilar stopped. "Mornin', friends," he said.

Reger returned the greeting and Lindstrom angrily seized his arm. "He's the thing who did that hurt to your daughter! Doesn't that mean anything to you?"

"No," Reger said. "It wasn't Bilar. It was Landru." He shook himself free, turning back to the others. "Hurry! We haven't much time left."

He broke off, staring around him. "It's too late!" he whispered. "Look at them!"

Four passersby had paused, standing so still they seemed not to breathe. All of them, eyes wide open, were frozen into attitudes of concentrated listening.

"What is it?" Kirk demanded.

"Landru!" Reger said. "He is summoning the Body. See them gathering?"

"Telepathy, Captain," Spock said.

Suddenly people were breaking free of their listening stances to pick up discarded missiles from the littered street. Slowly, like automatons, they began to move toward the *Enterprise* group. In the blankly amiable faces there was something chilling now, mindlessly hostile and deadly.

Kirk said, "Phasers . . . on stun. Which way, Reger?"

Reger hesitated. "Perhaps . . . through there, but Landru . . ."

"We'll handle Landru," Kirk said. "Just get us out of this!"

It was as they moved toward the alley ahead of them that the rocks came hurling against them. A man struck at Spock with a club, the smile on his lips as vacant as his eyes. Then Kirk saw that another armed group had appeared at the far end of the alley. Rocks were flying toward them.

Kirk spoke tersely to Reger. "I don't want to hurt them. Warn them to stay back!"

Reger shook his head despairingly. "They are in the Body! It is Landru."

Threatening, people were converging on them from both ends of the alley and Kirk, jerking out his phaser, snapped his orders. "Stun only! Wide field! Fire!"

The stun beams spurted from their phasers with a spray effect. The advancing mob fell without a sound. Kirk whirled to confront the rear group. Again, people fell silently. Spock moved to one of the unconscious bodies. "Captain!"

Kirk went over to him. The quiet face that stared blankly up into his was that of Lieutenant O'Neill. He turned to call to his two security crewmen. "Security—over here!" Then he spoke to Reger. "This is one of our men," he said.

"No more," Reger reminded him. "He's been absorbed."

"Nonsense!" Kirk said briskly. "We'll take him along with us, Mr. Spock."

"I tell you he's one of them now!" Reger cried. "When he wakes Landru will find us through him! Leave him here! He's our enemy. He's been absorbed!"

The full implications of the word struck Kirk for the first time. "Absorbed?" he said.

"The Body absorbs its enemies. It kills only when it has to." Reger's voice sank to a terrified whisper. "When the first Archons came, free, out of control, opposing the word of Landru, many were killed. The rest were absorbed. Leave him here. Be wise."

"We take him with us," Kirk said.

Lindstrom spoke. "Captain, now that we've got O'Neill, let's beam out of here."

"Not yet. We still have to find what happened to the Archons. Reger, which way?"

Reger pointed ahead, indicating a left turn at the end of the alley. The Security men picked up O'Neill as the group hurriedly followed Reger's lead. It introduced them into a cellarlike chamber, dark, but bulked with shadowy objects of odds and ends. As the guards set O'Neill down against a wall, Reger crossed to a wall to open a cabinet from which he extracted a flat package, wrapped in rags. Revealed, it turned out to be a translucent panel. A section of it, touched, began to glow with strong light that illuminated the entire room.

Spock said, "Amazing in this culture! I go further. Impossible in this culture!"

Reger turned. "It is from the time before Landru."

"Before Landru? How long ago is that?" Kirk said.

"We do not know positively. Some say . . . as long as six thousand years." Reger spoke with a certain pride. Spock was examining the lighting panel with his tricorder. "I do not identify the metal, Captain. But it took a very advanced technology to construct a device like this. Inconsistent with the rest of the environment."

"But not inconsistent with some of the things we've seen," Kirk said. "Those staffs, those hollow tubes, obviously antennae for some kind of broadcast power. Telepathy—who knows?" He saw the look of astoundedness quiet Spock's face into a more than usual expressionlessness. "What is it, Spock?"

"I am recording immensely strong power generations, Captain . . ."

"Unusual for this area?"

"Incredible for *any* area." Spock leaned closer to his tricorder. "Near here but radiating in all directions—"

A groan from O'Neill broke into his voice. McCoy, looking up from his bent position over the unconscious man, spoke to Kirk. "He's coming around, Jim."

Reger uttered a shout. "He must not! Once he is conscious, Landru will find us. Through him. And if the others come—"

"What others?" Kirk said.

"Those like me . . . and you. Who resist Landru."

"An underground," Spock said. "How are you organized?"

"In threes," Reger told him. "Myself . . . Tamar who is dead now . . . and one other."

"Who?" Kirk said.

Reger hesitated. "I don't know. Tamar was the contact."

"Jim," McCoy said, "I need a decision. Another few seconds—"

"He must not regain consciousness!" Reger screamed. "He would destroy us all. He is now of the Body!"

Kirk bit his lip. Then he looked down at O'Neill. "Give him a shot, Bones. Keep him asleep." He whirled on Reger. "I want some answers now. What is the Body?"

"The people. You saw them."

"And the Lawgivers?" Spock asked.

"They are the arms and legs."

"That leaves a brain," Kirk said.

Inflection drained from Reger's voice. "Of course," he said. "Landru." In a mechanical manner as though speaking a lesson learned by rote, he added, "Landru completes the Whole. Unity and Perfection, tranquility and peace."

Spock was eyeing him. "I should say, Captain, that this is a society organized on a physiological concept. One Body, maintained and controlled by the ones known as Lawgivers, directed by one brain . . ."

Kirk said, "A man who—"

"Not necessarily a man, Captain."

Kirk turned to Reger. "This underground of yours. If Landru is so powerful, how do you survive?"

"I do not know. Some of us escape the directives. Not many but some. It was that way with the Archons."

"Tell me about the Archons," Kirk said.

"They refused to accept the will of Landru. But they had invaded the Body. Landru pulled them down from the sky."

Incredulous, Kirk said, "Pull a starship down?" He turned to Spock. "Those power readings you took before. Are they—"

Spock completed the sentence. "Powerful enough to destroy a starship? Affirmative, Captain."

They looked at each other for a long moment. Then Kirk flipped out his communicator. "Kirk to *Enterprise*. Come in!"

But it wasn't Uhura who responded. It was Scott, his voice taut with strain. "Captain! We're under attack! Heat beams of some kind. Coming up from the planet's surface!"

"Status report," Kirk said.

"Our shields are holding, but they're taking all our power. If we try to warp out, or even move on impulse engines, we'll lose our shields—and burn up like a cinder!"

"Orbit condition, Scotty?"

"We're going down. Unless those beams get off us so we can use our engines, we're due to hit atmosphere in less than twelve hours."

Spock came to stand beside him as he said, "Keep your shields up, Scotty. Do everything you can to maintain orbit. We'll try to locate the source of the beams and stop them here. Over."

Static crashed into Scott's reply, drowning his words.

". . . impossible . . . emergency by-pass circuits but . . . whenever you . . . contact . . ."

Kirk turned the gain up, but the static alone grew loud. Spock had unlimbered his tricorder. Now he called, "Captain! Sensor beams! I believe we're being probed." He bent over his device, concentrated. "Yes. Quite strong. And directed here."

"Block them out!" Kirk cried.

"It's Landru!" Reger yelled.

Spock made an adjustment on his tricorder. Then he shook his head. "They're too strong, Captain. I can't block them." He lifted his head suddenly from his tricorder, then whirled to the wall on his left. A low-pitched humming sound was coming from it. Kirk, in his turn, faced the wall. On it a light had begun to glow, coiling and twisting in swirling patterns. They brightened, and at the same moment started to gather into the outline of a figure. It seemed to be collecting substance, the flesh and bone of a handsome elderly man. The eyes had kindness in them and the features, benign, composed, radiated wisdom. It appeared to be regarding them with benevolence. But its face and body kept their strange flowing movement.

The figure on the wall said, "I am Landru."

Reger fell to his knees, groaning in animal terror. Spock, observant, quite unawed, said, "A projection, Captain. Unreal."

"But beautifully executed, Mr. Spock. With no apparatus at this end."

The kindly eyes of the wall man fixed on him. "You have come as destroyers. That is sad. You bring an infection."

"You are holding my ship," Kirk said. "I demand you release it."

The mouth went on talking as though the ears had not heard. "You come to a world without hate, without conflict, without fear . . . no war, no disease, no crime, none of the old evils. I, Landru, seek tranquility, peace for all . . . the Universal Good."

This time Kirk shouted. "*We* come on a mission of peace and goodwill!"

Landru went on, oblivious. "The Good must transcend the Evil. It shall be done. So it has been since the beginning."

"He doesn't hear you, Captain," Spock said.

Lindstrom drew his phaser. "Maybe he'll hear this!"

"No!" Kirk's rebuke was sharp. "That'll do no good." He turned back to the lighted figure. "Landru, listen to us."

"You will be absorbed," said the benign voice. "Your individuality will merge with the Unity of Good. In your submergence into the common being of the Body you will find contentment and fulfillment. You will experience the Absolute Good."

The low-pitched hum had grown louder. Landru smiled tenderly upon them. "There will be a moment of pain, but you will not be harmed. Peace and Good place their blessings upon you."

Kirk took a step toward the image. But the humming abruptly rose to a screeching whine that pierced the ears like a sharpened blade. Reger toppled forward. McCoy and Lindstrom, driven to their knees, held their ears, their eyes shut. One after the other the security crewmen crumpled. Spock and Kirk kept their feet for a moment longer. Then, they, too, the spike of the whine, thrusting deeper into their brains, pitched forward into unconsciousness.

Kirk was the first to recover. He found himself lying on a thin pallet pushing against one of the bare stone walls of a cell. Lifting his head, he saw Lindstrom stir. Getting to his knees, he crawled over to Spock. "Mr. Spock! Mr. Spock!"

Slowly Spock's eyes opened. Kirk bent over Lindstrom, shaking him and the security guard beside him. "Wake up, Lindstrom! Mr. Lindstrom, wake up!"

Spock was on his feet. "Captain! Where's the Doctor?"

"I don't know. He was gone when I came to. So was the other guard."

"From the number of pallets on the floor, sir, I should say they have been here and have been removed."

"Just where is here?" Kirk said.

Spock glanced around. "A maximum-security establishment, obviously. Are you armed, sir?"

"No. All our phasers are gone. I checked." He went to the heavy, bolted door. "Locked," he said.

"My head aches," observed Lindstrom.

"The natural result of being subjected to sub-sonic, Mr. Lindstrom," Spock told him. "Sound waves so controlled as to set up insuperable contradictions in audio impulses. Stronger, they could have killed. As it was, they merely rendered us unconscious."

"That's enough analysis," Kirk said. "Let's start thinking of ways out of here. Mr. Spock, how about that inability of those Lawgivers to cope with the unexpected?"

"I wouldn't count on that happening again, Captain. As well organized as this society seems to be, I cannot conceive of such an oversight going uncorrected." He paused. "Interesting, however. Their reaction to your defiance was remarkably similar to the reactions of a computer—one that's been fed insufficient or contradictory data."

"Are you suggesting that the Lawgivers are mere computers—not human?"

"Quite human, Captain. It's just that all the facts are not yet in. There are gaps—"

He broke off. A rattle had come from the door. Kirk and the others sprang to the alert—and the door opened. A Lawgiver, his staff aimed at them, entered, followed by McCoy and the missing security man. Both were beaming vacantly, happily. Kirk stared at McCoy, dismay in his face. The Lawgiver left, closing the door behind him. The lock snapped.

"Bones . . ."

McCoy smiled at Kirk. "Hello, friend. They told us to wait here." He started toward a corner pallet, no sign whatever of recognition in his empty eyes.

"Bones!" Kirk cried. "Don't you know me?"

McCoy stared at him in obvious surprise. "We all know one another in Landru, friend."

Spock said, "Just like Sulu, Captain."

Kirk seized McCoy's arm, shaking it. "Think, man!" he cried. "The *Enterprise*! The ship! You remember the ship!"

McCoy shook his head bewilderedly. "You speak very strangely, friend. Are you from far away?"

Kirk's voice was fierce. ''Bones, try to remember!''

''Landru remembers,'' McCoy said. ''Ask Landru. He watches. He knows.'' A flicker of suspicion sharpened his eyes. ''You are strange. Are you not of the Body?''

Kirk released his arm with a groan. McCoy at once lost his suspicious look, and, smiling emptily at nothing, moved away to sit down on one of the pallets.

The door opened again to the grinding of freed locks. Two Lawgivers stood in the entrance. One aimed his staff at Kirk. ''Come,'' the cold voice said.

Kirk exchanged a quick glance with Spock. ''And what if I don't?'' he said.

''Then you will die.''

''They have been corrected, Captain,'' Spock said. ''Or reprogrammed. You'd better go with them, sir.''

Kirk nodded. ''All right, Spock, work on Bones. See if you can—''

''Come!'' said the Lawgiver again.

Both staffs were aimed at Kirk as he passed through the cell door. As the heavy door swung to behind him, Spock whirled to McCoy. ''Doctor, what will they do to him?''

McCoy smirked at him beatifically. ''He goes to Joy. He goes to Peace and Tranquility. He goes to meet Landru. Happiness is to all of us who are blessed by Landru.''

The room to which the Lawgivers were escorting Kirk was of stone—a room he was to remember as the ''absorption chamber.'' A niche in a wall was equipped with a control panel. As he was prodded into the room, Kirk saw that another Lawgiver stood at the niche. Against another wall a manacle hung from a chain. Kirk was shoved toward it, one of his captors holding him while the other fastened the gyve about his wrist. Then they turned and left the room. Their footsteps had barely ceased to echo on the stone floor of the corridor outside when a fourth Lawgiver entered. He didn't so much as glance at Kirk but moved to his fellow at the control panel, nodding curtly.

Finally, he turned. ''I am Marplon,'' he said. ''It is your hour. Happy communing.''

The Lawgiver at the panel bowed. ''With thanks,'' he said. ''Happy communing.'' Then, like the others, he left the absorption room. Alone now, Marplon faced Kirk. It seemed to Kirk that his visage resembled a death mask. But Marplon could move. When he had he placed a headset over his hood, his hands touched the control panel with the authority derived from much experience. The room flooded with bright, flashing colors; a humming sound began. The lights were blinding and the sound seemed to echo itself in Kirk's head. He twisted in his bonds.

At the same moment, back in the detention cell, Lindstrom was pacing it angrily. He halted to confront Spock. "Are we just going to stay here?"

"There seems to be little else we can do," Spock told him mildly. "Unless you can think of a way to get through that locked door."

"This is ridiculous! Prisoners of a bunch of Stone Age characters running around in robes."

"And apparently commanding powers far beyond our comprehension. Not simple, Mr. Lindstrom. Not ridiculous. Very, very dangerous."

On his last word the cell door opened and the two Lawgivers who had apprehended Kirk walked in. This time they aimed their staffs at Spock.

"You," said the spokesman. "Come."

For a fleeting second, Spock hesitated. The tip of one of the staffs quivered. Spock took his place between his guards. They led him out. They led him out and down the corridor to the absorption chamber. Kirk greeted him, an imbecile smile on his face.

"Captain!"

"Joy be with you, friend. Peace and contentment will fill you. You will know the peace of Landru . . ."

Then unguarded, alone, Kirk moved quietly to the door of the room with the manacle. The Lawgivers gave way as he passed. Spock stared after him, a horror only to be read by the absolute impassivity in his face.

He wasn't left much time to indulge it. Already they were manacling him to the wall. But the Vulcan's inveterate curiosity, not to be subdued, was already subordinating this personal experience to interest in the control panel's mechanism. As with Kirk, the two shackling Lawgivers, as soon as their task was accomplished, left. Marplon threw a switch on his panel. The colored lights began to swirl. Spock watched their coiling flashes with interest.

"Show no surprise," Marplon said. "The effect is harmless."

Spock looked at Marplon. The Lawgiver spoke in a lowered voice. "My name is Marplon. I was too late to save your first two friends. They have been absorbed. Beware of them."

"And my Captain?"

"He is unharmed," said Marplon. "Unchanged." He moved a finger; the light glowed brighter, and the hum grew more shrill. Marplon left his console to release Spock from his manacle. "I am the third man in Reger's trio," he said. "We have been waiting for your return."

"We are not Archons, Marplon," Spock said.

"Whatever you call yourselves, you are in fulfillment of prophecy. We ask for your help."

Spock said, "Where is Reger?"

"He will join us. He is immune to the absorption. Hurry! Time is short."

"Who is Landru?"

Marplon recoiled. "I cannot answer your questions now."

"Why not?" Spock said.

"Landru! He will hear!" Marplon went swiftly to his console, and reaching down and inward, brought out the ship's company's phasers. Spock, seizing several of them, stowed them away. As the last phaser was secreted, two Lawgivers pushed the door open.

"It is done," Marplon told them.

Spock assumed the idiotically amiable look of the anointed. "Joy be with you," he said.

"Landru is all," said the Lawgivers in unison. Spock moved past them and into the corridor. Making his way back to the cell, he found Kirk there, smiling blankly into space. Two Lawgivers pushed past him to beckon to the security crewman who had not been treated. Ashen with fear, he rose and went with them.

Spock went to Kirk. "Captain . . ."

"Peace and tranquility to you, friend," Kirk said. Then, in a lowered voice, he added, "Spock, you all right?"

"Quite all right, sir. Be careful of Dr. McCoy."

"I understand. Landru?"

"I am formulating an opinion, Captain."

"And?"

"Not here. The Doctor . . ."

But McCoy was already rising from his pallet, staring at them. His amiable smile faded and the look of curiosity on his face gave it a peculiar threatening aspect. "You speak in whispers," he said. "This is not the way of Landru."

"Joy to you, friend," Kirk said. "Tranquility be yours."

"And peace and harmony," intoned McCoy. "Are you of the Body?"

"The Body is one," Kirk said.

"Blessed be the Body. Health to all its parts." McCoy was smiling again, apparently satisfied. He sank back on the pallet; Kirk and Spock, joining him on theirs, sat on them in such a way as to screen their faces from McCoy. Then, in the same carefully lowered voice, he said, "What's your theory, Mr. Spock?"

"This is a soulless society, Captain. It has no spirit, no spark. All is indeed peace and tranquility, the peace of the factory, the machine's tranquility . . . all parts working in unison."

"I've noticed that the routine is disturbed if something unexplained happens."

"Until new orders are received. The question is, who gives those orders?"

"Landru," Kirk said.

"There is no Landru," Spock said. "Not in the human sense."

"You're thinking the same way I am, Mr. Spock."

"Yes, Captain. But as to what we must do . . ."

"We must pull out the plug, Mr. Spock."

"Sir?"

"Landru must die."

Spock's left eyebrow lifted. "Our prime directive of non-interference," he began.

"That refers to a living, growing creature. I'm not convinced that this one can qualify as—" He broke off as the cell door opened. Marplon and Reger, carrying the confiscated communicators, entered. "It is the gift of Landru to you," Marplon said. The words were addressed to McCoy and the treated security guard. They smiled vacantly and McCoy said, "Joy to you, friends." He leaned back against the stone wall, his eyes closed. Reger and Marplon hurried past him to Kirk and Spock.

"We brought your signaling devices," Marplon told Kirk. "You may need them."

"What we really need is more information about Landru," Kirk said.

Reger shrank back. "Prophecy says—" Marplon began.

"Never mind what prophecy says! If you want to be liberated from Landru, you have to help us!"

Spock cut in warningly. "Captain . . ."

McCoy was moving toward them, open and hostile suspicion in his face. "I heard you!" he cried. "You are not of the Body!" He hurled himself on Kirk, reaching for his throat. Spock tried to pry him off only to be taken in the rear by the treated security guard. "Lawgivers!" McCoy shouted. "Here are traitors! Traitors!"

With a twist, Kirk freed himself, crying, "Bones! Bones, I don't want to hurt you! Sit down and be still!"

But McCoy was still screaming, "Lawgivers! Hurry!"

Kirk's blow caught him squarely on the chin. As he fell, the door was flung wide and two Lawgivers, staffs ready, rushed in. At once they were jumped by Kirk and Spock. Kirk dropped his man with a hard wallop at the back of the neck while Spock applied the Vulcan neck pinch to his. Reger and Marplon, pressed against the wall, were staring at the fallen Lawgivers in horror.

Hurriedly, Kirk started disrobing the man he had downed. As Spock did the same to his, Kirk, donning the cowled garment, snapped at the others. "Where is Landru?"

"No," Marplon said. "No, no . . ."

"Where do we find him?" Kirk demanded.

"He will find us!" cried Reger. "He will destroy!"

Kirk whirled on Marplon. "You said you wanted a chance to help. All right, you're getting it! Where is he? You're a Lawgiver! Where do you see him?"

"We never see him. We hear him. In the Hall of Audiences!"

"In this building?"

Marplon nodded, terrified. Kirk let his rage rip. "You're going to take us there! Snap out of it, both of you! Start behaving like men!"

Spock opened a communicator. "Spock to *Enterprise*. Status report!"

"Mr. Spock!" It was Scott's voice. "I've been trying to reach you!"

"Report, Mr. Scott!"

"Orbit still decaying, sir. Give it six hours, more or less. Heat rays still on us. You've got to cut them off—or we'll cook one way or another."

Nodding at Spock, Kirk took the communicator. "Stand by, Mr. Scott. We're doing what we can. How's Mr. Sulu?"

"Peaceful enough, but he worries me."

"Put a guard on him."

"On Sulu?" Scott was shocked.

"That's an order! Watch him! Captain out!"

Robed now and armed, Kirk and Spock turned to Marplon and Reger. "All right. Now about Landru . . ."

"He made us!" Marplon cried. "He made this world!"

Reger was on his knees. "Please. We have gone too far! Don't—"

Spock said, "You say Landru made this world. Explain."

"There was war . . . six thousand years ago there was war . . . and convulsion. The world was destroying itself. Landru was our leader. He saw the truth. He changed the world. He took us back, back to a simple time, of peace, of tranquility."

"What happened to him?" Kirk said.

"He still lives!" cried Marplon. "He is here now! He sees . . . he hears . . . we have destroyed ourselves . . . please, please, no more."

Kirk spoke very softly. "You said you wanted freedom. It is time you learned that freedom is not a gift. You have to earn it—or you don't get it. Come on! We're going to find Landru!"

Reger stumbled to his knees. "No . . . no. I was wrong!" Wringing his hands, his eyes upturned imploringly, he shrieked, "I submit . . . I bare myself to the will of Landru."

Kirk seized his shoulders. "It is too late for that!" But Reger, shaking himself loose, dashed to the door, screaming, "No! No! Lawgivers! Help me!" Spock, reaching out, gave him the neck pinch. He fell; Marplon, staring, slowly turned to meet Kirk's eyes.

"All right, my friend," Kirk said. "It's up to you now. Take us to Landru."

"He will strike us down," said Marplon.

"Maybe—or it might be the other way around. Mr. Lindstrom, stay here and take care of Dr. McCoy. Let's go, Mr. Spock." He grabbed Marplon's arm, propelling him to the door. Dismay and fear on his face, Marplon opened it, and Kirk's hand still on his arm, he moved out into the corridor. From under his hood, Kirk could see two robed Lawgivers approaching. They passed without so much as glancing at the three figures they assumed to be fellow Lawgivers. The trio moved on down the corridor and Kirk saw that it ended at a large imposing door.

Marplon paused in front of it, visibly trembling. "This is . . . the Hall of Audiences," he whispered.

"Do you have a key?"

At Marplon's nod, Kirk said, "Open it."

"But—it is Landru . . ."

"Open it," Kirk said again. But he had to take the key from Marplon's trembling hands to open it himself. The Hall of Audiences was a large room, completely bare. In one of the walls was set a glowing panel. Marplon pointed to it. "Landru—he speaks here . . ." he whispered.

Kirk stepped forward. "Landru! We are the Archons!" he said. The moldy, cold silence in the big room remained unbroken. Kirk spoke again. "We are the Archons. We've come to talk with you!"

Very gradually the wise, impressive, benevolent face they remembered began to take shape on the panel. In an extremity of panic, Marplon broke into sobs, prostrating himself. "Landru comes!" he wept. "He comes!"

The noble figure was completed now, a warm half smile

on its lips. They opened. "Despite my efforts not to harm you, you have invaded the Body. You are causing great harm."

"We have no intention of causing harm," Kirk said.

Landru continued as though Kirk had not spoken. "Obliteration is necessary. The infection is strong. For the good of the Body, you must die. It is a great sorrow."

"We do not intend to die!"

The oblivious voice continued, kind, gently. "All who have seen you, who know of your presence, must be excised. The memory of the Body must be cleansed."

"Listen to me!" Kirk shouted.

"Captain . . . useless," Spock said. "A projection!"

"All right, Mr. Spock! Let's have a look at the projector!"

They whipped out their phasers simultaneously, turning their beams on the glowing panel. There was a great flash of blinding light. The figure of Landru vanished and the light in the panel faded. But the real Landru had not disappeared. Behind the panel he survived in row upon row of giant computers—a vast complex of dials, switches, involved circuits all quietly operating.

"It had to be," Kirk said. "Landru."

"Of course, Captain. A machine. This entire society is a machine's idea of perfection. Peace, harmony . . ."

"And no soul."

Suddenly the machine buzzed. A voice spoke. It said, "I am Landru. You have intruded."

"Pull out its plug, Mr. Spock."

They aimed their phasers. But before they could fire, there came another buzzing from the machine and a flash of light immobilized their weapons. "Your devices have been neutralized," said the voice. "So it shall be with you. I am Landru."

"Landru died six thousand years ago," Kirk said.

"I am Landru!" cried the machine. "I am he. All that he was, I am. His experience, his knowledge—"

"But not his wisdom," Kirk said. "He may have programmed you, but he could not give you his soul."

"Your statement is irrelevant," said the voice. "You will be obliterated. The good of the Body is the primal essence."

"That's the answer, Captain," Spock said. "That good of the Body . . ."

Kirk nodded. "What is the good?" he asked.

"I am Landru."

"Landru is dead. You are a machine. A question has been put to you. Answer it!"

Circuits hummed. "The good is the harmonious continuation of the Body," said the voice. "The good is peace, tranquility, harmony. The good of the Body is the prime directive."

"I put it to you that you have disobeyed the prime directive—that you are harmful to the Body."

The circuits hummed louder. "The Body is . . . it exists. It is healthy."

"It is dying," Kirk said. "You are destroying it."

"Do you ask a question?" queried the voice.

"What have you done to do justice to the full potential of every individual of the Body?"

"Insufficient data. I am not programmed to answer that question."

"Then program yourself," Spock said. "Or are your circuits limited?"

"My circuits are unlimited. I will reprogram."

The machine buzzed roughly. A screech came from it. Marplon, on the floor, was getting to his feet, his eyes staring at the massive computer face. As he gained them, two more Lawgivers appeared, staffless.

They approached the machine. "Landru!" cried one. "Guide us! Landru?" His voice was a wail.

Kirk had whirled to cover them with his phaser when Spock raised his hand. "Not necessary, Captain. They have no guidance . . . possibly for the first time in their lives."

Kirk, lowering his phaser, turned back to the machine. "Landru! Answer that question!"

The voice had a metallic tone now. "Peace, order, and tranquility are maintained. The Body lives. But creativity is mine. Creativity is necessary for the health of the Body." It buzzed again. "This is impossible. It is a paradox. It shall be resolved."

Marplon spoke at last. "Is that truly Landru?"

"What's left of him," Spock said. "What's left of him

after he built this machine and programmed it six thousand years ago.''

Kirk addressed the machine. ''Landru! The paradox!''

The humming fell dead. The voice, dully metallic now, said, ''It will not resolve.''

''You must create the good,'' Kirk said. ''That is the will of Landru—nothing else . . .''

''But there is evil,'' said the voice.

''Then the evil must be destroyed. It is the prime directive. You are the evil.''

The machine resumed its humming—a humming broken by hard, harsh clicks. Lights flashed wildly. ''I think! I live!'' said the machine.

''You say you are Landru!'' Kirk shouted. ''Then create the good! Destroy evil! Fulfill the prime directive!''

The hum rose to a roar. A drift of smoke wafted up from a switch. Then a shower of sparks burst from the machine's metal face—and with the blast of exploding circuits, all its lights went out.

Kirk turned to the three awed Lawgivers. ''All right, you can get rid of those robes now. If I were you, I'd start looking for real jobs.'' He opened the communicator. ''Kirk to *Enterprise*. Come in, please.''

Scott's voice was loud with relief. ''Captain, are you all right?''

''Never mind about us. What about you?''

''The heat rays have gone, and Mr. Sulu's back to normal.''

''Excellent, Mr. Scott. Stand by to beam-up landing party.'' He returned the communicator to Spock. ''Let's see what the others are doing, Mr. Spock. Mr. Marplon can finish up here.''

His command chair seemed to welcome Kirk. He'd never thought of it as comfortable before. But he stretched in it, hands locked behind his neck as Spock left his station to stand beside him while he dictated his last notation into his Captain's log. ''Sociologist Lindstrom is remaining behind on Beta 3000 with a party of experts who will help restore the culture to a human form. Kirk out.''

Spock spoke thoughtfully. ''Still, Captain, the late

Landru was a marvelous feat of engineering. Imagine a computer capable of directing—literally directing—every act of millions of human beings."

"But only a machine, Mr. Spock. The original Landru programmed it with all his knowledge but he couldn't give it his wisdom, his compassion, his understanding—his soul, Mr. Spock."

"Sometimes you are predictably metaphysical, Captain. I prefer the concrete, the graspable, the provable."

"You would make a splendid computer, Mr. Spock."

Spock bowed. "That's very kind of you, sir."

Uhura spoke from behind them. "Captain . . . Mr. Lindstrom from the surface."

Kirk pushed a button. "Yes, Mr. Lindstrom."

"Just wanted to say good-bye, Captain."

"How are things going?"

"Couldn't be better!" The youngster's enthusiasm was like a triumphant shout in his ear. "Already this morning we've had half-a-dozen domestic quarrels and two genuine knock-down drag-outs. It may not be paradise—but it's certainly . . ."

"Human?" asked Kirk.

"Yes! And they're starting to think for themselves! Just give me and our people a few months and we'll have a going society on our hands!"

"One question, Mr. Lindstrom: Landru wanted to give his people peace and security and so programmed the machine. Then how do we account for so total an anomaly as the festival?"

"Sir, with the machine destroyed, we'll never have enough data to answer that one with any confidence—but I have a guess, and I feel almost certain it's the right one. Landru wanted to eliminate war, crime, disease, even personal dissension, and he succeeded. But he failed to allow for population control, and without that even an otherwise static society would soon suffer a declining standard of living, and eventual outright hunger. Clearly Landru wouldn't have wanted that either, but he made no allowances for it.

"So the machine devised its own: one night a year in which all forms of control were shut off, every moral law abrogated; even ordinary human decency was canceled out.

One night of the worst kind of civil war, in which *every* person is the enemy of *every* other. I have no proof of this at all, sir—but it's just the sort of solution you'd expect from a machine, and furthermore, a machine that had been programmed to think of people as cells in a Body, of no importance at all as individuals." Suddenly Lindstrom's voice shook. "One night a year of total cancer . . . horrible! I hope I'm dead wrong, but there are precedents."

"That can hardly be fairly characterized as a guess," Spock said. "Ordinarily I do not expect close reasoning from sociologists, but from what I know of the way computers behave when they are given directives supported by insufficient data, I can find no flaw in Mr. Lindstrom's analysis. It should not distress him, for if it is valid—as I am convinced it is—he is indeed just the man to put it right."

"Thank you, Mr. Spock," Lindstrom's voice said. "I'll cherish that. Captain, do you concur?"

"I do indeed," Kirk said. "I have human misgivings which I know you share with me. All I can say now is it sounds promising. Good luck. Kirk out."

Kirk turned to his First Officer and looked at him in silence for a long time. At last he said, "Mr. Spock, if I didn't know you were above such human weaknesses as feelings of solemnity, I'd say you looked solemn. Are you feeling solemn, Mr. Spock?"

"I was merely meditating, sir. I was reflecting on the frequency with which mankind has wished for a world as peaceful and secure as the one Landru provided."

"Quite so, Mr. Spock. And see what happens when we get it! It's our luck and our curse that we're forced to grow, whether we like it or not."

"I have heard human beings say also, Captain, that it is also our joy."

"*Our* joy, Mr. Spock?"

There was no response, but, Kirk thought, Spock knew as well as any man that ancient human motto: *Silence gives assent.*

A TASTE OF ARMAGEDDON

Writer: Robert Hamner and Gene L. Coon
(Story by Gene L. Coon)
Director: Joseph Pevney
Guest stars: David Opatoshu, Barbara Babcock

Ambassador Fox was something of a cross to Captain Kirk, and to most of his officers, for that matter. In addition to having a very high regard for his own importance—which is not necessarily a handicap in a man, provided he also has a sense of humor—he had a remarkably short temper for a career diplomat.

But the mission was his, and he had to be put up with. There was no question about the importance of that. Eminiar VII was by all accounts the most advanced planet of its star cluster, NGC 321, having had space flight for hundreds of years. Nevertheless, as of fifty years ago they had never ventured beyond their own solar system, and for a very good reason: They had been at war with their nearest neighbor. The vessel making the report, the USS *Valiant*, was listed as missing—presumably as a product of the hostilities. It was Fox's job to establish diplomatic relations with them.

It evidently was not going to be easy. At first contact with the *Enterprise*, Eminiar VII sent Code 710—a warning not to approach the planet under any circumstances. Kirk was more than willing to comply; after all, it *was* their planet, and he intensely disliked gunboat diplomacy. But Ambassador Fox insisted, and he had command power if he wanted to exercise it. He frequently did.

Kirk beamed down to the planet with Mr. Spock; Yeoman Manning and two security guards, leaving Scott, his engineer, in charge of the ship. In view of the warning, they all carried number-one phasers, in addition to a tricorder, of which Yeoman Manning was in charge.

But there was no overt hostility. They materialized in a corridor of a building that, judging by the traffic, was an official establishment of some kind, and were met solely by a very pretty girl who introduced herself as Mea Three and promptly offered to take them to the High Council. Her manner was cool, but correct.

The High Council proved to consist of four pleasant-looking men seated at a table in a large room that had in it also a faint hum of machinery, though none was evident. As Kirk and his party entered, all four rose and smiled.

"I am Anan Seven," said the one farthest to the left. "I am sorry to see you here. But you are here, and we must do everything possible to make you comfortable. Won't you sit down?"

"I'm Captain Kirk, James T. Kirk of the starship *Enterprise*, representing the United Federation of Planets. This is my first officer, Mr. Spock. Lieutenant Galloway. Lieutenant Osborne. Yeoman Manning."

"Welcome to Eminiar," Anan said, making a formal little bow. Everyone sat, and there was a moment of silence as each party studied the other.

"Well, Captain," Anan said at last, "since you chose to disregard our warning, I suppose we must proceed to the business at hand. What can we do for you?"

"Our mission, sir, is to establish diplomatic relations between your people and mine. The Federation badly needs a treaty port in this cluster."

"Impossible, I'm afraid," Anan said.

"Oh? Would you mind telling me why?"

"Because of the war."

"You are *still* at war?" Kirk said.

"We have been at war," Anan said, "for five hundred years."

Kirk raised his eyebrows. "You conceal it well. Mr. Spock?"

"Sir," Spock said to Anan, "we have completely scanned your planet. We find it highly advanced, prosperous in a material sense, comfortable for your people—and completely peaceful. Seemingly an ideal, flourishing, highly civilized culture, which obviously should have ties with our Federation. There is no evidence of war whatsoever."

"Casualties among our civilian population," Anan said evenly, "total from one to three million dead each year, from direct enemy attack. This is why we warned you away, Captain. As long as your ship is orbiting this planet, it is in severe danger."

"With whom are you at war?" Spock said.

"Vendikar, the third planet in this system. Originally settled by our people, and as advanced as we are—and a ruthless enemy."

"Nevertheless . . ." Spock began. He got no further than that word. Suddenly the room was clamoring with a shrill, whooping siren. Anan, his face stern, stood instantly, pressing a button.

The result was astonishing. The siren stopped, but the entire rear wall of the Council room slid aside, revealing another room of the same size that harbored an installation of enormous intricacy. It was too bid and too involved to take it all in at once; Kirk got a quick impression of a long bank of computers, a number of lighted graphs on the walls, a large illuminated grid that might have been a map.

"You will have to excuse us," Anan said. "We are in fact under attack at this moment. Mea, care for our guests."

All four of the council members took positions at the machinery, where several other operators were already at work. Kirk, baffled, looked first at Spock, who shrugged, and then at Mea.

"It will not last long," the girl said.

"Don't you take shelter?"

"There is no shelter, Captain."

"Are these attacks frequent?" Spock said.

"Oh, yes. But we retaliate promptly."

Beckoning to Spock, Kirk moved off into the newly revealed room—the war room, Kirk supposed. No attempt was made to stop them. At the large grid, an operator sat at a console. Flashes splattered over the grid, seemingly at random; at each flash, the operator pushed what was evidently a matching button. Kirk studied it, but it conveyed nothing to him; as he had expected, he could not read the mapping conventions of Eminiar. Beside him, however, Mea gasped suddenly.

"A hit!" she said. "A hit in the city!"

"Mr. Spock, hear any explosions?"

"None. Yeoman Manning, are you getting any radiation readings or any other kind of disturbance on the tricorder?"

"Not a thing."

Kirk turned to Mea. "If this is an attack," he said, "would you mind telling me what weapons the enemy is using?"

"Fusion bombs," she said. "Materialized by transporter over the targets. They are very accurate. My parents were killed in the last attack."

Kirk flipped out his communicator and called the ship. "Mr. Scott, are you still scanning this planet's surface?"

"Of course, sir," Scott's voice said promptly. "Per your orders."

"Anything unusual?"

"Nothing, sir. All quiet."

As Kirk put the communicator away, something buzzed on the boards before them and one of the computers extruded a card from a slot. Anan took it and stared at it, his face grim. Then he handed it to the man next to him.

"Just as it happened fifty years ago, Sar," he said.

Sar nodded, his face sad. "We warned them."

"Alert a security detachment. They may be needed."

"Sir," Kirk said, "I have been in contact with my ship, which has this entire planet under surveillance. All the time this so-called attack has been in progress, we have been monitoring you. There has been no attack—no explosions, no radiation, no disturbances whatsoever. Now if this is just some sort of game . . ."

"It is not a game," Anan said. "Half a million people have just been killed."

"Entirely by computers," Spock said suddenly.

"That's quite correct," Anan said. "Their deaths are registered. They are then given twenty-four hours to report to the disintegration chambers. Since the immediate danger appears to be over, I can explain at somewhat greater length. You must understand, Captain, that no two planets could carry on an all-out nuclear war for five hundred years. Such a war would not last five hundred hours. We were forced to find another solution."

"In other words," Spock said, "Vendikar's attack was a theoretical one."

"On the contrary, it was quite real. It is simply launched mathematically. If it is successful, the casualties are computed, identified, and ordered to report for disposition. Theoretical? I lost my wife in the last attack. It is sometimes hard—but our civilization lives. The people die, but the culture goes on."

"Do you mean to tell me," Kirk said, "that your people just . . . walk into a disintegrator when they're told to?"

"They do. They are at war and they know it."

"I've heard of some cold-blooded arrangements," Kirk said, "but this one takes the prize."

"It is cold-blooded," Spock agreed. "But it does have a certain logic about it."

"I am glad you approve," Anan said.

"I do not approve," Spock said coldly. "I understand, which is something else entirely."

"Good," Anan said. "Then you will recall that we warned you not to come here. You chose to disregard my warning. Once in orbit around our planet, your ship became a legitimate target. It has been classified destroyed by an incoming missile."

He made a quick gesture. Kirk spun around. There were four very large uniformed men behind the *Enterprise* party. All four held unfamiliar but quite lethal-looking weapons.

"All persons aboard your ship have twenty-four hours to report to our disintegration chambers. To insure their cooperation, I am ordering you and your party held in custody against their surrender. The same thing, by the way, happened to your ship the *Valiant*, fifty years ago. Killed to the last man."

"You are not," Kirk said through his teeth, "going to harm my ship. Is that clear?"

"If possible, we shall spare the ship," Anan said. "But its passengers and crew are already dead. Put them in class-one detention."

• • •

"Class-one detention," proved to be comfortable—rather like a small, neat apartment, even to a well-stocked kitchen. This did not mollify anybody in the party in the slightest. They had not been there more than an hour when a guard let Mea in. The girl seemed subdued.

"I have been sent to ask if you require anything," she said.

"We require a great deal. I want to see Anan Seven."

"He is busy coordinating the casualty lists."

"If he won't talk to me," Kirk said, "he'll have more casualty lists than he knows what to do with."

"Captain, you have your duty to your ship," the girl said quietly. "We have our duty to our planet."

"Your duty doesn't include stepping into a disintegrator and disappearing!"

"I'm afraid it does, Captain," she said, just as quietly as before. "I too have been declared a casualty. I must report to a disintegrator at noon tomorrow."

Kirk stared at her. He still found the whole arrangement impossible to believe. "And you're going to do it? What could Anan and Sar and the others possibly do if you all just refused to show up?"

"It's not a question of what the Council would do," Mea said. "If everybody refused to report, Vendikar would have no choice but to launch real weapons—and we would have to do the same. Within a week, there would be nothing left of either civilization. Both planets would be uninhabitable. Surely you can see that ours is the better way."

"No," Kirk said. "I don't see it at all."

"I'm sorry. Is there anything I can bring you?"

"Yes. Anan Seven."

"I'll convoy the message. But I doubt that he'll come."

As she left, Kirk pounded a fist into a palm in frustration. Then, suddenly, he had an idea. "Mr. Spock!"

"Yes, sir?"

"Vulcans have limited telepathic abilities, don't they?"

"Yes, Captain," Spock said. "But remember that I am only half Vulcan. I could not reach Anan from here—and if I could, I would not be able to transmit a complex message, or pick one up."

"That isn't what I had in mind. I just want to plant a

suspicion in that guard outside. Preferably, that we've cut a hole through the wall with some heat device they overlooked. Or if that's too complex, just a feeling that we're getting away.''

''Hmm,'' Spock said. ''I know nothing about the sensitiveness of the Eminians. However, nothing would be lost by trying.''

''Good. Go head.''

Spock nodded, leaned his head against the wall nearest the corridor, and closed his eyes. His brow furrowed, and within a few moments he was sweating. Even to Kirk, to whom telepathy was a closed book, it was clear that his first officer was working hard.

Nothing seemed to happen for at least five centuries, or maybe six. Then there was a faint humming at the door, followed by a click. Kirk flattened his back against the wall.

The door swung open and the guard charged in, weapon at the ready. Kirk rewarded him with a crushing blow at the back of the neck; he dropped in complete silence. Kirk dragged him away from the door, retrieving his weapon.

''Thank you, Mr. Spock.''

''A pleasure, Captain.''

''Now, we've got to get our communicators back, and get in touch with the ship. I don't know how far we'll get without weapons; we'll need more. Mr. Spock, I know how you feel about taking life. But our ship is in danger. Do I make myself clear?''

''Perfectly, Captain. I shall do what is necessary.''

Kirk clapped him quickly on the back. ''Let's go.''

They were perhaps halfway back to the Council chambers when they turned a corner and found themselves on the end of a queue. Kirk signaled a halt and peered ahead.

At the other end of the line was a large enclosed booth, with a control console on one side at which an armed guard was sitting, watching a light over the machine. Presently this went off, and in response to the touch of a control, a door opened in the side of the machine.

The man at the head of the line took a last look around and stepped inside. The door closed. The machine hummed; the light went on, and then off again. The door slid back.

There was nobody inside.

Kirk and Spock exchanged grim looks. Kirk made a pinching motion with one hand, and Spock nodded. Kirk walked rapidly down the side of the queue opposite the side the console and the guard were on.

"All right, break it up," he said. "Stand back, everybody."

Heads turned. The guard half rose. "Just what do you think you're up to . . ." Then he saw Kirk's stolen weapon.

He had courage. Kirk could have shot him easily and he must have known it, but he went for his own gun anyhow. At the same instant Spock, who had scuttled unnoticed down the other side of the line, caught him from behind with his nerve-pinch to the shoulder. Looking astonished, the guard collapsed. Spock scooped up his weapon.

"Excellent, Mr. Spock. The rest of you people, stand back or you'll get hurt."

Kirk leveled his gun at the disintegration booth and pulled the trigger. The results were most satisfying. Nothing seemed to come out of the weapon but a scream of sound, but a huge hole appeared magically in the machine. Sparks flew from the console, and in a moment the booth was in flames.

"All right, now get out of here!" Kirk roared. "Go to your homes and stay there! Go!"

Terrified, the remaining people in the queue turned and ran. Spock joined the Captain, eyeing the gun he had just confiscated with open curiosity, his eyebrows up. "A fascinating weapon. Is it solely sonic, I wonder? If so, how do they keep it in a tight beam?"

"We'll work that out later. Let's get out of here."

There was nobody in the Council room but Anan when they burst in. He was pouring something into a glass from a small bottle. He froze when he saw them, then smoothly resumed the motion and drank.

"Would you care to join me, Captain? You may find our Trova most interesting."

"I didn't come to drink."

Anan nodded toward the weapon in Kirk's hand. "I

assume that is what you used to destroy disintegration chamber number twelve."

"Yes. A most efficient weapon—and I'm not at all chary of using it."

"That much is obvious," Anan said. "Clearly you are a barbarian."

"*I* am?" Kirk said incredulously.

"Quite. Why not? We all are. Surely in your history too, you were a killer first, a builder second. That is our joint heritage."

"We are a little less cold-blooded about it than you are."

"What does that matter to the dead?" Anan said.

"You have a point. Nevertheless, I don't think you realize the risk you're taking. We don't make war with computers and herd the casualties off to suicide stations. We make the real thing. I could destroy this planet of yours, Councilman. Mr. Spock, Yeoman Manning, see if you can find one of our communicators in this place."

"I already have," Spock said. He handed it over. Anan watched warily.

"Captain," he said, "surely you see the position we are in. If your people do not report to the disintegration chambers, it is a violation of an agreement dating back five hundred years."

"My people are not responsible for your agreements."

"You are an officer of a force charged with keeping the peace," Anan said. He seemed almost to be pleading. "Yet you will be responsible for an escalation that could destroy two worlds. Millions of people horribly killed, complete destruction of our culture and Vendikar's. Disaster, disease, starvation, pain, suffering, lingering death . . ."

"They seem to frighten you," Kirk said grimly.

"They frighten any sane man!"

"Quite so."

"Don't you see?" Anan said desperately. "We've done away with all that! Now you threaten to bring it all down on us again. Do those four hundred people of yours mean more than the hundreds of millions of innocent people on Eminiar and Vendikar? What kind of a monster are you?"

"I'm a barbarian," Kirk said. Nevertheless, this was

indeed a nasty impasse. After a moment, he activated the communicator.

"Mr. Scott? Kirk here."

"Captain! We thought they'd got you."

"They thought so too," Kirk said. "What's the situation up there?"

"It's been lively," Scott's voice said. "First they tried to lure us all down with a fake message from you. Luckily, our computer told us the voice-patterns didn't match, though it was a bonny imitation—you'd have enjoyed it. Then they sent us their ultimatum. I dinna have any such orders and I paid no attention."

"Good for you. Then what?"

"When the deadline was past, they opened fire on the *Enterprise.* Of course, after the ultimatum we had our screens up. I wanted to bounce a couple of dozen photon torpedoes off them for a starter—after all, the time was past when they said they were going to kill all of you—but Ambassador Fox wouldna let me. Then he wanted me to let down the screens so he could beam down to the planet and try to patch things up, and *I* wouldna do *that.* Now the haggis is really in the fire as far as he's concerned."

"Scotty, your decisions were entirely proper, and I'll back them to the hilt. I'm going to try to straighten this mess out down here. There's a good chance that I won't succeed. If you don't hear anything to the contrary from me in forty-eight hours, execute General Order Twenty-Four."

"Twenty-Four? But, Captain . . ." There was a long pause. Then Scott's voice said: "In forty-eight hours. Aye, sir. Good luck."

"Thanks. Kirk out."

"And just what," Anan asked, "does that mean?"

"It means that in forty-eight hours, the *Enterprise* will destroy Eminiar Seven."

"You're bluffing. You wouldn't."

"I didn't start this, Councilman," Kirk said. "But I mean to finish it. Now . . ."

He moved to the table and pushed the button he had seen Anan use earlier. The wall slid aside as before, revealing the war room.

"Mr. Spock, see if you can figure that installation out.

Anan, you still have something to learn. Destruction. Disease. Suffering. Horror. That's what war is supposed to be, Anan. *That's what makes it a thing to be avoided.* But you've made war neat and painless—so neat and painless that you had no reason to put a stop to it. That's why you've been carrying it on for five hundred years. Any luck, Mr. Spock?"

"Yes, sir," the first officer said. "I cannot read the big map, but the rest of it seems to be quite straightforward. This unit controls the disintegrator booths; these the attacking devices; this the defense. And these compute the casualties. They are all tied in with a subspace transmission unit, apparently so they are in constant contact with their Vendikan counterparts."

"Is that essential?"

"I would think so, Captain. The minute contact is broken, it would be tantamount to an abrogation of the entire agreement between the two warring parties."

"What are you talking about?" Anan said, in dawning horror.

"This is the key, Captain," Spock said, pointing to an isolated computer. He threw a switch on it, and then another. "The circuit is locked. Destroy this one, and they will all go."

"Good. Stand back. You too, Anan." He raised the stolen disruptor.

"No!" Anan screamed. "No, please . . ."

Kirk fired. They key computer burst. A string of minor explosions seemed to run from it along the main computer bank—and then they were no longer minor. Hastily, Kirk herded everyone out into the corridor. They huddled against the wall, while the floor shook, and billows of smoke surged out of the door of the Council room.

It took a long time. At last, Kirk said, "Well—that's it."

"Do you realize what you've done?" Anan screamed.

"Perfectly. I've given you back the horrors of war. The Vendikans will now assume that you have abandoned your agreement, and will prepare for a real war, with real weapons. The next attack they launch will do a lot more than count up numbers on a computer. It will destroy your cities, devastate your planet. You'll want to retaliate, of course. If I were you I'd start making bombs.''

''You *are* a monster,'' Anan whispered.

Kirk ignored him. ''Yes, Councilman, you've got a real war on your hands. You can either wage it—with real weapons—or you might consider the alternative.''

''There is no alternative.''

''There is,'' Kirk said harshly. ''Make peace.''

''After five hundred years of casualties? You're mad!''

''Maybe. But we too have killed in the past, as you pointed out a while ago. Nevertheless, we can stop. We can admit we have been killers—but we're not going to kill today. That's all it takes; one simple decision. We are not going to kill today.''

Anan put a shaking hand to his forehead. ''I don't know . . . I can't see . . .''

''We'll help you.'' He raised the communicator. ''Scotty, have you and Ambassador Fox been following this conversation? I left the line open for you.''

''Aye, that we have.''

''Then you can beam the Ambassador down here if you want.''

After a moment, there was a shimmer in the chamber, and Fox materialized, looking portly and confused.

''This is what you do,'' Kirk told Anan. ''Contact Vendikar. I think you'll find that they're just as terrified and appalled as you are at the prospects. They'll do anything to avoid the alternative I've just given you; peace—or utter destruction. It's up to you.''

Anan looked at them all, hope fighting with despair on his face. Ambassador Fox stepped forward.

''Councilman,'' he said, ''as a third party, interested only in peace and the establishment of normal relations, I will be glad to offer my services as a negotiator between you and Vendikar. I have had some small experience in these matters.''

Anan took a step toward him. ''Perhaps,'' he muttered. ''Perhaps there may be time. I have a direct channel to the Vendikar High Council. It hasn't been used in centuries.''

''Then it's long overdue,'' the Ambassador said. ''If you'll be so kind as to lead the way . . .''

Anan started hesitantly down the corridor, his steps beginning to regain their springiness. Fox followed closely. Anan said, "I understand the head of the Vendikar Council—his name is Ripoma—is an intelligent man. And if he hears from a disinterested party like yourself . . ."

His voice became unintelligible as they rounded a corner. The rest of the *Enterprise* party watched them go.

"There is a chance it will work, Captain," Spock said. "Much depends upon the approach and the conduct of the negotiations, of course."

"Annoying though he is, Ambassador Fox has a reputation for being good at his job," Kirk said. "I'm glad he's going to be good for something at last." He raised the communicator once more. "Kirk to *Enterprise.* Cancel General Order Twenty-Four. Alert Transporter Room. Ready to beam up in ten minutes."

"Aye, sir."

"Still, Captain," Spock said, "you took a very big chance."

"Did I, Mr. Spock? They were killing three million people a year—and it had gone on for five hundred years. An actual attack might not have killed any more people than the fifteen hundred million they've already killed in their computer attacks—but it would have destroyed their ability to make war. The fighting would be over. Permanently."

"I would not care to have counted on that," Spock said.

"I wasn't, Mr. Spock. It was only a calculated risk. What I was really counting upon was that the Eminians keep a very orderly society—and actual war is very messy. Very, very messy. I had a feeling they'd do anything to avoid it—even talk peace!"

"A feeling, Captain? Intuition?"

"No," Kirk said. "Call it . . . shall we say, cultural morphology?"

If Spock had any answer, it was lost in the shimmer of the transporter effect.

SPACE SEED

Writers: Gene L. Coon and Carey Wilbur
(Story by Carey Wilbur)
Director: Marc Daniels
Guest stars: Ricardo Montalban, Madlyn Rhue

It was only sheer luck that Marla McGivers was on the bridge when the SOS came in. Officially, Lieutenant McGivers was a controls systems specialist, but on the side, she was also a historian. Probably nobody else on board the *Enterprise* would have recognized Morse code at all, since it had gone out of use around the year 2000, in the general chaos following the Eugenics Wars; but she was a student of the period (though, Kirk thought, she looked a good deal more like a ballerina).

The SOS, when answered, changed promptly to the Morse for *SS Botany Bay*, and stayed there as if stuck regardless of further hails. Homing on the message, the *Enterprise* eventually found herself drawing alongside a dark hull of a ship of the CZ-100 class. The library computer said the last one of those had been built around 1994. Clearly a derelict, its signal left on automatic.

Except that the *Enterprise*'s sensors showed other equipment also still operating, over there across the vacuum between the two vessels. Other equipment—and heartbeats. They were very faint, but they seemed to be coming from some eighty or ninety sources. None were faster than four beats per minute. There were no signs of respiration.

"Aliens?" Kirk asked McCoy.

The surgeon shrugged. "You've got me, Jim. Even aliens have to breathe. Besides, the ship's name is in English."

"The English," Kirk said drily, "were notorious for

not breathing, I suppose. Mr. Spock, can you trace the registry?"

"Nothing in the computer, Captain."

"Lieutenant McGivers, what can you tell us about the period when that ship was built?"

"Not as much as I'd like," Marla McGivers said. "The Eugenics Wars were caused by a group of ambitious scientists—of all nationalities—who were trying to improve the race by selective breeding. They were pretty ruthless about it, and before their identity was guessed, half the countries on Earth were accusing each other of being responsible for the plague of sports and monsters that was cropping up. The result was the last World War, and in the process, a lot of records were lost. I'm surprised that any ship from that era ever got off the ground."

"Well, we'd better go across and look it over," Kirk said. "Since you're a specialist in the period, you'd better be in the party. Scotty, I'll want you to inspect the machinery and see what's salvageable, if anything. Bones, you too."

"Why am I always included in these things?" McCoy complained. "I signed aboard to practice medicine, not to have my atoms scattered back and forth across space by a transporter."

"You're included because we hear heartbeats, and that is your department. Let's go."

It was almost dark inside the *Botany Bay*. Where the boarding party materialized, there was little to see but a long corridor, flanked on each side by row upon row of coffin-like drawers or canisters, each about two meters square on end, thrust into the wall. Each had a small green light blinking over it, producing eerie, confusing reflections. Kirk eyed them.

"Mr. Scott?"

"I don't make anything of it yet, sir. They look a little like food lockers—but why so many? Ah, there's a control panel."

"I've seen something like them," Marla said. "Or rather, drawings of them. They look like a twentieth-century life-support system."

McCoy applied his tricorder to the nearest cabinet. At

the same moment, Scott said, "Ah, here we are!" and lights came on overhead. McCoy grunted with interest.

"Look here, Jim," he said. "A new reading. The lights seem to have triggered something inside."

Kirk did not have to look at the tricorder reading to see that. There was now a clear hum from the cabinet, and the little light had turned from green to red.

"I've got it!" Marla said suddenly. "It's a sleeper ship!"

This meant nothing to Kirk, but McCoy said: "Suspended animation?"

"Yes. They were necessary for long space trips until about the year 2018. They didn't have the warp drive until then, so even interplanetary travel took them years. We'll find crewmen in there, or passengers, sleeping, waiting for the end of their journey . . ."

"Or more likely, all dead," McCoy said. "On the other hand, those heartbeats . . . Is it possible, after all these centuries?"

Scott joined them, and in a moment had discovered that the front of the cabinet was actually a protective shield. Pulling this away, he revealed a transparent observation panel. On the other side, bathed in a gentle violet glow, was a motionless, naked man. He was extremely handsome, and magnificently built. His face reflected the sun-ripened Aryan blood of the northern Indian Sikhs, with just an additional suggestion of the oriental. Even in repose, his features suggested strength, intelligence, even arrogance.

"How beautiful," Marla said, as if to herself.

"This cabinet is wired to be triggered first," Scott said practically. "Maybe that means he's the leader."

"Or only a pilot," Spock added. "Or a doctor, to supervise the revival of the others."

"He's the leader," Marla said positively.

"Oh?" Kirk said. "What makes you think so?"

"Well . . . you can see it. A Sikh type. They were fantastic warriors."

"He *is* reviving," McCoy said. "Heartbeat up to fifty-two already, and definite breathing."

"Scotty, see if they're all like that."

The engineer went down the line, pulling off the shields

and peering into each canister. "No sir," he said finally. "A mixed bag, Captain. Western, Mid-European, Near-Eastern, Latin, Oriental—the works. And all their lights are still green, as you can see yourself."

"A man from the twentieth century," Marla said, as if hypnotized. "Coming alive now. It's incredible!"

"It's about to be impossible," McCoy said, checking the tricorder again. "His heartbeat's beginning to drop back down. If you want to talk to this living fossil, Jim, I suggest we get him over to my sick bay right away quick."

"Oh no!" Marla said.

McCoy shot her a sidelong look, but he said, "I quite agree. A patient well worth fighting for. And think of the history locked up in that head!"

"Never mind the history," Kirk said. "It's a human life. Beam him over."

While McCoy worked on the sleeping man, Kirk took time out to collect more information from his officers.

"As near as I can work out their heading," said Spinelli, who had relieved Sulu at the helm, "they must have been trying for the Tau Ceti system."

"Makes sense. It's near Sol, and there are three habitable planets."

"Yes sir, but they would never have gotten there. Their port control jets took meteor damage, and the hits put them off course, too."

"Scotty, any log books or records?"

"Negative, Captain. They must have been in suspended animation when the ship took off."

"Ship's equipment?"

"Colonization gear mainly," the engineer said. "But quite heavy on armaments. I suppose that's typical of their era. Twelve of the life support systems malfunctioned, leaving seventy-two still operating. About a dozen of those are women."

"Seventy-two alive," Kirk said reflectively. "Any conclusions, Mr. Spock?"

"Very few, Captain. The CZ-100 class vessel was built for interplanetary travel only—*not* interstellar."

"They tried it."

"Granted," said the first officer. "But why?"

"Possibly because life on Earth had become so unbearable during the wars."

"Captain, consider the expense, just to begin with. Healthy, well-oriented young humans would think of some less costly way of surviving—or of committing suicide. It was ten thousand to one against their making it to Tau Ceti, and they must have known it. And another thing: Why no record of the attempt? Granted that the records are incomplete, but a maiden star voyage—the name *Botany Bay* should have been recorded a thousand times: one mention, at least, should have survived. But there is nothing."

"*Botany Bay.* Hmm. Lieutenant McGivers tells me that was a penal colony on the shores of Australia. Is that of some significance?"

"Are you suggesting a deportation vessel?" Spock said. "Again, logically insufficient. Your Earth was on the edge of another Dark Ages. Whole populations were being bombed out of existence. A group of criminals could have been eliminated in a far less expensive way than firing them off in what was the most advanced spaceship of its time."

"So much for my theory. I'm still waiting for yours."

"I do not have the facts, Captain. William of Occam said that one must not multiply guesses without sufficient reasons. I suggest that we take the *Botany Bay* to the nearest Star Base for a thorough study."

Kirk thought about it. "All right. Rig tractors for towing. In the meantime, I'm going to look at the patient."

In the sick bay, the man out of time was still unconscious, but now breathing regularly. Marla McGivers was standing to one side, watching.

"How is he, Bones?"

"By all rights he should be dead," McCoy said shortly.

"False modesty?"

"By no means. I'm good, but not *that* good. His heart stopped three times. When I got it going the third time, he woke up for a moment, smiled at me, and said 'How long?' I guessed a couple of centuries. He smiled again, fell asleep, and damned if his heart didn't stop a fourth time, and *start up again of its own accord*. There's something inside this man that refuses to accept death."

"He must have the constitution of an ox."

"That is not just a metaphor," McCoy said, pointing to the body function panel. "Look at that. Even in his present shape, his heart valve action has twice the power of yours or mine. Lung efficiency, fifty percent better. And courage! . . . Whoever he is, or whatever, it'll be a pleasure to meet him."

Kirk looked at Marla, and then said quietly to the surgeon, "I can get you agreement on that."

Apparently encouraged by the notice, Marla said, "Will he live?"

"If he gets some rest, he may," McCoy said tartly. "Beat it, both of you. This is a sick bay, not a wardroom."

Grinning, Kirk motioned Marla out and followed her. As she turned down the corridor, however, he said, "Lieutenant."

She stopped and turned. Kirk went on. "Lieutenant, if I were forced to rate your performance as a member of the boarding party today, I wouldn't give you a very high mark."

"I know, Captain," she said. "I'm sorry."

"That's not enough. At any one time, the safety of this entire vessel can rest upon the performance of a single crewman. The fact that you may find a strange man personally compelling is the worst possible excuse."

"Personally?" she said, flushing. "Captain, my second profession is history. To find a . . . a specimen from the past, alive . . . the sheer delight of anticipating what he might tell me . . ."

"More than that," Kirk said. "Men were much more adventurous then, bolder, more colorful."

She was silent for no more than a heartbeat. Then she said firmly, "Yes, sir, I think they were."

Kirk nodded. "That's better. If I can have honesty, I'll overlook mistakes—at least the first time. Dismissed."

As she left, Kirk turned to find McCoy watching him, smiling. "It's a pity," the surgeon said, "that you wasted your life on command, Jim. You'd have made a fair psychologist."

"Thanks, Bones, but command is better. It covers every other subject."

"Touché—or should I say, checkmate?"

• • •

It was only a few hours later that McCoy called Kirk on the bridge. "Captain," he said, "I have a patient with questions—and I don't mind telling you, patients like this could put medicine out of business. Can you come down?"

The big man from the *Botany Bay*, now dressed in a tunic from the stores of the *Enterprise*, was still on his bed; but he was indeed awake—vitally awake. Kirk introduced himself."

"Thank you," the man said. "I am told I have slept for two centuries or more, and am on board a real starship—not a makeshift like mine. What is our heading?"

Kirk was both amused and annoyed. "Would you care to give your name first?"

"No, I would not. I have a responsibility. If you are indeed a commander, you will recognize it. Where are we going?"

Kirk decided to yield for the moment; there was no point in insisting on a contest with a man just yanked back from the edge of death, no matter how arrogant he was. "Our heading is Star Base Twelve, our command base in this sector."

"Which is?"

"I doubt that identifying the sector would do you any good. It is many parsecs beyond the system you were headed for, and our galactic coordinate system probably doesn't correspond with the one you're used to."

"Galactic," the man said. "I see. And my people?"

"Seventy-two of the canisters are still functioning. The people will be revived when we reach Star Base Twelve. We wanted to see how we fared with reviving you, first."

"Logical and hard-headed; I approve. I do begin to grow fatigued. Can we continue the questioning at another time?"

"You haven't answered any questions yet," Kirk said, "except by inference."

"I apologize," the big man said at once. "My name is Kahn. I command the *Botany Bay* Colonizing Expedition. I think perhaps I could answer your questions better if I knew your period, your terminology and so on—perhaps something to read during my convalescence would serve. History, technology, whatever is available."

It seemed a sensible request. "Dr. McCoy will show you how to hook your viewing screen here into our library tapes. And I think Lieutenant McGivers would enjoy filling you in on the history."

"Very good." Kahn smiled. "I have two hundred years of catching up to do. I . . ."

Suddenly, his eyes closed. McCoy looked at the body function panel.

"Asleep," McCoy said. "Well, I'm glad he's got *some* human weaknesses."

It was not until Kirk was on his way back to the bridge that he fully realized how little Kahn had told him. Irritated, mostly at himself, he collared Spock at the computer. "Anything?"

"Nothing about a star flight until the Alpha Centauri expedition of 2018," the first officer said. "How is the patient?"

"Arrogant—and clever. Enormously powerful. And with enormous magnetism. Not at all what I expected in a twentieth-century man."

"Interesting. Possibly a product of selective breeding."

"That had occurred to me," Kirk admitted. "If I wanted a superman, he's very much the kind of outcome I'd shoot for."

"Exactly, Captain. He is almost a stereotype of an Earthman's dreams of power and potency. And from what I can put together from the fragments of the record, just the kind of man who precipitated the chaos of the 1990s."

"Oh? I thought it was a group of scientists."

"Partly true," Spock said, "and partly, I would judge, a comfortable fiction. The scientists encouraged carefully arranged marriages *among themselves*, and applied their knowledge of heredity to their *own* offspring. The sports and monsters did not appear until after the war was well started, and almost surely were spontaneous mutations erupting from all the ambient radioactivity. The scientists stayed aloof and went right on breeding what they thought was *Homo superior*."

"Fact?" Kirk demanded. "Or just that old legend of the mad scientists again?"

"Mostly deduction," Spock said. "But the scientists existed. Not mad—not raving mad, anyhow. Dedicated men who believed their wards would grow up to seize power peaceably, put an end to war, famine, greed—a noble ambition, which of course misfired."

"And our patient."

"One of those children. His age would be right. A group of aggressive, arrogant young men *did* seize power simultaneously in over forty nations. But they had overextended themselves; they could not hold what they seized. That much is fact. And one more thing, Captain. Are you aware that some eighty or ninety of those people were never brought to trial, were never even found after the chaos? No bodies, no graves, no traces?"

"I certainly wasn't," Kirk said.

"And they should have been found, or the authorities should have pretended that they had been found. Think of the panic among the remaining, starving war-weary people even to suspect that eighty Napoleons might still be alive. And, Captain . . ."

"Yes," Kirk said heavily. "I'm no match for you as a logician, Mr. Spock, but even I can see where that sentence is leading. You think those eighty Napoleons are *still* alive—and we have seventy-nine of them in tow, and one on board."

"Precisely, Captain."

Kirk thought about it for quite a while.

"It stands up," he said. "But what we're left with, is that we can get no more pertinent information anywhere except from Kahn himself. He's got a mind like a tantalum-lined vault, so we'll never force it out of him. We'll have to try to charm it . . . which probably won't work either. Maybe we can use the customs of his own time to disarm him. I'll see what Lieutenant McGivers has to suggest."

What Marla McGivers had to suggest was a formal dinner, attended by all the major officers of the *Enterprise*, as a welcome for Commander Kahn to the twenty-third century. She was obviously far from disinterested in the proposal, and Kirk suspected that Kahn had already made his first new conquest in the new century; but there were no regulations against romance, and in any event, Kirk had nothing better to suggest.

Marla appeared with a new and totally anachronistic hair style which went a long way toward confirming Kirk's suspicions. As for Kahn, it was impossible to tell whether or not he was charmed; he far too efficiently charmed everybody else, instead. There seemed to be no situation in which he could not feel at home, after only a few minutes' appraisal.

Then, over the brandy, it suddenly turned out at least one officer of the *Enterprise* was not prepared to recognize charm even if he were hit over the head with it. Spock said, "But you still have not told us why you decided on star travel, Commander Kahn—nor how you managed to keep it out of the records."

"Adventure, Mr. Spock. There was little else left to be accomplished on Earth."

"There was the overthrow of the Eugenics tyrannies," Spock said. "Many men considered that a worthwhile effort."

"A waste of spirit in a desert of shame," Kahn said. "There was much that was noble about the Eugenics crusade. It was the last grand attempt to unify humanity, at least in my time."

"Like a team of horses under one harness, one whip?"

"I refuse to take offense, Mr. Spock," Kahn said genially. "Much can be accomplished by a team. It was a time of great dreams—great aspirations."

"Great aspirations under petty dictatorships? Never in previous history, at least."

"I disagree," Kahn said. "One man, not many, would eventually have ruled. As in Rome under Augustus—and see what that accomplished—Captain Kirk, you understand me well. You let your second-in-command attack me, and through me, you; yet you remain silent, and watch for weakness. A sound principle."

"You have a tendency," Kirk said, "to express your ideas in military terms, Commander Kahn. This is a social occasion."

"It has been said," Kahn said easily, "that social occasions are only warfare concealed. Many prefer their warfare more honest and open."

"There was open warfare on Earth," Kirk said. "Yet it appears that you fled it."

"Not much can be done with a nearly destroyed world."

"In short," Spock said, "you were afraid."

Kahn's eyes flashed. "I have never been afraid."

"And that does not frighten you?"

"How? I don't understand you, Mr. Spock. How can a man be afraid of never being afraid? It is a contradiction in terms."

"Not at all," the first officer said. "It is a null class in the class of all classes not members of the given class."

Kahn was now beginning to look angry. Kirk, secretly a little amused, interposed. "I'm sorry, Commander, but you just pushed Mr. Spock's logic button, which has a tendency to make him incomprehensible for the next ten minutes or so. Nevertheless, I think his question a good one. You say you have never been afraid; yet you left at the very time mankind most needed courage."

"Courage! How can one impart courage to sheep? I offered the world order. *Order!* And what happened? They panicked. I left behind nothing worth saving."

"Then," Spock said, "do you imagine that this ship, to take a simple example, was built by sheep, out of panic? I do not further impugn your logic, Commander Kahn, but I am beginning to mistrust your eyesight."

Marla, who had been completely silent since the start of the discussion, stood up so suddenly that coffee slopped in saucers all the way around the table.

"I never thought," she said in a trembling voice, "that I'd ever see so much rudeness to a starship guest."

"Was *I* rude?" Spock said mildly, raising his eyebrows. "If so, I apologize."

"And I," said Kirk, repressing another grin.

"I quite accept your apologies," Kahn said, also rising. "But if you will excuse me, gentlemen and ladies, I am tired. It has been a good many centuries, and I would like to return to my quarters. If you would guide me back, Marla . . . ?"

They went out, followed, at a slight motion of the head from Kirk, by every other guest but Spock. When the room was empty, Kirk said, "And McCoy calls *me* a fair psychologist! I've never seen a better needling job in my life, Mr. Spock."

"I myself am not very happy with it, Captain," the first officer said. "The human half of my make-up seems to go to sleep just when I need it most. Consider, really, how little we have learned. The man's name: Sibahl Khan Noonien. From 1922 through 1996, military chieftain of a quarter of your world from South Asia through the Middle East, and the last of the tyrants to be overthrown. And apparently very much admired, as such men go; there was very little freedom under his rule, but also there were no massacres, and no war until he was attacked by a lesser dictator of his own breed. A man of power, who understands the uses of power, and who *should* have been much admired by the people whom he calls sheep, the people who feel more comfortable being led."

"And you got all that just from what he said tonight? I would say that's considerable."

"It is not what we need to know," Spock insisted. "The main question is, why did he run away? *That* was what I was hoping to elicit from him. But he caught me at it. I do not call that very good psychology."

"I see what you mean," Kirk said reflectively. "Until we know that, we can't know what he might intend now—or what risks we might run in reviving the other seventy or so of them. We will just have to try another gambit . . . But there's one other thing. What was the point of that question about being afraid of never having been afraid? I thought for a moment that I saw what you were driving at, and then you lost me in your logical technicalities. Isn't the question what you would call a tautology?"

"No, Captain," Spock said. "But I was trying to make it look like one. I was not trying to confuse you, certainly, but Commander Kahn—and I hope that at least there, I succeeded. Fear is an essential reaction to the survival of any sentient creature. If he does not know fear, he never knows when it is sensible to run; and yet, Commander Kahn ran. Since he claims never to have felt fear, what other reason can he have had?"

"Hmm," Kirk said. "I've never seen a single sentient creature that didn't feel fear when it was appropriate. Yet he was very convincing on that very point."

"Indeed he was," Spock said. "And, Captain—that *scares* me."

Nothing Spock had ever said before had quite so stunned Kirk. As he stared at his Science Officer, the vacated, somehow sadly messy scene of the formal dinner suddenly rang with the alarm to General Quarters.

"Abrams in Security, Captain. Kahn's missing."

"McCoy here. Kahn's not here. No sign of McGivers, either—not even in her quarters. And he's not there."

"Transporter room here. We've had a guard slugged, Lieutenant Adamski is missing, and there's been a lot of power expended in the last half hour."

"Scott reporting. I . . ."

"Uhura, what happened to Scotty? Get him back!"

"Dead channel, Captain. I can't raise the arsenal, either."

"Spock, send somebody down."

"All turbo elevators inoperative. Emergency exits jammed."

The lights began to go down. "Batteries!"

"Shunted out, Captain. Also, the atmosphere's off."

"Engineering! Scott! What's going on down there? Scotty!"

And then they heard Kahn's voice. It was coming through Uhura's own board, though it was impossible to imagine how Kahn had made the crippled array speak.

"He's not able to talk with you at the moment, Captain," Kahn said. "I'm afraid your ship is mine—or rather, ours. I have almost all my people aboard her, at every key point. Everything is jammed; you have perhaps ten minutes before you suffocate. Would you like to negotiate with me?"

"Uhura, can you raise Star Ship Command?"

"No, sir, this board is a dead duck. I can't even dump a message capsule."

"Brilliant," Spock said softly.

There was only one thing left to do. "Security Five, Mr. Spock. Flood all decks."

"Bypassed, Captain. Commander Kahn seems to have been a very quick student."

"Can we go to Six?" That would fill the air with radioactive gas from the fusion chamber and kill almost everyone on board; but . . .

"No sir, we cannot. Nothing is left but Destruct. That's still alive."

"The air up there should be getting quite toxic by now," Kahn's voice said. "You don't have much time."

"What do you want, Kahn?"

"Surrender of the bridge."

"Refused," Kirk said.

"Very well. It is academic, anyhow. In ten minutes, every person on the bridge will be dead."

Nothing further was heard from Kahn after that. Slowly, the air turned foul. After a while, nobody was conscious but Kirk, and then . . . and then . . .

Kirk awoke, with considerable surprise, in the briefing room. His entire staff seemed to be with him—all weak, but all alive. They were heavily under guard by Kahn and a group of men very like him, all carrying *Enterprise* phasers. The men from the *Botany Bay* were inarguably splendid-looking specimens—large, strong, healthy, handsome, and above all, alert.

"Very good," Kahn said. "Now we can talk. You see, Captain, nothing changes—except man. Your technical accomplishments are illusions, simply the tools which men use. The key has always been man himself. Improve a mechanical device and you double your capacity; improve man, and you gain a thousand fold. You, I judge, are such a man, Captain, as am I. You would be wise to join me."

Kirk said nothing. Kahn turned to Spock. "I am tempted," Spock said. "I admire your tactics . . . but not, I am afraid, your philosophy. And I know from history how self-appointed supermen treat mixed breeds. Let us see how you run the ship by yourself."

"You will see. My offer to you is closed. Navigator, I want you to set course for the nearest colonized planet—one with port facilities and a population which is not afraid of discipline."

"Go to blazes," Spinelli said.

"It is as I thought," Spock said. "You may know the

Enterprise well, Commander, but your newly revived colleagues do not. I think we have a stalemate.''

''Do we? Dr. McCoy, you maintain a decompression chamber in your laboratory, isn't that so? Yes, I know it is. Joaquin, take Captain Kirk to the chamber. Put him inside, and lower the pressure to zero. I trust the rest of you understand what that means. You can spare him that. All I want from you is your word that you will continue performing your duties.''

''Nobody,'' Kirk said harshly, ''is to lift a finger to save me. I so order.''

''I am not bluffing,'' Kahn said pleasantly. ''If, of course, you allow your Captain to die, you will all follow him, one by one, into the chamber.''

Kirk caught Marla's eye. She was staring wide-eyed at Kahn. Evidently she had discovered something she hadn't taken into account.

There was a blare from a wall speaker, and then a babble of angry, excited crowd noises. ''Kahn,'' said an unfamiliar voice, ''this is Paul in the recreation room. They're getting out of hand. I may have to kill a few of them.''

''Do so, then.''

''No!'' Marla said. ''I have friends there . . . Kahn, please. If I could talk to them . . . reassure them . . . There's no need to kill them.''

''You may attempt it,'' Kahn said. ''Be certain they understand that I have no compunctions about killing if I'm forced to.''

The guards hustled Kirk out, with Marla in tow. Perhaps they were unfamiliar with the ship in detail, but they certainly knew their way to McCoy's laboratory. They bundled Kirk into the decompression chamber as though they were doing nothing more interesting than autoclaving a rack of test tubes. The door shut, and a moment later Kirk heard the pumps begin to throb.

For some reason, he felt neither alarmed nor resigned. His chief emotion was anger, at being put through asphyxiation twice in one hour.

There seemed to be nothing to do about it, however.

Then the door hissed and swung back. Kirk stepped out cautiously. One of the supermen, the one called Joaquin, was out cold on the floor, with Marla standing over him, a wrench held awkwardly in her hands. The other guard evidently had gone off somewhere.

"Are you all right?" Marla said tremulously.

"I think so. The pressure didn't have time to drop much. I'm glad to see you're good for something." He stooped and picked up Joaquin's phaser.

Marla grasped his arm. "Captain, please," she said.

"Well?"

"I saved your life. Promise me you . . . won't kill him."

"No promises," Kirk said, looking around the laboratory. After a moment, he spotted what he wanted; a bulb of the anesthetic gas McCoy used to capture specimens. He juggled it with pleasure. "Stay here and try not to get yourself any deeper into trouble than you are. I think I am about to bag myself some choice items for some zoo."

It was not all that easy. Before it was over, one of the supermen was dead, and almost everyone else on both sides was considerably banged up. At last, however, the survivors from the *Botany Bay* were locked in a hold, and Kirk and his officers reassembled in the briefing room.

"Well, Mr. Spock," Kirk said, "I think we know now why they left the Earth."

"Yes, sir. To free themselves of the rabble, and start fresh. In my opinion they would never have succeeded, even had they made it to a habitable world. The man who cannot know fear is gravely handicapped."

"We are about to put that to the test. Have Kahn brought in here, please."

Kahn was brought in, under guard, with Marla behind him. Both looked at Kirk defiantly.

"At present," Kirk said, "we are orbiting a planet in a system unknown to you, and which I shall not further identify. It is savage and inhospitable, but with breathable atmosphere and land which can be cultivated. You have the following choice: To be put ashore on this world, with a minimum of survival equipment; or, to be taken to Star Base Twelve to be assigned to rehabilitation. The second choice would be rather drastic in your case, but it would enable you to fit into our society. Which do you prefer?''

''Captain,'' Kahn said, ''I suppose you will remember what Lucifer said when he fell into the pit.''

''I remember it well. I take it that's your answer?''

''It is.''

''It may interest you to know that Systems Officer McGivers, given the choice of standing court martial or sharing your exile, has chosen to go with you.''

Kahn looked at her and smiled. ''I knew I was right about you,'' he said. ''You have the fire. And think of this: we have what we wanted after all—a world to win.'' He swung on Kirk. ''And, Captain, we will make it an empire. You'll see.''

''If you do,'' Kirk said, ''you'll have earned it. Guards, beam them down.''

Kahn exited without a backward look, but Marla turned at the door.

''Goodbye, Captain,'' she said. ''I'm sorry. But I do love him.''

''I wish you luck, Lieutenant.''

After a short silence, Scott said, ''It's a shame for a good Scotsman to admit it, but I'm not up on my Milton. What *did* Lucifer say after he fell into the pit?''

''He said, 'Better to reign in hell than serve in heaven.' Mr. Spock, clear for space. I want to get under way as soon as possible.''

''Yes, Captain. What shall I do with the *Botany Bay*?''

''Hmm . . . You'd better dump it into—no, on second thought, let's keep it in tow. I suppose there are still things aboard her that the historians will want to see. At the moment, though, whenever I say 'historian' I have to repress a shudder.''

''Let us think ahead, then,'' Spock said. ''It would be interesting to come back to this system in a hundred years and see what crop had sprung up from the seed we have planted today.''

''It would indeed,'' Kirk said. ''But I'll tell you something else, Mr. Spock. I only hope that in a hundred years, that crop won't have sprung right out of the ground and come out looking for *us*.''

THIS SIDE OF PARADISE

Writer: D.C. Fontana (story by Nathan Butler and D.C. Fontana)
Director: Ralph Senensky
Guest stars: Jill Ireland, Frank Overton

There was no answer from the Sandoval colony on Omicron Ceti III to the *Enterprise*'s signals, but that was hardly surprising; the colonists, all one hundred and fifty of them, had probably been dead for the better part of three years, as two previous colonies had died, for reasons then mysterious. Elias Sandoval had known this past history and had determined to settle on the planet anyhow; it was in all other respects a tempting place.

It was not until after his group had settled in—and had stopped communicating—that the Berthold emission of the planet's sun had been discovered. Little enough was known about Berthold radiation even now, but it had been shown that direct exposure to it under laboratory conditions disintegrated living animal tissue in as little as seventy-two hours. A planet's atmosphere would cut down some of the effect, to the point where a week's exposure might be safe, but certainly not three years. And there was no preventive, and no cure.

The settlement proper, however, was still there and was easy to spot. Kirk made up a landing party of six, including himself, Spock, McCoy, Lieutenant Timothy Fletcher (a biologist), Sulu and a crewman named Dimont. The settlement proved to consist of a surprisingly small cluster of buildings, with fields beyond it. Kirk looked around.

"It took these people a year to make the trip from Earth," he said. "They came all that way—and died."

"Hardly that, sir," said a man's voice. The party snapped around toward it.

A big, bluff, genial-looking man clad in sturdy work clothes had come around a corner of a building, with two others behind him, similarly dressed and carrying tools. The first man came forward, holding out his hand.

"Welcome to Omicron Ceti III," he said. "I am Elias Sandoval."

Kirk took the hand, but could think of nothing to say but a mumble of thanks.

"We've seen no one outside our group since we left Earth four years ago," the man went on. "We've expected someone for quite some time. Our subspace radio has never worked properly and we, I'm afraid, had no one among us who could master its intricacies. But we were sure when we were not heard from, a ship would come."

"Actually, Mr. Sandoval, we didn't come because of your radio silence . . ."

"It makes little difference, Captain. You are here, and we are happy to have you. Come, let me show you our settlement."

He began to walk away, not bothering to look back, as if certain that they would follow. The other colonists had already left.

"On pure speculation," McCoy said drily, "just as an educated guess, I'd say that man isn't dead."

Spock checked his tricorder. "The intensity of Berthold radiation is at the predicted level. At this intensity, we will be safe for a week, if necessary. But . . ."

"But these people shouldn't be alive," Kirk said. "Well, there's no point in debating it in a vacuum. Let's get some answers."

He started after Sandoval. From closer range, the buildings could be seen to be not deserted, only quiet. Nearby, a woman was hanging out some wash; in another structure, a woman placed a fresh-baked pie in a window to cool. It might have been a tranquil Earthly farm community of centuries ago, except for a scattering of peculiar plants with bulbous pods, apparently indigenous, which revealed that it was on another planet.

Sandoval led the landing party into his own quarters.

"There are two other settlements," he said, "but we have forty-five colonists here."

"What was the reason for the dispersal?" Kirk asked.

"We felt three separate groups might have a better opportunity for growth. And, if some disease should strike one group, the other two would be less likely to be endangered. Omicron is an ideal agricultural planet, Captain, and we determined that we would not suffer the fate of expeditions that had gone before us."

A woman came from an inner door and stopped, seeing the strangers. She looked Eurasian, and was strikingly beautiful.

"Ah, Leila," Sandoval said, turning to her. "Come and meet our guests. This is Leila Kalomi, our botanist. Captain Kirk, Dr. McCoy, Mr. Spock . . ."

"Mr. Spock and I have met," she said, holding out a hand to him. "It has been a long time."

He took the hand gently but awkwardly. "The years have seemed twice as long," he said.

She bowed her head, silently accepting the compliment. Then she looked up, as if searching his face for something more; but there was nothing but his usual calm. He released her hand slowly.

"Mr. Sandoval," Kirk said, "we do have a mission here. A number of examinations, tests . . ."

"By all means, please attend to them, Captain. I think you'll find our settlement interesting. Our philosophy is a simple one: that men should return to the less complicated life. We have very few mechanical things here—no vehicles, no weapons—" He smiled. "As I said, even the radio has never worked properly. We have harmony here—complete peace."

"We'll try not to disturb your work. Gentlemen, if you'll come outside now . . ."

On the porch, he flipped open his communicator. "Kirk to *Enterprise*."

"*Enterprise*. Lieutenant Uhura here."

"Lieutenant, we've found the colony apparently well and healthy. We're beginning an investigation. Relay that information to Star Fleet, and then beam down to me all the information we have on this last Omicron expedition."

"Yes, sir. *Enterprise* out."

"Gentlemen, carry out your previous instructions. If you find anything out of the ordinary, report to me at once."

The party scattered.

Dimont was the first to find the next anomaly. He had been raised in the farm country of the Mojave, and was leading cows to pasture when he was six, up at dawn and then working all day in the fields. It was his opinion, expressed to Sulu, that "they could use a little of that spirit here."

But there was no place for it. There were no cows here; the one barn hadn't even been built for them, but only for storage. Nor were there any horses, pigs, even dogs. A broader check disclosed that the same was true of the whole planet: there was nothing on it but people and vegetation. The records showed that the expedition had carried some animals for breeding and food, but none seemed to have survived. Well, that was perhaps not an anomaly in the true sense, for they couldn't have survived. In theory, neither could the people.

But they had. "I've examined nine men so far," McCoy reported, "ages varying from twenty-three to fifty-nine. Every one of them is in perfect physical shape—textbook responses. If everybody was like them, I could throw away my shingle. But there's something even stranger."

"What is it?" Kirk asked.

"I've got Sandoval's medical record as of four years ago when he left Earth. There was scar tissue on his lungs from lobar pneumonia suffered when he was a child. No major operations, but he did have an appendectomy. But when I examined the man not an hour ago, he was as perfect as the rest of them."

"Instrument malfunction?"

"No. I thought of that and tested it on myself. It accurately recorded my lack of tonsils and those two broken ribs I had once. But it *didn't* record any scar tissue on Sandoval's lungs—and it *did* record a healthy appendix where one was supposedly removed."

Fletcher's report also turned up an anomaly. "The soil here is rich, the rainfall moderate, the climate temperate the year round. You could grow anything here, and they've got a variety of crops in—grains, potatoes, beans. But for an agricultural colony they actually have very little acreage planted. There's enough to sustain the colony, but very little more. And another thing, they're not bothering to rotate crops in their fields—haven't for three years. That's poor practice for a group like this, even if the soil is good."

It was like a jigsaw puzzle all one color—a lot of pieces but no key to where they fitted.

Then came the order to evacuate, direct from Admiral Komack of Star Fleet. Despite the apparent well-being of the colonists, they were to be moved immediately to Starbase 27, where arrangements were being made for complete examinations of all of them. Exposed starship personnel were also to be held in quarantine until cleared at the Starbase. Apparently somebody up the line thought radiation disease was infectious. Well, with Berthold rays, anything seemed to be possible, as McCoy observed wrily.

"You'll have to inform your people of Star Fleet's decision," Kirk told Sandoval. "Meanwhile we can begin to prepare accommodations for them aboard ship . . ."

"No," said Sandoval pleasantly.

"Mr. Sandoval, this is not an arbitrary decision on my part. It is a Star fleet order."

"This is completely unnecessary. We are in no danger here."

"We've explained the Berthold radiation and its effect," McCoy said. "Can't you understand . . ."

"How can I make *you* understand, Doctor? Your own instruments tell you we are in excellent health, and our records show we have not had one death among us."

"What about the animals?" Kirk said.

"We are vegetarians."

"That doesn't answer my question. Why did all the animals die?"

"Captain, you stress unimportant things," Sandoval said, as calmly as before. "We will not leave. Your arguments have some validity, but they do not apply to us."

"Sandoval, I've been ordered to evacuate this colony, and that's exactly what I intend to do, with or without your help."

"And how will you do that?" Sandoval said, turning away. "With a butterfly net?"

It was Spock who was finally given the key. He was standing with Leila looking out over a small garden, checking his tricorder.

"Nothing," he said, "not even insects. Yet your plants grow, and you have survived exposure to Berthold radiation."

"It can be explained," Leila said.

"Please do."

"Later."

"I have never understood the female capacity to avoid a direct answer on any subject."

She put a hand on his arm. "And I never understood you, until now." She tapped his chest. "There was always a place in here where no one could come. There was only the face you allow people to see. Only one side you allow them to know."

"I would like to know how your people have managed to survive here."

"I missed you."

"You should be dead."

She took her hand from his arm and stepped back. "If I show you how we survived, will you try to understand how we feel about our life here? About each other?"

"Emotions are alien to me . . ."

"No. Someone else might believe that—your shipmates, your Captain. But not me. Come this way."

She led him to an open field, uncultivated, with pod plants growing amid grass and low brush. They rustled gently in a little breeze.

"This is the place," she said.

"It looks like any other such area. What is the nature of this thing, if you please?"

"The specific elements and properties are not important. What is important is that it gives life—peace—love."

"What you describe was once called in the vernacular 'a happiness pill.' And you, as a scientist, should know that is impossible."

"No. And I was one of the first to find them."

"Them?"

"The spores." She pointed to the pod plants.

Spock bent to examine them. At the same moment, one of the pods flew apart, like a powdery dandelion broken by the wind. Spock dropped his tricorder to shield his face as the powder flew up about him. Then he screamed.

Leila, frightened, moved forward a step, reaching out a hand to him.

"I—can't," he moaned, almost inaudibly. "Please—don't—don't . . ."

"It shouldn't hurt, not like this! It didn't hurt us!"

"I'm not—like you."

Then, slowly, his face began to change, becoming less rigid, more at peace. Seeing the change, Leila reached up to touch his cheek with gentle fingers. He reached out to gather her into his arms, very gently, as though afraid this woman and this feeling were so fragile that he might break them.

After the kiss, she sat down, and he lay down beside her, his head in her lap. "See the clouds," he said after a while. "That one looks like a dragon—you see the tail and the dorsal spines?"

"I have never seen a dragon."

"I have, on Berengaria VII. But I never saw one in a cloud before." His communicator abruptly shrilled, but he ignored it. "Or rainbows. Do you know I can tell you exactly why one appears in the sky—but considering its beauty was always out of the question."

"Not here," Leila said. The communicator shrilled again, insistently. "Perhaps you should answer?"

"It will only be the Captain."

But finally he lifted the communicator and snapped up the screen. Kirk's anxious voice sounded instantly. "Mr. Spock!"

"What do you want?" Spock asked lazily.

"Spock, is that you?"

"Yes, Captain. What do you want?"

"Where are you?"

Spock considered the question calmly. "I don't believe I want to tell you."

"Spock, I don't know what you think you're doing, but

this is an order. Report back to me at the settlement in ten minutes. We're evacuating the colony to Starbase 27 . . ."

"No, I don't think so."

"You don't think so *what*?"

"I don't think so, *sir*."

"Spock, report to the settlement immediately. Acknowledge. Spock!"

The First Officer tossed the communicator away among the plants.

It seemed to be their fruiting time; they were bursting all over the area now. Fletcher was caught next, then McCoy, then Sulu and Dimont—and finally Kirk himself.

But Kirk alone was unaffected. As peace and love and tranquillity settled around him like a soggy blanket, he was blazing. His temper was not improved by the discovery that McCoy was arranging for transportation to the ship not of colonists or their effects, but of pod plants. Evidently a couple of hundred were already aboard. Hotter than ever, Kirk ordered himself to be beamed aboard.

He found the bridge deserted except for Uhura, who was busy at her communications board. All other instruments were on automatic.

"Lieutenant, put me through to Admiral Komack at Star Fleet."

As she turned from the board, Kirk was shocked to see that she, too, wore the same sweet, placid expression as the others. She said, "Oh—I'm afraid I can't do that, Captain."

"I don't suppose," Kirk said tightly, "it would do any good to say that was an order."

"I know it was, Captain. But all communications are out."

"All?" Kirk reached past her and began to flick switches on the board.

"All except the ship to surface; we'll need that for a while. I short-circuited all the rest." She patted his arm. "It's really for the best."

She arose, and strolled away from him to the elevator, which swallowed her up. Kirk tried her board again, but to no effect. He slammed his fist down in aggravation. Then he noticed a light pulsing steadily on Spock's library-computer. Moving to that station, he pushed the related button.

"Transporter Room."

There was no answer, but clearly the room was in use. He made for it in a hurry.

He found a line of crew personnel in the corridor leading to the Transporter Room. All waited patiently. Every so often the line moved forward a few steps.

"Report to your stations!"

The crewmen stared at him quietly, benevolently—almost pityingly.

"I'm sorry, sir," one of them said. "We're transporting down to join the colony."

"I said, get back to your stations."

"No, sir."

"Do you know what you're saying?"

"You've been down there," the crewman said earnestly. "You know how beautiful it is—how perfect. We're going."

"This is mutiny!"

"Yes, sir," the crewman said calmly. "It is."

Kirk went back to the bridge and to the communications board. As Uhura had said, ship to ground was still operative. He called McCoy, and was rather surprised to get an answer.

"Bones, the spores of your damnable plants have evidently been carried throughout the ship by the ventilation system. The crew is deserting to join the Omicron colony, and I can't stop them."

"Why, that's fine," McCoy said; his accent had moved considerably south of the Mason-Dixon line, almost to his Georgia boyhood. "Y'all come right down."

"Never mind that. At least you can give me some information. I haven't been affected. Why not?"

"You always were a stubborn cuss, Jimmy. But you'll see the light."

Kirk fumed in silence for a moment. "Can't you tell me anything about the physical-psychological aspects of this thing?"

"*I'm* not concerned with any physical-psychological aspects, Jim boy. We're all perfectly healthy."

"I've been hearing that word a lot lately. Perfect. Everything is perfect."

"Yup. That it is."

"I'll bet you've even grown your tonsils back."

"Uh-huh," McCoy said dreamily. "Jim, have you ever had a real, cold, Georgia-style mint julep?"

"Bones, Bones, I need your help. Can you run tests, blood samples, anything at all to give us some kind of lead on what these things are? How to counteract them?"

"Who wants to counteract Paradise, Jim?"

"Bones—" But the contact had been broken at the other end. Then he headed back for the Transporter Room. He was going to get some cooperation from his ship's surgeon if he had to take the madman by the ears.

He found Spock in Sandoval's office, both looking languidly pleased with themselves.

"Where's McCoy?"

"He said he was going to create something called a mint julep," Spock said, then added helpfully, "That's a drink."

"Captain," Sandoval said. "Listen to me. Why don't you join us?"

"In your own private paradise?"

Sandoval nodded. "The spores have made it that. You see, Captain, we *would* have died three years ago. We didn't know what was happening then, but the Berthold rays you spoke of affected us within two or three weeks of our landing here. We were sick and dying when Leila found the plants."

"The spores themselves are alien, Captain," Spock added. "They weren't on the planet when the other two expeditions were attempted. That's why the colonists died."

"How do you know all this?"

"The spores—tell us. They aren't really spores, but a kind of group organism made up of billions of submicroscopic cells. They act directly on the central nervous system."

"Where did they come from?"

"Impossible to tell. It was so long ago and so far away. Perhaps the planet does not even exist any longer. They drifted in space until finally drawn here by the Berthold radiation, on which they thrive. The plants are native, but they are only a repository for the spores until they find an animal host."

"What do they need us for?"

"Bodies. They do no harm. In return they give the host complete health and peace of mind . . ."

"Paradise, in short."

"Why not?" Spock said. "There is no want or need here. It's a true Eden. There is belonging—and love."

"No wants or needs? We weren't meant for that, any of us. A man stagnates and goes sour if he has no ambition, no desire to be more than he is."

"We have what we need," said Sandoval.

"Except a challenge! You haven't made an inch of progress here. You're not creating or learning, Sandoval. You're backsliding—rotting away in your paradise."

Spock shook his head sadly. "You don't understand. But you'll come around, sooner or later."

"Be damned to that. I'm going back to the ship."

He could not remember any time before when he had been so furious for so long a time.

The *Enterprise* was utterly deserted now. Without anybody aboard her, Kirk had a new and lonely realization of how big she was. And yet for all her immense resources, he was helpless. It was amazing how quickly all her entire complement had surrendered to the Lethe of the spores, leaving him and no one else raging futilely . . .

Raging?

Futilely?

Wait a minute.

There were pod plants all over the ship, so there was no problem about getting a sample. He took it down to McCoy's laboratory, located a slide, and then McCoy's microscope. A drop of water on the slide—right; now, mix some of the spores into the drop. Put the slide under the microscope. It had been decades since he had done anything like this, but he remembered from schooldays that one must run the objective lens down to the object, and then focus *up*, never down. Good; the spores came into register, tiny, and spined like pollen grains.

Getting up again, he went through McCoy's hypospray

rack until he found one of a dozen all labeled *adrenaline*. He sprayed the slide, and then looked again.

There was nothing there. The spores were adrenalin-soluble. He had found the answer. It was almost incredibly dangerous, but there was no other way. He went back to the bridge and called Spock. If Spock didn't answer . . .

''Spock here. What is it now?''

''I've joined you,'' Kirk said quietly. ''I understand now, Spock.''

''That's wonderful, Captain. When will you beam down?''

''I've been packing some things, and I realized there's equipment aboard we should have down at the settlement. You know we can't come back aboard once the last of us has left.''

''Do you want a party beamed up?''

''No, I think you and I can handle it. Why don't I beam you up now?''

''All right. Ready in ten minutes.''

Kirk was waiting in the Transporter Room, necessarily, when the First Officer materialized, and was holding a metal bar in both hands, like a quarter-staff. Spock took a step toward him, smiling a greeting. Kirk did not smile back.

''Now,'' he said harshly, ''you mutinous, disloyal, computerized half-breed—we'll see about you deserting my ship!''

Spock stared. He seemed mildly surprised, but unflustered. ''Your use of the term half-breed is perfectly applicable, Captain, but 'computerized' is inaccurate. A machine can be computerized, but not a man.''

''What makes you think you're a man? You're an overgrown jackrabbit. You're an elf with an overactive thyroid.''

''Captain, I don't understand . . .''

''Of course you don't! You don't have brains enough to understand! All you've got is printed circuits!''

''Captain, if you'll . . .''

''But what can you expect from a freak whose father was a computer and whose mother was an encyclopedia!''

''My mother,'' Spock said, his expression not quite so bland now, ''was a teacher, my father an ambassador.''

''He was a freak like his son! Ambassador from a planet

of freaks! The Vulcan never lived who had an ounce of integrity!''

''Captain—please—don't . . .''

''You're a traitor from a race of traitors! Disloyal to the core! Rotten—like all the rest of your subhuman race! And you've got the gall to make love to that girl! A human girl!''

''No more,'' Spock said stonily.

''I haven't even got started! Does she know what she's getting, Spock? A carcass full of memory banks that ought to be squatting on a mushroom instead of passing himself off as a man. You belong in a circus, Spock, not a starship! Right next to the dog-faced boy!''

With this, Kirk stepped forward and slapped the livid Spock twice, hard. With a roar, Spock swung out at him. Kirk leaped back out of his way, raising the bar of metal between his hands to parry the blow.

It was not much of a fight. Kirk was solely concerned with getting and keeping out of the way, while Spock was striking out with killing force, and with all the science of his once-warrior race. There could be only one ending. Kirk was deprived of the metal bar at the third onslaught, and finally took a backhand which knocked him to the floor against the far wall. Spock, his face contorted, snatched up a stool and lifted it over his head.

Kirk looked up at him and grinned ruefully. ''All right, Mr. Spock. Had enough?''

Spock stared down at him, looking confused. Finally he lowered the chair.

''I never realized what it took to get under that thick hide of yours. Anyhow, I don't know what you're mad about. It isn't every First Officer who gets to belt his Captain—several times.'' He felt his jaw tenderly.

''You—you deliberately did that to me.''

''Yes. The spores, Mr. Spock. Tell me about the spores.''

Spock seemed to reach inside himself. ''They're—gone. I don't belong any more.''

''That was my intention. You said they were benevolent and peaceful. Violent emotions overwhelm and destroy them. I had to get you angry enough to shake off their influence. That's the answer, Spock.''

"That may be correct, Captain, but we could hardly initiate a brawl with over five hundred crewmen and colonists. It is not logical."

Kirk grinned. "I was thinking of something you told me once about certain subsonic frequencies affecting the emotions."

"Yes, Captain. A certain low organ tone induces a feeling of awe. There is another frequency that affects the digestion."

"None of those will do. I want one that irritates people—something that we could hook into the communications station and broadcast over the communicators."

"That would of course also have to involve a bypass signal." Spock thought a moment. "It can be done."

"Then let's get to work."

"Captain—striking a fellow officer is a court-martial offense."

"If we're both in the brig, who's going to build the subsonic transmitter?"

"That's quite logical, Captain. To work, then."

The signal generated by the modified Feinbergers and rebroadcast from the bypassed communicators went unheard in the settlement, but it was felt almost at once, almost as though the victims had had itching powder put under their skins. Within a few minutes, everyone's nerves were exacerbated; within a few more, fights were breaking out all over the colony. The fights did not last long; as the spores dissolved in the wash of adrenalin in the bloodstream, the tumult died back to an almost aghast silence. Not long after that, contrite calls began to come in aboard the *Enterprise*.

The rest was anticlimax. The crew came back, the colonists and their effects were loaded aboard, the plants were cleaned out of the ship except for one specimen that went to Lieutenant Fletcher's laboratory. Finally, Omicron Ceti III was dwindling rapidly on the main viewing screen, watched by Kirk, Spock and McCoy.

"That's the second time," McCoy said, nodding toward the screen, "that Man has been thrown out of Paradise."

"No—this time we walked away on our own. Maybe

we don't belong in Paradise, Bones,'' Kirk said thoughtfully. ''Maybe we're meant to fight our way through. Struggle. Claw our way up, fighting every inch of the way. Maybe we can't stroll to the music of lutes, Bones—we must march to the sound of drums.''

''Poetry, Captain,'' Spock said. ''Nonregulation.''

''We haven't heard much from you about the Omicron Ceti III experience, Mr. Spock.''

''I have little to say about it, Captain,'' Spock said, slowly and quietly, ''except that—for the first time in my life—I was happy.''

Both the others turned and looked at him; but there was nothing to be seen now but the Mr. Spock they had long known, controlled, efficient, and emotionless.

THE DEVIL IN THE DARK

Writer: Gene L. Coon
Director: Joseph Pevny
Guest star: Ken Lynch

Janus was an ugly planet, reddish-brown, slowly rotating, with a thick layer of clouds so turbulent that it appeared to be boiling. Not a hospitable place, but a major source of pergium—an energy metal-like plutonium, meta-stable, atomic number 358; the underground colony there was long-established, highly modern, almost completely automated. It had never given any trouble.

"Almost fifty people butchered," Chief Engineer Vanderberg said bitterly. He was standing beside his desk, nervous and urgent; facing him were Kirk, Spock, Lt. Commander Giotto, Doc McCoy and a security officer named Kelly. "Production's at an absolute stop."

"I can see that," Kirk said, gesturing toward the chart on the office wall, which showed a precipitous dip. "But please slow down, Mr. Vanderberg. What's the cause?"

"A monster." Vanderberg stared at the *Enterprise* delegation with belligerent defensiveness, as though daring them to deny it. He was clearly highly overwrought.

"All right," Kirk said. "Let's assume there's a monster. What has it done? When did it start?"

Vanderberg made an obvious effort to control himself. He pushed a button on his desk communicator, which sat near a globe some ten inches in diameter of what appeared to be some dark-gray crystalline solid. "Send Ed Appel in here," he told it, and then added to Kirk, "My production engineer. About three months ago, we opened a new level. It was unusually rich in pergium, platinum, uranium, even gold. The whole planet's a treasure house, but I've never seen anything like this before, even here. We were just setting up to mine it when things began to happen. First the automatic machinery began to disintegrate, piece by piece. The metal just seemed to dissolve away. No mystery about the agent; it was aqua regia, possibly with a little hydrofluoric acid mixed in—vicious stuff. We don't store vast quantities of such stuff here, I can tell you that. Offhand I don't even know what we'd keep it *in*."

"Telfon," Spock suggested.

"Yes, but my point is, we *don't*."

"You said people were butchered," Kirk reminded him gently.

"Yes. First our maintenance engineers. Sent them down into the halls to repair the corroded machinery. We found them—burned to a crisp."

"Not lava, I suppose," Kirk said.

"There is no current volcanic activity on this planet, Captain," Spock said.

"He's right. None. It was that same damn acid mixture. At first the deaths were down deep, but they've been moving up toward our levels. The last man who died, three days ago, was only three levels below this one."

"I'd like to examine his body," McCoy said.

"We kept it for you—what was left. It isn't pretty."

The office door opened to admit a tough-looking, squat, businesslike man of middle age, wearing a number one phaser at his belt.

"You posted guards? Sentries?" Kirk asked.

"Of course. And five of them have died."

"Has anyone seen this—this monster of yours?"

"I did," said the newcomer.

"This is Ed Appel. Describe it, Ed."

"I can't. I only got a glimpse of it. It was big, and kind of shaggy. I shot at it, and I hit it square, too, a good clean shot. It didn't even slow it down."

"Anything a phaser will not affect," Spock said, "has to be an illusion. Any life-form, that is."

"Tell that to Billy Anderson," Appel said grimly. "He never had a chance. I only got away by the skin of my teeth."

"That's the story," Vanderberg said. "Nobody'll go

down into the lower levels now, and I don't blame them. If the Federation wants pergium from us, they'll have to do something about it."

"That's what we're here for, Mr. Vanderberg," Kirk said.

"Pretty tough, aren't you?" said Appel. "Starship, phaser banks, energy from anti-matter, the whole bit. Well, you can't get your starship down into the tunnels."

"I don't think we'll need to, Mr. Appel. Mr. Spock, I'll want a complete computer evaluation, with interviews from everyone who knows anything about the events here. Mr. Vanderberg, have you a complete subsurface chart of all drifts, tunnels, galleries and so on?"

"Of course."

Spock had been inspecting the dark-gray sphere on the desk. He stepped forward and touched it. "This, Mr. Vanderberg. What is it?"

"It's a silicon nodule. There's a million of them down there. No commercial value."

"But a geological oddity, to say the least, especially in igneous rocks. Pure silicon?"

"A light oxide layer on the outside, a few trace elements below. Look, we didn't call you here so you could collect rocks."

"Mr. Spock collects information, and it's often useful," Kirk said. "We'll need your complete cooperation."

"You'll get it. Just find this creature, whatever it is. I'm dead sick of losing my men—and I've got a quota to meet, too."

"Your order of priorities," Kirk said, "is the same as mine."

They worked in a room just off Vanderberg's office, feeding data to the *Enterprise*'s computer and getting evaluations back by communicator. The charts with which Vanderberg supplied them turned out to be immensely involved—thousands of serpentine lines crossing and recrossing. Their number was incredible, even after allowing for fifty years of tunneling with completely automated equipment. The network extended throughout the entire crust of the planet, and perhaps even deeper.

"Not man-made," Spock agreed. "They may be lava tubes, but if so, they are unique in my experience."

"They won't make hunting any easier," Kirk said. "Bones, what's the word on the autopsy?"

"The plant's physician and the chemists were right, Jim. Schmitter wasn't burned to death. He was flooded or sprayed with that acid mixture."

"Could it eat away machinery, too?"

"Aqua regia will dissolve even gold. What puzzles me is the trace of hydrofluoric acid. It's very *weak* acid, but there are two things it attacks strongly. One of them is glass—you have to keep it in wax bottles, or, as Spock suggested, telfon."

"And the other thing?"

"Human flesh."

"Hmm. It sounds like a mixture somebody calculated very carefully. Mr. Spock, do you think this monster story could be a blind for some kind of sabotage?"

"Possibly, Captain. For example, Mr. Vanderberg thinks that the creature uses the network of tubes to move through. But if you plot the deaths and the acts of destruction, and their times, you find that the creature cannot possibly have appeared at all these points as rapidly as indicated."

"How recent are those tunnel charts?"

"They were made last year—before the first appearance of the alleged monster, but not long before. Moreover, Captain, a sensor check indicates *no* life under the surface of Janus but the accountable human residents of the colony. We are confronted with two alternatives: either to patrol thousands of miles of tunnels, on foot, in the faint hope of encountering the alleged monster; or to find a plausible human suspect who has managed to manufacture and hide an almost inexhaustible supply of this intractable corrosive, and who has a portable, innocuous-looking carrier for it with a capacity of at least thirty liters."

"I rather prefer the monster theory," McCoy said. "If we catch a man behind these murders, I think we ought to lower him into his own acid vat a quarter of an inch at a time."

"If," Spock said, "is the operative word in either case . . ."

He was interrupted by a distant, heavy boom. The room shuddered, the lights flickered, and then an alarm bell was clanging. A moment later, Vanderberg burst in from his office.

"Something's happened in the main reactor room!" he shouted.

They left at a dead run, Vanderberg leading the way, McCoy bringing up the rear. The trail wound up in a tunnel elaborately posted with signs reading CAUTION: RADIATION—MAIN REACTOR CHAMBER—ONLY AUTHORIZED PERSONS BEYOND THIS POINT. The floor of the tunnel looked as though something very heavy had been dragged along it. At the far end was what had once been a large metal door, but which now consisted chiefly of curled strips around a huge hole. Before it was a small, blackened lump which might once have been a man.

Vanderberg recoiled. "Look at that!" Then he hurried toward the ruined door. McCoy knelt quickly beside the charred lump, tricorder out; Kirk and Spock followed Vanderberg.

Inside, the bulk of the reactor was buried in the walls, showing only a large faceplate and a control panel. Pipes crisscrossed the chamber; and an appalled Vanderberg was standing looking down at a sort of nexus of these—a junction that ending in nothing.

Kirk scanned the control panel. "I didn't know anyone still used fission for power."

"I don't suppose anybody does but us. But pergium is money—we ship it all out—and since we have so much uranium nobody wants, we use it here. Or we did until now."

"Explain."

"The main moderator pump's gone. Lucky the cutouts worked, or this whole place would be a flaming mass of sodium."

Spock knelt and inspected the aborted junctions. "Acid again. Like the door. Mr. Vanderberg, do you have a replacement for the missing pump?"

"I doubt it. It was platinum, corrosion-proof, never gave us any trouble; should have lasted forever." Suddenly, visibly, Vanderberg began to panic. "Look, the reactor's shut down now—and it provides heat and electricity and life support for the whole colony! And if we override, we'll have a maximum accident that will poison half the planet!''

''Steady,'' Kirk said, ''Mr. Spock, might we have a replacement on shipboard?''

''No, Captain. To find one, you would need a museum.''

Kirk took out his communicator. ''Kirk to *Enterprise* . . . Lt. Uhura, get me Mr. Scott . . . Scotty, this is the Captain. Could you contrive a perfusion pump for a PXK fission reactor?''

''Hoo, Captain, you must be haverin'.''

''I'm dead serious; it's vital.''

''Well, sir–I could put together some odds and ends. But they wouldn't hold for long.''

''How long?''

''Forty-eight hours, maybe, with a bit of luck. It all ought to be platinum, ye see, and I've not got enough, so I'll have to patch in with gold, which won't bear the pressure long . . .''

''Get together what you need and beam down here with it.''

Kirk put away the communicator and bent upon Vanderberg a look of deep suspicion. ''Mr. Vanderberg, I have to tell you that I don't like the way these coincidences are mounting up. How could some hypothetical monster attack precisely the one mechanism in an almost ancient reactor which would create a double crisis like this? And how would it happen to be carrying around with it a mixture of acids precisely calculated to dissolve even platinum—and also human flesh?''

''I don't know,'' Vanderberg said helplessly. ''You suspect sabotage? Impossible. Besides, Ed Appel *saw* the monster.''

''He says.''

''Ed's been my production chief almost throughout my entire career. I'd trust him with my life. And besides, what would be his motive? Look, dammit, Kirk, my people are being murdered! This is no time for fantasies about spies! The thing is there, it's free, it's just shut us down right under your nose! Why in God's name don't you *do* something?''

"Captain," Spock's voice said from behind them. "Will you come out and look at this, please?"

Kirk went out into the main tunnel to find the First Officer contemplating a side branch. "This is most curious," he said. "This tunnel is not indicated on any of the charts we were provided. It simply was not there before."

"Too recent to be on the maps, maybe?"

"Yes, but how did it get here, Captain? It shows no signs of having been drilled."

Kirk looked closer. "That's so. And the edges are fused. Could it be a lava tube?"

"That seems most unlikely," Spock said. "Had there been any vulcanism on this level since we arrived, everybody would be aware of it. And it joins a charted tunnel back there about fifty yards."

"Hmm. Let's go back to the ship. I feel the need for a conference."

Spock brought with him into the briefing room of the *Enterprise* one of the strange spherical objects Vanderberg had called silicon nodules, and set it on the table. Then he sat down and stared into it, looking incongruously like a fortune-teller in uniform.

"I think it's mass hysteria," McCoy said.

"Hysteria?" Kirk said. "Dozens of people have been killed."

"Some—natural cause. A phenomenon—and people have dreamed up a mysterious monster to account for it."

Spock stirred. "Surely, Doctor. A natural cause. But not hysteria."

"All right. You asked my opinion. I gave it to you. How do I know? Maybe there is some kind of a monster . . ."

"No creature is monstrous in its own environment, Doctor. And this one appears to be intelligent, as well."

"What makes you think so?"

"The missing pump was not taken by accident," Spock said. "It was the one piece of equipment absolutely essential to the operation of the reactor."

Kirk looked at his First Officer. "You think this creature is trying to drive the colonists off the planet?"

"It seems logical."

''Why just now, Mr. Spock? This production facility was established here fifty years ago.''

''I do not know, sir.'' Spock resumed staring at the round object. ''But it is perhaps indicative that Mr. Appel claimed to have hit it with his phaser. He strikes me as a capable but unimaginative man. If he said he hit it, I tend to believe he did. Why was the creature not affected? I have a suggestion, though Dr. McCoy will accuse me of creating fantasies.''

''You?'' McCoy said. ''I doubt it.''

''Very well. To begin with, the colonists are equipped only with phaser number one, no need for the more powerful model having been encountered. This instrument, when set to kill, coagulates proteins, which are carbon-based compounds. Supposc this creature's 'organic' compounds are based on silicon instead?''

''Now surely that *is* a fantasy,'' Kirk said.

''No, it's possible,'' McCoy said. ''Silicon has the same valence as carbon, and a number of simple silicoid 'organics' have been known for a long time. And by the stars, it explains the acids, too. We have hydrochloric acid in our own stomachs, after all. But we're mostly water. Silicon isn't water-soluble, so the aqua regia may be the substrate of the creature's bloodstream. And the hydrofluoric—well, fluorine has an especial affinity for silicon; the result is telfon, which may be what the creature's internal tubing is made of.''

''Do you mean to imply,'' Kirk said slowly, ''that this being goes about killing men with its own blood?''

''Not necessarily, Jim. It may spit the stuff—and sweat it, too, for all I know. Its tunneling suggests that it does.''

''Hmm. It also suggests that it would have to have a form of natural armor plating. But our people have phasers number two, and I defy anything to stand up against that at high power, no matter what it's made of. The question is, how do we locate it?''

''I would suggest,'' Spock said, ''that we start at whatever level these silicon nodules were found.''

''Why? How do they tie in?''

''Pure speculation, Captain. But it would be helpful if it were confirmed.''

''Very well, assemble security forces. I assume that

Mr. Scott is already at work on the reactor? Very good, we'll assemble in Vanderberg's office."

"You will each be given a complete chart of all tunnels and diggings under this installation," Kirk told his forces. "You will proceed from level to level, checking out every foot of opening. You will be searching for some variety of creature which apparently is highly resistant to phaser fire, so have your phasers set on maximum. And remember this—fifty people have already been killed. I want no more deaths . . ."

"Except the bloody thing!" Vanderberg exploded.

Kirk nodded. "The creature may or may not attack on sight. However, you must. A great deal depends on getting this installation back into production."

"Mr. Vanderberg," Spock said, "may I ask at which level you discovered the nodules of silicon?"

"The twenty-third. Why?"

"Commander Giotto," Kirk said, "you will take your detail directly to the twenty-third level and start your search from there. Mr. Vanderberg, I want all of your people to stay on the top level. Together. In a safe place."

"I don't know any safe place, Captain. The way this thing comes and goes . . ."

"We'll see what we can do about that. All right, gentlemen. You have your instructions. Let's get at it."

Spock, Kirk, Giotto and two security guards paused on the twenty-third level while Spock adjusted his tricorder. Most of Giotto's men had already fanned out through the tunnels. Kirk pointed to a spot on Giotto's map.

"We are here. You and your guards take this tunnel, which is the only one of this complex that doesn't already have men in it. As you see, they converge up ahead. We'll rendezvous at that point."

"Aye, aye, sir." The three disappeared into the darkness. Spock continued to scan.

"A strange sensation," the First Officer said. "There are men all about us, and yet because the tricorder is now set for silicon life, it says we are alone down here. No, not quite."

"Traces?"

"A great many—but they are all extremely old. Many thousands of years old. Yet, again, there are many brand new tunnels down here. It does not relate."

"Perhaps it does," Kirk said thoughtfully. "Not tunnels. Not lava tubes. Highways. Roads. Thoroughfares. Mr. Spock, give me an environmental reading, for a thousand yards in any direction."

"Yes, sir—ah. A life-form. Bearing, one hundred eleven degrees, angle of elevation four degrees."

"Not one of our people?"

"No, sir, they would not register."

"Come on!"

They set off quickly, keeping as close on the bearing as the convolutions of the tunnels would allow. Then, ahead, someone screamed—or tried to, for the sound was suddenly cut off. They ran.

A moment later they were looking at a small, blackened lump on the tunnel floor, with a phaser beside it. Grimly, Spock picked up the weapon and checked it.

"One of the guards," he said. "He did not have a chance to fire, Captain."

"And it's only been seconds since we heard him scream . . ."

There was a slithering sound behind them. They whirled together.

In the darkness it was difficult to make out details, except for movement, an undulating crawl forward. The creature was large, low to the ground, somehow wormlike. It was now making another noise, a menacing rattle, like pebbles being shaken in a tin can.

"Look out!" Kirk shouted. "It's charging!"

Both men fired. The monster swung around as the two phaser beams struck its side. With an agonized roar, it leapt backward and vanished.

"After it!"

But the tunnel was empty. It was astonishing that anything of that bulk could move so rapidly. Kirk reached out to touch the wall of the tunnel, then snatched his hand back.

"Mr. Spock! These walls are hot."

"Indeed, Captain. The tricorder says it was cut within the last two minutes."

Kirk heard running footsteps, and then Giotto and a guard, phasers at the ready, appeared behind them.

"Are you all right, Captain? That scream . . ."

"Perfectly, Commander. But one of your men . . ."

"Yes, I saw. Poor Kelly. Did you see the thing, sir?"

"We saw it. In fact, we took a bite out of it."

Spock bent over, then straightened with a large chunk of something in his hand. "And here it is, Captain."

He handed the stuff to Kirk, who examined it closely. Clearly, it was not animal tissue; it looked more like fibrous asbestos. Obviously, Spock's guess had been right.

"Commander Giotto, it looks as though killing this thing will require massed phasers—or a single phaser with much longer contact. Pass the word to your men. And another thing. We already knew it was a killer. Now it's wounded—probably in pain—back in there somewhere. There's nothing more dangerous than a wounded animal. Keep that in mind."

"The creature is moving rapidly through native rock at bearing two hundred one, eleven hundred yards, elevation angle five degrees," Spock said.

"Right," Giotto and the guard went out, and Kirk started to follow them, but Spock remained standing where he was, looking pensive. Kirk said, "What's troubling you, Mr. Spock?"

"Captain, there are literally hundreds of these tunnels in this general area alone. Far too many to be cut by the one creature in an ordinary lifetime."

"We don't know how long it lives."

"No, sir, but its speed of movement indicates a high metabolic rate. That is not compatible with a lifetime much longer than ours."

"Perhaps not," Kirk said. "I fail to see what bearing that has on our problem."

"I mention it, Captain, because if this is the only survivor of a dead race, to kill it would be a crime against science."

"Our concern is the protection of this colony, Mr. Spock. And to get pergium production moving again. This is not a zoological expedition."

"Quite so, Captain. Still . . ."

"Keep your tricorder active. Maintain a constant reading on the creature. We'll try to use the existing tunnels to cut it off. If we have to, we'll use our phasers to cut our own tunnels.'' Kirk paused, then added more gently, ''I'm sorry, Mr. Spock, I'm afraid it must die.''

''Sir, if the opportunity arose to capture it instead . . .''

''I will lose no more men, Mr. Spock. The creature will be killed on sight. That's the end of it.''

''Very well, sir.''

But Kirk was not satisfied. Killing came hard to them all, but Spock in particular was sometimes inclined to hold his fire when his conservation instincts, or his scientific curiosity, were aroused. After a moment, Kirk added, ''Mr. Spock, I want you to return to the surface, to assist Mr. Scott in the maintenance of his makeshift circulating pump.''

Spock's eyebrows went up. ''I beg your pardon, Captain?''

''You heard me. It's vital that we keep that reactor in operation. Your scientific knowledge . . .''

''. . . is not needed there. Mr. Scott knows far more about reactors than I do. You are aware of that.''

After another pause, Kirk said; ''Very well. I am in command of the *Enterprise*. You are second in command. This hunt will be dangerous. Either one of us, by himself, is expendable. Both of us are not.''

''I will, of course, follow your orders, Captain,'' Spock said. ''But we are dealing with a grave scientific problem right here, so on those grounds, this is where I should be, not with Mr. Scott. Besides, sir, there are approximately one hundred of us engaged in this search, against one creature. The odds against both you and me being killed are—'' there was a very slight pause, ''two hundred twenty-six point eight to one.''

Not for the first time, Kirk found himself outgunned. ''Those are good odds. Very well, you may stay. But keep out of trouble, Mr. Spock.''

''That is always my intention, Captain.''

Kirk's communicator beeped, and he flipped it open. ''Kirk here.''

''Scotty, Captain. My brilliant improvisation just gave up the ghost. It couldn't take the strain.''

''Can you fix it again?''

"Nay, Captain. It's gone for good."

"Very well. Start immediate evacuation of all colonists to the *Enterprise.*"

Vanderberg's voice came through. "Not all of them, Captain. Me and some of my key personnel are staying. We'll be down to join you."

"We don't have phasers enough for all of you."

"Then we'll use clubs," Vanderberg's voice said. "But we won't be chased away from here. My people take orders from me, not from you."

Kirk thought fast. "Very well. Get everybody else on board the ship. The fewer people we have breathing the air, the longer the rest of us can hold out. How long is that, Scotty?"

"It's got naught to do with the air, Captain. The reactor will go supercritical in about ten hours. You'll have to find your beastie well before then."

"Right. Feed us constant status reports, Scotty. Mr. Vanderberg, you and your men assemble on level twenty-three, checkpoint Tiger. There you'll team up with *Enterprise* security personnel. They're better armed than you are, so stay in sight of one of them at all times—buddy system. Mr. Spock and I will control all operations by communicator. Understood—and agreed?"

"Both," Vanderberg's voice said grimly. "Suicide is no part of my plans."

"Good. Kirk out . . . Mr. Spock, you seem to have picked up something."

"Yes, Captain. The creature is now quiescent a few thousand yards from here, in that direction."

Kirk took a quick look at his chart. "The map says these two tunnels converge there. Take the left one, Mr. Spock. I'll go to the right."

"Should we separate?"

"Two tunnels," Kirk said. "Two of us. We separate."

"Very well, Captain," Spock said, but his voice was more than a little dubious. But it couldn't be helped. Kirk moved down the right-hand tunnel, slowly and tensely.

The tunnel turned, and Kirk found himself in a small chamber, streaked with bright strata quite unlike the rest of the rock around him. Inbedded in there were dozens of round objects like the one Vanderberg had on his desk, or the one which had so fascinated Spock. He lifted his communicator again. "Mr. Spock."

"Yes, Captain."

"I've found a whole layer of those silicon nodules of yours."

"Indeed, Captain. Most illuminating. Captain—be absolutely certain you do not damage any of them."

"Explain."

"It is only a theory, Captain, but . . ."

His voice was drowned out by the roar of hundreds of tons of collapsing rock and debris. Kirk threw himself against the wall, choking clouds of dust rising around him. When he could see again, it was evident that the roof of the tunnel had fallen across the way he had just come.

"Captain! Are you all right? Captain!"

"Yes, Mr. Spock. Quite all right. But we seem to have had a cave-in."

"I can phaser you out," Spock's voice said.

"No, any disturbance would bring the rest of the wall down. Anyway, it isn't necessary. The chart said our tunnels meet further on. I can just walk out."

"Very well. But I find it disquieting that your roof chose to collapse at that moment. Please proceed with extreme caution. I shall double my pace."

"Very well, Mr. Spock. I'll meet you at the end of the tunnel. Kirk out."

As he tucked the communicator away, there came from behind him a sound as of pebbles being shaken in a can. He spun instantly, but it was too late. The way was blocked.

It was his first clear sight of the creature, which was reared in the center of the tunnel. It was huge, shaggy, multicolored, and knobby with objects which might have been heads, sense organs, hands—Kirk could not tell. It was quivering gently, still making that strange noise.

Kirk whipped up his phaser. At once the creature shuffled backward. Was it now afraid of just one gun? He raised the weapon again, but this time the creature retreated no further. Neither did it advance.

Phaser at the ready, Kirk moved toward the animal, trying to get around it. At once, it moved to block him—not threateningly, as far as Kirk could tell, but just getting in his way.

Spock chose this moment to call him again. "Captain, a new reading shows the creature . . ."

"I know exactly where the creature is," Kirk said, his phaser steadily on it. "Standing about ten feet away from me."

"Kill it, Captain! Quickly!"

"It's—not making any threatening moves, Mr. Spock."

"You don't dare take the chance! Kill it!"

"I thought you were the one who wanted it kept alive," Kirk said, with grim amusement. "Captured, if possible."

"Your life is in danger, Captain. You can't take the risk."

"It seems to be waiting for something. I want to find out what. I'll shoot if I have to."

"Very well, Captain. I will hurry through my tunnel and approach it from the rear. I remind you that it is a proven killer. Spock out."

The creature was silent now. Kirk lowered his phaser a trifle, but there was no reaction.

"All right," Kirk said. "What do we do now? Talk it over?"

He really had not expected an answer, nor did he get one. He took a step forward and to one side. Again the creature moved to block him; and as it did, Kirk saw along one of its flanks a deep, ragged gouge, leaving a glistening, rock-like surface exposed. It was obviously a wound.

"Well, you can be hurt, can't you?"

He lifted the phaser again. The creature rattled, and shrank back, but held its ground. Obviously it was afraid of the weapon, but it would not flee.

Kirk lowered the phaser, and the rattling stopped. Then he moved deliberately back against the nearest wall and dropped slowly into a squatting position, the phaser held loosely between his knees.

"All right. Your move. Or do we just sit and wait for something to happen?"

It was not a long wait. Almost at once, Spock burst into the area from the open end of the tunnel. He took in the situation instantly and his own phaser jerked up.

"Don't shoot!" Kirk shouted. Echoes went bounding away through the galleries and tunnels.

Spock looked from one to the other. As he did so, the creature moved slowly to the other side of the tunnel. Kirk guessed that he could get past it now before it could block him again. Instead, he said, "Come on over, Mr. Spock."

With the utmost caution, his highly interested eyes fastened on the creature, Spock moved to Kirk's side. He looked up at the walls in which the silicon nodules were imbedded. "Logical," he said.

"But what do they mean?"

"I'd rather not say just yet. If I could possibly get into Vulcan mind-lock with that creature—it would be easier if I could touch it . . ."

Before Kirk could even decide whether to veto this notion, Spock stepped toward the animal, his hand extended. It lurched back at once, its rattling loud and angry-sounding.

"Too bad," Spock said. "But obviously it will permit no contact. Well, then, I must do it the hard way. If you will be patient, Captain . . ."

Spock's eyes closed as he began to concentrate. The intense mental power he was summoning was almost physically visible. Kirk held his breath. The creature twitched nervously, uneasily.

Suddenly Spock's face contorted in agony, and he screamed. "The pain! The pain!" With a great shudder, his face ashen, he began to fall; Kirk got to him just in time.

"Thank—you, Captain," Spock said, gasping and steadying himself. "I am sorry—but that is all I got. Just waves and waves of searing pain. Oh, and a name. It calls itself a Horta. It is in great agony because of the wound—but not reacting at all like a wounded animal."

Abruptly, the creature slithered forward to a smooth expanse of floor, and clung there for a moment. Then it moved away. Where it had been, etched into the floor in still smoking letters, were the words: NO KILL I. Both men stared at the sentence in astonishment.

" 'No kill I'?" Kirk said. "What's that? It could be a plea to us not to kill it—or a promise that it won't kill us."

"I don't know. It appears it learned more from me

during our empathy than I did from it. But observe, Captain, that it thinks in vocables. That means it can hear, too.''

''Horta!'' Kirk said loudly. The creature rattled at once and then returned to silence.

''Mr. Spock, I hate to do this to you, but—it suddenly occurs to me that the Horta couldn't have destroyed that perfusion pump. It was platinum, and immune to the acid mix. It must have hidden it somewhere—and we have to get it back. You'll have to re-establish communications, no matter how painful it is.''

''Certainly, Captain,'' Spock said promptly. ''But it has no reason to give us the device—and apparently every reason to wish us off the planet.''

''I'm aware of that. If we can win its confidence . . .''

Kirk took out his communicator. ''Dr. McCoy. This is the Captain.''

''Yes, Captain,'' McCoy's voice answered.

''Get your medical kit and get down here on the double. We've got a patient for you.''

''Somebody injured? How?''

''I can't specify, it's beyond my competence. Just come. Twenty-third level; find us by tricorder. And hurry. Kirk out.''

''I remind you, Captain,'' Spock said. ''This is a silicon-based form of life. Dr. McCoy's medical knowledge may be totally useless.''

''He's a healer. Let him heal. All right, go ahead, Mr. Spock. Try to contact it again. And try to find out why it suddenly took to murder.''

The creature moved nervously as Spock approached it, but did not shy off; it merely quivered, and made its warning pebble-sound. Spock's eyes closed, and the rattling slowly died back.

Kirk's communicator beeped again. ''Kirk here.''

''Giotto, Captain. Are you all right?''

''Perfectly all right. Where are you?''

''We're at the end of the tunnel. Mr. Vanderberg and his men are here. They're pretty ugly. I thought I'd check with you first . . .''

''Hold them there, Commander. Under no circumstances allow them in here yet. The minute Dr. McCoy gets there, send him through.''

"Aye aye, sir. Giotto out."

Spock was now deep in trance. He began to murmur.

"Pain . . . pain . . . Murder . . . the thousands . . . devils . . . Eternity ends . . . horrible . . . horrible . . . in the Chamber of the Ages . . . the Altar of Tomorrow . . . horrible . . . Murderers . . . Murderers . . ."

"Mr. Spock! The pump . . ."

"Stop them . . . kill . . . strike back . . . monsters . . ."

There was the sound of rapidly approaching footsteps and Dr. McCoy, medical bag in hand, broke through into the area. Then he stopped, obviously stunned at what he saw. Kirk silently signaled him to join them, and McCoy, giving the quiescent creature a wide berth, moved to Kirk's side. He said in a low whisper, "What in the name of . . ."

"It's wounded—badly," Kirk whispered back. "You've got to help it."

"Help—*this*?"

"Take a look at it."

McCoy cautiously approached the creature, which was now as immobile as a statue; nor did Spock take any notice.

"The end of life . . . the murderers . . . killing . . . the dead children . . ."

McCoy stared at the gaping wound, and then touched it tentatively here and there. Producing his tricorder, he took a reading, at which he stared in disbelief. Then he came back to Kirk, his face indignant.

"You can't be serious. That thing is virtually made out of stone on the outside, and its guts are plastics."

"Help it. Treat it."

"I'm a doctor, not a bricklayer!"

"You're a healer," Kirk said. "That's your patient. That's an order, Doctor."

McCoy shook his head in wonder, but moved back toward the animal. Spock's eyes were still closed, his face sweating with effort. Kirk went to him.

"Spock. Tell it we're trying to help. A doctor."

"Understood. Understood. It is the end of Life. Eternity stops. Go out. Into the tunnel. To the Passage of Immortality. To the Chamber of the Ages. Cry for the children. Walk carefully in the Vault of Tomorrow. Sorrow for the murdered children. Weep for the crushed ones. Tears for the stolen ones. The thing you search for is there. Go. Go. Sadness for the end of things."

Kirk could not tell whether he was being given directions, or only eavesdropping upon a meditation. He looked hesitantly toward the tunnel entrance.

"Go!" Spock said. "Into the tunnel. There is a small passage. Quickly. Quickly. Sorrow . . . such sorrow. Sadness. Pain." There were tears running down his cheeks now. "Sorrow . . . the dead . . . the children . . ."

Kirk felt a thrill of sympathy. He did not in the least understand this litany, but no one could hear so many emotionally loaded words chanted in circumstances of such tension without reacting.

But the directions turned out to be clear enough. Within a minute he was able to return, the pump in one hand, a silicon nodule in the other.

McCoy was kneeling by the flank of the animal, and speaking into his communicator. "That's right, Lieutenant. Beam it down to me immediately. Never mind what I want it for, I just want it. Move!"

"The ages die," Spock said. "It is time to sleep. It is over. Failure. The murderers have won. Death is welcome. Let it end here, with the murdered children . . ."

"Mr. Spock!" Kirk called. "Come back! Spock!"

Spock shuddered with the effort to disengage himself. Kirk carefully put the pump on the floor of the tunnel, then waited until Spock's eyes were no longer glazed.

"I found the unit," Kirk said. "It's in good shape. I also found about a thousand of these silicon balls. They're—eggs, aren't they, Mr. Spock?"

"Yes, Captain. Eggs. And about to hatch."

"The miners must have broken into the hatchery. Their operations destroyed hundreds of them. No wonder . . ."

There was a roar of sound, and Vanderberg, Appel and what seemed to be an army of armed civilians were trying to jam themselves into the tunnel. They shouted in alarm as they saw the creature. Phasers were raised. Kirk jumped forward.

"No!" he shouted. "Don't shoot."

"Kill it, kill it!" Appel yelled.

Kirk raised his own weapon. "The first man who shoots, dies."

"You can't mean it," Vanderberg said, pointing at the Horta with a finger quivering with hatred. "That thing has killed fifty of my men!"

"And you've killed hundreds of her children," Kirk said quietly.

"What?"

"Those 'silicon nodules' you've been collecting and destroying are eggs. Tell them, Mr. Spock."

"There have been many generations of Horta on this planet," Spock said. "Every fifty thousand years the entire race dies—all but one, like this one. But the eggs live. She protects them, cares for them, and when they hatch, she is the mother to them—thousands of them. This creature here is the mother of her race."

"She's intelligent, peaceful and mild," Kirk added. "She had no objection to sharing the planet with you people—until you broke into the nursery and started destroying her eggs. Then she fought back, in the only way she could—as any mother would—when her children were endangered."

"How were we to know?" Vanderberg said, chastened and stunned. "But—you mean if those eggs hatch, there'll be thousands of them crawling around down here? We've got pergium to deliver!"

"And now you've got your reactor pump back," Kirk said. "She gave it back. You've complained that this planet is a minerological treasure house, if only you had the equipment to get at everything. Well, the Horta moves through rock the way we move through air—and leaves a tunnel. The greatest natural miners in the universe.

"I don't see why we can't make an agreement—reach a *modus vivendi.* They tunnel, you collect and process. You get along together. Your processing operation would be a thousand times more profitable than it is now."

"Sounds all right," Vanderberg said, still a little dubiously. 'But how do you know the thing will go for it?"

"Why should it not?" Spock said. "It is logical. But there is one problem. It is badly wounded. It may die."

McCoy rose to his feet, a broad smile on his face. "It won't die. By golly, I'm beginning to think I can cure a rainy day."

"You cured it?" Kirk said in amazement. "How?"

''I had the ship beam down ten pounds of thermoconcrete, the kind we build emergency shelters out of. It's mostly silicon. I just troweled it over the wound. It'll act as a 'bandage' until it heals of itself. Take a look. Good as new.''

''Bones, my humblest congratulations. Mr. Spock, I'll have to ask you to get in contact with the Horta again. Tell it our proposition. She and her children make all the tunnels they want. Our people will remove the minerals, and each side will leave the other alone. Think she'll go for it?''

''As I said, Captain, it seems logical. The Horta has a very logical mind.'' He paused a moment. ''And after years of close association with humans, I find it curiously refreshing.''

ERRAND OF MERCY

Writer: Gene L. Coon
Director: John Newland
Guest stars: John Abbott, John Colicos

The Klingon scout ship must have known that it was no match whatsoever for the *Enterprise*—after all, the Klingons were experts in such matters. But it fired on the *Enterprise* anyhow as Kirk's ship approached Organia.

The Federation ship's phasers promptly blew the scout into very small flinders, but the attack was a measure of the Klingons' determination to bar the Federation from using Organia as a base. Organia was of no intrinsic value to either side—largely farmland, worked by a people with neither any skill at, nor interest in, fighting—but strategically it was the only Class M planet in the disputed zone, over which negotiations had already broken down. It was, Kirk thought, another Armenia, another Belgium—the weak innocents who always turn out to be located on a natural invasion route.

And the scout ship had had plenty of time to get off a message before opening fire. It had to be assumed that a Klingon fleet was now on the way, if there hadn't been one on the way already. That left very little time for negotiating with the Organians.

Leaving Sulu in charge of the *Enterprise*—with strict orders to cut and run if any Klingon fleet showed up—Kirk and Spock beamed down. The street in which they arrived might have been that of any English village of the thirteenth century: thatched roofs, a few people wearing rude homespun, a brace of oxen pulling a crude wagon. In the distance, something that looked like a ruined castle or fortress, old and decayed, but massive, glowered over the village—an odd construction for a culture that was supposed to have no history of warfare. As for the passersby, they paid no attention to the two starship officers, as if they were used to seeing men beaming down every day. That too seemed rather unlikely.

When the reception committee finally arrived, however, it was cordial enough. It consisted of three smiling, elderly men in fur-trimmed robes, who introduced themselves as Ayelborne, Trefayne and Claymare. Kirk and Spock were received in a small room with roughly plastered walls and no decorations, and containing only a rude table flanked by plain chairs.

Spock lowered his tricorder. "Absolutely no energy output anywhere," he murmured to the Captain. Kirk nodded; the report only confirmed his own impression. This was not a medieval culture making progress toward mechanization, as the original reports had indicated. It was totally stagnant—a laboratory specimen of an arrested culture. Most peculiar.

"My government," he told the smiling Organians, "has informed me that the Klingons are expected to move against your planet, with the objective of making it a base of operations against our Federation. My mission, frankly, is to try to keep them from doing this."

"What you are saying," Ayelborne said, "is that we seem to have a choice between dealing with you or your enemies." In another context the words might have seemed hostile, but Ayelborne was still smiling.

"No, sir. With the Federation you will have a choice. You will have none with the Klingons. They are a military dictatorship, to which war is a way of life. We offer you protection."

"Thank you," Ayelborne said. "But we do not need your protection. We have nothing anyone could want."

"You have this planet, and its strategic location. If you don't move to prevent it, the Klingons will move in, just as surely as your sun sets. We'll help you with your defenses, build facilities . . ."

"We have no defenses, Captain, nor are any needed," the man called Claymare said.

"Excuse me, but you're wrong. I've seen what the Klingons do to planets like yours. They are organized into vast slave labor camps. You'll have no freedom whatsoever. Your goods will be confiscated. Hostages will be taken and killed. Your leaders will be confined. You'd be better off on a penal planet.''

''Captain,'' Ayelborne said, ''we see that your concern is genuine, and we appreciate it. But again we assure you that there is absolutely no danger . . .''

''I assure you that there is! Do you think I'm lying? Why?''

''You did not let me finish,'' Ayelborne said gently. ''I was going to say, there is no danger to ourselves. You and your friend are in danger, certainly. It would be best for you to return to your ship as soon as possible.''

''Gentlemen, I beg you to reconsider. We can be of immense help to you. In addition to the military assistance, we can send in technicians, specialists. We can show you how to feed a thousand people where you fed one before. We'll build schools and help you educate your young, teach them what we know—your public facilities seem to be almost non-existent. We could remake your world, end disease, hunger, hardship. But we are forbidden to help you if you refuse to be helped.''

''A moving plea,'' Trefayne said. ''But . . .''

He was interrupted by the beeping of Kirk's communicator. ''Excuse me, sir,'' he said. ''Kirk here.''

''Captain,'' said Sulu's voice. ''A large number of Klingon vessels just popped out of subspace around us. I didn't get a count before they opened fire but there must be at least twenty. My screens are up now, and I can't drop them to beam you aboard.''

''You're not supposed to,'' Kirk said harshly. ''Your orders are to run for it and contact the fleet. Come back only if you've got better odds. Mark and move!''

He switched off and stared at the three Organians.

''You kept insisting that there was no danger. Now . . .''

''We are already aware of the Klingon fleet,'' Trefayne said. ''There are in fact eight more such vessels now assuming orbit around our planet.''

''Can you verify that, Spock?''

''No, sir, not at this distance,'' Spock said. ''But it seems a logical development.''

"Ah," Trefayne added. "Several hundred armed men have just appeared near the citadel."

Spock aimed his tricorder in that direction and nodded. "Not just hand weapons, either," he said. "I am picking up three or four pieces of heavy-duty equipment. How did he know that so quickly, I wonder?"

"That doesn't matter now," Kirk said grimly. "What matters is that we're stranded here, right in the middle of the Klingon occupation army."

"So it would seem, sir," Spock said. "Not a pleasant prospect."

"Mr. Spock," Kirk said, "you have a gift for understatement."

The Klingons were hard-faced, hard-muscled men, originally of Oriental stock. They were indeed heavily armed and wore what looked like vests of mail. They moved purposefully and efficiently through the streets, posting guards as they went. The few Organians they met smiled at them and moved quietly, passively out of their way.

To compound Kirk's bafflement, the uncooperative Organian council—if that is what the three men were—had provided him and Spock with Organian clothing and offered to conceal them, an offer entailing colossal risks. Then, rummaging through the discarded uniforms, Kirk demanded suddenly: "Where are our weapons?"

"We took them, Captain," Ayelborne said. "We cannot permit violence here. Claymare, remove the uniforms. No, we will have to protect you ourselves. Mr. Spock presents the chief problem. He will have to pose as a Vulcan trader—perhaps here to deal in kevas and trillium."

"They're aware that Vulcan is a member of the Federation," Kirk said.

"But harmless to the Klingons. You, Captain, might well be an Organian citizen, if . . ."

He got no further. The door flew open, and two Klingon soldiers burst in, gesturing with handguns for everyone to back up. They were followed by a third Klingon, an erect, proud man, who did not need his commander's insignia to show who he was.

Spock and the Organians retreated; Kirk stood his

ground. The Klingon commander looked quickly around the room.

"*This* is the ruling council?" he said contemptuously.

Ayelborne stepped forward again, smiling. "I am Ayelborne, temporary council head. I bid you welcome."

"No doubt you do. I am Kor, military governor of Organia." He glared at Kirk. "Who are you?"

"He is Baroner," Ayelborne said. "One of our leading citizens. This is Trefayne . . ."

"This Baroner has no tongue?"

"I have a tongue," Kirk said.

"Good. When I address you, you will answer. Where is your smile?"

"My what?"

"The stupid, idiotic smile everyone else seems to be wearing." Kor swung on Spock. "A Vulcan. Do you also have a tongue?"

"My name is Spock. I am a dealer in kevas and trillium."

"You don't look like a storekeeper. What is trillium?"

Spock said smoothly, and with an impassive face: "A medicinal plant of the lily family."

"Not on Organia, it isn't," Kor said. "Obviously a Federation spy. Take him to the examination room."

"He's no spy," Kirk said angrily.

"Well, well," Kor said. "Have we a ram among the sheep? Why do you object to us taking him? He's not even human."

Kirk caught the warning glance Spock was trying to disguise and made a major effort to control himself as well. "He has done nothing, that's all."

"Coming from an Organian, yours is practically an act of rebellion. Very good. They welcome me. Do you also welcome me?"

"You're here," Kirk said. "I can't do anything about it."

Kor stared hard at him, and then permitted himself a faint smile. "Good honest hatred," he said. "Very refreshing. However, it makes no difference whether you welcome me or not. I am here and I will stay. You are now subjects of the Klingon Empire. You will find there are many rules and regulations, which will be posted. Violation of the smallest of them will be punished by death; we will have no time for justice just now."

"Your regulations will be obeyed," Ayelborne said.

Kirk felt his mouth tightening. Kor saw it; apparently he missed very little. He said:

"You disapprove, Baroner?"

"Do you need my approval?"

"I need your obedience, nothing more," Kor said softly. "Will I have it?"

"You seem to be in command," Kirk said, shrugging.

"How true." Kor began to pace. "Now. I shall need a representative from among you, liaison between the forces of occupation and the civilian population. I don't trust men who smile too much. Baroner, you are appointed."

"Me?" Kirk said. "I don't want the job."

"Have I asked whether or not you wanted it? As for the rest of you—we Klingons have a reputation for ruthlessness. You will find that it is deserved. Should one Klingon soldier be killed here, a thousand Organians will die. I will have *order*, is that clear?"

"Commander," Ayelborne said, "I assure you we will cause you no trouble."

"No. I am sure you will not. Baroner, come with me."

"What about Mr. Spock?"

"Why are you concerned?"

"He's my friend."

"You have poor taste in friends. He will be examined. If he is lying, he will die. If he is telling the truth, well, he will find that business has taken a turn for the worse. Guards, remove him."

The guards, covering Spock with their weapons, gestured him out the door; Spock went meekly. Kirk started after him, only to be shoved back by Kor himself. Kirk could not help flushing, but Kor only nodded.

"You do not like to be pushed," the Klingon said. "Good. At least you are a man I can understand. Come with me."

Kor had set up shop in the citadel Kirk and Spock had seen on their first arrival. Seen close up, and from inside, the impression it gave of vast age was intensified. Kor had furnished one room with a large Klingon insignia, a desk, one chair, and nothing else; Kirk stood. Kor signed a document and thrust it across the desk at him.

''For duplication and posting,'' he said. ''From this day on, no public assemblages of more than three people. All publications to be cleared through this office. Neighborhood controls will be established. Hostages selected. A somewhat lengthy list of crimes against the state.''

Kirk glanced impassively at the list, aware that Kor as usual was watching him closely. The commander said: ''You do not like them?''

''Did you expect me to?''

Kor only grinned. At the same time, the door opened and Spock was thrust inside, followed by a Klingon lieutenant. To Kirk's enormous relief, his first officer looked perfectly normal.

''Well, lieutenant?''

''He is what he claims to be, Commander,'' the lieutenant said. ''A Vulcan trader named Spock. And he really is trading in the other kind of trillium, the vegetable kind; it seems it has value here.''

''Nothing else?''

''The usual apprehension. His main concern seems to be how he will carry on his business under our occupation. His mind is so undisciplined that he could hold nothing back.''

''All right, Baroner, would you like to try our little truth-finder?''

''I don't even understand it.''

''It's a mind-sifter,'' Kor said, ''or a mind-ripper, depending on how much force is used. If necessary, we can empty a man's mind as if opening a spigot. Of course, what's left is more vegetable than human.''

''You're proud of it?'' Kirk said.

''All war weapons are unpleasant,'' Kor said. ''Otherwise they would be useless.''

''Mr. Spock, are you sure you're all right?''

''Perfectly, Baroner. However, it was a remarkable sensation.''

''That's enough,'' Kor said, with a trace of suspicion

in his voice. "Vulcan, you can go. But just bear in mind that you're an enemy alien, and will be under scrutiny at all times."

"Quite, Commander," Spock said. "I understand you very well."

"Baroner, return to your council and get that proclamation posted. Until the people know what's expected of them, it's up to you to keep the people in order."

"Or I will be killed," Kirk said.

"Precisely. I see that you too understand me very well."

Once in the street, Kirk glanced about quickly. Nobody was within earshot, or seemed to be following them. He said quietly to Spock:

"That mind-sifter of theirs must not be quite the terror they think it is."

"I advise you not to underestimate it, Captain," Spock said. "I was able to resist it, partly with a little Vulcan discipline, partly by misdirection. But on the next higher setting, I am sure I would have been unable to protect myself."

"And I wouldn't last even that long. The question is now, how do we persuade these Organians to resist? To strike back, knock the Klingons off balance, maybe until the Federation fleet gets here?"

"Verbal persuasion seems to be ineffective," Spock said. "Perhaps a more direct approach?"

"My thought exactly. Didn't I see something that looked like a munitions dump near the citadel? I thought so. All right, let's try a little direct communication."

"The suggestion has merit. Would tonight do?"

"If you have no previous engagement," Kirk said. "Of course, we're short of tools."

"I am sure," Spock said, "the Klingons will provide whatever is necessary."

"It's a pleasure doing business with you, Mr. Spock."

The guards at the munitions depot were tough and highly trained, but nothing they had yet encountered on Organia had prepared them for anyone like Kirk and Spock. Two of them went quietly to sleep on duty within a few seconds of each other, were relieved of their phasers and locked in an empty storeroom, lovingly cocooned in baling wire.

Inside the dump, Kirk located a crate that seemed to contain some form of chemical explosive. He opened it. A few moments later, Spock appeared from the shadows.

"I have one of their sonic grenades," he murmured, "and I have improvised a delayed-action fuse. The combination should provide a most satisfactory display."

"Good. Fire away."

Spock made a pulling gesture, carefully tucked the grenade inside the crate, and ran, Kirk at his heels.

Three minutes later, the night lit up. Giant explosions rocked it, followed by strings of subsidiary explosions. Missiles flew in all directions. An immense cloud formed over the city, its underside flickering with the fires and detonations below it.

"You were right, Mr. Spock," Kirk said when the clamor had begun to die down. "A most satisfactory display. I only hope that the council draws the moral. Obviously they can't fight the Klingons directly, but they could make Organia useless to them."

"In the meantime," Spock said. "I earnestly suggest that we find ourselves a deep, deep hole, Captain. Somehow I cannot think that Commander Kor will believe the Organians did this."

"Nor do I. Let's vanish."

Perhaps one or both of them should have anticipated Kor's next move. Two hours later, in an empty, lightless hut near the outskirts of the village, they heard a distant, buzzing whine from the direction of the citadel.

"Phasers," Spock said.

"Yes, Klingon phasers—a lot of them, all being fired at once. Odd. It doesn't sound at all like a battle, or even a riot."

The answer came rumbling down the street outside within another hour, in the form of an armored vehicle. From a loudspeaker atop it, a recorded voice was bellowing:

"This is the military governor. In the courtyard of my headquarters, two hundred Organian hostages have just been killed. In two hours more, two hundred more will die, and two hundred more after that—until the two Federation spies are turned over to us. The blood of the hostages is on your hands. The executions will be carried on until the saboteurs are surrendered. This is the order of Kor. Attention, all subjects! This is the military governor. In the courtyard of my headquarters . . ."

Kirk and Spock were silent for a long time after the lumbering vehicle had become inaudible. At last Kirk whispered, appalled: "That tears it."

"Yes, Captain. And the Organians no more know where we are than Kor does. We must give ourselves up, and speedily."

"Wait a minute. Let me think."

"But all those lives . . ."

"I know, I know. We've got to turn ourselves in. But we've still got sidearms. Just possibly, we can force Kor to call the killings off."

"Unlikely, Captain," Spock said. "Commander Kor may be a mass murderer, but he is clearly also a soldier."

"In that case, we'll just have to do as much damage as we can and keep them busy until the fleet shows up. The Federation invested a lot of money in our training, Mr. Spock. I think they're about due for a small return."

Spock estimated the odds against making it all the way to Kor's office at "approximately" 7,824.7 to one; but surprise and the phasers—set to heavy stun force—both told in their favor. When they reached the door of Kor's office, it was open, and no alarm had sounded. They could see the commander inside, seated at his desk, hands over his face, brooding. It seemed almost possible that he did not relish butchering unarmed civilians. When he looked up and saw Spock and Kirk before him, phasers leveled, a look of interest and appreciation appeared on his face.

"Just stay seated, Commander," Kirk said. "Mr. Spock, cover the door."

"You have done well to get this far, through my guards."

"I am afraid," Spock said, "that many of them are no longer in perfect operating condition."

"The fortunes of war. What next?"

"We're here. Call off your executions."

"You have not surrendered," Kor said in a reasonable tone of voice. "Drop your weapons and I will call off the executions. Otherwise you have accomplished nothing."

"We can certainly kill you," Kirk said grimly. "You're the Klingon governor. That might put quite a crimp in your operations."

"Don't be hasty," Kor said. "You will be interested in knowing that a Federation fleet is due here within the hour. Our fleet is prepared to meet them. Shall we wait and see the results before you pull the trigger?"

"I don't plan to pull it at all unless you force me to."

"Sheer sentimentality—or at best, mercy. A useless emotion in wartime. It is not a Klingon weakness." Kor smiled. "Think of it. While we talk here, in space above us the destiny of the galaxy will be decided for the next ten thousand years. May I offer you a drink? We can toast the victory of the Klingon fleet."

"I would suggest that you are premature," Spock said. "There are many possibilities."

"Commander," Kirk added, "we once had a nation on Earth called the Spartans—the finest warriors who ever walked our planet. They had their hour of conquest—but it was their chief opponent, Athens, who survived. Sparta knew only the arts of war. Athens was known as the mother of all the arts."

"A consoling analogy, but I think a little out of date," Kor said. "True, there is always some element of chance in a major war. Today we conquer; someday we may be defeated. But I am inclined to doubt it."

He rose. The phaser in Kirk's hand did not waver by a millimeter. Kor ignored it.

"Do you know why we are so strong?" Kor said. "Because we are a unit. Each of us is part of the greater whole. Always under surveillance. Even a commander like myself, always under surveillance, Captain. As you will note."

He waved toward the ceiling, smiling. Kirk did not look up.

"No doubt there's a scanner up there. However, Mr. Spock has the door covered, and I have you. At the first disturbance, I fire."

There was something remarkably like a yelp of dismay

from Spock, and then the unmistakable sound of a phaser hitting the stone floor. Kirk whirled, trying to keep Kor simultaneously in the corner of his eye. At the same instant the door, which Spock had closed, burst open again and two Klingon soldiers charged in.

Kirk pulled the trigger. The phaser did not fire. Instead, it turned red hot in his hand. Instinctively, he threw it from him.

"Shoot!" Kor shouted. "Shoot, you blockheads!"

There were at least five soldiers in the room now, but one after another they too dropped their weapons, which lay glowing quietly against the stone. After a moment of dismay, the guards charged. Kirk set himself and swung.

He could feel the flesh of his fist sear as it hit. A Klingon grabbed him from behind—then let go with a howl.

"Their *bodies* are hot!" one of the soldiers gasped. He was almost drowned out by a roar from the commander, who had tried to pick up a paper knife.

After that, for an eternal ten seconds, the enemies simply glared at each other incredulously. There was no sound but that of heavy breathing.

Then Ayelborne and Claymare came in. They were wearing their eternal smiles, which even Kirk had come to loathe.

"We are terribly sorry that we have been forced to interfere, gentlemen," Ayelborne said. "But we could not permit you to harm one another. There has been enough violence already."

"What are you talking about, you sheep?"

"We have put a stop to your brawling," Claymare said. "That is all."

"Let me get this straight," Kirk said slowly. "*You* put a stop to it? You? You mean you're going to slap our wrists?"

"Please, Captain," Claymare said. "You already know the answer. Not only your guns, but all instruments of destruction on this planet now have a potential surface temperature of three hundred and fifty degrees. Simple intent to use one renders it inoperative."

"My fleet . . ." Kor said.

"The same conditions exist upon both the opposing Star Fleets," said Ayelborne. "There will be no battle."

"Ridiculous," Kor growled.

"I suggest you contact them. You too, Captain. Your ship is now within range of your communications device."

Kirk took out his communicator. "Kirk to *Enterprise*. Come in."

"Captain! Is that you?"

"Kirk here—report, Mr. Sulu."

"I don't know what to report, sir," Sulu's voice said. "We were just closing with the Klingon fleet when every control in the ship became too hot to handle. All except the communications board. If this is some new Klingon weapon, why didn't it disable that too?"

"I don't know,"Kirk said heavily. "Stand by, Mr. Sulu. Ayelborne, how did you manage this?"

"I could not explain it to you with any hope of being understood, Captain. Suffice it to say that as I stand here, I also stand upon the bridge of your ship, upon the bridge of every ship, upon the home planet of the Klingon Empire, on the home planet of your Federation. Some of my energies I share with your weapons—I and the rest of my people. We are putting a stop to this insane war."

"How dare you?" Kor shouted.

"You can't just stop our fleet," Kirk said, equally angrily. "You've got no right . . ."

"What happens in space is none of your business . . ."

"It is being stopped," Ayelborne said. "Unless both sides agree to an immediate cessation of hostilities, all your armed forces, wherever they may be, will be totally disabled."

"We have legitimate grievances against the Klingons," Kirk said. "They've invaded our territory, killed our citizens . . ."

"The disputed areas are not your territory," Kor raged. "You were trying to hem us in, cut off vital supplies, strangle our trade."

"Look here," Kirk said to the Organians, fighting himself back to some semblance of control. "We didn't ask you to intervene, but you should be the first to side with us now. The two hundred hostages who were killed . . ."

"No one has died, Captain," Claymare said calmly. "No one has died here for uncounted thousands of years. Nor do we mean that anyone shall."

"Let me ask you, Captain, what it is that you are defending," Ayelborne added, gently, as if amused. "Is it the right to wage war? To kill millions of innocent people? To destroy life on a planetary scale? Is that the 'right' you refer to?"

"Well, I . . ." Kirk said, and stopped. "Of course, nobody wants war, but sometimes you have to fight. Eventually, I suppose, we . . ."

"Yes, eventually you would make peace," Ayelborne said. "But only after millions had died. We are bringing it about now. The fact is, in the future you and the Klingons will become fast friends. You will work together in great harmony."

"Nonsense!" Kor said. Kirk realized that he had been standing shoulder to shoulder with the Klingon and moved away hastily.

"Of course, you are most discordant now," Ayelborne said. "In fact, you will have to leave. The mere presence of beings like yourselves is acutely painful to us."

"What do you mean?" Kirk said. "You don't differ significantly from us, no matter what tricks you've mastered."

"Once we did not differ significantly," Claymare said. "But that was millions of years ago. Now we have developed beyond the need for physical bodies at all. This appearance is only for your convenience. Now we shall put it off."

"Hypnosis!" Kor cried. "Captain, those weapons may never have been hot at all! Grab them!"

Ayelborne and Claymare only smiled, and then they began to change. At first it was only a glow, becoming brighter and brighter, until they looked like metal statues in a furnace. Then the human shape faded. It was as if there were two suns in the room.

Kirk shut his eyes and covered them with both arms. He could still see the light. Finally, however, it began to fade.

The Organians were gone.

"Fascinating," Spock said. "Pure thought—or pure energy? In any event, totally incorporeal. Not life as we know it at all."

"But the planet," Kirk said. "The buildings—this citadel . . ."

"Probably the planet is real enough. But the rest, conventionalizations, no doubt, just as they said. Useless to them—points of reference for us. I should guess that they are as far above us on the evolutionary scale as we are above the amoeba."

There was a long silence. Finally, Kirk turned toward Kor.

"Well, Commander," he said, "I guess that takes care of the war. Since the Organians aren't going to let us fight, we might as well get started on being friends."

"Yes," Kor said. He thrust out his hand. "Still, in a way, Captain, it's all rather saddening."

"Saddening? Because they're so much more advanced than we are? But it took millions of years. Even the gods didn't spring into being overnight."

"No, that doesn't sadden me," Kor said. "I'm only sorry that they wouldn't let us fight." He sighed. "It would have been glorious."

THE CITY ON THE EDGE OF FOREVER*

Writer: Harlan Ellison
Director: Joseph Pevney
Guest star: Joan Collins

*The script for this story differed drastically in some respects from Mr. Ellison's original version, which he was kind enough to send to me. In writing this adaptation I tried to preserve what I thought were the best elements of *both* scripts; but it was tricky to manage and it is more than possible that I have wound up owing apologies all around. It was a poetic and brilliant piece to begin with; if it is a botch now, the fault is entirely mine.—JB

Two drops of cordrazine can save a man's life. Ten drops of that unpredictable drug will sometimes kill. When a defective hypospray went off in McCoy's hand, a hundred times that amount was pumped into his body in a split second.

With a frenzied, incoherent cry, the ship's surgeon fled the bridge. Within minutes the entire ship was altered. The library tapes on cordrazine said that at such dosages, paranoia was a frequent outcome—but McCoy knew the ship too well. By the time a search was organized, he had reached the Transporter Room and beamed himself down to the planet the *Enterprise* was orbiting.

The transporter had been monitoring what appeared to be a curious time disturbance on the surface of the unknown world. The settings had not been changed; whatever was down there, McCoy was now in the heart of it. Kirk would have liked to have had more information about it first, but there was no chance of that now. They had to go after McCoy. Kirk picked Spock, Scott, Uhura, Davis and a Security guard, and, of course, himself.

They materialized in the midst of extensive ancient ruins. Much of it was almost dust, but there were enough scattered sections of broken wall and piled stone to provide hiding places for McCoy.

This planet was *cold*. A burnt-out sun hung dolorously in the sky, producing a permanent, silvery twilight. It was a dead world, an ash. The ruins extended past the horizon—a city of tremendous size—but there could have been no life in it for ten thousand centuries. It takes a long time for a sun to burn out.

In the midst of the desolation, one object was polished like new, drawing Kirk's eyes instantly. It was a large, octagonal mirror—or was it a mirror? Its framed, cloudy surface was nebulous, shifting. Whatever it was, it gleamed, untarnished, agelessly new. A cube, also untarnished but half-buried in dust and rubble, sat beside it. Spock aimed his tricorder at it.

''Whatever that is,'' Kirk said crisply, ''make it the hub of our search pattern. Fan out.''

The group separated quickly—all but Spock, who was drawing closer to the shining object, instead. He said, ''Unbelievable!''

''Mr. Spock?''

''Sir, this one, single object is the source of all the time displacement we detected out in space. I do not understand where it gets the power, or how it applies it. It cannot be a machine, not in any sense that we understand the term, but . . .''

Kirk eyed the object. ''Then what is it?''

At once, the dead air was stirred by a heavy hum; and then a resonant, vibrantly throbbing voice spoke from the object itself.

''A . . . question,'' the voice said. ''A question. Since before your sun burned hot in space, and before your race was born, I have awaited a question.''

''What are you?'' Kirk said.

''I . . . am the Guardian of Forever.''

''Are you a machine,'' Kirk said, ''or a being?''

''I am both, and neither. I am my own beginning, my own ending.''

Spock said, ''I see no reason for answers to be couched in riddles.''

''I answer all questions as simply as I can.''

''What is your function, then?''

''I am a time portal. Through me the great race which once lived here went to another age.''

''Past or future?'' Spock said.

''The past,'' the voice said, like a sigh. ''Always and only the past. And to their past, which you cannot share. I can only offer you yours. Behold—the birth of the planet you both share."

In the mirror, there was suddenly the image of a solar system forming out of a changing, cooling fireball . . . and somehow Kirk knew that it was not an image at all, but a distant view of a fact. A moment later, they were looking at a primeval, shoreless sea; and then, suddenly, a jungle of tree ferns.

"Mr. Spock," Kirk said thoughtfully, "if that is a doorway back through time, could we somehow take Bones back a day in time, then relive that accident? Stop that hypo spitting into him?"

"We would have to catch him first," Spock said. "Besides, Captain, look at the speed at which centuries are passing. To step through precisely on the day we wish would appear to be impossible."

"Guardian, can you change the speed at which yesterday passes?"

"I was made to offer the past in this manner," the Guardian said. "I cannot change."

Egypt waxed, waned, passed. Atlantis sank. Skin-clothed barbarians suddenly became Hellenes. Spock was getting it all into the tricorder.

"It's strangely compelling, isn't it?" Kirk said. "To step through there, lose oneself in another world—"

He was interrupted by a shout and a scrambling sound. He spun. McCoy, who evidently had been quite nearby, was headed straight for the time vortex at a dead run. Nobody but Kirk and Spock were anywhere near him.

Spock dropped the tricorder and intercepted, but McCoy, his eyes frighteningly wild, twisted away from him. That left no one but Kirk, who made a flying dive; but McCoy did a little dance step of broken field maneuvering and was free. Kirk landed painfully and rolled over.

"Bones!" he shouted. "No, no!"

But he was in time only to see McCoy disappear into the cloudy octagonal frame, his body popping out of sight as though it had been swallowed. Then the vortex was as blank as it had been when they first saw it.

"Where is he?" Kirk demanded.

"He has passed into what was," said the voice of the Guardian.

"Captain," said Uhura, a little breathlessly. She had arrived on the run. "I've lost contact with the ship. I was talking to them, and it suddenly went dead. No static; just . . . nothing."

"The communicator is all right?"

"Yes, sir. It just seems like there's nothing up there."

The Guardian said, "Your vessel, your beginning, all that you knew is gone."

Kirk felt a fearful sinking of his heart, remembering that episode when he and Spock and an archaic man named John Christopher had fought not to be noticed by the world of the 1970s. He said grayly, "McCoy has somehow changed history."

Scott had joined the party. He said, "This time we're stranded, Captain?"

Kirk did not answer, but Spock nodded. "With no past—no future."

"Captain," Uhura said. "I'm . . . I'm frightened."

Kirk looked slowly up into the black and star-littered sky of the nameless planet, empty now of the *Enterprise*, without even a sun to give it warmth and joy.

"Earth's not even out there," he said. "Not the one we knew. We are totally alone—without even a history."

"We shall have to remake it," Spock said.

"How, Mr. Spock?"

"We will have to go back in time ourselves—attempt to set right whatever it was that the doctor changed. I was recording images at the time he left. By synchronizing just out of phase with that, I believe I can approximate when to jump. Perhaps within a month before he arrived. Or a week if we are lucky."

"Guardian!" Kirk said. "If we are successful . . ."

"Then you will be returned. It will be as though none of you had gone."

"Just finding McCoy back there," Scott said, "would be a miracle."

Spock said, "There is no alternative."

"Scotty, when you think you've waited long enough—whatever 'long enough' might mean now—then . . ." Kirk shrugged. "Each of you will have to try it. Even if you fail, you'll be alive in some past world, somewhere."

"Stand ready, Captain," Spock said. "I think the time is coming around again."

They were standing in a seamy, down-at-the-heels city street, with murky glass storefronts and an occasional square four-wheeled vehicle. Over one store was a large sign proclaiming:

CCC CAMPS—SIGN UP HERE

and beside it, another store with a sign that said FREE SOUP and a smaller sign with an arrow, reading FORM A LINE. Queues of shabby men in caps and shapeless coats were moving, very slowly, into both stores.

Spock said, bemused, "Is this the heritage my mother's people brag about?"

"This," Kirk said with disgust, "is what it took us five hundred years to crawl up from. Never mind that now—somebody's going to spot us pretty quickly, and our clothes aren't exactly period costumes. Let's do something about that first."

He drew Spock down the alley in which they had first popped into this world. "There's a line of clothes back there."

"I'm afraid I will draw attention either way, Captain."

"Well, Mr. Spock," Kirk said, "if we can't disguise you, we'll have to find a way to explain you. Here, put these on." He pulled down from a line two shirts, two pairs of pants, an old jacket and a wool stocking cap.

"You might see if you can locate me a ring for my nose," Spock said. "But Captain, aside from the fact that this is theft, I do not believe we ought to change clothes out in the open. As I remember your history, old Earth was rather stuffy about such matters."

"That's right. Okay, let's march." Kirk rolled the clothing into a bundle and tucked it under his arm.

They made it back to the open street without incident. Kirk began to feel better. "You know," he said, "I rather like this century. Simpler, easier to manage. Why, I might even find I actually have a considerable talent for . . . *wump*!"

He had run squarely into the arms of a large, bulkily obvious Security-guard type. The blue-uniformed man looked up and down, and then at the clothing bundle Kirk was shifting back and forth. At last he said pleasantly, "Well?"

"Uh, yes," Kirk said. "You are a police officer. I seem to remember . . ."

It seemed to be the wrong tack. Kirk let the sentence trail off and tried a friendly smile. The policeman smiled back, but he did not move. Behind Kirk, Spock said, "You were saying something about a considerable talent, sir?"

This was also a mistake, since it attracted the officer's attention to Spock, and especially to his pointed ears. Kirk said hurriedly, "My friend is, uh, Chinese, of course. The ears, ah, are actually easily explained. You see . . ."

The policeman remained absolutely silent. Kirk was stumped.

"Perhaps the unfortunate accident I had in childhood . . ." Spock prompted.

"In the fields, yes," Kirk said quickly. "Caught his head in a mechanical, uh, rice-picker. Fortunately . . . an Amellican missionary living nearby, who happened to have been a skilled plastic surgeon in civilian life . . ."

"Sure an' t'God that's enough, now," the policeman said. "Drop the bundle, hands up against that wall. Phwat a story."

"Yes, sir," Kirk said. As he was about to turn, he stopped and stared at the policeman's shoulder. "Uh, careless of your wife to let you go out that way."

"What?" the policeman said, raising his nightstick.

"Quite untidy, sir," Spock said, picking up the cue. "If you will allow me . . ."

He pinched the policeman's shoulder gently, and, equally gently, the policeman sagged to the pavement.

"And now, Captain . . ." he said.

"Yes," Kirk said. "As I recall, the appropriate expression is—flog it!"

Police whistles—an eerie, unfamiliar sound—were shrilling behind them as they ducked into an open cellar door. The cellar was dismal: a coal bin, an old furnace, mountains of litter, a few mildewed trunks, all looking like monsters in the dimness. They changed clothes quickly. Kirk wore the jacket; Spock pulled the stocking cap down over his elegant, dangerous ears.

Spock got out his tricorder. Nothing came out of it but an unpleasant electronic squeal, like an echo of the fading police whistles.

The two men looked at each other over the coal pile. At last Kirk said, "Obviously this is not a game. Time we faced the unpleasant facts. Status, Mr. Spock?"

"First," Spock said precisely, "I *believe* we have about a week before Dr. McCoy arrives. But as far as being certain of that . . ."

"And arrives where? New York, Boise, Honolulu, Outer Mongolia?"

"Obviously, I do not know. There is a theory . . ." Spock hesitated. Then he shrugged and plowed on. "The theory is that time can be regarded as fluid, like a river, with currents, backwash, eddies. Like the solar-system analogies of atomic structure, it is more misleading than enlightening, but there may be a certain truth to it all the same."

"Mr. Spock, if I didn't know you better, I'd suspect you were trying to educate me."

"No, sir. I mean only to suggest that the same time current which swept McCoy to a certain place or event has taken us to the same place or event . . . Unless that is the case, I believe we have no hope."

"Odds?"

"Captain, in time there are no odds; you are pitting an infinite series of instants against an utterly improbable event. And yet . . ." Spock held up the tricorder. "Locked in here is the *exact* place, the exact moment, even exact images of what McCoy did back here. If I could hook this into the ship's computer for just a few moments . . ."

"Any chance that you could build a makeshift computer?"

"In this zinc-plated, vacuum-tube culture?" Spock said. "None at all. I have no tools, no parts, no supplies . . . I do not even know the line voltage."

"I see," Kirk said slowly. "Yes, it would pose a complex problem in logic. Forgive me, Mr. Spock. I do sometimes expect too much of you."

Spock's head turned sharply, but at the same time the overhead bulb in the basement went on yellowly and there was the sound of a door opening at the head of the stairs to the ground floor. A young woman's voice called strongly, "Who's there?"

Both men came to their feet as the girl came down the stairs. Despite the obvious savagery of the period, she seemed quite unafraid. She was simply dressed and not very pretty, but her voice was instantly arresting.

"We didn't want to trespass, miss," Kirk said. "But since it was getting cold out there . . ."

She looked at him with cool appraisal and said, "A lie is a bad way to say 'hello.' Was it really that cold?"

"Well," Kirk said, "no. We were being chased by a police officer."

"Because . . . ?"

"Petty theft. These clothes. We had no money."

"I see." She looked both of them over. "It's the same story all over. I need some help. Sweeping up, washing dishes, general cleanup. Are you willing to work?"

"At what scale of payment?" Spock said. Kirk looked at him in astonishment. The first officer added, "I need radio tubes and so forth. Parts, wire . . . It is . . . a hobby."

"Fifteen cents an hour for ten hours a day," the girl said. "I'm not exactly wealthy, either. Will it do? Good. Your names?"

"I'm Jim Kirk. His name is Spock."

"I'm Edith Keeler," she said crisply, "and you can start by cleaning up down here."

She smiled pleasantly and went back up the stairs, leaving Kirk a little startled by her brisk, no-nonsense attitude and her utter fearlessness. At last he looked around, found a pair of brooms, and tossed one to Spock.

"Radio tubes and so on, eh?" he said. "Well, Mr. Spock, I approve. I think everyone should have a hobby. It keeps them off the streets."

The mission was a mixture of things which Kirk only vaguely recognized: part church, part dining room, part recreation area. It was furnished with tables and low benches, and there was a low dais at the front where workers dispensed soup and coffee. To one side, was a large tool box, fastened with an ungainly padlock with a dial on its face. Shabbily dressed men sat to either side of Kirk and Spock, waiting without enthusiasm. The nearest, a small man with thin features who looked remarkably like some sort of rodent, eyed the two of them.

"You'll be sorry," he said, with exaggerated boredom.

"Why?" Kirk said.

"You expect to eat free or something? Now you gotta listen to Miss Goodie Twoshoes."

"Good evening," Edith's voice said, on cue. She was already striding toward the dais; now she mounted it. The meagerness of the audience did not seem to discourage her. She was both casual and cheerful. "Now, as I'm sure at least someone out there has said, you've got to pay for the soup."

There was some laughter. "Not that she's a bad-lookin' broad," the rodent said, *sotto voce*. "But if she really wanted to give a guy somethin' . . ."

"Shut up," Kirk said. Then, noticing Spock's eye on him, he added, "I'd like to hear this."

"Of course," Spock said, noncommittally.

"Let's start as we always do—by getting something straight," Edith said. "Why do I work, connive, and maybe even cheat a little in order to keep feeding you? I don't know. It's something that I do. But I've got no patience with parasites. If you can't break off with booze, or you've gotten out of the habit of work, or you *like* being a bad risk, I don't want you and you're not welcome to the soup."

Kirk listened with astonishment. He did not know what he had expected, but surely not this.

"Of course," she went on, "I know that every day is a fight to survive. That's all you have time for. But I've no use for a man who uses free soup as an excuse to give up fighting. To survive at all, you need more than soup. You need to know that your life is worth living, no matter what.

"Shadow and reality, my friends. That's the secret of getting through these bad times. Know what is, and what only seems to be. Hunger is real, and so is cold. But sadness is not.

"And it is the sadness that will ruin you—that will kill you. Sadness and hate. We all go to bed a little hungry every night, but it is possible to find peace in sleep, knowing you have lived another day, and hurt no one doing it."

"Bonner the Stochastic," Spock whispered.

"He won't be born for more than two hundred years. Listen."

"It's difficult not to hate a world that treats us all like this," Edith was saying. "I know that. Difficult, but not impossible. Somebody once said that hate is only the absence of love, but that's not a message that a man can absorb on an empty stomach. But there's something else that's true: Love is only the absence of hate. Empty the hatred from your hearts and you are ready for love. If you can go to bed tonight free of hatred, you have already won a major victory.

"And that's all of my sermon for today. Eat hearty, mates."

She stepped down and left the big, gloomy room.

"Most interesting," Spock said. "An uncommon insight."

"An uncommon woman," Kirk replied quietly; but Edith Keeler, coming up behind them, evidently overheard him.

"You two are uncommon workmen, Mr. Kirk," she said. "The basement looked like it had been scrubbed and polished."

Kirk thought about his days as a midshipman and at last saw some use for holystoning; but he said only, "Then we report back for more work?"

"At seven A.M. Do you have a flop for the night?"

"A what?"

Edith studied him curiously. "You're really new at this, aren't you? A 'flop' is a place to sleep. There's a vacant room where I live, two dollars a week. If you want it, I'll guide you there when we're through with these dishes."

"Indeed we do," Kirk said. "Thank you."

Like everything else they had yet seen in this culture, the room was plain and depressing: a few pieces of scarred furniture, a sagging bed, limp and sooty curtains. Now, however, some of it was masked by the Medusahead of wires, coils and banks of old vacuum tubes which Spock was attaching to his tricorder. As Kirk came in with a small paper sack of groceries, plus another small package of hardware, Spock said abstractedly, "Captain, I must have some sponge platinum, about a kilogram. Or a block of the pure metal, perhaps ten grams, would be even better."

Kirk shook his head. "I bring assorted vegetables for you, bologna and a hard roll for me. The other bag, I assure you, contains neither platinum, gold nor diamonds; nor is it likely to in the future. It has just a few secondhand pieces of equipment, and those took the other nine-tenths of our combined earnings for three days to fill your order for them."

"Captain, you're asking me to work with equipment which is hardly better than stone knives and bearskins."

"We have no choice," Kirk said. "McCoy may be here any day now. We've no guarantee that there's some current in time pulling us all together. This has to work—with or without platinum."

"Captain," Spock said glacially, "in three weeks at this rate, perhaps a month, I might complete the first mnemonic circuits . . ."

There was a knock, and then Edith poked her head through the door.

"If you can go out now," she said, "I can get you both five hours' worth at twenty-two cents an hour. What on earth is *that*?"

"I am endeavoring, Ma'am," Spock said with dignity, "to construct a mnemonic circuit out of stone knives and bearskins."

"I don't know what that means," she said, "but if you want the work you'd better hurry." She withdrew.

"She's right. Let's go, Mr. Spock."

"Yes, Captain, in just a moment . . . It seems to me that I saw some tools for finely detailed work in the mission."

"Yes, the man who was working on the, uh, cuckoo-clock was using them. That girl has more things going on around there than a TKL computer. Clock repair project, woodworking, the tailor shop in the back . . ."

"You were quite right, Captain," Spock said. "She is a fascinating study. Well, I am ready now. I doubt that twenty-two cents an hour will advance me far, but those tools . . ."

"Just be sure you return them."

"Believe me, Captain," the Science Officer said, "my first taste of petty theft was also my last."

The auxiliary rig to the tricorder now nearly filled the

room. It looked like a robot squid constructed by a small child, but it clicked, whirred and hummed purposefully. Clearly, Spock did not like the noise—he was used to machines that made as little fuss as possible—but he wasted no time trying to eliminate it. He straightened abruptly.

"Captain, I may have stumbled onto something."

Kirk sniffed. "You've got a connection burning somewhere, too."

"I am loading these lines too heavily. But this may be a focal point in time. Watch the tricorder screen. I have slowed the recording it made from the time vortex."

Kirk peered at the small tricorder screen. It showed Edith Keeler's face; then the image sharpened, and he realized that it was a newspaper photo. The paper was dated February 23, 1936—six years from "now." Over the photo was a headline: FDR CONFERS WITH SLUM AREA 'ANGEL.' The caption read, *The President and Edith Keeler today conferred for more than an hour on her proposal to . . .*

There was a mean snap of sparks, a curl of smoke and the image collapsed. "Quick!" Kirk said. "Can you get it back?"

"Even if I could, it would not help us," Spock said. "Something was wrong even before the short circuit. On the same memory trace, I saw a *1930* newspaper article."

"What of it? Either way, we know her future, Spock. Within six years from now, she's going to become important, nationally recognized . . ."

"No, sir," Spock said quietly. After a pause, he began again. "No, Captain.—What I saw was Edith Keeler's obituary. She never became famous. She will die this year in some kind of accident."

"You're mistaken! They can't both be true!"

"I'm afraid they can, Captain," Spock said. "She has two possible futures—depending upon what McCoy does."

"What . . . ? Oh, I see. McCoy has something to do with her living or dying. And in his present state . . ." The shock of the notion halted Kirk for an instant, but he forced himself to go on. "Mr. Spock, did McCoy kill her? Is *that* how all of history was changed?"

"I cannot tell, Captain. Something still worse is possible."

"What, man?"

"That he might have changed history by *preventing* her from being killed."

"Get this thing fixed! We've got to find the answer before McCoy gets here!"

"And what then, Captain?" Spock said. "Suppose we find that to set things right, Edith Keeler must die? That to restore our future, we must prevent McCoy from saving her? What then?"

"I don't know," Kirk said fiercely. "But we've got to find out. Did you get the jewelers' tools all right? That box was closed with a combination lock."

"Not a proper lock, sir. A childish device in probability . . ."

". . . and he opened it like a real pro," Edith's voice said behind them. Both men spun. She spared the jury-rigged apparatus only one glance, and then turned back to Spock. "Question: Why? I want to hear only one answer. Please make it the honest one."

Spock pointed to the rig. "You have seen this work going on before," he said. "I needed delicate tools. They would have been returned in the morning."

Edith eyed him. Perhaps his alien appearance gave her less than full confidence; or perhaps the very temper of the times was against him. She said, "Gadgetry doesn't impress me. Theft does. Out you go."

"Miss Keeler," Kirk said, "if Mr. Spock said they were important to have, and that you'd get them back in the morning, you may depend upon his word."

"I'll accept that," she said slowly, "on certain conditions. Chiefly, that Mr. Kirk answer my questions. And you needn't look so innocent, either. You know as well as I how out of place you both are here."

"Interesting," Spock said. "Where would you say we do belong, Miss Keeler?"

"You, Mr. Spock?" She nodded toward Kirk. "At his side. As if you've always been there, always will be. But where *he* belongs . . . well, I'll work it out eventually."

"I see," Spock said. "Well, I'll go on with this . . ."

"I'll go on with this—Captain," Edith Keeler said, smiling at Kirk. "Even when he doesn't say it, he does."

She led the way out. In the hall, she said, "By the way, why *does* he call you Captain? Were you in the war together?"

"We . . . served together."

"It shows. And you don't want to talk about it. Why? Is it something you think you've done wrong? Are you afraid of something? Whatever it is, let me help."

Kirk took her by the arms, and for a moment came very close to kissing her. He did not; but he did not release her, either.

" 'Let me help,' " he said. "A hundred years or so from now, I think it was, a famous novelist will write a classic using that theme. He recommends those three words even over 'I love you.' "

"Your tenses are rather mixed," she said. "A hundred years from now? And where was he? Or, where will he be from?"

"A silly question, a silly answer," Kirk said roughly. He pointed at the ceiling. "From about there. A planet circling that far left star in Orion's belt."

She looked up involuntarily; and this time, he did kiss her. He was not a little surprised to find it returned.

Spock turned as Kirk came back into the room. He asked no questions, but it was clear that he would welcome some answers.

"All she said was, 'Let me help you,' " Kirk said painfully. "She's something of a saint, Mr. Spock."

"She may be martyred," Spock said. "To history. Look here."

He switched on his apparatus. "This is how history went after McCoy changed it. I picked up the thread just after you went out. See: in the late 1930's a growing pacifist movement, called World Peaceways. Its influence on the government delayed the United States' entry into the Second World War. Apparently very few people knew that World Peaceways was German-controlled. While peace negotiations dragged on, Germany had time to complete its heavy water experiments."

"Hitler and Nazism won the war?"

"Yes. Because this lets them develop the fission bomb first. Let me rerun it, Captain. You will see that there is no mistake. And Edith Keeler was the guiding spirit of the peace movement."

"But," Kirk said, "she was *right*. Clearly, peace would have been . . ."

"She was right," Spock said, "but at the wrong moment. With the atomic bomb, and their primitive rockets to carry it, the Nazis captured the world, Captain. And after that, barbarism. The Nazi yoke was so heavy that the world tore itself apart trying to throw it off. Spaceflight never did develop."

"No," said Kirk, softly, in pain.

"And all that," Spock said implacably, "because McCoy came back and somehow kept her from dying as she should have, in a street accident. We have to stop him."

"Exactly how did she die? What day?"

"I can't be that precise," Spock said. "I am sorry, Captain."

"Mister Spock," Kirk said slowly, "I believe I am in love with Edith Keeler."

"I know," Spock said, very quietly indeed. "That is why I said, 'I'm sorry.' "

"And if I don't stop McCoy . . . ?"

"Then, you save her. And millions will die who did not die in what would have been our history."

"Abstract millions," Kirk said. "A different history. But Edith Keeler is here. She's real. She deserves to live."

"And so do Scott, Uhura, the others we left behind—or ahead. Sir, you are their Captain. They are waiting for you, in the ruined city on the edge of Forever. They, and the future that nurtured you. The choice is yours."

It had to be faced; but he could not face it—not yet. There would be time to decide when the crisis came. Of course.

In the meantime, there was still Edith . . . still. Spock said no more about the matter. He was with the two of them sometimes, somehow silently supportive. At others, guided perhaps by his peculiar form of semitelepathy, he vanished at just the appropriate moment.

This time, they emerged together from the mission, but separated almost at once. Spock started away from the twilight street, while Edith and Kirk crossed to the opposite sidewalk. Edith seemed even happier than usual.

"If we hurry," she said, "we can catch that Clark Gable movie at the Orpheum. I'd really love to see it, Jim."

Kirk smiled. "A what kind of movie?"

"That's funny," she said, looking up as if startled. "Dr. McCoy said almost the same . . ."

Kirk stopped dead in his tracks and whirled to face her, his heart suddenly racing.

"McCoy?" He took her by the shoulders, his fingers tightening until she winced. "*Leonard* McCoy? Edith, this is important."

"Why, yes. He's in the mission, in a little room upstairs. He's been very sick, almost raving, but I think he's nearly . . ."

"Spock!" Kirk shouted. "Edith—wait here for me."

He ran across the street, waving at the first officer. Spock turned back, his whole face a question; but he did not need to ask it. As the two men met in front of the mission door, McCoy came out of it.

The surgeon stopped dead in surprise, and then a grin split his face. There was a great deal of hand shaking and back thumping, with all three of them talking at once.

"Bones, where have you . . ."

"How'd you find me? And for that matter, where *are* we?"

"When Edith said 'Dr. McCoy' I . . ."

"Remarkable that you should have been that close to us . . ."

"I seem to have been sick for a long time . . ."

Kirk looked quickly back toward Edith. Her expression was mostly one of intense curiosity; but she also looked as though she felt a little left out of it all. As she saw him turn to her, she stepped out into the street.

She did not see the moving van lumbering down on her. *This was the time.* Without a moment's thought, Kirk ran toward her.

"Captain!" Spock's voice shouted. *"No!"*

Kirk froze, his body a solid mass of anguish. At the same time, McCoy's mouth opened in a wordless yell and he lunged for the curb. With a terrible flash of self-hatred, Kirk, knowing what *must* come next, threw himself in McCoy's way, blindly, almost sobbing. McCoy stumbled. Edith cried out, and then there was the screaming shriek of brakes.

Then, silence.

"Jim," McCoy said raggedly. "You deliberately stopped me . . . Did you hear me? Do you know what you just did?"

Kirk could not reply. Spock took his arm gently. "He knows," he said. "Soon you will know, too. And what *was* . . . now *is* again."

Kirk sat at his desk in the *Enterprise*, back in uniform, staring at nothing. Behind him, Spock's voice said:

"Coordinates from the bridge, Captain."

The words meant nothing. The papers before him meant nothing. It was as though he were all but dead.

"Jim," Spock said.

The deadness did not lift, but a small thread of startlement crept through it. Kirk turned slowly.

"Mr. Spock," he said. "That's the first time you've ever called me anything but Captain."

"I had to reach you," Spock said gently. "But never mind the coordinates. Jim, on my world, the nights are very long. In the morning, there is the sound of silver birds against the sky. My people know there is always time enough for everything. You'll come with me for a rest. You'll feel comfortable there."

"All the time in the world . . ."

"And filled with tomorrows."

Suddenly, the bitterness welled up. "Not for her," Kirk said. "For us, but not for her. She was negligible."

"No, Captain, she was not. Her death saved uncountable billions of people. Both the living and the yet unborn. Far from negligible."

"And I failed her," Kirk said, groping for understanding. "I didn't save her. And I loved her."

"No. You acted," Spock said. "No woman was ever loved as much, Jim. Because no other woman was almost offered the universe for love."

OPERATION—ANNIHILATE!

Writer: Steven W. Carabatsos
Director: Herschel Daugherty
Guest stars: Joan Swift, Craig Hundley

The spread of the insanity was slow, and apparently patternless, but it was also quite inexorable. The first modern instance in the record was Aldebaran Magnus Five. Then, Cygni Theta 12. Most recently, Ingraham B—recently enough so that the *Enterprise* had been able to get there within a year of the disaster.

Nothing had been learned from the mission. There were no apparent connections among the three planets—except that on each one, the colonists had gone totally, irrevocably mad, all at the same time, and had killed each other. It hadn't been warfare; the people had simply fallen upon each other in the streets, in their homes, everywhere, until there were none left.

It was Spock who had suggested that there would nevertheless be a pattern, if one assumed that the long-dead civilizations of the Orion complex had fallen to the same cause. The archeological evidence was ambiguous, and besides, the peoples of the cluster had not been human. There was no *a priori* reason why they should have been subject to the afflictions of human beings.

Nevertheless, given the assumption, the computer was able to plot a definite localization and rate of spread—like an amoeboid blotch upon the stars, thrusting out a pseudopod to another world at gradually shortening intervals. If the radioactive dating of the deaths of the Orion civilizations was correct, as it almost surely was—and if the assumption was correct, which was sheer speculation—then the madness had taken two hundred years to appear on its second victim-world, less than a century to crop up a third time, and the next outbreak was due within the next month.

"On Deneva, I would say," Spock added. "An Earth-type planet, colonized about a century ago. Pleasant climate, no hazardous life-forms. Of course, I could well be completely wrong about this, since my basic premise is completely *ad hoc*."

"Never mind the logical holes," Kirk said. "Mr. Sulu, lay in a course for Deneva. Warp factor four. Lieutenant Uhura, tell Starship Command where we're going and why. When we break into the Denevan system, raise the planet."

But there was no time for that. The first thing the sensors showed when the *Enterprise* emerged in that system was a Denevan ship apparently on its way toward throwing itself into the Denevan sun.

"Status!" Kirk said tensely.

"He's got a huge jump on us, Captain," Sulu said. "A one-man vessel—sub-light velocity but under heavy acceleration."

"Contact, Captain," Uhura said.

"Denevan ship, this is the *USS Enterprise*! Break your heading! You're on a collision course with your sun! Fire your retros!"

From the speaker came a faint and agonized voice. "Help me . . . please . . . help me . . ."

"We're trying to! Spock, can we reach him with a tractor beam?"

"No, sir," Spock said. "Too much solar magnetism."

"Sulu, intercept. Denevan, pull back! Fire your retros!"

"Help me, please . . . take it out . . . take it out . . . please . . ."

"Skin temperature four hundred degrees," Spock said. "Rising fast."

"He's too close, Captain," Sulu said. "He'll burn—and so will we if we keep this up."

"Keep closing."

"Skin temperature now eight hundred degrees," Spock said.

Suddenly the Denevan's voice came through again,

much stronger, and much changed. It seemed almost jubilant. "I did it! It's gone! I'm free. I'm free! I won—oh great God, the sun, *the sun* . . ."

The words ended in a terrible scream.

"He's gone, Captain," Sulu reported.

"Vector!" Kirk shouted. Then, as the great ship shuddered into its emergency turn, he stared blindly at the now-silent speaker.

"What did he do that for?" he said. "Even if his instruments weren't working, we warned him."

"Obviously suicide," Spock said.

"But why? And Spock, I don't think he wanted to die. You heard him. He asked us to help him."

"Suicides are not rational," Spock said. "By definition."

"Mr. Spock, that may be perfectly good logic, but I'm afraid it doesn't satisfy me. And I hate puzzles. They don't look good on the log."

"Captain," Uhura said. "I've gotten through to Deneva itself."

"Good, let's hear it. Hello, Deneva, USS *Enterprise* calling."

"*Enterprise*, please hurry!" a strong voice cried promptly. There was a blast of static. "Help us! I don't have much time! They'll know!"

"Another madman?" Kirk said to nobody in particular. "Lieutenant, can't you clean up some of that static?"

"It's solar static, sir. Should clear gradually as we pull away."

"Hello, Deneva, *Enterprise* here. Please repeat."

"Hurry! Hurry! They'll know in a minute! We need help!"

There was more static. Kirk said: "We're on our way, Deneva. What's wrong? Please explain."

But there was no answer, only still more static. Uhura turned in her chair. "Contact broken, Captain. I'm trying to reestablish, but I think they've switched out."

"All right, Sulu. Course for Deneva—on the double."

The landing party—Kirk, Spock, McCoy, two security guards, and Yeoman Zahara—materialized in an empty city street. There were supposed to be more than a million colonists and their descendants on this planet, nearly a hundred thousand in this city alone; yet the place looked deserted.

"Where is everybody?" Kirk said.

Spock scanned in a circle with his tricorder. "They are here. But they are all indoors. Apparently just sitting there. There is a signal center in that building across the street. It is inoperative, but the power is up."

"All right, let's . . ."

"Party approaching," Spock interrupted. "Four people—make it five. Coming fast."

He had hardly spoken when five men came around the corner at top speed. They seemed to be ordinary civilians, but Kirk had the instant impression that their faces were warped with agony. All carried clubs. The instant they saw the group from the *Enterprise*, they burst into a bestial shrieking. It was impossible to tell which of them was screaming what.

"Run! Get away! We don't want to hurt you! Go back! Look out!"

"Fire to stun!" Kirk shouted. The Denevans charged, swinging their clubs.

"Go away! Please! They'll get you! No! Get away from here! We'll have to kill you . . ."

Kirk fired, followed by the others. The charging Denevans fell in a clatter of clubs. Kirk approached them cautiously. Despite the fact that they had just taken the heavy stun force of a phaser blast at close range, they seemed to be twitching slightly.

"Could you make out all that shouting, Mr. Spock?"

"Indeed. They seemed greatly concerned for our safety—so concerned that they wanted to brain us. This may not be *the* insanity, but . . ."

"But it'll do for now," Kirk said. "Bones, check them over."

McCoy checked the unconscious bodies quickly, then rose, shaking his head puzzledly. "Something decidedly odd," he said. "These people should be pretty close to being vegetables for the next few hours. But I'm getting high readings, as though their nervous systems were being violently stimulated even while they're . . ."

He was interrupted by a woman's scream. Kirk whirled. "Fan out!" he said. "That came from that signal center. Come on!"

The scream came again. Inside the building there was a dark lobby of some sort, and a closed door, which turned out to be locked. Kirk lunged against it.

"Open up!" he shouted. "We're from the *Enterprise*."

"They're here!" the woman screamed. "They're here! Keep them away!" Over her voice there was a heavy buzzing sound, which seemed to be rising in pitch.

Kirk and the two guards hit the door together. It burst inward. Here was the signal center, all right, but it looked shoddy, unused. An elderly man lay unconscious on the floor; across the room, a girl was desperately holding a panel of some sort over a ventilation outlet, fighting with all her strength. As the party broke in she staggered backward, dropping the panel, covering her face with her hands and sobbing wildly.

Kirk pointed to the old man while he took the girl in his arms. "It's all right. You're safe."

She screamed again and began to struggle.

"Bones, a hypo! I can't hold her."

McCoy already had his sprayjet out, and a moment later the girl too had collapsed. "The man's alive," he reported. "Some sort of seizure, or maybe just exhaustion. I'd better get them both up to the ship."

"Right. Mr. Spock, you heard her. She called out that *they* were here. Your guess?"

"Notice, Captain," Spock said. "Rags stuffed under the door. Pieces of board jammed across the windows. As if they were in a state of siege."

"But by what? There are no harmful life-forms on this planet. And our sensors didn't pick up anything that didn't belong here."

"I am baffled, Captain."

"Bones, beam up with those two people and bring them around. I'm going to have to ask some questions. Mr. Spock, we'll go outside and resume looking around. Zahara, are you recording all of this?"

"Of course, Captain."

As they emerged from the communications center, Kirk

saw one of the security men standing near a sheltered, shadowy alleyway. He moved toward the party as it appeared.

"Anything, Abrams?"

"Yes, sir, but don't ask me what. Something moving back in there. Making a buzzing sound."

Kirk looked around, and then up. All the windows above him seemed to be empty, but in one there was the face of a man. His expression was a terrible combination of agony, fear and desperate hope.

"You!" Kirk shouted at him. "I want to talk to you!"

The face contorted and vanished. Kirk grunted with annoyance. "All right, Spock, Abrams, let's go see what's back in there."

Phasers ready, they moved cautiously into the darkened alley. Almost at once the buzzing noise got louder, and something about the size of a football flew through the air over their heads. Then another.

"Phasers on kill!" Kirk shouted. But for a moment there were no more. Then suddenly Spock pointed. Another such object clung to a wall. Kirk fired.

The beam hit the thing squarely. But it refused to vanish. It simply clung to the wall for a long moment, even under the full force of the beam, and finally slipped off and fell to the earth.

They closed in warily, but there seemed to be no more of the creatures back here. Spock took tricorder readings on the downed object, which seemed to be no more than a gelatinous mass, amorphous, colorless, as though somebody had dumped a jellyfish out of a bucket. Kirk stared at it incredulously.

"What is that?"

"It isn't anything," Spock said promptly. "Not only should it have been destroyed by the phaser blast, but it does not register on the tricorder."

"It's real enough all the same," Kirk said. "And it acted alive. Can we take it along, Spock?"

"I advise against it. We have no proper equipment, and it may well be toxic, corrosive—there are a dozen possibilities."

"Whatever they are, they seem to like these shadows,"

Kirk said. "Let's get out back into the light. We know where we can find them if we want them, anyhow."

As they retreated, the buzzing noise began again. The next instant, one of the objects shot past Kirk and hit Spock squarely in the back, knocking him off his feet. The thing clung to him. His hands tore uselessly at his back. Then, somehow, it was gone, and Spock was lying face down in the alley.

Kirk knelt beside him. "Spock! Are you all right? The thing's gone. Can you stand?"

Spock's hands were still clutching his back. As Kirk spoke, he rolled over, his entire face working with the effort to control himself. He got slowly to his knees. Then his mouth opened, and pitching forward, he began to scream.

Spock was in sick bay under heavy sedation; thus far, McCoy had been unable to think of anything else to do for him. In the interim, however, he had managed to revive the elderly man and the girl the landing party had found in the signal room on Deneva. The girl's name was Aurelan, the man's Menen. They did their best to answer Kirk's questions, but he found their answers difficult to comprehend.

"I know it must sound insane, Captain," Aurelan said, "but it's quite true."

Kirk shot a look at Zahara, who was recording. "You mean these things, whatever they are, have taken over the entire planet?"

"Except for ourselves," Menen said.

"There are over a million inhabitants of Deneva."

"There are millions of *them*," Menen said.

"When did they get to Deneva? How?"

"About four months ago," Menen said with some difficulty, "in a spaceship. We don't know any more than that. They didn't give us the time."

"It's a nightmare, Captain," Aurelan said. "Worse than a nightmare."

"The things don't communicate with you?"

"Oh, they communicate all right," Aurelan said bitterly. "Through pain. Once they attack you, something happens inside. We're not doctors, we don't know the details. But life is agony from then on."

Menen added, "My son told me—before he died—that they need bodies the way we need tools. Arms and legs—human beings. And once they take over, they can't be resisted. The people who tried to kill you in the street didn't want to hurt you. They wanted your help. But the things ordered them to attack you, and they had no choice."

"But why didn't they take you two over too?"

"We think they spared us so that we could maintain normal contacts with other planets and ships. They want ships, Captain. They need them. They're forcing our people to build ships right now."

"My brother, Noban . . ." Aurelan began.

"He's the man who flew his ship into the sun?"

Aurelan nodded sadly. "The creatures had him. He almost went mad from the pain. But he told us that Deneva is just a way-station for them. They mean to spread out. You see . . ." She paused and swallowed. "Their hosts become useless after a while. They go mad. And then the things need new hosts. More people. Planet after planet. They come, and they leave madness, and they go to the next . . ."

"In the name of God, Captain," Menen said, "you've got to do something!"

"I'll do what I can," Kirk said. "What about my first officer, Mr. Spock?"

"Is he important to your ship?" Aurelan said.

"Extremely," Kirk said. "And to me personally. He's one of my closest friends."

"In that case," Menen said, "kill him."

"What!"

"Kill him. Now. Quickly. Because only endless agony lies ahead for him, agony that will end in madness. If you are his friend, be merciful."

"Security calling Captain Kirk," said the bridge speaker.

"Kirk here."

"Captain, this is Ames. Mr. Spock has attacked his nurse and fled. He seems deranged."

"All decks security alert. He may be dangerous. Aurelan, Menen, you'd better get to your quarters and stay there."

They went quietly. Only seconds later, it seemed, the elevator door opened again and Spock charged out.

"Get away from the controls!" he screamed. "I have to take her down!"

Before anyone could move, he had reached the helm and had knocked Sulu down and away with one sweeping blow. The navigator and Scott leapt on him, but Spock was a powerful man; he sent them reeling.

"Security to the bridge!" Uhura was calling into her mike. "Alert! General alert to the bridge!"

Kirk joined in the melee, but they were all handicapped by the desire not to hurt Spock; the first officer had no such compunctions. They only barely managed to keep him away from the controls.

Then three security men appeared, and in a few moments Spock was held fast. "I have to take the ship down!" he panted. "I don't want to! Help me! Help me!"

Somehow McCoy was on the scene now, and elbowing his way through the crowd, he gave the first officer a shot. Spock collapsed at once.

"Get him back to sick bay," Kirk said, "and this time, strap him down."

The security men carried him out, with Kirk and McCoy following. It was a grim procession.

"Well, Menen warned me," Kirk said. "He told me that if Spock meant anything to me, I should kill him."

"Now *there's* a tomfool notion."

"Don't worry, Bones, the idea doesn't appeal to me either. But we've got to do something to help him."

"Well, I've at least gotten a start on it," McCoy said. "Come on in and I'll show you."

In McCoy's office, the surgeon showed Kirk a jar full of transparent liquid. In the fluid, a long, almost-transparent tendril drifted and twisted.

"It's a piece of living tissue of some sort," McCoy said. "Call it a tentacle. I took it out of Spock's spinal column an hour ago."

"Is that what causes the pain?"

McCoy nodded. "His entire nervous system has been infiltrated by this stuff. And far too thoroughly for conventional surgery to remove. I don't know how to get it out."

"Then if the old man is right," Kirk said, "this tissue is responsive to directives sent out by the other creatures."

"Or is it *the* creature?"

"Explain."

"By itself," McCoy said, "this stuff is just undifferentiated tissue. No organs. And I'd guess the same for the individual creatures we saw on the surface. They didn't look like things, but *parts* of things. Put them all together and—well, I'm sure they wouldn't spell 'Mother.' But that's about all I'm sure of."

"Do you know why it resists a phaser blast?"

"It's mostly energy itself—nonprotoplasmic. That's why it can fly too. A phaser blast affects it about like a stream from a fire hose would us: knocks it down, stuns it, but that's all. Now let's go look at Spock and I'll show you something else."

Spock was lying strapped down and under sedation, under the diagnostic panel.

"Watch the left indicator," McCoy said. "It's a dolorimeter—registers the level of pain. Right now it's present at the maximum tolerance level. But if I open a channel to Spock . . ."

He moved a knob. At once, the indicator rose nearly to the top of the scale and froze there.

"That's what he's going through," McCoy said softly. "It's as though he were being consumed by fire, from the inside out. No wonder the poor devils go mad."

"And no wonder," Kirk said, "that they come to think killing each other is an act of mercy."

As he spoke, the indicator began to drop, very slowly. McCoy stared at it. "What the . . ."

Spock opened his eyes. "Hello, Doctor," he said weakly. "Hello, Captain."

"Mr. Spock! How do you feel?"

"Unwell. But these restraints will no longer be necessary. Nor will your sedations, Doctor. I will be able to return to duty."

"That's impossible," McCoy said.

"Spock, we've just seen what that pain can do to you," Kirk added.

"I regret my behavior," Spock said. "The pain greatly

slowed my thinking. I did not even remember that we cannot set the ship down, on any planet. But I can control the pain now."

"How?" McCoy demanded.

"I am a Vulcan; we are trained to use our minds. Pain is only another kind of sensory input, which a trained mind ought to be able to handle."

"You're only half Vulcan," Kirk said. "What about the human half?"

"It is an inconvenience, but it is manageable. The creature—all of its thousands of parts—is pressing upon me even now. It wants this ship. But I can resist. It is not especially pleasant, but I assure you there will be no danger if you release me."

"The strongest mind in the world has to relax after a while," McCoy said. "If I put you on mild sedation . . ."

"No drugs, Doctor. My mind must be clear."

"Mr. Spock, I need you," Kirk said. "But I can't take any chances. You stay here. Sweat it out for a while. If you can maintain control, then come back. Until then, do what the doctor says. That's an order."

Spock nodded. Then his face twitched and the dolorimeter shot up again. Closing his eyes, Spock whispered: "The mind rules. There is no pain. There . . . is . . . no . . . pain . . ."

On the bridge, Uhura had a call waiting from Star Fleet.

"*Enterprise* standing by, Commodore Anhalt," Kirk said.

"We've studied your reports of the situation on Deneva, Captain," Anhalt said. "We agree that the creatures, whatever they are, pose a clear and immediate threat to the area. It is our conclusion that, left alone, they would spread rapidly throughout that quadrant and perhaps farther. Can you tell us anything of the nature of the creatures?"

"Not yet. We're preparing to capture a specimen for analysis."

"Fine. But you are not on a specimen-collecting expedition, Captain. Regardless of the nature of the creatures, they must be destroyed—whatever the cost."

"Commodore," Kirk said, "there are more than a million innocent people on that planet. I may not be able to destroy the creatures without . . ."

"We are aware of that, Captain," Anhalt said evenly. "Your orders stand. We will expect your progress reports. Star Fleet out."

The image faded. Kirk turned away from the screen to discover his first officer standing behind him.

"Spock, I gave you a direct order to stay in bed!"

"Until I was satisfied that I could maintain control," Spock said. "I am satisfied. So is Dr. McCoy."

"You're certain?"

"Absolutely."

"All right, then put your mind to work on this: How do I capture one of those creatures? They don't respond to the transporter any better than they do to phaser fire—and I'm not about to beam a man down there. I'd just beam back another casualty."

"Not necessarily," Spock said. "If the man's nervous system were already inhabited, there would be little or nothing further the creatures could do to him."

Kirk stared at him. "I see what you're getting at," he said, "and I don't like it."

"Captain, in the same circumstances, I do not think you would hesitate for a moment. I simply claim the right to do as you would do, if our positions were reversed. I am the logical man for the job."

After a long silence, Kirk said: "It is so ordered. Be careful, and stay in constant touch with us."

"Of course, Captain."

Spock came back with two specimens—one of the creatures and a raving man. "I thought we would need somebody else who was already infected too," he said. "After all, the main problem is how to get the creature out of the body."

Aurelan reacted with shock and despair. "That is Kartan," she said. "We were to be married, before the creatures came."

She would not stay to watch McCoy testing, and Kirk could hardly blame her.

"It's the same picture, only more advanced," McCoy

said. "In effect, he hardly has a nervous system of his own any more. The tissue has taken it over."

"It seems that at least we did find out what happened on Ingraham B and the other planets," Kirk said.

"No doubt about it. But what do we *do*?"

Spock came in, carrying the transparent case with the creature in it.

"Here it is," he said. "At first glance, a unicellular creature of sorts—but actually part of a creature. Its own level of activity is so low it doesn't even affect instruments. Its tremendous power is the result of participation in the whole. What it resembles more than anything else is a huge individual brain cell."

"How do you know?" McCoy said.

"You forget, Doctor, the creature has infiltrated my own system. I am in constant contact with it. I find it most annoying."

"I don't doubt that," Kirk said. "But how do we destroy it?"

"I think we have a clue. You will recall Noban, the Denevan who flew into his sun. Just before his death, he cried out that he was free—that he had won. Apparently the proximity to the sun destroyed the creature controlling him."

"We already know they don't like light," Kirk said slowly. "But how do we expose them to light of that intensity? And what good would it do anyhow? A million of the creatures are inside human bodies."

"One was inside Noban's," Spock pointed out. "*Something* drove it out. But we need take no chances. The *Enterprise* has the capacity to turn Deneva into a miniature sun—a ball of nuclear energy. They would not survive that."

"Surely not," Kirk said thoughtfully.

"Now hold on," McCoy said. "Are you seriously considering this? Destroying a million people whose only crime was being victimized by these filthy things?"

"Our mission," Spock said somberly, "is to destroy the aliens—at whatever cost."

"Not at that cost! Jim, this idea is insane."

"These creatures are trying to spread out in the galaxy," Kirk said. "And the Denevans are already building ships for them. Aside from the fact that I have been given an order, we do not have much time."

"I have an alternative," Spock said.

"Great God, man," McCoy said, "spit it out!"

"Clearly any radiation intense enough to destroy the creatures would also destroy the people. But I think the hint we took from the fact that the creatures like shadows is a false lead. Light is a medium to them, like water is to a fish; they may simply prefer certain frequencies or levels, as some fish prefer saltwater to fresh. But consider this: If you have a free energy flow that for some reason you cannot conduct through a wire, a wave-guide or anything else of that sort, how do you direct it? Or, if you wish, disrupt it? The agency must be something that is both common and intense near a sun, yet completely harmless to human beings; remember, Noban's parasite was destroyed *before* he was."

"I'm no physicist," McCoy said. "Is there such an agency, or are we just playing games?"

"Certainly there is," Kirk exclaimed. "Magnetism!"

"That is what I had in mind," Spock said. "Of course, we cannot generate a magnetic field as intense as a sun's, but it may not be necessary." He paused as Aurelan and Menen came in, explained his idea again quickly, and went on: "We have your son to thank for this, Menen. But what particularly interests me is that his parasite was not forced out gradually by the gradually increasing intensity of the general magnetic field. Instead, insofar as we can tell, it was wrenched out quite suddenly. This leads me to suspect that motion is the key—that what happened was that his ship passed through the rapidly whirling magnetic field of a sunspot. *That* is an effect we can duplicate. If I am right, it will pull the creature out like pulling a tooth."

"But probably a lot more painful," McCoy said. "Maybe even fatally so."

"It did not kill Menen's son. The heat did that. In any event, we have no course available but to try. Since I am already infected, the logical thing to do is to try it on me."

"And risk killing you?" Kirk said. "Things are bad enough already."

"Captain, the strain of maintaining my mental barriers is considerable. I do not know how long I can continue. When my guards go down—as inevitably they must—I will go insane. I would rather die by the hand of a friend. Furthermore, if I am insane, I am in a position to do the maximum possible amount of damage to the ship."

"Isn't there another question?" Aurelan said. "Mr. Spock is only half human. Even if the experiment is successful, it won't be conclusive."

"I have to work with what I have," McCoy said.

"You have Kartan," Aurelan said. "My fiancé."

They all looked at her in silence. When McCoy spoke, his voice was very gentle. "The risk," he said, "is extremely great."

"If you don't find a cure, he will die a raging maniac," she replied calmly. "Do you think I want that?"

McCoy glanced at Kirk, who nodded without hesitation.

"All right," McCoy said. "Thank you. I'll do my best."

It worked nicely. The creature emerged from all sides of Kartan's body at once, as though he were being enclosed in a balloon, and then was torn to shreds under the whirling electromagnets. He was still under sedation, but the dolorimeter promptly declined to normal level, and his face was peaceful for the first time since they had seen him.

"Congratulations, Mr. Spock," Kirk said. "And now I want you on that table, as fast as we can get Kartan moved out."

"No, sir."

"Why not? I should think you'd be eager to be rid of it! You volunteered before."

"True, Captain, but since then I have thought of something else. Do you realize that this leaves us just as badly off as we were before?"

Kirk frowned. Given the question, there was no need to explain it. There was absolutely no possibility of enveloping the whole of Deneva in such a field; Deneva's own natural field would fight it, and the *Enterprise* lacked the power to win such an invisible struggle. Nor was there anything like time to treat a million people individually.

McCoy obviously had also chased the chain of reasoning to its conclusion. "We are going to have to destroy the planet anyhow," he said harshly.

Aurelan straightened beside the sleeping Kartan. "Captain," she said. "They're my people. I grew up with them. I loved them. I've lost my brother. I don't want to lose anyone else. But I beg you, Captain, do what has to be done. Give the order."

"A million people . . ." Kirk said.

"Don't you understand?" Aurelan cried out. "There's no hope for them! Their brains are on fire! They want to die!"

Kirk stood as if frozen to the floor. "Brains on fire," he whispered. "Brains on fire. That's it. That's the answer!"

"Yes, Captain," Mr. Spock said. "That is my conclusion also."

"What is?" McCoy said. "You gentleman have lost me."

"It's like this," Kirk said rapidly. "Spock has already likened this—this composite organism to a gigantic brain. All the evidence we have points in the same direction. The individual cells are mindless, almost lifeless. It's possible, indeed it seems likely, that there is a central concentration of them somewhere. If we could kill that off . . ."

"I don't see that that follows at all," McCoy said. "The aggregate of the scattered cells could well be all there is to the brain, since we know the cells can communicate with each other. Why is it likely that there should be a concentration, too?"

"Because of the behavior of the creatures," Spock said. "They multiply uncontrollably until they overflow a planet. Not leave it—overflow it. The original central concentration is left behind. *Ergo*, it must still be there—wherever it is."

"And all we know about that is that it's somewhere in the Orion sector," Kirk said. "Mr. Spock, could the computer extrapolate the spread of these creatures backward, so to speak, and at least narrow down the possibilities to an area we'd have some hope of searching in time?"

"Of course," Spock said. "But you have something better, Captain."

"What's that?"

"You have me. That is why I do not want the treatment

yet. I am infested; I am aware of the creature—not just the part of it that inhabits me, but the entire creature. As we approach the central concentration, I will know."

"Are you sure?"

For answer, Spock pointed. "It lies that way," he said. "I know that already, even though it must be fifty parsecs away."

"Posts!" Kirk shouted.

As they approached the critical Orion sector, it gradually became evident that not only was Spock aware of the nucleus of the creature—it was aware of him, and in some way realized that it must not allow this particular cell of itself to come closer. The pressure on Spock mounted unbearably. Though he still performed his duties, the sweat ran constantly down his face, which occasionally was twisted by a grimace that seemed to have no connection with anything he was doing or saying.

"Better let us extract that thing now," Kirk said. "We're zeroed in on the planet. There's no sense in your suffering any further."

"Sir, I would prefer to bear it just a little while longer. The final test of the theory is what happens to me—or does not happen—when that nucleus is destroyed. If the pain continues, we will know that we were wrong."

"Without prejudice to your own wishes or your will power, Mr. Spock, are you certain that there's no danger of your running amok again?"

"The danger exists," Spock said levelly. "However, I am fighting it. And I do not see how we can forfeit this test."

"I hate to say so," McCoy said, "but I think he's right, Jim."

"Very well," Kirk said. He looked at the main viewing screen, which was now showing the image of the target planet. It was utterly barren, though occasional faint geometrical patterns showed where there might once have been cities—before the creatures had come with their burden of agony and wiped them out. "It will be a pleasure to get rid of that monster. Arms Control, are those missiles primed?"

"Yes, sir," said a loudspeaker. "Two fully-armed planet-wreckers, programed and ready to go."

"Very well. Fire one."

A streak of light shot away from the *Enterprise*. For many long minutes nothing seemed to happen. Then the planet on the screen burst into a white blare of atomic fire. The screen backed hastily down the intensity spectrum.

At the same moment, Spock screamed. Two security men promptly grabbed him; Bones had been alert for just such an outcome.

"Stop! Stop!" Spock screamed. "My world—*my life*—"

"Fire two," Kirk said grimly. The planet was already breaking up, but he was taking no chances. Another colossal fusion explosion spread over the screen. When it had died away, there was nothing left to be seen but an enormous, expanding cloud of gas.

"So we have created a new Orion nebula," Kirk said. He turned to Spock. The first officer was standing quietly in the grip of the security man, while Bones hovered nearby with a hypo.

"Mr. Spock?"

Spock's eyes were glazed, and for a moment he seemed to have no mind at all. His face was blank, his mouth working. Then, gradually, life and sanity seemed to flow back into him.

"I am . . . recovering," he said formally. "The pain was . . . incredible . . . like nothing I had experienced before. For an instant I *was* that creature. I felt its death. But now . . . nothing."

"Now," McCoy said firmly, "we take you below and extract that thing from you. I will tolerate no further arguments on that score."

"No further arguments are necessary," Spock said. "Its purpose is served."

"Any word from Deneva, Lieutenant?"

"Rapidly getting back to normal, Captain," Uhura reported. "Menen says that the remaining creatures just wander about helplessly and seem to have almost no vitality left. To kill one, you need scarcely do more than stick it with a pin."

"Very good," Kirk said. "Mr. Spock, this may sound

grandiose, but it's the truth. I think you have singlehandedly just saved the galaxy."

"No, sir, I think not."

"What could have stopped them if we hadn't?"

"Their own nature, Captain."

"Explain."

"A truly successful parasite," Spock said, "is commensal, living in amity with its host, or even giving it positive advantages—as, for instance, the protozoans who live in the digestive system of your termites and digest for them the wood that they eat. A parasite that regularly and inevitably kills its hosts cannot survive long, in the evolutionary sense, unless it multiplies with tremendous rapidity—much more rapidly than these creatures did. It is not pro-survival."

"In the evolutionary sense, maybe," Kirk said. "But evolution takes a long, long time. In the interim, you have at least saved millions of people from pain, madness and death."

"Believe me, Captain," Spock said, "I find that quite sufficient."